THE TAMING OF A SIOUX

Taming of a Sioux
©2009 Peggy DePuydt

ALL RIGHTS RESERVED
No part of this book may be reproduced in any form, by photocopying or by any electronic or mechanical means, including information storage or retrieval systems, without permission in writing from both the copyright owner and the publisher of this book, except for the minimum words needed for review.

Taming of a Sioux is a work of fiction.
Any similarities to real places, events, or persons living or dead is coincidental or used fictitiously and not to be construed as real.

ISBN 13: 978-1-932993-93-6

Library of Congress Control Number: 2009928432

Edited by Janet Elaine Smith
Cover by Books and More http://bookcoversandmore.tripod.com/
Interior design by Star Publish LLC

A Star Publish LLC Publication
www.starpublishllc.com
Published in 2009
Printed in the United States of America

THE TAMING OF A SIOUX

PEGGY DE PUYDT

A Star Publish LLC Book

DEDICATION

This work of fiction is dedicated to the descendants of the hard-working Indian tribes that populated the Indian Village, aka *Indian Town* across the Sturgeon River from the timber town of Nahma (Nay-ma) located in south Delta County in Michigan's Upper Peninsula. There established about fifteen families, a composite of Sioux, Chippewa and Menominee Tribes. They found employment at the Bay de Nocquet Lumber Company (1881 – 1951) and were serious, dedicated servants of the endeavor.

Their heritage dated back to pre-Civil War days. Old burial grounds are yet detectable near the ballpark site and in earlier days, arrowheads were found in the clearing where the first sawmill and lumberyards were located.

INTRODUCTION

Creation is the storyteller's sustenance. The bits and pieces of life supply the pulled wool; refinement converts them into a fabric having its own design and excellence. I have sought to enact historical events and values through the characters. While some of the people contained in this book were real, the events surrounding their lives have been highly fictionalized, and the author assumes no responsibility for any *facts* that might have led to the *fiction* version of their story.

Situations and incidents described herein are pure invention. That they may have happened sometime somewhere dictates that the novelist must possess a perception and grasp of the era beyond that which history records.

By a happy circumstance of geography, Nahma, Michigan contains an essence of that moment in history suspended between World War I and the rich industrialization years of post-World War II in which timber loomed tycoon. The employment of the American Indian rested yet depressed in the U.S.A., and lumber mills found an inexpensive labor resource in these under-valued tribesmen.

ACKNOWLEDGEMENTS

The Delta Historian, Volume 31, Issue 2, Delta County, MI
Rosie Beauchamp for historical data and encouragement
Richard DePuydt for his patience and critiques
Violet Sargent, historical aficionado of Nahma, Michigan
Allen T. Mercier, Nahma Township Supervisor, 1935-1955, and Bay de Nocquet Lumber Company Office Manager
Nahma High Spots, High School Publication, Nahma, MI
Warren Hale, Historical Editor, Milan Area Leader, Milan, Michigan
The Delta County Historical Society, Escanaba, MI
The Nahma Historical Society, Nahma, MI
Something About Nahma, by Richard McClinchy, Nahma, MI
Microsoft Encarta Encyclopedia
Escanaba Daily Press, Escanaba, MI
Northland Publishers, Escanaba, MI
Arizona Republic, Phoenix, AZ
Life Among the Wolverines by Tom Hemingway with Bill Haney, Pub. Diamond Communications, Inc.
Bo, by Bo Schembechelr and Mitch Albom, Pub. Warner Books, Inc.
For the Glory by Ken Denlinger, Pub. St. Martin's Press
A Good Day To Die (The Story of the Great Sioux War) by Charles M. Robinson III, Pub. Random House
The Huntington Library, Art Collections and Botanical Gardens, San Marino, CA
The Pasadena Tournament of Roses Association, Pasadena, CA
Run to Daylight by Vince Lombardi, Pub. Prentice-Hall Int., Inc.
Sports Illustrated, *Football, A History of the Professional Game* by Peter King, Pub. Oxmoor House, Inc.
Natural Enemies, The Notre Dame-Michigan Football Feud by John Kryk, Pub. Andrews & McMeel
Football: They Call It A Game! But It's A Jungle Out There by Dan Jenkins, Pub. Simon & Schuster
30 Years of Pro Football's Great Moments, by Jack Clary, Pub. Rutledge Books, NY, NY
Football achievements and records are those of Don Hutson, a Lambeau early-on achiever

CHAPTER ONE

April 1942

At seventeen, Abe shook his head at how footloose a child he had been back when he was five years old, in the summer of his awakening. But his father, Fabian, living handicapped with crippling spondilitis, taught Abe many things to nurture self-confidence. He knew his full name: Abednego Matthew Miereau; his birth date: December 14, 1924; and his address: Old Beach Road, Nahma, Michigan as well as the names of various streets in this company-owned timber town.

Mulling the long ago, Abe threw another chunk of wood into the Kalamazoo space heater, the house cooling quickly under the torment of heavy winds. Flames quickly licked over the energy source and reminded Abe of how the sun had played high in a bursting blue sky that June day of his fifth year, the day of Old John Pedo.

As clearly as a rolled-back film, he saw the deliciously warm day. The steady hum of the lumber mill played on Abe's ears, and birds swooped lazily in springtime courting. Around a wild pear tree, Abe chased a monarch butterfly, while a cloud of fresh green like a watercolor blend covered the trees that leaned over the sawdust road. From his home near the beach of Big Bay de Nocquet, a south-facing body of water fed by Lake Michigan, Abe traveled in a bubble of dreamtime.

Dressed in high top boots and knickers, he wandered up the road that led him to the Village of Nahma, a prosperous lumbering town. Passing the wood-sided K-12 school, he watched as the buses unloaded country students for their last day of school. He fantasized on the kindergarten class with pretty Miss McClinchy as his teacher.

He'd not often seen ladies, but always wanted a mother. Why did he only have a father and no mother? Even though Fabian had explained that Abe's mother left him without notice when Abe was yet a baby, the thought rolled around in his head like a loose marble. Thinking that her leaving fell as his fault, he shed a river of Sioux Indian tears. With chubby fists, he wiped his eyes, but raven-like black hair entangled around his hand, loosening it from the ponytail that Fabian had brushed and tied with infinite care.

Staring now into the rich glow of the isinglass window of the space heater in the quietude of his lonely home, Abe surged with the injustices of that day. With the incessant wind scolding off the lake, the bias and inequalities of his life crept over him like a fall of mosquito netting. Emotions ran away with the bitterness he had experienced in the past three weeks since Fabian's sudden death.

Nonetheless, remembering his misadventure at five years old served as an antidote for loneliness. With small, leaden feet, he saw himself moving on from the school. He kicked along a rock, watching it roll ahead and stop dully in a crack of the wooden sidewalk. Tears again tumbled over the rims of his eyes, his shoulders shook and his nose ran. Leaning his head sideways, he wiped his nose on his sleeve. As often happened, tall white pines whispered in the freshening morning breeze, carrying to him a message of peace and better days.

Lingering spring fragrances filled the air: lilacs, bridal wreath and hanging snowball bushes. On Abe's small back, neck and shoulders, the sun grew kissing warm, but a nagging voice within alarmed him to an awareness that he strayed too far from home. Ignoring the agitation, he skipped peacefully along the sidewalk in his private bubble, shrugging off the knowledge that he wandered into uncharted territory.

Multiple streets ran to the inside of the Main Street "T". However, the only street leading back east off the top of the "T" was Wells Street, on the corner of which stood the Company Hospital. Exploration of Wells Street enticed Abe, even if his interior voice scolded. Walking by Old John Pedo's house drew him even though it stood a long way from home—long way—just a few doors from the Bay de Nocquet Lumber Company Hospital. In Abe's mind, he pictured the streets and the layout of the town, which he had mind recorded.

Passing Pedo's peeling vertical, one-by-four board fencing, he found himself beckoned by branches of green mint and pink wild roses, which were temptingly his height. Enticing redolence teased his nose as he gently brushed aside a fat bumblebee drunk on honeysuckle. Abe startled upon seeing Old John, grasping the weatherworn crossbuck of the garden gate. *He looks like an army man,* Abe thought. Behind Pedo, Abe saw small slices of the house, shingled, dingy-gray. Even the walls were made of shingles as if you could pick them off and—eat them!

Abe sniffed flowers as Old John Pedo stared eerily. His breath caught in his throat. M*aybe this man is a witch.* His dark eyes filled with fear.

Swarthy, square-faced, scruffy and seedy, Old John Pedo stared at Abe. His face deeply etched and wrinkled, he wore the hat of a sea captain. Salivating from the corners of his mouth, his jaw worked as if chewing a cud.

Breaking eye contact, Abe hastily turned and instinctively moved away.

"How would you like to have a penny to buy some candy at the Clubhouse?" Pedo's words were mellow honeyed tones that rolled off his lips.

Abe came to an abrupt and very surprised halt. The Clubhouse! His throat caught with excitement. *Penny candy, licorice whips, jellybeans, maybe even gumdrops!*

"Yeah!" Abe replied, showing no timidity now, but returned the gaze of this giant of a man. Abe *clicked* into the ugliest face he'd ever seen: heavily poxed nose, blue-red, bulging, with flared nostrils. Deeply imbedded facial rivulets ran on either side of his mouth, looking as if someone had pleated his face.

"Well then c'mon get your penny." He opened the garden gate and swept his arm in a command gesture for Abe to follow. He tagged along obediently as Captain Sea Legs walked in a shuffling gait, his heels making a dragging sound on the cracks between the boards in the sidewalk. He wore dusty bib overalls over which hung a loose-fitting denim jacket decorated with metal buttons.

"Just c'mon in and sit here in the kitchen while I get a penny," he said, as if everything spun hunky-dory. Pointing to a high-back chair with spindle spokes, Pedo disappeared into a dark dining room.

Abe complied, eager to please, but couldn't push out of his mind the rank smell: dank wallpaper, cooking odors and mildew—possibly a days-old chamber pot.

Returning with a shiny penny, folding and unfolding it enticingly in his big hand, Old John sat on another chair in front of which he positioned Abe with his back to Old John. Thumbing down Abe's knickers and shorts, Pedo proceeded to do funny things between Abe's legs, his hands rough, leathery, all the while grunting monosyllables and licking his fingers.

Abe turned his head around, sniffed loudly, his childish features wrung with fear. Raising his dark eyes to Captain Sea Legs, he tried to figure out this turn of events. Uncomprehending, his mind pulled to decipher yet more information for which he couldn't find a niche. The rebuking voice inside his head gnawed causing a deep keening within his throat. Nonetheless, it did make some kind of sense. He would gain a penny, would he not? And Captain Sea Legs wasn't hurting him.

Just the same, even to his befuddled five-year-old mind, Abe figured something kicked out of kilter. Just when he thought that he'd grasped the problem, it slipped away, like an elusive squirrel in an oak tree. How could he remember things he didn't understand in the first place? His tiny features taut, he couldn't think straight.

Shortly losing interest, Captain Sea Legs turned the penny over to Abe. Clutching the coveted coin, Abe buttoned his knickers and flew out of the house as if he had a cyclone at his back. His feet barely kissing the ground, he punished the wooden sidewalk but spun around to look back. Maybe the funny fella still watched him; maybe he wanted his penny back. Abe enthused to run even faster—zap away from what he'd just encountered, but his feet felt as if he walked through molasses. He had to think of something else—forget the old man—think of something else, quickly!

Sarah, his favorite sandbox friend!

He wished Sarah could see him now with a penny. All his own! Wished she could see him pounding down the sidewalk to the Candy Kitchen like a big kid. He had better spend it fast, or do some telling to Fabian.

"Where'd you get it?" Ruby Warren, the Candy Kitchen clerk, vented in villainous voice showing more sarcasm than solicitation. Her middle-aged cheeks were rouged, her hair in perfect circle curls created by twisting a small clump of hair around her index finger and slipping a bobby pin over the resulting tiny ring until it set up. Bright red lipstick accented her skinny-lipped mouth. *Click.* Abe recorded the look.

Scissor Bill, that's what Fabian called Ruby Warren. Lifting his chubby hand to his mouth, Abe had managed to stifle a giggle at the thought. He stood transfixed, face bloodless, mouth ajar, eyes drawn by the controlling fixation of Ruby.

"Did you get that penny from Old John Pedo?" she asked, her arms folded across her chest, eyes piercing Abe's very soul.

Ripping his eyes back to Scissor Bill, he replied softyly. "Yeah, he gave me the penny." His voice waxed wooden. He had a hard time saying the word. Many words Abe had a hard time saying; his fat tongue couldn't quite twist them into place. His lips felt anchored down with sinkers. Lifting his head, he inquired with his eyes about the status of the penny, too terrorized with the taunting to communicate.

Customers stared at him—giants all of them—right out of Gulliver's Travels: men drinking coffee with hands folded around mugs, women sipping through straws from softly curved ice-green bottles of Coca Cola all immensely proportioned in Abe's five-year-old mind. Their mouths appeared rubber; their eyes like giant marbles.

He swung his gaze to the glass counter and stared right into a pale blue and white display of Alka Seltzer, then figured he'd better cut his losses and tear out. Turning, he saw outside the glass entrance door a village dog bearing heavy collie genetic code watching the scene play out as if he'd paid admission.

"What did you do to get that penny?" Ruby pressed for on-stage performance.

Abe stiffened at the mean-spiritedness in her voice.

Leaning her elbows on the glass display counter to see him better, she continued unrelentingly. "Did Old John take off your clothes?"

Her queries were shards of glass that pierced his sensitivity. Silence hung heavily. Abe thought everyone in the Candy Kitchen could hear his heart thumping.

"No," he choked out softly. Somehow, what he hadn't felt ashamed of now made him feel guilty. "I buy some licorice whips?" he asked with reservation, head cocked, holding his penny tightly in his fist.

Instead, with tongue-in-cheek and a flare of satisfaction in her eyes for the benefit of her audience, Ruby wafted a small paper bag through the air with exaggerated deftness, resulting in a well-executed *pop*. With slow deliberation she gathered licorice whips, handed Abe the bag and took the penny as if it were a hot potato.

Walking home, stretching the long strands of licorice between his clamped teeth, Abe decided to shred the thoughts of Scissor Bill in her starched white uniform dress, peaked hat and peaked hankie sticking out of the peaked pocket of her peaked white smock. In the warm afternoon sun he'd again taken refuge in his bubble, listening to his own music. The sweet licorice stuck to his teeth and to the roof of his mouth, leaving a fuzzy feeling in his innocent *joie de vivre*.

The five o'clock quitting-time whistle from the lumber mill fell over the town. Its plangent echo grew legs and walked forever in the still warm air, bouncing off trees, circling the delicate green leaves of June and adding a peaceful finality to the day.

☙❧

A short hour before Abe's recollection into the day of Old John Pedo, his Sioux Warrior face strained to read the road between strokes of the windshield wipers. Abe had been on a heretofore forbidden visit with his Grandfather, Farley. For the first time since that fateful day three weeks ago, he'd ventured from the shelter of his home to hear the Sioux culture anecdotes of Farley. The sketches of Sioux history were as exciting and new to him as the warmth and hospitality of Farley's home, which resided on a black list drafted by Fabian for Abe's seventeen years of life.

The chiseled face drew into a sour frown, however, to hear how Suki, his mother and Farley's daughter, grew up there until marriage to Fabian. Within eight months, Suki brought Abe into the world, and ten months later abandoned them both, disappearing.

The newness of being part of an extended family gentled Abe's spirits. "Family," he said aloud. The word had been drifting in the margins of the stormy night. At last, he knew glue in this Village of Nahma tucked away in Michigan's Upper Peninsula. He ran a hand through his thick black hair.

A shudder shook him as he recalled the shock of Fabian's recent death, the thought never failing to crumble the ground beneath him. One day they were laughing together, and the next Fabian wrung from Abe's life forever like yesterday's wash water.

Abe adjusted his six-foot-two-inch frame to brace for the bump as he rolled onto the wooden Indian Town Bridge in his 1938 Ford. Hearing and feeling the familiar clunka-clunka of the dual planks, he eased back comfortably into the seat again. Forming tracks, the planks lay horizontally over open railroad ties girded by wooden truss support beams, easily fifty feet long. His face softened into rugged handsomeness hearing the roar of the Sturgeon River rushing in its quest for Big Bay de Nocquet. Windshield wipers clacked as they cleared the torrential rain scantily before yet another onslaught.

A wistful smile grew on Abe's face, his attention drawn by the whistling wing window. Opened and closed so many times, it failed to close properly any longer. Too many times Fabian had opened it to throw out cigarette butts that spat against the window, then flickered and dimmed as they ricocheted down the road.

Another mile and he'd be home. His long tapering fingers confidently guided the steering wheel. Heavy eyebrows nested his forehead as he recalled that just moments ago he'd been shivering with the wildness of wind tugging at his trench coat. Hastily, he had gathered the belt closely around his waist with one hand while huddling his Grandmother Norrhea's smoked fish as a football prized into the end zone. Norrhea, with her large, fluid brown eyes, Abe viewed as the youngest "grandma" he'd ever known. He affirmed that his association with his mother's parents had to be a gift from God. He worked his shoulders, aware he'd been sitting stiffly.

His home, standing quietly in the darkness on the Beach Road, stood forlorn when he arrived; he'd forgotten to leave a light burning. Abe sought some comfort in the fact that it didn't bother him so much recently to enter the house. Perhaps he'd outlived his nightmares, which a psychiatrist would undoubtedly claim indicated there hid something specifically nasty in the woodpile of Abe's hidden psyche. Pacing the three steps to the back door, he glimpsed across the street the cheer of warm lights of the Savin home pulsating through the sheets of angry rain. As his dark brown eyes squinted, his countenance softened. Maybe in time he could find ablution from the past, the pain that lived there, the rage and resentment that assailed him daily without warning.

Upon entering, the silence of the house settled around him like a fog. Abe felt smothered, frozen in time. His grief for his father lay crushingly upon his chest. Suddenly, the kitchen infused with an iridescent light, overpowering him with developing energy. Around him, the room brightened eerily, infusing him with a new essence. Unexplainably he felt taller. Angered at himself for feeling spooked, he shrugged it off. He no longer lived a child who snatched at the bed sheet and pulled it over his head, as if that youthful gesture could shelter him from the thoughts that intimidated his sanity.

Outside, the wind and rain continued to slash at the small house. He'd turn on the radio and suppress the sound of his own heartbeat. The signal from WDBC, Escanaba, came in clearly from across the bay. "On this blustery Friday, April 10, 1942, let's hear from a new young crooner who is reputed to be our next Bing Crosby: Frank Sinatra with "I'll Never Smile Again" accompanied by the Tommy Dorsey orchestra." Abe placed his palms on top the console radio, his arms bracing for a moment, his head cocked. Sinatra had a nice sound. Straightening, Abe found he liked Sinatra's sound. Sinatra. Yeah.

For a space, the only sounds were the diminishing drumbeat of water outside the window. An irresistible impulse seized Abe. He'd pack Fabian's belongings and store them away in the attic under the dormers. Running his large hands through thick hair, he understood that he desperately needed to get on with his life. His jaw tightened, working muscles in his temples. Fabian's wish for him to live a happy life lingered, he knew. Time demanded he shoulder the pain and press on.

Highly agitated with the appearance of the bright light and the subsequent dissipation of it, he wished to hell for the rain to cease altogether. He didn't need dancing-light tricks. Since Fabian's death, he wondered if he knew the time of day, but he knew with all certainty that he had to cease devoting his home to a shrine to his father. Drumming with persistency, the thought took life. He noted that the rain fell steadily now but less violently. A friendly fire in the stove would help.

After retrieving wooden crates from the garage, Abe rippled the rain off his shoulders. The heat thrown from the freshly lighted fire felt like a lifesaver. Into the crates, an endless stream of Fabian's life saw storage: his shaving mug and brush, toothbrush, a half-empty bottle of Wildroot Cream Oil, a hundred-year-old after-shave that had stood unused on Fabian's dresser for as long as Abe could remember.

Untold numbers of worn stockings he found as well as threadbare underwear, tattered shirts, seat-sprung trousers and coats as old as Joseph's jacket. Finding the bottom of another drawer, Abe stared into the fragile likeness of a beautiful lady smiling up at him in brown-gold tones as transient as she had become after the precious months Fabian had with her. Loneliness existed as a thing to which he had become accustomed with the austerity peculiar to the Sioux and their prairie way of life. Tonight it crept in on soft moccasins, causing his heart to thump with heaviness. His mother! How he wished that he could ransack some memories of her.

Seeking courage, Abe foraged on. Coming upon Fabian's one and only suit that remained after his burial, Abe pulled it to his face to smell one last time, squeezing his eyes against the burning tears of irreversible loss. He rubbed his thumbs reverently over two pair of shoes that he forced himself to cast into the crate. Worn and run over from the many painful miles Fabian had walked in them, they were a bond of familiarity to Abe. An old bathrobe hung behind the bathroom door where Fabian had last touched it, as if it were waiting to warm the debilitated body of his father. Gloves and felt boot-liners Abe drew from the closet, in addition to a black-and-red plaid deer-hunting jacket.

While folding Fabian's duck-hunting jacket, a soft feather lofted from a pocket. Slowly it floated to the floor on the warm air currents. Abe transfixed at the swimming feather as its lacy ends fluffed in and out imaging a living entity. Fabian's promise probed Abe's mind: *Whenever you see a falling feather, a glint of sunlight on the water, I'll be there.* The words came rushing in on him like a tidal surge.

It built the same bit of Sioux lore Farley had just related, and was too ominous to discredit. Shaken, it proved an epiphany to Abe of life after death. Startled realization crept over his face—the look of the pioneer edging up to the Grand Canyon.

The feather found its way into Abe's pocket without terror or superstition, yet his body tensed and he felt something warm and wonderful spread from his toes to his ears. Through the feisty rainstorm, a pale shaft of sun broke through the white pines, a shimmer of rays slanting through the living room window.

Having tackled the grim game plan, Abe disallowed himself to back off in the face of a floating feather. The wonderful happening didn't jibe with theoretical science, but he'd treasure the infusion of well-being.

Out of the dresser drawers he gathered a tumble of morose paisley-print handkerchiefs, undershirts, pajamas and sweaters with sagging weave having seen the inside of the Maytag too often. With a start, Abe came upon a dog-eared, daily missal with green, red and white silk ribbons separating the special passages to which Fabian wished to return. Under the red ribbon, Abe's tender eyes read from the Second letter of Paul to Timothy. *I have fought the good fight, I have finished the race and I have kept the faith.* Abe quieted at the relativity of the quote to the life Fabian had lived.

The green ribbon revealed a pummeled page bearing the Gospel according to Matthew. *Blest are the poor in spirit: the reign of god is theirs. Blest are those sorrowing; they shall be consoled...* Confined to the house for so many lonely hours, God only knew the comfort Fabian drew from these readings. Abe knuckled away tears.

A sudden gust of wind rattled the windows spewing a new deluge of unforgiving rain as if it wanted all in its path destroyed, as Fabian had been slowly destroyed.

A peculiar prominence of sorts met Abe's touch. Under the next page there lay a pressed wild rose in its fragile perfection, yet bearing delicate colors of subtle pink and pearl. Abe sunk with the feeling that he'd invaded the inner sanctum of Fabian's soul. Did the rose stem from his wedding day or something equally as memorable? A rose in keeping for so long spelled substantial meaning to Fabian when all else failed.

Did Fabian know treatment as a pariah in the community—a white man marrying an Indian maiden? He swallowed. Why had he not sought out his father's past: his life as a boy, his courtship of Suki, his love—his marriage? His heart ached with gripping fingers of pain. He counted so many days, nights and years when he could have known Fabian better. He'd let them all slip through his fingers like sifting beach sand.

After two hours of gathering every piece of disposable accumulation, Abe stood surrounded by the limp layout of Fabian's life—a sobering, insignificant collection. *See How His Garden Grows* struck Abe as an appropriate epithet as he packed away memories one-by-one and drove nails into the flip-top covers. Then fell the final act: the closing of a door, the putting away of his youth, his love, his protection and security. How badly he needed this time alone to quantify his life, to blame, to curse, to sort, to cleanse him from this tormenting pain, the rage. He recognized that his mind was a briar patch of self-imposed thorns—branches off branches off branches.

The final nail in place, Abe's sense of well-being cracked. He didn't realize how appalling the din of the pounding hammer was until it stopped. Loneliness and grief rolled over him like an avalanche, tumbling and burying him. Kneeling at the final box, he buried his head in his arms and wept. He wept in a tunnel of sorrow for the loss of his best friend, his father, his mentor, whom he knew to be a fine person with the decency of the Upper Midwest. He wept for the hard times he'd experienced all his life, and for Fabian's sudden death. He wept for what lay in his future.

Would he have enough money to buy food, clothing and gas for the car? How could he declaw the wolf at his door? Thank God for the little job he had stumbled upon at the Company Store and at the Company Office. His heaving shoulders were unmanageable. Maybe he could sell some of his oil paintings this summer at the Summer Art School Auction. He'd have to budget his time—stay focused. Devil voices beleaguered him. His six feet-two inch, one hundred and ninety-five pound frame sagged. What would he do without Fabian?

"Oh God," he moaned in terrible loss and frustration, "You need to help me." Emptiness surrounded him. Agony swept in like a black cloak, his knees too weak to stand. The luminescent aura he had witnessed earlier surrounded him again; peaceful reassurance rained down. Then it was gone as if rationed.

Strangely infused with self-control, Abe dragged the boxes to the attic, reining in his mind with thoughts of the glorious past of his mother's people the Sioux. They had a carefree, closely-knit life. Farley had imparted that the Sioux Braves were allowed sexual fulfillment while yet young men. It stood expected of them by the time they reached thirteen. Abe at seventeen hadn't given over to such thoughts.

Many times a surge of lust enveloped Abe when near Sarah Savin. It swamped him, driving him wild. He couldn't stand in her presence without becoming embarrassed with a rush of heat and hard desire. Being her soul mate since pre-school bonded them mysteriously. Feeling in depth the essence of her, Abe viewed the relationship as predetermined. Being with her was like having lunch with God.

Nevertheless, that bastard, Old John Pedo, had scared the hell out of her, and she'd never forgotten it. No one could get near her now, not even with gentle approaches. He'd get even with that old troll if it were the last thing he ever did. As he stored crates under the eaves of the dormer, he boiled with the remembrance.

Through Abe's bitterness, a warm thrill consumed him as thoughts of Fabian's tale pumped through him. Fabian had encouraged him to dream with his Sioux mother's predictions for him. *Revelations had come to her in a dream. She would bear a son who would accomplish great things.*

No matter how he hurt, Fabian never spoke unkindly of her. It was water over the dam, irretrievably lost. Abe, pushing the boxes to the end of the dormer, paused with the realization that Fabian had been hauntingly lost without Suki.

He digressed then in his thoughts. The Bay de Nocquet Lumber Company employed Fabian all his life and as a child looked as big as the whole world to Abe. While tracing geographical locations on a world globe, Fabian's hand showed age spots and his fingers shook while placing his finger on the 45th parallel. Encircling the globe there, he could sister city with Halifax, Nova Scotia, Bucharest, Romania, Hollaido, Japan, Portland, Oregon and Minneapolis, Minnesota.

As well as investigating the curves of the globe, Abe found the curious corners of town investigating every nook and cranny in his bump-around fashion, but he loved his small brown wood-shingled home on Old Beach Road. He cherished the porch that ran the distance of two sides of it. The big kitchen facing the south caught lake breezes. Abe warmed to snuggling into Fabian's lap as he sat in his big wingback chair in the living room, listening to the Saturday Night Barn dance from WLS, The Prairie Farmer Station in Chicago. Sometimes he padded into bed with Fabian in the bedroom off the living room. The nostalgia gripped at his chest with the remembrance of warmth and security.

Abe snapped mind-pictures and recorded them forever—*click*. He'd recorded Fabian with his dark eyes squinting in the morning sun, his bushy wild eyebrows forming a ledge over them like built-in protective sun gear. A permanently hunched back on the normally six-foot-tall man was his trademark. He wore long denim pants and blue chambray shirt over which suspenders ran the distance. Gray and black chest hair nestled under an unbuttoned collar.

On his feet he wore sloppy stockings and mangy morning slippers into which he could squiggle without bending over.

Fabian often reminded Abe that even at an early age he exhibited the same tendency to dream as Suki did. A product of Sioux, intra-family marriage, Suki's mother had married her father's brother—her uncle. The similarities between Abe and Suki were clear, how they both tended to drift into impenetrable fogs. Abe recalled how his eyes grew wide with the difficulty of processing even simple messages.

"It is nothing. Less than nothing," Fabian indulged Abe. Nonetheless, it *was* something, a big something that Abe would fight all his life.

CHAPTER TWO

Abe was up with the sun, although he'd lain for an indeterminable amount of time mulling the Old John Pedo affair and the trauma of packing on the previous evening. He devised a plan. It was his duty to avenge Old John's evils.

He didn't need to remind himself how badly things had gone at the Halloween Party last fall because of Pedo. A fierce determination thinned his mouth. He remembered all too well...

A new year had long since budded, bloomed and harvested at the time of the annual Halloween party—sophomore fund-raising event of the year. When he'd arrived that evening with Sarah, the school was tight with students leaking down hallways, buying concessions from various booths. It appeared a fast start to a long evening that would end with a Boris Karloff movie chosen to scare the beejeebers out of the student body: *The Bride of Frankenstein*.

It hadn't escaped Abe's notice that Sarah looked beautiful. She wore a black-watch plaid pleated skirt and a Kelly green wool-blend sweater accented by a white peter pan collar. Hugging above her black penny-loafers peeked rolled down white anklets. A fall of dark auburn hair swept her shoulders while full bangs accented her brown, upturned eyes—eyes that had the clarity of a child's—eyes that danced under long lashes as she glided with Abe to *Moonlight Serenade* by Glenn Miller.

Holding her made him feel vital and strong. The warmth of her body emanated into his like the outward ripples of a rock-strewn puddle. Bending down, he smelled her freshly shampooed thick hair that sparkled with highlights. Without expecting a reply, he breathed into her ear. "Remember when I thought I'd never catch on to dancing? Now, everything has come together; we're a team like Astaire and Rogers."

He didn't miss the fact that her eyes grew soft and shiny with his husky whispering while she snuggled into his protective bigness. Their whole world was wrapped in the nirvana of the moment. The hanging globe-lights in the study hall wrapped in orange paper pumpkins cast a surreal light upon the dancers.

Suddenly, and without warning, Neil Izcik swaggered toward them and seized Sarah, ripping her from the reverie of his arms. Abe pained with the startled look in her eyes. She was the obvious candidate, a beautiful woman. Were she plain, Izcik would probably never have taken a spade to this particular plot.

Exhibiting yellow saw teeth, Neil stared with beady green eyes, entrenched as deeply as citron in a bun. In slow assessment, they traveled up and down Sarah's legs, thighs, arms and breasts, undressing her with his gaze.

"You two got something straight between yourselves?" he asked loudly, disturbing the dancers around them. A circle of curious students stared, transfixed.

Abe could feel the tension building in Sarah. Her breasts were rounded and contoured in her sweater as Neil held her arm back and stared some more.

"It's my turn to dance with this lady, Miereau," his voice was freighted with truculence. Whipping her into his arms, he fought to move away, but Sarah's feet were terror-glued to the floor.

Livid, Abe's big hands worked in and out. Rage boiled. The muscles in his jaw worked as the firestorm broke. In one lunge, he corralled Neil by the back of the shirt and released Sarah. This started an argument that diverted attention from Sarah, to her unqualified relief. The fright spread contagious. Dancers felt themselves pulled magnetically into the mêlée like electropositive elements.

Abe rushed Neil to the wall. Hanging from Abe's gigantic grip, his feet flirted with the floor. Pinning him there, Abe tightened Neil's collar and squeezed while the offender kicked, choked and turned blue.

"You rotten piece of nothing. What a pain in the ass. You try that again and you're going to be history." Abe's hissing voice was barely discernible, spitting out words between clenched teeth—savage, violent, brutal.

Students had frenetically found Mary Krutina, the sophomore class advisor. Her eyes darkened at the incredible scene. Students gathered around, thunderstruck, while Neil faded fast, a fine drizzle of sputum emanating from his mouth. The energy suffusing the air was murderous. Had one a black light it would have shown in terrifying colors.

"Abe! Release him! Right now. Step back!" Krutina ordered.

Now Superintendent Bernard Tobin was there, pulling the two apart with a strength no one expected of him. "Abe, let it go," he said softly.

Somehow, Abe heard the quiet command and released Neil from his deadly grasp, where he collapsed into a clump on the floor, choking and gasping.

A murmur of conversation sprung from the students, at first at a modest level, then more bravely as they compared notes and related the incident.

"It was him," they said, pointing to Neil. "It was all his doing."

"Yeah, he started the whole thing."

"He grabbed Sarah and dragged her away from Abe; he's a rotten apple."

Tobin had heard enough. "Out!" he bellowed at Neil. "Out, out, out! You're never to attend another high school function. Your goofups allow no further consideration. Out!" he repeated red with rage.

"I'm going, I'm going, but I'm not forgetting this." Neil's voice took on the cutting edge of vindictiveness. "I'll get you for this Miereau. I'll get you but good," he veritably hissed." Leaving the building, he turned, shaking his fist at the students who were now crowding to assess the violent situation. "I'll get allaya!"

Abe was shaking. That sonofabitchin' Izcik, he'd get his. He'd see to that, one way or another. Abe only needed time; he'd think of something—right time, right place.

Neil had less than a year to *get alllathem*. He was found drowned in the millpond the next August, the millpond—the forbidden fruit of the town. He drowned in response to a challenge made by a party or parties, unknown to this day.

Drawing Abe aside, Mary Krutina, arms on hips, stood looking up at the height of him, her eyes troubled. "Abe, you need to control that temper. You don't want to worsen Neil's pathetic life. You could have killed him. You need to let go of that anger, just let it go. It's a lesson in taking the high road." Krutina had an uncanny depth perception into young people, profound and understanding. From inside the study hall drifted the sounds of *Pennsylvania 6-5000*. The song had a calming effect on Abe.

"Izcik is headed for a life of nothing, Abe. Don't let the likes of him interfere with the rest of your life." Her eyes traced the darkness of his, which she found now softening.

"I have good news for you," Krutina smiled broadly. "I've been researching your problems with learning-from-reading. Research has uncovered understanding of eidetic memories, photographic, like yours. The Delta County Traveling Library sourced material available for teaching by visual aids. There's a dismally small amount on hand, but they're ordering more from the state library." She paused, eager for him to absorb the impact of what she was offering.

Abe focused on what she was saying, concentrating on her message with searching eye contact—his big hands stuffed into his pants pockets.

"What I propose to do is offer you special tutoring after school for forty-five minutes every day. We'll use visual aids to education so you no longer have to *read* your lessons, but you'll view them in pictures and movies! How would you like that?" She was thumping his chest with her forefinger, thrilled with the possibility of bringing new hope to a learning-handicapped young man. Genuine concern danced in her eyes.

"Whah! Really?" He was comprehending, slowly a new door opening.

"Absolutely."

The smile that played around his mouth tugged at her heart. No one measured life's tribulations and successes the way Abe did.

"There's more. With your talent at creative painting and some personal tutoring, it might be possible to get an art scholarship to the University of Michigan when you graduate in '44. However, it's going to be a long, tough road. Working together, we're going to beat this thing. Work-work-work equals success-success-success for you-you-you." Smiling up at him, her enthusiasm lit up her face.

"You believe in this new technique—in me, in my ability?" Abe was overwhelmed, yet intimidated. His voice grew anxious, husky.

"Always have, Abe. Always have. You need to get back with Sarah. You've been gone far too long. She was sorely shaken by this incident."

When Abe found Sarah, she was being comforted by friends who encircled her with their presence and reassurance. His whole body relaxed at the sight, because all he could recall were the tiny details of each action, each remark, each abuse, until he had exploded out of control.

"String of Pearls" was the seventy-two rpm recording of the moment. Gratefully, he blended into the group, excusing himself and leading Sarah onto the dance floor. At the sight of him, relief ran rampant in her eyes. Compassionate students stood around in groups discussing the seamy attack that had been launched by Izcik.

He breathed her name—"Sarah"—just her name. His emotions ran rampant: regret, anger, embarrassment, love. Without further explanation, he felt her respond. Abe knew her reaction was that of life-long familiarity and trust. "I'm so sorry this happened," he said moving her closer into his arms.

She lifted her eyes to him, fear still reflecting in their depths. He felt the trembling of her slight body as if she were a rabbit caught in an open cornfield. "It's unforgivable that it took me so long to react. After that, it's hard to remember what happened. I'm sorry, Sarah. He's sick." Abe experienced a dichotomy of emotions: his *rage* with Izcik, his *gratefulness* to Mary Krutina.

Snuggling closer, Sarah felt secure once again. Words were difficult, but aloud she said softly, "It wasn't your fault, Abe, Neil was crass and crude. How fortunate you were there. Supposing he had found me alone? What else might he have tried?"

He pressed her tighter around the waist, his head down. "I love you, Sarah," he whispered compassionately, not trusting his voice.

"Abe?"

"Hmmm?"

"I need to tell you something—two somethings." Her voice cleaved hesitant, the words emitting slowly, her face fragile with lines of tension.

"Max is sending me away to Green Bay for my last two years of high school. He told me this afternoon." Her voice caught; her eyes flooded with tears.

"He *what*?" Abe nudged her from him to better study her face.

"Yes. I'll be leaving next August." She drew her mouth in, her chin quivering.

Never had he experienced such a heavy heart. It was a shattering kick in the head, dropping him right out of time and place. What would he do without her? Where would he turn for companionship, his homework? She embodied the very essence of his daily life. As if he were ten years old, his face sagged with vulnerability. How would he finish his last two years of high school without her encouragement?

"My God!" he said, pulling her back to him possessively, his heart thumping into his ears. "Unthinkable," he whispered, his heart stuttering and his mind numb. *You'll make it through, Abe. But how?*

The other thing is difficult to tell you." Sarah searched Abe's eyes.

He went weak in the knees with trauma overflow: the Izcik fight, the Krutina endorsement, and the absence of Sarah next year.

"If you have more news like the last bomb, let's go for a ride so I can handle it in privacy. No one will miss us." Abe felt as lifeless and cold as a chiseled chunk of stone.

After helping to re-align the study hall with chairs, and finding that the projector was humming with *Bride of Frankenstein* winding through, they descended five wide steps to the big double doors on the west side of the school.

The harvest moon shone orange as it threaded its way through the sprawling branches of leafless trees and white pine. Driving out the Nahma Junction Road, Abe took his time. How many times had he dreamed in his breakfast table fantasies of having Sarah in the car with him at night? Possession was a macho thing—driving around with Sarah sitting beside him. It was a man thing, and not boy stuff. Somehow, he felt like a kid again, wanting to impress a girl by popping wheelies on his fenderless bike.

Sarah relaxed in his presence and studied the size of him, his shoulders imposing and magnificent. She saw in him as a grand tree after a fierce storm, renewed and more commendable than ever—saw his chocolate brown eyes, and the way his dark hair grew strongly back from his temples. Her eyes digested his incredulous smile—wide and friendly, as he glanced over at her, saw the softness seized in his eyes. She thrilled at the thought of seeing him at his artist's easel, sitting on a stool in front of it, his tackle box of colors and brushes lying next to him. His long legs stretched out forever. The recollection sped back to her whenever her mind had a moment's inactivity, like a tune that rolls around inside your head repeatedly.

Abe felt again the possessive touch of her hand on his shoulder, his neck when they danced—the gentle, slim fingers. He remembered her warm breasts on his rib cage, her body moving poetically with his. Had she been as excited by touching him?

Sleeping leaves on the road swirled around the car making a rustling, clicking sound. The road was black top, but the moon cast the trees' shadows onto it, making elongated patterns that Abe drove in and out of producing ever-changing Picasso designs.

They'd only been in the car for ten minutes, but already he felt the straining of his pants. Was she frightened? Well, she may be, because he knew he carried a fiend between his legs.

Sarah turned quickly away in an involuntary gesture of quelling the rush of embarrassment that flooded through her—warm, exhilarating and unmistakable.

All there was to know about sex Abe had learned from his friends, who were older. They'd had steady girlfriends for a year already and had explained their intimacies to Abe in a how-to and when-to fashion. It was his turn. He cut a glance over to Sarah, who sat idly looking out the window at the passing moonlit scenery. A mild but gusty wind caught the car as the moon hid briefly behind clouds quickly scuttling toward some clandestine convention.

"Abe, you're my hero." She suddenly brought her hand to her mouth in a squelched gasp. "Every time I think of Neil's hands on my body, his eyes traveling over me, his greedy mouth grinning ..." Her voice trailed off as a shudder covered her body.

"Are you cold, Sarah?" He spoke solicitously. "Let's have a little heat." There was a quivering tenderness in his voice.

"That does feel good. Neil is crazy, absolutely crazy, scary and crazy, scary, dangerous and crazy" she said, her eyes wide.

"He's scary, dangerous, crazy, and a jerk—a badass jerk." It was a stretch to say that to her, but he guessed she could handle it.

"You can add bully to that too." Sarah laughed, feeling secure now.

"Bully, scary, dangerous. . ."

"O-kay!" Sarah fisted him. "Now you're poking fun at me," she said with a pout.

"Not really. I'm trying to make you feel better. You need to tell someone if he *ever* bothers you again—the bastard."

"Abe, you talk such talk!"

"Yeah, I know. What's to say? It's plain English. Now speak plainly to me, and tell me what else is bothering you." He turned toward her, inquisitively, frowning.

"It's hard to share. I never told anyone before." She bit her bottom lip in reluctance. A secret that she held locked away for so many years bereaved her soul and was going to be forthcoming with difficulty.

"You've cracked the door part way. Why close it again?" Abe encouraged, shooting her a kindly glance. He found a grassy parking spot near the river where leaves tumbled in the gentle breeze of the unusually warm night. Tenacious cedars lined the bank of the Sturgeon River, some dipping far out over the water like a nodding acquaintance. He rolled the window down part way. The water tumbling toward its destination with Lake Michigan made happy sounds, like a hundred orphans on a picnic outing. Sparkles danced lightly on the river while a gossamer ground mist gathered mystically in hollows and beneath dew-damp cedars.

"My mind feels like the movie projector at school, winding backwards, backwards. Seems like I can smell the magnetizing perfume of the flowers, the odiferous old man. Well," she preempted, spreading both her hands out, palms up, "it's like this. When I was a little girl, maybe six years old, Max and Ma left me with the Hruska family one weekend while they drove to Milwaukee on business. Through no fault of the Hruskas, I wandered down the street to where Old John Pedo lives. You know the place, over by the hospital, the house with all the pretty flowers and stuff." She hesitated.

Abe, leaning against the car door, stiffened as if he had been assaulted. His blood chilled. *No! Not Sarah. God forbid.* He moved over and put his arm around her shoulder, squeezing it. He closed his eyes. "Sarah," he choked.

"That old man took me into his house promising me a penny, and then he proceeded to pull down my panties and play...between my legs," she said softly, barely letting the words escape, her tone introspective, the memory so poignant as to cause her voice to ache in the telling.

"He didn't!"

"Yes." With the tightness of her small voice, the catch in it, Abe knotted up inside. A hand squeezed his heart. The single word breathed so lightly carved through him like a butcher's knife.

Wordlessly, Abe pulled her to him, pressing her into his chest, stroking her hair. *What a scuzz. He'd get his.* He felt her crying with the telling, crying with the release of telling, soundlessly and brokenheartedly. *He'd string up that bastard.* He couldn't shake the dark image of the dirty old man touching her intimately, something he wanted to do since she was thirteen years old, but he'd never been able to get close to her.

"Sarah, how awful for you," Abe said huskily. He could feel her fierce vulnerability in the telling. "It's all right. It's more than all right. Just close your eyes for a while. You'll see, everything will be all right, all right—all right—all right." His voice a soft whispering sound barely murmured. Silently, she nodded against his big shoulder. He tucked her head against his chest, his large hand encompassing her whole face.

A caressing breeze found the open car window, raising little wisps and tendrils of curls around Sarah's temples. In it was a message of hope, caring and time-passages. The moonlight played in the trees on the far side of the river.

"If it's any comfort to you," he said haltingly, "that same thing happened to me when I was five years old. All this time I've been thinking that maybe the old geezer only liked little boys. I had no idea he was making a heyday of it with any kid in town." Abe released her, looking down into her velvety, glistening eyes. His voice deepened. "You see, you aren't the only one that was molested. God only knows how many kids he touched and fondled with his dirty hands. He obviously has the morals of a vegetable."

Wide-eyed, Sarah reacted with a lurch. "Oh, to think I could have told you a thousand years ago and you'd have understood. It was difficult to speak of it. Can you understand that?" The tears brimmed over in her searching eyes.

Strong and caring, Abe held out his hand. Slowly and insecure as a child, she placed her small hand in his. Abe drew it to his mouth, brushing the back of it with his lips. "Shhh, it's in the past now." He feathered his mouth over her tiny nose, her delicate nose of the purest lines. "You're my girl only, always have been, always will be. Wait and see. You can't let something like that become a nightmare." He kissed her ear, nuzzling her hair and breathing warm breath into it. His fingers soothed her neck. He craved the smell of her, the flavor of her. She was wholesome and well-brought-up and would be his wife someday. He sensed it as if by spirited epiphany from his ancestors.

Demurred, she bent her head.

Cupping her chin in his fist, he turned her face up to him, studying her lethal, eyes, long lashes—the moonlight resting on her profile. His gaze moved to her mouth, her even teeth and sought-after smile. He couldn't hide the look of wanting long repressed, love unrequited.

Slowly, he moved his head down and kissed her lightly on the mouth, nibbling on her lips. She didn't move away, but closed her still-wet eyes for more. *She wanted him.* This was so good. She trusted him. He'd go slowly so he wouldn't frighten her. If she felt gratitude for his protection, that was fodder for his furnace. He loved her so much that he wanted her complete dedication, but he'd accept gratitude.

He moved in on her mouth again, this time more demanding, his kiss quickly becoming passionate, crushing into her teeth. He was nearing seventeen and wanted *his* woman desperately. He salivated profusely, which embarrassed him because it only happened when he was nervous. Could Dr. Whittaker help him? He'd ask sometime.

He left her mouth, nibbled at her ear lobes, licked her ears, feathered her cheeks and her eyes with his kisses and back to her mouth again, coaxing, working it until she opened to him, albeit slightly. Running her fingers through his hair sent electrical shivers through his body with the sensuousness of the trailings. He probed with his tongue, forcing her mouth open more, explored, his tongue darting and investigating. A whimper escaped her throat, setting his libido ablaze. Biting on her bottom lip, he breathed hard, drawing her to him, urgently.

His pulse pounding, his throat hot and dry, he surprised himself with the cool presence of his voice. "Let's get into the back seat where we have more room, Sarah. This is too confining. I can hardly move."

"I'd have to think twice about that, Abe," her tone hesitant. "Everything is running wild in me." Her heartbeat was warm and gliding like a well-oiled engine. *Was that a shake in her voice?* He clearly detected it as he ran his hand caressingly up and down her back, lifting her sweater a little higher with each stroke, letting his big hand ride on the bare skin of her shoulders.

"No, Abe." Her words were soft on his ears. "I don't trust myself. You have me wrapped in such warmth."

He was startled to hear himself say, "Don't tell me 'no,' Sarah. It's time, our time." His hands pulled her sweater over her arms and onto her shoulders. Hungrily, he looked at her slip, the nipples of her breasts proudly exhibited. He kissed them through the garment, finally pushing the straps off her shoulders, revealing the small sixteen-year-old breasts. Hearing the sound of her indrawn breath filled him with need. He felt her breasts, lifting them gently as if they'd break. He wanted more—the taste, the feel of her yielding. His eyes closed with the pleasure she aroused in him.

He needed to slow down, needed to leave her feeling dignified. She knew molestation by that old bastard. He needed to make her feel good about herself.

"Sarah," he expelled a long sigh. "I love you so much that I can't handle it; I need you. I need all of you." He knew that nothing could tear his heart out more than a negative response from her—his woman.

His big hands smoothed under her skirt with purpose, feeling the satin of her thighs, feeling the warmth of her belly, the softness of her nylon panties. He drew her to the length of his hips, pressing his need into her belly. He played with the elastic waistband of her panties, moving it down and kissing her mouth. He'd never been this far before. His strength of purpose was positively potent—powerful.

He could feel her lurch into his hardness now. The heat coursing through her had him trembling with control. He deepened his kiss disallowing her to protest, her half-hearted denials flagging. He could sense it in his male aggression.

Her eyes searched his face. "I can't possibly do this." Her voice caught.

"Yes you can, Sarah. It's terrific, I understand. It'll make you feel filled, warm and committed." His voice was rusty with need, barely getting the words out. "I've wondered what loving you would be like since I was thirteen. He had her panties worked down to her knees where he pulled them to the floorboard in one deft move. She slipped out of her shoes; the panties lay on the floor.

"C'mon Sarah, we'll get into the back seat. I have a condom." He was floating his hand back up her thighs, her bare thighs, felt her pubic hair, fine and lacy.

He unbuckled his belt, unzipped his trousers and pulled them to the floor. Sarah could now see the hardness of him. She looked away, aghast.

He discovered the topography of her body without further courtesies, his aggressiveness the reigning order of the day. This was not gratitude, he realized. Gratitude didn't make her breath catch, didn't give carte blanche to a man, and didn't make her heart beat against his chest.

He shrugged all thoughts of honor or courtesy or patronage. He pressed into her thigh, wanting the whole nine yards.

She reached out tentatively, placing only her thumb and forefinger on him. He stopped breathing. His body went rigid. He gasped, his head thrust back. "Ohhh," he groaned while he spent himself repeatedly, his whole body convulsing.

Sarah stared in disbelief and ultimate shock. "I didn't mean to…I don't know what I did wrong, Abe." She stammered apologetically, her voice catching.

"*I'm sorry*, Sarah." He didn't want to look at her. "I'm so embarrassed." He reached for his handkerchief from his trouser pocket. "You didn't do *anything* wrong. I ran at 'Hi' cook for too long." She had promised to consider doing this more than a year ago—forever to him. He'd lain in bed thinking about her in this situation, and it was all over before he got started. He needed to take it slower and not scare the hell out of her.

"It was good, Abe. I felt good. I've never felt like that." She'd lifted her hand to the back of his neck, massaging.

"It'll be better next time, little lady. I promise," he drawled like John Wayne, a grin in progress across his face with her favorable comment.

The next time—the next time? No. She shook her head. She couldn't. The price would be too high, far too high.

Returning a small smile, Abe realized her eyes were still wide with the revelation of him. He withered as she lowered her lashes, turning her head to look out the window.

Maybe…someday.

CHAPTER THREE

The memories he'd just revived should have been long dead; however, they surfaced with the thought of the abuses doled out by the village pedophile. He knew he needed to stuff them or they'd walk with him the rest of his life. Abe anticipated vengeance with all the eagerness of Joshua exploiting Jericho.

Spending the morning cleaning Fabian's bedroom, he made a dozen trips up and down the stairs to move his personal belongings into his new bedroom off the living room. Tackling the bathroom, only Abe's favorite towels remained. Out with the old, in with the new. Only the breath of essence-of-Abe remained.

The rain had let up and the sky had lightened in the west. A growl arose from deep within his throat with the thought of what he planned for Pedo. He was undefeatable today—a Crusader, his strength at full tide.

Whatever the cost, all the window coverings were going to the dry cleaners. Quick work was made of placing rag carpets onto the line after running them through the Maytag. Furniture flinched as he soared over it with the hand vacuum and sudsed down Fabian's favorite chair. After wet mopping, he found he had cornered himself in the kitchen, but felt like an anointed one and not an orphan. Last night, as dark as coal, he had looked like *The Last Judgment*. This morning he looked like *The Creation*—marked by careful calculation and filled with personal pride.

"How about a cup of coffee, Abe?" he said aloud. "Don't mind if I do, thank you," he chortled. Maybe he was cracking up, living alone. One thing he knew, he wasn't cracking up about Old John. As the day grew around him, he stood leaning against the cupboard staring at his cup that was steaming with invigoration, enjoying the quietude to dream—scheme. The desire for retaliation waxed insistent and primal.

After lunch he sought his biology text and studied the human nervous system. Abe was acutely aware that this class was giving him trouble, even *with* tutoring by Krutina. He riffled through the pages as he gathered his thoughts. The Old John Pedo get-even scheme could even be better than he had first thought.

The nervous structure of the earthworm consists of a main nerve cord, which acts as a primitive brain.

Yeah, sure. A worm brain must be the relic on which Old John ran, the scum.

In homo sapiens, twelve pair of nerves emerges from the brain; the tenth, or vagus nerve, affects muscles found in the walls of the trachea, stomach, and intestine.

Abe wondered if he could find Pedo's vagus nerve, fool around with his trachea, and force him to swallow his tongue.

Neuron cells are a receiving and transmitting unit capable of transferring information from one part of the body to the other.

Yeah, well. Abe would see to it that Old John's neurons acted highly efficiently. He'd transfer *lots* of information from one part of his body to another.

Each nerve cell consists of axons and dendrites. Dendrites are short extensions of the cell body and are receivers of stimuli. Axons, by contrast, are transmitters of nerve impulses to other cells.

Abe pondered if he might stimulate Sarah's dendrites and axons to the point where she could be seduced. He'd not known there was a pathway.

Free nerve endings are sensitive to pain and are directly activated, such as fingers and toes.

Maybe that's why Fabian said his nerves were right at the ends of his fingers.

Actions of the neurons of interconnected nerve cells are stimulated at one end and bring about glandular secretion at the other end.

Abe wondered if he kissed Sarah on the ears, the lips, and the neck, would she get glandular secretions where he needed them?

The sympathetic and the parasympathetic systems control the functions of the respiratory, circulatory, digestive, and urogenital systems.

Abe figured if he stimulated Sarah's lower back and abdomen, maybe he could arouse her like the women in Fabian's girly magazines.

With biology tedium settling in, Abe easily turned his thoughts to more exciting challenges. Studying was getting to be a pain in the ass.

Upon sunset, Abe glanced at this watch and then excitedly rose to his feet. His eyes grew hard. Wrinkles rippled back into his dark hairline, skin pulled tightly over his high cheekbones. He headed out to the car tossing the keys into the air and catching them. The picture Farley imaged for him of the Sioux

Indian braves ritualistically thrumming around the Sun Dance tree sapling with their chest flesh tethered to the trunk, swept back to him. Rituals and rites, who could say they were out of line? Different times, different rhymes. Perhaps patterns of hereditary predispositions were made of iron ore, deeply buried and minable.

Abe had found several pairs of rawhide shoelaces in Fabian's closet and slipped them into his jeans pocket. Together, the laces were easily fifteen feet long. He acknowledged that he had turned savage himself to think of this. Maybe it was his genetic role in life.

Acceptance or rejection didn't make much difference to him anymore. He answered only to himself. The worst thing that could happen was to fall flat on his ass. The choice was there—sometimes easy, sometimes decidedly difficult. For Abe it was "no contest." "Power grows from knowledge and strength," Fabian had told him repeatedly. He was imbued with strength; knowledge he was gaining.

The night throbbed with a chorus of frogs in nearby sloughs, but he scantly heard. The moon puffed orange, but he scantly saw. Head at slant, footsteps robotic, he made his way through the breathingnight.

Arriving at Old John Pedo's house, he parked in the alley. Troublesome thoughts struggled to germinate. Did he really want to do this? Was it worth the price he might have to pay? He didn't need the confusion of second-guessing.

For the first time since he'd been defiled as a child, he opened the garden gate he had once passed through so innocently, as did Sarah. He opened it quietly, with amazing calm. Silent leather hinges held the gate to the fence post.

Did he care if he made noise? *Not this kid.* The time had come for him to assert his heritage and take care of himself. Perhaps for some it was just not possible, but for him, the plot posed sizzlin' hot.

Walking down the yet-rotting planks of the wooden sidewalk, he felt the muscles rippling in his neck, his shoulders. It was past dusk, and a sallow flow of light filtered into the back entrance from the misty kitchen window. Hell, the window is sick—suckin' dirty, as dirty as the old troll who lived here. Bam! Bam! Abe's fist pounded on the door.

Pedo appeared, scraggly eyebrows angling, cloudy eyes intent and glistening. Here was the snake pit of the earth, the stench of all cesspools. Abe studied the gears turning in the old man's eyes. Bitterness boiled within him.

The two men stood, their eyes locked. By perception, Abe's strength and message of hatred permeated them. If Abe hadn't seen Old Pedo in a hundred years, he'd have recognized him—square jaw working, saliva dripping, bulbous nose prominent and vacant eyes staring. Retribution roared through Abe's veins—savagery in the inception. He broke through the Whiteman's barriers that denied him his Sioux heritage.

In an artful move doing justice to a ballet star, Abe stepped into the house, closed the door, grabbed Old John by the throat, and thrust him bodily against the wall on the other side of the room as if he was a partner in some kind of macabre dance. The man shrieked and kicked like a stuck pig at butchering time; his face purple.

"Shitbag!" Abe groaned, hardly recognizing his own voice, genderless as if some strange entity had invaded his body. If his great grandfather, Crazy Horse, practiced far left in his culture, Abe was farther.

The smell of the place was like a bear's den. Early spring flies crawled out of the woodwork and buzzed around a black iron skillet on a stove that created nightmares in its own right. The sink was molded, a stinking tar pit. Musty cooking odors hung heavily in the air...something rotten in the cupboards. The mixture swirled in his nostrils, tasted in his throat. Abe gagged.

"You kick me one more time and I'll punch out your lights permanently, you rotten letch! Remember me? I'm the little kid whose balls you twaddled twelve years ago." With that, Abe hammered him in the jaw, causing his head to loll against his shoulder. Slowly, Pedo slid down the wall into a heap on the floor.

With lightning speed, Abe whipped out his jackknife and opened it. Exhibiting the deftness of a surgeon, he cut two short side-by-side slices in the flesh of Old John's upper chest. Slipping the rawhide through the incisions, he tied a knot. The remaining length he circled around his hand and stuffed into Old John's front pant pocket for later reference.

He pulled another length of rawhide from his pocket in readiness for the second operation. With adroitness born of reprisal he jabbed a hole through the soft flesh at the ends of both thumbs and forefingers, pulling a stretch of rawhide through them, tying Old John's hands behind him.

Nerve ends, nerve ends, nerve ends. "In the history of human culture, there perhaps have never been greater devious tortures devised than that of the Tribal Sioux." Farley's words echoed in his ears.

Abe cut off with a snap the excess length of rawhide from Old John's tied hands. With a cruelness born of diablo genetics, he loaded the old geezer onto his shoulder, hefted him out to the car and dropped him onto the floor in the backseat like a newly purchased sack of seed. Whistling, he backed the car out of the alley.

Behind the giant blue spruce in Farnsworth Boulevard, Abe parked the car carrying his stinking cargo, laid him on the ground near the flagpole and removed the rawhide from Pedo's pants pocket. Tying the rawhide to the flagpole, he re-fastened the other end securely to his chest flesh. Old John had two to three yards of freedom before he tore a chunk of chest flesh, and could not loosen his hands unless he tore off his skin.

Aware that he'd never be the same again, Abe couldn't stop, driven by some fury deep within his soul. The elemental steering mechanism of some adults like Pedo never ceased to amaze Abe, so if someone must mete out punishment, why not himself?

He stood over the pitiful pile of humanity at his feet, plying his brain as to whether he wanted to go through with the rest of his plan—to kill him.

Suddenly, very low in the west, he saw that iridescent light again, dazzling, galvanizing, creeping as if it were some ground fog, lighted from within. He tore his glance from Old John and concentrated on the strange phenomenon.

"Abe." A strong reverberating voice resounded, in command.

"Yes." Barely a whisper.

Slowly materializing before him was a handsome wholesome image of Fabian, the light of centuries and wisdom in his eyes.

"You need not kill him," he said, his tone that of thunder. "Much is planned for your future." He possessed an openness and honesty that shown wax-like through his very countenance, brilliant beyond description. His eyes pierced like lightning, wide and gravely sober. "Take greater cautions with your life, Abe," he admonished as the entity of him faded back into the last ribbons of sunset, his golden luminescence growing dim until it was gone. Abe stood staring after the illusion until it was a mere pinpoint. Did he really see and hear this? Was he losing his mind? Did he have a brain lapse?

Looking down, he kicked Old John in the foot and moved away without remorse, then spun around and walked back, hunkered down, and slit the end of Old John's tongue with his jackknife. As if poetic ballast, the warm April evening wafted sweet smells of forsythia, daffodils and hyacinth.

Mechanically, he drove home, numb. Home—all re-arranged for his new life except for the kitchen and the loft, and he promised himself he'd do that tomorrow.

Maybe things *were* looking up. He had needed to pay back Pedo. He owed it to himself. Now, however, he really had to stay in control, get a grip, and stop dreaming of bright lights and apparitions. They were just that, fantasies.

He hoped that it wouldn't rain tonight and loosen the rawhide tied to Old

John's body. He laughed to himself, his chest convulsing, making small sounds that reflected his heartbeat—stuttering sounds. He should've stuck his jackknife into Old John's neck, but that would have been too easy for him, too quick. Besides, there was the appearance of Fabian. Was he going whacko? *Naah*, he shooed his hand. He had simply suffered too many sorrows and had hallucinated.

Death would have been too fast for that old reprobate anyway. He needed to suffer as Sarah and he had suffered for years. He knew Clyde Tobin would find Old John early in the morning when he checked the doors of the company store and raised the flag before he went to eight o'clock mass. One thing Abe knew, he wasn't going to be playing with any kids' genitals from now on. Nor would he be able to tell anyone what happened to him or who was the culprit. Pedo knocked out cold, his tongue slit, Abe might as well have been the headless horseman!

He chuckled at the ingeniousness of his scheme. He could still see Old John in the dark under the flagpole, his eyes shocked as if he'd been heavy on drugs. His pain would be his existence overnight, and a punishment for the rest of his life. Best he hadn't killed him. Fabian was right.

Maybe he should go back and torch that shack in which Old John lived. Why hadn't he thought of that? He could still hear himself laughing during the whole thing, as if it was someone else and not him at all. *Again*, he wondered if he was losing his mind, doing something so outrageous. Fabian would have chewed his ass.

Fabian!

Naah. *Oh yes, Fabian unquestionably would have done that.*

But didn't it disturb him at all, in retrospect?

Naah.

Still and all...naah!

For a few moments after he arrived home, Abe scanned the new arrangements and the freshly scrubbed look of the place. He pulled off his shirt while walking to the shower, and noticed for the first time the wetness of it—*blood,* and his trousers trailed with *blood.* His shoes revealed spatters. He had to wipe down the car tomorrow.

The shower spray soothed as the warmth washed away his involvement with the old man. He was a free man, free to make his own decisions and to carve his future on purely his merits. The reality of it filtered into his mind, filling him with want, desire, a chin-setting aggressiveness. No one was ever going to hang him out to dry again. The little wheels cogged with the big wheels in his mind and kept clicking forward.

He recalled the quote from Thomas Jefferson, third President of the United States: "The most valuable of all talents is that of never using two words when one will do." Abe wondered what Mr. Jefferson would think of the value of using *no* words when actions would suffice. He smiled with vengeance and felt the purge of the actions of the past few hours; they dribbled down the drain with the shower water.

In the distance, the Nahma Northern locomotive lost speed as its whistle sounded, then sighed into silence upon entering town and crossing the Indian Town Road. The sound hung forever on the heavy damp air, finding its way into every nook and cranny in town then died a slow death just as Old John moaned while leaching life.

Over the next few weeks he would accept and reject many times the fact that he had carved on that old man, but he was washed clean of the past. A hornet's nest of savagery had been building inside him. His early childhood violation by Old John, the tormenting cruelty of kids, and his father's recent death had all been ordnance stored away to serve as artillery on that bleak early April night.

A new day dawned as bright and brisk as the previous day had been gloomy. Abe was out of bed early, his mind on washing the car. The tailings of Old John's demise stained the car but not Abe's mind. Old John *needed confinement*, preferably somewhere that had therapy and shock treatments.

His hand slipped into his jeans pocket, his fingertips floundering over the leftover strip of rawhide, remembering the shock quality of Old John's eyes. It was *his* time at bat, he reminded himself as he turned the hose on the car, wiping it down in wide arcs.

Abe found that he needed a brush to remove the bloodstains from the car seat.

Why hadn't he thought of covering them? Did he have to be told everything? He'd spent the last seventeen years of his life with few directions. He'd lived in a kaleidoscope kingdom with changing patterns and scenes, constantly doubting himself.

He scrubbed the floor mats harder—leaving them to dry over the split-rail fence. The water thrummed at the hollow door panels, the sound receding as he splattered a sharp spray of water across the windshield. Splashed wet with hose water, Abe admitted that while flowing down the stream of life, he'd tumbled over boulders. Like the early June evening when twilight lasted forever and he was eleven years old sitting on the top step of the front porch. Thoughts of a mother he'd never known tormented his mind, blowing through it like the bent trees in the woods. From the lake came the boisterous sound of screeching gulls. He turned his mind and eyes to Fabian.

"All the other kids have a ma *and* a dad but me. Why did Ma disappear?" Abe asked struggling to find the right words. He saw his father's eyes narrow.

Fabian sat in an old cane rocking chair peeling an apple in a perfect circle with his jackknife. Silently, Fabian ate the circle as well as the apple, seeming not to hear, his head bent, his posture stooped. Abe turned farther around in askance.

"I knew I'd have to explain this to you some day. The past eleven years have slipped through my hands like water running from a tap." Fabian sighed long, leaning back in the rocker, eyes searching the rosy sunset as if he could find an answer there. "I've questioned myself about how much I can tell you." Having finished his apple, he paused for breathing space, smiling dryly down at his clutching hands.

"Well, son, your mother chose to leave us when you weren't yet a year old." Fabian shifted uneasily, his shoulders hunching and flexing, his chin worrying his collar. "She never came back, never *asked* to come back. Even yet, it hurts like hell," Fabian reflected with a frown, his voice catching. "She's full-blooded Sioux Indian—there's a bit of nomad in those people. She left a mighty fine boy, however. I want you to remember that." His words wound down to soft syllables.

Abe had read the love in Fabian's eyes, making him feel like a prince. Thick silence hung in the air while he stared at him with great recording eyes, the tally sheet between his ears sucking hard. Although revitalized with Fabian's love, a tiny doubt took seed. Maybe his mother hadn't liked *him*, and that's why she left.

Leaning forward on the porch chair, Fabian whispered, "I think you're the best thing that ever came into my life." Reaching out, he ruffled Abe's hair. "I realize that the years have disappeared one by one since you were a child and uninformed. What's more, you need to know that I'm growing slower in mobility every day. Thank God that Dr. Whittaker comes to the house once a week."

Fabian had leaned far back in the chair, closing his eyes, changing the conversation. "Since Roosevelt introduced the Social Security Act in '34, it has shown great progress for retirees. There is talk of including Americans with disabilities and dependents, too. It'll provide for you, too, Abe, if anything shortens Fabian Miereau's life before you're eighteen years old or as long as you're a student."

Abe shifted his feet uncomfortably, not accustomed to handling the overload of death and dying. Turning his head back to the trees, he realized that many things bothered him. He wondered if his brain was in his head, or if it was in his ass like the kids teased.

No! No! Then maybe, maybe, there is such a thing as brains in the ass. Was that everything? Brains? Doesn't being big and strong mean anything? Moreover, how about the pretty pictures he painted when Max allowed him to use a canvas and some oils?

Abe was aware that the kids snickered at him in class, calling him "the class dummy," the words hurting and grating on his ears. He had trouble recognizing words because he couldn't figure out the sounds. Then he didn't understand and remember what he had read! Sometimes he just wanted to laugh and laugh, but didn't know why.

He realized that even when he knew the right answers it was difficult to find the exact words quickly. As if that wasn't bad enough, they wanted him to write his ideas down on paper. How could he spell a word when he couldn't figure out the sound?

He'd always been able to solve problems on the chalkboard, however. His head dropped in small pride. Things he could see, he could solve. Things he could see he could paint, sketch and draw.

Embarrassment hung heavily when at thirteen years old he was kept back in seventh grade for a repeat year. He veritably trudged to school through the sawdust alley with Sarah and his neighbor Betty Hebert, his shoulders scrunched up forcing every step.

Sarah was conciliatory. "It's okay, Abe. Now you're in the same grade as I am. I can help with your homework too!" Her dark eyes swam with silent messages.

"I didn't fit into those desks last year, what am I going to do now that I'm five feet seven and weigh more than last year? I balanced the desk on my knees then!"

"We have a different homeroom teacher this year for seventh grade—Mr. Bramer. Maybe he can do something about your desk." Her gaze was full on him, a smile playing at the edges of her mouth. Nonetheless, Abe fed himself no fantasies about how well he'd do that year as opposed to the year before. School was just plain difficult.

~~

Lou Bramer, a tall, kindly, robust-looking, brown-eyed teacher intelligentsia, paused for effect. "The first known Township Government in Nahma was in the year 1862. At that time, Nahma Township comprised about four times as much territory as it does today. In the year 1863, ten townships, each six miles square, were given to the Village of Garden."

Abe gazed out the window. The trees in the boulevard were a showpiece of green to gold, from red to rust, some lazily taking their last flight from the trees. His focusing abilities vanished in a blink, and his thoughts scattered like the falling leaves.

"In the year 1868, a county road was built through Nahma at one hundred dollars per mile and finished within a year. The following year, the State Highway Department ordered built through Nahma Township a road, now known as Highway U.S.-2."

Abe flirted with fantasies of the magazines he'd found under Fabian's mattress. He wondered if Sarah would ever look like that. He got a hard knot in his stomach when he thought about her—she made his heart hammer.

"There was a Sioux Indian Tribal Council Trail that began near Munising and for the most part followed the Sturgeon River." Lou Bramer pointed to the pull-down map of the Upper Peninsula now hanging over the chalkboard. "The trail ran to the Tribal Council here in Nahma on the west side of the Sturgeon River."

A sudden gust of autumn wind rattled the windows while Abe mulled over his feelings toward Sarah. They were new and wonderful. She was changing.

"Forest products are Nahma's most important asset, just as they were when the town was founded fifty-seven years ago. The word 'Nahma' means sturgeon and the town named after the Sturgeon River that empties into the bay here." Lou Bramer moved away from the map and perched on the corner of his desk.

Abe shut out the information with thoughts of last summer. Sarah had gone into the beech woods to change out of her bathing suit, and Neil Izcik, Buster Tobin and Owen Menary hid in the bushes to peep at her. He ached for her embarrassment as she told him the sordid story. He wanted to kill them. No one peeped at his Sarah.

"In 1881, George Farnsworth and his associates acquired timber lands in Delta and surrounding counties and decided to build a mill here, a desirable spot because of its location on the river and at the head of the bay. The Indian Point Sioux, Menominee and Chippewa were very instrumental in starting the mill and making a success of the endeavor. The Red Man traveled miles in search of food and clothing materials, either on foot or in open Mackinaw boats. These boats were of an unusual type, long, very fast, and seaworthy when properly handled, and the Indian was an expert boatman.

"The Bay de Nocquet Lumber Company yet employs residents of a small Indian village across the river from Nahma. Their chief vocation is piling lumber and loading the lumber boats, which frequently visit the town in the summer months."

Abe hung on seeing the unholy "Sarah Peepers," snickering, poking each other, proud of their prowess. Rage riveted him as he reflected. Sarah's heart turned broken, her shoulders shaking, releasing a torrent of tears. Abe, in a thrust of energy, lunged at the three boys and he sent them toppling like dominoes when he picked them up one at time and slugged them. No one, but no one touched *his* Sarah, not even with their eyes.

"In those early days of 1882, Nahma was a typical lumber town with typical lumberjacks which one so often reads about. The trees saw cutting in the winter, landed on the banks of the river, and drove down to the mill as soon as the ice went out.

The log drive was one of the most dangerous of all lumbering operations. A real man's job it was with every minute full of thrills, danger and hard work with hours that knew no sunup or sundown. But gone are those days, gone is the timber and gone are the happy-go-lucky, carefree 'River Hogs,' a race of men we'll see no more."

Rain carried by the fretful north wind spackled at the windows, but it stayed cozy within the classroom. Abe, seated in the back, raised his entire desk off the floor with the sheer size of him. His thoughts were in free-fall as he dreamed vigorously of owning a pocketknife—a jackknife. He had seen some dandies at the Company Store. The thought spun a punch in the stomach.

"When the first of the drive reached the mill ponds, it was the signal to start making lumber. In the early summer of 1899 when the mill revitalized after damages of a fire, the season's supply of lumber sold in advance with a specified time of delivery. A penalty for delay followed with no fire clause in the contract. And, yes, the mill was struck by lightning and totally destroyed." Lou Bramer paused, testing for attention span.

"There was no time to buy a new mill and deliver the lumber within the contracted time and not to do so would entail a big financial loss in penalty. Fortunately, for the company, they were able to buy a mill at South Manistique. It was set up in record time to cut their season's supply of logs with but little delay."

Abe chewed on the fact that Fabian wouldn't allow him to have a jackknife yet, because he was too young. We-elll, he was both old enough and big enough to wear men's boots with a special pocket for carrying one. A mischievous smile crossed his face.

"In 1887 the present Soo Line Railroad was built through from Gladstone, putting in a station at Nahma Junction, five miles north of Nahma. This allowed for shipment by rail as well as water. The Bay de Nocquet Lumber Company decided to log by rail and started construction on their own logging railroad to be known as the Nahma & Northern." Bramer walked around the room, checking the windows against the onslaught of the maverick fall storm. "The company now operates about 65 miles of track and markets a large part of its mill and forest products by rail."

Abe pondered the enchantment of the jackknife. He couldn't remember when he'd wanted something so badly. Maybe, he thought...after school. Things would never be the same again without owning one.

"With the change from river to rail logging, logs could be delivered at the mill all year around. This gave steady employment both in the woods and in town for a large crew, the payroll averaging 800 men.

"On the evening of October 5, 1923, the night watchman discovered fire in the front of the mill and in a few minutes, the whole mill was a mass of flames. The volunteer fire department kept the lumberyards from burning too. This was one of a series of fires, which have continually hampered Nahma. In 1921, nearly the whole town burned to the ground and twice, the Club House has been destroyed by fire."

Abe considered the jackknives displayed in cases at the company store, near the hunting and fishing supplies. The company store had lots of 'em. They wouldn't miss one lousy jackknife. Wouldn't Sarah think him grownup to have a jackknife in his boot holder—the one with the metal snap on it? He passed the palm of his hand straight back over his hair, tasting the triumph of such a possession.

"The new mill which was begun immediately after the destruction of the other in 1923 is still operating. It runs entirely by electricity. The Nahma mill is one of the most modern plants in this section of the country. In addition to the lumber mill, there is a shingle mill and a lath and wood mill under the same roof. There is also a planing mill with the most modern equipment and completely separate boiler and engine houses.

"To accommodate shipping of the lumber by boat, the company built seven docks with a capacity of over twenty five million feet of lumber. With a requirement of ten thousand board feet of lumber for an average three bedroom home, that's enough lumber on hand to build twenty-five hundred homes." Bramer paused to let that staggering number sink in. "Since then, the Bay de

Nocquet Lumber Company has settled that much more yard space exclusively for rail shipment."

Yes sir, by tomorrow, he'd have a new jackknife.

"You're all aware that the town includes a company office, general store, post office, hotel, boarding house, hospital, community building, barber shop, garage, and one hundred and ten comfortable homes, all with such modern improvements as running water and electric lights. There is also a K-12 school, in which you're all sitting. A golf course and tennis courts added to Nahma's recreational facilities, and on the hard beach sand, an airport sits equipped with hangar and all modern facilities."

The dismissal bell rang. Done at last! The class made a move en masse to leave.

"Hold it just one minute everyone." Bramer shot a lead ball across the bow, his voice loaded. "Mr. Miereau, just what did you get out of the history lesson today?" His tone hummed with hidden meaning as insidious as the soft shining cocoon of the banana spider. Abe found himself in a clutch to remember.

Abe's eyes fell on the map. Relief flooded him. "I found interest in that Indian trail. I could draw you a detailed enlargement of that area." *Click!* His eyes glittered with mischief, darting from east to west at the other kids, looking for comedic relief.

He got it. Snuffled laughs and giggles ensued.

"All right. Let's see it on my desk tomorrow morning and no later." Bramer's index finger thrummed the desk, his irritation covered with a thin veneer of courtesy.

He'd be busy tonight. He'd have to forget the jackknife—for now.

CHAPTER FOUR

Abe shook his head in disbelief at the nincompoop experience of seventh grade. A shudder pinked its way up his back while he completed cleaning the car. His mouth was tight with the knowledge of how important this car was and how poorly he managed to survive. His stomach was pinched with the uncertainty of what the future held in store. One truth struck Abe—he knew he wasn't a Whiteman. He'd need to make his own breaks. Uh-huh.

For now, he promised himself to clean the kitchen and loft today. A new life beckoned him. Head up and shoulders squared, he remembered that he had nurtured one cranky kid that January of '39. The second semester had started, his birthday and Christmas had come and gone, and still no jackknife.

The next day at school, Abe had a shiny new jackknife in the pocket of his high top leather boots. His memories strayed to the pride he felt in the knife, one with a steel shield emblazoned on the side and boasting two blades, a big one, and a small one.

Within the next few days the school experienced a rash of carvings on the outside of the building, on Abe's desk, and in the boys' bathroom where one of the metal doors now read "School Stinks." Also, Homer Beauchamp, custodian and bus driver, reported that someone had carved up the side of one of the buses.

Lou Bramer observed how Abe repeatedly snapped the leather strap attached to his boot knife-pocket. Resultantly, Abe appeared at the superintendent's office. He sat facing Bernard Tobin, whose back was cast to a large mullioned window, placing his face in a shadow, while the light shined directly into Abe's eyes. Blinking, Abe felt a clammy chill—could feel his stomach freezing over to ice.

Bernard Tobin wasn't a tall man and tended toward being pudgy with coloring high enough to earn the nickname of "Pinkie" among the students.

His fingers and hands, of a size to fit his smaller stature were plump and neatly manicured. The eyes fixed on Abe were hard marble-blue, assessing. He wore a medium blue suit, white shirt, and a navy and white tie. Folding his hands on top of the desk and exhibiting a fragile smile, Bernard Tobin plunged right in. "Okay, Abe. Now let's find the underlying cause of the defacing going on in the school. Do you have a jackknife?"

Abe shook his head.

Bernard picked up a rubber band and stretched it between his two hands. "Have you ever had a jackknife?"

Abe again shook his head.

Bernard steepled both hands, encircled by the rubber band, to his chin. "Have you used someone else's jackknife and carved up the school?"

Abe, silent to the end, again shook his head. He figured that by now his nose had grown ten inches long and his hair stood at attention in scary peaks.

All Bernard Tobin could hear was the biblical cock crow thrice. "Your 'no' neurons are hard-wired today, Abe. If I take a look in your boot, do you think that I might find a jackknife?"

Abe's heart stopped dead, then started racing in place like his old bike on ice. His head shook back and forth, his long black ponytail whipping from side to side.

Bernard arose from his chair and studiedly walked around the desk, stooped, found and retrieved the jackknife from Abe's boot. Standing in front of him, he flipped the knife from one hand to the other.

"Where'd you get it?"

Abe wept, his head down, his hands folded between his knees.

"From the Company Store?"

Abe nodded, couldn't look up.

"You stole it?" His voice settled as soft as a confessor's.

Abe nodded again, his head still lowered—tears running down his face.

"Okay young man, we're going to the Company Store." His eyes revealed no disgust, just the acquiescence to multiple experiences such as this with maturing students. As an educator and counselor, he often walked on thin ice with a young man's future. In this case, a strange young man—one for whom he felt compassion and detected an element of potential.

Upon arrival at the store, Abe was marched into the office of Clyde Tobin, store manager and Bernard Tobin's brother. Again, just as he had been the center of confrontation in the Candy Kitchen as a child, he was the focus of the gossiping rumor mill of the All-American Company store.

Clyde looked up from invoices as if he were withdrawing from another world. A green transparent visor enhanced the same blue eyes that Abe had felt in the inquisition with Bernard. Clyde was not as rotund as Bernard was, but carried the same power.

"You know, Abe, sit down...sit down," he said. "You need to understand that when you steal from the store, you steal from everyone—the store, the company and the people in this town. When you reduce inventory through theft, you interfere with everyone's life-style. Don't you agree?"

"Yes," Abe breathed out, barely perceptible, his forefingers making small invisible rings around and around on his knees.

"Do you also understand that this is very risky behavior?" Clyde never raised his voice, twisting Abe's stomach into a prize-winning square knot.

"Yes," Abe sighed, head still down.

"Losses such as this pass on to the consumer. Did you know that?"

Abe shook his head so hard that tears flew off his cheeks with the effort.

"I want you to come here every day after school and work until you pay twice the price of the jackknife, which I'll hold here." He ticked the points off on his fingers. "You'll stock shelves, clean and sort produce, and unload shipping trucks." His tone was one of dismissal.

For an endless month, Abe worked for one and a half hours after school, walking home in the dark with blowing snow and cold his companion for the long mile and a half out to Old Beach Road. Warm lights showed from frosty windows of homes. With the last misty streetlight left behind, Abe trundled through the shadows of gnarled winter oaks, towering white pine, and the ever-present lonely wind pushing at his back.

Sometimes he knew tasking to shovel snow from the steps of the Company Hotel. He remembered how happy he was when the temperature warmed up to ten degrees below zero. How the snow squeaked under his boots, his boots that never really kept his feet warm when it was that cold. Tantalizing aromas of rich roast beef, honey-baked ham, and aromatic fried chicken greeted him through the opening of the double doors of the Company Hotel. For the last few years it had seemed like he was hungry all the time.

Finishing the job for the day, Abe huddled inside his jacket and headed for home dreaming of a hot dinner with Fabian. All about him fell the never-ending snow garnished with the ghostly shadows of the dark pines. Turned out, Fabian served stewed chicken and green peas on baking powder biscuits relieving Abe's endless penance.

Upon completion of his obligation at the Company Store, he received instruction from Bernard Tobin to redeem the error of his ways by sanding down his desk top and re-varnishing it. The boys' restroom door had already seen remedy by Homer Beauchamp.

The school bus had to be professionally painted. Abe again felt stomach flutters when Bernard sermonized. "Just you count your lucky stars that I don't soak you the price of re-painting that school bus, mister. Remember that!" Tobin's pointing finger was unrelenting—his office the scene of another one-on-one with Abe.

Motioning for Abe to sit down in the hot seat, Bernard eased himself into his judgment chair. The wan February light assailed him with a silhouette of saintly proportions. Driven snowflakes landed on the panes of the mullioned windows and slowly slid down as they melted. Leaning back, his arms resting on the chair sides, he locked onto Abe's eyes. "So far, you haven't shown me what I want to see in a young man, and that's a mirror of America: optimistic, happy, hard-working and honest."

Pausing for a minute, he went on, leaning forward on his desk. "You can *be* that, Abe. Don't pursue dead-end endeavors. They're anchors, and you can't move forward dragging an anchor. Instead, you need to be a shining example of accomplishment. I have complete faith in you."

"You do?" Abe's slow drawl revealed the wonder he felt at the offer. He nodded affirmatively as Bernard leaned over the desk and shook his hand.

Abe walked away taller, ingesting the encouraging words, realizing that Tobin had offered him a buffer zone between his shortfalls and the endless advantages of school. He'd never steal or lie again, ever.

❧

Coming back to the here and now, Abe removed the cupboard contents and washed all the shelves. Grateful that childhood days lay behind him, he suddenly closed his eyes and leaned his forehead against the counter, grief overcoming him in a surge of remembering the good times he'd shared with Fabian, the only person in his life who had nurtured and loved him no matter what he did.

"You're going to have to learn to drive the car, Abe. It's getting more difficult for me to get around, sometimes almost impossible."

Abe's eyes flashed wide, remembering.

"Today you learn to drive!" He envisioned the scene as if it were a vapor winding through his mind's paths. Only fourteen years old, and he'd be driving the family car.

Chomping at the bit like an Iditarod lead dog too long in the kennel, he'd coaxed him. "Whaddaya say, Dad? Let's get going. Time's a-wastin.' Let's go, let's go, let's go!" he said excitedly, flouncing around the kitchen feigning shadowboxing punches.

"You don't just jump into a car and become an Indy 500 race-car driver," Fabian snorted, snapping his fingers. "First you'll have to learn to back the car from the driveway. With your height, however, you'll have good command of the shifts, the rearview mirror, and the steering wheel."

Fabian stepped with care down the three steps of the back porch to the vehicle that was parked near the kitchen entrance. "Now all I need to do is get my skinny old ass into that passenger seat," he said while chucklng.

The late spring sunshine was warm on Abe's head, and the breeze from the copse of hardwoods across Old Beech Road filled with spring scents of new shoots and ripening woodland. "Okay, Dad, I'm ready," Abe said with undisguised exuberance.

Fabian viewed Abe sitting behind the steering wheel. "Abe, you're as good as a grown man. I trust your responsibility to drive this vehicle, but you aren't ready to join the Indianapolis 500 yet, so pay attention."

"All right," Abe agreed, eagerness emanating from every pore.

"See those two foot pedals?"

"Yeah, I know. I watch you all the time, Dad." Abe swallowed tension.

"Well, okay. The left one is the clutch. Push that in with your left foot. Now step on the brake with your right foot—that's the pedal next to the clutch."

"All right!" A giddy giggle escaped Abe's throat, neither a laugh nor a whimper.

"Over to the left of the steering column is the starter button. Push that."

The motor made an *eeerch, eeerch, eeerch* sound then turned over. Abe's eyes brightened, his back struck rigid, and both hands grasped the steering wheel.

Fabian shook his head. "Don't go into that bubble again, Abe."

"It's okay. I'm here. Don't be afraid. I'll do it!"

Fabian's scrutiny swept him, detecting the cloud-nine quality in Abe's eyes. "Now you know where the shift knob is. See it?" Fabian pointed with enouragment. "You see the pictue on the knob that looks like an *'H'*?"

"Okay, I see it."

"The top of the *'H'* on the left is reverse. The bottom on the left is first gear. The top on the right is second gear, and the bottom right is high. You must take it through all the gears before you get to 'high'."

Abe studied the knob diagram. "I like pictures, not *reading* about something."

"Now, remove your right foot from the brake and place it on the gas pedal—the long one on the right."

Abe adeptly moved his size ten shoe over to the gas pedal.

"Now with the shift as is you'll see how freely it moves. That's neutral. Now move the knob up into the reverse position," he said, motioned, pointing 'H'.

"Don't remove your foot from clutch!" Fabian cried as the car stuttered and stalled.

"Okay. Start from square one. Give the accelerator a little gas as you slowly let out the clutch, and we'll back 'er out of the driveway."

Whir, whirr, whirrr, the engine raced and nothing happened. Abe frowned.

"That's okay, son. Just let the clutch out some more—it'll grab soon. You need to be light on the gas now."

Shudder, shudder, shudder. Shut down...*ka-lump.*

Abe's shoulders wilted. "That didn't take any prizes, did it?"

"That's okay. Start over again, no harm done. You should've seen me driving Dad's old Model A. Damn near ground forty pounds of hamburger out of 'er." He shook his head and laughed. "And every time I got 'er up to forty-five, it shimmied like my sister Kate, or so the song goes."

Abe scratched his head, grasped the steering wheel, and repeated his efforts. The car purred into action. Letting the clutch out slowly, he gave the car a little gas. Nothing. More gas. Nothing. The car whined. Some more gas.

With the clutch engaged, the car charged backward toward the Old Beach Road, shot across it and into the woods, where it stalled out again.

Small beech wood branches scraped mockingly on the outside of the car window. In the blink of an eye—from hysteria, from fright, from relief, from pure hilarity—they both began laughing. Fabian's eyes watered over, his caved-in chest shook as he glanced at Abe affectionately. "If not meek, it was matchless." His voice soothed Abe.

Abe, finding Fabian's levity contagious, slapped his hand on the steering wheel, trying to tell Fabian between shaking convulses, "This—this—this Fuckin' car just took off so fast it steered itself!"

Fabian's eyes grew grave. "What did you say?"

"It just slipped out. You say that all the time, Dad." Abe felt pinned to explain.

"I guess I do, at that. However, you s*hould* have known that it's going to be a long time before you can talk that way, if ever. Just remember that. Okay?"

"All right Dad," he agreed, his laughter taking on a nervous edge.

"Now let's start from the top and get the car back into the driveway."

Eeerch, eeerch, eeerch, the engine turned over and purred. "I know what to do now." Abe was convincing and confident, each word a declaration.

This time it went more smoothly, Abe getting the feel like a sorcerer, engaging the clutch and the gas to make contact at about the same time. Slowly, the car rolled back into its resting place near the kitchen door.

"Now we'll try it again. This time go slowly, as you did in forward."

Abe liked the feel of the gas pedal under his foot. It meant power, and power meant control. Control meant he was taking his rightful place in the world as a man.

His left foot responded well to an ease-off the clutch as he pressed on the accelerator. Harder. Nothing. Harder yet. Still nothing! "Whaat?"

"Ease up, ease up," Fabian's voice sounded strained as tensions built.

The reverse gear engaged with the gas pedal halfway down. Again, the car took off. Abe looked out the rearview mirror, awed, as the ranch-style fence around the yard was approaching at devious speed.

Out of the corner of his eye, Fabian caught sight of the railing and ducked, expecting it to come right through the window.

Crash! Snap!

The end of the fence post broke off in smithereens, flying over the top of the car as the Ford once again zapped across the road and into the woods, parking immediately next to where they had been before as if they had been assigned a parking spot at the ball park. *Shudder, shudder. Die.*

"For cryin' out loud, Abe, drive this car back in the driveway and start over again," he said, splaying a hand on Abe's shoulder. "Get your suckin' feet in sync." Fabian growled—his dark eyes snapping; he'd give Abe no quarter.

Abe unconsciously drew back at the annoyance he saw on Fabian's face, and maybe more than that. There was frustration, growing disappointment and maybe even pain. A half hour later, Abe had successfully backed the Ford out of the driveway a dozen times and positioned it on the Old Beach Road. Life took on new blushes.

"You're doing just great!" By heaven, he remembered how tough it was to be a kid, to find torment in small peccadilloes and bliss in a penny stick of gum. Fabian's face grew reminiscent. "Let's take 'er for a spin over to Hebert's house, turn 'er around in their driveway, and then take the alley all the way to the school." He cut Abe a silent look of admiration and confidence.

"You mean it? Let's do it!" Abe was hoping that Sarah would see them in the car together, with *him* driving. Whah! What a happening!

Giggles bubbled up from Abe's throat, a reaction that had Fabian's hands rubbing together in anticipation. "Go for it!" Fabian could feel the once-in-a-lifetime thrill of this rite of passage. It was something to which one never came back. It was a monster paragraph in a long book.

"You really know how to make me feel good, Dad." Abe's face split into a wide grin, his beautiful teeth like his mother's—his secret weapon.

"My God, Abe! How you look like Suki!" Pride burst from Fabian's eyes, which suddenly clouded. "Son, you're going to have a tough road ahead of you with your speech handicaps, your excessive salivation and your lack of focusing qualities." His voice broke, then stilled for control. "If anything happens before I have a chance to contact Dr. Whittaker about help for these physical hang-ups, then you must approach him yourself. You understand?" He simply looked at Abe and smiled, a jagged spur running up his back like a sudden crack in the ice on a pond.

Abe heard the ache in his voice as he turned around in the Hebert's driveway. It had been an experience in endurance for Abe, both the ache and the maneuver.

"Just ease that clutch out now, son," Fabian said, half under his breath. "Ease it," he breathed, motioning easily with his hands. "Ease it..." he motioned for more.

The clutch had miraculously engaged with the gas, and Abe gracefully backed out of the driveway. Now he'd drive the alley to school and back home through town, and *everybody* would see him driving!

Fabian frowned, shaking his head. Rolling down his window, he found a warm spot in the sun, confident that his son was taking to driving like a robin to worms. Suddenly he smiled. An exaggerated sigh of relief heaved from him as he wiped non-existent sweat from his brow with his forearm for Abe's benefit.

"By the end of June you'll have a special permit to drive the car due to my incapacity," Fabian said gruffly, staring straight ahead in his pride and delivering the portent of the good news with watery eyes. His glance traveled from the sharp angles of his face, the firm set of Abe's chin to his heated brown eyes that burned with accomplishment. Fabian saw in him the determination and endless drive that would make him a man, perhaps even a man's man. Pride showed through as he brought his red swollen fingers to his mouth to wipe away a grin.

Gaining new pride and confidence, Abe molded mule-skinned toward the teasing and buffeting of the rest of the herd. He'd fallen ass-over-teakettle plenty of times in these early years, but he had always landed on his feet—so far.

CHAPTER FIVE

A fresh wind picked up through the long needles of the white pine in the yard, and shadows danced along the ground. It was a good day for Abe to shake himself back to reality and sponge down the walls before he proceeded further with the floor. He stopped in mid-swipe where the dormer wall met the ceiling. Pulling his arms down and reflecting, he couldn't shake off the intrusive delights, sights, smells and the sounds of the summer of 1939.

To some people, retirement was a time to curl up and die or vegetate in the land of the not-yet-dead, but not Sarah's daddy, Max Savin. At six-foot-three inches, he exhibited a scarecrow appearance, his long-stride-gait identifiable anywhere in town.

Maxwell Savin spent all year round digging up new challenges for the Summer Art School at Nahma, which drew artists from all over the country. Surely he had been a charter member of the Society for the Prevention of Boredom. A talented canvas artist in his own right, he supervised the tutoring and further education of a variety of arts for six weeks, from July 1 to August 15, ending with the gala Sadie Hawkins Day Festival.

As a professor at the School of Art and Literature at the University of Michigan in Ann Arbor, he had eagerly anticipated retirement. With long legs stretched out at his easel in the yard, he painted for hours, his straw Katy no detriment to the lucidity of his color choices. A full white mustache and silver hair decorated his head. He looked more like Mr. Monopoly than Mr. Monopoly did.

It didn't take Max long to notice that the kid from across the road had an inherent talent for painting. He was a half-breed—not white, not red, but some kind of woody color. What kind of a future did a kid of that caliber have? He didn't want Sarah mixed up with the likes of him.

Abe was startled as if he'd been stung when Max spoke from out of nowhere. "What're you painting today, Abe?"

"Sweet Peas in the Sand."

"Where the hell did you see those? They're beautiful."

"Right over there in the sand dunes—growing wild on the beach."

"I've been walking this beach since before you were born, kid, and I've never seen those flowers." Max's voice was thrown over his shoulder as he walked toward the dunes created by old high water tides of Big Bay de Nocquet. There, crawling along on vines bearing dark green leaves, grew a myriad of periwinkle flowers in full bloom.

"Well, I'll be damned!" Max muttered. Returning, he watched Abe trace the creeping vines right out to the end of the picture instead of centering them on the canvas. Putting both palms up to his temples, his arrogance burst through.

"Abe, where are you going with that plant—to Escanaba? You need to have some scope of finiteness." Max tapped the frame of the canvas scolding, always the mentor.

"That'll be on the next one," Abe said looking up, squinting at Max in the morning sun. "You see, I'll pick up in another picture where I left off with this picture, and then I'll hang them near each other on the wall at home. Fabian will like that."

Max swallowed. "It's called 'anecdotal painting'—painting a story in a series. I was *taught* the theory and in turn *teach* the theory, but only because it is scholarship. However, you seem to have popped right into it." There twanged in Max's voice an irritation. Trying to remain dispassionate, off came the straw Katy, against his leg banged the straw Katy, on went the straw Katy.

"Sometimes you're the windshield—sometimes the bug." Abe laughed, and then cleared his throat figuring he might be on caving ground.

Rankled with inexplicable irritation, Max reached up and rubbed his forefinger under his eye. "Abe, your canvases can only describe as art in its purest form. I've never reached that plateau of wonder you add to a picture. Sarah shows only the rote nuances of an art student. Nonetheless, I feel satisfied because every Saturday she gets piano lessons in Escanaba from the Notre Dame nuns at St. Joe's. That young lady will accomplish much in life." He cleared his throat.

If it were true that the meek would inherit the earth, Max would die landless. Abe gained awareness of Max's pedestal picture of Sarah as compared to his own lowly inadequacies. He swallowed an inner agony—lumber piles of self-doubt.

Late that afternoon Abe stood in his yard and observed Sarah in the flower garden snipping a fresh bouquet for Ma. "Want to pick clams tonight after supper?"

"Sure thing. Around six o'clock is fine." Her voice was tinkling wind chimes.

Dressed in shorts and sleeveless shirts, they left their footprints as they walked the length of the beach on an unfolding summer evening, their buckets swinging side by side.

"You've grown, Abe. How tall are you now?"

"Height claimed is five feet ten inches now. Dad said he can't keep me in clothes anymore." Abe laughed.

Sarah waved him off in the futility of his earthly requirements.

"Here, right here, I saw a whole slew of clams bubbling in low tide the other evening," he shouted upon reaching the Point.

Bending over side by side, he noticed her long tan legs reflected in the rosiness of the late-day sun. Her blouse gaped at the top, revealing her growing breasts just like in Fabian's magazines, but smaller. An emotional hurricane swept over him.

Abe was already well into manhood. He'd long since experienced erections and dreams in the night. The big guys, however, spoke of girls and the thrill of it all. This beach exposure was more than he could handle. Taking a break, he sat in the warm sand watching Sarah as she stood bathed in the setting sun. A flood of warmth rushed through him. Maybe he was going to need oxygen or something.

Sarah sensing his absence turned around to see where he'd disappeared.

"Quit already or just resting?" she asked over her shoulder.

"Just watching the sunset. Come sit and talk to me for a while." He'd come armed with a treasured roll of Life Savers and peeled a bright green one for Sarah.

"For me?" She pressed her chest with her hands and chuckled nervously.

"Of course." Abe wrinkled with laughter.

Sitting, she sighed, holding the Life Saver on her tongue, its flavor bursting. "Mmm-mmm," she said, swallowing. "The sunset is like a ball of fire tonight, redder than cranberries." She dragged a damp hand through her mahogany pageboy.

Abe dragged out uncertainties. "I'll be fifteen years old in December, and still in the eighth grade. Do you think any less of me, Sarah, because I stayed behind a grade?" His voice unveiled his humility of how years had grown from distressing to calamitous.

"No, I like it. You're my best friend. I hope you don't mind me telling you that."

"Why would I mind you telling me that?" he asked softly, finding her eyes hypnotic. "There are times when I feel *you* are my only friend." He reached out and put his arm around her shoulder. "You've changed so much this past year."

Pliable, she leaned into him, warm and snuggly. "Girls *do* get different, Abe. I'll be fourteen in another month. Everything changes, people, times and looks. You're very handsome and so big," she added in a moment of inspiration, her tone soothing.

"Sarah, I don't think you know what you do to me when you say things like that." His hand tightened involuntarily on her shoulder. After two attempts at getting his nose out of the way, he kissed her lightly on the lips. They were soft and warm.

"That was nice Abe Miereau—my *first ever* kiss," she said looking up into his deep brown eyes.

Abe slipped to the other side of Saturday. Squeezing her shoulder, her blouse gaped revealing her new small breasts. A squeak rose from his throat. Struggling with conscious effort to maintain control, he brushed himself off and assisted Sarah to rise.

"You've been hanging in my life as long as I can remember. I don't know what I'd do if you ever disappeared." Laughing uncomfortably, he staggered through the warm sand, his arm around her waist. "Will you always be my girl?"

"I'll always be your girl, Abe. Always."

❦

Abe had the walls washed as he remembered with realism how that summer had slipped away as it always did in Michigan, curled up and blew off like an autumn leaf, almost unnoticed. Another school year had been accomplished. Clyde Tobin approved of his performance at the Company store and offered Abe a steady job after school.

Late in the spring of 1940 when sunlight sparkled on the lake and the new leaves radiated like emeralds, Abe noticed a marked decline in his father's health. At fifteen years old, he stood six feet one inch tall and he had taken over most of the household duties as well as holding down his after-school job. He worried constantly. Was Fabian taking his medication as directed? Was he getting quality rest? He made the decision to inquire further into his father's health.

Situated on the boulevard downtown, the Whittaker place was an awesome mansion compared to Abe's home. The local landmark was a two-story structure of white with dark green trim, boasting broad steps leading up to the front porch, which in itself encompassed the full width of the home. White pillars supported the overhang.

Dusk had settled in and an impenetrable fog rolled off the lake churning misty circles around the post lantern in the yard, which looked like a pinpoint under a sheet. A warm yellow glow emanated from the side window units adjacent to the double front door. He felt like Oliver Twist ogling through a window of the toney home.

Dr. Whittaker himself responded to the door chimes. "Abe Miereau! Come in. Is your dad all right?" An eyebrow shot up, his voice holding genuine concern.

Abe nodded, out of his element in the presence of this distinguished man in the grandeur of such rich appointments. The home was furnished with expensive furniture and costly eclectic canvases. He viewed the solid oak stairway rising from the left and designed with two mezzanines before disappearing upstairs. The broad wall in front of him supported the upper portion of the stairwell and stood decorated with a magnificent oil copy of John Singer Sargent's "Boats at Anchor," presented in a gold rococo frame. Below it on a pedestal stood a giant vase composed of polished clamshells, which contained a tasteful arrangement of beige pods, brown cattails and orange bittersweets.

"Come in. We can talk in here," Doc said, closing the door and leading Abe off to the right of the foyer where satiny oak French doors opened onto his home office. Abe's feet sunk into the deep uncut loops of yarn forming the surface of the carpet. It was as silent as his ancestors in their moccasins. Inside grew rich oak paneling, a roll-top oak desk with a hundred pigeonholes, and an oak chair built to suit the size of someone as large as Dr. Whittaker. On top of the desk were the usual accouterments kept warm by a photograph of his parents upon emigrating from England and a small oval Faberge frame holding a loving picture of Liz, his wife.

Two oak visitor chairs accompanied by end tables bearing Tiffany lamps graced the room. A partial portion of the south wall was dedicated to a library stacked with handsome leather-bound burgundy medical books and the New England Journal of Medicine. On Doc's desk lay a gray and white marble-designed ledger. Abe figured it bulged with the names of just about everyone in town who owed him. Abe also knew that most would keep on owing him until death did its part.

Doc wore an unbuttoned white smock over a white shirt and paisley print tie, shoes of rich Moroccan leather under creased navy blue trousers, showing lightly knit argyle stockings. Abe studied his neatness—dark, impeccably groomed hair perfectly parted on the side, slightly graying at the temples, heavily lashed dark brown eyes under contoured eyebrows. His aristocratic nose was set over a well-manicured mustache complementing a mouth that was not wide, not thin but bearing a wet-look. Abe guessed him to be Fabian's age, but he looked at least ten years younger.

Standing uncomfortably, his hands stuffed into his jacket pockets, Abe was uncertain of the prescribed posture in such a grand setting.

"Sit down, Abe. Have a chair," Doc indicated with a sweep of his hand. "You've grown into a big guy." Easing comfortably into his own desk chair, he leaned back. "Now, young man, what can I do for you on this nasty night?" He gestured waving the back of his hand toward the window behind him, which overlooked the front porch.

Abe was unnerved and quickly tucked his scuffed boots under the chair as he leaned forward. "Well, I'm wondering if something else could be done for my dad." He hoped he didn't sound like a babe in the woods. "He's growing worse every day."

"Yes, of course." Doc said, nodding with his signature half-smile—his bottom lip wet and poutie. Although his face remained friendly, he presented his professional shroud. "He *is* growing worse every day," Doc acknowledged, allowing his hand to slap the arm of chair, sighing long. "That's the natural progression of his disease; he has irreversible spondilitis. That's inflammation of the joints linking the vertebrae—backbones. In ankylosing spondilitis, the inflammation recedes but leaves behind hardened joints that fuse together the separate bones of the spinal column."

Abe nodded, his eyes, as well as his ears, drinking in the words. A fierce buzzing commenced inside his head, gnawing at his tear stash.

"This may sound like medical mishmash to you, but I trust you can understand it. You don't have to be Swiss to enjoy cheese." He leaned forward in his chair, folding his hands between his spread knees. "The first joints to be affected are the sacroiliac joints, bones which line the base of the spine to the pelvis, or hipbone. Bony growths fuse the separate bones together, and the resultant stiffness may move slowly up the spine until it affects many, if not all of the joints between the vertebrae. In Fabian's case, it's *most*." Doc paused, mentally scrutinizing this young man—this fine young man.

Abe's heart hammered; his body tensed. He'd been seeking *good* news. He shuffled his withdrawn feet, trying to think of words to say to hold up his end of the conversation, but he'd have needed a wheelbarrow.

Observing Abe's rigid posture, Doc sat back and placed a hand along his cheek, index finger over the length of his mustache. "The patient suffers loss of energy and weight, a poor appetite and a slight fever. In addition, his eyes may become red and painful. The causal agent is unknown. The disease is much more prevalent in men and occurs mainly in the twenty to forty age groups and often traces back to the crib. I wouldn't worry about it in your case, Abe. You seem to have not inherited Fabian's traits. You look so much like your mother. By the way, what do you hear from her?"

Mother! The word joined the ever-increasing buzzing in his brain. "My mother?" The subject of his mother as opposed to his father's illness was light years apart, but he trusted the genuineness of the question. "Nothing at all. Funny. *No one* hears from her, not even Farley and Norrhea. Fabian says that it's a mystery."

"I'm sorry to hear that." Doc exhaled loudly. "Your mother is a beautiful woman. I expect that someday we'll hear from her again. I worked very closely with her years ago when the Sturgeon River overflowed about this time of the year. She and her parents, Farley and Norrhea, helped me set up a temporary shelter and inoculation program at the Indian Point Trading Post." Dr. Whittaker's reflections were disquieting to him for a moment.

Scrubbing his face, Doc bolted back to the here and now. "I'm not going to minimize the seriousness of Fabian's disease, Abe. Although the affliction does not usually progress very far up the spine, it *has* in Fabian's case. It has left him with a stiff spinal column that may soon cause his head to bend permanently onto his chest. The ribs may also become involved where they join the spine, and that would reduce his ability to breathe because of constriction of the lungs. Chest infection could then become a danger. His jaw may become stiff, which would cause difficulty in eating and speaking." Doc folded his hands prayerfully over his chest. "He's definitely in a downward spiral."

Abe lowered his head trying to close the gap between what *was* and what *may be*. It all sounded like hell to him. Could Doc feel Abe's outrage? It was as tangible as a searing wind. He drew a long breath. Swiping his hand across his face, he could yet smell the carrots he had recently packed into the cooler. He'd just about had it.

A smile that was slow growing but disarming moved over Doc's face. "Now Abe, we can't give up. Fabian needs to breathe deeply, sleep on a hard mattress, and not use a pillow. Try to get him to rest on his stomach rather than on his back or side. Those are measures to keep back muscles strong and prevent his spine from a bent position."

"He's in pain, I know. I wake up at night and hear him groaning." In Abe's anxiety lived a presence, that of his Indian spirits weeping.

"I have him on anti-inflammatory drugs *and* painkillers, but I can't be sure that he's taking them. *You* could oversee that. Doc was pensive. Some lumberjacks lived to be ninety-five after leading a killer life. Others, like Fabian, were stricken in their prime.

"What we need to do is try to make him comfortable." Doc gathered his foot on his knee, completely at home with his medical mumbo jumbo as a shaman of Abe's ancestors. "An educated guess is that he'll have difficulty breathing within a year. I'm hoping that we can ease him along for a while yet, but it'll be a handful." Empathy was evident in Doc's eyes.

Abe absorbed the brutal news internally. At fifteen, he didn't know if he could handle the extra care for his father, but he didn't want anyone else doing it either. He wished that somehow he could repel out of this situation. The buzzing in his head had entered his tear stash; a lump rose in his throat, and his eyes burned with held-back tears.

"I'll try to get him to carry out your instructions." Abe choked, stopped and pulled himself together. "I think that if *you* told him all those things, he might do them."

Dr. Whittaker discreetly looked away, noticing Abe's run-away emotions.

"Believe it or not, Abe, I've advised your father repeatedly about what he has to do for self-help. You might check to see that he *takes* his medication every day. It's critical."

"Yes, sure, I'll watch that," Abe said rising to leave after regaining some degree of composure. Glancing up at the bookcase, Abe caught a glittering reflection of light on what appeared to be a dazzling framed collection in the bookcase.

Doc followed his gaze. "You know what those are, Abe?" He went on, not really posing an academic question. "That is my Krugerrand collection. I started it shortly after I finished medical school and I now have twelve of them. They're one-ounce gold coins of the Republic of South Africa. Every year that passes makes them more valuable," he said, unlocking the bookcase door, taking out the embedded folder.

Registering the strange markings on them, Abe felt the glossy finish of the coins. His wondering eyes met Doc's in an aura of breathlessness. "Whah! Never saw anything like it." His eyes sliced from the Krugerrand to Doc's face.

"That's what I thought, too, when I first laid eyes on them at a fine jewelry store in Ann Arbor while I was in college. I always knew I'd own some one day. If you ever have extra money, it's a good way to invest in the future," he said returning the Krugerrands back to the safety of the cabinet.

Abe flashed an amused smile. "I'm not likely to ever see that day," he said walking to the door, appreciating the giant steps Doc had taken to ease his mind.

"Oh, I think that ownership is a distinct possibility, Abe. As far as Fabian is concerned, I'll start swinging by your house twice a week now." Clasping Abe on the shoulder, he found fitting advice. "I *have* discovered definite relationship between curing and caring, so let's both try harder at caring." His smile skewed Abe into wanting to see more of this man, wishing to be a greater part of his life.

"Thanks Doc. Thanks a lot." Abe moved slowly, reluctant to leave the warmth of this man for some reason indefinable. He felt a kinship in the caring.

"You're welcome." Doc smiled, filling the open doorway with his magnificent size. "You come any time." he said, shaking Abe's hand.

The decision to do so solidified in Abe's mind; it was irrevocable, and almost as cathartic as this insightful visit with Doc.

CHAPTER SIX

Abe couldn't believe now that it had been that same summer, a mere two years ago, when he'd spent so much time at the beach with Sarah. The heavy moist heat of July settled in, scintillating the bay with heat inversions. Sailboats on the horizon appeared and disappeared as if in a mirage, and the slow surge of the waves licked at the shore.

The past school year had been good. Sarah drew Abe along with her evening treks to study at the kitchen table while Fabian savored the evening news with Gabriel Heater who intoned his *baaad news tonight*. The advancement of Axis forces into Belgium and Austria had been foreboding. The English Prime Minister, Neville Chamberlain, had promoted the Munich Pact with Adolph Hitler, finding in him a fine example of leadership, courage, and diplomacy. This perception would soon be reversed.

Abe and Sarah found time in the evening to sit in the warm sand and enjoy the end of the day. She was a pampered personage of fifteen, while Abe neared his sixteenth birthday. He exhibited a degree of manhood reserved for the head of a household as he took on greater responsibility for Fabian. Having grown to six feet two inches, he was a commanding personality.

"Beautiful evening, Abe. Aren't we lucky to have all this?" Sarah posed with a graceful sweep of her tanned arm indicating the spectrum of the vista.

"Let's walk farther down the beach," Abe said with studied enthusiasm. "It seems everyone and their brother is out here this evening."

"All right," she agreed, sending shivers over Abe's skin. He readily acknowledged that Sarah was a beautiful young woman. At five feet four inches and long legs, he felt a sexual tug seeing her in a navy bathing suit. She wore her mahogany hair in a single French braid while energized tendrils of wispy curls hugged her temples. Dark brown eyes with sweeping lashes became animated when she spoke. A tiny nose and plucky chin framed her full ripe mouth as she smiled up at Abe.

With an adventurous laugh she suggested, "Let's go sit in the cove at the end of Stony Point. The water comes into the shallows as warm as a bath tub."

"Yeah." His voice was but a whisper that hung on the air as he pulled her to her feet. Abe liked the idea of some privacy. He felt like an early American water buffalo.

They watched the sun dip into the far western horizon in a galaxy of grandeur. Lightly kissing the cove was a teasing breeze. Searching for their evening meal, gulls flew in slow tangents. Fireflies glowed in the growth lining the curve of the cove.

Abe was alive with awareness of the satiny vellum texture of Sarah's tanned arms and legs. Her maturity in the past few years had been dramatic. She was the music of worship, the essence of his life. His hunger to touch her never diminished.

For only the second time in his life, he reached over to kiss her. Her head moved away. Commandingly, he drew her chin up to him, his long fingers controlling her. This time he kissed her without interference from his nose.

She pulled back gasping, her eyelashes heavy. "Ohhh, Abe. That was so nice. Every day you get older, you're more handsome. I love your five o'clock shadow and your smile that flashes just like that," she said, snapping her fingers.

As she spoke, he did it again—flashed that devastating smile. He ached listening to her voice that resembled pouring Aunt Jemima syrup over pancakes. He wished she were a jigsaw puzzle that he could store in a box on the shelf in his loft, take her apart, and put her together again.

She'd become an unshakable obsession, her mouth nubile and fiery in the setting sun. Speechless, he kissed her again, this time lingering bravely, tasting her lips with his tongue. His hand dropped from her shoulder, ran down her ribs, under her arm, feeling the soft side of her breast.

She gasped again. "No Abe, we shouldn't," she said, leaping up and moving to a windswept pine standing at the back of the cove, her legs not quite steady.

Abe followed her with his gaze, her timid rejection starting his juices flowing anew. He unfolded, dug his heels into the sand sending spewing tailings of sugar sand into the air, and easily closed the distance between them.

He was uploaded into another land, another land she'd soon come to recognize as his retreat, where he couldn't be reached by any means. Her eyes flew wide with fear as she backed up and found herself against the tree.

She took a deep breath. "Don't!" It was barely a squeak, uncertainty leaking through. Abe was exhibiting about as much finesse as a fan-tailed shark.

His head bent, kisses brushed her eyes, her cheeks, barely rubbing his lips over hers and found her quivering. He kissed her hungrily, his mouth curling, devouring hers.

When she melded into him, he picked her up and laid her onto the warm sand. "Chrise, Sarah, you're driving me crazy. I've wanted to do this for so long." Her smooth white breasts, still small, round and pink-tipped peeked above her bathing suit.

"Ohhh, they're so nice," he breathed excitedly, glancing up from her breasts to her eyes and back again. He kissed them and salivated with the succulence. He found her mouth again, consuming it.

His chest hair crinkled on her breasts. She could feel the hardness of him against her thigh and with the shock value, recovered.

"No, no, Abe! We mustn't," she cried, her voice softly husky. She was weak with his aggressions. She could hardly urge her legs to function when she stood and adjusted her bathing suit.

Abe, releasing her, was hoarse. "Okay, Sarah. Okay. I'm not going to hurt you." His arms were outstretched, hands splayed in contrition. He sat in the sand, his head resting on his knees, his hands wrapped around his head. His voice was thick as he raised his eyes to hers. "I love you, Sarah. I love you as deeply as my life."

"You say one more half-baked thing Abe Miereau, and you're going to regret it," she said somewhere between a sigh and a sob. "You need to give me at least another year to think about this. I'm not just *any* girl." The tears coursed down her cheeks in release. After a while, Sarah managed a small smile.

He used it as a study. So many emotions ran rampant being near her: self-esteem, sensitivity, empathy, and deep desire. Still shaken with desire, he plowed a large hand through his hair. Here he was in yet another dilemma with no one to coach him about what to do, what to say! That crazy kindergarten lump rose in his throat, stifling, choking. He couldn't let her think that he was a crybaby. Instead, he merely squeezed her around the shoulders, feeling their fragile structure under his huge hands.

After seeing her into her yard with a click of the gate, he ran his fingers through her hair, feeling it between his thumb and forefinger, bent and kissed her lightly on top of the head. "I hope you dream of me when you lay in your bed tonight, Sarah." His dark eyes charged, a puckish humor settled around his mouth. He'd learned quickly that a polished personality got as much honey as a powerful presence.

Abe ambled across the road where the glow of Fabian's floor lamp shined warmly out through the east window of the living room. There he sat near the Bendix radio listening to the "Saturday Night Barndance."

Nevertheless, he couldn't enter the house until he roused relief from his horrific, hard-pressing problem. He stopped by the tall white pine behind the house, where he could find support as he entertained thoughts of her, taking her apart, putting her back together again. Sweat rolled off his forehead.

Another year! *Then*...he could only *hope*.

"Abe, where have you been? It's been dark for close to an hour." Fabian sat next to the mahogany console radio. "Heart and Soul" by Hoagie Carmichael was being fought with banjos, mandolins, fiddles, and drums by the Carter Family.

"I was just on the beach with Sarah, out by Stony Point. It took us a while to get back." A strange flippancy lay in his voice, and a shambling stretch lay in his long body.

Fabian in the wisdom of his years heard the freighted implications of the swollen vowels, the stressed voice, and the labored casualness.

Abe sank into the soft embrace of the sofa across from Fabian, coupled his hands behind his head, and listened to the music, his long legs extended in front of him.

"Hey. You still with me?" Fabian asked, trying to reel in Abe before his line took him out to sea.

"Hmmm?"

"Look son, are you trying to seduce Sarah? It is not without notice that you have been inseparable. You need not to be touching her sexually. Save her for dessert, Abe." Fabian wondered how far he could comfortably go with this conversation. Abe had been a grown man for more than three years now. "You need to treat her as a good friend—smart as a whip, easy to look at and very insightful."

"No, Dad, I can't get near her. I make some progress, but she pretty much holds me at arm's length." Abe sighed and turned it into a tickled laugh upon seeing the exhilaration in Fabian's eyes.

"Listen, Abe. I understand that a young man your age has needs." Fabian leaned forward. "You know who the girls are." He waved his hand through the air. "I've bought you some condoms," he said, reaching into the drawer of the end table and motioning Abe to come get the box of Trojans. "You take these, and *use* them."

As though in slow motion, Abe arose, reached out and accepted them.

"You don't want to spoil your young life by getting some woman pregnant while you're still in high school." *Am I one lucky sonofabitch that Sarah has a good head on her shoulders!* "I don't want to overcharge this lecture, but sometimes I think that not *enough* is said." Fabian leaned back in his chair. "When you're around Sarah, keep your pants zipped. Give her time to grow up."

"Thanks Dad," Abe stammered, still leaning forward gazing at the box of condoms, running his thumb over the Roman Centurion on the cover, confused and surprised. "Eddie Arsenault said that I could sleep with Abby, his sister. He says she's good in bed." Looking up at Fabian, a small smile edged the corners of his mouth.

"For Chrise sake, Abe! I can't believe the way you kids talk." Fabian, with his elbow on the arm of the chair, put his hand to his chin. "I would rather not have you gallivanting with the Indians from Indian Point. I know you're half Sioux, but you need to stay on this side of the river. The Arsenaults are a very clean family, but evidently loose. You can pick up all kinds of junk from sleeping with the wrong women."

∽⌒∽

Abe hurried to finish the upstairs cleaning. He mulled on the mountains he'd climbed in the past seventeen years as he worked. Placing his bucket on the steps working downward, he swished the mop over each one. He ran his right shirtsleeve across his forehead, feeling the dampness of his shoes and jeans resultant of washing the car then the whole upstairs. He heard voices— old voices—as of that fateful Sunday. The resonance yet echoed in his ears, the stifling fear that lay upon him.

It was Sunday, December 7, 1941. Abe hazed back to that morning. He heard Fabian's radio playing loudly, the tone no-nonsense and pressing. Bouncing downstairs barefooted and wearing only a pair of sweatpants tied loosely at the waist, he feigned the flick of a towel at Fabian on his way to the shower. "You look very intent on the news for such a beautiful day. How're you feeling?"

"I'm okay. I'm fine. The news coming over the radio doesn't sound good, however. I knew it. I just knew it," he said, scrunching up his face. "The whole world's been going horseshit, and now there are early reports of a bombing in Pearl Harbor."

"Where's Pearl Harbor? And who's doing the bombing?" Abe stopped at the bathroom door shrugging, his posture benevolent.

"Go ahead; take your shower," Fabian said and waved him on. "It'll take a minute or so to tell you about it." Fabian, leaning nearer the radio, was closer to the bare bones of war than he ever wanted Abe to know. He dialed other stations, hearing a stream of static and strident voices, some overlaying the others. Finally, a clear signal.

"Ladies and gentlemen. This is Walter Winchell. I'm signing on early today to keep you abreast of news trickling in from Pearl Harbor. Good Evening will not be the starting words today, but good afternoon Mr. and Mrs. America, from border to border, and coast to coast, and all the ships at sea. Let's go to press."

"It's been confirmed that the Japanese exercised a devastating, air attack on Pearl Harbor, on the Hawaiian Island of Oahu early this morning, which was only a short while ago Eastern Standard Time. It is now 1:30 p.m. Information is sketchy."

"What's with the Pearl Harbor deal, Dad?" Abe whisked from the bathroom toweling his hair.

"It's all just breaking. This is a terrible national disaster, Abe." Fabian's eyebrows knit together forming a continuous briar patch across his forehead.

"This appears to be the climax of a decade of rising tensions between Japan and the United States." Walter Winchell went on. "Throughout the 1930s, Japan has been steadily encroaching on China, and the United States has been trying to contain Japan's expansion. Since America supplies more than half of Japan's iron, steel, and oil, Japan has been reluctant to push the United States too far. On September 27, 1940, Japan joined the Triple Alliance with Italy and Germany and began to expand into northern Indochina. The United States, in response, placed an embargo on aviation gasoline, scrap metal, steel, and iron. After Japan's seizure of the rest of Indochina in July of this year, President Franklin D. Roosevelt closed the Panama Canal to Japanese shipping. This past October, General Hideki Tojo, became premier."

"I knew it." Fabian hissed, slapping his knee. "It's Tojo. He's nothing but a half-ass troublemaker. It's all his doing!"

Winchell's overriding voice continued, somber, and grave. "Negotiations seeking a peaceful settlement are going on in Washington. On November 25, 1941, though continuing the discussions, the Japanese dispatched aircraft carriers eastward toward Hawaii and began massing troops on the Malayan border."

"Sure, sure enough. Just like the trusting husband, the United States is always the last to know and recognize the wayward wife. Son-of-a-bitch!" Fabian drew out the words as he leaned forward, his head cocked towards the radio.

Winchell thrummed on. "American military leaders have been expecting a Japanese attack on Malaya, but have given only general warnings to U.S. Forces in Pearl Harbor. Word that reaches us is that Admiral Herbert E. Kimmel and General Walter C. Short, in command on Oahu, were ordered to take only few precautions; no effective air patrol was set in place, and neither ships nor planes were safely dispersed."

"For those of you just tuning in, Japanese planes attacked Pearl Harbor at 7:55 a.m., this morning, December 7. Now we are informed that a second wave has hit. Early reports have it those eight battleships, three destroyer, and three cruisers have been put out of action. Two battleships, the Oklahoma and the Arizona, were destroyed. It is estimated that over 2,000 U.S. servicemen have been killed."

"It sounds like a fiery hell to me, one in which only Shadrach, Meshach, and Abednego would have survived—worse than the fiery furnace of Babylon. Sneakin' Japs!" The last words were merely a gasp from Fabian as tears coursed down his cheeks. Painful memories consumed him with the awareness that war was a terrible sacrifice of that which was beautiful, decent and good.

Abe's mind swirled with foggy fear and confusion.

"It is expected that within the course of the next couple of days, President Roosevelt will address the American people before a joint session of Congress. It is expected that he will request Congress to recognize the state of war that exists between the United States and Japan. With that vote, America will enter World War II," Winchell concluded.

"This is tragic," Fabian said, wiping his eyes with a red paisley print handkerchief. "With all the *baaaad* news I've been hearing in the evening from Gabriel Heater, I knew that the situation had escalated. The devil is in deciphering the daily details. Son-of-a-bitches. War! It's a damnable thing." With his head down, he shook.

"Does that mean I'll be drafted?" Abe's eyes darkened as he leaned toward Fabian, his voice chilled.

"They don't take kids out of school, and you have two more years." His mind crawled back to when he was in the First World War—Belgium—the heavy fighting he'd encountered near Ypres, the horrors, the fires and the sun a red ball in a gray haze of smoke-filled air. Fabian's nose and eyes had stung with the pungent smell of wood smoke and sulfur. Torturing his memories were the unending nightmares of men screaming and German flares over trenches. He shivered in the cold, pinned down for days by enemy fire and wondered when it would be his turn.

Fabian visibly convulsed at the vacuum of loneliness he felt in the folding waves of smoke that hung over the smoldering forests, and the sounds of artillery pounding day and night as incessant beating jungle drums. The acrid metallic smell of blood stayed in his nose for months. Rotting body parts strewn over the battlefields laid an indescribable stench on the land and flies collected as if for a communal buffet. He'd watched it, felt it—the heat on his face and his hands—smelled it in his dried-up nose and burning throat, tasted it in the windblown ash.

He didn't want that for Abe. He didn't want Abe in Camp Oglethorpe, Georgia near a run-amuck swamp. He'd never erase from his mind how sick he'd been with influenza in 1918 while in basic training. He'd come down with the acute, highly contagious disease, and had the delirium of fever, muscular aches, and inflammation of the respiratory mucous membranes ending in pneumonia. The pandemic that year decimated over twenty million people worldwide.

He'd been in a tent with seven other soldiers—all stricken. He recalled the magnitude of the situation as the tenants changed daily. His delirium had him only partly focused, and he didn't really care if he lived or died. When he *did* have periods of lucidity, the reek of urine and loose bowels permeated the very canvas of the tent. The air lay heavy and oppressive, hanging like a three-day fog.

Perhaps death was the better option. If he had to go through as much to get well as he had gone through to deteriorate in this wasting disease, he would say, "no thank you." His head exploded with pain, his eyes on fire. There was no person-to-person care and nurturing. The convention was survival of the fittest.

No, Fabian didn't want that for Abe. Ostensibly, he had fought for a better world of peace and order, and here, only twenty years later, the world was at it again. Fabian's eyes spilled over with tears, his head dropped, and his shoulders shook. May God have mercy on this country and all their young men—their greatest resource! The profanity of seeing them wasted wrenched at the depths of his soul.

Images of war danced in Abe's mind as he drank of the disappointment in Fabian. "Tell me what you're thinking, Dad." In his closeness to Fabian, Abe didn't want him re-visiting hell fire, but he felt alienated when silence soaked the space between them.

"When we went over to Europe we were happy soldiers standing around a piano singing "Pack up your troubles in an old kit bag and smile, smile,

smile." Then the nightmares wormed in. All told, more than nine million men died, plus thousands more who were captured and tortured." He sighed deeply. "And what did we have to show for these trips into hell?"

"When the war was over, the veterans of WW I felt that they were overdue for a bonus so three hundred of them out of Portland, Oregon went to Washington D.C. seeking legislation for this bonus. In a tent camp outside Washington their numbers grew to a coalition of over five thousand possessing extreme solidarity—a rag tag bunch. At this time was initiated the saying, 'Buddy, can you spare a dime?'"

"God, Dad. Is there anything worse than to have fought for your country, stared death in the face, then have to beg for subsistence?" Abe put his hand to his head and nodded in slow disgust.

"It was bad, as you said. They'd hit bottom. In that session, the legislature closed in the dead of night. President Hoover called out the Army to squelch the hullabaloo; Generals MacArthur, Patton, and Eisenhower were in charge. On orders from Hoover, they quieted this crowd with tear gas and hoses. That was not enough for MacArthur, however, who took it upon himself to burn Bonus City, which was now occupied by men, women, and children. It was a tragedy and a holocaust. Nothing seemed to faze MacArthur. I still ache, remembering." Fabian stared, eyes glazed.

"On that premise, Franklin D. Roosevelt was elected to office in 1932. We should have finished off the Germans after the First World War. Instead, we gave them short-term interest and fluffed them off as an innocuous entity. Now that high falutin' Hitler is committing the same old sins in the newest ways."

"Then the dog days of depression daunted our country." Fabian's voice suddenly went flat. "It was like a terrible Upper Peninsula thunderstorm— one with continuous flashing lightening and soul-shaking thunder that reverberates forever and ever. We have lived through some bad times together, but you don't remember all of them. People were lonely and puzzled with the turn of events. They stuck together, melding as if a single pink cell had split and proliferated commonizing all of them into a single presence. I remember back in the late twenties and early thirties that people were so poor and hungry that they ate their cats and dogs. Store shelves held little more than some canned goods and dried fruits. Meat, sugar, and dairy products were coveted."

Fabian's eyes stirred as he hoisted himself laboriously from his chair and walked to the window. Clasping his hands behind his back, he stared out into the brilliant sunshine of this December Sunday. The thermometer read a toasty forty-two degrees, a far cry from the normal twenty-nine degrees below zero.

Abe could feel the misery and desolation overtaking Fabian as floodgates suddenly opened. Maybe another chunk of wood in the Kalamazoo would help.

"Red Cross handouts were prevalent—people fought for them," Fabian explained. "A drought hit the nation. Farm prices dropped. Bankers couldn't meet withdrawals. All of America was for sale. Farms were auctioned for give-away prices.

"Hoover felt that by giving industry a boost it would create jobs; jobs would create paychecks; paychecks would create purchasing power; purchasing power would keep the factories humming, and the country would once again prosper. He called his new proposal the 'Reconstruction Finance Corporation.' It didn't work." The silence in the room suddenly grew loud interrupted only by the snapping of the burning wood.

Turning back to Abe, he motioned him into the kitchen where he poured two mugs of coffee. Fabian curled his hands tightly around his mug, eyes fiery.

Abe felt Fabian trudging through a self-imposed purgatory, the price of which was never to be paid. He sipped his coffee slowly, allowing the hot liquid to trickle down his throat feeling nurtured as Fabian recalled his inventory of incisive incidents.

"Charles 'Pretty Boy Floyd' robbed banks and gave the money to farmers. He was a Depression Robin Hood. He worked the banks from Oklahoma to Ohio and back, stealing more than twelve thousand dollars in five months. Oklahoma led the nation in bank robberies with six people being killed in 1932."

Abe wore crinkly lines of strain around his eyes as he listened to the horrors that had populated Fabian's past. How many little deaths had he already died in his lifetime?

"Well, sir, don't you worry about this war." The deep lines around Fabian's mouth curved outward to produce a reasonable facsimile of a smile, realizing he was laying a heavy trip on Abe. "I have a feeling that we'll be pretty much unscathed here in this tiny town. Chances are that in two years when you graduate the war will be over." His expression softened.

"But how about the Soo Locks? Wouldn't that be a prime bombing target?" Abe's heart was still stuttering in his chest. *War! What to expect. Would he be in it and have memories like Fabian? Would he not, and be blamed because he didn't take part?* It was like tossing a hot potato from one hand to the other—it burned either way.

"It could be a target, that is if enemy planes could get that far inland. The only other way it could be destroyed would be by sabotage. It's the great waterway for shipping iron ore, copper, and silver from the mines in the north on Lake Superior to Lake Huron, Lake Michigan and the factories of the industrialized areas."

"How do those locks work? Maybe someday we can go up there and see them, Dad." Abe was taking some downtime to feel Fabian out about his interests. Untold knowledge was stored here, gnawing to gain the freedom of good air and sky.

Fabian felt a sameness with Abe, a mutual benefit of knowledge. "The Sault Sainte Marie Canals, popularly called the Soo Canals, are two toll-free ship canals on the U.S.-Canadian border. Bypassing rapids in the St. Mary's River between Lakes Huron and Superior, they are a vital link in the Great Lakes Waterway."

"Yeah, but just how do they get ships through those canals without having rapids in the water?"

"The ships pass through the canals by means of sluice gates that are opened and closed allowing a ship from Lake Superior to enter, and then the gates are closed. The water level is then dropped by opening a sluice gate, bringing the level commensurate to that of Lake Huron. Then the opposite *lock* is opened to allow safe passage at the lower level. The opposite procedure is repeated for ships traversing from Huron to Superior."

Abe registered understanding, his eyes intent on Fabian.

"It's really quite an operation. I imagine that it'll be guarded night and day now that war is about to be declared. Awful thing war—brings a country to its knees." Fabian pressed his fingertips to the tensions at his temples and tried to forget war. "We'll go there someday, son, you and I. It's only a four-hour drive from here. Let's do it." He reached out, clasped Abe's hand and felt the responsive press of Abe's big hand.

"Yeah, I'd like that." Abe was daydreaming of a trip with Dad. Love didn't thicken by hoarding his time. Abe wondered how well Fabian would travel. What the hell—he'd do it!

CHAPTER SEVEN

As Abe tipped the bucket into the sink, the water swirled and disappeared with all the accumulation of soil he'd removed from his home. He had washed away part of his life—the cold, the mistakes and the jackknife—ah yes, the jackknife.

He resurrected his birthday of last December and how close he had felt to those who were dear to him. Would he ever forget the vacuous days after the jackknife episode? The teasing, the whispers, the learning disabilities, and the on-going speech and salivation problems?

December 14, 1941 dawned gray and bleak. Sleet spewed from out of the leaden sky with a wrath. Abe awoke late to watery winter light and the sumptuous smell of baking cake. Rushing down the loft stairs, which he always took sideways now because his feet were too big for the steps, he cried, "Dad! What do I smell? It even took precedence over a dream about Sarah." He laughed as he negotiated the last of the steps.

Fabian turned to check the seriousness of his grown son's remark and realized that Abe was teasing him. "You, you, you Abe. You're going to be the life of me yet with your *Sarah*. You need to leave her alone. She's a little lady and not fully matured. You hear me?" His eyes snapped.

"Yeah, Dad, I'm only teasing. I can't get within ten feet of her. What a woman!" Abe had an arm about Fabian's shoulder. "She's just as you said—a lady." Fabian's stooped shoulders shook with laughter. "You're all man, Abe. You'll seduce her but only on *her* terms. I'll chalk one up for Sarah."

Fabian switched his thoughts one-hundred and eighty degrees to the morning's endeavor. "I have a maraschino cherry cake baking in the oven." The oven door opened and Fabian poked a toothpick into the center of the fragrant creation.

"Will it have cherry nut frosting?" Abe blurted. "You're the best, Dad.

That's my favorite. Mind if I ask Sarah to come over after supper to have cake with us?"

"No, go ahead. You'll need to duck over there quickly," he said closing the oven door. "It's as freezing as the soul of Siberia today and twice as scourging."

Darkness descended early that night, a week after Pearl Harbor. Sarah arrived, unbuttoned her coat and shook her mahogany hair loose.

"For you," she said handing Abe a smartly wrapped gift, while a special light grew in her deep brown eyes. "It's from Max and me."

She smelled of springtime lilies-of-the-valley. Abe stirred with a throbbing pulsation in his throat that denied him speaking for a moment. He wished that he could control these sudden fevers that seized his good sense. His self-examination jolted him back to extending courtesies. "We'll have some birthday cake, Sarah. Dad baked it this morning. Then I'll open your gift." He adjusted a chair for her at the kitchen table, which, covered with a floral-designed oilcloth, invited happy talk and laughter.

"It sure looks good, Mr. Miereau," Sarah gurgled, her eyes lighting up. "Did you take all the calories out?" She laughed and reached over to squeeze his hand.

Fabian loved this young lady. He grunted out something between a spoken smile and a groan. "Not only did I take all the calories out, but I replaced them with walnuts." His very being warmed with her presence, as it had since she was a small child toddling across the Beach Road to share a sunbeam with him.

Suddenly, bright lights bounced through the living room windows and into the kitchen as a car swung into the yard and parked at the kitchen door.

"See who that is, Abe, and I'll move the coffee to the back of the stove." Fabian, stooped but undeterred, moved the blue galvanized percolator, twisting his head to see who was at the door. The storm door swung open revealing Bernard Tobin and Doc Whittaker smiling through the window of the inside door.

Pushing his chair back quickly, Abe moved to greet the visitors. "Welcome to our home. Come in." He smiled, fixated. The whipping wind and stinging sleet accompanied the superintendent and the doctor as they entered the warm kitchen.

Abe was suddenly aware that his home must seem dreadfully dingy compared to the lovely Tobin and Whittaker homes on the boulevard uptown. He didn't allow it to detract, however, from the pleasure he felt at their visit.

"Let me take your coats. Have some cake and ice cream with us." The words tumbled one over the other, Abe unable to conceal his pleasure. He carried the heavy coats into the living room, laying them on Fabian's chair.

Bernard and Doc drew chairs from the kitchen table and sat while Fabian poured them each a steaming mug of coffee.

"I was working on school records this week when I came upon your birthday, Abe, so I thought that I'd come over and wish you a big seventeen. I picked up Doc on the way." Tobin's bright blue eyes glittered.

They wore upscale clothing that smelled of wool blends and real leather. On their feet rested tasseled loafers covered with over-the-shoe rubbers. Rib-knit turtleneck sweaters layered over shirt and tie and corduroy sport coats—they wore them as easily as Fabian wore a flannel shirt. They counted among the Cadillacs and Packards of the Timber Society of this fiefdom, and wore an air of affluence.

Would he ever reach their status? Probably not, but he would learn from them, study them. There was no diminishing the rising tide of pride he felt in knowing these men-among-men. The old feelings of gratitude, love and respect ran deeply inside Abe's rib cage. He lifted his mug to disguise his admiring eyes.

The hot coffee raised steam ghosts from the hot brew, smelling always better than it tasted, Abe thought. The pink cherry cake with ice cream served on Fabian's best dessert dishes he carried off with ease and without embarrassment. He'd grown accustomed to his curved body.

"Bet you can't guess what Max and I got you, Abe. Open it. Open it!" Sarah squeaked with excitement, flipping the hair from her neck with the back of her hand. "We spent some time on these choices." Her eyes glowed with anticipation.

Abe tore into the wrappings, his big hands making shreds of the paper in just seconds. *Art Treasures of the Centuries* was the book that fell into his hands first. It was captivating: prehistoric and ancient paintings executed deep within caves of southern Europe during the Paleolithic period, some fifteen to twenty thousand years ago. Cave paintings leaped from the pages tracing back to 28,000 B.C. from Spain and southern France. Stark were the paintings from the pharaohs' tombs. Paintings of scenes on Greek pottery popped from pages. Early Christian and Byzantine paintings from the third and fourth centuries lay in brilliant colors. Abe was so awed at the deep, rich history of art throughout the centuries that he didn't know what to do first—sink into the book, or into Sarah's glowing eyes as she sat with her chin cupped on her hands.

"Thank you Sarah. This is outstanding." Abe glanced up from the book as he peeked at the pages. "I'll refer to this book forever and ever. Thanks so much." A quick smile sent highlights into his eyes, conveying a private message.

"And this one," she breathed, pointing to *Football for Even You.* "It's a collaboration of several sports writers. In as much as we don't have football at our high school, Max thought it would round out your sports education." Her arms were now folded in front of her, elbows resting on the table, lifting her eyes from the book to Abe.

"He's right about one thing. I *don't* know much about football. The book will be invaluable. Thank you again; both were good choices." He found his breath coming in short supply. After sharing special glances with Sarah, Abe turned his attention to the new books, enjoying the magical moments.

"It's not over yet, Abe," Bernard said, reaching into his jacket pocket for a small box, curling ribbon cascading from it like sleet outside the window. "This is for you from me," he went on slowly, laying emphasis on each word, his blue eyes mischievous.

Abe's eyes shifted snappily from Bernard to the gift as if he were a cocker spaneil waiting for a ball to toss into the air. Untying the ribbons and pulling off the wrapper with a trifle more delicacy than he had shown with Sarah's gift, he lifted his eyes and smiled. Bernard nodded in anticipation, encircling his mug with his whole hand, encouraging Abe's big hands to conquer the testy task.

Abe's eagerness had reached a feverish pitch by the time he found under the wrapping paper a gift box boasting silver and white diagonal stripes. Would it always be this exciting and adventurous? People need to be rich to gift such as this! Lifting the cover, his eyes fell upon a bone-handled jackknife bearing an emblazoned stainless steel crest. His hands clenched on the small box accompanied by a quick intake of breath.

The knife sparkled under the ceiling light while the memories it evoked played mayhem in his mind. Abe stared incredulously, going stiff as the frozen tree branches outside. Thoughts of the stolen jackknife come flooding in on him—the longing, the nefarious act of removing the knife from the store, lies and confession all followed by punishment sanctioned and served. It changed him forever.

How'd Bernard know that he never *did* get that jackknife…even after he'd paid his debt to society? He could no longer stand the sight of it. It had been private—a special kind of knowledge. Only he knew that. Magnetically, Abe raised eyes to Bernard, where he found a cornucopia of warmth and smiling blue eyes, the crinkles spreading out as wide and far as the ripples on a pond.

Permeating stillness shrouded the kitchen as if the winter storm had ceased its onslaught to add decisive influence to the occasion. Down the beach, a dog nagged at the nasty night, and the Nahma Northern train entered town from the north sounding two long plangent whistles, then two short staccato bursts. Silence stayed the room; only the coffee pot perked in slow gulps at the back of the range. Abe knew he was running out of reaction time, but his head felt as full of cotton batting as the little gift box.

"Think, t*hink,*"Abe whispered almost under his breath. He finally breathed, "Thank you. Thanks so much. I've always wanted to have a jackknife of my own. I guess that I'm old enough to own one now." There was a sensitiveness about his soft statement, but it did not lack humor, trying unsuccessfully to tether his lips to his teeth. "I can't think of anything I would have wanted more," he said, his hand shooting across the table to shake Bernard's firmly.

A smile of acceptance blossomed big on Bernard's face. He uncomfortably raised his shoulders, working his neck in a gesture of apology for the myriad of doubts that had swarmed on Abe's face.

Doc having finished his cake, held his mug by the ear, his shoulders hunched around his elbows resting on the table. "I wasn't prepared with a birthday gift for you, Abe, but I do have something that will be beneficial. I know you want to go to the University of Michigan when you graduate, and to get admitted you'll need a foreign language." Out of his coat in the living room he produced a Spanish textbook and placed it in front of Abe. "Now you'll have a chance to look over the first few chapters, and next fall we'll start Spanish lessons—you and I." Smiling down at Abe, he reached out and massaged his shoulders and neck.

Sarah observing him closely, for the first time noted his gentle eyes that shouted trust. His thick mustache was groomed in spades over his wholesome white teeth. She awed at his presence, his prestigious and confident presence.

Abe sat overwhelmed by the text and the offer of tutelage. He didn't know what to say so he murmured a husky "thanks" and raised his eyes from the book to Doc. How could he ever repay these people? Again, his hand peeled into the pages of a book bearing uncharted information.

"You don't know how much this means to me. Thank you again," he said making eye contact with both benevolent men who had befriended him a hundred times in the past few years. Tightly under the chair, Abe tucked his Big Chief company store boots, pulling in the reins of that part of himself he held private, that small part of himself that would always be just his.

"You're entirely welcome. You've earned that jackknife. I hope you enjoy it for the rest of your life and think of me whenever you use it."

"Also, think of me when you read my books!" interjected Sarah, her hand reaching out to cover Abe's. He gathered her fingers close within his. She felt the whip end of an emotion course through her. It hadn't dimmed since that evening on the beach.

"And think of me whenever you grow weary of conjugating the Spanish verbs," Doc added, smiling his vintage thin wet smile.

"I surely will. I'll never forget it, never." Abe's emotions mixed so that he knew he'd never forget this birthday, never forget the people sitting at his kitchen table while the wind howled outside like screaming banshees sweeping sleet before their assault...he never did. In times of future adulation, the humbling scene moved across his mind.

Deep in thought, Abe tugged at his shirt readying himself for a warm shower, chilly after washing the car and cleaning the loft. He remembered that he'd wanted to do something for Bernard Tobin to show his appreciation for the many courtesies he'd extended to him, but there were only ten days remaining until Christmas break.

The soothing shower relaxed the anxieties, the time limitations, and the wan loose light of the past December. As if it were yesterday, the surreal memory rolled in on him. He remembered debating if ten days was enough time to paint a picture of the school to present to Bernard for a Christmas gift. *Just do it!*

Tobin was a standup icon for today's world, and what a brilliant tactician, someone who pulled him through things thick and thin and instilled in him confidence. A vertically underprivileged man, Tobin lived big inside and spunky. Was he an extraordinary person? The answer, of course, was that there are no ordinary people. Abe possessed personal knowledge of treatment as a sub-culture, but he refused to allow himself be adjudged as ordinary.

Abe's eyes glazed over as he transported himself into his private bubble.

Aching to create, he decided to do it. His ancestral spirits stirred an inspiring concept. Abe never thought of himself as a particularly talented artist, or even that his canvas would be any more than a token way of saying "thanks" for all the favors received in the last five years from this irreplaceable superintendent.

Towing down, Abe remembered that he'd picked up a forty-by-fifty inch canvas from Max, and in the early morning light he tackled the project in the living room. Daylight hours shrunk with the fast approaching winter solstice, so by the time he arrived home in the evening from his job at the Company Store it was too dark to paint.

Fabian observed the angst skimming just below the surface of Abe's skin. "You're never going to get that picture done in time for Christmas at this pace. You take these twenty dollars," he said, slapping them down on the cupboard.

"Buy yourself a bright lamp at the company store for greater clarity of your color blends."

Abe, recovering from seeing twenty dollars in front of him, adamantly refused. "I can't do that; that's a whole lot of money. It was a stretch to start the project at this time of the year. The shadings are so delicate because the snow on the ground is only a few shades lighter than the gray school. It's as if I'm defining the color difference between the bay ice and puddle ice. I don't want them to be homogenous; they need to have contrast." Abe set his paintbrush down.

He drew the back of his wrist over his brow. "This is pure frustration. I know what I want to paint, but I don't have enough light. When I have enough light, I'm not able to paint." Glancing up at Fabian, his dark brown eyes cloudy, he confessed. "I can't ask you for anymore expenditures, Dad. We're barely getting by now. Thank you for the offer, however." Getting out the turpentine, he cleaned his brushes, wiped them on a stretch of gauze, and set them aside for the night—maybe for the duration. Squeezing Fabian's shoulder, he said goodnight

The next night when Abe came home from work, Fabian had one of his favorite dinners waiting for him: pot roast, oven baked with small potatoes and carrots simmering in thick gravy. The rich beefy aroma skittered throughout the house.

"How did you know that I was starving to death! Now this is a dinner!"

Fabian laughed, his eyes twinkling up at Abe from his stooped shoulders and bent head. "As soon as you finish dinner, go start on your Tobin canvas." He nodded toward the living room. "I'll kick around in the kitchen and do up the dishes. You'll never get that painting ready for Bernard if you work all the time."

Fabian, with his back turned, grinned from ear to ear.

Abe sighed. "Thanks Dad. I'll give it another whirl." He wanted Fabian to feel good about his offer, but it didn't solve Abe's problems. Moving reluctantly away from the table, he combed back his hair with his fingers looking like someone living with a bottomless problem.

The sky, smudged with somber gray ash, gave small encouragement. Upon entering the living room, he saw not one but *two* new lamps next to his canvas, both of photographer quality and intensity, just waiting to blow into action.

"What did you do, Dad?" Abe barely breathed. "You didn't go out and buy those lights for me? I told you not to do that but they're ever so nice. I'm *glad* you did it," he choked. "Thanks so much!" He didn't know whether to laugh or cry.

Abe's reaction was as Fabian had expected. Standing at the kitchen sink, he blustered and sniffed. "Well, if you think that you can finish that picture in dim light and have everything hunky-dory, your mind has pooped out."

"Dad, you old fox. Did you get into that car and drive all the way downtown?" His lips parted in pure surprise, hanging there. "How'd you do that? You can hardly get in and out of the car." Abe was suddenly aware of the explosiveness in his voice, the tears bright in his eyes. "You shouldn't have done that," he said more calmly. His eyes glistened with excitement—contentment and gratitude. "Is there nothing I can say to have you take these back? It's too much." His voice cracked.

Fabian turned back to the sink to give Abe a minute to recover with dignity. "Well, I did it. My heart was hammering, but I knew *you* wouldn't buy them. I didn't care what it did to me, how it made *me* feel. Now you can finish your project with colors that are exactly as you want them to be. Now don't flubbadub it!"

Fabian snorted as he moved slowly around the kitchen in his floppy slippers, making scuffing sounds across the linoleum. Sneaking a peek at Abe, Fabian stood immobilized, fully aware of the sense of accomplishment that trip to the Company Store had given to both of them—fully aware of what the lamps meant to his son, and his son's future. No one had to tell him that his own future was growing bleak.

There existed between them a bond beyond blood. It was carved deep within his caving chest. He'd live on through him, his boy child. He had been a perfect baby. Fabian found every aspect about baby Abe to be remarkable, especially the way he opened his fingers and then curled them around his fingers. From the very moment Abe nestled his mouth to Suki's breast, Fabian knew his feelings for Abe were cast in stone.

As for Abe, nobody had ever promised him rainbows and roses for the rest of his life or for even a small part of it. Nevertheless, this gift of lighting had come close. Turning on the lights, he nearly froze in the glare of clarity it created on the canvas.

"Dad, every little nuance jumps out at me. I can see screaming skirmishes where my colors weren't blended well; they're drifting." A shudder of disappointment ran through him, realizing his fallibility without sufficient light to attend the thousand details that were now brilliantly unmasked. He had a completely new feeling about the picture. He imagined himself across the boulevard north from the school—no, somewhat east. He flashed his memory at that angle. This would allow for two buses in the driveway on the east side, and the entire front of the school with all the windows.

He added the U.S. flag whipping in the stiff winter wind—students hurrying down the sidewalk to the west entrance carrying books and huddling their shoulders against the cold. The exhaust from the two buses burst straight up in the cold, dry air, forming ice crystals. Reverting to his vantage point, he peeked through the sturdy branches of a giant white pine laden with snow to get all the windows of the study hall into the picture. Alternatively, should he use an early-morning winter fog off the lake fraternizing with the trees, teasing, lifting and blending? Yes, he would.

The evening of the twenty-second found Abe putting the final changes on the effort. "Come see Dad. Tell me what you think. Hope Mr. Tobin likes it. It *does* look just like the school. Think it has enough color?" Abe had crawled into and lived within this picture for the past ten days and could no longer be critical—no longer offer an appraisal—no longer trust his judgment. He respected Fabian's discerning eye.

The restless winter wind whipped around the corner of the house creating background sound bank in the stove and causing windows to shudder. Shuffling over to the canvas with the floods on it, Fabian lost his breath. Drinking in the elixir of the scene, his stomach felt butterflies in full flutter. A rapid measuring of his son swept over him—*he had raised a gifted child.* The work moved with indolent cold yet stirred the viewer to seek the shelter and warmth waiting inside the schoolhouse.

Fabian studied Abe's profile—the bony cheeks and jaw line of the Sioux, the anticipatory emotions he was tucking away pending his judgment call. Fabian knew at that moment in time. He knew his son was grown and in control. He'd be able to maintain himself on his own. He also knew that the clock was ticking away for him—that he'd probably never ever see another finished canvas. No one had to tell him that recovery for him was out of the question. He allowed the indulgence of weariness to creep over him, never before tolerated.

He stared at the completed work with the fixation of a statue, standing in awe at the school-come-to-life in this singular offering. The focus of the building stood in symmetrical balance to the waves of white snow driven by the north wind that had banked up in front of it. Silver gray, the building stood stark in the shivery setting, its black roof showing only here and there through the mantle of snow. The tactile quality of the shades of gray, white and silver were viewed with a fine distribution of tones and shades. To the snow banks in front of the school Abe had applied the oil with an impasto, projecting the drifts from the picture's surface. Fabian's eyes blazed with the recording of the scene, as much frozen in time as the wondrous work before him.

The multiple large windows in front of the school stood highlighted with an intense brightness that inclined Fabian to squint and blink. Standing as a sentinel to education, the louvered cupola on top the school climbed valiantly against a winter sky. Fabian had a visceral feeling to dawdle there and climb into the warp of the scene before him. He could do it—the picture creating a rising pull of power, clutching him in its presence. He imagined he could live there, forever young and healthy.

A staunch white pine nearest to the artist had discernible needles hanging long, identifiable and deep rich green against the charcoal bark of the trunk. Abe's values of the greens, grays and browns were alive. The USA flag sprung awash in a fresh northwest breeze. Students wore coats in primary and secondary colors splashed against the white of the snow and the silver gray of the building. From their mouths escaped clouds of frosted air.

Abe had worked magic on the scene. Fabian's dreamy smile faded as an overwhelming seriousness superseded. "Son..." He swallowed hard. "It's outstanding," he whispered, not trusting his delivery. "Don't *ever* stop painting, Abe," he said while tousling his son's hair. "It's truly a gift from God." A great smile spread across his mouth. "Whatever self-doubts you entertain in your lifetime, don't ever doubt your talent as an artist. I wish that I had a trophy or a gold medal to give you."

The heat of admiration shimmering in Fabian's eyes was food for Abe's hungry soul. He flashed Fabian one of his deepening, irresistible grins.

The gentle pride in Abe's deep eyes ripped a hole in Fabian's gut, knowing that time stood limited in which he'd receive more of those smiles. What a source of solace to know that Abe had this talent to fall back on in life. Fabian readily recognized the young man's shortfalls. He'd need this talent for sustenance. Although his head was in a bubble most of the time, his body was perfect, alive with easy suppleness, health and strength. *God adds and subtracts.* In him he saw himself, years ago: clean, wholesome and unscathed by the world. His hands trembled with gratification, while his heart chugged to push life's blood through his diminishing lungs.

On the twenty-third, the last day of school before break, Abe wrapped the canvas in an old sheet, tied binder twine and red curling ribbon around it and transported it to the school in the back seat of the 1938 Ford. The road there seemed like a surreal ribbon, seemingly smooth and flowing, carrying him to some manifest destiny. Parking in the east driveway next to the buses, he slipped in through the grade school door. Bernard's office door stood closed; Abe knocked lightly.

"Yeah, it's open. C'mon in." Bernard sounded preoccupied. "Abe!" He said looking up from his desk. *Why does that kid always make me smile?* "What are you selling today? Whatever it is, I don't want any." His laughter was so genuine that his eyes crinkled.

"Got a present for you for all the nice things you've done for me, simple as that." Abe's eyes were warm, bright, his gaze direct and honest. Standing the canvas on a guest chair, the very one he'd sat in for his jackknife interrogation, Abe, with the sleight-of-hand movement of a magician, tugged the twine, ribbon and sheet from his creation and smiled his devastatingly best, standing even taller than his six feet two.

Bernard's face dropped. His jaw unfolded. Fighting with a desire to sob, he bobbled his ear lobe. "My God, Abe," he gasped. "That's absolutely outstanding—gripping. It's alive! I shiver at the cold emanating from that picture." His voice was as dusty dry as a desert. "It's for me?" he asked, his voice still in low gear, his glance traveling over the revelation of the picture. "I think it should hang in the hall at school."

Abe for a moment lost some of his assurance, feeling a strange mix of elation and disappointment. "No. It's for you to take home for yourself." He blinked with concern.

"A beautiful piece of work like this?" Bernard was undaunted. "Hanging at home? No one will see it. It needs to hang in a prestigious place out in the hall with all the annual pictures of the graduates. That's what we'll do. Then *everyone* can enjoy it. This is too good to keep to myself." Bernard's adrenaline was flowing. He hauled himself to calm down, still breathing heavily.

Abe could see that his project was very touching for Bernard, causing undue duress. "Well, sure, that's okay," he said shifting his feet, "but I just want you to know that I painted it for you, if you ever want to change your mind." Abe was smiling, his misgivings disappeared about Bernard taking the painting home.

"This is the nicest gift I've ever received, Abe. Thank you again. I hope our association is long and productive." Bernard sat back in his chair. "My God, Abe. You have textures to your personality that show through in this rendering—layers and layers of exquisite textures."

Abe stood without words for a moment, engrossed in the flow of words from his superintendent. He anticipated years of association with this venerable man.

There are times when the past closes over like shifting sand dunes, buried and flattened forever, but this association would swirl and remain windborne in spite of the global war raging outside their insular domain.

CHAPTER EIGHT

Dressed in warm forest green sweats after his shower, he turned on the radio and executed a lazy sprawl in Fabian's old chair, lifting his feet to the ottoman. With the house freshly cleaned and furniture rearranged, some of the ghosts had vanished, but the spirits curled around his mind like smoke from a doused campfire. "Apple Blossom Time" greeted his ears from the Bendix radio, soothing his mind with images of impending spring.

Closing his eyes he remembered the fracturing of his whole world. He remembered the weight of his burden as if he walked sluggishly in metal boots. Nausea nibbled triple-fold with the recollection of the trauma of the past month.

A leaden afternoon affected churning clouds; rain spattered in intermittent sheets. Abe was eternally grateful that he had taken the '38 Ford to school that day instead of walking soaked and shivering the long mile and a half home.

Curiously, he felt an urgency about getting home as he stared through the flip-flop of the windshield wipers. Two hours later than usual due to Friday hours, he was hungry. His hunger was a cauldron of trolls that trooped around endlessly in his belly gnawing and gnashing. Frequently, Fabian reminded him that he grew faster than Topsy.

His thoughts of food vanished upon entering the driveway. There were no lights on in the house. Opening the garage door, he drove the vehicle into its stall. If not, a sheet of ice would cover it by morning. Abe ran with his head down for the back door.

Jingling his keys, he walked into the house and placed them onto the counter top. "Dad, I'm home!" The words struggled from a constricted throat. Silence hung heavy. "Hey, Dad," Abe shouted jovially. Stillness, reverberating stillness, he could taste it.

"Dad," his voice thickened as he walked into Fabian's bedroom and found him laying on top the made-up bed, breathing with difficulty. His blue chambray shirt was buttoned crooked, as if he had wrestled with the intricacies of the shirt closure.

"Dad! What happened?" He massaged Fabian's chest. "Talk to me, Dad, please." Bending over the bed, Abe flung his arms over him, his mouth gone dry.

Fabian, shoring himself up with a shot of adrenaline, doggedly whispered between deep gasps, "under mattress—envelope." His eyes opened only partly and frighteningly as those of a shark, empty of emotion, his mouth slack and loose.

Abe gulped air. His shoulders slumped. The hush of the house was ringing in his ears like a quadrant of telephones, his heart stuttering, pulling. His mind galloped, grasping, accepting, rejecting.

Quickly, he ran to the kitchen plucking the key ring from the cupboard. Darting outside, he lifted the garage door, warmed the car. All his thoughts were contained in a common thread of urgency. Decisions took only a matter of seconds but they seemed uncomfortably long.

Flying back into the house with feverish energy, he lifted Fabian off the bed. With precisioned fluid movements he carried him to the car and set him upright in the passenger seat. Fabian emitted a long, low groan from deep within his chemistry, animalistic, as his hazy eyes closed completely.

Abe hardly remembered driving to the hospital, could hardly remember abducting the nurse for assistance, returning to the car and carrying Fabian into the examining room.

Nurse Quigley assisted, directing him with her arms. A plain, heavy woman, she had a nervous habit of wrinkling her nose in times of stress. Her white nurse's stockings made a swish-swish sound as she walked, her bulging thighs rubbing together.

Abe experienced a palette of raw emotions as he sat on an examining stool near Fabian, listening to Quigley call Dr. Whittaker on one of only five phones in the village. Dr. Whittaker probably hadn't been home for more than an hour. He wished for better timing in this urgent cry for assistance. Fabian's breath came in shallow gasps, his chin bent down to his chest, his body not conforming to the symmetry of the table.

What happened to him? He was talking to me as usual this morning. How could he have deteriorated so badly in just those few hours?

"Can you do something for him, Quigley?" Abe intensified his gaze from Fabian to the nurse. Her small green eyes escalated to double magnification by her thick glasses. Abe's folded hands were agitated, his eyes filled with divisions of hope and despair.

Quigley shook her head, a veil pulling down over her eyes viewing Abe with her mouth open as though to hear better, her nose wrinkling. "We need to wait for Doctor Whittaker's orders; it'll be just a few minutes." Her facial muscles worked as she fought to arrange them in a look of cool calmness.

Standing on the opposite side of the examining table, she proceeded to remove Fabian's shirt, button-by-button. Her eyes traveled back and forth between Abe and Fabian as she tried to comprehend the puzzle of Fabian's buttoning eccentricities. Abe assisted her, the moment having timelessness in its commonizing endeavor.

A shiver ran through his body as the rain cut at the windows in spasms. He thought he could feel the chill breeze blow about the window sash. How he hated the sound. It made him want to lash back. This had to be the nightmare from hell.

"Dad!" Abe's voice was elevated, demanding. "Dad!" he shouted, breathing hard and fighting to control himself. His voice stuck in his throat as Dr. Whittaker filled the examining room with his tall, quiet dignity. "Evening Abe. What do we have here?" His eyes wrinkled as he took a narrowed look at Fabian.

For the first time, Abe viewed Fabian as Doc did, in silence, evaluating his shrunken body, his faded muscles. He swallowed a lump in his throat, as his face grew pale. Slowly he eased himself back onto the three-legged chrome stool.

Glancing appraisingly at Abe, he handed his coat to Quigley, his shoes making soft sounds on the floor. The aura of authority that he emanated was so self-assured that it was a foregone conclusion that Quigley would accept his coat without abusiveness or arrogance on his part. Abe observed how elegantly he dressed, even at this late hour, in a hundred-dollar suit that fit him like that of a meticulous monarch.

Abe watched Doc make a sweeping analysis of the degradation of the patient, while tapping his chest. Making eye contact with Abe, he proposed firmly, "Why don't you wait out on the sunporch, Abe? We'll call you as soon as we have Fabian situated." Doc's British accent was clipped, the command in his voice superseding his suggestion.

Without hesitating, Abe stood to leave, but as he unfolded, he was consumed by a swirling suffocation that overlaid and devoured him. For a brief moment, the sounds of the room and the wind on the window echoed in his ears and seemed far removed. The floor pitched like the deck of a ship.

Dr. Whittaker was at his side instantly. "Okay, young man. Now let's not move for a minute while you regain some equilibrium. When did you last eat?"

Doc wore an air of watchful judgment and assisted Abe to sit down, lowering his head gently.

"I had a sandwich and a glass of milk for lunch, whenever that was," he breathed heavily, his voice husky. Abe reeled with anxiety and hunger to which he'd not given a passing thought for the past two hours.

"Quigley, have your aide prepare for Abe whatever the patients had for dinner tonight." Slowly, Doc helped Abe advance out into the hall and onto the sunporch, which served as the waiting room for the families of critical patients. "We'll call you as soon as we have Fabian settled," he promised in his executive manner. "I'll take the best route for him that holds solid, Abe. The Man upstairs has a master plan by which He molds our destinies. Sometimes, nothing I do is of great consequence." Doc rested his hand on Abe's shoulder, giving it a comforting squeeze.

The contented sunporch was secure from the echoing spats of sleet that assaulted the heavily windowed room. Abe stared absently at a calendar hanging on the wall near the door bearing a charcoal sketch from the *Saturday Evening Post*. The caption underneath read: "MARBLE CHAMPION, 2 SEPTEMBER 1939, by Norman Rockwell." There he saw a determined looking young girl kneeling, aiming her marble into the middle of a mumbly-peg circle while two boys watched.

His concentrated presence in the marble picture abruptly halted when Quigley brought him a meatloaf sandwich and a bowl of hot vegetable beef soup from the kitchen. It was pheasant under glass. His knees spongy, he felt frayed around the edges with shock, hunger and tragedy. He could feel a granddaddy of a headache coming on, wondering ironically if he could get an aspirin in this place.

"Thanks so much. How's Dad? Is he ready to see me yet? Can I go in there now? I can eat later. I need an aspirin, too..." His voice thinned out.

"Soon, young man, soon. You eat something now, and yes, I'll get you an aspirin." The veil drew down again. Abe, warmed by the soup and sandwich, envisioned the rest of the hospital. He'd been here at times with Fabian. This room was his favorite with wicker furniture wearing brightly flowered, pink and maroon cretonne padding.

Hanging with vines and feathered fronds of delicate greenery, two jardinière ferneries stood along the wall. Abe sat attentive to the magazines on the wicker tables and the straw rug which ran from the outside double doors to the inside double doors and across the foyer to the seven-foot-wide stairway leading upstairs to the patient rooms. Immediately at the top of the stairs and off to the left grew a cook's delight kitchen.

Downstairs and off to the left as one came in from the sun porch was a two-bed emergency/critical care room. Off to the right was the surgery/delivery room. In the middle of the downstairs there existed examining rooms, the doctor's office, a pharmacy and at the very back, a waiting room. Fabian had told him on a recent visit that the total square footage was approximately eight thousand square feet.

"Okay, Abe." Dr. Whittaker rubbed his hands together and sat on the wicker couch near him folding his hands between his spread knees, studying this handsome young man, wondering how far to delve into his fractious state.

"Where did you come from? I've been sitting here all the while, and I didn't see you come in." Abe had been shaken out of his bubble dream of the hospital layout, not in small degrees, but in one obtrusive invasion.

Doc smiled at the mix of doubt and dismay registered on Abe's face. "It's magic, I guess." Doc's caring eyes made direct eye contact, smiling.

With the heel of his hand, Abe slapped his forehead. "I'm losing it!" But he didn't sound very convincing; a visible shudder ran through him.

Doc smiled then set his jaw a flicker off plumb. "Actually, when I'm called out at night I come in through the pharmacy. So, you see, it really isn't a mystery at all."

Abe nodded, always in awe in the presence of this premier person. He fought to hold back the surge of questions he had for Doc, knowing he was barely coherent.

"I've examined Fabian. He's bad, Abe." Doc paused uneasily, looking down. Couching his message in medically understandable terms, he drew an implicit picture for Abe. "It's his lungs. He's not been able to get enough oxygen and he's developed an infection. I've given him something to reduce the fever, but he's not regained consciousness. I have him in the critical care room across from surgery." He paused.

The silence quickly brought Abe's pensive attention slicing to Doc.

Lifting his eyes to Abe, Doc went on evenly and with one-on-one intimacy. "Even though the malady started way the hell gone and back, this turn for the worse surprised me. With proper medications, I've added years to Fabian's life, but not life to his years. These spondilitis infections are insidious and perverse. Unpredictable." Doc studied Abe closely for signs of comprehension and level of anxiety. He knew he was leading the young man down a cold path where the walk steadily darkened.

Abe's face collapsed in confusion. "You mean that...are you saying..." Abe exhaled a distressful moan sensing the assaulting news, feeling strangely indignant. It just couldn't be! His face worked—struggling—struggling to take in this information, decipher and understand it. The analysis came like a roaring avalanche—one that had come silently to rest and left an overwhelming hush. It was the end of life, the junking of an earthly body. He wanted to swear; he wanted to go into hysteria of pent-up laughter; he wanted to whap a hole in the wall. A roaring in his ears established itself.

Doc stood and nodded, shoving his hands into his pockets. "This is a judgment call, but I really don't think you should expect him to last the night. You might try talking to him. Sometimes messages get through even though the patient doesn't respond. I'll check on him once again before I leave for the night." Doc turned away, indicating for Abe to come with him.

Fabian lay propped against three pillows, desperate for every breath, his chin frozen in a down position. If not comfortable, he looked fresh in his hospital gown. Doc looked at Abe with scarcely concealed empathy, took a breath as if to convey a message, then paused, uttering not a word. Managing a small smile, he nodded, turned, and walked quietly away. The wind clamored at the north-facing window, rushing at the building, as if it had backed off, gone in a complete circle, and attacked again with renewed vigor.

Abe lumbered to a chair and lowered himself into it. Closing his eyes as if to shut out the scene, the night, the terror, he swallowed hard. Dying. Fabian couldn't die! This must be some cruel joke. He was just sick. He'd get better. Abe opened his eyes; the lamp on the table in between the beds cast shadows into the corners of the room. *God! Are you listening to me? Don't take my dad. I have no one else!*

"Dad, Dad, can you hear me? It's me, Abe." Walking a deep chair over to the side of the bed, he drew Fabian's hand into his own. He wondered if this was real, as if he was riding the edge between a nightmare and reality. This morning was just another Friday in March, and now damn it, it grew into an old day that looked at death too. Abe lowered his head to Fabian's hand. He wished he were a small boy again, with Fabian sitting by *his* bedside. Strange, how fast the journey from June to December in one's tenure on earth. It wasn't the pace of life that brought Fabian to this sudden stop, but his gene pool where there were no lifesavers.

He stared at the clock on the wall moving in its path around the hours in herky-jerkies, *a-click, a-click, a-click*. It sounded like a time bomb to him...thirty seconds to hell...measuring the ending of a day, the closing of a life.

Abe leaned forward in his chair, his elbows on his knees, his chin cupped in his hands. The hair stood out on his arms as he shivered; a phalanx of fear marched through his body. His toes contracted. Chasing one another for first place, memories flooded in upon him. He sorted them, one at a time, savoring, examining.

"Remember, Dad, when we used to go fishing for perch off the docks by the mill? We could do that again, you and me. How about all the great summer nights we sat on the front porch until dark? You told me stories while the fireflies blinked in the bushes, and I shed my childhood worries with just one of your hugs. I never *said* I liked hugs, but I did. I always worried that you might leave me, too, like Suki. Seemed to me that if it happened once, it could happen again. I thrilled to the long gliding paths you took me on into the interior of Rumplestiltskin and Pinocchio. And did I ever tell you that I liked the white alyssum and lilies of the valley we had growing around our front porch?"

Fabian's hand stirred in minutia, but Abe felt the electricity. Could it be? A surge of intense emotion pulsed through his body, starting in his chest and shooting clear to his fingers and toes like lightning.

Rejuvenated, he reached deeper into his memory reserves while still squeezing Fabian's thin hand. "How about that pair of hockey skates you bought for me when I turned ten years old? You were the fox, placing a *Wanted* sign in the store, and then bought them for fifty cents. I can't tell you how many times I prayed to have hockey skates, as if my Guardian Angel, maybe, would bring them. I used to think that would do it...just pray and it would become reality. Ain't that the berries? Just send up those prayers, and the next morning all of them would be answered. However, *you* did it, Dad. *You* answered my prayers."

Fabian's breathing became barely discernible at times. Abe reached out and straightened his gown, smoothing, caressing, the gesture a subtle ownership of this man, the most important person in his life. He struggled to hang on to that edge he rode.

The logging train wailed into town. Abe knew it wore an umbrella of white steam accompanied by the mundane clack and roll of the cars as it irreverently passed by to the west of the hospital. The storm cushioned the lonesome whistle as it approached the Indian Town Road.

Abe's attention stumbled back to his driving lessons. "I'll never forget learning to drive the car. That took the cake, and didn't we laugh? You're the best, Dad. You gotta stick around to cook me more of your famous meals. I'm going to starve to death if you don't. You hear me Dad?"

Fabian lay inert and unresponsive as Abe stomached reality. He envisioned an hourglass slowly losing its contents through a narrow channel, hitting him with the knowledge of how finite the flesh, how numbered our days.

He pushed the chair back and walked over to the north window in a vacuum of loneliness. Piercing his pockets with hands that felt useless, the enormity of what transpired came crashing down on him. Framed in the window stood trees lashed by wind, streetlights a muffle of pale light twisting and dancing a macabre rhythm to the driving sleet. Abe pulled the shade down as a barrier to the depressing weather. He could hear his own tattered breathing. Tears threatened.

Get a hold on yourself! You'll be alone now. In the end, you only have yourself, maybe Farley and Norrhea, but don't bank on it. No one's going to explain this to you so it makes sense. What is, is. Can I handle it? Can I climb another mountain, this time without my best friend? Oh God! Please, don't take him. He muffled a sob.

Doc Whittaker came by, listened to Fabian's breathing, recorded his blood pressure, observed Abe—the beaten expression, his dark eyes a mixture of hurt and hope.

He spoke kindly yet firm. "You use that other bed tonight, Abe. I told Quigley to bring in whatever you need such as pajamas, toothbrush, whatever. I'll return in the morning before seven. Try to get some rest." He paused for a moment, but it seemed there was nothing more to say.

Abe paled, his shoulders hitching. As if in a dream, he watched Doc walk over to him, close his hand over his own, pat him on the back. He recognized the gesture of sympathy that matched the care written on Doc's face, easing the grief somewhat.

The room grew instantly quiet again upon Doc's departure. Through Abe's head flew scraps of flitting thought: only yesterday he was five years old, only yesterday Fabian took him to the beach and taught him to swim. A cold fist out of nowhere wrung at his heart. Easing himself further into the empty chair, Abe postured himself for another attempt to communicate.

"Dad," he said, folding Fabian's hand again. "You gotta stick around...we haven't gone to Sault Ste. Marie to see the locks yet, you and I, remember? Besides, I haven't painted a picture just for you since I did the beach sweet peas." The guilt hit hard and low. Thoughts produced teeming words tumbling out like spilled Bingo beans. "Remember you always told me I lived a survivor? And that if I wanted to know what time it was to just listen to my stomach? All good stuff, Dad."

"Really funny stuff too. Like the time you told me about Tom Tweetie, the game warden. You pointed out how bow-legged he looked in his jodhpurs. You always made me laugh. Geez! We used to go fishing on the Sturgeon River where the meanders had eddies and the brook trout gathered. How frightened I was the first time we startled a great blue heron into flight. But you were there, and that's all that mattered."

The thoughts hung mindless in the small room that contained his father's withered body—thin, skeletal, the skin on his cheeks taut as if covered by wax. His last ticking moments. *So little is needed to die*, he thought.

The hospital sank sodden with pervasive silence that hung in the air. It developed as if there were a black hole that sucked out the essence of the moment, his energy, Fabian's life and the very light in the room. He could smell methanol and cleaning agents, could hear now the susurration sounds of night movements from upstairs. He felt lost in this dark maze as the clock continued its endless clicking. He wanted to pound it with his fist and muzzle interminable time forever.

He had felt so all-together and strong when he'd arrived at the hospital, but now the hopelessness of the situation bathed him in sweat. He sat spent, and could think of nothing more to say, his mouth dry as an old sock in the sun. Leaning his head atop Fabian's hand, Morpheus, the god of dreams swept him into the land of forgetfulness until the shift change at six thirty.

He awoke with a start in a strange room, his mind muddled. Darkness clung outside, and a howling wind knocked at the windows. Disoriented, his tongue sleeping, he slurred, "Dad!" Fabian's face viewed no longer flushed with fever, but ashen, his jaw slack. How still he lay, his eyes closed, his breathing raspy.

"Dad! Talk to me, Dad." From sleeping hours in a chair, his legs hardly functioned as he tried to stand. He churned sick at his stomach; a bug crawled around in his mind, and his confidence waned. The bug in his mind found the little boy lost.

"Dad, you need a shave. Would you like for me to do that for you?" he urged, wanting to do something, some small thing. Grabbing Fabian's shoulders, he shifted him up straighter on the pillows. "Don't leave me now, Dad," he breathed hoarsely. *Oh, God let me wake up from this nightmare*. His mouth felt as if he'd been eating beach sand.

Doc Whittaker came around early, just as promised. Abe could hear him talking to Quigley, who had come back for the day shift. Together they whisked into the room. Quigley quickly opened the shade to another day of rain and sleet. The wind still complained against the small windowpanes, ice built up in the corners like the snow on a Currier and Ives Christmas card.

Abe backed off from the bed. Words couldn't get past the boulder in his throat. Tears coursed down his cheeks, his body registering what his mind still rejected. He felt robotic drifting in a vacuum of time indeterminable. He understood none of this as his heart thudded high in his throat.

Doc had the stethoscope to Fabian's chest, his back, re-arranged his pillows, and stared down at the lingering humanity that had been passing on in pieces for years—down to his last piece to give. Doc's eyes were a mixture of sorrow and relief.

Fabian took two shallow breaths. Then nothing... His chest sank and stilled.

"No!" Abe cried, "No!" The words were guttural.

Doc listened once more—chest, back, checked Fabian's eyeballs, and shook his head. "He's gone, Abe. He's at peace now. No more pain. No more pills."

Abe froze, stricken dumb where he sat, impoverished for words. Not dead. Not alive. Not feeling anything. Numb. Dumb numb. He stooped in overload. Just one more thing, one more thing, and he would snap. He breathed in a deep rush that sounded like a growl. *Let it go. Just let it go.* The unwanted tears burned in his eyes. They found free flow. Then the dam broke with unspeakable grief accompanied by soul wrenching sobs that tore him apart as he placed his head in his hands and wept. How he hated the slashing rain at the window. His house of cards had blown down.

A myriad of miniature thoughts moved in his mind like motes in a sunbeam. *I've lost my best friend, my dad. Why did I not see it coming? Now what will I do?* It was too late to ask, too rotten late. *Too late to tell him how much he loved him. Too late. Too late to tell him how much he'd miss him. Too late for everything.*

Having pulled his chair closer to the bed in weary abandonment, he sat with his head over Fabian's dead hand, flung his arms over Fabian's belly, and leaked his grief, remorse, loneliness and fear. They were touching with the last thread of love. Together for the last time, he could feel it.

The great mill in Abe's mind lay as dank and dismal as the weather. He kissed Fabian, kissed him for the last time. Hadn't kissed him since he was a little kid. "I love you, Dad," he choked. "Will forever and ever."

Rounding the bed, Dr. Whittaker kneaded Abe's shoulders and neck, administered an avuncular pat and quietly left the room with Quigley. Alone now to deal with unspeakable grief, Abe collided with the yin and yang of his relationship with Fabian. He wore yin holding murkiness within, where untamed fervors raged. Fabian wore yang, brilliant reality enlightening fresh minds such as his. There lay a huge leap of logic between what Fabian construed as life-lessons and the reckless inclinations of Abe. Would he now fall into one deep chasm after another?

"I'm going to call Father McKevitt. I'll call Farley and Norrhea too," Doc confided to Quigley, hoarseness in his normally commanding voice. "I'm aware that Fabian never kept in touch with them, but they *are* Abe's grandparents and they could be of considerable comfort to him. Fabian was as stubborn as a mule and so was Farley. They butted heads like an irresistible force and an immovable object."

"Sounds like a plan to me." Her nose wrinkled; she blinked prejudicially at him through thick glasses, and then a look of pleased surprise spread over her face. "Yes."

With blurry eyes, Abe looked out the window and saw the gray day but night strung along behind, determined not to be thrown away. It remained dreary and dowdy.

It wasn't a half hour and Abe's grandparents were in the room with him, as well as Father McKevitt wearing his black surplice and berretta, a purple stole about his neck, an Extreme Unction Kit in hand.

"We'd have been here sooner, had we known, Abe." Farley, apologetic, cold and wet as he hurried into the room, was appalled that this young man, his grandson, should have witnessed his father's death with no family support. "From now on you won't be able to shake loose of us. Remember, the Great Spirit is already welcoming Fabian. He has traveled the Hanging Road to the Spirit Land by now." Stepping over to the bed, Farley enfolded Fabian's hand and chanted in guttural tones, "*Nimeaseoxzheme.*" May your journey be a good one. "*Hoka hey*! It's a good day to die!"

Eyebrows raised, the priest competitively solemnized the final anointment. "*In nomine patre, et spiritu, sancte, Amen.*" The holy oils in finality were administered to Fabian's head, his lips and his heart.

Farley stood a tall good-looking cuss. Abe hadn't seen many Indians with curly hair, but then he had never seen much of *him* or Norrhea. It occurred to him that if Suki were as beautiful as everyone says, she came by it naturally. Farley owned sculptured features and Norrhea with her dark hair and eyes had the look of an Indian princess.

"We want you to come with us back to your house." Norrhea extended solace putting her arm around Abe's waist. Her face reflected a choke as she observed Abe's pathetic posture, broken and embattled. "I'll fix breakfast while you take a shower and put on a new day. You'll see. You'll feel better afterwards." She held him closely, noting that his body dwelled tall, lean and hard.

Doc Whittaker inquired as to which funeral home Farley wanted to use. "I'll call them for you," he said softly in deference to Abe's vulnerability.

"Hallo Funeral Home in Gladstone." Farley, while standing in the room of death with Doc, Abe and Norrhea, settled firm and became a take-charge person. "Thanks. We may be a while over at Abe's, and there's no phone there. Thanks, too, for calling us. We had no idea, none whatsoever," he said shaking his head in atonement, "but I should have expected bad news. The great owl hooted many times in the early hours."

Wordlessly, Whittaker nodded, well aware of the Sioux Tribal strong belief in the omen of birds, especially the owl, as a sign of death. One did not trifle with their rites and rituals. Instead, he clasped Abe firmly on the shoulder as the Indian family left. The wind drove through the door as they opened it, and a slant of sleet blew in.

At home, Abe showered while thoughts pinged in his head like sonar feedback. The last twelve hours were an intolerable horror. Fire and heat had been applied to his very existence with the diligence of Sioux vindictiveness. Life would be unendurable without Fabian. Would he become an orphan? His worry roster ended with where would he get money to live? *From Social Security, Abe! Remember this. Legislation of 1939 provided benefits for dependents under eighteen if regularly attending school.* Fabian's words came sliding in on one of the sonar feedbacks.

Where are you, Fabian? Behind closed eyelids, Abe imagined him walking away with slow bent steps, diminishing into the distance, never looking back. He let fly his thoughts after him, desperate and demanding. *Come back. Come back.*

Slowly his mind cleared with the drumming of hot water on his exhausted body. New perspectives nudged their way into his bearing. He recalled Fabian faintly whispering to him of an envelope under his mattress. Did he mean girlie magazines? But why would Fabian expend the last of his energy and breath on something so trivial?

Abe found the cache of publications between the mattress and the box spring. Wait just a minute! There *was* an envelope lodged way under there. He grunted, giving the mattress an extra lift and pulling out an 8 X 10 manila envelope with a string twister, the thin red strand forming a figure eight around two north/south, thick paper buttons. Sitting alone on the edge of Fabian's bed, he sagged in spirit and body. The air hung still and the loneliness an entity. Undoing the envelope, his eyes calmed in disbelief. Money!

There dwelled a smell to money, and old money resided ever so much more pungent. Spilling it out on the bed, he counted seven hundred and fifty dollars. What the hell! His eyes went wide enough to consume the better part of his face. Fabian must have been saving it for years and years. It banked his life's savings! *And a note.* "A note," Abe squeaked. He'd had doubts in his life, but never doubted his father's love, his allegiance, his dedication.

He read. "Abe, I know that it won't be long before I'll be leaving you forever. My disease is rampant and my constant companion. But I want you to know that I've always loved you, and will continue to love you into eternity. I'll be with you—in the sunny warmth of a summer day, in the turbulence of an autumn storm, in the sound of snow thudding off cedars, and when the lilies of the valley bloom early in the spring. I'll be there. Forget about the plans that don't work out quite right, just cherish dreams."

Slipping to the floor near the bed, Abe died a thousand deaths. His shoulders slumped over the note from heaven. He couldn't stop the tears, the desolation, and the emptiness. Finding rubber legs, he plodded out to the kitchen. The tantalizing smell of bacon and eggs greeted him as well as his grandparents. His eyes burning, meeting theirs, he took a chair across from Farley, turning it around and straddling the seat.

"Look at this," he said chokingly as he dumped the money out onto the oilcloth with a smooth swish, plop—plop, shaking the envelope upside down. Abe secured the note contained in the manila envelope for his own personal refuge. "When I came home from work last night and found Fabian semi-conscious, he willed himself enough spunk to reveal this envelope, but I forgot about it until now." His voice cracked and tears poured down his face again, tears from a fresh reservoir of sorrow.

Norrhea's heart in her eyes, she swung her gaze to Farley capturing an instant reinforcement. "Abe, we want you to know that we were never close to Fabian after he married Suki, but he never wanted the Indian element in his home. Nevertheless, do you have any idea how much we love you?" Leaving the bacon sizzling slowly in the cast iron frying pan, Norrhea placed her arm around Abe's shaking shoulders. "Even if you didn't have this money, we'd be there for you. We'd even sell our holdings in real estate if we had to, and if you knew how much that land meant to us, you'd know that's a whole lot of love." She looked to Farley for verbal reinforcement.

Struck by his grandson's grief, it took a minute for Farley to compose himself, speaking ever so softly. "You'll be all right, Abe. Every day that goes by will be better." He swallowed to reinforce his own convictions. "It's just going to take time. You're allowed to sorrow and grieve; it's the natural progression of things." His hand reached out across the table patting Abe's arm.

Resolution flickered in his eyes. "We need to make some decisions about the funeral arrangements." Farley continued crisp but cautious not wanting to interrupt the delicate balance of Abe's momentary containment. "We'll go slowly here." He cleared his throat of the ball of tanning leather growing there. "We could drive to Gladstone this morning, and get the whole thing settled, have the wake Monday night and the funeral Tuesday morning at St. Andrew's. Does that sound proper and fitting to you?"

Abe made no answer to bend toward funeral arrangements lest he break down.

"Say something, Abe. We're here for you." Farley rubbed the young man's arm soothingly while Norrhea served breakfast with freshly brewed coffee effusive in the room, giving comfort of home and hearth.

"Yes. Yes, we can do that," he responded in a dry scratchy voice. "It's just that it's so much to handle all at once." The tears slid down Abe's cheeks, this time silently. "I want to have his wake at home. We'll put...place him...in front of the big double north window in the living room. It's back-to-back with the front porch where we spent so much time there together."

"He devoted his whole life to making me feel good about myself—told me once that when two people loved each other they could never separate, ever, even by death. Said Suki told him that. One feels the presence of the other in a soft spring breeze, in a feather falling gently from the sky, in the first star of the evening, in a sunlit glint on the snow, or the dancing-diamonds of sunshine on water." He could feel Fabian's very breath over his shoulder, his touch, his love.

Instant joy sprang to Farley's eyes. "That's an old Sioux Indian belief. Suki *must* have taught him that," he said in dismay. "It's a good thought to hang onto, Abe. You'll find comfort in that forever. My faith in Fabian is renewed because he gleaned insight into the Sioux traditions before Suki left him. We must all live with the past and walk on into the future. Now let's move on and get over to Gladstone so we can get back at a decent hour," he said, not too subtly. There hung a long pause as Farley wished he could take back the insensitive words.

"I'm sorry, Abe," he said. "That sounded crass, but the weather isn't with us, so we need to allow ourselves time, *kola*, my friend."

CHAPTER NINE

At the time they entered the funeral home it had been raining for three days. Abe was immediately ill at ease. The somber music in the background and the dark conservative colors laid morose to him. Lenny LeVine, a slightly-built man, directed them into a private office. He had piercing black eyes, disciplined eyebrows and sunken cheeks with a cookie-duster mustache skimming plump pink lips. Dressed in a black suit, he emerged as dour as his funeral home. Upon introductions, his handshake fluttered cold and fleeting. As though it were a tedious task serving these Indians, he sighed theatrically.

"Please be seated," he said waving agitatedly at the guest chairs, which accommodated bereaved families and were in alignment as if planets in orbit. LeVine dropped into a very large chair behind his mammoth mahogany desk. He reminded Abe of some child Oriental king. The lack of ardor in his voice besieged Abe.

"We're prepared to take care of the funeral for Mister, ah, Mister. ...Let me see here," he said with hard eyes peering through pince-nez at the pertinent papers.

"Fabian Miereau," Abe interjected impatiently, growing a great amount of difficulty finding common ground with this man, Lenny LeVine. He'd never before had anyone make him feel so much a minion, a pilgrim.

"Yes, yes, indeed. Fabian Miereau," he said tasting his bristly mustache. Bearing pre-printed information, he handed each one of them a folder containing various funeral plans. "As you can see, we offer a one hundred-dollar funeral, which you will find listed at the top of the page." He pointed across the desk to see if these people were following his simple instructions. "That provides for a wake at the funeral home, a decent casket and two attendants at the church." Again, he looked up and grunted.

Abe shuddered in his sorrow. *Was death and dying reduced to this? Was there nothing in life that didn't equate to dollars and cents?*

"The two hundred-dollar funeral provides for an organist at the wake at the funeral home, my wife as a hostess, an upgrade on the casket and, of course, the attendants." He looked up, waiting for reactions. "Just speak up when you fall into a comfortable slot." He skinned his lips back in facsimile of congeniality.

No response.

LeVine went on. "The three hundred-dollar funeral provides for a wake in *your* home with soft downlights at either end of yet another up-graded casket, a vault, transportation to the church, transfer of flowers and a hostess." Again, his gaze swept this unusual element in his funeral parlor.

No response.

"The four hundred-dollar funeral provides for an up-graded vault, all the above with a further up-graded casket, all church expenses including sexton fees, and my wife as a hostess." Lenny LeVine sat back in his leather chair. He knitted his fingers together and twirled his thumbs around forward and reverse, waiting for the family to make their choice, savoring yet more pieces of gold in his coffers, be it ever so little in this instance.

Mrs. LeVine came into the room to check on the morning mail. She was a big woman wearing heavy glasses held up by a generous nose. Her wide liberal mouth pursed into place as she slid the morning mail one behind the other, ignoring the visitors and retreating with a swish, swish, swish of her black water-moiré taffeta skirt under which her bread-dough butt hung like an elephant's.

Abe viewed the scene as chaotic and cold, miserable and miserly. He felt himself slipping into a deep drop-off from a sandbar in Big Bay de Nocquet. Was he going to hide in the depths as a bottom feeder or uphold some kind of principle? Suspicion seeped into his regard for this primate sitting in front of him. Abe assumed the posture of a man who had a sudden revelation of the species: LeVine excessed as a baboon.

He and his wife were two unresponsive dollar bills who showed the concern of a doorknob. He couldn't be hearing these words, making these decisions. He felt so alone in the dark cavern of the drop-off, but a fierce light now pierced the darkness with dazzling sunlight that shimmered in waves down to his depth.

A new emotion rumbled under his skin. It polarized disrespect from dignity. Thorniness lay just under his skin, pulsing, born of the secondary importance visited upon him. Abe kept his own counsel, sorting the insults to his intelligence.

He viewed himself as a prime example of Boy Meets World, his intense loss aggravated by the insensitivity visited upon him by this Napoleonic dictator. He studied his Big Chief boots for the moment.

"Predicated on my past experiences with your people, I think that the two hundred-dollar funeral is best suited to your needs." His nostrils pinched in officiousness. With his bent forefinger he smoothed his mustache to the right and then to the left, impatient. "We have an easy payment plan that you can stretch over five years with an interest rate of only one percent per month on the unpaid balance." He leaned back, pleased with his offer, restlessly thrumming on the desk. The blue-white diamond ring on his little finger did not go unnoticed by Abe.

LeVine's superior expression never deviated as his eyes swept the faces of all three of them, feature by feature. Feeling that the process crept at a snail's pace, he gathered the pre-printed material, tamping the sheets on the desktop, adding a touch of finality to the transaction. "Now, I have the contract right here. My wife, Abbie, will serve as witness to your signature, ah Mister, Mister, ah yes, it's right here, Mr. ..."

Abe leaned forward, tapping the desk with his index finger, eyes flashing, and voice staccato loud. "Miereau. It's Miereau. That's M-i-e-r-e-a-u. Got that? What's more," he went on, his face livid, his words coming more easily than he'd ever known. "My first name is Abednego. That's A-b-e-d-n-e-g-o. Got that too? I've had a day sent to me straight from hell, and you sit there blowing smoke up my ass about what I can afford, about contracts, about the kind of performance you can put on for the price of a few pieces of silver—the more silver the better the performance!" Abe paused, his expression appalled. Abe's eyes did not conceal the contempt he felt for this baboon, whom he'd now mentally reduced to a snake.

Abe's free-flow of words were unstaunchable. "What's more, what do you offer for *five hundred dollars*? That's what I want." Abe's gaze froze, unflinching.

LeVine only thinly disguised the thin curve of his lip forming on his face. "Yeah, sure, and if wishes were horses, beggars would ride."

Abe bristled. "This beggar is riding you, skinflint. I want the finest casket, the finest vault, two attendants present for the wake as well as the funeral, transportation for all my guests without cars, my living room stacked with roses, total church expenses picked up, sexton fees included, and a breakfast after the mass for all my guests at the Nahma Hotel!" If he leaned any farther over the desk he and LeVine would be eyeball to eyeball, that is, if he could stand LeVine's foul breath any longer.

"And how do you propose to pay for that, Mr. Miereau?" LeVine waved a silencing hand at him, the I-can-handle-your-kind, Buster, lazy wave.

This time Abe couldn't stop the vulnerable tears. Seeing the smarmy smile on LeVine's face, laid back in his over-sized desk chair that established big enough to accommodate two skinny asses as his was more than he could bear.

"Cash!" he spit out between the tears. "As in c-a-s-h. Cash money." Abe's giant hulk of a body dwarfed LeVine. "You'll get half today and the other half upon the performance of *my* needs. Now draft a contract for that for your wife to witness. And I don't want her sad ass at my dad's funeral. She's obviously socially bankrupt when she can't extend a courtesy 'hello' to mourning families!" White-hot anger roiled.

The diminutive funeral director pushed farther into his chair wearing a tormenting look of skepticism. Wordless!

The silent standoff produced a magician's verve in Abe. He flourished Fabian's stash of money grandly, counting out two hundred and fifty dollars in dog-eared tens and fives, just as Fabian had saved them. He sent the paper money sailing across the desk where they fluttered and fell at random.

LeVine scurried to pick them up, greed glinting in eyes that endeavored to deceive with a smile, teeth showing under his mustache. Shuffling the bills together, he placed all the tens together and all the fives together in neat piles without raising his eyes from the two stacks. He had skin as thick as January frost when it came to money.

"Very good sir. Yes. Very good," he said upon counting the exactness of the bills. Looking up and brushing his mustache again, he quibbled over the last battle in this war. "Picking up the price of a breakfast for the mourners, however, does not mirror the policies of this mortuary. Maybe for a slightly higher fee…"

"To-hell-you-say. Don't test me." A wave of hostility washed over Abe with such impact that he gasped. Hard and confident, he had his hand on LeVine's tie, leaning so far over the desk he blanched at the bad breath. He warned the snake. "I'm as unpredictable as Crazy Horse and Sitting Bull put together. Savagery that they never dreamed of, I practice routinely."

LeVine lurched as if he had been bit, and then stiffened, barely breathing. Around and around he twirled the solitaire diamond on his ring finger.

The little pissant, Abe thought. *One more objection from him, he's dead meat.*

Farley and Norrhea eased Abe back into his chair.

"Yes, of course." LeVine having stared into the eye of unpredictability, chose condescendingly to address Farley. "We'll arrange everything as you have indicated. Monday night the wake in your home, Tuesday morning the funeral at St. Andrew's, and breakfast for your guests immediately following the graveside blessings." Stepping his skinny ass lightly around the desk, he offered a tight smile and loose hand. Abe chose to ignore it. He left before he knocked the wind-up toy into the middle of next month.

❧❦

With no apologies, the sun continued to hide behind the clouds for the fourth day. Fog hung in thick layers making dancing haloes around the streetlights. Abe wished the wake was over; he could barely get past the kitchen table in his sorrow and could hardly bear to view Fabian in the casket at which military watch guard stood. He had to clamp his mind over his aching heart to fulfill the responsibilities expected of him—responsibilities that society imposed upon families at times of bereavement, impositions that were siphoning him dry and empty.

The small brown house burst full, every chair taken and every free surface covered with food. Neighbors were still coming up the front porch steps with cakes, casseroles and bowls of fruit. In the kitchen, Abe sat with his hands pressed to his temples. He viewed most of the visitors as white-bread friends and himself as unleavened in a world where class dictated hindrance or happiness.

Then there appeared Sarah, a sweet bread filled with citron. With Ma beside her, she busily tended the buffet, which ordinarily Abe would have devoured but now the very smell of food fisted his stomach—might as well be serving boiled boots. Oh, but Sarah, dear Sarah! Abe observed her as fresh and crisp as a new dollar bill. Treasuring every moment he spent with her, he viewed her as his angel of mercy, his woman, his salvation. She set up the perfect package of wisdom, grace and beauty. With an ambivalence of gratitude and bitterness, he envied the security of her home life.

How could he be thinking these things? He would later come to feel both pride and shame at his reactions that evening, as to what he did and what he failed to do. He hadn't slept but a few hours since Fabian died. Constantly, he questioned himself. What had he overlooked that morning? Was he too deeply involved with himself to care? There were no quick answers to his quest. His throat felt choked, and his digestion rolled nil. He was sure his stomach must be bleeding.

Most difficult was the triteness of the visitation guests. Their efforts at solace were ever-present as a creeping fungus and twice as unwanted, which prompted his responses inadequate. Trailing his tongue slowly around the inside of his mouth, he tried to find enough saliva to talk. Courtesies were out of reach. He was embarrassed of himself. No one pushed him to change direction, somehow gleaning that he barely clung to sanity. He took a buttressing breath, trying to digest how his life had changed in the span of just a few days—changed irreversibly.

Levity immediately enveloped him as Doc approached. Abe could smell his damp wool topcoat, his after-shave, saw his noble soft brown eyes, smelled his strength. Raw and tense, he pushed back from the table to greet him, ill at ease upon taking on the role of a man. He never did remember who made the first move, but with sensitivity and compassion he found himself gathered closely to him, Doc sinking his hand into his hair, cradling Abe's head on his shoulder. A soft whisper escaped Doc into the muffled collar of Abe's first suit that he hardly remembered buying with Farley's assistance. Tears squirted from Abe's eyes as he shook, at last allowing himself to be comforted by the extraordinary man in whom he felt such inexplicable magnetization.

෧෨

Tuesday dawned wrapped in rapidly rolling clouds as viewed only over the Great Lakes with the changing of a weather front. Alone in the early morning, the small Indian contingency went back into the living room for the final viewing. Fabian lay with a full day's growth of beard! He appeared as yet a living entity. Yet, it was not Fabian's face that moved Abe most; it was his hands. Clutching a rosary, they folded below his chest, transparent and waxy with fingers as flat as Abe's intake of breath. Were they really that gnarled or was it because the undertaker had overlooked cosmetic niceties? Hands—the vehicle that curved to soothe Abe's childhood scrapes, to hoe the vegetable garden, to pile thousands of board feet of lumber, to place dinner on the table, to kill in time of war, or open to stroke with a gentle palm. All the confused web of Abe's perception and inflexible foolishness—everything, all of it that constituted Abe and all that he contained throughout his life lies here without life.

The next minute he held his head; his eyes squeezed shut, groping the edge of the coffin for support. Standing on either side of him, Farley and Norrhea lent him support.

Abe watched in horror, his mouth a rictus, eyes wide, as attendants closed Fabian's casket with a dull thud and click, sounding to Abe like a cannon— the last time he would ever see Fabian. His whole body shook with great spasms of sorrow, his tears unrestrained. Farley and Norrhea flanked him more closely, struggling for their own self-control. They had stayed at the house with him since Fabian's passing, urging him along, getting him over the rough spots.

At the church service, the dolorous chords of the church organ, played by Margie Tobin, Clyde's wife, struck into "My Soul Is Longing For Your Peace." Father McKevitt read the epistle, a letter from Paul to the Romans. "We know that affliction makes for endurance, and endurance for tested disappointments, because the love of God has been poured out into our hearts."

The ritual flowed one part into another without Abe physically witnessing the purity of the celebration of the Mass of the Dead. It didn't surprise him one bit to find himself in his bubble.

"*Requiescat in pace,*" intoned as the pastor sprinkled holy water on the flag-draped casket. Father Epoufette, the Indian Point missionary priest assisting at the mass, responded, "*In nomine patri, et filii, et spiritui sancti, Amen.*"

Just as Lenny LeVine had promised, two attendants were there after the service to wheel the casket out of the church where the pallbearers carried it down the front steps to the hearse that would drive around back to the cemetery where the winterkill grass looked sickly and rotten. The air hung heavy in the silence, broken only by the call of two blackbirds shifting through the clearing air over the cemetery.

Farley and Norrhea held Abe's elbows. Their eyes locked with his, conveying assurance and wholesome strength. His hands shaking, his throat constricting, he stood at the graveside scrunched into the collar of his trench coat. The great lurch his life had taken encompassed his very senses outlawing a single redeeming thought.

The fog lifted steadily; a contrasting ray of light played lightly among the cedars in the cemetery. Abe watched the patterns of light and shadow lift and shift as if some spatial entity searched for a suitable place to land, as did Abe—a land of peace and love.

> *The distance that the dead have gone*
> *Does not at first appear;*
> *Their coming back seems possible*
> *For many an ardent year.*

Why did he remember this particular passage from Emily Dickinson? He didn't even like literature classes. His reason didn't have to be a *why*. It could be a *where* or even a *when*. His jaw clenched at the roaring rage that ate at his bowels. He felt that everyone was watching him, him with his papier-mâché insides. Abe felt the emptiness of his soulless body. There evolved nothing left of the old Abe; he'd died, too.

Father McKevitt blessed the casket again with holy water as he read the 23rd Psalm: *The lord is my shepherd; I shall not want. In verdant pastures, he gives me repose. Beside restful waters, he leads me. I fear no evil; for you are at my side, with your rod and your staff.*

Abe could feel himself fading fast, his throat filled with spring slush. Feeling the silence and stillness of death in himself, he started counting the legs around the grave: one, two, three and four, start all over, there were more. He felt the silence and stillness of death within himself. Memories washed over him clear and coherent: mannerisms, smiles, warm eyes, shared pleasures, ceased forever in the finality of death.

The bugler, Clarence Menary, sounded taps on his dented bugle, a relic of World War I. The plaintive notes, reluctant to dissipate, hung in the heavy air, cleaving onto every cedar branch. The color guard folded the flag in its intricate, precise triangular folds. Abe accepted the flag robotically, an out-of-body experience. The acid bile in his stomach had jelled to a steel ball. Too many demands were suddenly pressed upon him. The young man's eyes once alive with light, dimmed. His Huckleberry days were over. He'd never be the same. A feeling of violence and savagery invaded his very being.

Mourners in attendance clasped Abe's hand, patted his shoulder, as they stood awkwardly awaiting the arranged transportation to the hotel. Scuttling clouds broke open and a brilliant ray of sunshine flooded the church cupola where the crucifix on top reflected dazzling brightness.

In a ray of sunshine, I'll be there. Fabian! Abe chose to take comfort in this surreal setting, leading him to consider that burying his father had dealt him a rite of passage to a new personage. He had left behind an era of lost innocence. As his great- great grandfather, and great grandfather, both named Crazy Horse, had done repeatedly, Abe would move on to another hunting ground never to be the same again.

֍

Why was *business as usual* the order of the day? Abe arose in the morning, went to school, and found the same old hubbub. Few acknowledged his lingering loss. The rain swept back like the wrath of God. With an iron-gray sky, March went out like a lion.

Coming home after school circled even worse. The house was eerily empty. Everything lay silent and sagging as though weighted down, faulted to function never again. The refrigerator, the stove and the coffee pot were all dead. Dead. The curtains and drapes hung limply at the windows as if in mourning.

Abe went on only because night turned into day, as turmoil boiled inside him. Was it anger—frustration? It became difficult to explain away this overwhelming sense of loss. Sitting in Fabian's wingchair, he entwined his fingers behind his head, stretched out his long legs, and crossed his feet one over the other at the ankle. The late afternoon sunlight filtered through the windows, dull and lacking enthusiasm. The house slept as a cavern, cold and barren.

Flashes of Fabian's last moments migrated across his mind in endless succession like trudging demons chained together. It was three weeks ago, a thousand years ago, and a lifetime. Still, he couldn't put it behind him. The thoughts tugged at his stomach, tearing and burning. They floated through his consciousness one after the other like a series of interloping ellipsis. Details, gestures, words, smiles and loving eyes came alive.

He realized that his struggle for dispassion wasted him, consuming him like an invasion of proliferating cancer cells.

Realizing that he could not go on like this, he determined to visit his grandparents. Perhaps Farley and Norrhea could bring some levity to his enormous burden of loss, weighing him down, making every step seem as if he mucked through winter molasses.

It was only three miles out to Farley's Mission Trading Post. Abe found himself actually *seeing* the tall stands of native timber, growing proud and straight in the thick forest. The scrawny birch and sweet maples stood proudly like detailed designs among the pines. After drowning in his grief-ridden whirlpool he started to see again outside his self-imposed bubble of bereavement, even if it measured a snick at a time.

Farley greeted him at the Indian Point Trading Post. "Well, look who's here," Farley welcomed Abe with pleasure, his eyes springing to light. "C'mon in and take a load off." Farley immediately recognized need while gazing at Abe. The hollow cheeks, the sunken eyes, the withdrawn manner and hunched shoulders told the whole story. His heart ached to see this incredibly handsome young man falling apart before his eyes.

The rain continued to whip against the windows, the gusts rattling the door, making the inside of the Trading Post a haven. The smell of rawhide and tanned leather bearing images of a hunt permeated the air. Beaded jackets, vests and leggings hung along the wall. Beautiful quilted moccasins stood like soldiers at attention in a pale-green-tinted plate glass and oak showcase.

"I suppose that it's been the best of days, but the worst of days too," Farley said softly, still exploring the geography of Abe's face. "Come sit by the fire. It's raw and chilly this afternoon," he encouraged, leading the way to the potbellied stove that stood in the center of the trading post. He glanced sideways at Abe trying to identify his needs.

Standing taller than Farley stood, Abe shivered as he followed while unbuttoning his trench coat. "Just can't seem to glue my life together since Dad died. Everything seems so meaningless. There's no way to go back and spend more time with him...to say the things left unsaid..." His voice cracked.

"Don't weigh yourself down with blame, Abe. That time is past but *wakan*, sacred. Accept your burdens and move on. We can always heap on the shortfalls. I've been there, wondered why the moon still rose and the sun came up in the morning. When my brother Burton died it seemed as though time should stand still until I could make up for the tons of tripe that I tossed his way, but it didn't. Life goes on. We grieve; we get angry, then numb. We overcome, and go on with making a life for ourselves as best we can." Farley shoved his hands into his pockets, rocking back on his heels, sighing with the subtleties of dealing with a young man's rough road.

"You have a great future, Abe, and can be whatever you want to be. You've a gifted heritage that few young men have known so must persist in seeing it through. Besides, Fabian wouldn't want you moping around." Farley's eyes searched with consciousness every move Abe made, even the way he breathed.

Leaning over the end of the display case, Abe had his chin in his hand, his elbow resting on the smooth surface. "Well yes, but when the loss hits me it's like a tidal surge. As far as my heritage goes, I hardly know it myself. Dad never said much."

Farley's face grew hard at Fabian's disregard of Abe's Sioux genetic influence, but decided to pass over this foible. He quickly determined it rectifiable.

"Consider your skills as an artist; they're part of your heritage." Farley's voice picked up in enthusiasm and pitch. "There were great artists among the Sioux—Take a look at the inspired work here," he gestured. "They carved, they sculpted, they designed intricate feather and beadwork on deerskin. I've seen detailed burnishments on deer hide so realistic that you'd think they were going to jump right off the scroll. You have that flair. You have a gift of creation that bridges from your mind-pictures onto canvas." Farley took a straight-back chair, turned it around and sat straddled on it near the stove, his arms now folded comfortably over the tall back.

"Do you know how you're going to eventually learn of art? Books! Social situations! Study only the pictures that draw you to them. You must see and hear only the best in architecture, sports, theater, music and books. View only the best, the most arresting and beauteous, and before you know it, you'll *want* only the best. That's cultivation. That's enlightenment."

Finding a jolt of contact in Farley's words, Abe shed his coat, placed it on the end of the display case, walked over to a nearby chair to join Farley while pushing up the sleeves of his sweater. He admired the way Farley remained so self-effacing when he obviously lived as a very successful man with a rich heritage.

"Dad never talked much about my Sioux ancestry, but he *did* push knowledge, as well as painting and creating on canvas the things that I see with my eyes. It seems, however, that I *have* been rather starved of my mother's heritage." He paused, tilting his head to the side and folding his hands in his lap.

"I don't think Fabian did it as a concerted effort, Abe. Terrible hurt pervaded him when Suki left and he never shed it. It was as if he closed a door and locked it." Farley bit his bottom lip, studying on this. "He tucked her away in some secret corner of his heart, and if he ever unlocked that door and took out the memories, we'll never know."

The quiet import of his message told Abe more than the content of his words. "I think that perhaps he did, many times." Abe paused, thinking. "He told me once that Suki taught him old Indian adages. Whether or not it sealed true isn't terribly important. He *thought* it was true, and that kept him going."

Farley's eyes flickered with the pleasure of Abe's quicksilver grin. "He did a yeoman's job at raising you, Abe. He doted all his life on your welfare. Norrhea and I just stayed away. We thought it best." Emotion filled his voice.

"Do you ever hear from Suki?" Abe asked, his eyes searching Farley's face.

"No. We're just as much in the dark about her whereabouts as you are. When she left your father, rumors hopped around town like rabbits in a cornfield, but none of them materialized." He reached for a handkerchief in his pants pocket and wiped it over his face. "When she wants us to know where she is, she'll get in touch."

"You trust that?" Abe asked, his voice cracking, a trickle of excitement seeping through. With the speculation, his eyes came alive.

"Always have. Yup. Always have." Farley pondered this, pulling on his bottom lip. "I don't know what prompted her to leave Fabian with a small baby boy. Maybe she found that living with him wasn't all wine and roses, but she wasn't wearing gunnysacks, either. One doesn't really ever know the secrets in someone else's heart." Farley's eyes grew distant, remembering.

"Was she as beautiful as Dad said?" Abe's eyes showed small licks of sparkle, feasting on the positiveness of his grandfather.

"Yes, she blossomed fresh, bronze, dark-eyed, delightful, and soft as cornstarch."

Norrhea breezed in from their home across the road, a cardigan sweater thrown hastily over her shoulders. "Hello there, Abe, my favorite grandson!"

"Hey, Norrhea!" Abe stood, showing some enthusiasm, which had been absent without leave for more than three weeks now.

"Can you stay for supper? We'd be pleased to have you join us." She pulled the sweater more tightly around her hunched shoulders with a shiver. Liquid brown eyes swept assessingly over Abe, registering with honesty the changes the past three weeks had wrought: weight loss, hollow. A painful pulse flashed over her countenance. "I'm fixing Swiss style venison steaks and mashed potatoes. I even made an apple cobbler for dessert," she said, walking over and reaching up to pat Abe's thick black hair.

Circling his arm around Norrhea's waist, he gave her a tug. "You bet. I'd like that. I kind of catch as catch can now that Dad isn't around. Besides, I'm going out for the track team this year, so I don't get home until late in the afternoon, and then I'm too tired to run anything down." He smiled at his play on words.

"Okay! I have half a dozen things going over at the house, so I'll see you both later," she said over her shoulder. As she left, a heavy draft of rain-laden air invaded the warmth of the cozy post then deteriorated into a wimpy *whoosh* against the overlapping shields of heat from the fire.

"Glad you're going to be on the track team." Farley returned his attention to Abe. "That's good exercise and good therapy. Challenges will keep your mind occupied."

"Something has to do the trick, but my grandfathers, both named Crazy Horse, tell me about them." Abe flashed a nervous smile. "Although the history books report the Plains Indians were savage and treacherous, they surely didn't live in violence before the settlers went west. There must be more to the story than what we read." Abe tilted back on the wooden spoke chair, his feet propped up on the chrome ledge that found its way around the bottom of the potbellied heater.

Farley squiggled his butt on the chair and settled for the duration. "I think you know that Crazy Horse the Second was actually my father, but he died before I was born. He exemplified one of the Sioux's greatest warriors. You, too, could be a warrior for the Sioux—not a painted warrior but a *painter* warrior—a Renoir Warrior. Paint things as you see them just as Renoir did.

He was a French impressionist. You'll learn all about the history of the arts when you go to the University of Michigan."

Rising, he moved to the deep red cooler with the flip-back lid behind the counter and shook out two cold Coca Colas. At the end of the counter he uncapped both bottles on the opener attached there. A smoking whoosh exhaled from the bottles like genies.

Handing a bottle to Abe, he remained standing, gazing off into space. "I think you should also know that Norrhea's father, Burton, was my brother—she was my niece. At twenty-three years old I arrived to live with them back in 1900. Upon my arrival, I got a job with the Bay de Nocquet Lumber Company."

Abandoning his Coke for the moment, Farley stood up and strode over to the front window as if the stove area had grown too confined for his thoughts. Staring out, he poked his hands into his back pockets. Silent now, he studied the fast approaching night. Gusts of wind shook the panes, scolding like tireless blue jays.

Abe stared after him. At sixty-five years old, he figured a fine man with wavy, graying hair and light complexion. Except for his broad nose, one would hardly take him for an Indian. He stood six feet tall and possessed a commanding presence.

Abe stirred from his chair and joined him by the window. He observed Farley's eyes squinting, and his body struck rigid. Taking a deep breath as if to say something, Farley mentally reversed his decision, stiffened, his eyes becoming impenetrable.

Turning around, Farley urged Abe back to their chairs by the stove where he continued in a studied voice. "A person just can't fight one thing leading to another. Norrhea and I got to fooling around, fell in love and, resultantly, she became pregnant with your mother. We were married right here at the mission church and have managed just fine ever since." An adoring glow pervaded his eyes.

"Your mother was a very fine child—dark, big eyes, blessedly white teeth like yours, Abe, and she was never any problem. She had trouble focusing, however, such as you've had all your life—so you come by it naturally. With what we know about incest today, we're lucky that Suki turned out as well as she did." His eyes twinkled with pride. "Her problems certainly weren't compounded in *your* case as you can see by the looks of you. Seventeen years old, and you've been a man for years already. I think it was heaped upon you all too soon, son, *all too soon.*"

Abe observed the bony harshness of Farley's cheekbones, identifiably Sioux. Unseating himself, Farley captured two chunks of wood from a woodbox in the back of the post, winter wood split from great slabs of giant white pine timbered off his land. Using the dangling coil spring on the door handle, Farley chucked in the two pieces of wood. "Klunk-a-klunk," they dropped into the bed, sparks flying upward and coals scintillating with the breath of new air introduced through the open stove door. Closing it, he brushed his hands together shaking off the sawdust.

Abe, following his every move, found himself obsessed with an insatiable greed to know everything about his family history. "Didn't your brother Burton know about your relationship with Norrhea?" Abe fell enamored with a situation that would have been considered taboo in *his* social structure.

"Oh sure he did." Farley struggled with the truth in a scenario that was polarized from Abe's. "Burton and his wife Winona were very pleased about it. You see, that setup wasn't all that unusual in the Tribal Fire Councils," he said, leaning his elbows back against the countertop. "They encouraged it. At that time, Burton and I both observed fertility dances exercised at the Council Fires, and we'd perform them in our loincloths on hot summer nights on the beach. It emerged as our own sacred cow." He crossed one foot over the other at the ankle. "Winona taught Norrhea all the tribal dances, too. By the time I arrived, Norrhea was well-versed in Sioux traditions."

"That's an interesting approach to living—different and primitive, but understandable when you consider the great distances involved among the Plains people." Abe raised his eyebrows in delving this situation. "What do you know of the life of Crazy Horse? Did he have more than one wife?" Abe searched Farley's face, his enthusiasm glistening.

"Actually, Crazy Horse only married one woman—my mother. Other women came and went as the mood struck him. My mother said he surfaced as the Oglala Lakota's wisest wanderer; his masculinity flourished well-renowned." Farley laughed, enjoying the adulation of a new audience.

"She issued the daughter of the medicine man, someone of strong influence at that time. Of course Burton and I are the products of that marriage. So you now know how you came by your strong and early manhood," Farley added in good spirits, ready to share more Sioux folklore.

"The scuttlebutt on Crazy Horse is endless. Your great-great grandfather lived the life of a notable warrior in the Great Sioux War in 1876, which was different from other American conflicts. Despite the fact that the government won, the war is remembered primarily for Custer's defeat at the Little Bighorn. We have faced hatred and persecution for generations because of that battle. Disagreements become arguments, then battles, then war, however. It's a piss-poor truism, I'm afraid."

Farley walked over to the counter where he picked up his meerschaum pipe from the ledge that ran around the side of the pipe holder. Packing it with tobacco from the thin green can with "Half and Half" printed diagonally down the front in large red letters, he held it between his thumb and forefinger, tamping it down with his finger. On the end of the counter sat a box of Diamond wooden matches, one of which he stuck headfirst onto the side of the hot stove, watching as the end popped into flame with a snap. Lighting the pipe, he made a few cursory puffs, sending the smoke around his head like a muslin cloud. He shook the match repeatedly, as if stuck in the rote of doing so.

"Given the public outrage after Little Bighorn," he said between puffs, "and the glorification of Custer that lasted an additional eighty plus years, only a few Indians spoke of their roles in the war. When they did, they were careful to tailor their remarks according to what they thought the Whiteman wanted to hear. White people looked at an amoeba incident and tried to tell us that it puffed a fire-breathing dragon. Our people offered only passive resistance to the many miscarriages made by the military."

Abe struggled with a grimace of anger. "You mean that no one willed to speak out in truth of what the Indians had endured or what their reasons *were* for making a stand against the Whites?" Abe's voice imparted a supply of empathy.

"They were afraid to do that." Farley stood stiff as a monument. "The Whiteman positioned himself as unstoppable; their numbers were undefeatable."

Abe nodded, encouraging in his focus an undisguised interest. "It all seems so clouded with the passing of time."

"Not for me," Farley grumbled. "The Black Hills, dark and cool on the horizon, overlapping the boundary between South Dakota and Wyoming is where I lived before I came to Michigan. There were several tribes in that area. My mother told me often of the annual meeting of the Seven Tribes representing the basic national cohesiveness of the Lakotas, regardless of where they might be the remainder of the year. They would hold a great Sun Dance in June of every year at the time of the summer solstice. The chiefs and elders would meet to act on matters that affected them as a whole. Living was easy; the forests abounded in wild game. The lakes and rivers were alive with black bass and trout. No reigning monarch ever had the thousands of acres we had to roam, live, hunt and call home.

"But as we stepped forward to live and let live through it all, the turning of time brought the eternal Whiteman who marauded and massaged the native Indian to lesser than North Dakota pyrite.

"The Indian Nations were on a respirator."

CHAPTER TEN

Objectively, Farley viewed himself. He looked through a telescope, back to the end of a long, long corridor of time, during which his people had deteriorated, scattered and died. "The Sun Dance endured as the great spiritual event, and the Council of the Chiefs of all tribes, their legislature."

"Was your father one of these?" Abe now sat on the floor next to the cozy stove, absorbing with eagerness all the information he could record from his grandfather. He felt twisting in his stomach, anger that this genealogical field had fallen hidden. Hardly containable, his excitement swelled as he urged Farley to continue.

"Yes, Crazy Horse was a Council Chief, and traveled far for these meetings. Look, the majority of the Sioux migrated north and east when the Chinook wind blew out of the Rockies. They settled in the marshes and lakes of northern Minnesota and at the headwaters of the Mississippi River, including the Western Upper Peninsula of Michigan. There they lived in permanent lodges, raised crops, hunted, gathered food such as cranberries and wild rice in the bogs, and traveled in birch canoes."

The fire in the stove slowly died down as the wind dashed splattering rain against the windows and doors. Having little insulation, the old building cooled rapidly without the assistance of the pot-bellied stove. Darkness slowly swallowed the day. It was soon time to move to Farley's tight cozy home where Norrhea had a hot supper waiting.

"I'll just close things down here and we can leave," he said, spanking his pipe bowl against the inside of the stove. "Norrhea will think that we fell off the earth."

Absorbed by Abe, the scope and dimension of his ancestors grew. "So actually, you and your ancestors were never very far from where you are now, right?" Abe added, trying to mentally tally the miles between Nahma, Michigan, the Mississippi River and the Black Hills.

"Uh-uh, not far at all." Farley nodded.

Greeting them outside, slanting sheets of rain from blew off the bay at a temperature reading of thirty-eight degrees. Shoulders to the wind, they hurried across the St. Jacques Road to the lakeside of the highway—land Farley and Norrhea inherited. This land they'd have and hold forever without fear of the Whiteman.

As they entered the warm home, the smell of slow simmering venison and onions and crisp apple cobbler greeted them. Abe hadn't had such a warm feeling since the time Fabian had left him on his own. He really *did* have family, *did* have love, *did* have heritage. The ambience wound him in a web of wonder and fulfillment.

"Got time for a beer before dinner?" Norrhea asked from the kitchen.

"How about that, Abe? Wish to have a beer with me? The evening is young; it's Friday night, and you don't have school tomorrow."

"Yeah, don't mind if I do," Abe said eagerly, falling into step with the mode of the home. "That is, if you tell me some more about your—*our* ancestors." He sat in the living room rubbing his hands together in anticipation.

Norrhea served up two bottles of Schlitz, ice cold and dripping condensation. Placing a glass and napkin down for each of them, she quickly disappeared again into the kitchen, enjoying the presence of both *her men.*

On the coffee table in front of the couch, Abe read a caricature cartoon of Franklin Delano Roosevelt on the front page of the *Escanaba Daily Press.* With his monocle in place, his cigarette holder clamped between oversized teeth, from his mouth grew the ever-present balloon. The message contained therein read, "I hate Warrrh. Eleanor hates Warrrh, and my dog Falda hates Warrrh!" Abe filled with a sense of security in this warm comfortable home with loved ones—the war seemed far away.

Farley studied the bottle of beer for a moment; then he sipped disregarding the glass. Eyes recalling—widening then blinking—he slowly and with deliberation placed the bottle on the coffee table. "It's estimated that in the 1830s the Sioux population existed at somewhere between forty and fifty thousand, of whom eight to ten thousand were warriors. At least half those warriors were six feet tall or more."

Abe, sitting across the room from Farley, who was encamped on the living room couch situated directly under the big bay window overlooking the lake, thought of Fabian before he became ill—tall, robust and husky. The comparison led him to believe that either way, Abe had come by his size naturally. The window behind Farley let in the last light of the day, ashen and subtly blackening by the minute.

"Yes, you certainly have the Sioux genes—just a roll of the dice," Farley's voice faded with a sniff of unanticipated pride.

"I can't believe all this. Why did I not know this before? Fabian never gave me even the slightest hint of so much history in our family."

"You'll know it all now." Farley gave him a palm upwards shift of the shoulders and shook his head. "My mother told me that no one who ever saw Crazy Horse could fail to be impressed by him. He was the finest looking Indian she'd ever seen. In repose, his face and figure were as clear-cut and classical as a bronze statue of a Greek god—like yours, Abe. He moved as light and graceful as a panther, and on the warpath he bred as bold as a lion and as bloodthirsty as a Bengal tiger. "

"C'mon you guys, supper is ready." Norrhea called, interrupting them. "Enough already of the historical highlights of your father and his fire-eating fanatics. Maybe you're boring Abe, and we want him to come back," she said, a smile creasing her eyes.

"No! Don't stop. This is the first time I've heard all this. I want to hear more," Abe added, taking his bottle of beer with him to the table.

A canon could not curtail Farley at this point. "Crazy Horse matured into a solitary mystical figure, who distanced himself from most of his people. He generally was acknowledged as 'the strange man of the Oglalas.' He had sandy hair, and a very light complexion. He didn't have pronounced cheekbones as Indians generally have. About five feet ten inches tall, with a slight build, he shrank smaller than Sitting Bull, but those who knew him considered him more striking. Later in life, a bullet inflicted by my mother's jealous former husband scarred his cheek. Crazy Horse was a woman's man."

"How old was he when his first child arrived?" asked Abe, eager to view the legend in full color, rerunning the scenario preferably in small details.

"My brother Burton was born to Crazy Horse at only twenty years old, so who knows how many children he sired before that time. He had the sexual maturity of the Great Turtle, who, legend has it, said that he'd support the whole planet on his back and proliferate his species. His baby name, Curly, referred to his light wavy hair. Although some people mistook him for a white captive, he was in fact Lakota.

"His father, also named Crazy Horse, escalated to an Oglala Lakota holy man. A Brule Lakota, his mother was the sister of the great chief of that tribe. He birthed in the early 1840s near Bear Butte, which is the present site of Sturgis, South Dakota. He had seen Lakotas carried off in chains for violations of the Whiteman's law, so declared it better to die a fighting plains Indian than to live in chains under the Whiteman."

Farley had been speaking between eating. "Mmm, good supper, Norrhea. This venison is cuisine for a king!" His eyes fixed on his wife spoke a feel-good statement.

"Sure is good. I don't know whether to eat or talk." Abe, feeling as much at home at their supper table as a pigeon in a roost, continued. "But I think that Crazy Horse was accurate in his philosophies. Why should he live in chains or be surrounded by fences when the land was his in the first place?" Abe found that the ingestion of nutrition and new information made for good bedfellows.

Farley nodded. "Crazy Horse's father and the other elders built a sweat lodge and invited the boy, Crazy Horse, to sit with them. You see, a sweat lodge was identified as an isolated place in the hills where braves went to meditate until they cultivated a vision. Sometimes it took them two, three days to get a vision. Curly told them of a vision he'd had. He deliberated near a small lake. A man on horseback came out of the lake and talked with him. He told Crazy Horse not to wear a war bonnet; not to tie up his horse's tail, so Crazy Horse never tied his horse's tail and he never wore a war bonnet. He didn't paint his face like the other Indians. The man from the lake told him that a bullet would never kill him. Instead, his death would come by being stabbed while restrained. He was also given his father's name: *Crazy Horse.*"

"Did you go to a sweat lodge when you were young?" Abe asked.

"Yes, I did. It is part of my heritage."

"And did you see a vision?"

"Yes. It took some time, about a day and a half. You'll have to remember that I deliberated in the plains. But positive as a pine stump, I viewed sea gulls flying steadily east, far to the east and then dropping down into dense timbered land near a great water, which I now know had to be Lake Michigan. And here I am, led by the vision."

"No! You didn't really..." Abe stared incredulous at the unfolding story.

"Yup. It's all true. A historic thing happened then. Lt. Col. George Armstrong Custer led an expedition into the Black Hills to consider sites for new military posts. The discovery of gold there in 1874 had led to an influx of white prospectors into Tribal Territory, resulting in attacks on the prospectors by the Sioux under Chief Crazy Horse."

Abe broke to attention, a river of interest registering in his eyes.

Farley smiled with the joy of relating to his grandson about his heritage. "The Sioux had acquired extensive wealth in ponies, buffalo hides, robes, food stores and trade articles. The loss of that was to be felt most deeply. The army hoped to hammer away at the Indians, harassing them, destroying their villages and pony herds. They would wreck their economy and thus their ability to wage war. Manipulation was rampant—turned an idea or event into what the military wanted it to be."

Abe sunk down, appalled, slapping his forehead. "So by whittling away at their ability to be independent, the U.S. Army hoped to bring them to their knees." He gestured with his open hands.

"'Twas their strategy exactly." Farley's voice roughened with the memory. "But they really didn't care to take any prisoners, either, because it would put a hole in the Whiteman's economy to support thousands of dependent Tribal Plains Indians. I think it was Mark Twain who said, 'There's no distinct American criminal class except for Congress.'"

Abe quickly cleared away a blossoming grin when observing the stark realism on Farley's face.

"In 1876, the army planned a campaign against the hostile Indians who were then centered in southeastern Montana Territory. Custer's regiment of six hundred and fifty-five men formed the advance guard of a force under General Alfred Howe Terry. On June 25, Custer's scouts located the Sioux on the Little Bighorn River. Unaware of the combined strength of the Sioux and the Cheyenne, between two thousand five hundred and four thousand men, Custer disregarded arrangements to join Terry at the junction of the Bighorn and Little Bighorn Rivers and prepared to attack at once."

Abe leaned forward, his dark eyes fathomless, as if he'd hear more by closing the distance between himself and Farley.

"In the hope of surrounding the Indians, he formed his troops into a frontal assault force of about two hundred and sixty men under his personal command and two flanking columns. The center column encountered the numerically superior Sioux and Cheyennes. Cut off from the flanking columns and surrounded, Custer and his men fought desperately but all were killed, the wipeout inevitable. It proved a numbers game.

"Later, Terry relieved the flanking columns. The site of the battle exists now as the Custer National Monument. Better, the plaque read 'Crazy Horse-Sitting Bull Monument.' These brave Indian leaders were *not* exactly nobody. They had more reason to fight and they fought the better battle, and for all the right reasons." He leaned his elbows on the table and folded his arms, shaking his head.

"How about another beer in the livingroom, Abe?" Farley offered, taking great pride in his analysis to this young man, who knew nothing of his ancestors.

"You bet. That'll be good. I haven't had beer since Fabian treated me at Christmas time," Abe replied comfortably.

Farley further explained. "The Annual Sun Dance and Fire Council was primarily why there were congregated so many tribal peoples at the Little Bighorn. It was a ritual to cut a hardwood dance pole. This then stood in the center of the tribal dance area. Young braves who wanted to become warriors saw testing by means of stringing long tethers of rawhide through a slit in the skin on their chest, which was carved by the tribal chiefs. The other end of the tether was tied to the dance pole. The young braves danced frenetically around the dance pole to the beat of the drums until either the rawhide snapped from tautness or the skin tore from their chest. In either event, the young brave realized his acceptance as a warrior." Farley shot Abe a quick assessing look.

"What a rite of passage!" Abe breathed a rush of air. "That's more than dedication." Abe shuddered recording the imagery to his memory.

"You'd be interested to hear the final chapter in his life." He took another sip of beer, waiting for Abe's tensions to settle.

Farley ran a hand over his face as he thought. "The Great Sioux War was finally over. It is perceived as perhaps the most costly of all Indian conflicts. No one knows how many private citizens, settlers, Black Hills miners and others died. They succumbed at the hands of northern plains Indians from 1875 through 1877. It awakens the imagination. The government spent more than two million dollars defeating the Sioux." Farley slapped the armrest of the couch. "They used inoffensive words such as 'reconnaissance missions' and 'topography surveys' for their dastardly deeds."

"That had to be a helluva lot of money back then, and all just to practice genocide." Abe spun mesmerized as the story unfolded; his hands turned cold, his stomach constricted like an oxbow on the Sturgeon River.

"The Indian losses will never be accurately determined. Many died of starvation and exposure after their villages saw destruction by the army. Their historic way of life swirled away forever."

A sound of outrage escaped from Abe as the atrocities left him weary and drained. "There were more victims involved in the Indian quelling than the warriors. Cemeteries had to have been filled with women and children, too." Abe sighed in disgust.

Farley's jaw bulged with the indignities he remembered. "Yes, the thread of violence was woven into the Sioux tapestry, but sewed into the lives of many an innocent. But the life of Crazy Horse was rife with resentment. Although viewed as a potential leader, some feared him and were jealous of the psychological hold he had on the Whiteman. Rumors were seeded among the troops that Crazy Horse intended to break out of the agency in which he saw captivity. He was dogged by jealous informers—his own people. With growing suspicion, the government mistrusted him immensely."

"However, Crazy Horse declared that he had grown tired of war and wanted to live in peace and help the great White Father 'to go north and fight until there is not a hostile Indian left.' The translator said, 'We should go north and fight until not a Whiteman is left.' With that kind of translation, Crazy Horse's stated intentions ceased to track. This misunderstanding punctuated the turning point. Crazy Horse was arrested and returned to Camp Robinson in Nebraska and taken to the guardhouse."

"What a rigmarole to go through to have a conversation! No wonder there were so many misunderstandings," Abe rationalized aloud.

"That's it exactly. Nevertheless, once inside the rough log building he saw the cells and several prisoners in irons, and suddenly realized what had developed. With a shout he drew his knife, slashed at the officer of the day, and dashed out the door. One of the sentries instinctively lowered his rifle to the challenge position. Another, a jealous Indian, grabbed Crazy Horse, trying to pinion his arms behind him and force him to the ground. Thrown off balance, Crazy Horse fell against the sentry's bayonet. The blade slicked through his side, piercing both kidneys."

Abe audibly gasped at the ripping realism of the scene.

"Blood trickled out of his mouth. His pulse already weak and missing beats, the wound was mortal. Moved to the post adjutant's office, he died about midnight. Only then did his spreading rage cease against the Whiteman. The boyhood prophecy saw fulfillment. Crazy Horse died by the knife, while his arms were cramped behind him by one of his own." Farley melted back into the cushions.

"So after the Whiteman took everything from him, all he had left was his spirit, and they took that, too." Abe's voice vibrated with agitation, his feelings intense as he reflected in the awful light of the truth of the plight of his ancestors.

"They took everything!" Farley grew intense.

"Settle down, Mr. Horse," Norrhea interjected sharply from the kitchen.

With obvious effort, he calmed himself. "The remaining Indians were forced to gather east to a new Agency near the Missouri River confluence with the Mississippi. While enroute, some of the northern bands, primarily those associated with Crazy Horse, slipped away and managed to move farther north and east into Michigan's Upper Peninsula. That's when my brother and his wife settled in Nahma as part of the Menominee Council Fire."

"Many of the alarmed Indians stampeded to what is now the Badlands

National Park, some fifty miles to the northwest. A large band of Lakota refugees, including my mother and myself, saw interception and were escorted to Wounded Knee Creek. With the lonely wind blowing in our faces night and day, there ensued a seemingly endless journey. We suffered confinement to wickiups—flimsy accommodations made of bent willow saplings and elastic twigs. These we covered with reed, mats, grass or brushwood. They were crude temporary shelters. You might think of them similar to a tipi, but far less durable—far less secure and warm."

"At least one hundred and six warriors with their dependents were on an open plain west of Wounded Knee, just north of a dry ravine that led into the creek. I can still see the Sioux squaws, their braves and their children, like me, sitting outside the Wickiups. There always seemed to be someone cooking in pots over open fires. Many nights yet I go to bed lying awake imagining I can smell the pungent wood smoke, re-hear their voices and laughter. Horses tethered nearby neighed in the sun as it shone through the mist of the smoke. To make certain they would remain, the camp was banked on three sides by soldiers with a fourth line of troops facing the Indians from the opposite side of the ravine."

Abe sat forward; a shiver ran through him even though the room was comforting.

"We managed to kill some deer. We tanned the hides to soften them and then made moccasins, leggings, jackets, dresses, shirts, vests and gloves. That's where I learned the skills I use today to keep the Trading Post open. When we painted our leatherwork with scenes from life, plants and animals, the predominant color was red for all the bloodshed we had seen. We gained the red dye from the plain's bottlebrush plant.

"In the evening the men played their flutes as the women compared their beadwork accomplishments in a rich variety of colors. The heavily beaded garments were worn only on special occasions. We sang sad songs to our god, Wakan Tanka, whom we found in all nature, no matter how barren. The entire encampment was permeated with only minimal expectations."

Abe sank back in the chair and laced his hands together behind his head, stretching his long legs. His eyes watered with empathy for his once-strong people.

"What a God-forsaken life for a people once free and strong and independent. How did you tolerate it?" Abe fumed—mind pictures vivid. Bewildered anxiety and frustration gripped him. *The Whiteman remains yet hard on the Indian*, he reflected.

"But wait...there's more!" Farley said.

"Four heavy-caliber, hotchkiss, rapid-fire guns, each capable of firing fifty rounds a minute were placed on a nearby rise and trained directly into the camp where we had hoisted a white flag. There were four hundred and seventy soldiers and scouts. Shortly after eight in the morning on December 29, 1890, a command was issued to the warriors to assemble and turn over their weapons. As the soldiers searched, a young warrior named Black Fox pulled a rifle from under his blanket and opened fire. Instantly, a line of soldiers moved forward, raised their rifles, and fired point blank into the crowd, their muzzles almost touching the Indians immediately in front. That first volley killed about half the warriors. The survivors rushed the troops."

Abe froze, his eyes wide, as though comprehension could only be seen and not heard.

Farley leaned forward in an effort for impact of delivery. "For a few minutes there continued a terrible hand-to-hand struggle, where every man's thoughts turned to killing. Although many of the warriors had no rifles, nearly all had revolvers and knives in their belts under their blankets, together with some of the murderous war clubs still carried by the Sioux. The very lack of guns made the fight bloodier, as it brought the combatants to closer quarters."

Abe could see the war waged in Farley's mind between re-living the passion of the morning and continuing the story as a gauze memory.

"The women and children rushed up to see what was happening." Farley's voice turned raspy. "At that moment, the four Hotchkiss guns opened up with two-pound shrapnel shells. The flying fragments and exploding steel literally tore the spectators to pieces. Within minutes, sixty soldiers and two hundred Indians were dead. The surviving Sioux fled into a ravine. The Hotchkiss guns then shifted and swept the ravine with shrapnel, raising great clouds of blue-gray smoke, the smell of which I'll never clear out of my nose.

"It lingered as a maelstrom of the greatest proportions, a massacre where fleeing women, with infants in their arms, were shot down after resistance had ceased and after almost every warrior was either stretched out dead or dying on the ground. It emerged as simplicity in itself—*just kill every Indian in sight.*"

Abe edged forward, incredulous; he felt an icicle slip deep into his chest. "It sounds as if the order of the day was established before the first shot was even fired."

"I'm sure. While history has noted that an Indian fired the first shot and that the soldiers behaved correctly in returning fire against the warriors, the wholesale slaughter of women and children stands unnecessary and inexcusable. I don't feel that they acted correctly, either, although that is how history records it. One Indian drawing a gun generated no excuse to wipe out a whole tribe. Wounded Knee has remained a bloody stain on the national conscience, the very name coming to mean an atrocity, a massacre."

"So what I hear you saying is that when it ended, it was treated as the three monkeys—see no evil, hear no evil, speak no evil—and probably, 'Don't ask any questions.'" Abe fully understood that all the terms were interchangeable and relayed the same message.

"That's right. Any means justified the end of gaining the west. For all practical purposes, the Indian Wars ended on that frozen windswept plain in the newly created state of South Dakota on December 29, 1890. Can you believe that one of the last sounds I remember hearing while lying there in the ravine was the cheerful call of the chickadees high in the naked hardwoods?"

A low moan escaped from Abe. "You were there?" The idea swam in his head.

"*I was there.* I yet smell the acrid stench of blood and the stink of the dying, hear the pain-filled groans, bodies ripped apart, stomachs exploded and the terrorized muffled sobbing. At thirteen years old I knew safety by the weight of dead and dying fellow tribesmen as they lay on top me in that fateful ditch. My mind is battered with the sights and sounds of holocaust." His voice tightened for control.

"I'm sorry," Abe said incredulously. He could see the history of his people written in his grandfather's strong face. "I'm so sorry. It's such a ruthless story. Every time you speak of it, it must get scarier." Abe's eyes were tar-pit black and awash.

"*Scarier?* Does water get wetter or a full moon rounder? I could hardly move, or walk or talk for days as I slogged on dog-tired to yet another council site, my mother dead, and my friends gone. It echoed of hell and not something to plow under and let lie fallow. I know what it is to not to want to go on living.

"To add to the heedlessness of the whole affair, that same year the superintendent of the census declared that the American Frontier was no longer a relevant factor in national development."

"Damn! The Whiteman killed the sacred cow then didn't need the beef!" Abe smoothed a hand over his stomach to cut the cruising. He reached for Farley's hand. "Thanks so much for the history lesson no matter how hideous it is. Now I need to be leaving, Farley, but I can't tell you how much this evening has meant to me. Your personal recall is better than *anything* I've ever *read* in the history books."

"You come back anytime, Abe. In fact, if you'd like, you could stay out here for the rest of the school year. Think about it. It might serve a need. You could run the three miles to school in the morning for track practice—and along the bay shore, too."

"I'll consider that. Thanks very much. Thanks for dinner, Norrhea," Abe said, moving toward the kitchen.

"You come back to see us soon now," she said as she smiled warmly, coming out to administer a hug, her smile soothing and radiant. Abe lived as part of her quiet years, her reward forever. "Here's a package of smoked white fish—enjoy!"

Abe flashed a blue ribbon smile at Norrhea while slipping into his trench coat. "Thanks so much," echoed back over his shoulder as he ran for the car.

Farley stood at the door hugging Norrhea to him—his treasure forever, his beautiful swan—as the rain dripped steadily from their overhead stoop roof.

Much of the Sioux pride was vested in their gifted, magnificent grandson.

Abe arrived home experiencing the dichotomy of need for change yet he also needed to hang onto the old and established. How things had changed since Fabian's death. He roused from his memories and walked into his new bedroom—*his* bedroom. He sighed as he slid between the dried-outside sheets and freshly laundered blanket. A piece of April air gently stirred the curtains above his bed. For the first time since Fabian's death, he slept the sleep of the weary without the mental floggings, the "I should haves" and "I could haves."

CHAPTER ELEVEN

Had Abe been asked what he felt, he could have said it was not vengeance, it was not comfort, it was not bitterness and it was not resentment. It was all of those things—and beyond them. Farley had whirled him through the long days of suffering so quickly related, but never lost.

In this small village plopped down among the farms, fields and forests of other breadwinners, he was determined to make his mark. The sap seems to go out of things if you wait too long for them. He needed to remember that the laughter of the future and tears from the past are closely related. As quickly as he reasonably could, he would excel, and the Nahma High School Track Team would be his key to achievement.

Coached by Leo Pintal, the track team loomed large and enticing to Abe. *Clinical and cold*, that was what he thought of Pintal, even though the man epitomized an avid sports enthusiast. A little town big shot, Pintal was of medium height, and slim to skinny; his dark eyes darted hither and dither like a turkey vulture mulling his next meal. A heavy mustache split in the middle and bushy eyebrows bore hints of premature graying. Pintal had a habit of digging in his ear habitually; it irritated the hell out of Abe.

Nonetheless, Abe's focus ratcheted as to why he had gathered here at track indoctrination. He wanted to run! Run in the 440 relays and the distance events, move with the speed of a gazelle, feel the wind in his hair, experience the natural high of over-oxygenation, fill the tremendous void in his life resultant of Fabian's death. He'd be the Sioux redemption of Wounded Knee.

Pintal lined up his team: a slump block crew of neophytes ranging in age from fifteen to eighteen. Abe sighed. What a hopeless, helpless sight—short, tall, skinny, fat.

Pintal's shout sounded like a rasp on hard metal. "All right you guys. Let's do it. You, Beauchamp, eyes forward. You, Ritter, knock off the dumbass jokes." He paused, making eye contact with each one of them.

"I'm only going to tell you this once, so hear me well. 'Track and Field' is a term denoting a group of athletic events held as contests between individuals or teams at both indoor and outdoor meets. We will participate in outdoor meets only. Track events are runs and walks. Running events constitute the largest number of Track and Field sports."

That's what Abe wanted, the runs—whatever kind. His eyes shifted to Sarah, who patted the grass near her for tall Betty Hebert and short Mary Nolan to sit and listen to the indoctrination. Betty's outstanding features were her black hair and topaz blue eyes; while Mary's dark hair was accentuated by Snow-White skin and highly colored lips.

"Field events are jumps and throws. Meets usually are held in a stadium or athletic field built around a cinder, clay or synthetic-compound track. The tracks are usually a four hundred and thirty-seven yard oval with two turns and two straight-aways. The Meet Track is in Escanaba and is built of macadam." Pintal jerked his gaze to include each one. "Most Field events are contested in the area enclosed by the oval.

"The shortest and swiftest running events are Dashes, also known as Sprints. The distances are one hundred and nine yards, two hundred and nineteen yards and four hundred and thirty-seven yards. We'll concentrate heavily in this area."

He moved his stance to the south to avoid the late afternoon western cycle of sol. In addition, he found that he could study the reaction of the girls at a greater advantage.

Abe's eyes followed the path of Pintal's, discovering Sarah sucking air through a stem of quack grass. Sweet Jesus, she was beautiful!

"Hurdling events are actually dashes in which competitors must clear a series of ten wooden barriers called 'hurdles.' In our athletic program we use carpenter horses.

"Middle Distance Runs are races ranging from six hundred and fifty-six yards to three thousand two hundred and eighty-one yards. That's approximately one-third of a mile to close to two miles. The mile run, for which no one has ever broken the four minute time barrier, is one of pounding endurance."

A murmur of agreement rumbled across the team. Abe knew he could ace this one. Excitement traveled through him like a midnight express, his muscles aching to run.

Checking off his clipboard, Pintal continued. "Relay Races are events for teams of four in which an athlete runs a given distance, called a 'leg,' then passes a rigid hollow tube, called a 'baton,' to a succeeding team member within a given zone.

"The Broad Jump we'll compete in this year. The contestant dashes along a runway and springs into the air from a point called the 'takeoff board,' with the aim of covering the greatest possible distance. While still in the air the jumper throws both feet far forward of the body to increase the distance and to prepare to land."

Abe knew he could try that one, too, and itched to have at it. The light behind his eyes boosted up extra wattage.

"The Shot-put is an old standby. The aim in Shot-putting is to propel a solid metal ball through the air for maximum distance. It weighs sixteen pounds."

Abe knocked back a sprout of an idea; he'd ask Farley if he could find something for practice similar to a Shot-put that weighed sixteen pounds.

Pintal spoke low and persuasively. "The Discus Throw is never left out of our program. The discus is a steel-rimmed hardwood or metal platter that is thrown from inside a circle eight feet, two and one-half inches in diameter. The Discus measures from eight to nine inches across and one to two inches in thickness and weighs four to four and one-half pounds. The one we'll be use is hardwood ringed by metal.

"Just one more thing, guys." Pintal's usual imperious smile showed some warmth. The Pole Vault will be incorporated into our competition this year. You'll attempt to clear a high crossbar with the aid of a flexible bamboo pole about sixteen feet long. Pole Vaulting requires good running speed, powerful shoulder muscles, and all-around gymnastic ability. It's not for everyone."

Abe immediately recognized this wasn't for him. He knew this particular aspect of track traced to smaller, lighter men than him.

Pintal turned up the volume, his eyes becoming intense. "I want you to know that Track and Field events are the oldest organized sports in history, and have been held for thousands of years. Organized by the Greeks, they played out for the Olympian Games.

"Since 1896, the Olympic Games roll out in various countries at intervals of four years, except in time of war. With headquarters in London, the International Amateur Athletic Federation completed its organization in 1913. The federation establishes rules and proves world records. In example, if one of you good-looking jazboes ran the three-minute mile, we'd have to prove it to the IAAF for accreditation.

"Every day after school you're to come directly out here prepared to practice for two hours. You'll find that lightweight clothing and sturdy gym shoes will best serve your needs. I'll see all of you out here every week day from three-thirty until five- thirty." Pintal pinched pages onto the clipboard and headed for the school slapping himself on the leg with the clipboard. Was it pride or a paycheck that prompted him to accept the challenge of a lifetime?

Abe practiced running on the beach, the sand unrelenting in its hold on his heels. Kenny Ritter, his friend and partner in many an escapade, joined him. Ritter was sandy-haired, tall and handsome with a nose so perfect Abe thought that it must have been molded of clay. Running out to Indian Point and back—three miles each way—gave him three more weekends to spend at Farley and Norrhea's homestead. He familiarized himself with every bend in the road, every landmark: The old lightning-struck oak with a hole in its trunk stuck in his mind, as well as the copse of white birch, the intimidating white pine with arms stretching and beseeching. His weight dropped to one hundred and eighty-six from his usual one hundred and ninety-five. Like a panther, he was all-lean.

It wasn't long before word spread about the beach practice sessions of Ritter and Miereau. The track team members joined them running through the tough sand. For hurdles, they fashioned obstacles out of felled trees and cleared them like white-tailed deer. On weekends they built bonfires after dark and roasted whatever fare pilfered from the family pantries: wieners, potatoes, marshmallows, even popcorn posed a treat.

On a night just before the Mid- Peninsula Track & Field Meet in Escanaba, they built a tripod and made hobo stew. The cuisine was created from a concoction of potatoes, carrots, green beans, onions, garlic, beef bouillon, fresh water, and celery. Sitting around the fire, wolfing down the hot stew, vegetables yet half-cooked, the conversation grew as heated as the stew pot.

"Hey, O'Brian, are you getting anything from Mary Nolan? Huh? Huh? How does it feel to have your *regular* living next door?" Arsenault, a wiry Sioux with fox-like features, paused over the spoon that was resting halfway to his mouth, mentally feeding on the supposition of his friend's delights.

A stunned silence ensued crammed with each-his-own thoughts, intuitive and tangible. The very air sputtered with charged tension. The campfire crackled.

"You'll never know, Arsenault. One of these days your mouth is going to get your ass in trouble." O'Brian sluiced him off, his intense blue eyes like a bit of sapphire, blazing above the rim of his cup.

"Well, go figure. Abe and Sarah, Ken and Betty, you and Mary, all these twosomes. Something's going on." Arsenault scraped the bottom of his cup, making grating sounds as he picked up the last piece of potato.

"That's for us to know and for you to find out when you're old and gray, stooge." Ken kicked back the retort placing Arsenault on the defensive. He had finished his stew and sat on a felled log washed clean by timeless tides, his hands folded in prayer fashion and tucked between his knees.

"Well, I get all I want right at home." Instead of squirming, Eddie bragged, placing his cup in the sand and brushing his hands one against the other. "My family is so big that no one ever knows who's sleeping where," he chuckled, riding life like a Green Bay fly, flitting here and there, always looking for a brighter light.

"That's bull!" Beauchamp grunted. "If the track team had a foot-in-the-mouth award, you'd be the leading contender."

Standing near the fire, relaxing with flame hypnosis, Abe's jaw became rigid as he felt the discussion on the cutting edge of an argument. He pulled his bottom lip between his teeth. They had not come here to dig into each other's personal lives.

Since Fabian's death, he'd grown up so fast that he'd surfaced as someone of authority with his peers—someone judicious yet compassionate. He needed to seek some semblance of accord. Although he lived in a small town where people grew narrow-minded and put residents into slots, he knew he existed as "that half-breed Indian," but somehow he had risen to leadership in this motley crew.

"Hey, guys. We all have our place in life. Some get more, and some get less. What the hell! I've never been able to figure out why I'm always the one to get lesser than least and more of the less than most!" He gesticulated broadly with both his arms sweeping widely in a defeated gesture.

The play on words struck the right chord, re-establishing harmony in the key of C. Laughter scaled around the fire bouncing off the logs and the yet-bare beechwoods that grew thickly above the high tide line. The highly charged undercurrents bent equalized, the faces around the fire placid again with no hovering ghosts of intimidation. They bantered easily, wanting to keep their fire circle forever.

The dry wood from a fallen tree was parched for the flames that beset it, tonguing high into the anxious air and licking into the dark night, throwing light and shadow onto the faces around the fire. Eyes shone brightly, cheeks red, young bucks in their prime feeling energy pulsing through their veins, sharing deep thoughts.

"Hey, you guys!" Eddie Arsenault called through the silence that ensued. "Did you know that different kinds of wood produce different kinds of colors?" The sound of atonement hung heavy in his voice. Standing, he held his hands out toward the warmth of the fire. Gaining no encouragement from the replete runners, he continued.

"Yeah, well, they do. Pine burns a yellow flame. Cherry is blue. Oak glows orange. Tamarack gives off the most sparks. Green wood of any kind creates the highest hissing frequencies. My dad taught me that. He learned it as a kid from *his* dad who worked as a seasoned Sioux hunting guide."

"Let's try it next time we come out," LaBrasseur said.

"We can all bring a different kind of wood," Bobbie Thibault agreed, brushing sand off the back of his pants.

Abe took a mental picture of the scenario, capturing the silent but present ambiance of camaraderie as the firelight played over the team. A burst of warmth flooded him as he saw a bright star peek from a skimming cloud. *When you see the first stars of the evening twinkling in the sky, I'll be there.* The thought coasted across his mind, soothing and receptive. "Hi Dad," he breathed.

෴

Leo Pintal drilled in the schoolyard in preparation for the Mid-Peninsula Track Meet. "Remember, in running the dashes, the athlete crouches at the starting line, leaps into full stride when the starter pistol is fired and races to the finish line at top speed. Use high knee lifts, free-swinging arm movements, and a forward lean of about twenty-five degrees at all times. Achieve top speed for the first half of the race, float for the next thirty percent, and then finish the race with a final burst of speed."

Pacing in front of the gathered team, he continued. "The hurdles are thirty-six inches high, and are the ones that you will be jumping at Escanaba in the Mid Peninsula Track & Field Meet. You know there are ten of them, all about one–hundred and fourteen feet apart. Stay focused. Don't leave your balls on top of the hurdles."

Abe's mind blinked in a blur with the covey of instructions. He wished he could use the beach woodpiles at the Meet. A guy's gotta figure there'd be more comfort in something that they'd become accustomed to.

Pintal moved again, head down and arms in back of him, with his hands locked together with fingers sticking out as in "open the door and see all the people." "To excel in the mile race, keep knee action slight, arm movements reduced to a minimum, and the strides shorter than those used in sprinting."

The late afternoon sun broke through the clouds, spreading a God-like haze over him creating the sheen of molten gold. The aura captured standup attention from the team members, who could have been spooked but instead stood there hypnotized.

Placing his clipboard on the ground in front of him, Pintal emphasized with a broad sweep of his arms, looking more like Moses by the minute. "The relays are a big event for smaller schools. It gives everyone a chance to participate regardless of athletic prowess. When you finish running your leg of the relay, pass the baton into the hand of the receiver while the receiver is facing forward." He postured himself to receive the imaginary baton. "You receivers *remember that*—you receive it facing *forward*. Upon completion of each leg the runner enters a zone, called the "passing zone," enabling the baton receiver to start running in preparation for the baton exchange. You're good; you're *all* good. Your times are excellent!" He laughed, pleased and excited as he scrubbed his hand across his mustache.

As the last-leg receiver, Abe received from Ken. They'd done it so many times that he could do it in his sleep, and that quite summed it up he thought, pleased with his mind picture.

Pintal nodded gravely, making deep eye contact with everyone, seeking comprehension. While not holding out false promises for the team, Abe realized that sometimes nothing a coach did succeeded: talent, hard work or application. Pintal *had* to be packing a tonnage of doubt.

"The arena of most success is broad jumping. You're all capable of coming in with first places in this event." Checking the clipboard again, he removed his glasses, flipped the stems down and returned them to his jacket.

"Now the Shot Put isn't everyone's cup of tea, but I insist that we all participate in this event. Let me remind you. You must begin at the back of the circle, face back, hold the shot in the fingers of the throwing hand, and rest the hand against your shoulder with the shot under your chin. Then bound or hop across the circle in a half crouch, turning and building up speed. Upon reaching the opposite side of the circle, face forward, straighten suddenly and *put* the shot with an explosive uncoiling of the arm and body." Everything he said filled the need of the moment and summarized what he'd been teaching for more than a month.

"Your discus circle is marked off by a metal rim or white line. Two straight lines extend from the center of the circle at a ninety-degree angle, and all legal throws must land in the area between these lines."

Abe had found the discus throw not as much to his liking as he did running, but he'd give it his best effort. His feet shifted restlessly.

Pintal managed a light laugh at the agitation exhibited by the team. There proved a sound philosophy to humor, and the moment was right. Spreading his hands in a parody of concession, he carried on in amusement. "I know you've all heard this shit before, but every time I remind you guys of proper procedures, you pick up something that you've forgotten, so bear with me. Only eighteen survived the spring training session, and I'm proud of all of you. I've never before had such promise on a team!"

Abe, standing with his hands in his pockets was strangely affected by the closing remarks. This wasn't the smart-ass coach with whom they'd started. *This* man enthused with pride in the team—pleasured. He could feel it in his gut.

"Abe, are you taking the crew out on the beach tonight?" Pintal asked.

"Yeah, I am." *I'm taking the crew? Whah! They just show up voluntarily.* "We'll all be out there tonight until dark." He sure didn't want the coach to think they were a bunch of wienies who ran home to mama at the first signs of dusk.

"That's fine," Pintal said reflectively. "I think it's paid off more than you know. However, I don't want anyone running the beach on Friday night. The bus leaves from the school at 7:30 Saturday morning and I want everyone there on time and fully rested. We have at least an hour's drive to Escanaba, and the Meet starts at nine." Gripping Abe's shoulder with a squeeze, he walked toward the school.

SHOW TIME!

The brilliance of a May-blue sky stirred a fixation for the mind as well as the eye. Like a giant sphere of a fixed dome, it went on forever, punctuated by the uncertainties in Abe's mind—the questions, the qualms. The track and enclosed area at Escanaba were a hundred times more sophisticated than the ball diamond in Nahma. It swelled professional and smart, reducing their beach practices to a farce.

The team gathered around Abe at their designated dwelling on the bleachers. Adrenaline welling in a common heartbeat, they carried a goal-oriented demeanor. Although aspirations were as high as their spirits, the sports complex was intimidating.

"Whaddya think, huh, Abe? Do we have a chance on this track? Never saw anything like it. Is it going to be hard to run on that tar?"

"Look." Abe turned full into them, raising his hand in a silencing gesture and nodding his head. "For Chrise sake, don't lose your gonads now. A fancy track doesn't make a winning team. Pintal says our times are second to none." His eyes squinted in a conspiratorial wink, adding more coal to the exuberant furnace.

Jim Vidal, Athletic Director of the Escanaba Public Schools, provided

Pintal with the starting lineups, exhibiting an off-handed air of efficiency and condescension as his eyes slid quickly over the Indian element.

Leo Pintal shoved one hand into his trousers pocket while he read the clipboard roster showing the teams that would be competing: Trenary, Perkins, Nahma, Cooks, Bark River/Harris, Rock, and Hermansville, all Class E Schools according to the Michigan Athletic Association.

Showing the finesse of a gentleman, Pintal introduced the Athletic Director to Abe as Captain of the team. Abe's hand shot out to shake on introduction to the tall, forever-Joe-college director, noting his lack of eye contact under the bill of a sweat-lined baseball hat. Vidal touched Abe's hand but briefly with four fingertips, nodded his head and moved on to the next group. "Be ready when you're called," he barked.

Abe froze, feeling like he'd been stung. It was difficult while yet young to learn that there were people in the world who didn't like you. But then, there were people *you* didn't like either! Pompous know-it-alls who hesitate between words, have bland responses and dirty fingernails. Abe wasn't always strong on politeness, but he'd practiced respectfulness, and after long years of struggle to earn respect, he grew to expect the same in return. He'd had nationality bias up to his ass. Vidal had just failed the first impression test.

Maybe that gave him the ultimate boost. Gathering around Leo Pintal, who wore a green sun visor in addition to sunglasses, the crew reflected Abe's squared shoulders and head held high.

"Listen up. We're not here to make friends with the Athletic Director." No one failed to notice Vidal yukking it up with the team from Bark River/Harris.

What Abe wanted to do was try out his jackknife on the guy.

Pintal kept his eyes fixed on the team. "When we have to make a choice between currying the hierarchy and good manners, we'll choose the latter every time. We all know our objectives—FIRST PLACE! Stay focused. Remember who your relay receiver is and don't drop the baton *or* the vaulting pole *or* the shot put *or* the discus." He felt he couldn't lecture enough on this, but his voice remained full of warmth.

"We're going back to Nahma with the horn blaring all the way into town, the windows rolled down and cheering the full distance. "A hot fudge sundae is waiting for everyone at the Candy Kitchen for taking first place!" Pintal projected his voice over the noisy flight of fancy his soaring crew exhibited. You're the best I've ever had! DO IT! Just get out there and DO IT!"

Dumbfounded, Andy Vidal and his assistant timers were bare faced in awe as the Nahma team of only eighteen contenders knocked down one record after another. The 440 Relay surfaced first in a record-setting time of 54.2 seconds without a hitch, Abe closing the last leg in lightning speed. He ran the one-mile race in 4.8 minutes, breaking the old record by 0.4 minutes. Kenny Ritter took the broadjump at 22.2 feet, smashing the long-standing record of Bark River/Harris by half a foot. The pole vault was won clear and away by Del O'Brian, whose agility took him smoothly over the bar at eighteen feet. Eddie Arsenault, whose uncanny muscle coordination was a piece of art, threw the discus blithely into the circle. Jimmy Weberg took the hurdles so easily that every team competing in the tournament stopped their activities to watch him. He had three attempts at perfection and out-perfected himself every time.

Every school had an entry in the two-mile endurance run and considered it their own *coup d'état*. Abe swiped his hand over his dry mouth as the starter gun fired. He had a good lead off the gun and kept his pace steady for the first mile. As instructed, he slowed and coasted for the next half mile or so, other entries passing him, sweat staining the backs of their jerseys, faces red, panting for breath. In the last stretch, Abe shoveled on the coal, producing short, measured strides. Relaxed from his floating time, his elbows fairly feathered near his body without excessive motion, head high, chest out full. At 8.6 minutes he passed the finish line, smoothly and princely, his ponytail coming in behind him, applauding his neck.

Out of the vacuity of the mind-numbing race, he now heard the crowd—not just the Nahma fans, but all the teams entered into the tournament—cheering and whistling. Time had stood still. All events had ceased and desisted as the captivating new runner out-distanced by a wide margin every other contender. Abe maintained unawareness.

Before the cheering stopped, a large hand gripped his and shook it firmly. Sunglasses propped atop his head and his face slit in a wide grin, Athletic Director Andy Vidal pumped his congratulations. He returned the handshake vigorously and visibly, wanting no hard feelings to fester over Vidal's earlier iciness. Pintal approached like a rock, wrapping his arm around Abe's waist to lead him to a seat on the bleachers where the team gathered.

Abe took a deep breath and released it slowly. There were no words for it. All the millions of words that had been written came down to nothing. He'd known the team would make a good showing, but *all the firsts!* Not one team member had exhibited a faint heart at winning the fair prize, including team first. An electrical delight sped through his body as the impact of the win hit home.

The bus driver, Homer Beauchamp, a squat wiry man who rarely ever smiled, promptly produced a handshake, with tears in his eyes, recalling the gross amount of mischief Abe used to get into when he was younger—shaking his head with the incredulity of the whole tournament. Viewed upon arrival at the Meet as assholistics, they were not individuals, but a holistic unit as the sunny day led them closer to home.

"Aw, c'mon you guys," Abe mumbled. "Some people can run, some can jump, and some can throw. Indians can run, don'cha know?" Abe started to get that kindergarten knob in his throat, lowering his eyes, focusing on his feet.

The thirty-five mile drive home breezed by in the aftermath of victory. Arsenault, with a mouth bigger than the Sturgeon River, kept their spirits up all the way home, an impudent glow emanating from his eyes. "We're number one. Let's have fun!"

Just as promised, Beauchamp drove the bus through town with the windows down, harassing the horn and calling attention to the fact that the team *was* NUMBER ONE. The hot fudge sundaes were especially good, and Abe thought the price right. He didn't need a penny from Old John Pedo.

"More nuts! Need more nuts on mine!" Eddie hollered, as if he'd just crawled out from under a bridge with an over-sized head, stringy hair and a long beard.

"Give the kid more nuts." Leo grinned at Ruby Warren.

She cut him a look of askance, annoyed with the *Indian's* dissatisfaction of her work of art. She sniffed loudly, her face a frozen mask, eyes cold, body tense. "God only knows who is going to pick up this bill," she demanded icily.

Pintal bit his tongue and rolled his eyes as he stood behind Ruby. That won loud cheers from the team and slaps on the back. "Give all of them anything they want: bananas, cherries, whipped cream, the works, but especially nuts." Pintal laughed with a puckish twinkle. People, as water, seek their own level, but Ruby Warren forfeited her uptown level with this downtown squad.

From out of nowhere appeared the Clubhouse Manager, a burly ton of a man, with a cauliflower nose, a monster chin, and the name of *Shirley!* "Give the kids anything they want, Ruby. It's on the house!" he shouted. His pugilistic lips ripped with a grin.

The celebration strung a heady experience for Abe. Until today, his life experiences had been second place. He'd endeavored to succeed, and he'd found it in the Nahma High School Track Team. Would Abe ever again find the exaltation of this moment? He thought not.

The fates had more in store for this humble athlete, however.

CHAPTER TWELVE

The Mid-Peninsula Championship Track Team put to bed their successes for another year. Abe viewed with anticipation this summer of 1942, his seventeenth summer that was stretching before him. After his full workweek, he could paint as much as he desired. He found himself charged while a myriad of canvases mazed through his mind where he had stored them in pigeonholes from which he could retrieve them quickly, in living color and animation.

His gift of a recording memory served him well and transported him through spooky spots at school. Although he couldn't always grasp the oral reading of a printed page, he competently envisioned it. Pictures and graphs sunk in well-digested so he wished that he could have all his classes in the form of screen animations.

Social Science class had taught him that persistent modification of behavior produced a person's life experiences, especially successful experiences. In addition, good judgment sprang from experience. He learned in Earth Science that materials have a memory, a capacity to return to a previous shape after deformation. He found that rocks didn't have any memory. Split into a thousand pieces, they'd never recover. Mercury possessed a remarkable memory and could re-assemble with only a slight nudge. However, these facts were memorable because they were evident pictorially.

He'd learned to control his annoying problem of excessive salivation through sheer concentration. Still, it interfered with extended conversation, sometimes *spitting* words out. It lived with him every day. At night he drooled on his pillow and woke up choking. Sometimes his ears burned and ached. The epitome of a man's man, lean and muscled, broad shoulders and big hands, yet, he drooled!

Abe never missed a chance to be reticent, reluctant to contribute because the words didn't always spill out correctly. Damn it all, it didn't take long for a goat to stand out in a herd of sheep! Frustrated, he had difficulty getting his tongue around syllables such as *sh, ch, en* and *ja,* but *wishing* and *doing* were as different as cherries and cheese.

Although an Indian with physical shortfalls, pride was the last thing to prevent him from a good meal. Abe often had dinner invitations to the Savins, the Heberts, Farley and Norrhea's, the Tobins and the Whittakers.

"Have some more roast beef, Abe. That's a big body you're supporting," Dr. Whittaker urged, his booming voice equal to his intimidating size. It carried the length of the exquisitely appointed oak dining table where Abe sat to the right of Liz Whittaker and across the table from Bernard Tobin. Trixie Tobin, Bernard's wife, sat to the right of Dr. Whittaker. Hattie Acker, the bovine wife of Bill Acker, saw seating near the center of the table; her husband sat directly across from her. Abe understood that Bill Acker was employed as Executive Vice President of the Bay de Nocquet Lumber Company. A slightly-built discerning man, Acker had gold hair and eyebrows. His eyes, ever assessing, prevented people from guessing his thoughts.

The dining room was directly north of Doc's living room, which was situated back-to-back with his office. Abe had never seen such rich rugs on hardwood floors, but heard someone mention Bukhara...*Bukhara?* Rugs and tapestries hung sumptuously; Abe thought that surely one should be able to eat them. In *his* house, everything he and Fabian owned was either functional or edible.

Entering the dining room, he found it conveniently located off the east side of the kitchen. Above the dining room table hung a triple-tiered Waterford crystal chandelier with a thousand dancing elliptical prisms that sent roaming reflections around the room at the slightest provocation. Under the table, on the polished hardwood floor, lay a mauve and pink area rug. He found the outer dimensions of the rug spreading nearly to the corners of the room, the fringes of it sweeping the hardwood.

Set high into the north end of the dining room were a set of wide windows done in leaded glass, also generously splashed with mauve and pink. Below stood an eight-foot-long oak buffet boasting a hutch with four etched-glass doors. Delicate bone china pieces were so tasteful that Abe had to discipline himself not to stare at them. Squinting at the wine tripod next to Doc's chair he read *Piñot noir* on the bottle, wondering what that meant. Someday he'd have all these things too. However, he knew he wasn't going to gain them by kicking dried cow chips on a hot day.

Observing the ambience, Abe became uncomfortable. He'd have declined the invitation had he known the guest list. But nuts, he liked the Whittakers and the Tobins, and even Mr. Acker showed him respect. Besides, when he accepted Doc's invitation, his intention was to seek help for his physical problems, but it didn't appear the opportunity would present itself. A tug of anxiety knotted in his stomach.

Observing Liz Whittaker, Abe recorded her refinement. She had classic femininity that shone through—broad forehead, wide-set gray eyes, and a sincere smile with one of her front teeth overlapping the other ever so slightly, giving her a down-home uniqueness. Her short blonde hair fluffed softly.

Abe cut his glance to Hattie, a raw, loud, self-indulgent woman. He recalled clearly his complete captivation with the ornately-framed picture that greeted him in the foyer as he entered the Acker home as a kid after Christmas caroling with the CYO, the Catholic Youth Organization. Hattie Acker invited them in for hot chocolate with a great sweep of her arm rising out of a generously cut sleeve of an authentic Chinese kimono.

"It's a remarkably accurate reproduction of 'The Judgment of Paris' by Peter Paul Rubens, the Belgian baroque master of the seventeenth century," Hattie told the carolers.

He remembered vividly the bright-red silky fabric of the robe Mrs. Acker wore. Designed with fire-breathing dragons and stitched with scalloped brocade; it tied at the waist and had no other means of staying on or staying together. Every time she bent over with a tray of goodie cups, her ample bosoms rushed to ripple their way out of her robe. He'd been so enamored of the scene that he burned his tongue on the hot chocolate. He stared down the table at her now, the memory burning in his bones and stirring along his electrical neuron highway.

Bill Acker's appreciation of fine art, music, and women was commonly known among the townspeople. Although a slightly-built man, his position with the company and his insatiable desires made him a giant. His wife of many years, long-suffering Hattie was known as a heavy smoker and thus earned the nickname "Hackin' Hattie." Word on the street had it that Bill had a twinkle in his eye. He probably wasn't the idol after whom Abe would pattern his life, but he wouldn't judge, especially with all the problems he had with that devil between his legs.

"Have you tackled any new paintings this spring, Abe?" Bill Acker, holding his knife and fork poised over his roast beef, nudged Abe out of his reverie.

He knew Bill lived and breathed not as a bogus art expert but actually owned a small Whistler painting, a landscape done in the Japanese manner. These paintings James Abbott McNeill Whistler called "nocturnes," and dated back to 1877.

Acker continued cutting his roast beef, choosing to ignore Abe's mental vacation. "I'd like to have a large canvas done to hang in the lobby of the Clubhouse. Think you could do that for me this summer?" He winked at Bernard Tobin. "I could convince the Company powers-that-be to spring two hundred and fifty dollars for it."

Stunned, Abe stared unbelievingly at this powerful man. A mix of unease and disbelief stirred deeply inside him. Abe turned to Doc, eyes filled with angst. He cut a glance at the others, trying to get a reading from them.

Bill, not only a judge of good art but of good people, recognized the stiffening in Abe. "You don't have to commit this very minute, but give it some thought. It would be good exposure for you, and perhaps other commissions will follow," he pointed out. "People taste good whiskey and they know it won't be followed by water, that is, unless you run out of good whiskey!" A great laugh resulted, putting Abe at ease.

Feeling a great amount of anxiety, he folded his hands in his lap. "What?" Abe's perplexity fell full on the one word.

Doc smiled with reassurance, working magic on Abe.

Excitement started small in his stomach, a little pollination that created a cell bulging with reproduction. "Of course, I'll start on a picture right away. How large a picture do you want?" *Take your time Abe.* He wanted to drop quietly through the floor and land squarely in hell. Abe's innards ached, but the pollination cells generated more seeds of hope. *Two hundred and fifty dollars!* That would buy food and clothing this winter. Pay for maintenance of the car and buy wood for the stove. *Stupid-ass luck!*

Bill easily read Abe's facial reactions to his offer. "The canvas should be large, say forty by fifty inches. The subject matter can be of your choice. I would prefer, however, if it were about our nice little town, some event or whatever. It's your call." Acker looked up from under his light eyebrows.

Were his eyes gray or light foggy green? Abe couldn't tell, but he saw business insight mixed with a suppressed fondness, which Acker endeavored to separate, unsuccessfully, his warmth seeping through.

Abe looked around the table, riddled with incredulity. *Is he serious?*

Liz laughed placing her small hand over his resting on the table, the touch as scintillating as cool water on a hot summer's day. "I think that is a fine offer, Abe, commendable for the community as well as yourself." The throaty sound of her voice saturated his senses. *Someday I'm going to have a wife like Liz. Yes. Sarah will be like Liz.* His gaze traveled from her hand to her face, where he found the benevolence of a queen, someone who lived above reproach. His stomach wanted to cry.

Thunder rumbled in the distance, the harbinger of a gentle spring rain. "There, see?" Doc interjected. "It's settled. Thor, the god of thunder has spoken. There are two theories to arguing with a woman; neither one works."

Liz wrinkled her nose at Doc, while everyone enjoyed the quip.

"Congratulations on your first paying contract, Abe," Bernard Tobin said, easing the fragile moment while sitting back in his chair, hooking his chubby thumb into his belt, his eyes intent. He had shown off his "Beach Wildflowers" many times to guests in his home, as well as the "School in Winter" that hung in the hall at the school. Abe had presented the two-set series of "Wildflowers" to him after Fabian's death, not wanting any more reminders short-circuiting him day and night.

"A few commissions such as that and you can start yourself a nice little savings account for your college years. I'll see what I can do to send more business your way too." His expression spoke of pride and enthusiasm for his protégée.

Around the table started a covey of conversation, reinforcing the need to continue to support art in the community, and how much Abe, the only local artist besides Max, could help in this area. "Sorely lacking commodity"..."Must shore up this interest in the arts"..."Why don't we...?" Abe felt warmly rewarded with the formal comments and the easy smiles. His wan smile reached ripeness, glistening in its wholesomeness.

With his feet more firmly planted, Abe grew in confidence and enthusiasm. "I'll talk to Max about getting the materials I need for the project," he said, looking from one to the other... *Did he say "proyect"?* "But here it gets tricky." He squinted thoughtfully. "I hope he doesn't get miffed because I have a commission instead of him."

Dr. Whittaker shook his head. "He's had a highly successful career of his own and deeply admires your talent. He'll be happy for you, I'm sure." Abe hung on his soft "r's," his sporty and scathing adjectives, his *petrol* for gas, his *naught* for not. When he finished something, he *packed it in*. His car didn't have a *hood*—it had a *bonnet*.

"Dear," Liz interjected, her mouth curving into a smile. She propped an elbow on the table, cushioned her chin on the heel of her hand and smiled conspiratorially. "Why don't *you* explain to Max that Abe was approached on this challenge, and that it wasn't *his* idea?" Her smile curled secretly and seductively—the message being sent to Doc.

Doc, on the receiving end, felt an overwhelming need to please his wife. Flipping his hand back and forth in a gesture of neutrality, he agreed. "It wouldn't hurt. Flavored medicine makes it more palatable."

The dinner party moved to the living room for liqueurs, and Abe headed for home, but he managed to get Doc alone for a moment. "I need to talk to you about something after work tomorrow." His eyes darted. His feet shifted. "Is it okay if I stop on the way home, maybe just after five o'clock?" Sincerity grew in his dark eyes.

Doc raised an eyebrow, a signature of his facial prose. "Sure, you do that. I'll be home by then unless one of my expectant mothers decides to pop a delivery on me," he added, chuckling.

Abe felt a melting inside him. The small anxious grin faded from his face, and his whole body relaxed, having been unaware of how tightly he'd been sitting scrunched, contained. It was as if he suddenly gained breathing room after suffocating.

His long walk gave way to more distant rumblings of thunder from the southwest. *A comforting sound*, thought Abe. A freshening wind spoke to him of the approaching storm. The air smelled of soft rain, reminding him of the pending summer with all the promise it held. The leaves stirred in the beechwoods, assuring him the comfort of his home, the security there, the legacy of Fabian and Suki. He knew Fabian watched over him. Abe acknowledged it without being spooked any longer.

❧

The Company Store had longer hours on Friday nights, so Abe ran late getting to Doc's. Stocking newly arrived produce into the glass refrigerator cases had kept Abe busy until nearly seven o'clock.

"Hope it's okay to see you at home instead of at the hospital." Abe again took in the rich patina of oak, uncertain as to where Doc wanted to talk to him. "It seems that with going to school and having a job, there's no time to get sick!" Abe shook his head, looking regretful.

"Ah, now, everyone's allowed a moment or two to get sick. However, you look healthy to me, Abe. C'mon into my office, and we'll discuss it. I am a doctor first. Secondarily, I am a scheduled robot."

Abe again found himself behind French doors, the same ones he had entered what seemed like a hundred years ago to get help for Fabian.

"Sit down, sit down, Abe." Doc's brow creased with concern. "Now, what can I do for you?" It didn't take a clairvoyant to sense the unease in this young man. "I'd wager that it's something we can medicate or *fixicate* so swiftly that you'll wonder why you haven't mentioned it earlier." His head cocked to the side with quiet laughter. "I've thought about you all day." Still wearing his white smock from the office, he sat down with the ease and confidence of one who had found his niche in the world.

Abe felt a trickle of sweat accumulating behind his ears as he sat uncomfortably across from a man who epitomized everything he held dear in his gender: strength, success, intelligence and compassion. "Well, it's like this." Taking a deep breath, he opened up the terror-ridden issue. In a gesture of helplessness, his hands spread. "There's always too much saliva in my mouth; it gets embarrassing. My ears burn and ache sometimes, too. I can't sleep all night without waking up two or three times, choking." He waited out a heart flutter. "I used to tell Dad about it, but he thought I'd outgrow the problem. Another thing, if I talk too fast, I spit!" Abe faked an off-handed smile, unsuccessfully.

Leaning forward in deference to this man, Abe swallowed with spunk, shifting gears. "I have another problem, too. If I don't concentrate on what I'm saying, I don't quite pronounce 'd's' and 't's' and sometimes 'n's, 'j's' and syllables such as 'cha' and 'ish.' I've been teased about my speech since I was a kid, and it's made me cranky." He slapped his knee. "Enough." Abe sat back, no longer attempting levity.

Doc clasped his hands between his spread knees. His head lowered slightly, awareness flickering in his eyes. Having analyzed Abe, he knew what his young friend could and could not accept—a dent to his ego, a blind-side remark—yet Abe needed to know that everyone has barbs in life and adjust to a less-than-perfect world.

"I'm glad that you mentioned it, Abe. Yes, I've noticed the speech hang-ups, and I've been hoping they'd go away, too, just as your dad did. But they aren't going to disappear like summer fog." Taking a quick breath, he stood, washing his hands together. "Let's go out to the kitchen and grab a roast beef sandwich. I'm the cook tonight; it's Liz's night out with her bridge club."

Abe somehow had a difficult time imagining Doc in the kitchen with his scrupulous professionalism and faultless clothing. Abe's eyes followed him as he slapped together whole wheat bread with thin stacked slices of flaky roast beef. He added horseradish and mayo, then grabbed a giant jar of homemade pickles from the refrigerator—a payment in-kind from one of his patients.

"You like pickles?"

"Yeah, I do." Abe shuddered. "But *they* make my ears ache, too." Abe shook his head in confused perplexity. "Sounds stupid, ay?" Sitting at the kitchen table, his glance shifted only shortly to Doc, not wanting to reveal the pain in his eyes, but he didn't miss the enormous apple pie resting on the counter.

"No, it doesn't sound stupid at all. I'll bet your ears ache just *looking* at this jar of pickles or an orange or a grapefruit or even lemon pudding. Right?" Abe spotted a smile around the corner of Doc's lips, his eyes gentle and caring.

How'd he know that? Even tomatoes made his ears ache. Abe laughed uncomfortably. "That's right. Yes!" He pushed his chair back, sitting sideways so he could cross his legs, and flipped his arm over the back.

"You're having a problem with your salivary glands, which secrete saliva, a somewhat alkaline fluid that moistens the mouth, softens food and aids in digestion. The largest of the glands are under the lower jaw; beneath the tongue; and the ones in front of each ear. Glands near the front of the mouth also secrete saliva. These glands contain enzymes, which aid in the digestion of carbohydrates." Doc had put the sandwiches on plates setting one in front of Abe and the other one in front of himself.

Snapping a napkin over his lap, Doc waved for Abe to go ahead and start on his fare. "The salivary glands, especially the parotid, of human beings are affected by a disease called 'mumps.' I know you had the mumps when you were five years old.

"I've always been your doctor and I don't mind telling you that I've taken a special interest in your welfare. Maybe it's because I spent so much time with Fabian and I realized he had a very limited life expectancy." He shifted uneasily for a moment. Perhaps he tampered too far with the boy's feelings, but he did want to lift his burdens.

"Getting back to your problem, the mumps are an acute contagious, viral disease whose symptoms include pain, fever and swelling of the salivary glands. Mumps usually affect young people and rarely last more than three days. I remember, however, that we were concerned about your recovery time, which was double the norm. Nonetheless, you did rise above it, and I deduced that all's well that ends well." Doc got up and retrieved a half-gallon bottle of milk from the refrigerator, pouring it into glasses for each of them.

"It appears you've suffered deterioration of your parotid glands, causing them to secrete an abundant flow of saliva at all times instead of only when you're eating.

Abe hung on every word Doc said, his hands, and mouth taking a walk on the delightful side, deeply engrossed in the roast beef sandwich while he ingested Doc's knowledge as if eavesdropping into the coveted and cloistered.

"What I'd suggest is that we remove those parotid ducts. Your remaining exocrine glands will be ample for you. Of all the exocrine glands, however, those two are the ones that produce the enzymes to digest carbohydrates, as I said before. No remedy is perfect, but it's better to light one little candle, etcetera, etcetera. After the surgery, if you're having any difficulty with digestion, we can place you on a medication that substitutes the enzymes."

Clearing the plates from the table and placing them onto the cupboard, Doc advised, "As for your difficulty with pronouncing some words, let me check here." He felt under Abe's chin, his neck. "Now, let's take a look at your mouth and your tongue." He produced a penlight and a tongue depressor from the breast pocket of his smock. Flashing the small light into Abe's mouth and throat area, he checked under the tongue, as well as the interior mouth surfaces. "Hmm, uh-huh, okay. You did a good job on that sandwich—left no traces," he teased, hoping to put Abe's worries to rest.

Maybe in the darkness of a few months ago, when he sunk deep in grief, Abe would have felt hopeless. Somehow, on this fast-fading evening in late May, his blood pulsed as if he were reborn. No more teasing, no more whispers. He wondered if Crazy Horse ever had speech problems, or ever had the mumps. Even if he did, he'd still have been a leader. Leadership was *his* inheritance also.

Doc again sat across from Abe at the state-of-art chrome and Formica kitchen table, waiting for Abe to return from his bubble trip. "So, are you ready for a little surgery? What do you think of a week from today? Then you'll have time over the weekend for recuperation. By the way, you have an overextended, soft-flesh tie between your tongue and the bottom of your mouth. I'll snip that just a trifle to allow you more latitude with your tongue. What do you think of that?" Doc laughed with British conservatism, his eyes twinkling with warmth, slapping his hand over Abe's.

Nodding involuntarily at Doc's suggestion, Abe's eyes glazed over like an early freeze on the rain barrel. "I think it's nice." His voice was no more than a whisper. "It's unbelievable." He sighed, shaken with the new knowledge, but then stiffened. "Is this going to be very expensive?" Distress crept into his voice. "I don't have any extra money now, but when I finish my picture for Bill Atkins I'll pay you in full. Okay?" Abe rose to his feet, pushing his chair back under the table.

"Sit down, Abe, and don't worry about it. Now, how about a hunk of that apple pie, hmmm? I'll make arrangements for everything to be handled by the B.A.R.E., the Benevolent Association of Railroad Employees, the insurance your father carried, and still covers you until you're eighteen years old, which will be in December, right?" An understanding arm slipped around Abe's shoulder.

"Uh-*huh!*" Abe nodded, his smile disbelieving that Doc remembered the apple pie as well as his birthday. His heart did a cadence, feeling special.

"I can tune in that night you were born," Doc said. "There blew a helluva storm off Lake Michigan, and I had to walk the last yardage on the Beach Road. Your mother is not a very big woman and you were a chunk of a baby. Nevertheless, she did all right, and you sailed into the world hollering and protesting. Beautiful woman. Ever hear from her?" His frown lines shook a leg.

"No, but Farley says that he's confident she's alive and well. It's been hard not having a mother, but I sure am glad I had Fabian." Satisfied with the evening's turn of events, Abe spread his hands with an all-embracing gesture.

He shook Doc's hand, strong in the belief that his wobbly youth had taken a walk. He shouldered a man in a man's world now. "Thanks for supper and all the advice." He melted like the puddle of a candle at the look of gentle concern in Doc's eyes. "I'll be there next Friday morning, six o'clock!" His arms spread again in incredulity.

The hand on his shoulder as he left triggered a transmission of energy and well-being. Under the umbrella of the newly leafed hardwoods, Abe could hear the world breathe. For tonight, he would crawl into his old bed under the sloping roof of his attic room with the sweet scent of wood shingles and the weight of the world off his shoulders.

Abe recuperated quickly just as Dr. Whittaker had predicted. There was no more reluctance to speak up and speak out. The surgery gave him new faith, new gusto so dominant that it electrified the very air around him. Maybe even Vidal would give him recognition some day, even though he was half Sioux Indian.

CHAPTER THIRTEEN

Each night Abe hurried to the beach to catch as much daylight as he could before the sun disappeared. He could depend on eighteen hours of daylight in late June. After discussing with Sarah the venture of a canvas for the Clubhouse, the idea of painting the Nahma landmark Burner won out. A receptacle for unusable wood by-products, the monolith Burner had held court on this point of land since the first mill was established in 1881, thus the signature Burner was in step with Bill Acker's wishes.

Abe chose to offset the Burner to one side, not being someone to brood over the balance of symmetry. Daily, the picture took on greater tones of life; the waves licked the shoreline near the point and arched in a white line into the curve of the bay. The setting sun half concealed itself farther to the right on the canvas. Gauzy clouds grew salmon and mint, the Burner dusky-colored and shadowy the first one-third of its height, then becoming scintillatingly blue/white, then yellow-orange and vividly red at the top, where its screened dome protected the environment from flying sparks and chips.

The scene beyond the Burner lay in shadow, the lumberyard trams superimposed minutely against the backdrop of the setting sun. A fishing boat created a lazy wake approaching a lumber company dock. As the scene drew closer, the sandy beach stretched in luminescent gold and ivory, with clusters of courageous Indian paintbrushes, buttercups and stark-white daisies. The sky beyond *all* this appeared eerily blue-green and coral in the last throes of the fiery setting sun. For Fabian's sake, Abe stylized one single star far to the dark side of the picture—Venus rushing to follow the setting sun.

After four weeks Abe sat back and released an audible sigh. "Yesss." He'd captured the essence of slow-rolling whitecaps as they neared the shore, the lap lines curved and rounded to leave no doubt as to where they had last stalked. Abe felt such tenderness for the finished canvas, as if it were his child.

Would the picture be shuttled from place to place like an orphan looking for a home? Old childish concerns surfaced—the hurts of rejection, the secret fright of being cast aside and never realizing the prophecies of his Sioux ancestors.

This evolved as his summer solstice Sun Dance—his recognition of the rituals of the Plains Indians. He felt their magnetization to the summer moon, the long days, the warm nights. His people had seen for generations what he had painted. They viewed it all again through his eyes. He shook his head, towing him back to the here and now his hands trembling with the revelation.

The Fourth of July celebration would be in full swing soon, and Bill Acker would want his painting hung for holiday homecomers. Abe, on lunch break, called on Max. The noonday sun cast rainbows in the fine mist hovering over the garden hose that he held on his hodgepodge of hybrid flowers.

"Hey there, Max," he said, crossing the expanse of lawn. "My canvas for the Clubhouse is finished, but I don't want to trust it to the backseat of my car. I wonder if you could drive me down to the Company Office in your pickup truck. I'll ride in the back and hold it until we get there."

Max moved his jaw as if trying to scare up a gumball of patience. "I'll just set this aside until we get back." He wore a light blue cotton shirt that vanished into a pair of dark-blue putter pants with an elasticized waist that rode loosely on his shapeless hips.

Max and Abe carried the canvas tacked tightly onto a wooden frame, into the Company office, a homey-type brick building that stood just a stone's throw from the Company Store. Self-doubt squiggled in Abe's throat. What if Acker thought the sunset too vivid or the water too prevalent? What if… Yeah, but…maybe. Hell, Acker was nothing if not politically correct; he would suggest corrections without biting Abe.

Abe felt as if he were moving from a jail cell to the gallows. He rubbed the backs of his fingers across his dry mouth. This could be the beginning of the end, or something that held great promise. Would the door slam shut with a reverberating thud, or would it stay forever open? Fabian had told him years ago that the only difference between a rut and a grave was the depth.

"Well, look who's here!" Acker stepped out of his glassed-in office. There hovered a welcoming wariness in his expression, which sent the temperature in the room skyrocketing. Standing the canvas on the floor next to the water cooler, Abe and Max shook his hand before removing the protective sheet covering the canvas.

Abe studied the knot of office personnel gathered around: Bill Acker, First Vice President; Alan Mercier, Operations Manager; Fern LaBrasseur, secretary; Bunny Bennette, stenographer; Rudy Jehn, cost analyst; Bill Brophy,

Pay Master; and John Zimmerman, bean counter. As he glanced at each of them, he caught widened eyes as they stared at the picture, then at each other—the atmosphere taut.

Silence. The very air stirred electrically with unspoken words.

Hold it together, Miereau. You've been through tougher spots than this. Hold on. Abe sucked in a deep breath as if he were coming up for the third time.

Complete absorption of each individual was evident. They stood sucked into the vortex of the rendering, absorbed softly into the terrain, blending them into the sheer magnetism of the picture, its dramatic seascape, marked variations of light and shade, its composition of forms blending with colors. Peering closely, they marveled at the clarity of the close-up objects as opposed to the blur of the setting sun in the distance, the highlighted intense heat generated by the Bay de Nocquet Lumber Company Burner. The impasto of the tide lines on the shore of the beach stood touchable and uplifted.

Slowly, Bunny reached out, the tips of her fingers caressing the bold, thick strokes along the shoreline, the pearlescent finish on the daisy petals facing the setting sun, the vivid orange of the Indian paintbrushes. Hesitatingly, she moved her fingers to the top of the intensely heated wood-chip Burner, allowing her fingers to float just above it, as if avoiding the high temperature. With the palm of her hand, she ever so lightly swept over the sunset where Venus followed the sun obediently off the end of the earth.

Her hand fell slowly to her side. She sighed softly and lifted her eyes to Bill Acker, who yet hadn't said a word, but had followed every move Bunny made with electric hypnotism. "It's beautiful," she whispered as though the spell shouldn't be broken. This idolatry to God's existence needed the calm and comfort of a cathedral.

Acker studied the way in which the brush had been affected, the manner in which color could be applied to hold the life of daylight!

Max stood back, leaning his shoulder against the wall. His pride in his protégé begged to break out, to shout, to publish and declare to everyone in earshot, "Long live this talent." Would it be too much if he said it aloud? This was one walkin' piece of work, but he could not bring himself to say it, and the moment passed.

Abe stood several steps back toward the door, experiencing a Freudian fancy to flight. The old familiar icicle-chest reasserted itself. He had a bad case of the heebie jeebies, the horrors and the creeping crud of self-doubt.

Bill Acker, in the silent heavy air, maneuvered closer to Abe, put his arm around his shoulder, and squeezed it. "Brilliant," he said, softly. His head nodded several times in confirmation, his eyes filled with pride in this young man. "It has an iambic pentameter; whereas some pictures that I view are simply blank verse."

"I'll tell you what, young man," Alan Mercier declared in a sober inflection, clutching Abe's arm. "I have a feeling that there's going to be some damn happy text to your life between the Once-Upon-A-Time and The End." There was something enthusiastic in his wide grin for the young man who'd walked many a weary road—alone.

"I would like to take you to one of our lumber camps to have you paint a picture of the lumberjacks outside the mess hall, but not until this winter. Many of the jacks go home for the summer months where they put in hay, wheat or alfalfa and have a money crop in addition to working for us." He allowed the message to gravitate for a moment, a slow smile spreading across his ample face. "Besides, there's a certain beauty about the winter woods." Affection danced in his eyes.

"Sure. I can do that." Abe sighed and laughed at the same time, his world turning a little brighter. "I'll have to take a day off from school though."

"Yes, of course. I'll arrange it with Bernie. You and I'll ride up on the train early in the morning; it's about thirty-five miles due north of here. You can take a look at our operations and we'll return the same night when the train hauls in the recent cut."

Abe shot a quick look at Max, excitement burning in his eyes like incandescent bulbs. For all Max's personal containment, Abe sensed that he had grown taller with the work. He tried to keep his voice level, but enthusiasm kept oozing through it. "Sure would enjoy a trip to a lumber camp. Thanks for asking." He wanted to spin around the room like a top, slip into the Sioux Indian Sun Dance. Instead, he contained himself, content with a non-stop smile.

The whole crew milled about the picture, studying it from different angles. The scene would be forever indelible in Abe's mind. The sun had slowly crept over midday and shone hugely warm into the southwest windows. Like God's own spotlight, it focused on the picture injecting an element of life and vibrancy, lightening shadows and bending the elements with elasticity. Was the moment life or a living thing? Had Crazy Horse met Fabian and encouraged the radiance?

"Well, son, where would you choose to do your banking?" Bill Acker roused Abe from his bubble, eager to reward him with a commission. "You can save with us. Our interest rates are commensurate with competitive banking fraternities, and we compound all earnings. What's more, you can borrow up to twice the amount you have saved with us." He portrayed a man who spoke within his depth, but not manipulative.

Abe stole a look at Max, who nodded his head in confirmation.

"Okay, let's do that. When winter comes, though, I'll need some of that money for food, clothing and wood for heating the house. My car needs some work too, if it's going to see me through a few more years. It crawls into the garage as if it's been injured on the street." Abe had to beat down an intense flirtation of giddiness.

"You're welcome to draw out of this account anytime and to deposit at any time. You work right here, so it'll be an easy transaction," encouraged Acker. "You'll be multiplying your possessions from here on out, Abe, but don't ever reduce your values." His lips spread in a well-intended smile. "Allow me to extend my deep appreciation of this offering for our Company Clubhouse. I'll do everything I can to get further commissions for you."

"And I," inserted John Zimmerman, pride in his tone. Consensus careened around the room like players fresh from a huddle.

Max covered his mouth with a hand to hide his smile. It was as if he was watching a come-from-behind duckling waddle to the head of the line behind his mother.

Standing in the molten sunlight streaming from the windows, Abe was stymied for words but eked out, "Thank you, thank you all." *They liked it! After all the gut-wrenching doubt, they liked it.*

Wearing his biggest sunshine smile, he and Max headed out the door.

Giving Abe's arm a firm grasp, Max winked. "I'll pick you up after work."

"Thanks." Abe was preoccupied with a savoring thought. He liked the way they had viewed his picture, not with estimating its worth. Rather, they saw attraction in the environment of the scene, the use of colors, the emotions it stirred within each of them.

☙❧

Summer Art School was in full swing when Abe replaced his "Burner" project with the one he really wanted to do: "The Sidetracked Track Team." The sky was draped Great Lakes Blue, sporting only a few sleeping cirrus clouds waiting to ship out. It was crunch time to master it as quickly as the last one. He needed to have the project completed in time for the auction, which would take place the third Sunday of August.

On his front porch in the cool of the evening with crickets tuning up, he pondered long on variations for his theme. He decided that what he'd do was to use the anecdotal method. The first one would measure thirty inches by forty inches and would feature the crew shooting the breeze around the bonfire. Smaller, the second one would measure twenty by thirty inches and show them melting down with yawns and such. The third one he estimated at eighteen by twenty-two inches and would pose the firepit as it was reduced to flickering coals. There remained someone's lingering feet walking away. His skin grew taut and unduly waxen as he transported himself into the creations.

Weeks flew by while absorbed in his summer endeavor until he found himself into a week before the auction. He caught a movement in his peripherals. "Sarah!" Abe shouted across the street as he saw her in the flower garden, the sun highlighting the sheen of her auburn hair, which fell forward as she cut fresh flowers.

"What's up?" she responded, rising and shaking her hair over her shoulders.

He closed the gap between them. "The final touches are on my pictures; they'll be ready for the auction on Sunday." He stood at the picket fence that surrounded her yard. "How about us going to the Sadie Hawkins Day Festival and dance on Saturday?"

"Sure!" She moved toward him over the nicely manicured lawn. "I'll go as Daisy Mae and you can go as Li'l Abner. Max and Ma are going as Sadie Hawkins and Joe Bpftsk." She laughed as she approached Abe, a large gathering of burnt-orange tiger lilies and bright-yellow day lilies in her arms. Pollen from the tiger lilies had brushed off on her chin. Reaching over, Abe wiped it off, stroking her cheek with the back of his fingers, which sent smoking tingles up his arm.

Her chin quivered, caught his hand and held it to her cheek. There quavered a distance about her. "What's the problem, Sarah? Is something wrong?" His knuckles now under her chin lifted her face to his.

Her long lashes closed down, her mouth working.

"Come sit on my porch and we'll talk about it," he encouraged her, opening the gate for her. Placing the flowers in the soft fringe of grass outside the fence, he walked her across the street, his heavy hand resting on the small of her back feeling the shadowy sway of her hips and the moist heat that diffused from her body.

"I don't know what you have in your pretty head, but I know what I see in your eyes, Sarah. It's disturbing. Come," he motioned widely.

Taking a deep breath, her voice barely above a whisper, Sarah blurted out, "Max and Ma really *are* sending me away to school—in Green Bay to Our Lady of the Lake Academy for Young Women." Her glance flew up to him seated a step above her. "They're determined that I should have a fancier education than locally." She buried her face in her hands. "This means that I'll have to finish my last two years of high school away from you and all my friends."

Abe sat speechless. Stiffened with deep resentment, his anger and pain showed in every muscle of his face. With arched thumb, he wiped the tears from Sarah's drowning eyes. Still without words, he pulled Sarah up and led her to Fabian's rocking chair that sat under the porch overhang. Attaching a dark green and white canvas-draped porch chair, he sat next to her. Searching for her hand, he pressed it to his cheek.

Sarah's shoulders heaved. "I had to tell you. I've been putting it off. It was easier to be brave when you didn't know."

He swallowed. "This is a bunch of bullshit, Sarah. Bullshit!" he repeated. His sympathetics and parasympathetics hammered against walls of confinement.

She agreed, nodding, knowing she needed the substance of him surrounding her as much as sustenance on the table and roof over her head. A gray squirrel ran a herky-jerky path across the lawn, standing to inspect with curious eyes the two intruders into his busy work-a-day world. Sarah studied the freedom of its life, its carefree existence living off the land, scampering in and out of the most unlikely places, its long fluffy tail sending messages of the moment.

Abe shook his head as if to throw off this new baggage. How uncanny. *How ironic!* Max drew a generous salary as Director of the Summer Art School, funded partially by public school moneys, but the public school was assessed unfit for his daughter. Now he'd heard everything.

Giving Sarah a few moments to sort her thoughts out, he went on. "It's impossible. They can't do that to us. It's always been you and me. Everything I do, I do for you. Everything I am, you've created. Sonofabitch," he growled, his voice tenuous. Crazy Horse must have felt like this when he was moved from one agency to another on the Great Plains that were originally his own home. His eyes took on a faraway look.

A faint quivering appeared around the edge of Sarah's mouth. She shrugged and toyed with the sleeve of Abe's shirt. "I leave a week from Saturday and I won't be home again until Thanksgiving. Then I get two weeks off for Christmas."

Abe, sitting in front of her and slightly to the side, stopped cold by the jarring jolt that for a moment stunned him as he caught the sheen of deep rich velvet in her eyes—the darkest color of brown, swimming in pools of white anxiety. Over her shoulders and down her arms, his fingers glazed gently, softly as if in memorization. "Impossible!"

"No, it's not. It's not impossible." Sarah's tone bespoke reality. "We'll just have to try to spend as much time together as we can while I'm home on breaks." It took more out of her than she'd thought to tell Abe of her family's plan for her future.

"I haven't told Betty Hebert or Mary Nolan yet." Her voice wound down like a debilitated calliope. She folded her arms in front of her, rubbing them.

"They can't do this to us, Sarah." He became belligerent. Sultry August air brought a mixture of surf mist from the lake and perfume from the wildflower mix on the upper beach. The waves rolled in slowly, with a rhythm—a-whoosh-ahh, a-whoosh-ahh. In the distance, seagulls screeched stridently breaking the enveloping silence.

"It won't always be like this, Abe." Sarah possessed an expression of hope, giving some radiating life to her face. "When we graduate, maybe we can go to the same college." She averted her eyes to her folded hands as they lay resting in her lap.

"Hang on, Sarah. I'll get us cold lemonade." Choking down his own tears, he used the moments alone to regain control of his shaking knees. Handing her the tumbler, his hand tremors rattled the ice.

She caught the moisture in his eyes. By sipping on the lemonade one swallow at a time, it helped hold back the tears. A small breeze stirred the birches across the road, leaves showing silver-white, then green—chattering.

Abe flowed with frustration. It was as if he'd had another death in the family. If he hadn't been so infuriated, he would have been flattered at Max's stand against his relationship with Sarah. He'd noticed that ever since he'd been ten years old Max had gritted his teeth at their close companionship. Sarah's news foretold of not being with her everyday anymore, maybe for always. He seemed wrinkled, like a man dying in the desert from lack of water, a drop of autumn rain metamorphosing into a cold snowflake.

"Sarah!" Ma Savin called from her backyard. "I need those flowers now, while I'm still young enough to put them into vases."

"Thanks for the lemonade, Abe." For the briefest moment, their eyes locked in a communion of need. "I'll talk to you some more about this later. Along about Wednesday, show me what you've painted on the Track Team series," she said while walking away backwards, reluctant to leave him alone in his devastation and she in hers.

Again, Abe knew that a heart could cry. In this small village, he knew that there were families that nurtured and loved. They provided places in the heart where a soul could find refuge. But all he owned ceased to be no more than a place inside four square walls that no longer provided day-to-day sustenance. He wasn't nobody, a cardboard cutout, but he might as well be just that.

Abe threw himself into his work to dull the pain of losing Sarah to a new world, one in which he'd never be a part. He hauled his easel and canvases to the beach and set them up for as long as the sun shed light. The large picture lent an image but it needed life. The campfire with a kettle of steaming stew hung on a tripod positioned in the middle. Flames leaped about the pot in a contest of endurance, slow bubbles appearing at the open top. Sitting around the fire was a menagerie of eight young men in various postures. Some lay in the sand; some faced sideways to the fire.

Jackets zipped and collars upturned, coolness showed in the picture. Eyes reflected the firelight and cheeks glowed rosy from the workout and heat generated by the fire. Kenny Ritter wore a shy smile, while Jimmy Weberg grinned broadly. Abe and Eddie sat on a log, both hypnotically staring into the fire as if genetically drawn to it.

Del O'Brian, with hands stuffed into his pockets, bent to sniff the stew. The background faded to purple, then black. Through ragged slits in their pants' knees, various shades of skin peeked out. Jackets were misfits of big, small, bright red to dark brown.

Yes, the colors were complete. Abe spread his hands and cocked his head. *Yes.*

The second picture showed bay water lapping in the firelight and empty stew cups strewn forlornly in the sand. Weberg yawned. Abe and Eddie sat with their backs against a log, hands folded on their stomachs. Del O'Brian lay on his back stretched out like a slug. At half-mast, Ritter's eyes faded fast. In varying shadows beyond the fire, the rest of the crew were slowly cranking down. Blackness encroached ever closer.

The third picture telescoped right down to the smoldering fire, the tripod gone and the kettle conked out. Glowing embers winked and sputtered in the fresh on-shore breeze. Surrounding the fire were empty footprints by the dozen, the sitting logs abandoned. Two pairs of feet were lifted off the picture leaving deep indentations in the soft sugar sand.

Abe laughed. Yes. He liked it. He bit his bottom lip and grinned.

It had taken him a month from concept to completion. The pictures would be displayed on three easels he'd borrowed from Max. Their captions would read, "The Off-track Team," "The Sidetracked Team," and "The Track Team Is Off." He found that he'd mixed tears with his paint during that miserable week of sinking hope for everything he had planned for his future.

As she promised, Wednesday evening Sarah came down to the beach to check out the pictures. She stared, awed. Literally bouncing from one picture to another she exclaimed, "Abe! These are terrific! How you've captured the faces around the fire and the fellowship in their eyes and the humor in their mouths." She glanced over at him in appreciation, her eyes wide. She put her hand to her mouth. "Look how you caught the last remnants of the sunset in the background on the big one! Max says that kind of shading is called "chiaroscuro"—variations of light and shade for dramatic effect." Her glance cut away to him, puzzled at his silence to her comments.

In his bubble, Abe hunkered down in the sand balancing on the balls of his feet, letting his eyes span over Sarah. He drank in her presence, her profile against the backwash of the bay, the offshore breeze catching her slacks against her legs and playing in her angel-soft hair.

Suddenly, she twisted the blowing hair around her hand and tucked it into the collar of her waistcoat jacket. *Click.* She froze in time into a cubbyhole for retrieval one day when he could bear to paint her from memory—her ingenuousness, her peachy-tan skin and her candidness.

"You ready for the big day on Saturday?" Abe asked,

"Yes, I am," she said turning from the paintings. "It's really quite simple. A pair of cutoff shorts, a peasant blouse and some huaraches is all it takes. How about you?" A dark glow in her eyes revealed warm interest.

"It'll be bibbies for me with a far-too-small cotton shirt. It's out of the question to wear heavy boots like Li'l Abner did, so I'm going to scruff along with my gym shoes." He managed one of his electric smiles while standing and brushing sand from his hands.

CHAPTER FOURTEEN

Abe awoke brighter and more energized than the gray squirrels in the windswept oak trees. Their chattering on this Sadie Hawkins Day placed him into high gear.

By ten o'clock Sarah flounced up to the front door and knocked. "C'mon Abe, let's go. I hope you're not sleeping yet just because it's your day off," she added with a throaty chuckle, standing outside the front porch door.

The door popped open. "Surprise! I'm all ready. I've been up for hours." He studied her costume intently. "Where did you scare up the red polka dot blouse?" Abe had all he could do to keep his tongue in his mouth. She looked good enough to eat—peasant blouse pulled off her shoulders, cutoff jean shorts hanging ragged just below her buns, long legs and squeaky huaraches.

She met his enthusiasm with lowered lids to conceal her pleasure and stepped back a pace. "I used some of Max's art paint and dabbed the red circles on one of my drawstring blouses." Her eyes sprang to life with the appeal of his powerful physique. "You're big, tall and husky, just like Li'l Abner. Those bibbies are far away without fault, and you look as if you're going to pop right out of that old tee shirt. Here, let me unbuckle one of the bibby straps so you'll look more authentic," she said, searching his face and seeking his approval. She lifted on tiptoe, balanced eight fingertips against his chest until she found the buckle.

Abe felt exhilaratingly disquieted.

"There, *Voilà*," she said, gathering her wits about her and patting his broad chest.

Abe felt the magic, too, his eyes alight with excitement looking down at her standing so close to him, possessively re-arranging his bibbies. He could smell the freshness of her. Around her forehead, tiny tendrils curled at her temples as the rest of her dark brown hair hung curled under slightly at her shoulders, her thick bangs complementing her long black lashes. Squeezing her shoulder, something told him to get out of there fast.

At the first stop they purchased cotton candy. Sarah entwined her fingers with Abe's as they watched the two-legged gunny sack races. Several times they talked to Doc and Liz in the open grassy lot behind the Clubhouse. Doc smiled warmly, proud to know Abe and Sarah to whom he always deferred with, "How's the best looking young couple in town?" All the while he spoke, his arm swept about Abe's shoulder, squeezing and releasing it. To Sarah, Doc shot an impish grin, taunting but flattering.

Sarah's eyes flew wide open, feeling as conspicuous as a mortician at a circus.

There were dozens of Daisy Maes and Lil Abners, Mammy and Pappy Yokums, Sadie Hawkins and Joe Bpftsk's; Shmoos and Kigmies ran all over the place. A real Hill Billy Band complete with washtub, ukulele, spoons, white lightning jug, banjo, guitar, fiddle and mouth organ provided the entertainment. The cacophony of sights, sounds and smells stimulated the senses and spurred the activities.

The greased pig races were held with a raucous crowd participating. Dave Phalen, a mid-sized Irishman and dressed as Stinky McCoy in tattered undershirt and pants cutoff at the knees made a final plunge at the pig near the finish line and brought it down with a flourish and roll that sent them both back into an upright position, the pig squealing as if he'd been stabbed. Dave held the pig's front feet up for a picture. The race area roared with laughter and jibes. Big bucks had been bet on the winning pig-catcher. A sweet deal, the *Escanaba Daily Press* was there to cover the event, and Dave's picture was sure to wind up on the front page of Monday's paper. Holding a corncob pipe between his teeth and wearing a mangy witch's wig, he hardly looked the part of the lumberyard foreman and secretary/treasurer of the local school board.

In the late afternoon, Abe and Sarah strolled hand in hand to the smorgasbord served by the Swedish Church ladies from Isabella, the farming furrows of the county.

Jostling through the buffet line, Doc and Liz joined them. "How would you kids like some company through this gastronomical delight?" Doc asked, approaching the long table of taste treats. Liz, smiling comfortably, placed her arm around Sarah's waist.

The meatballs tempted Abe, while Sarah chose the fried chicken and Doc and Liz sampled herring salad, pickled salmon and smoked whitefish.

"Skål!" Doc said as he held high a glass of Swedish schnapps. Abe returned the salute with a quick half-bow. Together, they tossed the drink back, the clear yellow-white liqueur with its flavor of caraway coursing gratefully through their receptive veins. The schnapps lined up elbow-to-elbow with ice cold beer in proper Swedish fashion.

"Do you really think you ought to be enticing Abe with alcohol, Danforth?" Liz's raised eyebrows generated concern, yet love and caring for her husband's toes on which she may be treading.

"For Christ's sake, Liz, he's almost eighteen years old. I'm sure this isn't the first time he's had a beer." Bending his head, Doc nuzzled her hair.

Sitting at cafeteria-style tables set up on the promenade porch, Doc poked Abe out of his intense concentration on the meatballs. "That little Sarah is the ripest peach I've ever seen—beautiful. Are you treating her well?" His eyebrows drew together in a straight line over his dark eyes, shot full with amusement and warmth.

Abe, embarrassed, poised his fork halfway to his mouth. Then it hit him that Doc simply shared a man-thing question in camaraderie. "Well if you mean what I think you're asking, the answer is *no*. Do you have any suggestions?" Abe's eyes traveled the terrain of Doc's face, looking for any hidden meanings.

Doc savored the smoked whitefish, contemplating, his eyes cast down. "Do you love her?" he asked, raising that signature eyebrow as he turned to Abe.

"Yes," he replied quietly. "She drives me nuts—on my mind constantly." Abe rested his forehead on the palm of his hand, his elbow propped on the table in an attempt to pull off this conversation as quietly as possible.

Doc stretched his arms upward and outward in an air of complete relaxation and turned to Abe. "Then you need to be more assertive and aggressive, but don't scare her," he said. "Furthermore, make sure to use a condom so we don't have a mini-World War II on the Beach Road." He poked Abe in the shoulder. "Gotta run and make some early evening rounds at the hospital. Enjoy your dinner."

People by the hundreds milled around the smorgasbord on the long porch, which ran parallel to the auditorium in front of the Clubhouse. Abe and Sarah entered through the large lobby adjacent to the auditorium on the east side, which stood lined with art exhibits for the auction tomorrow: watercolors, oils, etchings, pottery and sculpture stood cordoned off with theater rope, surveillance officers stationed every ten feet. Abe's anecdotal series of three paintings held a prestigious position, immediately viewed as soon as you walked into the lobby. Thick crimson velvet drapes cushioned their presentation. Sarah squeezed

Abe's fingers, whereupon he brought the palm of her hand to his mouth, gently kissing the warm center of it.

They wandered into the auditorium bumping into Ken Ritter and Betty Hebert as well as Dell O'Brian and Mary Nolan. The room was crowded and hot with sheer body count. "Let's get out for some fresh air, Sarah, before the band starts for the evening. Maybe it'll be cooler when we get back," Abe suggested.

Although they seldom had to run for shade in Michigan's cool pine forests, it made refreshing sense to Sarah. "I could sit down for a while. We've been going since this morning," she replied tenuously, but puckish flickers of amusement prevailed.

The soothing strains of "Twilight Time" reached them before they could clear the building. "The band's already playing!" Sarah nudged Abe. "Slow-dancing is my very favorite thing to do." She smiled warmly up at him, flexing her shoulders.

"You got it little lady." Abe drawled the words *better* than John Wayne did.

She leaned into him as if she were molded into a grommet on an assembly line. Abe's body flooded with satisfaction and desire. He observed people watching them, heads turning, aware that they posed a handsome couple—she so tiny and fragile, he looming large and protective.

"We're getting out of here as soon as this song is over." Abe was hot with hyperactive energy and had to get *her* out of there.

Struck by Abe's determination, Sarah cast no hidden meaning behind it.

The last light of day yielded to darkness; the tree line past the Sturgeon River hung barely visible upon leaving the Clubhouse. Crickets hummed as if tuning up for a festival, while Abe parked the car in his yard. He stood still for a moment drinking in the heavy air, redolent with fragrances. Through the birch copse across the road, the moon hung like a dabbled crescent in the evening sky.

Abe entered the house and turned on the radio; music drifted onto the front porch, mellow and soft. "Tangerine" *was* playing with a singing rhythm, a sexy sax getting the best of it. "There, now isn't that better than the noisy bedlam we've been hearing all day?" He was surprised to find that it was only nine o'clock. It seemed like he'd been gone for at least two days.

"It's so right to have you on my porch, Sarah." He sat a step above her massaging her shoulders, feeling the silkiness of her skin, her shoulders bare. He wanted to gently slide her sleeves down, down, and feel the smooth softness of her breasts...

Sarah smiled contentedly, hanging her head to the side, locking Abe's hand between her ear and her throat, where it felt so right. She would entertain that thought, tired of Max's constant forbidden-fruit lectures about Abe.

"I think you're seeing too much of that young man," Max advised as his Mr. Monopoly mustache stiffened. "Eventually, you're going to run out of conversation, and I hate to imagine what comes after that." His voice waxed irritable. "As long as he's only the kid from across the street, he's acceptable, but not as my daughter's boyfriend or fiancé, or husband!" He had shredded the words through his teeth. Words.

The words Max dredged up were words that stung and hurt. "He's nothing...less than nothing!" She hid her watery eyes at the recalling of Max's verbal attack.

"Perish the thought, missy. I'll spend a lot of time and money on your education so you can meet and marry a man of means, not that upstart Sioux Indian." He delivered the venomous racial epithet. "The relationship you have with Abe plays into intimacy."

Sarah acknowledged that Max wanted desperately to keep her sheltered—sheltered from a dead-end marriage and a prissy lifeless bedroom such as his own. The basic heart experiences and the deepest of human emotions that she'd always ascribed to a bedroom seated in the fire and fervor of love, the intoxication of ecstasy, birth, death, joy, grief and fear. She knew that these had all escaped Max in his marriage, leaving him no remnants to re-create and enjoy, left him only with a chilling incompleteness.

"I don't want to see you years from now being married and tied down to a recognized-too-late zero," he added as a knockout punch.

Sarah could feel rage pulsing through her at his high-handedness.

"Next year you'll go to the all-girl Notre Dame academy in Green Bay. I've already enrolled you and paid the tuition. This is your last year at Nahma High School. That half-breed kid chasing after my daughter, who does he think he is? Still wears his hair in a ponytail as if he's some kind of a western-plains pony rider."

Max used the power of parenthood for his personal imposition of tyranny. His rants were an exhibit of hysterics thus far unsurpassed in Sarah's lifetime—his messages venomous. Many times he'd reduced her to tears, quaking clear down to her toes.

Sighing with her memories, she grew clearly conscious of Abe blowing cool air into her hair, weaving his fingers through the length of it, creating tingling sensations. Supporting her elbow on her knee, she rested her chin on her hand and pondered. She'd never experienced such thrills as Abe had given her, had never burst with such love as she felt in his presence. Heaven couldn't be much different than being with him.

How far should she go with Abe, and when? Her eyebrows arched with the thought. Sarah knew that they had drifted to a more serious relationship and she couldn't put Abe off much longer. When she was with him, all her convictions of steadfastness melted the uncontrollable feelings that wore Max's objections threadbare.

"I'll be home for the summer months and Sadie Hawkin's Day next year," she said rising, and moving to the rocking chair that Fabian had called his "second home." But the reality for now was that she needed to leave for the academy in just one week.

Abe adjusted a chair to sit near her, found her hand, separated and kissed every fingertip. "I've been struggling with this business of you leaving," he empathized. "I guess that I've come to terms with it. This appears to be the next step for Max—to take you away from all the cedar savages. He's Freudian in viewing the locals as riffraff—ever notice?" A rueful smile tempted the corners of his mouth.

"Yes, I have," she admitted readily, bitten with fury that had been seething in her reverie. "He's a bit of a pain when he does that too."

He caught that hand and pressed it firmly to his cheek. "You're so beautiful. I want you to be mine for the rest of our lives."

Her eyes followed his mouth meeting her fingers. "I want that, too, Abe…with you, only you." Her voice was as smooth as dandelion fluff, her breath sweet.

He stirred with her words, her first commitment. "We *will* be married some day, Sarah. Just keep that in mind." Standing, he assisted her out of the rocking chair, folding her comfortably in his arms. He bent his head and was surprised to hear ready low acceptance in her throat.

In the mauve of the encroaching darkness, she turned her face up to him, her shimmering brown eyes and her heady half-smile. Abe wondered if the same electrical currents were running rampant through *her* body, the sympathetic and the parasympathetic in cut time, all stuttering in staccato.

He captured her tiny face in his hands, and with an incredibly tender kiss covered her mouth but briefly before breaking away and exploring her cheeks, her ears, whispering a husky and grainy, "I love you so much."

Receptive and clinging, she closed her eyes, exciting to the turmoil tumbling through his voice. "And I love you too, Abe," she admitted, her tone thick as she strived to project a voice that was unruffled and calm.

Drinking in the beauty of her petal-smooth skin in the half-light, he sighed.

How did she do this to him? Irresistibly overcome, he groaned, whispering her name, smothering her lips with the warmth of his kiss—his mouth hard, demanding.

Sarah was roused by the surge of surprise sensations that consumed her. Her mouth opened under his as his tongue tipped around her lips, then darted into the intimate softness, savoring her mouth for the first time. She shook with the invasion and stood as still as a rabbit in camouflage, indecisiveness at war in her head.

Standing yet on the front porch, Abe's arms encircled her slight body. He could feel her melting, her breathing becoming more rapid. His hand traveled the shallows of her spine. Seemingly with a mind of its own, his hand then slid down over the curve of her thighs, her flanks. Under the Daisy Mae shorts he could feel soft warm skin.

Holding her tightly, Abe knew that she could feel his stiffness as she took a hasty breath and pushed away, but to no avail. Holding her pinioned, he nurtured pride and not embarrassment. He stood back, as if re-assessing this wonder in his arms and drank in eyes that registered clearly a feverish rush of love for him. The muscles in his jaw flexed as he realized that for the past eighteen years this little wood nymph had been slowly seducing him, killing him with desire.

With her hands on his chest and a look of total surprise she breathed, "My God, Abe! You make me tingle all over. I'm going to get a drink of water to cool off," she called back over her shoulder as she walked into his house and back to the kitchen. Shaken, he watched her move away from him: her long legs, her curved hips, her tiny waist, her shoulders tanned to satin flowing freely out of the peasant blouse.

He found her in the kitchen, her back to him, standing at the sink.

"There, that's better," she said, turning around to find him right on top her. "Ohhh," rose from her throat, startled.

Placing an arm on either side of her, he backed her against the cupboard in front of the sink. "You have no idea how often I've dreamed of you in my kitchen."

The seductive strains of Glenn Miller's "Moonlight Serenade" floated through the night air. She melted when Abe took her in his arms and danced closely and slowly. She arched into him in some kind of a primal move she couldn't explain.

Abe swallowed a moan. This was his woman. His Sioux heritage entitled him to have a woman—many women. He was long overdue for fulfillment with the woman of his choice. The time for dessert had arrived. He needed to start attempting bases.

They danced their way into the living room. Warm night air, fragrant with blooming shrubs and flowers floated in through the front door: honeysuckle, alyssum, snapdragons, sweet peas, larkspurs.

Abe released Sarah and stepped back from her. Slowly and deliberately, he approached the front door, closed and locked it. He opened two windows instead, one in the bedroom and one behind Fabian's favorite wing chair. He advanced to where she stood smiling slightly, a mixture of amusement and enticement. Hypnotizing her with his eyes, he reached out, untied the drawstrings of her peasant blouse and moved her blouse down over her arms in a smoothness that was both both tender and depraved.

Sarah found herself tensing, his touch scintillating the fiber of her skin. She had a bad case of dry mouth, attempting to moisten her lips with the tip of her tongue. She promised herself she wouldn't be afraid.

He stood, transfixed, staring at the lacy bra covering her small breasts. She filled his senses with an unexpected repleteness. Yet, he saw the controlled panic in her eyes.

Slipping his hands under the straps, he smoothly slid them over her shoulders and down her arms, feeling her silken skin, his fingertips electric with the contact.

His words emitted in fractured confidence. "They're beautiful," he gasped, his eyes drifting to her face and back to his dessert.

She stood, immobilized. Wonder and trepidation appeared on her face. She had never known this part of him. Subtly, he moved the blouse and bra down off her arms, staring all the time at her bashful breasts, nipples elevated ever so slightly. *Don't scare her; she's been sheltered.* Gently, he moved her arms out of the blouse, whereupon it slipped slowly to the floor, followed by her bra.

With a strength she had come to expect, he lifted her by the waist, equalizing their height. His lips brushed her breasts. She nearly lost her breath with the newness of the explosive sensations sweeping her to a brainless stupor, and she was no longer able to control herself. She closed her eyes, acquiescing to this new-found plateau of penetrating passion, her head bending back, her throat pulsing.

Sweeping her into his arms, Abe carried Sarah, stopping to kiss her just inside the bedroom door, his tongue searching her mouth. Her arms slipped around his neck, reluctant to let go when he lowered her onto the bed to unbuckle his bibbies.

The Li'l Abner overalls fell to the floor. Tee shirt and shoes followed. He escalated so steeply into the here and now that nothing else existed. There existed no Sadie Hawkin's Day; there *was* no world outside. Time stood still. Sioux need and desire blinded his daily discipline of control. His hands palmed her calves, smoothed at her thighs, stroked her breasts, her waist and her belly in a smorgasbord of paradise.

Excitement sharpened acutely. He nibbled on her bottom lip to keep from going over the edge. Drawing back, he saw in her eyes trust, yet wariness, and deep in the irises he saw soft love, their honesty so real he wanted to weep. His mouth went dry. She seemed so tiny, her rib cage such a narrow gauge and slimming to such a small waist, his hands covered it. Sarah's willowy hips spoke to him of youthfulness, not like Abbie Arsenault's, that curved seductively.

Abe was grateful to Doc for the encouragement and for the surgery on his salivary glands. He didn't want Sarah to think of him as an animal. However, something nudged him to reality. He *was* an animal—a Sioux animal about to take his woman.

Submissive, Sarah knew that this was what she wanted right now: his strength, his hardness, his muscle and his conquest. She had seen this before while at the beach, but it seemed so much more dangerous now. Apprehensive, she knew she must decline.

She knuckled under her eyes.

He chuckled with an arrogance born of masculine destiny and reached for a condom. *Don't create another World War II on Old Beach Road!* Abe amused at Sarah's eyes squished closed. He knew he had to ease down beside her and not push this new venture too suddenly into her life.

"Don't be afraid, Sarah." His voice was rough with all the emotions running loose inside him—the lust, the longing. He wanted this first time to be good for her, his future wife, the mother of his children.

"You're doing fine, Sarah," he encouraged, his voice like a strained sign caught in the wind. Boosting up on one elbow, he gazed at the wonder of this beautiful woman in his bed. Aching grew and flared anew, like a breeze on white dusty coals, showing the intense life smoldering within. Reaching down, he tipped her head up to him. He'd been too long in dry dock; he needed to feel the smooth embodiment of her silky sea. With a gentleness born of need, he probed the waters, heat building to implode. He could feel her responding, squiggling under his touch, her fingers gracing the hair at the back of his head and neck, holding him to the promise of his hands.

"Relax, Sarah." His breath was shaky.

The pain ripped sharp. She cried out—pushing at his chest.

She held Abe's head in her hands, trying to read the demanding darkness that grew in his eyes. "No, Abe. No further." Her brows drew together in a frightful frown.

His sense of urgency clouded any other thoughts. Never had he felt such warmth, such smoothness, and such sensations.

"Unnhh," Sarah cried. Her body went limp. The color drained from her face. Her eyelashes fluttered as her eyes rolled back in her head. She lay under him, lifeless in his hands. Abe knew he must have killed her. She lay so still, so white. Pulling on his jockeys, he observed her eyes fluttering back to reality.

"No…" she cried, her voice a reedy thread, color slowly reappearing in her face.

He ached all over with remorse, choked with regret. She lay motionless; sweat beads forming on her forehead.

"Are you all right, Sarah?" His voice faltered. "Say you're all right…"

"Abe, I think you need a different girl. You have too much of everything for me." Her eyes were those of the repentant—the repentant who recognized her own shortfalls, blamed no one else and saw no light at the end of the tunnel.

"Don't say that. Please don't say that. Eventually, things always seem to straighten themselves out. He smoothed back the hair from her temples where moist curls were trickling onto her face. "You're mine forever now, Sarah. Will you marry me some day when I'm smarter, gentler and richer?"

Glancing up at the height of him, she searched the love in his face. "I will consider that very fine offer, Mr. Miereau," she said, tongue in cheek, for she never had considered marrying anyone else in all her life—never, ever.

CHAPTER FIFTEEN

The glorious sun rose, sparkling off the lake on auction day. At the other end of town St. Andrew's Parish bells rang with resonance, the sound loitering on the air like smoke wisps from a campfire. Thoughts of Fabian lying in the parish cemetery crowded Abe's mind. He wished that he were here today. But with piercing insight, his thoughts turned to Farley and Norrhea. He'd drive out to Indian Point and invite them to attend the auction.

"By golly, there he is!" Farley exclaimed, greeting Abe at the door, shaking hands. "We're just sitting down to breakfast. How about joining us?" he urged.

"I could smell French toast all the way to Nahma!" Abe said enthusiastically.

Norrhea served home-canned cinnamon apple chunks and maple syrup accompanied by crisp brown strips of bacon. Abe helped himself to everything without remorse. He could hardly contain the excitement in his voice. "I came to get you to attend the auction this afternoon."

Pouring more coffee, Norrhea asked graciously, "So what do you think your series of pictures will bring in, Abe?"

Abe flipped his hand back and forth in a gesture of indecision. "It's a gamble."

Farley smiled directly into Abe's eyes. "We're really proud of you having this ability to place on canvas what you see in your mind. That is definitely a Sioux trait."

Smiling and nodding in acknowledgment of Farley's Sioux comments, he speculated. "I'm hoping maybe a hundred dollars. It'll go right into my savings account at the Company Office. In only two years I'll be off to college, so I'd better have something stashed away. Being half Sioux Indian will get me nowhere on the huge Michigan campus—*less* than nowhere.

"Speaking of heritage, however, I feel strange insights at times when I'm painting. I feel as if I've seen the same scenes before—been in the same places before."

He sat forward, pointing a quick finger at Farley. "Curious. Sometimes I sense what's going to happen, and it does! It's spooky." He grew sober at the thought.

With barely concealed excitement, Farley arose and walked to the window, gazing over the brilliant bay, his hands clasped behind his back. "Sure as hell, Abe," he said, turning around, "you got 'em, the Sioux characteristics. The Plains Indians lived for thousands of years through instinct."

At one o'clock Abe and his grandparents were centered on the lawn in front of the open porch that ran half the entire side of the Clubhouse. Red white and blue buntings lay scalloped across the front railing of the long veranda. The sun continued to shine; only a few circumspect high cirrus clouds graced the sky. "Sentimental Journey," with Jo Stafford vocalizing, blared over the loud speakers and hundreds of voices buzzed in the cacophony of anticipation. Townies were there, as well as bargain hunters and gift shop owners. Surrounding counties attended *en masse*. A brewing of exuberance bubbled, spreading the yeast of excitement throughout the crowd.

The auctioneer was none other than Max Savin, who acted as an entertainer as well as Director of the Summer Art School. Abe knew Max as a master at one-upsmanship, a compelling auctioneer.

Sarah joined them on the colorful blanket Norrhea had spread on the grass. Turning his shoulders to her, Abe thought she looked restless and distraught. He put his arm around her shoulder and gently squeezed it; she responded with a warm snuggle.

"Good afternoon, ladies and gentlemen," Max's voice boomed over the mic. "We have no less than forty-eight items to ingratiate into your lives this afternoon. All entries are products of the Nahma Summer Art School and created by artists who came here to enjoy the discipline of learning new approaches to old artistic endeavors."

Abe whispered an aside to Sarah, "My pictures are number seven on the roster."

Max's voice droned on. "There are few things I can think of that are worse than long drawn-out windbag auctioneers, so we'll start right in." Anticipation etched his face; ghosts of successful past auctions were projected to the audience.

The first item shown was a generous vase, glazed in glistening white with exquisite cloisonné drawings spiraling around its unique, spittoon shape. At the final rap of the gavel it brought twenty-five dollars.

"Twenty five dollars!" whispered Norrhea, shocked at the high price. "But then, I have to swing with the times." Her dark-skinned hands crossed beneath her breasts with a harumph. "I paid *eleven cents* for a loaf of store-bought bread last week, if you can believe that!" Her shoulders dipped as she blew off demonstrative hot steam.

Scheduled second was a sand sculpture, fashioned in a fish bowl, with deep forest pines surrounding a path springing from the trees and down to a vividly blue lake.

Sarah spoke softly. "Each color and variation has been hand-set into this piece. It's a collector's item." In her eyes lay the bright sheen of pride in her father's appraisal.

"Going once...going twice...thirty-five dollars! Sold to the gentleman with paddle number one-one-seven," he instructed the runners as the gavel struck.

An eighteen-inch high hammered copper depiction of two lumberjacks wielding a two-man saw was presented next. Freestanding, it traced each man individually, the dedication to the job-at-hand showing on their faces. Alan Mercier was the highest bidder at fifty dollars. Conventional wisdom suggested that he would place this artwork on his fireplace mantel.

Abe built with insurmountable stinging of anticipation, yet found great pleasure in the escalating excitement. His hands swaggered between his spread knees, and the afternoon sun lit the soft expectancy on his cheeks.

The fourth piece displayed was a set of carved wooden partridges with feathers rich and velvety. The bidding closed at seventy-five dollars. They would be exhibited in the Company Hotel, right behind the check-in desk. Bill Acker paraded around as the high bidder, smiling and accepting congratulations and adulations from the high muck-a-mucks sitting around him on chaise lounges, including Doc and Liz.

Abe lowered his forehead into the palm of his hand, reminding himself that soon it would be *his* pictures on the chopping block. Pointedly, he made himself relax, but still had to thumb-under a shudder.

Carried out very carefully now was the fifth article: a set of eight hand-blown glass tumblers, each of at least a six-ounce capacity. They were of the deepest sky-blue color, with minute air bubbles captured within the housing. Small indentations were interspersed at various points around the glasses into which one could sink their fingers.

"Max tells me this is a special art taught this year by a tutor from Las Cruces, New Mexico," Sarah said, imparting another "ism" of information from her father. "The workmanship is so new and unique to this area that he said he wouldn't belabor the value of them. It should be self-evident." She hunched around the hulk of Abe to include Farley and Norrhea in her conversation.

Abe calmed when he saw the relaxed look in her eyes. Was it confidence in his work, or was it the satisfaction of sitting near him? He hoped it revealed the latter.

Thereafter, an assistant set an oil-on-canvas measuring 24" X 30" of the Indian Point Mission Church perched on a gently sloped hill above the bay. Proudly, its steeple and bell tower reached for the sky among tall virgin white pine, sending good tidings from earth straight to God. The small building had a wooden stoop and a dwarfed front door, adequate for admitting only one person at a time. The bay below blazed in the sun. A simplistic honesty graced the scene and lost the viewer in its depths.

"I've got to have that picture, Norrhea," Farley whispered hoarsely. "It beckons to me—speaks to me, if you will." His face glowed with enthusiasm and desire.

"Well, all right. However, I don't think that you should pay more than forty dollars for it, Farley. That's a lot of money." Norrhea had perception enough to acquiesce to Farley when he became flooded with the flames of gritty emotions.

"I hear ten dollars," Max shouted. "I hear fifteen dollars. There! Fifteen... fifteen. Do I hear twenty? Twenty it is. Do I hear thirty? Yes! Thirty it is. Then thirty, then thirty...then forty...Yes! Then forty...then...forty. Let's hear fifty...let's hear fifty...fifty it is...sixty it is. Sixty, looking for seventy, a do-si-do and around we go looking for seventy. Seventy it is! Seventy, can't wait for eighty..."

"Eighty dollars" shouted Farley, waving his paddle.

"Ninety!" came from the back of the crowd. Ruby Warren was the bidder.

"Ruby Warren!" Abe involuntarily squeaked, remembering his nemesis from the Candy Kitchen when he was a tender five-year-old. She whirled her way through the throngs, reminding Abe of the erratic lope of a black bear, dodging this way and that with unpredictability. Flashing her paddle, she had snapping greedy eyes and the vacuous smile of Reddy Fox.

Farley had to turn completely around to appraise his competitor. "Bullshit if I'm going to allow *her* to get this work. I want it. It's *my* parish, and I'm pissed," he groaned. "That woman is a pariah." He raised his paddle.

One hundred dollars it is. A hundred...a hundred I hear...a hundred ...going once, going twice...GONE." BAM sounded the gavel. "Sold to Mr. Farley Horse, the grand proprietor of the Indian Point Trading Post!"

Farley danced, both hands in the air, executing a ritual Sioux celebration.

Ruby Warren crossed her arms over her chest; her mouth puckered like a drawstring coin purse as she conceded the fight, giving up the ghost of any goodwill when she saw *who* had the highest bid. Bearing disgruntled anti-Semitism, she stomped off, planting primal jubilation in the crowd that cheered heartily for the highest bidder and the competitive direction the auction was headed.

The spirit spread with catching enthusiasm. Electricity hung in the air.

A flurry of activity arose on the long porch as the attendants ran with the three easels holding Abe's anecdotal series of "The Track Team." They were set up high to create excellent viewing for bystanders and just plain busybodies.

"Well lookit here; everyone gets an egg in their beer. Did you ever see so much cheer as these three pictures? Dear oh dear," Max set up the bidding with a rhyme, getting the juices flowing. Laughter spilled into the warm afternoon. "There's a story behind these paintings. They're our Championship Track Team. After practicing their runs on the beach they had a cookout. These pictures tell the whole story. Sad but true that even young people run out of steam, fold up their tents and trail off into the desert, so to speak." Once more he elicited laughter.

"I don't think that we should start with anything less than twenty-five dollars apiece for these memorable offerings." Max let the words sink in as he adjusted his hat, a white straw chapeau with red-white-and blue ribbon, one with which he could dip, sway and bow to the ladies. "They're to go as a single lot, so let's hear a starting bid of seventy-five dollars. Let's hear it…not ten…not twenty…not thirty…but seventy-five dollars. Yes! Seventy-five it is. Do I hear a hundred…a hundred…looking for a hundred…now—now—now…

"Yes! A hundred it is. Do I hear one twenty-five? Let's hear one twenty-five…Easy one twenty-five…just pocket change at one twenty-five…just pocket change, folks. Yes! I have one twenty-five!

"Looking for one fifty. Let's hear one fifty…hardly enough to cover the cost of the paint…let's hear one fifty. Yes! There it is."

Abe nudged Sarah to glance at the end of the porch where Bernard Tobin and Dave Phalen were in a heated discussion, head-to-head and nose-to-nose. Dave held the purse strings for the Board of Education. Tobin wanted to circle the wagons, protect the hometown production of "The Track Team" for posterity.

"One hundred and seventy-five dollars isn't far behind, it's right around the corner…I can feel it coming…like buffalo on the plains. Yes! There it is, one seventy-five…easy one seventy-five.

"Two hundred!" shouted Bernard Tobin. Dave Phalen, standing next to him had his arms folded over his chest, fearful of at what price ownership would come.

Before Max could take up the chant again, he heard, "Two fifty" from paddle number two-one-two—Andy Vidal, the Athletic Director from the Escanaba School District—standing at the back of the campus area! Bidding!

For a jerk of time, Abe stood immersed in the tall man outlined by the afternoon sun. "Saints in heaven!" Abe said, alternating his view between Vidal and Tobin, who viewed the new bidder with caution. Abe felt the thrill of competition titillating his nerve ends in wholesale surprise.

Hiding a smile behind a finger, Sarah laughed, sounding on edge with nerves.

Abe angled his shoulders toward Sarah, making inquisitive eye contact at the intrigue of an unanticipated bidder. He probed his mind for the whys and wherefores.

Max cut in with "two fifty, two fifty...just a pittance for this historical set of pictures, a once in a lifetime opportunity, your hometown boys on canvas, three hundred...let's hear it—three hundred dollars...let's hear it, a measly three hundred...fast now, fast now." His voice reflected the enthusiasm of the bidders. "It's gotta be three hundred to take it home!" Max's voice boomed across the breathless crowd. His tongue-defying prattle was where good auctioneers excelled; he couldn't lose the momentum.

"Three hundred!" shouted Bernard Tobin, while Dave Phalen prepared to faint. Bernard raised both his arms, flagging the paddle victoriously.

Abe's deep brown eyes flickered with the ageless mystery of involvement without being involved.

"Three hundred once, three hundred twice..."

"Three-fifty!" shouted Vidal, exuding an intoxicating challenge.

"Three-fifty it is! Loud and clear I hear...I hear clear...three-fifty now."

The great crowd grew quiet.

"Four hundred!" Tobin bellowed, even louder than before. Phalen slapped his forehead with the palm of his hand, bending over as if a severe abdominal pain had struck him. Four hundred dollars was more than enough to put on an additional teacher, at half time, for a *full* school year.

Abe, Sarah, Norrhea, and Farley, their eyes searching each other, sat dumbfounded at the fast-flying bidding, the scene changing quickly. Tobin must have received free rein on the checkbook; this bidding was not frivolous.

"Four hundred. I have four hundred...It's a steal for four hundred...It's a real steal...haul them away with your own wheels," he added as a bit of nonsense. "Four hundred dollars...four hundred...going once, going twice! SOLD!"

Dave Phalen's shoulders slumped. He looked at Bernard and shook his head. Bernard, grinning, affected a casual air. Both men moved in Abe's direction.

Abe, shaken and unsure, stood at their approach, driving his hands into his hair in a helpless gesture. A nudge would have slipped his lips into a perfect "O."

Reaching out, Bernard shook Abe's hand, as Dave did in turn. "Those pictures aren't going anywhere but into the high school where they'll hang in the hall along with all our trophies and other memorabilia," Tobin said.

Liquid lava poured through Abe's veins, keeping him upright.

"And the school board will underwrite the cost of it," added Dave, winking at Abe. "To whom shall I draft the check—to you or the Summer Art School?" Dave asked, uncertain of how the auction proceeds saw division.

"All the checks go to the Art School," Bernard said, laughing. "They in turn disburse the checks to the entrants." He reached out and patted Abe on the shoulder.

Abe hung there, too dumbfounded to speak for a moment—hazed, numbed, hearing nothing but silence and seeing the astonishing figure of four hundred dollars flash inside his head like blinking pinball lights.

"Thank you," he said to the two men, smoothing the front of his shirt with his hands. "I don't know what to say. I've never dreamed of anything near this. I never earned so much money in all my life!" His voice rose from baritone to tenor.

Caught up in the moment, Bernard smiled and patted Abe's back.

Abe found presence enough to reach out and accept Andy Vidal's *firm* hand in congratulation. There arose a round of excited voices, laughing, rehashing the bidding.

"Down in front there, you guys. You're having way too much fun," Max said, waving them to sit in the grass. "This show has only just begun. There's a gold mine of material here, folks, precious art right here in our small village." Max glowed as he excited with the success of the artisans, but he knew when to pause and when to push.

The rest of the auction seemed like a blur to Abe, who put his arm around Sarah.

Norrhea and Sarah exchanged looks of warmth for Abe, someone they both loved, but would never totally understand. Never. His warmth, his distance, his lack of focus, his brutality, his ambition, his inherent drive to excel, his downtime in a bubble, his dreamtime with his ancestors, his eidetic memory.

Never understand.

Chapter Sixteen

SPRING, 1943

On this dreary March 5, Abe drove to Indian Town to pick up Eddie Arsenault for the final basketball game of the season. The weather had been damp and rainy for days on end, and now the rain gathered on the car windows and slid down the glass in long snaky snatches. He scratched his head. Where had the school year gone? The '43 Michigan Athletic Association District Basketball Tournament would start next week already. He felt great pleasure because he'd gone out for basketball. Practice had started in November and it had helped pass the dark hours of winter without Sarah.

The thought stirred his senses, finding himself reflective of other interests. He took Eddie on as a close friend, and at times they spent the night together. Eddie was right about his house being an Indian Mecca. No one knew who slept with whom. A damn good thing it was, too. His mind surged with intimate thoughts of Abby.

Turning off Nahma's Main Street, Abe proceeded on the St. Jacques Road, which ran westerly out to U.S. Highway 2. His mind returned to the abandonment he'd experienced at Sarah's absence in his life. The meager four days she'd had at Thanksgiving were a whirlwind; Max never allowed her out of his sight. On her ten-day Christmas break Max kept her so busy that they'd hardly had time to talk, let alone found any time to be alone. Sarah stood taller now that she lived off on her own at the academy, putting him in mind of Elizabeth Whittaker. There was a cool aloofness and confidence about her.

Another year and maybe they could be at the same college. He'd accepted the fact that he would never be a Whiz Kid, but Krutina promised that if he maintained his "C" average, the University of Michigan would consider a scholarship under the gifted student policy. That thought kept him compellingly alive. Abe gnawed on his bottom lip while the windshield wipers clacked a rhythm: *swoosh, click, swoosh, click.*

Gifted. It came so naturally. People marveled, but it lingered in his mind, genetically inbred. Therefore, it *was* a gift. Abe eyed his huge hands warily and mulled on how those big mitts could hold an artist's brush and move it intricately through involved scenes. *A gift, lunkhead!*

He pulled up at Eddie's house and sounded the horn. Too wet to run inside.

"Hey Abe!" Eddie climbed into the car, throwing his satchel into the back seat.

"Hey Eddie. How goes it?" Abe found Eddie's voice receptive, as well as his looks—long, lean, reddish-brown skin, snapping brown eyes. His hair had a habit of flopping down over his left eye. It was easy to like him—Eddie and his upbeat attitude. Abe smiled broadly.

"Stayin' alive. Just stayin' alive," he smiled his *bell ringer*—got Abe in the gut every time with its warmth, its honesty, its camaraderie. Good Lord, he liked the sound of Eddie's voice.

"What the hell. Did you get a new jacket, Eddie? Nice!" Abe did a double take.

"Yeah, Sears & Roebuck catalogue—expensive, too, and all leather. Twenty-nine ninety-five. Look at all the buckles and tabs, even on the sleeves," he jingled the metal fasteners. "They're on the pockets and way up here under my chin in case it gets cold." Eddie smoothed his hands down the front of it. "Nicest jacket I've ever had. Pretty proud of it too!" He shifted his attention back to Abe, who smiled in approval.

"We'll stay on this road to St. Jacques instead of going around by Nahma Junction," said Abe. "I don't think it's ever going to stop raining so we'd better start measuring by cubits!" His eyes shone brightly in the shadows of the car.

"Yeah, man!" Eddie said. "I've never seen the water in the Sturgeon River so high. When the school bus came over the bridge this afternoon there were tree branches and old root systems tossing in the river; they were rolling and twisting like someone's nightmare. He made a tumbling action, rolling his arms in circles in front of him, his eyes galloping as he recalled the dangerous scene.

"That's for sure. On the way back we'll take the Nahma Junction Road just to make sure we have a bridge left standing," Abe teased, glancing over at Eddie. "This game tonight should be very interesting. We've each won one of the two previous encounters, so this game is fair game." He grinned at the word usage.

Eddie gestured a barf sign at the dumb pun, his finger pointing down his throat.

Disregarding Eddie's antics, Abe leaned closer to the windshield as the rain fell in torrents. His athletic prowess had not decreased in the past year, but instead had grown with increased sharpness. Even in close competitions, his luck superseded his ability.

"We'll take 'em," Eddie said, leaning back into the seat. "Did you read in tonight's *Escanaba Daily Press* about the new schedules being adopted by the Big Ten?" His eyes turned dark and smart as he flipped his stubborn hair off his forehead.

"Nah, I didn't have time. By the time I finish work after school then dash to Doc's house for my Spanish lessons there isn't time for reading the paper. If I don't have two semesters of a foreign language, I'll never get that scholarship to UM."

"Well, it seems that due to the war the Big Ten Coaches need to save on travel, so they re-arranged gridiron schedules for 1943 in the interest of easing rail mileage and to provide for games with service teams. Each team is limited to nine games, with a minimum of six within the Big Ten." Eddie rolled his eyes at the roof in dismay, his jaw resting on one fisted hand.

Abe nodded, urging him to go on.

"The Western Conference last spring voted to permit a maximum of ten games, provided that two were with service teams. Interesting?"

"Yeah, sure, you bet. Their athletic program is one of the advantages of attending a big school. I'm going to be living on a shoe string, so God only knows if I'll be able to afford a ticket to the games." Abe had survived the past year by the seat of the pants.

"All you need to do is paint another picture and *poof,* your bank account shoots up a couple hundred dollars. Don't give me those sad stories. That's a crock." Eddie popped Abe a fist in the shoulder.

"Your imagination runs rampant," Abe said, his gaze trapping Eddie's. "I can see it all now—me, standing on the corner in Ann Arbor, hawking pictures." Abe laughed, reached over and kneaded Eddie's cheek with his fist, treating himself to a quick glance at one of his closest friends—the depths of his dark eyes, and his wholesome honesty.

"What's new on the war?" Abe asked, settling down.

"Well, according to the paper, it appears that Eisenhower and Montgomery are getting ready to put the pinch on Rommel's rebels in North Africa."

Eddie slapped the dashboard in confirmation.

Abe squinted as another cloudburst spit at the car. "This sure isn't any garden variety downpour."

"Gotta stop sooner or later." Eddie pulled on his bottom lip and leaned against the passenger door, his shoulders almost full to Abe, a new thought growing, almost visibly, trapping his expression. "There's going to be a draft deferment for college students in scientific fields, but not art. But I found a way out for you." Eddie smiled, his eyes lighting with mischief. "The local draft boards can no longer draft fathers of dependent children. So if you don't want to be drafted while you're in college, you can always get Sarah pregnant." Eddie doubled over, laughing at his mind's-eye image of a pregnant Sarah.

"You dirty dog, Eddie. How am I supposed to get Sarah pregnant when I can't even get near her?" Abe's mouth quivered with a dry smile.

"Well, you need to be a more bodacious stud, like me. I've never met a woman that I couldn't bed if I really wanted to." Eddie's smile bloomed, both genuine and teasing. "Christ, I've been doing that since I was thirteen. I'm beginning to think that you're underprivileged or too civilized." His voice growled emanating power.

Abe waved his hand through the air. I know. I know. I know...nice work if you can get it." Their eyes connected in commonizing high spirits.

"I'll be drafted right out of high school, I suppose." Eddie clasped his hands behind his head and stared out at the rainy *blitzkrieg*. "This General Hershey, the Selective Service Director, said that at the first of the year there remained only six hundred thousand unmarried men subject to draft, and they've been drafting about four hundred thousand a month! That means that I'll probably be scarfed up by the middle of June." Eddie's voice rolled raw with acceptance. "Maybe it's time I get out and see the world. What the hell. I'll get to drive those rag-top army jeeps."

Abe's mind swept with a lingering sense of the injustices in this war. What an insane thought to carry around night and day—being drafted. How ironic that the devastating retention in seventh grade had won him a year's reprieve from the draft.

❧

The ballgame turned into a barnburner, with both teams lunging forward with hoops one after the other. Abe, watching the clock, shot off a last second Hail Mary attempt at the buzzer—it was good! Nahma won, thirty-four to thirty-two, but only because Rapid River ran out of time.

Abe and Eddie poured out of the locker room doors with the rest of the team and they headed straight for the car and home. The iron gray March night was bleak and raw in the steady downpour, but Abe and Eddie felt oddly warm and secure in the car.

"Weather's not fit for a dog tonight," Eddie said, shaking his hair like a canine.

"You keep shaking like that and I'll let you try it out," Abe said good-naturedly.

"Hey," Eddie said, remembering something else he'd read in the paper. "Did you know that this summer more than thirteen hundred U.S. Navy trainees will arrive on the UM campus and take over the entire west quadrangle section of dormitories?"

"No bull!"

"Yup. Together with Army trainees, this will give the Michigan campus a population of almost three thousand service men by the middle of August. You'll be lucky if you get a dorm room by the time you enroll in '44." Suddenly, he grinned with excitement. "Maybe, just maybe, I'll be one of those servicemen. Then we could be a team again, Miereau!"

"Are the dormitories co-educational?" Abe asked, moving his eyebrows up and down like Groucho Marx and tapping a fictitious cigar.

"Dammed if I know, but if I were you, I'd start asking questions. It doesn't hurt to have your trap line set up," Eddie said, entertaining wild, corrupt thoughts.

"Yeah, sure. Until then, let's stop at Mac's Station here at the junction. I'll spring for some potato chips and Coca-Colas. How does that sound?"

"Glad you're buying. I spent my last dime on some beads and mirrors at the Company Store." Eddie donned his Happy Indian smile and held up a finger for a feather behind his head. "I'll wait here; this old dog knows how to stay out of the rain."

Whoosh, the wind blew through the car as Abe opened the door to run into the filling station at the junction of Highway U.S.-2 and County Road 416, known to locals as the "Nahma Junction Road."

Whoosh, came the second rainy gust when Abe opened the door to get back in. "Screwball weather," he said, sailing the Coca-Cola and potato chips in ahead of him.

"Hey, Bink's sodas." Eddie flashed a pleasured glance at Abe as his hand tightened around the green bottle. "You got good taste, man. Yessirreee. I'm sticking with you, big guy. We make a great team." Eddie's voice reflected immeasurable pride as he tore into the chips.

"Couldn't do it without *you*, old buddy." He landed another punch into Eddie's shoulder.

"I'm going to do some *real* formidable faking when I get over to North Africa. I'm going to drive my jeep right past the kraut Mark IV tanks. Brrrh, Brrrrh, Brrrrrrrrrrrh" Eddie's lips vibrated as he took the imaginary Jeep through its gears. "Yes sir. I'm going to drive right between them with their pissant crews sitting at the guns and looking at me like a mouse getting away from the cat." He pulled a fake tremble.

Delaying his dialogue for a draw on his Coca-Cola, he swallowed and rushed on. "I read where a guy escaped by stepping on his Jeep and went soaring across the desert, flying over irrigation ditches you'd normally cross in low gear. German artillery got after him. They dropped an eighty-eight on his right and then one on his left and then one in front of him. They had him pocketed." Eddie's voice had turned to a no-nonsense level.

"When artillery does that, the next shot always gets a guy." A potato chip sat clenched in Eddie's fingertips, waiting for an opening to jump into his mouth. "But they never fired a fourth shell! It was just kind of a miracle. I know the luck I'll have. My Indian Spirits tell me. They've been bugging me all day: 'Do this. Do that. Hurry up,'" he said, at last downing the chip and taking an urgent glug of his soda.

"Like hell, Eddie! Just stay hidden. You don't have to be a macho Red man to kick ass over there. Jeeps don't tangle with tanks. You have a bit of Early American Warrior in you. Did your spirits tell you that?" Abe shot him a quick, frowning glance.

As Abe approached the Half-Mile Bridge, he noticed between windshield wiper sweeps that the structure appeared to be out-of-plumb. He questioned the blur. Nah. The bridge of steel extended fifty feet long and saw regular maintenance by the Delta County Road Commission. He'd seen how the steel girders elbowed and braced the bridge well on either end by concrete abutments strong enough to withstand the advancement of Rommel's tanks.

Slowing to a crawl, he again gained focus on the steel span, and this time the certainty of it hit him right between the eyes. Churning with foam, a stream of debris-ridden turbulence outstripped the riverbanks. Abe viewed the bridge ahead, constricted and humped, rising from a swirling lake that had overflowed the swollen riverbed.

"My God! Look at that, Eddie. Look at that!" he cried aloud. The forward end of the bridge listed into the water. Stumps, railroad ties and whole trees swirled about the braces, hugged the abutments, and even those were nodding and straining.

"Holy shit!" Eddie shouted. A streak of lightning revealed both the look of stark reality on his face and the whipping scene.

The car headlights searched through the windswept rain, revealing the holocaust. Abe and Eddie left the car and inspected more closely the havoc wrought by the violence of the turgid river. Abe felt a burning panic.

Standing next to him, Eddie became uptight. "No way is any vehicle going to get over that bridge, Abe. No way," he shouted over the din of the river. "We need to do something fast. What can we do? What? What? Think fast, Abe. What'll we do?" Uncontrollable fear flashed over Eddie's face; rain rolled down his new leather jacket and sparkled on the large zipper loops.

"We'll turn the car around and stop the first vehicle we meet, then we can close off the road together. Yes, that'll work." Abe waved 'c'mon' to Eddie.

"It's gotta work," Eddie said, the rain pouring off his hawkish nose.

Driving back to the junction in the blackness of the pouring-down deluge, the first vehicle they met had its headlights glaring at them on high beam.

"Good God, Abe! I think that's one of the buses coming back from the game, and it's loaded. All the kids wanted to go tonight because it was the last game of the season. There must be fifty, fifty-five kids on that bus." Eddie's voice cracked with overload.

"We're only about three miles from the bridge." Abe flashed his headlights repeatedly with staccato repetition, rolled down his window and waved, drawing only an appreciative blast of the bus's horn. Good spirit prevailed.

"That's Homer Beauchamp driving. He thinks I'm sharing in their good times. Abe stiffened as a bolt of lightning silhouetted the bus containing profiles of kids as thick as popcorn.

"My God, Abe...all those fans...*the river!*"

Abe hurriedly careened the car around in the middle of the road. In the new direction, he sped ahead, the car fishtailing and skidding. Overtaking the bus, he edged the car dangerously close. Again, Beauchamp avoided the *nutcase* and held a steady speed, bringing the vehicle ever closer to the crumbled bridge.

"Jesus H. Christ, Eddie, by the time Homer Beauchamp sees that bridge, he'll not be able to stop the bus in time to prevent the whole load of kids from sinking into the river. The current's too swift. The river's too deep. I barely stopped the *car* on time."

"I know. Do something, Abe. Anything!" Eddie shrieked, and then stopped abruptly, his hand clutching his throat with the horror of it all, his heart stuck there.

"Okay, Eddie. I'm going to slow down in front of the bus. The bus will have to crawl along behind me and maybe even stop." Unsettled, Abe gasped as the bus crawled past him and actually picked up speed.

"Oh no! Oh no, please, God." Eddie prayed, squirming in the seat.

Again, Abe accelerated, passing the bus in the same fashion as before. No luck. He shook his head, unable to find words, only thick muttering utterances.

"I'll get well up ahead of the bus, Eddie, then I'll swerve the car into the middle of the road and brake to a halt. It'll have to stop then."

"The bus can't stop in time to avoid hitting the car, Abe." Eddie sat far forward now, his eyes blinking rapidly.

"Yeah, that's the point, Eddie. We'll abandon the car and run to the side of the road. Let the bus ram the car. That's okay if it saves all those kids."

"Great idea. Great. We're far enough ahead of them. Good thinking, Abe. There's the bridge coming up. Do it now, Abe. We gotta do it now. What the hell! No more time. We're outta time! This is it!" The desperate sound of Eddie's voice fell fiercely on Abe's ears.

In the middle of the road, Abe stalled the car, jumped out, and heard an explosive crash of thunder as the sky danced with blinding blue-white arcs revealing the swollen river, poxed with rain. He ran like hell.

Eddie, holding the bottle of Coke in his right hand, used his elbow to open the car door to jump clear of the collision site. Slipping on the rain-slicked road, he caught the buckled sleeve-strap of his new leather jacket on the wind-down window handle. Eddie tugged and bent to unhook the restriction just as the bus collided with the car, carrying it at least thirty yards down the road.

Abe watched in horror as Eddie sloughed under the car, his body dragging the distance, with his arm still enjoined to the window crank. The wreckage came to rest uncomfortably close to the swirling water in front of the now-battered bridge.

The searching eyes of the bus headlights picked up not only the demolished car, but also the burgeoned black water of the river, depositing riverbank growth, churning and roiling with rocks and boulders.

In silent horror, Abe saw Homer Beauchamp sit transfixed as the reality of the situation crept into his soul. His hands froze on the steering wheel as he stared unblinkingly into the night. Steam poured out of the warm radiator, which drained water onto the road with a hiss. The precious cargo manifest of the flesh and blood of many village families was at least sealed safe.

Abe had seen the outline of Eddie, half in and half out of the car, as the school bus struck. Could he have survived? The question crowded into his throat with a choking, convulsive thrust. His chest turned into a wave of ice. Guilt pierced his innards.

Multiple cars now stopped behind the crippled bus, terrorized at the sight, seeking information on the condition of the students. Abe and others ran to the remnants of what had been a car where they found Eddie pinned upright between the car, the car door, and the unforgiving steel of the bridge. Small and vulnerable, Eddie's eyes stared vacantly into the drenching rain. Still clutched in his left hand was the bag of chips. With a gravitational pull of responsibility, Abe needed him to smile more than he needed his next breath. An industrial strength knot gripped his throat. Abe encircled his rib cage with both his arms, feeling queasy, gasping for air. He thought he had super strength whereby he could pry Eddie from the metal jaws of the car.

"Eddie," he screamed in stubborn insistence. *It was fast*, he told himself. *Eddie never felt a thing. He rose to the occasion. The occasion was his time.*

"No, Eddie. Eddie! Not Eddie. I can't go through this again. Oh God!" Abe stood in the riotous rain, superimposed against the lightning brightening the night with intermittent flashes. "Eddie. Talk to me!" He put the heels of his hands to the sides of his head as madness overtook him. Sounds without articulation spewed from his mouth. "Why didn't you run? Oh, Eddie, I don't want you to die. Come back! You hear me! You gotta drive that Jeep yet. We got more basketball games to win! You gotta get assigned to UM, you and I, Eddie...together..." Abe wept with the realization. *Eddie said his Indian Spirits bugged him all day!* "He's dead. He's dead. He's dead, dead, dead!" It struck at Abe, choked and ripped a hole in his heart. As he single-handedly attempted to free Eddie from his metal prison, great sobs escaped from his tightened chest, but Eddie wasn't coming back.

Mary Krutina, accompanied by Chi-Chi Chamberlain, a tiny butterfly of a woman who taught high school English, was driving one of the cars that had stopped to assist. Incoherent, trembling with leaden feet and spongy knees, Abe knew he should be grateful and revel in their warm comfort. Encircling him with their arms, they led him away and bundled him into their car. So he needn't be alone after this terrible trial, they drove him to Farley and Norrhea's home.

"You and Eddie did a valiant thing, Abe. What happened was simply an accident," Mary Krutina consoled him en route. "You were not responsible for that. Life plays funny tricks on us some times." She glanced over at him, feeling inadequate; he'd had so many curve balls thrown his way.

Shaking his head avidly back and forth, he responded mechanically. "I can't handle any more of life's funny tricks. I've had it," Abe cried, his head bowed, fists pounding his knees. He sat in the front seat, wet, cold, shivering, and forlorn. "Dad died. Sarah left and now Eddie's gone, too. Everything I love turns to horseshit."

"Now that's not true. You have an irreplaceable talent for painting. You have a thousand friends in this town—everyone loves Abe Miereau. Let that be a great consolation to you," Mary added, reaching out and squeezing his shaking shoulders.

"I'll never get over this, never! Eddie's eyes...Eddie's laughter...Eddie's stupid-ass jokes." His voice grew thicker. "His cockiness, his stubbornness, his pipe dreams—they were all threads that attached him to me in our Sioux brotherhood."

"You'll get over the pain, Abe," Chi-Chi Chamberlain whispered softly, "but maybe you don't want to ever shake his memory. It's a nice one; you hold onto it. There's really no need to repel out of all life's impositions."

Somehow, this made sense to Abe, but he knew he'd always blame himself.

༜༜

Such a number attended Eddie's funeral that the small Indian Point Mission Church overflowed out the door and onto the hillside like loose lava. The requiem heard the cracking and moaning of ice going out in the bay, heard the call of crows over distant hills, and the deep sighing of the wind in the centennial white pines.

Eddie would never see the world of the military; however, he had a send-off worthy of Arlington. He had the finest of everything—a superior casket, a snappy new suit—his first one, Abe knew, the fairest of flowers, the basketball team for pall bearers and the CYO Choir from St. Andrews Parish. Now at peace with the world, he found in death a respectable, acknowledged niche in his community, which was more than he'd been able to achieve in eighteen years of living. Had he been in the military, the Silver Star for gallantry in action and the Purple Heart for sacrificing his life would be his.

Perhaps most special of all, there was a plot of ground allocated especially for him at the site of the wreckage at the river, where a great granite monument was erected to the memory of Eddie, whose heroics saved the town's future. Wild roses grow near the monument and proliferate with an abundance not known anywhere else in the county.

Abe, having a difficult time handling the reality of the situation, nestled with Farley and Norrhea for the next month, unable to pick up the pieces and go home. He plunged headlong into every task—his Spanish lessons, especially.

He and Doc dealt with each other in an uptight and guarded silence. Abe struggled. Dr. Whittaker encouraged.

Doc submitted to an overwhelming desire to hug Abe without excessive conversation. He wore an armor for these occasions, but Abe had slipped ingenuously through. Another person, another time, and he would have sworn he'd been blitzed.

"You need to follow the dictates of your head right now. Let your heart heal." Doc witnessed amazement at the penetration he felt when talking to Abe—electricity, telepathy and hyperactive reality. He gently curved his arm around Abe's shoulder and delicately drew him in.

Abe, finding Doc avuncular and sympathetic, broke down in shaking sobs. It had all been too much. He kept Fabian in a special compartment...locked away, and now he needed to find another compartment for Eddie. He'd never forget them, ever.

Quietly, Doc motioned Abe into his office and closed the door behind them, a soft thudding finality that reminded Abe of theater drapes closing down at the end of a solemn drama. He sat down; two pairs of eyes met, yet no one spoke. A horn blew on the boulevard, and a dog yelped.

"Abe, you need to remember that Eddie lived as a generous and simple person. He made all our lives better by gracing our time."

Abe's attempt at a smile never reached his eyes, and his heart ached. He had had an abundance of Eddie's jokes, his disillusionments, his taunts and teasing growing up as an Indian. Strange, how such stinging blows to personal pride can occupy a niche in one's memories of a "simple" man. Life evolved not as simple as Abe had once believed it would be if only he had enough to pay his bills and face each new day with friends.

The shadows of the day were purple now, warm and closing in. Abe needed to remember that this was a good town to him and Eddie, in its own way. Abe silently left. It was a clear April night with the moon dazzling the sky dome and dimming the stars.

A wave of deep comforting silence engulfed Abe as if it were richest, warmest tapestry, and the moon drew his path home to Old Beach Road, the road he'd trudged for eighteen years.

CHAPTER SEVENTEEN

Graduation Day for the class of '43 loomed right around the corner. Motioning Abe out of study hall and into his office, Tobin circumspectly directed a weighted question. "We're going to set aside time to present the Arsenaults with a plaque to remember Eddie. I'd like you to be the presenter." Tobin paused, keying into Abe's expression. "Do you think you could carry that off for us?"

Abe eased into the chair of historical reprimands. He spread his arms and allowed them to flop a hopeless gesture. "All right, but I have so many regrets about that night," he mused. Yet he realized that this act of kindness posed an absolution that even Fr. McKevitt couldn't render him.

Bernard heard Abe's epiphany, with both hands folded in front of him. "You'll do just fine, Abe. The Arsenaults understand completely the variables of life." Tobin blinked his eyes rapidly. How many times could this kid get knocked on his ass? "I'll be plugging for you all the way," he said hoping he'd put a stake into the heart of the black hole into which Abe had fallen. The kid had balls.

☙❧

The ceremony lay less than an hour away. In the auditorium, Abe sat in the front row, indecisive. His elevator hit the ground with a thud, the doors silently slid open and all his dark thoughts flooded out into plain view: *unworthy, unqualified.* In union with that thought, he reminded himself that life was for the living.

The new clothes that he had purchased gave his confidence a nudge: a pair of wool, charcoal gray slacks, a white shirt, a new sport coat of light gray wool flannel, and a slate gray tie with stripes of baby blue, light gray and soft silver. A new pair of dark gray suede shoes shod his size twelve feet. Nonetheless, he reminded himself of a Michigan black bear in a man costume.

Voices buzzed around him in a riot of mingled laughter and conversation. Sitting back, he crossed his long legs and checked the program. There he noted that he was scheduled after the valedictory speakers: Del and Dave O'Brian. Both were whip smart, both going to Houghton Tech next year. They'd earned deferments because of their course of study: engineering, electrical and mechanical.

"Hello there," a melodic voice from heaven said. Looking up in total amazement, Abe found Sarah standing before him, dressed in a delicate pink suit with a waist-cut jacket sporting a white collar and cuffs. Small pearl earrings peeked out of a softly folding pageboy. Bright brown eyes swam in pools of white-white. She was as mesmerizing as the face of royalty in a coronation portrait, yet underlying the disciplined garb she conveyed to him a smoldering femininity. She smiled and time stood still. His eyes froze in disbelief. Yet here she stood, intelligent, sensitive and beautiful.

It was painful to see her and not touch her. He'd never kick the magic she worked on him. What happened to the buttoned-down cool he'd felt when he'd showered, shaved and dressed for the program? Suddenly he whispered hoarsely, "Sarah, where'd you come from? What a surprise! Sit down here. Sit down." Abe rose, gesturing with his program to the chair next to him. They stood alone, suspended in time, closing out the world, looking into each other's eyes.

"My, you cut quite the figure when you are duded up. Of course I've known that for years. *You* make the clothes whether it's a pair of cutoff shorts, old jeans or a tracksuit. Whatta guy!" She settled gracefully onto the chair he offered her.

"The academy runs for only another week, so I cut it short to be here with you for Eddie's presentation. It's only right that you're the presenter. We all miss Eddie." She reached out and squeezed his hand, moving her fingers to his wrists, and felt the strongly ribbed lines of tendons, the wide bones, the thick hair creeping from his cuffs.

Running his finger around his collar and adjusting his tie, he cleared his throat. "Yeah, it's hard to talk about him. I feel so responsible." His eyes swept to hers, giving full rein to his grief in the dark recesses.

"Hey, you two. Got room for two more?" Doc Whittaker's voice boomed just in time to waylay Abe's return of sorrow. Liz, smiling warmly, had her arm hooked into his in an affectionate manner.

"Sure thing," Abe said, standing and smiling headily. "Nothing would please me more. Hello, Mrs. Whittaker," he said cordially.

"And how about us?" Bill and Hattie Acker came around the other end of the row, looking for seating, as well as Clyde Tobin and his wife, Margie, and Alan Mercier and his wife, Rose. Abe climbed up and down like a yo-yo, greeting people who had befriended him for years. It warmed his soul to think that they chose to be present at this important ceremony. Max and Ma Savin saluted him coolly from farther back, not-so-subtly hammering home disapproval of their daughter's association with him.

Abe smiled brightly, concealing the vague defensiveness they produced in him.

"Pomp and Circumstance" was struck up on the piano by Olive McClinchy, the kindergarten teacher. The graduates slowly marched up the aisle and took their places on stage, leaving one chair vacant for their recently stricken classmate.

This was so difficult. Abe knew he skated on thin ice—knew his serene facade scarcely covered his deep anxiety. On the other side of the aisle sat Eddie's mom and dad. Abe felt his shoulders tighten. Would he always cringe when he encountered them? Maybe his presentation of the plaque today would replace these feelings of self-doubt.

After the valedictory and salutary addresses, Bernard Tobin continued the program. "Now comes a special moment in our ceremony. The hero of the senior class, Eddie Arsenault, saved the lives of fifty-three students on March fifth by giving his life." Bernard paused, allowing his gaze to travel slowly from east to west, encompassing everyone in the auditorium. Heavily hushed silence prevailed over the group.

"We can never adequately commemorate his sacrifice." Tobin's voice grew hoarse with emotion. "But we chose to start with a commemoration to turn the tragedy of March into the triumph of May." His face masked itself into self-control. "Thirteen years ago Eddie Arsenault entered kindergarten as a child, and today he should be exiting as an educated adult. It's the fundamental progression of life. There are times, however, when fate blows obstacles in our paths. We now invite Mr. and Mrs. Arsenault to come up on the stage, please, for a presentation from the senior class. The presenter is Abe Miereau, Eddie's closest friend." Bernard nodded to Abe.

It was his cue. Abe's brain thought his legs had been cut off at the knee. Doubt shot through him with gripping intensity. Standing up, he didn't move for a brief second, in an attempt at self-preservation. Somewhere in the soul of everyone who has ever been introduced from the podium their lies a doubt about himself—a pounding of pulse, an unquenchable fire of anxiety.

Abe prayed silently. *Please, God. Allow me to carry this off as a man, and not get that lolapalooza lump in my throat.*

Seeing the Arsenaults ascending center stage ahead of him, he advanced, overcome with stupefaction, when a golden aura appeared around them both, beckoning Abe to follow. Tall and regal, plaque in hand, Abe ascended the steps; his sweaty palms squeaked on the frame.

"*Stay focused Abe. I'll always be with you when the golden glow glints in the day—whenever friends seem far away.*" Abe lost himself in Fabian's promise, which urged him forward on rubbery legs.

Tobin positioned them gently on either side of the podium. "The dedication verse is a replication of the one that's engraved on the granite monument near the Half-Mile Bridge. Would you please read the inscription, Mr. Miereau?" Bernard stepped back, relinquishing the mic to Abe.

Abe's posture belied the quivering he felt inside. He wanted nothing more than to disappear, as the golden aura had. It took all his courage to measure up to Tobin's expectations. Would he croak like a bullfrog? Through some miracle, Abe's voice boomed over the mic, not shaky, but confident, a confidence born of necessity and support, renewing his sanity. Suspending any disbelief he previously had in himself, he summoned the necessary courage and strength to continue.

"In tribute to Eddie Arsenault, a hero,
May he know the admiration and grateful esteem,
In which he is held by all, forever, for saving,
The lives of fifty-three people on March 5, 1943,
By giving the greatest gift of all—*his life.*"

A faltering tremor shook within his voice as he delivered the last two words just above a whisper.

Abe screamed inside with relentless pangs of remorse. He saw the desperation and loss in Eddie's mother's eyes, so like himself upon losing Fabian. Memories freshened, causing him to lock his knees to maintain stability. He felt as if he'd been leapt upon and torn by a tiger—his very vitals running vagrant. Attempting to conceal his sorrow, he kept his eyes averted.

Tobin attached his sleeve with an infusion of support, transferring certain stability. He could handle standing there, his dedication reading accomplished.

"And now I'm pleased to introduce Mr. William Acker, Vice President of the Bay de Nocquet Lumber Company." Bernard smiled as he waited for the smart figure of the executive officer to come on stage.

Abe's mind shifted into high gear. That's why Acker was sitting in the front row! At this slow rate of deduction, he'd need to enter school next year in first grade.

"Graduates, Faculty, Board of Education, families and friends," Acker addressed the packed audience with masterful dominion in his eyes. "The Bay de Nocquet Lumber Company, as well as the townspeople in general, would feel remiss if we let this day slip by without special recognition of the Arsenault family and their irreplaceable contribution to this community." A glow spread across his face. "As a gesture of our gratitude, the company takes pleasure in presenting Mr. and Mrs. Arsenault with a three bedroom home in the heart of Nahma, rent free, for as long as they choose to live there." He jangled a set of keys, walked over and presented them to Mr. Arsenault, accompanied by a says-it-all embrace.

Gasping, Mrs. Arsenault placed her hand to her mouth.

Accepting the keys with a handshake, Mr. Arsenault took a handkerchief from his pocket and swabbed his eyes, his shoulders visibly shaking.

Abe looked away discreetly as a great round of applause sprung from the audience. What a tremendous gesture. The Arsenaults had little in life. Now, through the grace of the company, they had a new home. He felt a rush of headiness with the moment of retribution. *There is a God. Yes!*

Abe smiled widely, applauding with the rest of the tumultuous crowd in the auditorium. He grew with the thought that he at least looked presentable in his new suit and hoped his presence made a statement. The headache that had been trying to establish itself for the last hour backed off a notch.

Suddenly, Bill Acker turned to him. Abe froze, intimidated by the expensively clad Acker, who wore a black pinstriped Hart Schaffner & Marx suit and shining black leather shoes with perfect soles, hardly worn. A ten-dollar tie and Van Huesen full-fashioned crisp nylon shirt daunted Abe. He towered as the embodiment of leadership and business acumen. Acker mutinied, unlike the high muck-a-mucks from Chicago strutting around the Company office, such as Charlie *Perfect* and others of his ilk with their silk suits and expensive haircuts.

Abe stepped back—a Freudian glitch. He was aware that his breath appeared shallow. Surfacing as a bubble of air rising to the top of thick syrup, courage popped into his head. Miraculously, he recaptured the confidence he'd found to make the presentation. He sent off a hundred prayers of gratitude to his guiding Sioux spirit.

"And now, young man," Acker said with a timbre of triumph, "we have a set of keys for you too. No one can ever adequately measure the debt you're owed for your actions on that bleak night in March. It was up to you or no one to stop that bus, and you came through. You put your own life in danger as well." Acker took a steady step toward Abe. "This hardly seems enough to repay you for fifty-three lives, but we want you to have a new 1942 Ford V-8 to replace the car you lost. This vehicle is one of the last ones that came off the assembly line since the war. I know I speak for everyone here when I say thank you." Bill Acker grasped Abe's hand, dropped the keys into it, and covered the top of his hand with his other one.

The audience hushed with heavy anticipation and time stood still. Abe gripped the keys in his hand as though hypnotized. He backed up again. These people didn't owe him anything. Anyone would have done what he did. His heart skipped a beat, the skin on his face taut in amazement.

"Thank you," Abe said, his gaze sweeping the large audience. "Thank you very much." His voice quavered. "I'd never be able to save enough to replace my dad's old car. This is so unexpected." Abe flinched, aware that he needed to edit himself, but he was too swamped with disbelief to do anything but babble. "Thank you again," he said, shaking Bill Acker's hand, then Bernard Tobin's, the Arsenaults and the school board, getting an extra punch in the shoulder from Dave Phalen.

Everyone stood as the house burst into applause and whistles. Cradling the keys in his hand, Abe looked bewildered as he and the Arsenaults and Bill Acker left center stage to allow for the awarding of the diplomas. The names echoed in Abe's ears as if by rote. This was *his* class, the class with which he had started kindergarten.

Carter Bedard	David Phalen, Jr.	Marilyn Tureck
Evelyn James	Emery Menary	Neil Olmstead
Richard Moberg	Fritz Gemuenden	Dorothy Deloria
Betty Hebert	Mary Nolan	Kenny Ritter
Dave O'Brian	Del O'Brian	Kathryn Hruska
Camilla Bonifas	Robert Thibault	James Weberg

Betty Johnson ... the list rolled on.

Sarah squeezed his hand. "Congratulations, Abe," she whispered. "You deserve it. Let's go around to all the graduation parties in your new car," she said, her voice satiny smooth and seductive. She crept inside his skin, burrowed, and lived there as his own pink cells, proliferating, pulsating.

A keen awareness seeped into his soul, powerfully blocking out all other dimensions as he studied the porcelain qualities of her face. "You're a class act, Sarah."

"I heard that," Doc said as he chuckled softly. "You kids behave yourselves tonight or you'll have me to answer to in the morning." Slipping his suit jacket on, he cocked one eyebrow and grinned. "I think you'd rather answer to me than to Max."

Abe threw him an amused glance. *How did he know how Max felt?* Somehow, some way, Doc seemed to know everything. He sucked in his breath at the wild gamut of telepathy that played between them.

Acker, Whittaker, Phalen, Mercier, and Tobin all circled about the new car that was parked in front of the Clubhouse. Others milled around. "Congratulations! You deserve it, Abe. Lucky to get a car during the war. Yeah. Scarcer than hen's teeth."

Abe, smiling his thanks and waving, entered the car with Sarah, then sat back, sighing. They eyed each other a few seconds and then burst out laughing at the unbelievable turn of events.

Abe's face grew more hulking and powerful each time Sarah saw him after an absence. An unexplainable thrill crept through her body at the pale bronze cast to his skin and the clearly defined bone structure of his Sioux ancestry. She'd searched for this look wherever she went, but she never found one to match Abe's handsomeness. She was delighted when he drove out to the baseball diamond just north of the Catholic Church; at last they'd have a moment alone.

Abe swelled with the natural beauty of her and at her being in the car with him and giving him cause to feel alive. "Well, what do you think of 'er, little lady? Nice?" Would he always have these John Wayne intonations? Covert? Flipping his emotions off as a comedic comment?

"Sheww," she responded, exhaling slowly. "Very nice."

The soft reserved sound of her voice reminded him again of Liz. He couldn't help but register the changes in her in the past year. The undercurrent of electricity that coursed through him hadn't changed as he indulged in allowing his gaze to travel down the split of her jacket lapels, the flare of her hips and the length of her legs. He looked away before she caught him in this smoldering voyeurism.

If perfection could be perfected upon, she summed it up as a magical metamorphosis. He managed to croak a hoarse nothing as she moved closer to him, putting her arm around him and lightly kissing his cheek. He parked the car under ancient oaks spreading without measure along the river. There he drew her to him.

"I've missed you so much, Sarah. I don't know how I got through the school year." Nibbling her tiny ear, he kissed his way around her cheek to her nose by cupping his thumb and forefinger under her chin and lifting her face to him. He read the warmth of her deep brown eyes flecked with mosaic gold and framed by heavy lashes. Slowly he moved his mouth over hers, searching for entrance with his tongue.

Placing both hands against his chest, she pressed for release, which he gave reluctantly, breathing hard, his eyes closed.

"Sarah," he sighed. "You're all I want in this life. I need you to be mine, all of you to be mine." He leaned back behind the wheel.

"We've graduation parties now, Abe." Her eyes were dazed, her pulse racing.

"You're right, of course, but remember, there's more where that came from."

After making appearances at half of the graduates' homes and running out of enthusiasm and cordialities, they silently communicated a "let's bunch it" gaze.

"Let's get our bathing suits and go down to our cove for a swim, Sarah." Abe smiled broadly.

"Sounds good to me."

He bowed with a great sweep of his arm, holding a non-existent cowboy hat. "You're talking my language now, little lady."

The cove lay deserted and the warm lingering daylight of late May permeated the evening. In its first half, the moon hung low over Big Bay de Nocquet, pompous and orange, tossing a bucket of molten gold across the water. Hanging with bells of coral, orange and red, wild honeysuckle exhaled wafts of fragrance. The wetland irises of purple and yellow bowed in homage to the lake from whence they took sustenance.

"Last one in's a monkey's uncle," shouted Sarah, making a beeline for the cove water, warm and licking at the shore. She had kicked off her sandals and slipped out of her shorts. Pulling her tee shirt quickly over her head, she tossed her hair before Abe could decide if he really wanted to go for a swim. Her eyes glowed with the challenge.

The challenge was answered before the words had melded into the evening air. Even with a late start, Abe invaded the cove before she got her feet wet. He'd been maintaining his running during the long months since Eddie's sudden death. The beach strip at Farley's was perfect for wearing himself out.

He observed that Sarah wore a two-piece bathing suit, navy blue with white piping. Max and Ma provided the best and latest of everything, whatever the demands. She looked like Aphrodite with her mahogany hair, golden skin and brown eyes.

After the swim, they sat on the bleached trunk of a fallen oak, watching their silhouettes elongate in the path of the moon.

Abe reflected, "Do you know that Indians fished and loved here for centuries right where we're sitting? Makes you feel tiny, doesn't it? Farley has taught me to be proud of my Indian heritage."

"I'm proud of your Indian heritage too, Abe," she said, her eyes fastened on him with searching fixation.

He wished she wouldn't do that. She'd never know how it put him in overdrive. She knew nothing of the workings of a man's desires.

Spreading the beach blanket, he told Sarah of the fierce night Eddie met his death. "It's been tough for me." A long slow breath eased between his lips as he lowered himself to the blanket, his long legs stretching out forever in front of him.

Sarah listened, her hands folded between her knees, giving him her full attention. "Yes, I found a friend in Eddie, too." She felt inadequate to supply the magic words he needed in his reflective sorrow.

"Just when I think I've put it out of my mind, it drifts back silently without warning—and there he is, smiling at me, his eyes warm and crinkly. It keeps coming around like a haunting tune." He stretched slowly on the blanket.

"I can't even imagine what you've been through. But I want you to know that you're never out of my thoughts for very long, and there you are again." Rising from the log, she cuddled next to him, hugging her knees.

"I hate to heap any more on you, but I won't be spending the summer here either, as you and I had anticipated." She wore a frown line as she shifted her gaze to him.

"But why?" he gasped, bewildered. His deep brown eyes, filled with unspeakable misery, locked with hers.

Briefly, he saw a storm brewing in the depths of her eyes, which she managed to conceal quickly. Abe stirred, raising himself on one elbow, his face framed in shock.

"Max has arranged for me to spend the summer in Minocqua, Wisconsin with friends who own a cheese factory in Lena, but have a summer home there. Their daughter goes to school with me in Green Bay." Her voice grew thready.

Abe sat up and slumped, his head bowed, his spirit as limp as Fabian's old chambray shirts. "You've been gone all winter. Now he wants to uproot you for the summer months, too!" he exclaimed angrily, his fist slamming devilishly into the sand.

"I expect so, Abe. He's terribly jealous of anyone who gets too close to me. It appears that Max and Ma are arranging already for me to attend Mount Mary College in Milwaukee. I'll be cloistered there just as tightly as I am at the academy." Her voice caught on a short breath, her chin growing soft.

Abe was stymied. "We've waited all winter to be together. Now summer is here, and away you fly like some migrating fowl." Balancing himself with one arm on the blanket, he trapped her eyes then stared angrily out at the bay.

She smiled with cognizance of what he'd said, her look gentle. "There's a big hole in my life, too. Max can be a pain in the kiester." She laid her head on his shoulder. "But, you know I love him deeply; he's my father."

The waves washed softly onto the shore, foamed anemically and slipped back into the cove, making a lazy sucking sound. *Shooshh.*

Sighing, she said, "I guess that we all live with our mete of loneliness."

Abe placed an arm around her shoulder. "What're your goals in college, *milady*?" Abe funned her delicate ears as well as taking a stab at graciously acquiescing to the fact that there would be a long separation.

"It'll be Business Administration. Maybe I could work in management when I get my degree." She loosened her hair wet from the water, combing it with her fingers. Abe fell struck by the stream of dark brown velvet falling around her face and savored this significant quality of her personal attraction.

"When you get your degree," his voice getting deeper, "you won't have to work at anything, missy. By then I'll be in a position to take care of you." He smoothed back hair that had fallen into fine wisps around her face. "I've never wanted anything in my whole life as much as I want you."

"Me, too, Abe," she responded, her hand finding his neck.

The approaching night hummed warm and peaceful with a million stars decorating the eastern sky.

She quivered as he captured her mouth, a small kiss, barely brushing, tentatively easing her down on the blanket. Half her body disappeared under the sheer size of him—her upper breasts scintillating to the welcome matting of his chest hair.

Netting the back of her neck, kissing her more deeply, he leaned Sarah firmly against the blanket until he felt her yielding to his advances. Happiness choked his throat to feel her small tremors as her mouth opened ever so slightly.

Under her newly formed cool exterior, he detected a raging inferno. Her fingers fondled his coarse chest hair weaving and engaging, then down the length of his stomach, exciting and stimulating. Excitement bloomed through Abe's body.

His nostrils flared. His ego spoke. *Go for it, Abe. This is your last chance in God only knows how long. Take her. In his Sioux culture, there remained three primal instincts: to eat, to procreate, and to slay the buffalo (or any pain-in-the-ass competitor).*

Sarah, cloistered for long months, could taste and smell the man in him.

Feeling masterful, he leaned back and unbuttoned her suit in front. His hand slid up her rib cage tenderly fondling her small breasts. The skin sheltered under her swimsuit stood out white and luminescent. He sought this new feast with his tongue. Sensations traveled Sarah's body as never before, making her tremble with urgent desire that engulfed her and overflowed like a deluge. She couldn't get enough of him. Her hand fisted into his ponytail and pressed him further onto her chest.

"Mmmh," he groaned. Waves of electrical impulses clamored through his groin. His hand caressed her hip, her belly.

"We're going too far," she said suddenly, stiffening and gently pushing him away.

"Don't be afraid, Sarah. I'm not going to hurt you."

Over her bathing suit to her tiny waist, he moved his hands slowly up her thighs where he held her, caressing upward to her hips and then pulled her tightly to him.

She felt herself deployed by him—aroused by his posture. As a timeless natural reaction, she pressed back into him, before she realized this was the wrong move. Obeying the dictates of her body, she wanted to gather him within herself, but knew better. This was the dog bite. The bee sting.

"Your fear is unfounded, Sarah." He held his breath for a moment anticipating her further protest, but saw only love and trust in her eyes. He slipped his fingers under the waist of her bathing suit, not releasing her from his all-consuming kiss, not wanting her to reject him and become Catholic rational. Slowly he worked the suit down.

Sarah lay speechless. Nothing she could say would convey what she felt— the urging, the desperate need and the liquid fire flitting to her loins. She traced her fingertips down Abe's spine and over his hips.

He lay still. Gasped. It seemed that he stopped breathing all together. He became unplugged. "Sarah, promise me you'll marry me. Right now if you want to. I'd work in a lumber camp just to come home to you at night." His voice streamed with a flood of honesty and need only known in a relationship of commitment. He tightened.

Where the bathing suit landed, he couldn't be sure, but they could find it later. Unintelligible sounds escaped him when she clutched him ever more closely. Wrapping his arms around her, he pulled her to him. He feared he wouldn't endure much longer.

Insistently he ran his tongue down her belly.

The sensual gliding of his tongue directed painfully enrapturing for Sarah.

In the containment of the cove, the moist softness of their mouths led them down the road of a disappearing world. There were just the two of them, the surf, the moon and the star-filled fragrant night. She decided she'd been childish with her fears, fears that evaporated with his nearness and assurance. She marched toward him in demand.

Abe needed neither prodding nor tutoring to satisfy his drives.

However, Sarah's eyes were brimming tears. She gutturally whimpered feeling as if she lay overrun and forayed by a tank.

He moved to the side. "All right. All right! Damn it, Sarah, when are you going to grow up and be a woman? You're a spoiled bitch!"

Even if love mixed the major ingredient of what he felt, his fulfillment would have to wait. How could he be so jaded to the woman he loved? Make it up to her before he lost her forever.

He observed for the first time the trauma on Sarah's face. His heart broke to see her crying because of something that he'd enjoyed so much. Gathering her into his arms, he carried her to the cove, and sat in the shallows with her on his lap. Gently, he rocked in the brilliant moonlight, which played meticulously in the gentle ripples of the cove.

He felt the first burning prickle of tears after seeing her face defeated and drained. She had the look of someone who would never return from the void of disillusionment and fear—his woman of culture, cuisine and couture.

Did they sit there for ten minutes, or for an hour? Abe didn't know. But he knew he had egregiously violated the only thing in this world that he really loved. Abe could feel small tremors running up Sarah's back as she cried uncontrollably.

Standing, he pulled her up, fished her bathing suit out of the sand and helped her dress as well as pulling his shorts right over bare skin.

In a sudden move, Sarah made a fist, twirled in a wide circle and whopped Abe smack in the belly. "Why? Why did you do that? You big overgrown bull moose!"

Crestfallen, Abe stared after her, opening his hands in a gesture of futility.

"Don't say anything, Abe. Just don't say a darn thing. I can't believe this treatment, can't believe you talked to me that way—so uncaring." Underneath her chilling words swirled a current of strong emotions: betrayal and disenchantment reaching critical mass.

"Goodnight Abe," she said turning away quickly.

Abe's eyes followed her until she disappeared down the beach like a door closed in finality.

CHAPTER EIGHTEEN

Sarah's separation last May blended into the past as Abe viewed the upcoming Easter break of 1944 as a reprieve from his humdrum life. Just two eeks ago, he'd been lifted out of his doldrums after arriving at Doc Whittaker's home for Spanish lessons.

Leading the way into his office, Doc's eyes twinkled with the thought he entertained. Once seated in their customary chairs, Doc leaned back slowly, the coil spring under the chair protesting.

"*Yo voy a Ann Arbor por la Pascua. Te gustaría ir?*"

"*Sí! Me gustaría ir muchisimo! Sí.*"

"Go to Ann Arbor? Yes. Yes! I'd like that very much. Yes!" Abe dropped his Spanish textbook onto the end table with a plunk; the hard cover doing an open-up, flop-down trick. He sank into his chair, dropping his face into his hands in disbelief. Lord God, this man was good to him.

Doc chuckled. "I'm going to visit my brother Walter. He's retiring from the University Of Michigan Law Department with a full professorship, so his cohorts are throwing a celebratory farewell for him. Liz has been having some nasty headaches, so she doesn't feel she can handle the long trip. It's three hundred and fifty miles." Doc raked his mustache, first to the right and then to the left, as if lost in thought.

"I'm sorry to hear about Mrs. Whittaker's problem, but I'd be interested in going. It looks pretty solid that I'll be getting that scholarship to UM. I'll know for sure in just a couple of weeks. The announcements come out early in April. I'm still hovering at just above a "C" average."

Doc smiled understanding. "The University of Michigan board of directors acknowledges that they have an obligation to educate a core of underprivileged students who have a special forte in music, physics, art, or say, athletics. A student to enter this program must have a "C" average in eleven core courses in high school, and you've fulfilled that with your Spanish. With something to excel in, such as sports or art, the student doesn't have to feel inferior every time he enters a classroom. He feels proud. And maybe he realizes that these smart privileged kids are no better or worse than him."

He turned the table lamp on. "The phrase *student-artist, student-athlete* should not be a contradiction in terms, and it won't be in your instance. We're all very proud of you, young man." Making a grunting sound, Doc moved back to his Spanish text, thinking maybe he'd been less than sensitive by using the term "underprivileged" to this man among men. Silence filled the room as he mulled his comment.

Abe felt as if he'd swallowed a ping-pong ball. He viewed Doc in a different light. The man was handsome—a very handsome sonofabitch. Did it really take him nineteen years to figure that out? He wasn't an old man, either, as he used to think. He probably wasn't much older than Fabian. Of course, Fabian had been timeless until he got crippled from the spondilitis.

Doc's eyes brightened. "By the time we make the trip to Ann Arbor, you'll know with certainty about your scholarship. Easter is a little early this year—April ninth," he said, glancing at his desk calendar. "We'll leave on Thursday, the sixth. School is out on Wednesday; I already checked with Bernie."

"Do you need some of my gas rationing stamps? I don't use many traveling around town," Abe explained, stretching his hands palms up in a gesture of simple truth.

"I don't think so. I'm allotted extra stamps because I'm considered a critical service, but carry those stamps with you, just in case." His head nodded with affirmation.

"We'll be gone for five days, coming back on Easter Monday. There'll be parties to attend, so bring whatever you need for those affairs, and some knock-around clothes for touring the campus with Walter." Doc lifted an arm from the chair and let it fall again, smiling, amusement reflective in his eyes.

"I graduated from the University Of Michigan School Of Medicine so I know *my* way around there too, having spent nine years on that campus." Doc laughed. Dark brown eyes sparkled with life. He returned to smoothing his mustache with his forefinger. "You might give some thought to getting a short collegiate haircut sometime between now and next fall. I do believe you'll look right smart, using a side part." He did not convey insistence, but continued the conversation after allowing time for Abe to absorb the message.

"Because your hair is thick, it'll style nicely. Only *you* can decide, but you won't want to stand out from the crowd when you register." Doc's shoulders shook as he laughed. "I remember the tough times I had adjusting at Ann Arbor. I was an immigrant with only a year in this country."

Abe stiffened, yet a small glow of pleasure leaped into his eyes. "Fabian always liked my hair like this, so I never cut it in deference to his memory. It never occurred to me to have it re-styled. I *could* go to Bill Schwartz, the company barber. He'll probably drop over in a dead faint, but I'll think about it." Abe cocked his head sideways, staring, lost in deep thought. Get his hair cut? It echoed in his mind, persistent as a mosquito around a pillow. After all, the suggestion held value, and it was not that of a fool but that of a very knowledgeable person. Hmmm.

Driving home after his lessons, Abe found himself making mental notes of items to take on the trip. It would be a tear, riding in Doc's snazzy Packard Eight Club Sedan—maroon, with a fawn interior. He'd seen it parked around town. Whah! Sinbad had not had a better adventure. He viewed the trip as the highlight of a dark period, since Sarah had left without saying a word last June. He wondered how she would like to know what transpired the next day.

In a fit of rage, Max entered his home, his white hair cockeyed as if he were skewered to a light socket—deep, hard lines around his mouth. "Listen, you ungrateful whelp! I don't know what transpired between you and Sarah last night, but I don't have to be a German rocket scientist to figure it out. I know you spent some time together yesterday, which wasn't all at graduation parties. You goddamn stay away from her. You understand? You hear?"

Abe found the ferocious fire in Max's eyes volatile, and resisted the impulse to go nose-to-nose with him. Max could be as eccentric as hell. Abe had all he could do to keep from rolling his eyes, but he knew that would be catastrophic. Max must be the Sioux's third requisite for basic life: to kill a pain-in-the-ass, he thought.

"I purposely sent her away to school to remove her from your influence. She's getting a superior education and will marry someone her equal some day, and over my dead body would that be you." His tone was taunting and jagged.

Abe stared at him. It was incredulous that Max had blown in through the front door without as much as a "Mother May I?"' Incredulous that after all these years of helpful relationships, Max's words were beyond his grasp and out in left field.

Crestfallen, Abe gulped, his big hands tucked into sizable fists. "Sarah and I love each other. There's never been anyone else in either of our lives. By the time I graduate college I'll be just as worthy a husband for her as anyone else she might find in Green Bay, Milwaukee or anywhere else as far as that goes!" Abe found himself winding up as he spoke. Instilled with anger with himself as well as toward Max, he wished to hurt him. "And you can bet your skinny old ass on that!" Abe added, but all he accomplished was staring into the most bedeviled eyes he'd ever seen—mad, steely gray eyes.

"You sonofabitch! You'll never be fit to be her husband. You're nothing but a half-ass, half-baked half-breed. You have no heritage, no family, and no money. God only knows I've done what I can for you by giving you art instructions. What's more, I don't expect any more than a picture or two out of you for the rest of your life. You'll head down the same alcoholic path as the rest of the Sioux Indians across the river," he added with abusiveness.

Size for size, Max stood as tall as Abe, but he was lanky, hollow-chested, and breathing fire. Upon leaving, he swung around at the bottom of the porch steps and sliced him with a lethal glower. "You see her again and I'm gonna make you one sorry ass," he vowed, low enough so only Abe could hear, then turned away.

At the memory, Abe smiled faintly. All these years of security he'd felt from his neighbor exploded into a mist of surrealism. Was Max some kind of flim-flam man, one who changed patronage as the moment presented itself? The doomsday element, both physical and tactile, caused him to suck in air.

He stuffed his hands into his pockets, determined to look to the better day: running on the beach, good friends, Norrhea's applesauce, a fresh bed at the end of a long day. He needed to remember Sioux spirits that stayed in touch, even though physically separated. He had to discipline his over-reaction to Max's debilitation. It was *him* speaking, not Sarah. In addition, it was doubtful that he'd taken Sarah's innocence. Her innocence was a matter of soul that glowed in her eyes.

☙❧

This last year of school had crushed Abe with the courses he needed to complete the minimum curriculum for college entrance. Thank God for Krutina! How she ever obtained all those graphs, charts, training materials, etcetera, he'd never know. Undoubtedly, the Delta County Traveling Library was a boon for rural schools.

Life had indeed been bleak, but he'd held up just like he'd done after Fabian's death. Night turned into day and faith moved him along life's path. Faith in the future, he believed. He believed in the intangibles in his life:

Fabian's appearances, pictures that sprung to life in his mind, the happenstances in his life that weren't just luck. He believed in many things: the infinite vastness beyond the stars, life after death, the physics of the atom.

They were all as unexplainable as the weather, which turned bitterly cold in early December. The nights were brutal. Frost formed scratchy patterns on the windows. Abe went to live with Farley and Norrhea for the remainder of the cold months. Thus he found only pitiful tidbits of time with Sarah over the holidays, except for brief cordialities shouted through the stingingly cold air while checking on his home.

Seeing her was unsettling—painful. Max's warning had been a blow, making her untouchable. It was a sad commentary on the trust he'd put into their adult relationship. The one he'd previously considered a family friend turned out now to be a formidable foe. Many a night he'd been seized miserable in his isolation. *Some broken hearts never mend*, he reminded himself as he heard the Nahma Northern train whistle, plaintive and strung out, as it pulled into town every evening during the dark nights of winter.

But again, Abe's Sioux Indian spirits intervened. His athletic talent was not to be overlooked by the staff at Nahma High School just because he turned nineteen.

"How about taking on the assistant coaching position for basketball and track this year?" Tobin and Pintal approached Abe like a fork in the river, mixing and swirling with a common offer.

Abe offered no indecisiveness. "Sure thing. I will. The kids need to run more, gain conditioning to play ball, and compete in track." His dark eyes burned with a fiery glint at the proffered challenge.

"Good thinking. We'll leave that part up to you, Abe. We appreciate every minute you spend with them," they added, their eyes conveying considerable respect.

So, with the right breaks and a lot of hard work, he was honoraria *promoted* to one of the staff. He allowed the idea to marinate. Damn, but it felt good! The vote of confidence in the right stuff he'd exhibited in the last four years added up.

☙❧

The 1944 calendar pages flipped back. In the blackness of an early January morning, as promised, Abe accompanied Alan Mercier to Camp Five, situated thirty miles north of Nahma. The thermometer held at twenty-eight degrees below zero when the train chugged steam on its daily run to the camps. A wood-burning stove kept the caboose warm, giving off visible mirages of heat inversions. Abe sat back in the plush seat, his arms folded complacently over his chest, nodding and smiling, encouraging Mercier's chronicles of the camps.

A medium height and weight man, Abe often thought Mercier looked the part of an accountant with his wide forehead and intense eyes peering from over pinz nez glasses. Outside, ice crystals hung in the air, dancing dizzily as dawn broke, giving the deep green forest a watercolor appearance. It remained a picture forever. *Click.*

"Years ago in the spring," Mercier shared, "hundreds of thousands of logs were banked along the river or on the ice of the streams. Increasingly each day the warm sun morphed the ice and snow to water, allowing the River Hogs to send floating crashing logjams downstream by means of working with the peavy pole." Alan sat, looking out the caboose window as the train rocked over rough tracks, his face a study in yesteryear. "I've seen the peavey poles hanging in the lobby of Clubhouse," Abe mulled. "They're the long wooden rods with a curved spiked end on them. "

"They were mightily effective. In the springtime, cutting came to an end in the camps. River Hogs, a special breed of man we'll see no more, had to be agile, daring and strong. They wore caulked boots with spiked heels and soles with sharp points to work the logs downstream. The river can be a rigorous challenge that time of the year, unforgiving in its chase to Lake Michigan." Alan glanced over at Abe, his eyes crinkling in a thin-lipped broad smile as they moved over the rails in the booth-style seats.

"Number Five Camp covers twenty-two miles of rich forest land. This camp has not yet been depleted of its marketable timber. When we're done, only the hemlock, maple, birch and red oak will be left. That too will go. We call the collateral "slashings." Jobbers bid on these cutovers most of the time. This is one of our biggest camps ever—eighty-five men and twelve teams of horses. The timber here is plentiful along the river. In some sections it stands a million lineal feet to every forty acres. We establish the camp buildings halfway between the scene of the cutting and the railroad landings."

Abe realized that the railroad stabilized the main street of Camp Five, with the cookhouse, bunkhouses and office on one side of the track, and the horse barns and smithy shops on the other side. All the roads in between and trailing off into the woods were a slick of ice to make easy pulling for the horse teams, sometimes six of them attached to one sled, piled high in a pyramid of logs often times six feet in diameter, to be rolled off near the railroad tracks.

Alan pointed out the highlights. "The road sprinklers in winter are kept running all night long so that the roads are a sheet of ice from the woods to the landings. All the teams are in camp every night, half of them bound for the landings in the morning with full sleds, the other half bound for the woods with empty sleds." Alan became pensive as they drew near camp, the engine slowing with a chung, chung-chung-chung-chung, the cars echoing rat-tat-tat as the train slowed and came to a stop. While the two men walked down the plank landing, the engine puffed excess steam in a slow series of grace notes— sha-shooss, sha-shooss, sha-shooss. The vapor turned immediately to ice crystals.

Thin silvery strings of smoke from chimneys climbed straight into the air as if they were threads being pulled up into a giant vortex where they met finally and disintegrated into the cold air. Abe shuddered. *Maybe there is no hell; it's right here before my eyes.* The present was colorless and the future tenuous, tending to rely on timber supply and demand. The way the finite forests were being felled and massacred, the demands would far outlast the supply. The needs of every fast-growing city, the mamas the papas, the churches, the children and their Chihuahuas were obvious.

"Here we are inside a bunkhouse," said Alan, making a sweep of his arm as they entered a frost-heavy wooden door. "The big stove in the middle is called a 'caboose.' It heats the entire building. Suspended overhead you see the men's flannels and socks drying for another day's hard work. The bunkhouse has bunks for all the men where they may be sawing wood even as they sleep. They have real mattresses now, but they used to be made of pine boughs. You can work to keep these places neat and never quite get there." Mercier paused, envisioning the scene through the eyes of a first-time beholder.

"In the morning someone walks around, banging a pan with a wooden spoon and making an awful racket. He keeps bawling, 'Daylight in the swamp!' Men of every nationality grumble and start tumbling out of bed. It's about four a.m. The eastern horizon is barely being born."

"What a time to start the workday! *I'm* still sawing logs at that hour!" Abe laughed as they left the bunkhouse and walked through the camp. His voice vibrated in the cold, still air, his chin frozen, his mouth laboring to form words, but the adrenaline pumped steadily at this whole new world, a civilization of its own.

"The lumberjack's work attire is designed to keep him warm," Alan advised, walking briskly. "Long johns and several pair of heavy wool socks make up the bottom layer, topped by bright woolen shirts and pants cut off just below the knee. The exterior consists of heavy mackinaws, spiked boots and a knit chooks. And they damn well need every square inch of it." A wry smile turned up the corners of his mouth.

"I've seen some. How do they move with all that bulk on?" Abe whirled around and looked again at the party that had just passed. *Click.*

"By layering they can remove some of these articles of clothing as the day warms. Fully dressed, however, the lumberjacks head for the table. Heavy work demands a hearty breakfast. Lumber camps assure their men are fueled with baked beans, eggs, flapjacks, cookies, bacon, fried pork ends, potatoes, hash, cake, cookies, and trowels of churned butter. Add caldrons of coffee. The cook and his helpers need to arise around three o'clock to start the preparations. There are many different camps, but one rule at all of them is, 'No talking at the table.' After breakfast, when it's nearly daylight, the lumberjacks pick up their tools and head out to the woods."

In spite of Mercier's many years with the lumber company, Abe observed the sensitivity he exhibited toward the Jacks. Both followed the crew into the woods—men on foot and on sleds. The cutting site lay two miles from camp. Alan and Abe rode on the yet empty horse-drawn wagon. The horses whinnied, hooves stamped, and steam emitted from their nostrils in the frigid cold. Far off across the woods, a wolf howled in the half-light of the approaching day.

"There are many different jobs in the woods," Alan said as he picked up the seasoning lessons as though breakfast hadn't intervened. "Some chop. Some saw. Some lead teams of horses. Some load wood. It's tough physical work, and it lasts all day. At last, a triangular piece of iron called the 'gut hammer' is pounded. Lunchtime! A hot meal has just been delivered to the men in the woods. They eat and then go back to work. We'll join them today." Alan smiled at Abe from the back of the wagon, his beaver cap pulled well down over his ears; his Mackinac, lined with lamb's wool, gave him the look and feel of the woodsman.

Advised by Doc of the crude conditions of the camp, Abe mobilized the treasury of Doc's camp-visit clothes. He, likewise, dressed as Alan did. On his head sat an identical beaver hat, pulled clear down over his ears.

Alan and Abe watched the process of downing a tree, which was accomplished now by weighty power saws. Abe wore a controlled daze when, before his eyes, a giant white pine was unmercifully punished and slaughtered— a hundred years old, two centuries, three. They had seen the passing of the Indian, the Missionary Priest, Father Marquette, the early explorers. They had viewed hunters, trappers and cruisers. Its rings showed the scars of arrowheads and hatchets, knife-carvings, bullets, lightning and hail. The rings mapped out a living historical record of the region. The handiwork of God knew reduction to an abattoir, with blows inflicted by His greatest creation: mankind.

"It wasn't so many years ago that these trees were harvested by chopping and hand saws," Alan pointed out, standing a distance from the activity with Abe.

"Crack! The first scream of anguish from the pine. They looked at the great tree. It is trembling, swaying almost imperceptibly. It gathered all its strength in an effort to remain standing. Again they sawed, back and forth, back and forth. Crack!"

"Timber! There grew an awfulness in the sight of this great structure toppling, leaning and falling: a whine, a scream, a groan, a crash that resounded through the forest followed. There it lay, measuring its length on the ground, vanquished and dead. It took ten minutes to undo that which had taken two hundred years in the doing." Mercier deliberately paused in the still cold, allowing the ugliness of the harvested supply to equate to the greed of demand.

Abe began to understand, as few others do, something of someone else's sustenance, his way of life. The timberman knows he must do so as a stranger, without entering into the whys or wherefores of this industry. His is not to reason why. Abe lowered his head and idly kicked at a chunk of ice.

"How many acres does the Bay de Nocquet Lumber Company have for available cutoff?" Abe, in awe, cut his glance to Alan.

"Oh, I'd say handily five or six hundred thousand acres. They acquired it by means of actual buyouts, back-tax auctions, the Homestead Act years ago, and the U. S. government give-away to build railroads. This gave us the opportunity to take timber land—miles and miles of it—cut it down and send it to the sawmill. Besides, we cut the slashings and send it to the paper mills for extra income."

Abe didn't fail to notice the way Mercier's tongue curled around *extra income*, as if it were tossed off as incidental. He turned his thoughts to the slaughterhouses of Chicago; never let it be said that any part of the animal went to waste.

"The workday is governed by daylight, not the clock. When light starts to fade, it's time to head back to camp and the evening meal." Abe found that dinner was just as hearty as the morning meal. Afterwards, Mercier carried on his composite account of camp life. "The lumber camp's cook is an important person and stays busy, making all the meals, along with the bread, cookies and doughnuts, all in great quantity. A good cook is highly prized. He keeps lumberjacks well fed and satisfied and is paid handsomely for his efforts. After supper, it's time to relax. The men talk, play cards and tell tall tales. If they have a radio, they listen to that. Every camp has a fiddler and a jig dancer.

These he-men of the Northwoods sing and dance with each other while he plays. Some have handkerchiefs tied around their arm. They are the *ladies*."

Abe gave an appreciative laugh. His fingers drew small circles on the table while he absorbed the atmosphere of the log, moss-caulked dining hall.

"Festivities die down after a while. Before too long the bunkhouses will resound with their snoring. The only variety comes on payday. Some lumberjacks get checks, while others are paid in cash."

"Many of the Jacks are frugal men with wives and families. They save for the future. Other lumberjacks really don't have anything to save for, so they don't. But don't judge them too harshly. These are rough and ready guys, hard men who live a hard existence. They work hard, play hard and drink hard." He grinned a knowing smile.

"Does Father Epoufette ever come up to the camps to give services for the jacks—give them a chance to say their *mea culpas*? I thought that perhaps that could be a solution to carousing and absenteeism." Abe's voice sounded empathetic with the pitiful lot in life of the camp worker.

"As a matter of fact, he does at times. I've ridden up to the camps with him on our very train. But you might as well use a sling shot against the Golden Horde. Wish it were all that simple, but that suggestion took a lot of insight from a young man who has never faced these problems." Alan gave Abe an appreciative sideways glance as he circled his coffee mug with both hands.

"The part of the job that maybe has changed the least over the years is the work of the timber cruiser. His job is to look over the woods and decide on the best stands of wood for cutting. We have two men—Jake Runkle and "Peanuts" Sargent—both crackerjacks. They started in the woods while they were still young men, and they know their timber. Definitely one-of-a-kind. We're lucky to have them on our payroll."

Abe flashed a full-blown grin. One would never know Runkle and Sargent had skills to their names, to see their desks. He, himself, faced the challenge of straightening them at least once a week, but within a few days they looked like the wrath of God had torn through, chased by a blast of hot air from Mt. Vesuvius. But, what the hell, out of their chaos grew intelligent calculations.

"The timber cruiser is a key player. He estimates the volume of each kind of tree by species on a section of land. The bottom line is this: Is the land worth buying? Can the company make money on it? When the cruisers move on, the lumberjacks move in.

"We use power saws now. They're heavy. Weigh about one hundred and fifty pounds, and two strong men are needed to run them. The new saws greatly increase a lumberjack's productivity. The old two-man cross-cut saw has become obsolete.

"Well, do you think that you have a mental picture of places, dimensions and people so you can paint a series of pictures that we can hang in the lobby of the Clubhouse?" Mercier grinned with the tickle it felt to have shown someone something of such magnitude for the first time, and to observe his response.

"Many," Abe responded, his eyes trailing around the cook shack, redolent with damp clothing, food and a hint of wood smoke from the immense ranges in the kitchen.

Before boarding the train for the return trip, Alan breathed deeply of the forest air, his hands on the come-along rails of the caboose stairs. As a business man, however, he felt no qualms at the miles of pine forest turned into a wasteland of bleeding pine stumps left there to rot and dry like corpses on a battlefield. In fact, he found himself a fine citizen icon, providing jobs for sometimes upwards of a thousand people. In keeping with the times, his satisfaction in the part he played rested replete.

On the return train with Alan, Abe was sated with ideas. "It would be interesting to do a series of pictures such as a daylight-to-dusk anecdotal sequence, showing the life of the jacks."

"Great idea. Maybe you could do one of the train too, going out in the morning cold, empty, full of snow and coming back at night pulling eight, ten flatcars carrying a pyramid of chained logs crusted with snow that chunks off as the train runs the rough track. It should keep you busy for the rest of the winter," he said in a gale of laughter, as he and Abe and the trainman sat in the warm caboose drinking coffee royals, which Abe thought were pretty damn good.

CHAPTER NINETEEN

Indeed, the trip held enlightenment. In all, he now had seven pictures sketched and ready to put the final drama to each of them: "The Morning Train O' Need," "The Lumberjack Breakfast," "The Lumberjack Lunch," "The Lumberjack Supper," "Evenings Entertainment," "Sleeping Beauties" and the "Evening Train O' Plenty." He would have them completed for the Fourth of July Homecoming Festivities, just as he had completed the Burner picture for the same occasion last year. The thought wrapped him in the comfort and reassurance of his organizational skills.

Now he could relax and enjoy his Easter trip to Ann Arbor. Thursday, April 6, dawned as bright and clear as Abe's mind. Traveling Highway U.S. 2 East to St. Ignace where they'd catch the ferry to Mackinac City, Abe sat beside Doc. He'd seen his scholarship materialize as anticipated. *It's your heritage to excel, to learn and to aspire to even greater heights.* Many times Farley's words soothed his fuzzy brain.

"Your haircut is outstanding; you've created a whole new person. Do you like it?" Doc wore a half-smile, his eyes twinkling.

"Yeah. I have to admit that it's quite a change. I couldn't believe the difference when he finished. The left part doesn't want to fall into place, but he said it would in time. Combing it down on the sides feels like I'm swimming up-stream." He stopped to laugh richly. "All the guys in the barber shop applauded." It hadn't been an easy decision, but perhaps the benefits would far exceed any disappointments. He could hardly abide any more tormenting from on-lookers such as he'd endured as a child.

"There, you see? Another hurdle tackled and cleared. In just two months you'll be out of school. You must feel it's long overdue." Doc rolled down the window a crack and let the early morning air stream over his face.

Laughing indulgently, Abe acknowledged, "I wanted to get out of high school ever since I was in the seventh grade. Now it's all over and I'll be starting a new life. With the education I'm going to get, I can go just about anywhere and have a profession, even teaching fine arts. It's like striking a match to a fire on a bitter cold night."

"Yes, you'll have all of that and more." Doc re-postured himself, sitting higher. "You're lucky. There are a number of places right here in Michigan that use a degree such as you'll have." The thought whet his buried knowledge of opportunities. "The University of Michigan has a fine Museum of Art with extensive exhibits of Western African and Asian art. The Detroit Institute of Art is very impressive with art from America, Europe and the Orient as well. Then you have great cultural centers such as Flint, Grand Rapids, Kalamazoo, Lansing and Battle Creek."

Having left Nahma while it was yet dark, the drive took them into daylight, which awakened with with pink, orange and silver streaks. Lights went out in homes along the road as if the total population were going on vacation.

"Many of the young men coming out of high school go right to work in the woods or in the mill, and who can say that's bad? It's a needed profession. The demand for wood products is so great that the War Manpower Commission placed all woods and lumber workers on a forty-eight hour workweek, including the Bay de Nocquet Lumber Company. The mills around here producing veneer for aircraft manufacturers and shipbuilders have been operating more than forty-eight hours a week." Doc paused, viewing the early spring hardwoods that harbored just a hint of green.

Abe couldn't decide what he liked best about Doc—his all-abiding sense of humor, his sympathetic message on the lumber mill employees, or his crisp British accent in the delivery of it all. While mulling, the Packard drove into the belly of the car ferry, Pottawattamie, at the Port of St. Ignace and was immediately swallowed by the great hollow interior. "Let's go topside and take-in passing through the Straits of Mackinac," Doc encouraged. "There's talk of a bridge being built that would carry traffic over the Straits in just minutes instead of the hour it takes now. Imagine the engineering fete that will be: a five mile suspension span." Doc's eyes lit up with the coalescing thought of a magnificent bridge spanning the Straits of Mackinac.

"Well, I hope they don't wait for *me* to design it; we'll be using this ferry until the year 2000!" Abe smoothed his new haircut.

The water slipped past the huge black warehouse, taking them ever closer to the Mackinac City shoreline. The throbbing thrust of the engines from deep within the ship could be felt vibrating throughout the floor span. Coal smoke poured from her high thick stack, painted bright red, while a misty spray blew at them with the ever-changing wind patterns peculiar to the Straits of Mackinac.

Leaning on the rail, they scanned the outline of Mackinac Island that commanded the north Lake Huron end of the straits—a passage that connected Lakes Huron and Michigan between the Upper and Lower Peninsulas.

"The small, thickly forested island was long the center of an important fur-trading era dominated by the John Jacob Astor American Fur Company," Abe read from a brochure he had taken from a rack near to the interior cabin door. "It is now a popular summer resort. Attractions include Fort Mackinac (built by the British in 1780) and a house (now a museum) used by the Astor Fur Company. The island, once inhabited by Native Americans, passed to U.S. control in 1783." Abe grunted dryly.

Doc rested his elbows on the railing, his hands folded. "That was about one hundred years before your great-great grandfather died. Just another instance of the Whiteman infringing on Indian grounds and entitlements," Doc said reflectively. "It was genocide just as sure as what Hitler is now doing to the Jews."

"Who knows? Maybe I would now be heir apparent to a kingdom, had my people survived the Indian Wars," Abe said, smiling at Doc, his voice filled with humor. "Who owns all those huge white homes I see?"

"Most of them are privately owned. Some are owned by corporations and some by the State of Michigan. There's the governor's mansion over there, up toward the Grand Hotel. See it?" Doc pointed in a south-southeast direction. It's the one with the American flag flying in the front yard and the State of Michigan flag below it. That means that Governor Van Wagner is now in residence on the island—probably took his family there for Easter break." He glanced at Abe, his eyes intelligent brown.

Abe leaned sideways on the rail, turning his full attention to Doc, his trench coat unbuttoned on this April morning with the temperatures hovering in the sixties—atypical for a Michigan early spring day. He stuffed one hand casually into his trousers pocket. "Pretty nice place to vacation, I'd say." Abe couldn't imagine the impossible distinctions between the life he led and the lifestyle of the governor.

"Speaking of vacations. How are you and Sarah getting along now that you've had a long dry spell?" A small smile crept around the corners of his mouth as he turned to Abe.

"Well," Abe said shyly, glancing at Doc, then away. "I've hardly talked to her since last year at graduation time. Max doesn't want me to see her anymore." His color rose to the roots of his hair. A cold lump plunked in his gut like a bag of steelies.

"What?" Doc smiled uncertainly. "What happened? I've never seen two people more perfectly matched than you two are. Like Samson and Delilah—tea and crumpets. What's gotten into old Max?"

Abe adjusted his stance against the rail, his hip resting easily on the double bars as he relived the events leading to Max's tirade. "He doesn't think I'm good enough for her. He told me I wasn't fit to marry his daughter. I had no future, no heritage, no money, and he didn't think I'd ever amount to a row of beans." Abe's voice faded at the end, becoming gravelly and his neck prickling with frustration.

"No! You've gotta be..." Doc spit out, his eyes blazing from under heavy eyebrows. He tapped his hands on the rail as he contemplated this. *More people are hurt with words than with guns and bombs. Oftentimes, the wounds ache for the rest of their lives. Max had all the finesse of a doorknob.*

"You know what's wrong with Max? He thinks that people are like the water down there. They seek their own level. That's never going to happen in a free society. Cupid strikes in strange places."

Yeah, sure, Abe thought, *but a man can get nervous dancing on eggshells around an irate father.*

The loudspeakers on the ship blared, "Five minutes to docking. Please return to your cars. Do not start engines until the gate is lowered. Thank you."

Turning toward the metal stairs, Abe sighed, grateful for the interruption. "Yeah. He might as well have beaten me with a stick. I had to use all my self-control not to knock him into the next county." Abe recalled how overwhelmed he had felt with Max's message—torpedoed and sunk.

"When did all this happen?" Doc tried to shake the nebulous imagery of Max's verbal attack from his mind.

"Right after the graduation parties last spring, a year ago already. Max came marching over to the house the next day and said that Sarah didn't feel well, and he knew that the fault was mine."

The perforated metal steps in the stairwells rattled, reverberating to the sound of descending feet.

"Well, what was the nature of her illness?" Doc asked as they entered the car while the ferry docked.

Damn! The guy was uncanny with his leading questions. It mattered not what Abe said to him, it triggered his synapses like light bulbs. It was as if Doc had a key to unlock the door to Abe's soul. Scary, that's what it was. How could he explain?

One thing for damn sure, he would take his time about revealing the sordid end to that beautiful day. Abe remembered clearly every detail—every ache, the longing, the desperate desire, and Sarah trembling delightfully in his arms. The memories would never fade away. He fired up with fuel in the furnace of remembrance as he recalled the first time he'd discovered that she had grown breasts, the breathlessness and wonderment of the moment when he first undressed her, the uncontrollable gnawing in his groin to make her his own at any cost.

It wasn't an attack, he admonished himself; it was an act of love. She was his woman. He had a right to her—to her mind, to her body and to her spirit and soul. He grunted with the arrogance of the thoughts

"I'm going to duck into that Curious Kettle," Doc said, nodding off to the right. "I'll grab us a couple of quick sandwiches for the road, saving close to an hour, and putting us into Ann Arbor before dark." He grinned with the feasibility of the idea.

Abe accompanied Doc into the restaurant, his knees feeling like a loose goose. All the while, he browsed the network of his mind, recalling the events of that fateful evening. She conceded to try one more time at the supreme act of love.

Returning to the car, Abe shifted uncomfortably, bending over slightly and cupping his hands, his elbows resting on his knees, momentarily ignoring lunch. His stomach fired up some fantastic flipping.

"So, where were we now? Oh, yes, you were telling me about what happened after the graduation parties last year. Sorry for the interruption." Doc peeled back half the napkin that held his burger and lit into it, shifting it to his other hand on the steering wheel and reaching for his coffee. The car filled with the appetizing aromas of fresh coffee, burgers and fries.

Abe changed his mind, and peeled into his burger too. With a long breath, he tried to control the bedlam of emotions inside him. "Well, Sarah and I went for a swim in that cove off Stony Point." Abe shot an uncomfortable glance at Doc over the rim of his coffee container.

"If you remember, it was a beautiful night, the moon shining across the lake as if someone had spilled out a can of gold paint, full and running." Abe took a long, bracing swallow of his coffee.

"Yeah, I remember that. Liz and I sat on the front porch until late, enjoying the crickets and the 'Thousand and One Arabian Nights' ambiance. But don't let me interfere with your story," Doc said, taking a contemplative bite of his burger.

"We enjoyed the swim, and *the company* of course. One thing led to another and the first thing you know a kiss led to fondling, and that led to everything that followed."

Abe slipped into an easy comfort zone, finding a measure of relief by confiding in Doc in the privacy and warmth of the car. The late morning sun coming in from the east outlined Doc's profile. He established one handsome toney icon. This stylized car captured his image perfectly. Abe crushed the coffee container, depositing it into the carryout bag. He hoped that Doc would not be disappointed in the rest of the story.

Doc held his coffee in his hand, only taking teasing sips, his teeth nibbling on the rolled edge of the paper cup. His face was unreadable. Abe wished that *the rest of the story* could be disclosed by psychic transference. He rapped his knuckle lightly against the car window, taking a deep breath.

Abe shifted, sitting up straight, looking out the side window. He wondered, as he had many times in the past year, if he were certifiably insane or simply insensitive to Sarah's needs. He took a deep breath, then gradually explained what had materialized. When he finished, he shook his head sadly.

"You mean to tell me that after all these years of being the *Bobbsey Twins At The Seashore,* that the first time you had carnal knowledge of her happened just last year?" Doc's face softened as he nodded in Abe's direction. "I wish you would have consulted me about this instead of keeping it to yourself for such a long time. It must have been like sitting on a grenade with a loose pin!"

Abe shrugged. How does a guy confide these things in someone else? Maybe Fabian. Fabian would have been advisory, but no, he'd not thought of Doc.

The Lower Michigan radio stations suited Abe just fine. "And now here's Les Brown and his band of renown with Doris Day with 'Sentimental Journey.'" The familiar strains circled the interior of the comfortable Packard. Day's vocal sincerity grappled with his imagination.

There arose such a beating and fluttering in his chest that he couldn't shut himself down; Abe recaptured his subject. "As a child, the town jerk-off, Old Pedo, enticed her into his home and molested her to a point where it hurt. Now, she's frigid." His fists opened and closed. A small sound escaped from his throat.

"Yes, I knew that, but I'd forgotten. I'm so sorry. Damn letch!" Doc adjusted the radio to a lower volume. "Old John Pedo molested a number of children in town before someone gave him his just desserts a few years ago. It was a nightmare. Old John had nearly lost his mind by the time someone discovered him. I had to put so many sutures into the tips of his fingers that he'll never have normal sensations again."

"It was downright savage! Someone...someone...w-a-n-t-e-d," his voice trailed off. "Someone wanted...retaliation...big time...someone personally involved." His words were a mere measured whisper.

Abe could discern a growing awareness in Doc—an awakening. His gut tightened. His heart knocked like a worn-out engine.

"Speaking of involved—Abe! Was it you?" His face took on shades of darkness, his voice demanding with harshness. He shook a reproaching finger. "It was *you* with your Sioux Indian traditions and Tribal Rites? What were you thinking of?" He tossed a sharp, accusing look at Abe. "You need to buffet those beliefs and adjust your disciplines to today's world." Doc visibly softened. Given some thought, it did not surprise him. "I'm sorry, Abe. It was my shock speaking. It adds up. That's exactly what your tribunal would have done in that instance, but it's not a socially acceptable practice in our society, and that's where you live." Folding the whole thing aside to re-examine at another time, he tossed his crushed coffee cup into the bag. He found himself wildly territorial with Abe since Fabian's passing. He could no longer deny or camouflage it.

Abe rested four fingers against his lips and leaned an elbow on the car window, studying Doc. His eyes lightened and darkened with undercurrents of anxiety. "You'll never be sure, though, will you? That's a deduction on your part. It could have been any number of people." He caught his bottom lip and chewed thoughtfully. "I've never felt any compassion, however, about the old codger's comuppins."

"So," Doc pre-empted. "You were unsuccessful with Sarah due to the pain she experienced? That's strange. But her experience is not unprecedented. There *are* some things you can do to remedy that." The confidence, silently spoken by the movements of his shoulders, was articulate.

Abe's mind meandered like a riverbank, convoluting here and there, trying to anticipate Doc's full explanation. His dark eyes blazed with expectancy at being offered a solution to his frustrating problem. The spin-off seemed staggering; he'd be able to lie with Sarah, make her see how love shared was love pleasured.

"So why *did* Sarah not feel well the next day?" Doc gave Abe a solicitous glance. "In fact, so out of sorts that Max picked up on it? He has an inane insensitivity to people. He's quite a boor, to be specific."

Abe's comfort zone grew thinner. He punched his knee with his fist. "I promised her I'd go gently and not hurt her, but...Abe's voice started to squeak. He lowered his forehead into the cup of his hand.

Doc glanced over at him with alarm. The words *taming* and *civilizing* formed on his lips like a mime. The young man relived a visit to hell, his eyes contrite.

"Christ, Abe! You must control your libido; you're no goddamned jackrabbit. You love this woman, yet you can't be sensitive to her needs. You don't want to dismantle a mountain to realize a rock. Did you use a condom?" He threw a quick query at Abe.

A pitiful sound of remorse and hopelessness slid from deep within Abe's chest. "No. She's my woman," he said with feigned ease. It gave Abe a heady dizziness to think of the masculine power that came with Sioux entitlements. He limply let his hand slap at his knee. "Then she stood up, made a fist, spun around and laid a slugger right in my belly...called me a big over-grown bull moose."

Doc swallowed a grin at the pluckiness of Lady Sarah. "You're damn lucky that you didn't get her pregnant." Doc's mouth curved upward at the imperiousness of this young Sioux, shaking his head in disbelief.

Houghton Lake and Claire had slipped away almost unnoticed while the intimate conversation continued.

"Liz and I have been married for twenty-four years, and there are yet times when I need to be especially cognizant to her needs. Women are the gentler sex and need coddling, not coercing. You want Sarah to be the queen of your home, not a tipi transient." Doc's big hand reached out and squeezed Abe's knee. "You need to cool it and polish the rough edges off the diamond you are. Just stay focused."

Doc reminded himself that of all the mammals in the world, human beings are the only living entities that can act irrationally and find a rational reason for their actions. He also knew that empathy and acceptance were the keys to being humane. Condemnation and punishment never were successful roads for the encouragement of floundering intellects. Actually, this kid had spunk; he possessed quickness, had a Spartan composure and an intangible dignity about him. He was by definition the sort of young man he would have been proud to have as a son.

"This is WKXY in Flint. The time is two o'clock." Abe's beautiful music station broke for an on-the-hour newscast. "Before this year is out, Michigan's passenger cars will be dangerously near the point where they'll be inadequate for essential transportation. Passenger car registration is down and cars are going off the road at a rate of approximately six percent a year from old age alone."

"Michigan produces one-sixth of the implements with which this country is waging war. And seventy-six percent depend on automobiles to get to and from work. Every car owner today is the custodian of a vehicle as vital to the war effort as tanks, planes and guns. Mileage rationing must be supplemented by the most scrupulous care of our cars and tires."

Abe could feel his future fading. He mulled aloud, "After listening to all this gloom and doom brought on by the war, it seems questionable to aspire to a college education. I only have a one-year deferment for college. If my grades aren't equal to the Delta County Draft Board expectations, I'll probably be drafted next year at this time. War!"

"War mongers are users. They persuade whole nations into the most contemptible acts for the sake of a superior society. Don't let it get you down. I have a feeling that your grades are going to be just fine. This too will pass, and our country will need educated cultural enthusiasts like you."

Doc detected the strange depression that had overtaken Abe. "I wasn't really listening to the entirety of that broadcast. I mentally searched for a solution to your problem with Sarah. You know Sarah well enough," Doc persisted, "to understand that she would need a long, convincing buildup before she could possibly even consider your tactics. Her maturity has everything to do with her sexual growth. I've noticed that her figure is more youthful than it should be for a woman her age, so she may just need longer to blossom. Don't rush her, or things will go from sachet to shinola."

Save her for dessert, Abe. Save her for dessert.

Pondering, Doc bobbled his bottom lip into a vee with his thumb, index finger and third finger. "Sarah needs medical attention." Doc's interest picked up. "There are many conditions that can make sexual activity painful for women. Without examining her, I'd say she lacks natural lubrication, and the lower vaginal muscles tighten into spasms. The problem occurs when natural arousal is somehow inhibited for psychological reasons."

The glow of delight in his eyes was replaced by an undercurrent of surprise as something surfaced of his genealogical training. "This condition of Sarah's *can* be relieved by working with a physician or therapist trained in treating sexual disorders of women. The physician or therapist may prescribe a series of treatments to be supplemented with exercises that are designed to teach a young woman to relax. I would personally rule out infections and diseases," he said softly.

"For chrissake, Doc, that may be the lifeline I need to save our relationship. I've walked around like a tightly wound coil, blaming myself, blaming Sarah." He shrugged, gesturing, *what can I do?*

"You're so well matched, that is, except for size. You're the biggest of the big and she is the smallest of the small. Curious." Doc laughed, trying to bring some levity into Abe's dark trauma. "A man's chemical attraction to a woman will forever be inexplicable. I hope you get the chance to make all this up to Sarah some day, Abe, for your sake and for hers."

Now driving through Lansing, Abe's shoulders sagged. "It doesn't seem likely. I can't get near her without Max around, and he's a madman. I worship the ground she walks on. I never wanted to hurt her," he added, looking away, his strong chin getting soft, "but I appreciate your advice." He felt better—a whole lot better—the disintegration of the hairball of all hairballs. Sharing his story equated to freedom.

They passed a sign that read, ANN ARBOR—63 MILES. The notice brought them from their particular immersion with each other back to the commonplace world.

"In about an hour and a half we'll be in Ann Arbor," Doc sighed with an end-of-the-day weariness. "It'll feel good to get out and stretch. It's hard to abide by this thirty-five-mile-an-hour speed limit."

CHAPTER TWENTY

The Michigan Stadium was warm and inviting. Lazy clouds of early September were superimposed against a sky so blue Abe figured he must have painted it himself with wild trumped-up colors. Tranquilized with the day, he rough-sketched the Michigan football team working out. In the back of his mind, he recorded the colors, activity and dimensions. He'd do a series of canvases—three of them, one for each term of his freshman year. Yes.

His thoughts had legs that wandered the length and breadth of Nahma as he had as a child, thanking God for all the beautiful people who had contributed to his being here. He'd give it his best shot. He'd had enough already of *Max referring to him as a schlemie*, enough already of the man's gelding criticism. The Bachelor of Fine Arts degree loomed distinctive and functional in his mind.

Holding his paintbrush idle for a moment, he rested his elbows on his knees, staring down at his feet. Among those nice people was Doc, with whom he'd had a terrific tour of the campus last spring. The heart of Central Campus social environment he found situated on the "Diag." This long walkway, diagonally slicing through a square block of University buildings, thrummed with students on their way to classes, throwing catch balls, campaigning for causes or lounging under the trees. "Loose Lips Sink Ships!" one placard read as a young Naval officer paraded up and down the Diag.

Impressive stood the Michigan Union where presidents actually came to speak. Abe felt a good measure of button-bustin' pride just being here. Imagine, actually having the opportunity to see and hear a president speak in person! Incredible! Plain old dumbass luck—him, Abednego Fabian Miereau walking the corridors of higher education. His appetite grew. As Doc would say, "It is no ordinree university."

From Central Campus he could walk to the Medical Center, which was adjacent to University Hospital. He could take a free maize and blue University bus to the south campus, where the Michigan Stadium stood and where he presently sat sketching.

"The University of Michigan consistently ranks among the very best universities in the country, and it's in the classroom where this excellence is particularly evident," he was told during orientation.

Abe developed a bad case of second thoughts. He didn't assume by any stretch of the imagination that he'd find any Mary Krutinas here who would provide private tutoring. The evidence surrounded him—thousands of students. Who would have time to further one little Indian in this sea of intelligence? The thought produced yet another mind-abrading doubt to play with.

Most students take four classes per term for a total of fourteen to sixteen credit hours. Classes range in size from fifteen students to large lectures for two hundred to five hundred students.

Abe couldn't complain about his classes: English Literature, Math, History of Art, and Comparative Studies.

The College of Literature, Science, and the Arts—LSA—has a mission. It includes developing intellectual attitudes and skills. The School of Arts is where students prepare for a career in the visual arts or in design.

Abe found himself restless with the odyssey of Orientation—kicked back.

The School offers the Bachelor of Fine Arts degree with concentrations in a multitude of things as well as art. Within all concentrations are opportunities to study applications of art and design, as well as the relationship of the visual arts to other academic disciplines.

You'll be interested to know that students at the University of Michigan represent diverse social, ethnic and economic backgrounds, originating from all forty-eight states and more than ninety-six foreign countries. Minorities registered are at nineteen percent. Because the kind of academic depth and personal growth achieved by our students is unique, Michigan graduates are prepared to assume leadership role.

Abe figured he'd been counted in the nineteen percent of minorities. He couldn't help but wonder if that number tallied academically explosive or just dawdled along, but his interest piqued at far less than a terrifying mystery.

"We've already received your enrollment deposit, or you wouldn't be here for orientation."

Abe sagged in his chair with the banal statement, but figured it must be a lead-in for another landscape. Since his deposit submitted last April, he swelled with the fact that he possessed the ability to pay for it himself. He could thank Max for his training in art for that, bastard that he was.

Freshman students who don't have their parents' permission to live off-campus are required to live in University housing.

Abe still couldn't believe the good fortune of living with Walter and Anne, Doc's brother. They offered to have him stay in their home for the entire academic year. They'd been so gracious—leaving for Florida soon. From 2871 Geddes Road, he would have to travel only trivial minutes from the campus. It was like living in a small town.

His mind floated to the pastoral setting of the brick, ranch-style home with white shutters and a wrought-iron safety door with the letter "W" meandering through the middle. A breezeway ran between the matching brick, two-car garage, also with white shutters, which stood only thirty feet from the house. A beautifully manicured lawn equal to half a football field crept out to Geddes Road, gently sloping and planted to intermittently staggered blue spruce. A patriotic flagpole stood near the large, fifty-foot spruce growing in the middle of the lawn.

❧

He allowed his mind to drift back to the graduation parties he'd attended last spring with Doc and Bernard Tobin. It warmed Abe to remember how welcome he'd felt at all the homes.

"Abe, I have an offer for you," Doc said after graduation, slapping him on the back while they milled around the yard at Jimmer Hruska's. "We'll fly down to Ann Arbor for your orientation in August, just you and me. Why the hell should anyone spend two days on the road for a one-day orientation? What say you?" Doc had that half-smile on his face, his thick eyebrows raised devilishly.

A Texas tornado formed in Abe's mind, sweeping everything in its path. "I'd say that's unbelievable. I've never flown before!"

"Okay. It'll do me good too. Nurse Quigley can hold down the fort for that short period," he spoke with his tongue-rolling English accent. "I'll visit with Walter while you go to orientation; however, we won't stay with Walter this time. We'll stay at the Allenal Hotel on the corner of Huron Street and Fourth Avenue, not far from the campus. Now that Eisenhower has invaded Normandy successfully, it looks as if you'll be able to enjoy your four years of college without military duty interrupting."

"Thanks, Doc. I'd like that a whole lot. Sometimes I think that it would have been an experience to see some active duty myself, but as it turns out, it'll be all over soon. I'll look forward to that trip with you." Abe's shoulders rose and fell, agitated with anticipation. Doc loomed the ultimate icon in his life, like a redwood on steroids.

"You know, Abe," Bernard Tobin contributed, standing at vertical disadvantage between the two big men, "We're all proud of your accomplishments of the past six years. Since Fabian died, we know life hasn't been easy for you, but you came through with unprecedented flying colors—colors between colors! Mary Krutina said that she doesn't regret one minute of the time she spent tutoring. She veritably lights up when she mentions it as if she baked the best spice cake in town!" Bernard's eyes twinkled with delight in passing on the message.

"I don't really know what I'd have done without you both," Abe replied shaking his head. "You've been Yin and Yang to me, offsetting all the bad times: the jackknife episode, Dad dying. You got me the job at the Company Store, leaned on Dave Phalen to buy those track pictures for the high school, and fed me a hundred meals. You made me feel okay about the Eddie trauma. I'll never forget it. It's thanks to you and your school system that I'm even going to college. I feel like a rogue rock that wandered into your education system, became polished and spun out. Kinda nutty, ay?" Abe blinked before a full smile infiltrated his face, shaking his head as an afterthought.

Bernard rapped him lightly on the shoulder with a folded hand. "Your contributions *ain't* too bad either, kid." Words of depth came too hard in regard to the young man who had found a way into his heart years ago.

Abe wondered if it were just the light, but Tobin's eyes were phenomenally blue; they matched the sky itself with such depth you could see the altruism in his soul.

"I need to share something with you since you have your diploma." Tobin sniffed, with a hitch to his shoulders. "I've wanted to enlist in the Navy for two years, but I was afraid that if I did you'd feel scuttled and wouldn't finish school."

"Well, I can't thank you enough for your supportiveness and for those two years you waited. I had no idea. You've always been there for me. I wasn't aware of your military bent." He stumbled over the words, taking a sip of the soirée punch to cover himself. "Sometimes my lips get overly excited and my tongue doesn't keep up," he said, humbling himself, flicking an apologetic glance at Tobin.

"I've bent all right. I leave July 12 for Milwaukee, where I'll be sworn in as a Lieutenant Junior Grade. My indoctrination courses will be at Fort Schuyler, New York in August. I'll never forget the great years that I've had in Nahma as superintendent and coach. You're a great athlete, Abe. Keep it up at college. I've never seen anyone run like you do. Remember, you have great leadership qualities too. People don't follow leaders with great titles; they follow leaders with courage, and you are strong in that category."

"Geez," Abe uttered in a queer, strained voice. He felt as if he were having an out-of-body experience in which he was looking down on himself and Tobin. "This town is sorely going to miss you." Abe nodded his head firmly. "I personally will miss seeing you and Mrs. Tobin, and having dinner at your house when I come home next summer. I feel like it's the bottom of the ninth, and the school system has struck out."

Bernard waxed reminiscent, at a loss for words. A moment such as this would never come again. Students as memorable as Abe were not plentiful, like the mosquitoes that were starting to relish him.

Abe recorded forever how thin Tobin's Irish skin was, the crinkles around his eyes as blue as topaz, and his veracity. He was one lucky pup to have had this man in his life. He hoped God would keep him in his tour of duty.

In Abe's heart, it grew late early. He quietly released a long breath as his shoulders flagged.

The graduation parties slowly faded as Abe brightened to the here-and-now. He sighed and watched the sun slant across the stadium. Still etching in the highlights of what he imagined to materialize, Abe took a double breath when he thought of Farley and Norrhea inviting him to their home after the graduation ceremonies for a "Special Moment."

"Norrhea and I are so proud of you, son, very proud." Farley greeted Abe at the door, after searching the road for a half hour as he awaited his arrival. "Sit down, sit down, Abe. Norrhea will get us a beer. This is a special day, very special. I don't have to tell you that you're one of the few Indians that ever graduated from Nahma High School." Farley eased himself onto the couch near Abe, sitting restlessly on the edge of the cushions.

"Our Sioux Nation has lost so much of its pride since the Whiteman took our land from us, except for Agency and Reservation areas. Nonetheless, you, son, are going places. This is a big break, getting that Art Scholarship to Michigan, and even being *considered* for a one-year deferment from the Delta County Draft Board. Don't *blow* it. Don't mess up with being seduced into parties and extra-curricular activities that one finds on big campuses. Keep your eye on the sparrow and your objectives in focus." Farley stretched his arm up along the back of the couch and with the other hand accepted a cold Schlitz from Norrhea.

"Thanks, Norrhea," Abe said, wrapping his big hand around the brown bottle. "Yeah, I know I'll have to be *plenty* in focus. The class load will be heavy, but thanks for the encouraging words. If I don't get my deferment again next year, I'll join the Navy. I don't think I want any part of the Army after what Dad went through—freezing in fox holes in the First World War."

"We'll always be here for you, Abe, no matter what you decide to do." Farley's hands folded around his beer and dangled it between his spread knees. "Of course, our fondest wish is for you to be able to stay in college, but many other young men would desire that too. Our country is going through terrible times right now with this damn war.

"Norrhea and I don't want you to have to work even *part* time while you're in school, so we have a financial security gift for you. It's an entitlement from your Sioux heritage and has been handed down to me by my mother, your great-great grandmother, the wife of Crazy Horse. And here's some advice handed down by me. There are three great powers: learning, money and success. Bet on those and let it ride." Rising, he opened a drawer in the end table and pulled out a soft, tan-colored suede pouch with rawhide strings woven through loops cut into the top. Bright blue, red, yellow and orange beads intricately stitched onto the bag hugged together below the drawstring. Moving to Abe, Farley held the tautly hanging pouch, his hand trembling so that he nearly dropped it, giving Abe an even deeper bond with his grandfather.

After hanging on every word from Farley, Abe held the amazing piece of leather art, glancing quizzically up into Farley's eyes. Slowly, he loosened the rawhide string, slipping it smoothly through the loops, thoroughly reminiscent of the beans that Jack traded for the family cow. There lay a myriad of gold nuggets. G*old nuggets*! Large, small, round, every geometric shape under God's sun.

"Whahh, what, what is this?" Abe breathed out in a belly whisper.

"That's gold from the Black Hills in South Dakota. There may be mineral deposits on some of them because of the raw quality of the ore. The pieces that are polished are those that were stolen from prospectors during Indian raids. My mother carried many of these pouches tied under her Indian robes as she was driven from one agency to another before she was killed at Wounded Knee. What remained, I brought to Michigan with me." Farley remained standing in front of Abe, studying his reaction, bursting with pride in this young man, and in his own ability to provide him with this perfect present— an ancestral cultural gift. Raw gold could never be devalued in terms of scarcity, as well as *wow* value.

Crossing his arms over his chest, Farley sighed. "I presented gold to Suki when she married. Whether she shared it with Fabian, we'll never know, unless she shows up again." A complacent smile spread over his face at his daughter's circumspection.

"My God, Farley! There must be ten, twelve ounces of gold in here. It'll be a nest egg for all four years. This is so unanticipated. You've already done so much, taking me in, consoling me, getting me through the post-Fabian days and the post-Eddie days, cooking meals and encouraging me to run to town instead of walking to train for the track team. You urged me to run on the beach in the sand, barefoot, in the evenings and let the wind blow through my hair—to watch the waves roll in and the sea gulls coast on the air currents for a back-to-nature trip. It produced my very own vision quest. I got a grip on my life, changing it dramatically. I'm so beholden to you both," Abe said, unable to go on, his breath catching hot in his throat.

"Hey, big guy, what's family for?" Farley returned to sit near Abe, placing an arm around his shoulder in a celebratory embrace. "I have a thousand regrets about not being closer to you in your youthful years, but Fabian never promoted our presence. He proved to be the power broker of your time and energies." Farley sank back into the couch becoming more comfortable now that Abe had been presented his prize.

"On balance, gold retains and gains in its value, being presently traded at thirty-seven dollars an ounce. There must be somewhere between three hundred and seventy and four hundred and forty-four dollars worth of gold in that bag. Considering of the average household income of thirty dollars a week, what you have there is approximately fifteen weeks worth of the working man's wages. That should see you through the thick and thin of any pinches you may run into. What you need to do with it is take it to the Delta County Assay Office in Escanaba. There they'll analyze the value and notify the bank of your choice. You then take the bag of gold to that bank and they'll convert the amount to paper money for you.

"It's illegal to hold gold right now. It's been legislated that citizens must convert it to legal tender of the USA. Gold is to our nation's financial engine what religion is to the redeeming engine to heaven. Before 1933 you could present paper money at a bank and exchange it for pure gold, because every dollar was backed by gold reserve. Since that time, however, it has come under the Precious Metal Act and must be converted according to law. But I'm not about to bend to every whim of legislation and turn in all my gold." Farley chuckled richly. "It's mine."

Abe stared in awe at the dazzling divulgence, which now rested in his care. His! He'd gone from a struggling student to King Tut in thirty seconds.

"I'm aware that you have your savings in a Bay de Nocquet Lumber

Company savings account. That's fine. They pay comparable interest to other banking fraternities and give you life insurance double your investment as an incentive." Farley was relieved to have passed on the gold heritage, doing what was expected of him as a grandfather in the architecture of the Whiteman's social system.

"Remember, Abe, the three great powers in life are the same today as they were yesterday and will be forever: learning, money and success. I know that I may sound repetitious, but never stop striving for all three."

"We'd like you to feel welcome to stay with us on your break time from school instead of opening your home at the beach in Nahma. What a hassle that would be. You might want to do that for the summers, but break times are simply too short."

"I'd like that. Yes I would, and don't be surprised if I take you up on that offer. Yes, that sounds good to me." One thing Abe acknowledged was the reluctance to come home for a week or two and walk into a cold, unreceptive house in the middle of the winter. This plan sounded much better. *How lucky can a guy get?* The appreciation radiated from his eyes. "That'll work."

He'd forever hold dear the lasting pleasures of that memorable day.

༺༻

As the sun dipped behind the bleachers on the west side of the stadium, Abe folded his easel and rolled his brushes in gauze strips; he'd clean and tip them when he arrived home. The previously raucous sounds of the football players were ebbing as the players and player-wannabees jostled their way back to the locker rooms.

Reflective and yet mesmerized by the late afternoon sun from the stadium, Abe lulled himself with the camaraderie of the night that he and Doc had flown to Ann Arbor. He tipped the *maitre d'hôtel* for a quiet table. Their dinner served up delicious—a banquet of exquisitely prepared food accompanied throughout by vintage wine. While Doc enjoyed Lake Michigan white fish, Abe devoured a sizzling Porterhouse steak.

"May I bring you gentlemen something from the bar before dinner?" the unobtrusive waiter asked, smiling broadly.

Doc nodded. "Yes, it's been a long day; you certainly can. We'll each have a Brandy Old Fashioned as our aperitif." Doc smoothed his heavy mustache with his forefinger, leaning back and relaxing in the button-back soft leather chairs.

"Very good, sir. It'll be just a few moments. In the meantime, perhaps you would care to look at the menu and study the wine list." The waiter moved away as silently as a vapor.

"*Saluté,*" Doc said when the drinks arrived, his diamond-studded cuff links reaching out of his suit sleeves, coarse hair creeping onto the back of his hands.

"What was the name of that drink, Doc?"

"Brandy Old Fashioned." He smiled amusedly, his jaw slightly offset.

"My eyeballs feel like a Mickey Mouse clock," Abe chortled. "I can't handle too many of those. In fact, I think my new haircut just got singed!" The setting, grandiose and imposing, and Abe, in his new charcoal sport coat and gray trousers worn only for the second time, left him feeling out of his element.

As fine cosmetic retailers and clerks in better men's stores, wine stewards are the handmaidens of the elite, their nostrils flaring and clamping, they eternally lean on the unlearned, knocking them off their center of gravity, but not Doc.

"I'll have Bordeaux Sauternes and my friend will have Bordeaux Beaujolais. Please bring us each a bottle to sample," Doc said, his English accent purveying the ambiance, the sheer size of him commanding.

"What the hell is *Bordeaux,*" Abe whispered as the wine steward backed off into the midst of the diners.

"Bordeaux is a city in southwest France on the Garonne River with accessibility to the Atlantic—a region of exceptionally fine grape arbors. Their wine production is noted as commendable all over the world," Doc advised good-naturedly.

Flying this young man to Ann Arbor for orientation seemed like the best idea he'd had since getting married, and that had occurred a helluva long time ago—twenty-four years. Watching Abe exhilarated him, giving him a soaring sense of potency and youth. He couldn't believe how he'd grown to love this young man in the past five years or so.

"Fabian and I never had wine in the house. I can't even imagine being a connoisseur of a wine line." Abe felt himself shrinking into his chair.

He had never dined like this in his whole life where there were waiters right out of movie land—waiters in crimson bolero jackets and black trousers with black silk stripes running down the length of the outside seam, stiff white shirts and spotless white serving towels hanging handily over their arms. Accoutrements Abe had never seen surrounded him. Abe couldn't take his eyes off the elegance and affluence of the clientele. He felt rather like a doughnut hole in a French pastry shop.

Doc observed Abe's uneasiness. "Just relax, Abe. There's no one in this room that's any better than you are. Just remember that, and you'll always be comfortable. Don't let anyone intimidate you. You're a fine person, and that's to say nothing of your fine looks." Doc cleared his throat on the last gambit, grinning proudly for emphasis.

He reminded himself that somehow, Doc's lips always looked wet when he smiled. He had such great features and the most uncanny characteristics, similar to Abe's. However, Doc stood taller than Abe, had a British accent and dark, suave good looks that he would never achieve.

Abe smiled uneasily, hoping that it would relieve the sudden tension that wrapped his body. "I didn't know I was that obvious." He straightened his diagonal-striped blue, silver and gray tie and leaned back.

In a walnut humidor carried on a silver tray, the waiter brought Doc a Cuban Roitan. Doc bit off the end of the cigar, lit it and asked, "Have you seen Sarah at all this summer?" The words coming out in between quick puffs, he laid the lighted cigar into the gold rococo ashtray provided by the attentive waiter.

"No. She's not even around town. Max sent her off to Minocqua again for a restful summer with her cheesehead friend from Wisconsin. He wants her to meet the *right* people. This fall she enters Mount Mary College in Milwaukee. But if he thinks distance can keep us apart, he's mistaken. I'm going to marry her some day, whether Max approves or not." Abe sat back, folding his hands in his lap.

Doc cocked his head to one side. "When she comes home this summer to prepare for a new school year, try to get a few minutes to talk to her. Give her space and give her time. She's very adolescent and naïve. Max and Ma have sheltered her—in spades. Nonetheless, somewhere between the end of the sidewalk and the start of the asphalt she'll fall into step with your desires."

"You might suggest to her, however, that she *can* have treatments for her problem. She needs deep psychological analysis as well as an exercise regimen. Historically, you know you're good for each other." Doc blew blue curling smoke into the air, turning his head upwards to avoid the murk of misinterpretation between their facial geographies.

The wine settled Abe down to the intimacy of a private conversation. He no longer reacted to the atmosphere around him. "If for no other reason, I'll be successful at this university just to show Max that I'm a worthwhile candidate to be considered for her husband." His jaw hardened, the muscles in his temples flexing.

Doc studied this handsome young man for a moment—impulsive, master of his soul, brutal, in charge. *Yes, I believe every word he's saying. He's capable of just about anything, he's proven that. I hope college will polish him somewhat and remove the knee-jerk-decisions.*

Doc knocked the ashes off his cigar, twirling it around the end lightly, the tobacco glowing bright red. "The treatments aren't all that painful, mentally or physically. There are four of them. With some luck, I may be able to complete them in the time frame of Christmas break and Easter vacation." Doc folded his hands together, resting his elbows on the table, the cigar extending from the first two fingers of his right hand.

"You think so?" Abe showed enthusiasm. "But what if she refuses?"

"She'll think about it. At least plant the seed. It may take a little mulling."

"It's going to be a tough topic to approach, but I'll give it a full court press."

"I'd do the psychological analysis first, then the exercise regimen," Doc contemplated. "She has had some trauma in her life...not only from Old John Pedo as it turns out, but from you, too, inadvertent as it was." Doc smiled at Abe. "You need to treat this problem with gentleness, without bogging down in your Sioux philosophies."

The crazy kid seemed capable of anything. He'd need to stay on top of Abe's lifestyle to get him through the next four years.

∽∾

Abe slid back to reality as he swung into the long driveway of the Walter Whittaker home on Geddes Road. It hit him again—the grandeur of this peaceful setting, as opposed to his four-room home near the beach in Nahma. Small as it was, it was his, and he reminisced on his remorse at departing.

The car packed, the electricity and water turned off and the drapes pulled in the living room, he picked up his jacket, tossed it over his shoulder and stood with one hand on the kitchen doorknob. Surveying his little kingdom, he recorded: Fabian's favorite chair abandoned now for more than two years, the double north windows where he'd been laid out for the wake. The strong morning light permeated the closed drapes, sending beams of dancing motes in a long column to the floor. The silence surrounded him like a fog. Suddenly, a gust of a wind whipped up, shaking the screen door, beckoning Abe like Captain Ahab riding the ropes on Moby Dick, telling him it was time—time to leave. He was about to embark on a new leg of his life. He needed to close this door to open a new one—his future.

He felt comfort in his hometown. The main street gave him a smiling declaration. The Company Store flowed with humanity of the town, remarking on the weather and the newest batch of puppies. The school, as always, hung out a notice of starting dates in September. The Company Office continued to drift with paycheck patrons lending solace and nurturing to those in need, such as his own needs, had been met; the Company Hospital stood as a beacon of salvation. The undercurrents in a small town are what surprises and eventually hangs out at the Clubhouse as "Did-you-knows?"

But how could he forget the threads of his life here, woven into such a security blanket? Starting school with Sarah and the warm days and nights spent at the beach with her. Hailing shouts over the fence for nineteen years. Learning to paint and to drive. Stealing the jackknife. Getting the same knife for his seventeenth birthday. The long frosty walks from home to the school, store, and back. From out of nowhere came the dancing sound of Fabian's coffee pot perking slowly on the range—the smell that woke him on cold mornings.

Tapping on his mind came that nasty night, finding Fabian near death. He took a deep breath with the plunging pain of remembering the all-night vigil at the hospital, counting down to his last breath.

An electrical thrill sped through him, visualizing his first encounter with sex and Sarah, right here in his home. God, he missed her so much. Max leaped back into his mind and landed on both feet. Max had seen to it that she never returned to town this past summer. Abe would never shake the injustices and verbal bruising he'd suffered at his hands. He was an asshole from the word go, to the word stop and in between.

Nonetheless, this would always be home. Shaking his head to throw off the cobwebs of memories, he stepped outside into the clear August morning. In the east lay a low streak of early morning haze. The rest of his life lay ahead of him. Slowly, he closed the door and heard the lock click, closing off this part of his life. His footsteps on the wooden planks of the back porch echoed hollowly in his ears. Slowly, he descended the three steps to the driveway and to his waiting car. He sighed deeply. Leaving, he talked fast to his head not to turn, not to look back. Now he knew how Lot felt upon leaving Sodom and Gomorrah.

He'd come back again next summer. Had to have his summer job, sell his summer paintings and see Sarah again. He'd come back home to Nahma, home of the Upper Peninsula Art School, silver beaches, soaring sea birds, a model lumbering village, caring people and a summer wonderland.

CHAPTER TWENTY-ONE

The next day Abe again perched on a bleacher seat on the east side of the Michigan Stadium. His canvas and easel set up, he caught the same angle of the sun, the same routines, and the same brouhaha from the eager student players. Drifting conversations indicated there would be team cuts soon.

"Watch where you're going, Honky," echoed up to him.

"Watch it yourself, Boogie," flipped back the fresh retort.

A scuffle ensued.

Abe spotted a tall Mr. Touchdown stride quickly out to the melee. "You—and you!" He pointed to the two contenders. "Off the field and into the showers. I don't need your ilk out here for practice or for keeps. Out! Out! Out!"

Whah! This guy doesn't monkey around.

Abe continued sketching, trying to ignore the two humbled students as they headed for the lockers.

"Hey you!" he heard the same man hollering again.

That guy had a bad case of the grumpies today. Abe continued painting.

"Hey you…kid!" The voice got closer. Abe's eyes jerked up—saw the same clamorous man ascending the bleachers, bigger up-close, like a giant.

"Who, me?" Abe asked, pausing with his paintbrush in mid-air. His stomach did a somersault. He hoped to look calm at best, comfortable at the least.

"Yeah, you! Who gave you permission to be here during practice?" Grimness thinned his mouth, his tone woody, his lime-green eyes assessing.

Having the validity of his presence questioned by this powerful person was a scrotum shrinker. "Well…" Abe choked. *"Don't let anyone intimidate you…you're as good as anyone else,"* rolled around in his head. Swallowing, Abe plunged in. "I'm doing a three-picture series of the football team for art class." Stopped in his project, Abe's glance rested squarely on this impressive man.

"It'd sure be nice if your art instructor let me know when he's sending a student to my turf. Let me see what you have. My name is Kyle Kreiler," he said, offering his hand. "I'm the football coach here. And who am I talking to?"

"My name is...is...is Abe Miereau. Pleased to meet you, sir, er, Mr. Kreiler," Abe said, standing, the words coming out strong and sincere, surprising himself.

"Likewise, I'm sure," Kreiler said, still shaking Abe's hand cordially. "Hmmph. Doesn't look like much yet, does it? I mean, the picture is rather etchy sketchy, wouldn't you say?" Kreiler paused, his eyes switching quickly from the canvas to Abe as if he had second thoughts, wishing he had searched for better words.

"Yes. It is. But I do all my finish work at home. You see, I have what I've been told is an eidetic memory, so I don't have to be on the scene to complete a work, but I do need some actual happenings, tone and light shadings to record." If Abe was blown away by Kreiler's "etchy-sketchy" remark, he didn't show it.

"Interesting. I'll want to see this series when it's completed. Yes, indeed. Well, carry on, young man." Kreiler moved to the aisle from the stadium seats.

"Thank you. Pleased to have met you." Abe remained standing.

"Same here, err, ahh, it was Abe, wasn't it? Abe..." He raised two golden, sun-kissed eyebrows.

"Oh, it's a nickname that my father dubbed me with when I was just a little tyke." Abe smiled his warm and open smile.

"But what's your given name? I'll bet it's something splendid such as Abraham, Abner or Abel." Two steps down the bleachers, Kreiler paused, turning around.

"Well, no. It's not a special name; that's why I'd just as soon be called Abe."

Kreiler waited expectantly.

What the hell, Abe thought. *I'll probably never talk to him again.* "It's...it's..." he said, embarrassed. "It's Abednego," he murmured, his tone candid.

Kreiler, breaking out in a deep amused chuckle, walked back up the two steps to Abe and clasped him on the shoulder, instantly disarmed by Abe's candor. "Son, if my name were Abednego Miereau, I'd want to stick to Abe too. Forget I asked."

Son of a gun, the guy turned out to be a nice guy after all. Big, sure. Good looking—fine features, sand-colored hair that curled. Abe wished he had a big "M" sweatshirt like Kreiler's. Probably came with the territory. He'd bet the price of a picture that it had a price tag of a hundred bucks—probably a pint of blood too.

Abe found everything expensive at the university. He couldn't complain. His tuition was fulfilled by the scholarship, which was a Godsend. His books had been a whopping twenty-four dollars! Spense!

Arriving home on Geddes Road, he rang the Ann Arbor long distance operator and put through a person-to-person call to Mount Mary College in Milwaukee for Sarah Savin.

Abe heard the circuits clicking. His insides were a series of knots as he anticipated hearing Sarah's velvet voice. Crackle, hollow conch-shell sounds. Crackle.

"Hello. This is Sarah."

"Sarah! This is Abe. How are ya?" His whole being was suddenly transfused.

"Oh Abe, it's so good to hear your voice. Is everything okay?"

"Yeah, sure. I've missed you since I didn't get to see anything of you this summer." Abe's heart squeezed hard in the admission.

"It's Max. He figures that if you're out of sight you're out of mind. But you're not, Abe. I think of you every day."

"I can't' tell you how glad I am to hear that, Sarah. Will you still marry me some day?" Abe could never shake the angst and uncertainty involved with that question.

"Yes, of course. My *good spirit* longs for the peace I've known with you and screeches with the turmoil. I'm so glad you called."

A warm glow enveloped him with the promise of marriage and the renewed interest she showed.

"Things just shouldn't be this way for us. I feel as if someone has cut my umbilical cord."

"Speaking of umbilical cords, Sarah, I hope you don't mind, but I confided in Doc Whittaker about your problem of being unable to accommodate er, ah, sexual fulfillment." Abe fought to keep his tone casual, but angst seeped through like a spreading leak in a sun porch ceiling. "He said that he could help you." A small smile developed slowly. "Think it over. Doc figured he could start treatments over Christmas break and finish them during Easter break."

Sarah could hear Abe's sharp intake of breath. "I could, but I get so uptight about it. I'll need more information. Anyway, my phone time is up, so I'll get back to you."

"I love you, Sarah. Don't ever forget that."
"I love you too. Take care. Study hard. Get lots of rest. Bye."
"Bye...talk to you later."

She floated before him like a mirage, her long willowy legs and her dark brown hair that curled around the temples and brushed her shoulders when she moved. Her eyes! Her deep-brown eyes that slanted just a little on the outside, and lashes so long they held snowflakes. Her smile, so radiant.

Sometimes his memory of people leaked like a colander, but Sarah's presence hugged him like a snug mitten. He swallowed hard. "Goddamn Max—bastard!" he said, his voice hoarse. The void of her absence bit like a Siberian Express.

※

In the windless afternoon, not a twig stirred. A warm sun broke through the clouds, and above the Michigan stadium, they drifted like lazy fuzz balls. After a long weekend, Abe again decorated the bleachers, trying to capture the distance of the west side of the stadium—giving it an out-of-focus treatment. His concentration on this first canvas was the line of scrimmage. He identified that from the book Sarah had given to him on his seventeenth birthday.

It's the perfect place to start, he thought—an even playing field, symmetrically correct. It was an orderly world for a few moments before the field became chaotic with a panorama of figures moving aimlessly without any system or organization. *Well, that is until I see someone coming out of the backfield, running like hell with the ball!*

"How ya doing today, kid?" Coach Kreiler had crept up on him while he floated in one of his bubbles.

"Fine, just fine, thanks, Coach. You don't mind if I call you 'Coach,' do you?" Abe again was impressed by this man's carriage and demeanor.

"I'd be surprised if you called me anything else, even though there have been some choice words used in lieu of my name." Kreiler laughed, his eyes twinkling. "You have nice hands, son—big, nice fingers. Ever play football?"

"No. I never have. My hometown is too small, never had a football team."
"Where from?"
"Nahma, Michigan."
"Where the hell is Nahma, Michigan?"
"Well it's near Escanaba and Gladstone."
"Way up north, eh? I know the athletic director in Escanaba, Andy Pinal. Ever meet him?" Kreiler stood, his arms folded across his chest, his bottle green eyes riveting.

"Yes, our Upper Peninsula Track Meets were held in Escanaba, and Andy Pinal is the head honcho there."

"How'd you do in track while you were in high school?"

"Pretty good. I used to run a lot. Still do whenever I'm home...run on the beach. My last year in high school I helped coach the track team because I was too old to participate anymore."

"How old *are* you?" Kreiler put both hands on the stadium seat in front of him, leaning, ostensibly preoccupied with Abe's progress on the picture.

"I'm almost twenty years old now. Because of learning disabilities, I was held back in the seventh grade." Abe looked directly at the coach, lifting and then relaxing his shoulders. Memories of those years were still as painful as a double-blade sword.

Kreiler sat back, whistling his surprise. "You sure don't impress me as a learning disability student. How the hell did you ever get into the University of Michigan?"

"They have a special program for talented students with a 'C' average. I had a couple of teachers who helped tutor me over the hump. I showed some skill at painting, and here I am. Just lucky, I guess."

Coach Kreiler studied Abe, with arched eyebrows. "I'm familiar with the Special Admissions Program. We use it for athletes too. We allow twenty-five scholarships a year for the football program. Sometimes we need to bend on admissions, at least in premier universities like Michigan, to recruit topflight athletes. Well, it's too bad you didn't play any football. I'll bet that you'd have been plenty good. Play basketball? Baseball?"

Abe nodded. "Both. Liked them a lot."

"Figures. Well. Gotta go," Kreiler said, slapping his knees before he rose. "No one gave me a scholarship for excellence in art work, so I have to get out there and kick ass until I get a team in shape for the opening game in less than two weeks. See ya later." Patting Abe on the shoulder, a smile warmed his eyes.

No further questions were asked. That day.

༄༅

The sun sneaked slowly out of an innocent cloud and played tricks with autumnal colors, dazzling the eye. *Click.* In the stadium, Abe again captured the moment in his mind as work progressed on his canvases.

The first Michigan football game was scheduled for September 14; the fifty allowable players jelled in place. It was already the first part of September and Krieler was yet working with underclassmen, seniors, seasoned players and the freshmen wannabees. Because of the war, freshmen were allowed to play football this year. Abe had watched as the fifty players were divided into an offensive first string and a defensive first string, involving twenty-two players. They, as well as others likely to see significant playing time, wore Michigan-blue jerseys. Of these, the offense wore light blue jerseys; the defense wore dark blue jerseys.

Second-teamers wore maize, the offense light maize, and the defense dark maize.

Third-teamers were stuck with maroon. Those in disfavor were stuck with white.

His second canvas would be a defense pileup of blues.

A touchdown spiking churned in his mind as the third picture.

Glad he got that off his mind. One thing Abe prided himself on was that he learned from his mistakes, some tougher than others. Decision-making grew easier for him every week.

"The Line Of Scrimmage" canvas would be on a bright sunny September day. "The Futility," the defensive pileup, would be in mid-October. Perhaps he should do this in raucous primary colors: bright blues, reds and yellows to offset the overcast sky. "The Spiking" would highlight the Thanksgiving game. However, he still had only his first canvas drawn and quartered.

Mid-September had slid into place by the time Abe measured all three pictures in his mind and featured ghostly onto the framed canvases. The mumble-jumble of the second picture, with the pile of cordwood players imprinted, sat in his mind in a vapor. Should he make it surreal or realistic? Leaning toward the canvas, he concentrated.

A shadow flowed over him, and again he had a surprise visit from Coach Kreiler.

"Well, kid, how's it coming? I hope that after having you in the bleachers for a month that you aren't going to leave and enroll at Notre Dame. I'd lose my britches on what you've observed here." A smile pushed its way to full-blown.

Abe laughed heartily at the preposterousness of the thought. "Have no fear. I don't even know where Notre Dame is. You're talking to the candidate least likely to disappear." Abe couldn't help but feel that somewhere underneath these visits by Kreiler there hid more than justifiable concern over his team workouts. Imagine, such a busy guy taking time to talk to a nobody freshman!

Kreiler examined the outline of the defensive coup. "That's a good choice for one of your pictures; it's the one that people carry around in their minds.

"I came up here to ask you if you'd do me a favor. I've had to juggle players on the offense because of pre-season injuries, so I wonder if you'd catch laterals for one of the new quarterbacks, Bruce Hulk. Just stand on the sidelines and catch some spirals he'll throw downfield. They'll be twenty to thirty-yard passes. You'll need to return them. Have you ever thrown a football?" Kreiler eyes evaluated, always appraising.

Abe's heartbeat quickened. "Yes, sure, we used to throw footballs as part of coordination drills and exercise. If you figure that Bruce will settle for a greenhorn, that's fine with me. I'll just leave my art materials here until after practice." A flicker of fear mingled with the yearning Abe felt to participate.

On the field Abe met a player dressed in a Michigan dark blue jersey who stepped forward and introduced himself. "Hi, I'm Bruce Hulk." He had thick dark-colored hair and an even darker complexion. He flexed with a solid build that was not obtained by spending his Saturday afternoons piloting an armchair.

Smack. Abe caught the lateral. His first return went wild and off-line. Hulk retrieved it, leaping high inside the playing field.

Thud. Abe's long fingers coiled around the ball confidently and securely. His return spiraled closer to his objective this time, but still not in the direct line of the receiving Hulk, a freshman like himself.

Hulk ran over, whispered some tips on how to spin the ball so it had more direction. Being a quick study, Abe had the pigskin sailing back and forth readily, losing no practice time for the brilliant arm of Hulk.

Trying to stay unobtrusive, Coach Kreiler watched the two of them work out, instructing his assistant, Jim Funt, to do the same. "What do you think, Jim? Willing to do some grooming and training?" The words were tautly whispered to the assistant coach, a fireplug of a man, who knew chapter and verse of football—lived on football. "So far so good—good direction, good arm and good attitude. Let's do it."

Kreiler rubbed his chin, the line of his mouth relaxing. "Well, now I'll tell you that I called the athletic director at Escanaba High School, a guy by the name of Pinal, where this young man competed in high school track meets. Says the kid is a natural. Ran the mile in 4.6 minutes. He's like the wind. Name's Abe. *He* never told me this, but Pinal says he's half Sioux Indian and half French. Can you believe that he's the great-great grandson of Crazy Horse?"

"No shit!" Funt met the amused eyes of Kreiler.

"Abe never told me *that*, either. He's pretty much reticent and mostly answers only what you ask him." He returned to rubbing his chin again, this time adding some squeezes. "Maybe I need a lobotomy to get this rambunctious over an unknown, but nothing ventured, nothing gained…"

Funt could feel the excitement building in Kreiler. "We could try him for offense as a running back. I'd say he's six feet two or three, weighs roughly two hundred pounds. He stood with his legs at ease like a sumo wrestler. "Let's do it."

Abe saw Kreiler approaching him on the sidelines at a fast pace. He probably wanted Abe to knock off the practice with Hulk. He's seen enough mistakes for one day.

Kreiler gave Hulk a palm up *stop* motion. "Okay, Hulk. That's enough for now. See you out here tomorrow."

"Right, Coach. See ya later, Abe." Bruce waved in camaraderie as he ran off.

"You, Miereau, come over here a minute," Kreiler motioned, and then stuck his hands in his front pants pockets, hunching his shoulders as if he'd caught a sudden chill.

"Look Abe, do you think you could work out with the team every day after school for a couple of hours? Jim Funt and I think there's potential in your style. We're willing to spend some time with you." Again, Kreiler stood eye-to-eye with Abe, unflinching.

"You mean it? Never ever thought…maybe I can. I'd have to paint at home at night, but I hoped for the chance to participate in sports again." Abe, clad in a pair of shorts and polo shirt on the football field, felt incompatible talking team.

"Hell, you can do it. We'll suit you up in a maroon jersey, of course, as a beginner, but if you develop as I anticipate, you'll be wearing the light blue jersey soon."

"Okay, I'll give it my best effort!" Abe felt the scorching thrill of excitement churning in his stomach.

"I just know you will, son. I just know you will. I can feel it in my bones," Kreiler said, smiling at Abe, one hand coming up and clasping Abe's shoulder.

Although the dressing room at Yost Field House felt a privileged sanctuary, it had nothing but wooden two-by-fours bolted to the wall with intermittent nails sticking out. The nails were the lockers. A player's locker number was also his seat number in the team meeting room, which, with its rising rows of wooden seats, resembled a small lecture hall. For Abe's first pre-game lecture, the players sat waiting expectantly for the arrival of Kyle Kreiler and Jim Funt. Voices were lowered. Unrest pervaded the room.

The door opened and Kreiler entered. Not came in—He *entered!* Wearing a no-nonsense aura, his stride suggested someone forever bucking a powerful wind.

On the dais, he positioned himself behind the podium. "All right, guys. Now's the time to stop talking about the gaggle of girls and how many of them are gravitating toward you. It's time to take stock of why you're here, and who you represent."

"The first game of the season is against Vanderbilt, a school of traditions. We have traditions here at Michigan too. Tradition is something you can't bottle. You can't buy it at a quick stop, but it's there to sustain you. I've called upon it frequently and so have countless other Michigan athletes and coaches. There is nothing like it."

Was this the same man who had talked to him like an old daddy? He was spellbinding, knowledgeable—tough. *Fabian would have called him a 'straight shooter.'*

"One of our traditions is winning. *Winning!*" He pounded his fist on the podium. "I've never understood those who criticize winning. What should we play for—second place, fourth, sixth? I always hope that I am a gracious loser and have always instructed my team to be the same, but I also have the determination that the next time we meet, by God, *I* will be the *victor!*" Kyle's icy eyes browsed the team.

"You know what I want to see out on the field Saturday? I want winners. I want only young men who give thirty-six inches to the yard and thirty-two quarts to the bushel. I want young men who aspire to the possibility of becoming pro-football players. Do you know that only one in twelve thousand college grads become a pro-football player?"

Deadly silence. All eyes faced straight ahead. Ears strained now.

"You! You men!" He bellowed in a stage shout. "You are the chosen fifty. You enjoy a brother-brother relationship as well as the bruises, the pain, the mud, the pulled muscles, the chalk talks, the long hours. They're all worth it. Every minute you spend in this effort pays off. It pays off in character building, in dedication to something bigger than your own behinds.

"When you're part of a squad, you're better than you ever could be alone. The strength of the pack is the predator and the strength of the predator is the pack. That is the law of competitive sports. And don't you ever forget it. We all rely on each other for a finished product—*winning!*" Again he hit the podium in the silent meeting room. The players visibly jumped out of their intense mesmerization.

"None of you should be carrying more than twelve credit hours. Tops.

Each term. That amounts to three hours a day at the most in class. Even if you give me eight hours for football, that leaves thirteen hours. Sleep takes eight of those hours, so that leaves five free. It's entirely up to you what you do with those five free hours, but remember, the rest of the time belongs to academics and me. If that doesn't suit your fancy, you can just as well move on right now." Kreiler scanned his crew, making eye contact.

Abe figured the guy couldn't get any plainer than that.

"If football were like the educational system, with a credit given for every hour spent in class and in practice/labs during the week, it would meet the criteria of about a twenty-five credit hour course in the fall and spring terms. With the academic freight for most terms at twelve credit hours, a football player carries something like a thirty-seven credit hour encumbrance. But you can do it. Place your priorities. Just make up your mind who you're serving. You're not living with your mama and your daddy anymore. All decisions are yours. All mistakes are yours. All successes will be yours as well."

Abe sure as hell hoped he could live up to whatever this guy thought "success" meant. He had his faults, but stupid wasn't one of them. Successes, he liked.

"Another thing. I don't want any showboating out there when you make a touchdown or a good tackle. If it's done spontaneously, it *floats*, but if it's a grandiose gesture of being on-stage, it *gloats*. Forewarned is forearmed, and I don't want to have to expect the unexpected."

All fifty players felt the cold challenge of his intense eyes.

"I'm going to continue employing the platoon system this year. Each time the Michigan offense punts the ball away, only one man—a designated running back—will remain on the field. Ten players, better suited to play defense, then will join him."

It sounded like a good idea to Abe, even if it only meant that they'd get fresh horses for offense and defense.

"We'll start that with the Army game, which we play next week. Because of the war, we'll play both Army and Navy this year. "

"Another thing we'll need to contend with this year, as usual, is bigotry and anti-Semitism. I will not tolerate it on this team. Every Southern and Southwestern Associated Press voter objects to color—that is, black players. We have twelve black players that remain on the team after our roster cuts. We initially had eighteen. They're welcome here. They're outstanding athletes. The big schools down South have always closed their doors to blacks, and refused even to schedule any team that played blacks. We'll cling to our Northern principles here at Michigan. Do not bend them one iota.

"Speaking of minorities, I want all of you to meet Abe Miereau," he said, lowering his arm toward the freshmen front row. "*He* never told me this, but I am informed by a good friend of mine that Abe is half Sioux Indian and the great-great grandson of Crazy Horse, the Oglala Chief of the Great Plains wars. He shows tremendous promise, and will serve the team's best interests very well. Stand up, Abe, so everyone knows who you are."

Abe, sitting in the front row next to Bruce Hulk, slowly and reluctantly rose. Bruce jumped up, took Abe's hand and raised it into the air in a victory sign as if he were Two Ton Tony Gallento.

The upper classmen booed good-naturedly. Abe laughed, his wide honest smile beaming up at the rest of the team.

"Okay, guys, settle down," Kreiler interjected, waving his arm.

"We're going to continue to work. Work harder. Work harder than that.

"You'll find that nothing motivates you like your own failure. Nothing. No player is worth fifteen yards for a mistake. If it's mistakes we're talking about, I want my players to be afraid. If it's a violation of team rules, I want them to be petrified.

"All of you are sitting here because you were chosen for your natural ability, but mostly for your character and how well you fit into our program. Your speed didn't dazzle me, and neither did your strength. I can get that from an eighth-grade bulldozer. I'm looking for good character.

"I won't have any asses on this team. I take that back. We only need one ass on this team, and I have designated myself."

Abe chuckled. This Kreiler was Kublai Khan, a bloomin' military leader—*Colonel Kreiler.* Abe had a feeling that Great Grandpa Crazy Horse would have liked him.

Moving away from the podium, Kreiler stepped down from the dais and paced. "Motivation. It is quite simply the spark that makes someone do that which he might not otherwise do. You need a ton of it in football. Football is a tough bloody sport with contact so fierce it'll make you wince. I'll give you motivation, but you'll find your own too. Maybe it's your parents, maybe it's a friend or maybe it's your wife or a girlfriend."

Hot damn! Abe pondered, rubbing his chin. He wondered if Sarah would ever come to one of these games. That would be some motivation!

"Finally, in closing, here are your priorities: number one is academics, number two is football. And whatever is number three sure as hell had better not interfere with numbers one and number two.

"Now get out of here and kick ass tomorrow."

CHAPTER TWENTY-TWO

Funt looked out on a dull November sky, rubbed his chin and said, "I've never seen anyone on the football field with more raw ability than Miereau. Let's give him a gold jersey and move him up to second string so he gets workout time with a greater number of experienced athletes. I'd sure like to see him with a position on the second string when we start spring training." Antsy, he shifted his feet.

"I spoke to him just the other day about how he felt about being in the backfield. He said, "I'm nervous as hell being back there, but when the ball's in the air, it's everybody's. Once you get it, you use a full head of steam to break loose." Funt's eyes crinkled in delight.

"No shit!" Kreiler was impressed, but not surprised. "Can you believe that kid's attitude? Humble as hell, doesn't even know that he runs like a deer. I saw him catch an acrobatic fifty-three-yard catch on a wild pass from Hulk last week as if there were nothing to it but to do it." He removed his hat, combed his fingers through his hair and returned the hat to his head, shaking it in wonder. "And I've seen him knock players out of the way as if they were pickup sticks! He's seems to have some kind of inner torment that drives him." Kreiler stood with his arms folded across his chest, weaving.

Funt fidgeted with anticipation. "I saw him cut over the middle at the twenty-five-yard line like magic. He juked past one defender and left him in the dust. Cut past another. Lost him, too. Time ran out as he crossed the goal line, but he went in standing up and scored that touchdown; his scrimmage team won with zero point zero on the clock. Move him up now so he gets a workout with some tighter talent. Next spring we can keep him in the light golds. It's like finding a Renoir at rummage sale. Do it."

Kreiler reached for his clipboard. It was a done deal. They ended the season with seven wins, two losses.

"Don't think that's anything to write home about, you hoo-hahs," Kreiler advised at the last team meeting. "Even Roosevelt and Truman beat out Governor Dewey of New York State in the last general election. It was no closeout, but they won. That's what we want—*to win*. We'll make that nine-zip next year. Take care of yourselves, stay out of the bars, don't hustle girls to your dorms, and maintain your grade point average!"

So it was written. So it shall be.

Coach Kreiler kept in touch with Abe, encouraging him to raise his grade point average. The time he'd devoted to football had taken a toll on his studies. It was infinitely important to Kreiler to see that this young man had a chance. There always were students who stayed on his mind constantly. Abe was definitely one of those kids.

Kreiler visited Abe just before his twentieth birthday at home on Geddes Road, found him working on his canvases. A cold winter fog hung in layers and slices, snagging on the lower branches of the blue spruce in the Walter Whittaker's front yard.

"How about some coffee, Coach? Cold day out there." Abe grew conscious of the pleasure he felt at Kreiler's visit.

"Sounds good to me. You bet." Kreiler removed his trapper-style sheepskin hat, the woolly side flipped up above his ears, while Abe took Kreiler's Mackinac jacket of the same workmanship and hung them in the foyer closet. *Very outdoorsy,* Abe thought.

"I have a suggestion for you, Abe." Kreiler rubbed his hands together while Abe clattered in the kitchen. "My wife, Karen, does private tutoring for students who are grappling with their grades. What would you think of her hiking you up to speed with your math and English? We'd arrange the time frame to suit your schedule."

Abe turned to him, his eyebrows raised as the coffee perked. "I can't afford private tutoring rates. I understand that they charge anywhere from seventy-five cents to a dollar an hour! I live on a small Social Security check, by selling my canvases in the summer time and assisting in the Bay de Nocquet Lumber Company Office, but it really doesn't allow for private tutoring sessions." Abe poured coffee at the dining room table, which was separated from the kitchen by a tier of ceiling-hung etched glass cabinets, as well as a row of under-the-counter cabinets of rich cherry wood.

The line of Kreiler's mouth softened into a gentle smile as he stirred a lump of sugar into his coffee, feeling the frustration Abe fought to conceal. "I'll arrange with Karen for you to have free tutoring. She volunteers from time to time. You'll like her."

Abe stared from across the table at Coach Kreiler for a full minute in stark disbelief, his coffee cup hanging suspended between table and mouth. He wondered if he had a fairy godmother. It couldn't all be dumbass luck. "You mean it? Free tutoring?"

Kreiler chuckled with a nod of assurance.

"I'd take you up on that in a minute. *Until* Christmas break, I have late afternoons free. *During* Christmas break, of course, I'll have two weeks free. I'm staying here to catch up on all the slack I've given myself during football season." Well, he wasn't about to roll the situation around in his mind and analyze its many components.

"Okay," Kreiler said, resting the coffee cup in the saucer. "It's a deal. I'll want to see your football art series when you're finished. I've been telling my associates about the artist on my team. Jim Funt says that you're our Renoir Warrior. I figure the Wolverines can stand to have a few warriors, so carry on." Pulling on his Mackinac jacket and hat, Kreiler shook Abe's hand. "I'll be in touch soon."

The Christmas season flew by with busy tutoring hours. Christmas Day Abe spent with Bob Chapin in Milan, only a stone's throw from Ann Arbor. He'd been spending much time with the gold-jersey running back, his easy-going ways and all-encompassing sensitivity. Abe admired Bob's rust-colored hair, but the curly fur on his head irritated the hell out of Bob. Fluid blue eyes always took Abe off guard. They were like incandescent lamps. And acoss his nose and cheeks grew a freckle farm. With ruddy cheeks and pink lips, he stood almost as tall as Abe and just as common.

"Hey, you Injun, Abe," Bob shouted while pursuing the sidewalk after their last day of classes. "My mom says to invite you for Christmas dinner. The whole family will love it." Bob shifted his weight from one foot to the other. "I have a little sister too; she's seven years old. She thinks you're going to look like the Indians in Thanksgiving celebrations, the ones with feathers in their hair and loin cloths on their hips." Bob laughed like hell.

"I'll give you feathers and loin cloths! What a stretch, but I'll be honored and delighted, to show up at your house for Christmas dinner. I might just come over and spend all day with you," Abe said, reaching his car, opening the door and throwing his books onto the seat.

"That would be just fine. My kid sister has two front teeth missing and gets milk mustaches at dinner and my grandpa edges food onto his fork with a knife." A castoff shrug barely lifted his broad shoulders. "He'll probably ask you if you use wampum for legal tender. Gotta go," he said laughing, turning to leave. Still grinning, Bob walked backwards to his own car in student parking.

With happy memories of Christmas break, winter of the new year 1945 settled in as if it had always been there. Abe found that even though there were weight-lifting sessions three times a week and frequent conditioning drills, football was a back burner item in the winter and early spring.

During this down time Abe got to thinking about major league football. Why did it appeal so to him? There was the glory, no doubt, and the chance to excel and to have several million people acknowledge your good work. He mostly wanted to please one fan, Sarah, whose anticipated presence at a game meant more than Abe had ever revealed. Even if he didn't get to play first string, he'd be proud to watch with the serene patience of a Sioux Indian hunter, maybe get her to attend the University of Wisconsin game at Madison.

There was an attraction beyond fame and showing Sarah that her husband-to-be was a take-no-quarter man. He learned one of the universal truths about college football: what he'd joined was a fraternity. Why did he not join even the most prestigious Greek fraternities? Because he already held part of a better one. There was bonding between teammates. They didn't have a special handshake. They didn't have a hat to wear or a frat house to live in, but it was a fraternity nonetheless. They didn't have to prove anything to anyone.

Other than classes, Abe did negligible on-campus social magnetizing. He focused on keeping his head above water academically. Besides, he didn't have wampum to throw around on goofing off. He was sorry to hear on the radio one night in April that President Roosevelt had died in Warm Springs, Georgia. He wondered if Fabian had met up with him yet—his hero.

So far, what he'd heard about Roosevelt's successor, Harry Truman, was that he was a tough old bird. Maybe that was exactly what the country needed right now. America continued to juggle with the Japanese. It pressed time to stop. Get this slow-death-war done and over with! The whole world had gone horseshit, as Fabian had reckoned it would. Of indescribable relief to Abe was the fact that Berlin fell on May 7. Things were looking good; there remained only mop-ups and peace pacts now. That fairy godmother was still looking after him.

Spring turned into summer. In relation to his associate freshman class academically, Abe, with his 2.4 GPA, tested almost exactly in the middle scholastically at the end of the final term. Eight players had end-of-the-year averages of above 2.5; seven had averages below 2.0, or a "C."

One of the first places he stopped after arriving home for the summer was Doc Whittaker's. Abe waited until after five o'clock so Doc would be home and unwinding. The evening was soft and still, with a reluctant sunset hovering in the west.

"Well, look what the wind blew in," Doc said upon answering the door. "What a nice surprise, Abe Miereau. Come on in. Come in. Hey Liz! Abe is home." His voice flooded the house with its English accent.

Abe had forgotten how beautiful Doc's home was. It stood grand, *grande!* Doc's seventy-two rpm oak phonograph cabinet in the living room vibrated with Vivaldi—happy, light. "I enjoy that music, Doc. It speaks happy to me." Abe tried to stay emotionless while great waves of affection washed over him at seeing Doc again.

Doc quickly responded. "That's exactly why I play it, for happiness and peace. We had a bad accident on the trams today. One of the *bugs* went through a batch of bad boards, taking the driver and load of wood down about thirty feet to the ground. The driver's in bad shape and I don't know if we can pull him through. He has a broken pelvis, broken ribs, a concussion, a broken leg and a large splinter of wood entered his rectum as if it was a suppository. However, there were tears and some of the lower intestine had to be cut away." Doc's mouth held a bitter slanting.

Abe viewed the accident in deepening horror. "I heard about it at the office on the way in, but had no idea it was that bad." Aghast, Abe hung on Doc's every word.

"Abe!" Liz swept into the foyer, giving him a gargantuan hug. Her hair smelled like fresh sheets.

"Good to see you again, Mrs. Whittaker. There's something timeless about you, and you're so pretty." Abe smiled, licking his lips shyly, hoping he hadn't overstepped the bounds of courtesy.

"Aren't you just the sweetest young man? Please stay for dinner. We'll enjoy every minute. There is so much catching up to do." She smiled encouragingly.

"Well, thank you. Sure, I can do that." He wore a denim waist-cut jacket with gripper fasteners—his hands in the side slash pockets. It was the jacket and jeans he'd received from Doc and Liz for his birthday, and he intended for them to see that he *did* wear them. For Christmas they'd sent him a check for two hundred dollars, for which he had called and thanked them immediately. It was a million dollars to him.

Doc grinned from ear to ear. "Come sit in here," he said, motioning to the expensively-furnished living room with Queen Anne chairs placed strategically at the back corners of the thick carpet, while a deep leather divan and two matching chairs sat grouped near the fire place. Splendid paintings in rococo frames hung one on either side of the fireplace. Abe inspected them closely: an early Paul Jackson Pollack—a sketch depicting a river boat on the Mississippi River. The boat almost lost its significance in the southern migration of the river. Interesting treatment. The other was by Ben Shahn and portrayed city life during the Great Depression—somewhat morose.

Doc observed for a moment how engrossed Abe became in the paintings and moved to kitchen for two beers, which he set one on either side of the couch on oak end tables, shouldering solid brass table lamps large enough for the university library.

"Now tell me all about this football prowess that Coach Kreiler found in you. Football! That's the last thing I'd have imagined for you this year." His jaw slightly moved offset again as he awaited Abe's accounting of the school year.

In the telling, it occurred to Abe that he loved the presence of this man.

ཟ⌇

The summer seemed all too short to Abe. After a full day of work at the office, he ran three miles out to Farley's and back before he drove to his home on Old Beach Road, having left his car at work. He had to melt down; speed up. He alternated his runs to Farley's house at Indian Point on the west side of town, with runs on the stretch of beach from Burner Point to Stony Point on the east side, a distance of about a mile and a half. He grew wiry, strong and aggressive. Time was of the essence. He needed to report to school on August 5 for pre-season football training.

In addition, Abe wouldn't be home for the Sadie Hawkins Day Celebration.

"Sarah," he called on a hot day in late July, meeting her as they simultaneously left their homes. "Would you bestow me a favor, milady, and register two paintings at the Summer Art School Auction?" He managed a smile while walking toward her.

"Of course I'll do that for you. I don't go back to school until the end of August. Want to go swimming this afternoon? Ma might come along, but she's not as adamant about our relationship as Max is." She'd stopped before him, meeting him in front of her home, just past the white picket fence gate.

Abe thought he'd never seen her look more beautiful. He'd almost forgotten what she'd asked—deliberation dimmed as his desires escalated, rendering him pretty much completely batshit. "Sure, I'll just take the time."

"Let's be lazy and lolligag in the sun." Her dark brown eyes danced with laughter.

If she only knew how she affected him—seeing her—breathing the same air. He couldn't fight it! Goddamn! He wanted to reach out, touch her and hold her close.

On the busy Nahma beach, Abe lay near Sarah. Dark sunglasses covered his eyes, his arms crossed loosely on his swim trunks. He had always pictured Nahma's sky as bluer than all others. Oh, he would come back here every summer, bring his children some day, and absorb it year after year.

Soothed and relaxed, he visualized the two paintings he'd finished for the auction. One captioned "Landing a Coup," featuring a young Indian maiden and her buck pulling a canoe into the Stony Point Cove. Dressed only in soft tan leather pants, his hair plaited into two braids, he stood tall and strong. The maiden wore a three-quarter length deer-hide dress with a fringed bottom, which swayed with efforts at docking the canoe. Glowing blue-gray and streaked with ribbons of pink and mauve, the canvas stood horizontal, encompassing the vast arc of the bay in early evening. The young couple fleshed out as subtly entertaining the beating of their hearts.

The other one was titled "The Tragedy of the Trams," a painting of the pitiful accident that sent a young man to his eventual death. *But for the grace of God, there go I*, Abe thought. It depicted the stripped down Ford Model A on a frame and four wheels crushed under a load of lumber. Only legs angled out from beneath. Around the cataclysm glowed an aura of tender light injected with glitter of heavenly glory, as if Michael the Archangel had come to escort the mangled body to heaven. Abe hoped that someone would be struck enough by the rendering to create safer working conditions.

His paintings of the football anecdotal series never traveled farther than his instructors for grading. Kreiler and Funt convinced the athletic department to buy them for the briefing room. "The Spiking" turned out just as he anticipated. Under a dreary November sky, the colorful lone receiver stood triumphantly over the goal line doing a ritualistic dance, his knees bent, his head down, his hands raised in the air poised to spike the ball. It could only have come to life by someone who had been there, done that.

He still couldn't believe that they brought in five hundred dollars. If he could get a good price for his pictures at the Summer Art School Auction, he'd again start the academic year with more than a thousand dollars, and he needed every cent of it.

What was he doing daydreaming about his canvases when he lay nestled next to his woman? He had dreamed of this day and night and here he was wasting time gathering wool. Abe rolled over onto his stomach, sought and found Sarah's hands and linked her slim graceful fingers in his. One at a time, he separated and kissed them in reverence, feeling, tasting. "Have you given any more thought to Dr. Whittaker's offer to help you with your ah, er ...problem?" Abe had lowered his head close to hers, urging softly. "He says that it *is* a problem—there *is* help." Abe hoped he'd couched the proposal diplomatically, fully aware that he wasn't strong in this venue.

"Yes, I have, but I just can't subject myself to a cursory pelvic exam." She tittered uncomfortably. "It's terribly frightening." Water filled her eyes.

It hurt him to see her so distraught, but he knew her fears were grossly exaggerated. *All* women had to see doctors. It was almost requisite to being female. Why couldn't she see that?

"May I make the appointment for you?" he asked with an eagerness born of necessity. "I want to have you visit me in Ann Arbor this winter to see a couple of Michigan football games." His excitement accelerated, thinking of having her at a game—watching him play. He could feel the ebullience, the deafening roar of the crowd, the cheers and the spiffy Michigan marching band. *Don't get ahead of the game, preppie. You may not even play this year. I have to. I need to. She needs to see me as I am—in control. My own person. Husband material.*

"I desperately want you to be the mother of my children, and you know that can't happen if we have a platonic relationship. Please do it—for me," he went on relentlessly. "What say you, Sarah?" *Surely, she can't misconstrue what I've said; she has to see how reasonable it is, for both of us.*

"Okay, I shall, but I can't promise when. It has to be on my own terms and in my own time—when I'm comfortable with the idea." Her eyes looked up at him with their in-depth beauty and enchantment working magic.

"I guess that I can't ask for more than that. I love you so much. When I'm with other women, all I ever think of is you." He was frank and open; it was his heritage.

"What?" she asked hoarsely. "You're seeing other women? Why Abe Miereau! All the while that I'm curbing my social life you're waltzing around like some student prince. What are you thinking of?" She looked troubled.

"Well, Sarah, I *am* a man. I have needs and desires. But these women don't mean a row of beans to me. You're all I want. My grandest dream is of the day I marry you. You're my woman," he breathed softly into her ear.

In a universe of private nirvana, his voice stirred husky, yet a strange eerie feeling permeated Abe's body. He found the feeling annoying, just when, with tremendous effort, he had crawled inside Sarah's head.

But wait a minute! Something was wrong. Stirrings swirled in his head like nearly-set fudge. An electrical chill traced his nerve network. A seagull feather fluttered onto the sand.

Fabian! It was Fabian! He sent warning.

Something's wrong. Evil and wrong.

CHAPTER TWENTY-THREE

Ma's voice overrode the hubbub of the beach bedlam and the wash of waves licking the shore. "No! No! Max. Stop it!"

Max wasn't listening. "I'm going to kill you, Miereau...you leach!" His benevolent Mr. Monopoly face dissolved into a mask of hatred and rage— his eyes bulged, mouth twitched, as he approached wielding an oar above his head.

Pure visceral control galvanized Abe to roll like lightning to the side, landing with his knees in a "Start" position, the tips of his right hand touching the beach sand, his knees crouching, his body wired.

Simultaneously, Sarah moved to roll over, laying her right arm out over the blanket to support the rise to her elbow.

Taken from Max's rowboat anchored nearby, down came the oar, already in motion. With the intention of beating Abe into a nefarious Never-Never Land, Max landed the oar with maniacal force upon Sarah's forearm, tearing the flesh and cracking the bone with a sickening snap!

"Ohhh. Ohhh my God!" Sarah instinctively tried to push her skin together to spate the flow of blood, attempting to hold her bone together, like a child trying to mend a doll with pure love, goodwill and scotch tape. Turning ghastly white, she fused into the beach blanket, slipping into a deep faint.

Abe rushed Max, wrestling the oar from his hands with ease. Stunned, Max stared with vacant eyes at the panorama of people all locked into some kind of slow motion. He looked like an efficacy of madness, naked nuts and steeped in a self-made coventry, staring curiously at Abe as if he were a total stranger.

Abe's Neanderthal reaction rushed to mash Max with the oar, but he knew better. "You sad sonofabitch! Don't think you aren't going to pay for this, you mangy old goat."

Miereau, that was plain old luck from above that your mind isn't a piece of putty. Someone took a liking to you.

Max didn't move from the spot where he'd been relieved of the weapon oar. His face featured a blissful blankness.

"They were just talking, Max, just talking," Ma interjected, fluttering closer to Sarah, her voice but a scant squeak.

Battling the surge of adrenaline and anger, Abe hurriedly lifted an unresponding Sarah, her head lolling over his elbow. Tucking her arm between his hand and her body to secure it, barefooted, he carried her the hundred yards to his home and car, placing her in the backseat. Before he could back the car out of the driveway, Max again attacked. This time he hit the trunk of the car with the heavy oar, which he had somehow found strength and might to carry up from the beach.

Abe couldn't remember where he'd heard it, but he'd been told that the wily sense of lunatics shone more sharply than those of us who are sane. Here and now lay the proof. Max was out of his mind and strong as hell—a quart low on sanity, but a full tank of fury. His pallor florid, his eyes glazed over, he was lost in a madman's timewarp.

Maneuvering the car around Max, Abe quickly accelerated, leaving the deranged creature in the middle of the beach road, the sun beating down on his stiff white hair, which sprung up all over as though he'd been electrocuted.

Doc was in—the hospital busy with office visits. Abe didn't go in through the back door where the waged people entered for office visits. Instead, he parked outside the front door used for emergencies. Sarah's pulse must have been somewhere between thirty and zip. Her face white, her mouth open, breath shallow, he couldn't tell if she drew any oxygen at all. Blood spilled over himself, over Sarah, and in the car.

Quigley, hearing the commotion, shut off the patient treatment area to handle the emergency from the front entrance. She quickly admitted Abe into the surgical arena, where he laid Sarah on the examining table, her right arm askew like a trashed rag doll.

Abe could hear Doc, ushering out a patient in the next room. Entering the theatre, he looked at Abe and the patient appraisingly—bathing suits, blood and obvious broken arm. Nothing appeared reasonable to him as his eyes raced over Abe's face.

Quickly scanning Sarah, Doc inserted a stethoscope into his ears, checked her heartbeat, then opened her eyes with his thumb. Abe, anxious and on the verge of needing treatment himself, hovered over her, rubbing her left hand, smoothing the wispy hair back from her forehead where sweat beads, grew around her temples.

Dismayed, Doc queried, "What the hell happened?" His thick eyebrows raised, eyes wide in askance, he performed the cursory exam. His concentrated concern was evident. It brailed on Quigley and stamped on Doc, trying hard not to jump to conclusions, recalling fully Abe's capacity for cruelty, his Sioux ancestry and ritual-ridden culture. The carving on John Pedo for the childhood molestations of himself and then of Sarah sprang to mind, which threw Abe into a virtual Sioux séance.

Abe sensed the imagery railing in Doc's mind of the rawhide woven into Pedo's chest flesh; Pedo tied to the flagpole downtown bloody with rawhide tethers drawn through his fingertips. And Doc had no idea of the Neil Izcik incident.

"It was Max," Abe explained in a voice stronger than he thought he could muster. "He went nuts. Sarah and I were on the beach with at least a hundred other people, including Ma, when he attacked us with a boat oar. The hit was meant for me, not Sarah. By a fluke, her arm lay in the line of the falling oar. Help her, Doc. She's so important; she's the rest of my life." His voice failed him finally, as the powerful emotions of the afternoon's events succumbed to sobs as dry as the desert.

Quigley ushered him out to the wicker-furnished porch. "It's going to take a while to set that arm. Why don't you go home, dress in street clothes and we'll take care of Sarah? Good idea?" Her eyes squinted and blinked.

"Yes, sure. Of course. I forgot that I'm still in my bathing suit. Thanks," he stammered. He produced an unstable smile.

Abe's thoughts were tangents, flying out from a nucleus like Fourth of July fireworks. Thoughts illuminated and burned out before fruition as he drove home. *Pull yourself together; hold on, you're losing it, man. Settle down.* A formidable idea took a bite of his brain. *I'll kill that weird bastard. I'll take him out in his rickety tub of a rowboat and drown the sonofabitch. That's what I'll do. No way, Abe. Drowning's too good for him. Twist his balls uptight and tie them to his legs with rawhide shoelaces, then switch him with ever-so-thin beechwood branches and watch him dance. Grandpa Crazy Horse would be so proud.*

Everything was quiet at the Savin home. Was that good or bad? Quickly he showered and pulled on white cotton shorts, a navy and white polo shirt and a pair of leather thongs. Running out the backdoor, he saw Ma Savin coming up from the beach with Betty Hebert and her mother, one on each side. She staggered, sobbing.

Running to the women, Abe took over for Mrs. Hebert, assisting Ma.

The woodchip road roasting under the summer sun was dry and crackly under their feet. Everybody was talking at once.

"It's Max," Betty revealed to Abe. "He's dead. He just dropped in his tracks when he came back to the beach hauling that oar. He approached the boat, tried to push it off shore and collapsed." She blew hair off her forehead with her bottom lip.

"Dead on the spot," exclaimed Mrs. Hebert, her face waxen, eyes hollow.

Between deep breaths, Ma rambled on, her voice plaintive. "No! Not my Max. He needs to stay with me. Oh God, I don't want him to go!" she cried in total rejection, her words garbled.

The hair on the back of Abe's neck stiffened and rose. "Where's Max now?" he asked Betty. Bewildered and shaken, he couldn't believe the scene unfolding like an over-dramatized third act.

"Uncle Vital and Uncle Reggie carried him to their car and drove to the hospital just minutes ago. There's hardly anyone left on the beach. It's been a frightening afternoon." Betty's eyes were worried, her wet dark hair pasted to her head.

Abe literally envisioned Max's mind like the top coating off a golf ball peeling off and finding the minutia weaving of rubber bands that snapped and popped when he cut into it, like an overstuffed piñata. *Something snapped? He's been off his rocker for over three years now, and I'm the only one who's noticed? In dying, he cheated Ma. In dying, he cheated Sarah. And most of all, he cheated me out of retaliation. Sonofabitch!*

Out of nowhere, Ma remembered Sarah. "How bad is her arm, Abe? Did Doc say? I didn't see it up close." She trembled like a field mouse caught in an open field.

He lifted his eyes to look at her directly, trying to shore her up. "She's going to be all right. Her arm is broken, but Doc is setting it now. I'll go back to the hospital to sit with her. I don't know if he'll permit her to come home tonight. She'll be awfully groggy." Abe underplayed the seriousness of the fracture, afraid Ma would sink into overload.

When Abe arrived at the hospital, Vital and Reggie Hebert were leaving. "We're so sorry, Abe. None of us can figure out what moved Max into such a frenzy. They say that when a person gets tetched in the head, the first one they attack is a loved one." They offered condolences before leaving, with the sincerity of long-time neighbors.

Sitting down, Abe brought himself under control and realized that observers thought the oar was intended for Sarah. Only he and Ma would remember that Max had been shouting at *him*, which provided damn compelling evidence.

It was unsettling to realize that *he* survived as the one not injured. Was it possible that hatred could tunnel so terribly into the human heart?

Maybe Max was sane and he was the nut. Pity that one can't ever see oneself as others see them. Abe, however, did see his life as eddies that formed at the mouth of the Sturgeon River where it spilled into the bay. Like eddies, the flow of his life swirled around, dancing forever in-place and going nowhere.

Mahogany braids on the Currier and Ives calendar took Abe back to the time Sarah, at eleven years old, had gone into the beechwoods to change into her clothes after swimming. Neil Izcik, Buster Tobin and Owen Menary lay there, peeking from cover of nearby bushes. He'd laid them flat and sent them home with their tails between their legs. No one messed with *his* girl.

And how about the time he took her to Stony Point, clam digging, when she was thirteen, and he'd noticed for the first time that she had grown breasts. He'd been so excited. He'd never changed. They remained soul mates.

The Halloween Dance entered his memories: Neil Izcik making a move on her, treating her like a piece of fresh fruit ripe for…for…picking, he guessed. At seventeen, Abe was inclined to have killed him on the spot while he had him pinned to the wall.

He'd taken her parking that night; she was just sixteen. Chrise, that was as embarrassing as hell! How he ever muddled through that, he'd never know.

Crazy Neil got *his* a year later in the log pond down by the mill. *I dared him to swim. When logs came rolling into the millpond off that flat car, it scored logs ten, Izcik zip. I'd do it again.*

No one would ever know how exciting it was to see Sarah naked in his bed after the Sadie Hawkins Day celebration a year later. Holy Moses, she was beautiful, her skin satin sheets, her breasts silk mounds!

I should've known how unready she was for the experience. I was insane, really a dumb bull moose! I'll make the experience comfortable in the future. Doc will help us.

Abe's thoughts wavered, unconvincing. His huge body suddenly shook with sobs, his head in his hands. Viewing the truth of all the bad times he'd given her caused a hellish hurt.

"It won't happen again, Sarah." he spoke aloud to the ferns and the asparagus plants. The hospital wore the quietude of the tomb into which Max would soon be lowered, cold and stiff. The minutes stretched on and on, seemingly endless, like cold winter days when the unrelenting wind incessantly blew the searching snow.

But what's this? Abe heard the rolling of a gurney as the theatre doors opened and Doc and Quigley rolled Sarah across the hall to the same room where Fabian had died more than three years ago—a *thousand* years ago.

"One, two, three," Doc said softly, his tone and movements methodical and deliberate as he and Quigley moved in unison to slide Sarah onto the hospital bed. With anxiety, Abe followed them into the room, observing that she lay pale as a cave dweller, and highly sedated. Her right arm had grown a vast plaster cast.

What the hell? She wore a hospital gown. He couldn't qualify the hospital garb to a broken arm. Nakedness and a flimsy hospital gown were not acceptable!

Walking over to Doc, he stopped before him, reached out and squeezed his arm, not gently. "What's with the hospital gown? You never asked if you could undress her. You can't look at her." His chin grew soft. Why'd he say that? He was as crazy as Max, his mind nothing but a junkyard!

Doc nodded to Quigley, smiled, his teeth closing in the middle like some movie star on the silver screen. "Thank you for putting in such a long day. Feel free to go home now; the night nurse is here." He rationally chose to end this discussion and pocket Abe's last comment until they were alone.

"Thank you, Doctor; don't mention it. It *has* been a long day, however. It'll be nice to get home and apologize to my feet." Patting Abe, she left the room, her white hosiery singing *squish, squish, squish,* her gigantic thighs rubbing together.

Doc tore his glance from the patient and focused on Abe. "I say, let's you and I go to my house and have a sandwich and a quiet talk. Sarah won't be coherent for hours, so you can come back with me in the morning around six-thirty. Instead of going home, why don't you just stay in the guest room at my house tonight?" He was filled from the hectic day, and smoldering, his lips formed a thin line.

It took a few long hard minutes for Abe to respond. "Well okay. I didn't know she'd be out for so long." Abe promised himself that he would not weep, but he wept. He hadn't broken down like that since losing Eddie and Fabian.

When he raised his eyes, the anguish in them communicated itself to Doc, bringing sudden comprehension. Abe, in spite of his bravado facade, desperately needed the confidence and security held out to him.

Terrifyingly real, Abe felt it, too. He'd needed it intensely for the last five years or longer. He clung to the solace of Doc to ease the pain and suffering of his lifetime. Men like him didn't happen often. Once in a coon's age, among the pitch and roll of adept people, came someone with that special touch, a sort of cellular composition so blazing that nothing could ever douse it—not time, wealth, distance or even love.

Bending over Sarah, Abe kissed her forehead, smoothed his huge hands over her forehead, and eased back her thick bangs, wanting to drink in all of her face. He lightly dusted her cheeks with the back of his fingers and rubbed her now unhearing ears. Everything now lay within reach for them: the equinox of the years of their youth.

He couldn't lose her now. The future beckoned.

Abe tried not to think about Sarah lying inert in a hospital bed, but she always stuck there, as his past was there—his childhood bedroom with the dormer ceiling, his dad's voice, the giant white pine, the wide arc of the bay and all else that had made him what he was. He reconstructed his life and found it turned a full circle of unending toe-stubbers. His memories floated the bend of the orb way back to when he was five years old and had been molested by Old John Pedo, his bouts of frantic jealousy with those who interfered with his and Sarah's life and the heartache and grief of death! In another bend of the circle lay his academic failures, his roustabout Indian friends and the insecurities resultant from his Indian culture. Still, there surfaced the cruelties hidden in his heart for those he despised.

Seated in the security of Doc's living room, Abe felt comfortable sharing his fears, and he buried his cruelties in a beer. Doc chose one of the leather chairs in front of the fireplace, while Abe sat in the other. Brilliant flashes of heat lightening ran rampant outside, reflecting in the large bay window that overlooked the front porch. The stained glass insets in the four corners of the window stabbed prisms through the room. Upon arriving home, a Mozart Clarinet Concerto found its way onto the turntable of the phonograph. The year Abe had spent at college diminished none of the wrap-around warmth emanated by this room.

Doc studied the strength that had developed in Abe's face during the past year. "Abe, I've never known anyone who has been through as much trauma in his short lifetime as you have." It was an aggressive beginning to what he had to say—unhurried and systematic. He trusted that it wasn't too risky, considering Abe's fragile state.

"I couldn't believe it today when you brought Sarah in with a badly fractured arm. Given what I know about your explosive personality, I choked down the faint idea that you might have done it yourself—accidentally, of course." An alert smile sliced his mouth, but the cloud of doubt stayed in his eyes.

"You can't *possibly* think that, Doc! You know how much I care about Sarah." Abe knew he didn't rank among the world's intelligentsia, but he thought he had Doc figured out better than that. Of course a person's mind can get up to some stinkin' stuff sometimes. He folded his fist into the palm of his other hand.

Old reservations surged through Doc's mind. He remembered all too well the heat of Abe's vindictiveness, the taste of his explanations hard to swallow. He mastered his emotions, silencing his suspicions. "The thought never crossed my mind until that very minute but just came and went. It became practically anti-climactic when Max arrived dead. I was up to my ass in emergencies all day long. If heavy caseloads are combustible, I should have exploded about two hours ago. These two incidents were the detonation cap. When I graduated from medical school, I aspired to be Dr. Dualot, but today reached the pinnacle." Doc shook his head.

Sighing, he went on. "Max will be picked up tomorrow morning by the Hallo Funeral home, the same place where Fabian's arrangements were made. His life being snuffed out in such madness is going to be very difficult for Sarah to endure. This is no microcosm bump in the road for her. It'll take all of us to pull her through—Ma, too. Doc felt the closeness of family loss in this tragedy of tragedies. Nothing knit a hometown together more quickly than families in need.

"You and Sarah are the most important people in the world to me, Doc. If either of you hurt, I hurt." Abe drained his Pilsner glass, while feeling the loss all over again. He had only to close his eyes and see her lying on the beach blanket, her arm bloody and battered, with broken bone, cartilage, ligaments and muscle. He shuddered.

Doc arrived from the kitchen with two more beers. "Now, let me address the hospital gown question you raised. Every hospitalized patient wears a prescribed gown. You must remember that is one of the first things Quigley did with Fabian too. We don't leave patients in their bathing suits. You understand?" Doc extended his goodwill to the bare bones, and trusted that he didn't come off as sarcastic or mocking.

"I saw red to know that someone else saw her naked. Of course you had to do that. I don't know what got into me." Abe's eyes moistened. He'd had a day beyond comprehension. He was just inches from being the victim of a cracked skull—brained, decapitated and God only knows what else! But that was no excuse for what he'd accused Doc of perpetrating. His mind had gone on permanent leave for a few moments, making him Sioux-mean, but he'd be hanged by his heels before he'd acknowledge that.

Doc's mouth curved into a gentle smile at the distress this young man had been through today. He held empathy for his loss and fear, but no one, absolutely no one, could question his professionalism. "If I want extracurricular activity, I have no need to sneak a peek at my patients." Doc smiled broadly at Abe; his mustache bore just a wisp of foam on it that he wiped away with his cocktail napkin.

Abe nodded.

Doc began herding together his thoughts of the day. "Reggie and Vital told me what happened. I know you did the right thing. I could go to the bank on the fact that you'd do the right thing. That's because you're you. I never doubt what your intentions are. They're good—not mediocre, but good.

"Max has been falling apart for several years now. I've observed it. His eccentricities, his far-off trips, his trigger temper tantrums. It's always pitiable when someone professionally impressive begins to fall apart, like watching a monument collapse. His death has to be explained tomorrow morning to Sarah, however. I'll drive over to Ma Savin's to advise her on what she needs to do, just as I advised you when Fabian died. These are bad times for families. It's the land of murk for them. Even if they know what to do, it's a stretch from what they're motivated to do." Having said the words, Doc again envisioned the heart-rending moments after Fabian's death. Abe alone—collapsed over his father in complete surrender to hopelessness.

"It'll be a tough week for the Savin family," Abe said, his beer extending over his right knee, doing a balancing act. "They were there for me; I'll be there for them." After all these years, Abe felt the pangs of remorse brought sharply home again by Sarah's loss. And Max *did* have better days—treated him as one of his family for years, recognizing his failings and dreams. Max extended love, art instructions and hospitality.

After a weary and restless night Abe arrived at the hospital the next morning at six-thirty. How could he best tell Sarah about Max? He felt like a minion, Capt. John Smith delivering a marriage proposal to Pocahontas from Miles Standish.

Sarah was sitting up, her eyes bright.

It took tremendous effort to step forward with a smile. "Well there, little lady. Would you care to dance?" Abe offered in his best John Wayne replication. He swore he could still see Fabian's last moments in that very bed, smell the last vestiges of life, the disinfectants used by the night shift, hear the pelting of ice on the window. He shuddered and scolded himself because he could still be hit with a whip of sorrow he should have shirked by now.

Sarah's eyes shifted from the light of amusement to being dead serious; a frown stabbed between her eyes. "Abe, tell me what happened. Nobody will

The Taming of a Sioux   257

talk to me about it. How did this happen? I don't remember." Her eyes flooded with tears.

His gaze swept over her with warm attachment. *How to tiptoe through this?* Silence filled the room. He fixed a slow feature-by-feature study of her face, searching for a show of possible insight, but he saw nothing but lingering questions.

Mustering up courage from God only knew where, Abe plunged on. "Max came up from behind you with a boat oar. I was his target, but I moved too quickly, and he struck you across the arm, breaking it. I'm so sorry, Sarah. You're suffering on my account." Abe had drawn up a straight-backed chair, which he turned around backwards and straddled near the bedside. He held her hand and wished that he could again hear her carefree laughter, see her eyes dancing with excitement. This was hell!

Sarah's eyes grazed his face. "He can't stand for us to be together; it drives him crazy. It's absolutely unreal. I'm so glad that you're here. Where are Max and Ma? Why aren't they here?" She grew inquisitive; yesterday was a blank. Her fine eyes widened in honest askance.

Abe did not respond, could not respond, but sat motionless, studying her with a stone-set expression for a long while before beginning what would no doubt be a most unpleasant undertaking.

"What's wrong, Abe?" she asked in a thin, concerned voice.

His voice suddenly became soft and solicitous. "Ma will be here soon. Doc went to get her. But, Sarah, it's like this..." He was hesitant. "Max had a heart attack yesterday after he attacked you with the oar, and he...died...died right there on the beach. Nothing could be done for him. He went peacefully."

Abe experienced a hollowness like that of an executioner—nauseated. His stomach went into a quick knot, holding fast. His throat closed over.

Eyes shifting back and forth, she searched his face with uncertainty. "You're lying," she stammered, confused, skeptical, hesitating. "You never liked him after he stopped wanting you around. You're just saying that. It's not true!" She attempted to rise, but her gross loss of blood and resulting dizziness caused her to collapse.

Abe heard the rubber soles of Quigley's shoes doing a *squish, squish, squish* on the polished hardwood floors. He accommodated her reassuring presence. Somehow, her sheer size and humane sensitivities were consoling.

"Now there," Quigley soothed upon entering the room. "Don't shoot the messenger. Today is the first day of the rest of your life, Sarah. You're going to do just fine without your father. He's given you a good home and a good life.

You need to carry on for him." She pressed Sarah's shoulders gently against the backrest of the bed, fluffing the pillows. "It would be a terrible mistake not to acknowledge his passing."

"No!" She clasped Abe's hand tightly, feeling the comfort of his responding grip. Shock took over; she couldn't identify her feelings of fear, confusion, disbelief, rejection. Sarah had taken immeasurable pride in her father. Pride goes with infallibility, and infallibility nurtures longevity. He could not die. "No!" she repeated now as she wept—broken, as he'd wept when Fabian passed out of his life. Death was so final. No looking back. No bringing back. Her sorrow broke his heart, opening old wounds, surfacing forgotten emotions that bubbled up from some stinking tar pit. An oppressive stillness permeated the room as if time had no measure.

Abe could hear her rapid, terrified breathing, saw the pain and trepidation on her countenance. "Sarah, you've got to understand that we could both be dead. Max's mind snapped." Words came hard. Whatever Max's faults, and they were many and varied, Abe knew that Sarah would never forget her father. Out of his mouth came a strangled sob for her sorrow. Swinging his chair around, he folded his arms on the side of the bed and encompassing her hand, he wept tears he didn't know he had. "I love you, Sarah Savin," he whispered thinly. "Always and forever I'll be here for you."

And he was true to his word. Abe remained in town for Max's service, a brief simple send-off for a complicated man. His reporting time for the football team, however, pressed urgently upon him. He paced inside his tiny brown house as he had thousands of times as a kid, then slumped into the sofa and heard the sounds of those years—shouting, but laughter, too. He felt drained in meaning that went beyond being physically drained, in meaning that had to do with being the only surviving person in this house. He felt a sinking in the pit of his stomach. Now Max was gone too.

With an effort, he pushed himself forward. After a gut-wrenching apology, he parted Sarah's world and returned to Ann Arbor.

CHAPTER TWENTY-FOUR

Goddamn! The sun was burning hot today. Abe had been swearing since eleven years old, and he didn't know how to curb it. That nice Karen Kreiler did her best to improve his vocabulary and knew some jawbreakers, but sometimes just plain words wouldn't do. A guy just had to say something worse to make him feel better.

With Michigan's first game just a week away, Abe felt pumped. He'd been playing with the gold jerseys since last spring and began to see the results of a year's worth of torture. He was hard-hitting and crushing running.

The golds scrimmaged against the blues in the fourth quarter; the score teetered at twenty-eight to twenty-eight. They drove to the eight-yard line. Fourth down.

"Let's go for it, Hulk," Abe urged. "Let's go for the touchdown!"

"I'm going for the field goal!"

"No, Hulk. Let's get the touchdown!"

"I'm going for the field goal!" Hulk said, enunciating every word.

The golds kicked the field goal and sent up thirty-one to twenty-eight. The blues began their drive; Abe figured *there goes the ball game*. They were going to score.

He reckoned wrong.

They threw an interception; the golds took it in and won: thirty-eight to twenty-eight. That's where experience paid off with Hulk. He took the bird in the hand, not the one in the bush. He needed to work. Work harder. Work harder than that.

"They call that being the quarterback," Hulk razzed Abe as they ran off the field. "I win every argument, hands down," he said, slapping Abe on the shoulder pads and laughing as they headed for the showers.

"Hey Moose!" Hulk yelled from next to him under the showers.

"It's Abe, Bruce—Abe!"

"Yeah, I know, but every time I see you naked I think of a moose," he said. "Can't help it." He always reminded Abe of Gary Cooper—tall, lanky, dark, kind of sad eyes and slow with his words.

"How about Big Bear?" Chapin chipped in. "Wish I had half as much red hair as you have black hair. What hair I do have you can't see because it's so light. What can I say?" He grinned widely, shaking up his freckles under the shower.

"It's not the hair I wish I had half of," said Bump Ness, Abe's favorite offensive fullback—two hundred fifty-five pounds, six foot four inch, square shoulders to cuddle a ball securely, hips that swiveled down the field to the detriment of anyone who dared get within his cozy quarters.

Abe laughed and waved a get-outta-here arm at all of them.

The next day was just as hot—ninety degrees and seventy-two percent humidity.

On the first offensive play, the gold fullback, Bump Ness, broke free for ninety-nine yards and a touchdown. The gold offensive tackles draped the field with blue defenders. They kicked the extra point and the score was nineteen to thirteen, with about three minutes remaining. It was pretty much up to the defense now to hold onto that lead.

They did. Abe was totally impressed.

Kreiler didn't miss a thing, but rather appeared absorbed in other areas.

"I think we need to consider Hulk, Chapin, Miereau, Burgher and Ness for the first string," Funt told Kreiler later, sitting across the desk from him in his office.

"I hear ya. They're ready, all of them—and more. I worry about Miereau, though; he's a different breed, that one. Yet he's an excellent receiver and a great clutch performer. But during chalk talks you can see him staring at walls, looking out the window, drifting away. Sometimes you need an alarm clock to get his attention."

"Tell him to get his head back into the lecture. Once or twice of that should cure his nebulous thoughts." Funt would overlook small stuff for greater gain.

"Well, I'll dance with it. Hate to embarrass the kid, but it just might work." Kreiler rubbed his chin thoughtfully, leaning back in his deep chair.

Friday night, before the first game, the team awaited their motivational moment. Kreiler, a steamroller and master of bully pulpit politics, felt comfortably in command.

"Gentlemen! Many others have played this game before us. Tradition demands that you play as they did...like Michigan! That's why you're here! You didn't come here to play in a mediocre program, and if you did, you're at the wrong place. When I talk to you, I don't want some guy looking up into the sky, and I don't want him looking down at his feet or out the window. I want your eyes on me. *Hear?*" he shouted. "And that means you, too, Miereau. The lecture's in here, not outside the window."

The room hushed, a hurt-your-ears variety of hushed.

His voice barely above a whisper, Kreiler sighed, "I don't intend to shout to get your attention." The team almost imperceptibly en masse leaned forward.

"*Remember* my sermon on errors and mistakes. *Remember* your positions and don't jump the gun. During punting drills, I carry a yardstick to measure the distance between each player on the line. You'll all remember that I'll drop that yardstick between the players' legs, and if it doesn't measure up, you get whacked. *Remember* that during real action. Anyone out there being tagged with unsportsmanlike conduct will sit out for two games. I don't care who you are."

"You quarterbacks—don't think that you've been canonized as saints. It's all right to be conservative and use the rush, rush, rush instead of the long bomb, but *remember* that all you're going to get is three yards and a cloud of dust. Look for daylight. Look for your free receiver, even if it isn't the setup you called originally. Make your decisions quickly. It's not cast in concrete that you hang on the book-plays."

He paused, a deep scowl forming on his forehead, his lips thinned. "And don't think that I don't have a *temper*. Any player that has been here for a year has seen it. I have a *sideline temper* in the heat of the battle. I have a *practice temper* to get you motivated. I have an *office temper* between myself and a player, and a *staff-meeting temper*. When I say 'You're fired,' you're fired. I play for keeps."

Hell and damnation, yes! Abe had seen him kick garbage cans last year.

"I want all of you to play for keeps. We aren't playing marbles here. We're at war! It's a survival game out there. One battle does not win a war. I want to see you put together a string of winning battles until the war is over at Thanksgiving."

His face softening, his expression turned twinkly, mischievous. "Does everyone here have a girl friend, wife, someone you care about deeply?"

A knee-deep silence fell over the players. Their heads poked forward, ears alert. They heard a chord in the concert with which they could all connect.

"And you're aroused when you're near her?"

A low mumble of assent seeped through the team like a misty vapor.

"And it's the same thing every time you're around her?"

There surfaced more nodding and looking at each other for confirmation. Yes.

"That's passion. That's love. That's your male testosterone doing the Boogie."

Lusty laughter rippled through the players.

"That's what I want you to feel when you get out there and play tomorrow. Passion! Deep and serious and aggressive!

"Faint heart never won fair maiden, and faint heart never won fair football game. When you're passionate, it's no time for timidity. Go for it. Go for the tackle, go for that touchdown. *Score!* Just like you go for the gusto with your women. If you aren't scoring with your women, you're not aggressive enough. We want only scorers on this team. If you can't score with your women in private, you sure as hell aren't going to score with a football in public."

Yeah, Abe considered. A guy could get it on with the thrill of the chase, the anticipation of the reward at the end of the field. Good metaphor. Another word he'd learned from Karen!

"Your heart better be pounding, your pulse racing. I want you so locked into the strategy of the game that you wouldn't notice Betty Grable walking the sidelines. And if there is anyone here who wouldn't want to see Betty Grable walking the sidelines, please turn in your resignation first thing Monday morning!"

Belly laughs encircled the briefing room, forming a vortex over Coach Kyle's ears. "Liked that, huh?" Standing sideways, he rested one elbow on the podium.

"For those of you who've been out in the boonies and aren't aware of it, we're locked into nine conference games: Ohio State, Iowa, Illinois, Minnesota, Purdue, Indiana, Northwestern, and Wisconsin every year, and our choice of three non-conference teams: Michigan State, Miami of Ohio, Florida State, Washington, Army and Navy. Of course it's Washington, Navy and State this year."

Resuming his full front approach to the team, he flipped pages in his notebook.

"If anyone asks you why the Wolverines still wear those ugly black football shoes, tell them that Coach Kreiler likes black; it's the color of death and that's what we're dealing in—death to our opponents.

"Also, if I forget to mention it again this season, *remember,* I look to fine character from my players, my men. *Be men*! Don't bend your principles because someone on the other team is a scuzz. *My men* are principled. They speak, hear and see the truth. It's known as the Three-Monkey Principle. *Don't bend your principles!*" He shouted again, observing the players getting comfortable, slumping down in their seats. "As long as I live, I'll marvel at kids who lie so beautifully, they think they're telling the truth."

Abe knew the cost of lying, ever since he'd tried it in seventh grade when he'd stolen that jackknife from the Company Store and carved up the school. Bernard Tobin had him collared so fast he was tongue tied. He still didn't know how Tobin had figured he'd done it. Of course, he had.

"Tomorrow, Michigan State plays here. We have a target of opportunity to start the season out with a bang. The whole campus wants that victory. *Everybody!* I need you to perform forty inches to the yard! I'm hard to live with when State defeats us. I'm practically an alligator crawling out of the swamp…hungry…mean. I'm a bellowing behemoth. It's a pathetic existence. Don't try me on! I'll bust your asses all year, but when the season is over you'll find out that I'm really your friend."

MICHIGAN BEATS STATE BY 23-20 VICTORY, blared the Ann Arbor Daily News headlines in extra bold print. "The final two minutes told the story; victory came about through a blocked punt and a thirty-seven yard field goal in the final two minutes."

Abe saw no playing time, but exhibited passion while sitting on the sidelines. His eagerness took him to half-standing positions, to standing, to doing his Indian Ritualistic Sun Dance around the bench after a superior play. Pride. Great pride in a team he never ever expected to be a part of. He never expected to wear a uniform. Never expected to know Coach Kyle. *Never ever expected to go to college.*

Anne and Walter had attended the game and shared his excitement afterwards on their front lawn. September was unseasonably hot, extending outdoor activities to the appreciation of any Michigander. When Abe arrived home, they were having an early evening cocktail, re-hashing the game.

"Abe! Congratulations on today's victory. That was outstanding! I can't think of anyone we want to defeat more than Michigan State—that is, of course, unless it's Ohio State," Walter said, grinning as if he had just won the Irish Sweepstakes.

"Oh How I Hate, O-hi-o State*!*" Anne arose and extended her arms, cheering.

"Yeah, isn't that just something else?" Abe was filled with exuberance. "It wasn't any shoo-in, though. We had no cushy points to relax us for a minute. It was squeaky."

"Nah, you guys had things nailed down all along. Have a beer on me." Walter habitually included Abe as one of the family.

He glanced at Anne and Walter with a dichotomy of appreciation and respect. "Don't mind if I do. It's hard to settle down after a game like that. We have some terrific first-string players. Maybe...someday..." his voice trailed off.

Walter protested with enthusiasm "You bet *someday*, someday soon! I've asked around of my old cohorts out at the college, and the word is out that you're Kreiler's favorite son. You'll see play, m'boy, and probably soon. It'll have to be at Kreiler's choosing, however. He has a very strong personality."

Abe laughed. "You got that right." *Strong personality*, Abe thought. If Walter only knew! "He's been good to me, and has Karen tutoring me again this year, which is going the extra mile. *Lo necessito.* The University requires a foreign language, even in Art Majors, so she's refreshing me on my Spanish in addition to English. Next to Kreiler, she seems like a half-grown sibling. 'Sibling,' that's a new word that Karen taught me as part of my vocabulary enrichment." Abe leaned forward in his lawn chair and entertained a delicious thought. "I wonder if you'll excuse me for a few minutes while I call Doc. I want to share the good news with him."

"Yes, we would expect you to do that," Anne replied.

As Abe arose to leave, the radio on the front porch softly played "White Cliffs of Dover." It reminded him of the A-Bomb blast at Hiroshima on August sixth, right after he'd returned for the new school year. And then, as though that wasn't enough, there was another one at Nagasaki on August ninth. Old Give'Em-Hell-Harry wasn't fooling around any longer. The Japanese surrendered on August fourteenth, and made it official with signing the Unconditional Surrender on the battleship Missouri on September second, just eight days ago. It was over, but at what a staggering price.

෴

"Hello. Doc?" Abe was uncertain it was him. The line was noisy and awash with wave-like din.

"Yes. This is Dr. Whittaker." The tone sounded officious.

"This is Abe. How are ya? Did you listen to the game today? Did any of the local stations carry it? Did you like it?" Abe exploded.

"For cryin' out loud, Abe. Yes, I heard it. The Escanaba station carried it play-by-play. You bet. Any time we can defeat Michigan State, it's a feather in our hat. I say *our*, because I feel just as much a part of the school system as you do." Doc sounded inexplicably touched by the phone call. Warmth flooded his substance.

"What do you hear from Sarah? I haven't talked to her for two weeks." Abe's anxiety dripped through the dialogue.

"I talked to my associate at Milwaukee County General, Harry Burnson. He removed her cast two days ago, x-rayed her arm, felt she needed about three more weeks of stabilization with a cast, so he re-plastered her. She isn't happy to have it on again, but he said she was a lady about it. He was reluctant to allow her to go around unprotected when he saw significant signs of the need for additional bone growth in the area. The prognosis is good, however. By the way, he complimented me on setting that fracture. It was complex. Jagged. I never told you—or her." Doc paused, reflecting.

"I guess you didn't have to draw me a picture. It scared the hell out of me, but I knew you would do a good job. This Burnson shouldn't have been surprised one bit—nice of him to comment on it, however.

"How did he say she progressed mentally after the funeral and the trauma? I left so quickly. Football pre-season practice was critical. I never really had a chance to help her over the rough spots." Abe's voice seeded raw with the admission—and the guilt.

"We all understood that, Abe. Don't let it work on your nerves. Burnson's had her see a friend of his, a psychiatrist out in Brookfield. She's handled a terrible blow; Max was almost God-like to her. No one could ever be as good at anything as Max was at everything. She'll need a lot of support from both of us for the foreseeable future, at least. Ma is packing up the house to close it for the winter. She'll be spending the time in Milwaukee with her family, so Sarah won't be back in town until next summer either, if then. I hope that doesn't blow your mind."

"No, no. That's okay. She's told me about that possibility." He paused. "Doc?"

"Hmmm?"

"Do you think we're too young to get married? I could take care of her and give her the nurturing she needs. God only knows how much I love her." Abe released the words in slow breaths.

"I think so. Yes, very definitely. *You* aren't too young, but *she* definitely is. She's a fragile budding flower. Even though she's the apotheosis of an eligible young woman, she's nineteen, going on fifteen. After a very sheltered home life, she went to a near-cloistered Catholic high school. Now she's at Mount Mary, run by the Notre Dames, and she's still monitored, which doesn't promote worldliness. I know women who are adult at sixteen—at fourteen—but not Sarah. She needs your love and dedication, Abe, but she's not ready for marriage. Why don't you try to see her this winter? Break time over the Thanksgiving or Christmas holiday would work."

"Doc? Did she ever confide in you about her problem? You know," his voice dropped to a confidential low, "the one I explained to you. Did she?" Abe was anticipatory to the point of conveying his angst over the telephone line.

"No. She did not. She never mentioned it. I think she's frightened and juggling all she can handle right now. Give her a little space. She'll come around."

"Doc? How is Liz?"

"She continues to have headaches for no earthly reason. I've run every test I know on her, and nothing shows up. I need to sedate her at times because the headaches get so bad. Arrangements have been made at University Hospital for a complete physical next month. We'll fly down there and stay with Walter and Anne. It'll be nice to see all of you again." Doc spoke professionally in relaying the bad news. Abe knew, however, that if he could see his eyes he would see deep concern.

"Sarah tells me that you helped hike the price on my two canvases at the Summer Art Festival by raising the bidding three or four times. I want to thank you for that. Those five hundred dollars go totally for my education. Somehow or another, by spring it's all gone. I'll never be able to repay you for all the kindnesses you've shown me. Never." What more could he say? Can you tell a man you love him? Can you tell him that he makes you happy? I don't think so. "Thank you very much."

"Don't even mention it. You're deserving. Those paintings are keepsakes; a person can get lost in them. By the way young man, do you know that you've never painted anything especially for Liz and me? We'd be deeply honored if you'd do that."

Abe was taken aback. "Really? You have such significant paintings in your home, and you'd like one of *mine*? Sure, I'll think of something special, very special."

"Thanks, Abe. I'm sure you will. Now you stay with the program. Keep up your grades first, football second. We'll see you in about a month. You take good care of Walter and Anne for us." He laughed quietly. "Take care of Abe too."

Doc wanted desperately to tell Abe how much he meant to him. Is it okay to tell a young man you love him? His chest ached and pulled strangely with longing. His hand clung to the earpiece, reluctant to let it go. He could still feel and hear the warmth of Abe's voice. Why did he so concern himself with this young man? A thought knocked at the door but Doc denied admittance, then it simply slipped away. He acknowledged that a small percent of the population had varied psychic experiences, the ability to perceive things that are usually beyond the range of human senses, whatever. Communication from long distances. Sometimes Abe transmitted and he received.

Only three days into the next week and during scrimmage play, senior wide receiver Duke Johns stumbled over a teammate and fell clumsily to the ground. Jim Funt, with one quick glance, correctly assessed the damage: a broken leg. This sent senior Woody Zelinski into the role, leaving the backup position open. Funt enthusiastically hoped to place Miereau into the vacant slot.

"I still don't know, Jim." Coach Kreiler stroked his chin thoughtfully. "Some deep sensitivity resides in Miereau's psyche. I'm not sure we can release the dreamer in him. He had some trauma this summer with his girlfriend's father dying under most unpleasant circumstances. I often catch him in that dream world he slips into. Don't know where he goes, but he just seems to zap himself off somewhere."

"But you can't doubt his mental presence during a game," Funt rationalized. "Sometimes I think we need to put him on a leash to restrain him from running onto the field to rev up the receivers! Christ, Kyle, he's a tiger! It's only once in a lifetime that we get someone who flies higher, faster and farther than we ever thought possible and helps us do the same. We can't let this chance pass us by."

Kreiler felt a slow chuckle churn up in his throat. Funt must be in collusion with Karen. That's all he hears from her. 'Give him a chance. Give him a chance.'

"I've had him in mind for a long time, Jim." Kreiler still speculated, still what-iffed, still did the old yeah-but when he placed his hands in his pockets and let out a long slow breath. "I've pictured him as a wide receiver; he's good enough to be a cornerback or free safety on defense. His quickness and speed suggest thrilling possibilities as a kick-returner. He has that rare combination of instinctive reactions and headiness that makes a Heisman. We'll do it!" Kyle observed the smile that Funt tried to hide, knowing he'd made a good decision.

And so it came about that Abe went from struggling artist in the bleachers to a gopher catcher for the gold quarterback, to a gold jersey, then to the coveted blue jersey. Bam. Bam. Bam. In just one year. From rags to riches. From little town USA to the heights of glory. Just wearing the blue jersey turned the trick for him. The one with the big maize "M" on the front. The one that had to have cost a hundred dollars and a pint of blood. How'd he do it? God only knows. A feather fluttered to the ground in front of him when he ran onto the field with the first string for practice.

The highlight of practice that day consisted of an eighty-four yard punt-return for a touchdown in the third period by Miereau, pushing the advantage of the blue jerseys.

Kreiler put his head down, placing his hands in his pockets, and walked back to Funt, shaking his head and smiling.

Funt said not a word, but he felt like a million bucks inside with tickles of pleasure creeping all the way up his legs to his groin.

The next day Abe had a pass reception for forty yards, then a run from scrimmage for forty-eight yards.

Again, Kreiler shook his head as he approached Funt. "Crazy kid. No one can touch him. He runs like a goddamn gazelle, like a message bearer for General Lee, for Christ's sake."

Funt smiled, containing himself, but inside he danced the Teaberry Shuffle.

Kreiler displayed a professor's knowledge of the Civil War and its battles. "That's interesting," Funt prodded at the military analogy.

"I found that being a student of military campaigns is a definite aid to me as a coach. You need to know your opponents' combat tendencies. Some concentrate on your strengths, so sometimes by employing a quick thrust away from your main base you can surprise the opponent coach. Sometimes a coach will try to hammer at my weak points. I spot these tendencies in my rivals by studying the battle campaigns of Robert E. Lee." Kreiler was conscious of Funt's unusual absorption in his historical prowess.

"Then you need some more captains to execute your Civil War plans. How about Hulk, Chapin, Ness and Burgher?" Funt felt it was high time he pushed for quarterback Hulk, wide receiver Chapin, fullback Ness, and halfback Burgher to be plugged into the first string also. "Sort of like that good Macintosh apple you bought last week, firm and popping good with juice. This week you'll buy six of them."

"Actually," Kreiler responded, "I can afford to deepen my lineup since I'm using the platoon system. I can *use* more backup. Hulk is a heady quarterback. Chapin is clever as hell at getting himself into daylight. And Ness and Burgher are such all around players that they're valuable no matter where I play them."

"Move 'em out and move 'em up, Kyle." Funt's stomach rolled with angst. "Doit-doit-doit-doit-doit," he prodded Kreiler.

Kreiler rearranged the names on his clipboard. His own Mt. Sinai stone tablet, etched in fire. Kreiler didn't traverse into the unknown. He dealt in certainties.

The next game of the season, Michigan crushed Navy 40 to14. The Wolverines gained over 360 yards rushing.

"Listen you hoo-hahs." Kreiler was vexed from this victory. "You were just lucky this time. Rushing isn't going to win you a whole lot of games. You need to start passing that ball for the long bomb. You'll never get three hundred and sixty yards rushing when you meet Ohio State. Just put that in your pipes and smoke it!" His eyes were quickly veiled, lashes dropping, but the team knew it made sense.

The third game, non-conference, Michigan walloped Washington 45 to7.

The fourth game—Missouri, a nationally ranked team. Michigan fumbled the ball away four times and allowed seven sacks.

"MISSOURI SMACKS MICHIGAN SOUNDLY, 40-17," virtually vibrated from the "News."

"Kreiler's mad," Chapin told Abe. "He's moping. I saw him kick the bleacher seats the other day. I think he's staying up nights trying to figure out what went wrong. I hope he's not having second thoughts about moving the five of us up."

The boom lowered Thursday before practice. "Seven sacks, my ass. If I ever see that happen again I'll move up the complete gold roster and send you blues to the showers."

"Hulk! You're moving up to starting quarterback."

"Chapin and Miereau! You start next week against Purdue. You'll both be designated wide receivers. Goddamn it, Hulk! Use 'em! I've seen enough rushes to fill a career. I'm up to my ass with 'em."

"Ness! And Burgher! You start at fullback and halfback next week in that order. I want you to pick up the blitz on passing plays. Hit those holes on the line quickly and quit dancing around. *Help the quarterback!* He can't play the game alone. Snooze and you lose!"

The Mighty Wolverines chewed up Purdue 31 to 20 in a beautifully played game.

There were four intercepts by a solid, well-oiled defense. Abe made his first touchdown for Michigan on a toss from Hulk in the first quarter. It came at the right time, right place, and Abe had free sailing. People parted in front of him like the waters in the Red Sea. He made it look as if there was nothing to it but to do it. He held the ball to his stomach and danced around in his native Sun Dance before spiking the ball.

It was the fourth quarter and Kreiler was itching with anxiety. Purdue had possession and chose to punt a long one.

"You, Miereau, get ready. I'm sending you in as a punt-receiver as soon as the play is stopped." Abe caught and returned the punt seventy-eight yards for a touchdown on the second play of his career. He danced and maneuvered his way down the field like a hysterical kangaroo, dodging, jumping and evading as he did on the beach at Nahma, using driftwood piles, during track practice.

Minnesota was scheduled for the next week, playing there. Michigan lost 23 to 12 with more fumbles, stupid mistakes and poor defense.

"They rolled up yardage as if we were Aunt Emma's tatted pillowcases," Kreiler dunned the team. "What's the problem with you bunch of old ladies? Can't remember a thing I ever taught you? You're not playing schoolyard football here." Kreiler watched and analyzed every breath the team took—every nod, every eye contact. "It's war!" His eyebrows rose in emphasis; his green eyes sparked.

"I think it's elementary that you guys don't move on the line of scrimmage. I also think that it's mighty elementary that you don't get called for offside by being cute and moving your fingers to irritate the opposition scuzz. And, believe me, they're scuzz! I want you grinding-teeth hating them when you go out there. Eat 'em up! Annihilate 'em! We can't afford five-yard penalties every time you decide to get cute. You know the rules. *Now, let's play some grownup football!*" Kreiler shouted. His face looked a thousand miles from a smile, his voice demanding and riddled with emotion.

Indiana vs Michigan. At half time, Michigan trailed nine to seven. Kreiler was fed up with whiney-type injuries and left half the team home, many of them seniors.

During the second half, Michigan kicked the living daylights out of them by scoring three touchdowns, and they won thirty-five to nine.

"You guys can do it when you buckle down." Kreiler paced during his chalk-talk. "Miereau! You caught some incredible passes; those passes I thought were going down the tubes. In addition, you made two touchdowns—commendable.

"Chapin! Nice ball handling out there, nice assistance; nice tandem between you and Miereau."

"Hulk! I liked that last-minute decision to pass to Chapin on a previously called play for Miereau. Keep 'em guessing."

Wisconsin clobbered Michigan thirty-five to seven.

In the Iowa game, Michigan marched seventy-seven yards for a touchdown on the first drive, and never looked back. By the final gun, it ended with Michigan fifty-one, Iowa thirty-six.   Miereau danced twice.

Illinois at Champaign—no problem.

Northwestern. Breezed through it again.

Purdue and Ohio State were the two top teams in the conference. The team in the locker room chanted "Beat the Bucks" over and over and over again.

"I swear there's saliva dripping," Funt whispered to Kreiler.

At the motivational pre-game Kreiler put it damned basically. "Ohio has a twenty-two game winning streak. 'The Greatest Team of the Century,' they're hyped as. Usually, I only ask a player to outplay the man he's facing, but this Saturday, to pull off the upset of the decade, each of us has to perform *beyond* his Buckeye parallel as well."

CHAPTER TWENTY-FIVE

It was the big day in Ann Arbor. November 26, a cold cloudless blue sky hung over all. Kreiler motioned the players to follow him through the tunnel for their pre-game drills. There were entrances to the Michigan Stadium, and then there were *entrances*. The grand one had the coach out front among players in the blue and gold suits. Abe was part of that thrilling full-trot fist-in-the-air parade. He raised his eyes to the stands and saw a maze of colors and movement—a sell-out crowd.

The Ohio State team warmed up on the Michigan side of the field! It was obviously a mind game. Kreiler had seen the Ohio coach use this tactic before, countless times, but never on Michigan.

The team marched out there and took their spots. Kreiler approached the Ohio State coach. "You're warming up on the wrong end of the field."

"Okay, Kyle," he spewed, his jaw set. "Fine. Come on, men! Let's go."

While moving to the other end of the field, an Ohio State fullback feigned a bauble and pushed Abe catching him awkwardly off guard. Instinctivly, Abe turned around, and in his leopard-like speed raked the fullback off his feet. Other Michigan players joined in the melee, and there developed a rough and tumble involving both teams until the field was cleared completely by the officials.

It looked like war. Michigan was electric. Abe could hear the Michigan band encircling the perimeter of the field playing John Philip Sousa's "El Capitán." He understood that the band was as famous as the legendary fight song they played.

He'd observed that they wore blue uniforms consisting of tailored trim pants and white boots and spats. The jackets were spiffy cutaways with maize and white bibs bearing the letter "M" over the breast. Their hats were Princeton-style with an under-the-chin strap, gold braid over the bill, and the letter "M" superimposed on a blue band set on a maize-colored hat. A royal blue plume extended from the top of each hat, while white gloves were worn on the hands. The instruments glinted dazzlingly in the sun.

The moment the band started playing, the team came charging out again into the cold afternoon. The air was charged with momentum as if all the energy from a season's worth of tackles and body-slams had just been released. The stadium was packed—seventy-five thousand at least. With twenty-five thousand from Ohio State, it numbered the largest crowd Kreiler had ever seen in the stadium.

On the first play the Ohio State All-American quarterback scampered twenty-five yards. On the second play their All-American fullback, burst ahead for seven more.

"It looks like the Ohio State Team is picking up right where they left off last year," the WWJ radio announcer said.

"Stinkin' radio announcers, they stick with the glorious winner." Kreiler steamed when he heard of it from support staff. "This isn't last year. Not even close." Michigan stopped that drive on fourth and one at their ten-yard line. The Michigan defense nearly flew off the field.

"I knew they could do it!" Kreiler cried above the din of the crowd.

The Buckeyes scored first—a touchdown, but they missed the extra point. *Good, Goddamn it! Good!* Krieler was agitated.

Michigan returned the kickoff from thirty yards. Hulk threw three times—twice to Chapin, once to Miereau and got Michigan to the three-yard line, then scoring a touchdown for UM! They pulled ahead, seven to six.

"They're cooking, Jim. They're cooking." Kreiler said as he paced.

Ohio State scored again, but failed on the two-point conversion.

They shoulda gone for the kick and settled for one. It's that old elusive greed, Jim." Kreiler slapped his knee. "You can bank on it every time! Military strategists will tell ya that nine out of ten times the enemy is going to go for the whole enchilada."

Michigan drove to Ohio's thirty-three yard line. After the reception, Miereau twisted, turned, and broke tackles for twenty-eight yards all the way to the five.

Pandemonium broke out in the stands! Two plays later, UM punched through again. *Take that for last year!* And now they were ahead, fourteen to twelve.

Rick Volvo caught a punt and drove straight down the middle, busting tackles, gaining speed, and the sidelines went wild. "Go! Go!" Midfield, forty, thirty, twenty and all the way to the Ohio State three! A sixty-yard punt return!

Hulk took the snap, rolled around and sneaked over the goal line.

"We're ahead, twenty-one to twelve!" Kreiler went cockamamie nuts with the turn of events, his piercing green eyes glowing like lighted gems.

Michigan then intercepted a pass, drove downfield, scored another touchdown, and had it called back! Illegal procedure. After driving to the twenty-yard line they were stopped by the Ohio defense. Michigan then kicked a field goal.

Ohio State choked up, stung and stunned. With just over a minute left in the half, UM lead twenty-four to twelve.

"No other team has scored more than twenty-one points on the Buckeyes all year, and here we have twenty-four by half-time!" Kreiler preened like a peacock.

They left the field to an ovation that continued to ring in their ears as they poured into the locker room, the players roaring and coaches screaming. Michigan's defensive coordinator stood in front of the chalkboard and pounded it repeatedly, between each word. "They—will—not—score—again! Gentlemen, they will not score again!"

They did not score again.

"The second half established a defensive masterpiece," Kreiler said afterwards, while replaying the game. "The defensive back, Rick Volvo, was on fire out there." He intercepted three passes, made four unassisted tackles, and manhandled the great Jim Ellis. In a single afternoon he went from nobody to a fifth-round draft pick by the NFL St. Louis Cardinals. "He had heart, toughness, grit and grind."

Jim rehashed the fact that Ohio State pulled their star quarterback and went to the backup, who fared no better. "He threw an interception to Volvo!"

"That's it," Kreiler laughed.

"All she wrote." Jim gaped, super satisfied.

The mighty Buckeye offense had committed six turnovers, four interceptions, and two fumbles. Their defense had broken for twenty-four points, twelve of them attributable to Abe.

FIVE ... FOUR ... THREE ... TWO ... ONE ...

The field undulated with mobs of fans. The goal posts melted like a March snowman. The band blasted, "Hail to the Victors." Melding into a sea of arms, legs and helmets, the players went wild. Kreiler bounced on players' shoulders while the fans witnessed the upset of the decade. Michigan returned as a national football powerhouse.

Abe felt what deep, gut-twisting, all-you-got football was about.

Kreiler hurtled with Abe's performance. "He darted past two or three defenders, smokin'em." Kreiler's eyes shone. "He's broken the Michigan career touchdown record for receivers as a sophomore. The things he can do with a football are unreal—catching it at the oddest angles, twisting his body, and finding the best position against defenders."

"Abe, you are the best receiver in the NFL right now."

"But Coach, I'm still in college."

"I know. Doesn't matter. You're already the best."

"I relied on my instincts out there. Did what I knew how to do."

"Hulk, you're a special breed," Kyle went on. "You let go a bomb to Chapin a split second before that safety crunched him and they both went down. Chapin, you never saw where that ball went, but it landed in Abe's hands for a seventy-seven yard touchdown that clinched the game for us."

"That's our Sky Pass," Hulk said. "I had told Chapin and Miereau in the huddle: 'Sky Pass coming to you.' It's that quick zip over the middle, where you just split the linebackers. Our receivers have such great hands; it works nearly all the time!"

"Sky Pass…gotcha."

What a way to end the season—seven to two conference, ten to two non-conference.

Last year's shadows were now the substance.

※

Doc and Liz's visit in October had dealt Abe a dichotomy of emotions. Returning from the Purdue game victorious, Abe was ecstatic.

"Hey, guys, it's so good to see you!" Abe exclaimed with anticipation. He hoped his shock didn't show when he hugged Liz—thin, pale and quivering like a frightened bird. Her bones felt like twigs on a dead tree, her eyes round, swallowing her face.

Doc smiled encouragingly, however, putting him more at ease. Shaking his hand flooded Abe with the forgotten warmth of this man. Again, he rewound that perhaps he had known him in another century or on the other side of a great water.

"I see you're giving 'em hell out there on the football field, Abe. Walter says no one can match your speed or your footwork. Damn proud of you, boy! The whole town is! Everyone listens to the UM games just to hear your name!" Doc laughed, standing with a cocktail before dinner, looking eye-to-eye with Abe.

Abe, thrilled with Doc's approval, lowered his eyes as he smiled. "Well, I sure fell into it. I have to work like hell to get my course assignments completed though. I only took twelve credit hours this term—need to make up for it in the next two terms."

Turning to Liz, Abe tilted his head in interest. "What's the good word at the University Medical Center, Liz? Hope they found you a solution to your problems."

"Not yet. The diagnosis will come through later." Liz sank into a comfortable chair near the big bay window. Drawn for the evening, the gold brocade woven into the damask of the draperies contained the same color as her hair as if it were planned. A pale gold silk blouse graced her thin frame and highlighted the honey hue in her hair, her vivid gray eyes, and the rebellious highly-rounded cheekbones. *Click.* Abe captured her fragile radiance, her waning energies, and the ivory skin taut over her nose.

"Did we lose you, Abe?" Anne asked humorously, handing him a beer.

Shaking his head he explained. "No, just daydreaming, I guess."

"Say, Abe," Doc interjected, "how about taking me on a tour of the inner sanctum of the football arena tomorrow?"

"*No problema*!" Abe eagerly complied.

The grand tour du jour passed successfully, —even including the lecture pose by Kreiler at his pulpit.

On the return trip, Abe sat in deep conversation with Doc.

His chin slightly offset, Doc stared straight forward at the street ahead, seeing nothing. "I need to tell you something in the greatest confidence."

The raw sound of his voice triggered Abe's defense system.

"I told Liz that her test results weren't back yet. That's not true. I have them already, and they're bad. I won't tell her until we get back to Nahma—in the privacy of our own home, where she can collect herself. "She has a brain tumor." Doc expelled a short breath, his voice trailing off.

"What the hell…" Abe turned quickly to Doc, unbelieving. He moved off Forest and onto Washtenaw Avenue. The streets burgeoned with scuttling leaves that danced and weaved with the breeze as if in their last macabre toehold on life.

Hurt flickered in Doc's eyes. "It has been insidious as hell! It's malignant. They give her no more than three months." His shoulders heaved.

Abe shot Doc another rapid glance. *Incredulous! Beautiful vivacious Liz was to be rendered inert?* He felt a primeval icing and fumbled for words as he turned onto Geddes Road. "Doc. That's terrible. Three months! My God! How does a person get a tumor in their head?" Abe knew he was babbling.

A gust of October wind blew a cyclone of leaves against the car. Doc leaned back in the passenger seat. "Broadly interpreted, any abnormal local increase in size of a tissue or organ is called a tumor. However, with a microscope, you can determine whether or not the swelling is due either to the infiltration of cells from another part of the body or to the proliferation of cells originating within the affected site itself. In Liz's case, it is the latter. Her tumor originated in the brain and it's shooting off a whole series of crazy cells." He turned intelligent eyes to Abe.

"Medicine isn't my long yardage. Tell me more."

"Tumors are classified as either benign or malignant. The most important property rendering a tumor malignant is the ability to invade nearby or distant tissues. It's called 'metastasis.' Liz's tumor has not only metastasized, it has grown so large in a vital area that surgery is out of the question."

"Can't those metastasized cells and tumors be shot down?"

"Sometimes they can be 'shot down,' with radiation, but that is often just a stopgap measure. Proliferation usually occurs by means of the lymph vessels. Some benign tumors can kill without metastasizing. Chief among these is a brain tumor called 'glioma' which can grow large enough to exert pressure on nearby brain structures and destroy respiratory function."

"My God, Doc! Is Liz going to die because she can't breathe anymore?" Abe witnessed inner rage at the finality of Doc's dissertation, his voice a gasp.

"More or less, Abe. Her malignancy has grown and is crowding her available bone structure. The clearest examples of benign tumors are skin moles and warts. That's why you need to watch for any changes in their appearance. But you can hardly watch for a change in the appearance of a brain tumor."

Fields in fallow gently flowed by as they left the city behind, reaching out to the pale blue of a hazy sky, entertaining high cirrus clouds. A caprice wind scared more leaves from their last hold on the hardwoods across the fields.

"Physician, heal thy wife," Doc, a compendium of grief, whispered.

Abe reached over and clasped Doc's knee silently, words out of his realm.

～∽

During the two-week Christmas break, Abe concentrated on the here-and-now and pursued his studies of Italian Renaissance Art. He prepred a five-thousand-word research paper on Michelangelo, one of the most inspired creators in the history of art. His talent was a tremendous influence on subsequent Western art in general. Here, four hundred years after his death, he could still impress a young man.

Abe learned that it took Michelangelo four years to paint the Sistene

Chapel. This gifted artist devised a sequence system of nine scenes from the Book of Genesis, beginning with "God Separating Light from Darkness," "The Creation of Adam," "The Creation of Eve," "The Temptation and Fall of Adam and Eve" and "The Flood."

Abe acknowledged that his own infatuation with painting sequence canvases was not so innovative after all. He shook his head at the enormity of time that had passed since this great designer had implemented the series theory.

As was his custom, Michelangelo portrayed all of the figures nude, but prudish draperies were added by another artist, who was dubbed "the breeches-maker" a decade later, as the cultural climate became more conservative.

The bastards! Imagine that! Since the Michelangelo onset of brutal honesty in the High Renaissance era, his theories, ideas and strategies had been beaten to death time and again. Know-it-alls stood ready to trash the beautiful and the good.

Abe daydreamed while the late-afternoon winter sun filtered through the picture window facing Geddes Road. Sarah was beautiful and good, but he was ready to trash her memory. All the anxieties of the past four months became encapsulated again. She spent the holidays in Milwaukee with her mother. Same old shit. Something had to change. When he had invited Sarah to spend Thanksgiving with him in Ann Arbor and attend the Ohio State-Michigan game, her mother needed her in Milwaukee. *Needed her, my ass! Her mother has family and friends; he had no one.*

☙☙

Yeah, well, he needed to get a life without Sarah. With the campus on shutdown for two weeks, Abe and Bob Chapin hit student hangouts: Preketes Sugar Bowl and the Pretzel Bell. The juke boxes blared "Boogie Woogie Bugle Boy of Company B."

"Hi, guys!" Girls that Bob knew jostled up to their booth, disarmingly amiable.

"Hey, what's up?" Bob, the freckled-face, brotherly boy-back-home type always put Abe in mind of Van Johnson, one of his favorite movie stars. "This is my friend Abe. Abe, this is Jan and Nancy. They're in my Human Genetics class—both going for nursing." Bob gestured for them to sit down. Abe admired Bob's aspiration to be admitted to the Michigan Medical School after he earned his baccalaureate.

"Pleased to meet you, ladies. Get you a soda?" Abe proved affable, and the girls were way across town from being socially challenged.

"Sure thing. I'll have a cherry soda." There was not one minute of hesitation as she plopped down next to Abe.

"Same for me." Nancy was not hard to please either.

"So, just what does Human Genetics entail?" Abe rolled the words around.

"Well," Jan paused, taking a breath, "a guy named Gregor Mendel, an Augustinian Monk, during his genetic investigations on the pea, observed that characteristics of the pea plant could change between generations."

Bob, listening intently, added, "From such observations, Mendel concluded that those involved in biological mating transmitted factors that would alter their offspring. We now call these factors 'genes.'" A smile crept across his lips, nefarious and teasing.

Nancy, taking a quick swallow of her soda, interjected. "It shows the hereditary nature of humankind and the inheritance of human diseases."

Abe found himself captivated with the intensity of her round blue eyes.

Bob, taking it full circle, couldn't resist commenting. "Yeah. As Hitler is doing in Europe with the Jews—ruthless experimentation on them in Concentration Camps trying to genetically engineer a Superior Race."

Abe, intrigued with the genetic information, plunged on. "So if you and I had a baby, Jan, there's a reason why it would resemble you or me or my father."

Eyes flirting, Jan smiled. "Yeah, and it's a lot of fun making babies."

Nancy cocked one knee up on the seat in the corner of the booth. "You don't have to play for keeps, Jan. Fooling around is half the fun," she teased.

Covertly, Abe stole a glance at Bob, thrusting his head toward the door.

Bob smiled, reading the invitation in Abe's eyes. "How would you like to go out to Abe's and get a beer?" He reached out and put his hand on Nancy's shoulder.

"I hope it's not on campus," Jan said, eye-browed in askance.

"Actually, it's a home I have to myself during the winter while the owners are in Florida." His face was an open invitation.

Upon leaving the lights of the city, the umbrella of sky spun alive with glittering stars in the cold winter night. Abe built a fire in the fireplace, nurturing and nesty for the four of them to sit comfortably around, creating a reclusive romantic lair. Kreiler would have been proud of his two wide receivers scoring with fair maidens.

☙❧

Two years and twenty-three football plays into UM, it was early June 1946 when Abe sat in an empty meeting room and called most of his collegiate experience a whopping windfall. It was testy to put away the games of winter for the gains of summer, but he desperately needed his summer job and paintings to sustain him.

Time moved too fast. Max lay dead. Sarah had another year finished at Mount Mary. Liz died. Abe's world turned too quickly. Where'd the time go?

Abe's love for football consumed him. Between painting and football, he felt pretty much fulfilled. He dreamed of allowing Sarah into his world, but that looked fairly fruitless. Too much water over the damn. Too many separations.

Storing the football gear in Walter and Anne's garage, he bade farewell for the summer months. "If I said 'thank you' a hundred times, it wouldn't be enough for all the nice things you people have done for me in the past two years." Standing near his car, he gave Anne a hug and Walter a handshake.

"Don't be too busy and let the whole summer disappear without calling us," Walter admonished, shuffling his feet awkwardly. He fought to keep his voice even, his emotions buried. God, how much they were going to miss this new love in their lives!

"Here's a tin of oatmeal raisin cookies I baked while you were gone this morning. You can chow them down while you're driving home. There'll be a big hole in the house without you." Her vivid blue eyes snapped with love and care.

Abe carried a mental picture of them as he flew along the highway, north, with the radio cranked up. "As Time Goes By" almost appropriately played. "Woman needs man and man must have his mate, that no one can deny..." Ain't it the truth?" Abe said aloud to Jo Stafford, her voice soothing and soft.

The deep lush green found in the hardwoods of Washtenaw and Livingston Counties disappeared and yielded to the flatlands of Shiawassee and Bay Counties in mid-Lower Michigan. They were all a hazy swirl as Abe thought of Sarah's winter phone calls describing the blow-by-blows of Max's hysterics of the past few years. It was like a bad dream, filled with the bric-a-brac of someone else's nightmares.

Impossible! She'd been impossible! There remained no chance for them anymore. None. None at all. All the hurt and blame Sarah had heaped on him because Max had a heart attack and died. She'd been absolutely unreasonable. He couldn't forget the call she made to him in January.

"Abe, I'm so sorry for all the things I said after Max died."

Abe stood rigidly in the dining room at Walter's, holding the phone, wondering where this prelude would lead, steeling to hold indifference to her message.

"After spending the holidays with Ma, she told me of Max's terrible anxieties of the past few years. It was incredible." She took a deep breath audible to Abe.

"What the hell are you talking about?" His mind mulled on a hundred different facets that could have contributed to Max's madness.

Sarah recognized the impatience in his tone. "I don't blame you for being short with me in this department. It must all seem like yesterday's news, but it's not."

Abe reached over the countertop that separated the kitchen and the dining room and poured himself a cup of coffee. Taking a sip, he squelched his irritation with her. MaxMaxMax! Talk about being tired of hearing about it! How about AbeAbeAbe?

"Abe." She paused.

At least she remembers my name.

"Max was a Jew."

"Son-of-a-bitch!" Abe dragged out a long breath.

"I never had the slightest inkling. Ma said that when he took me to Escanaba on Saturday for my piano lessons, he'd go to temple. He even wore a yarmulke."

"Who'd have believed it?" Abe found the impact spin-offs ad infinitum: the fear of discrimination in a small town, the fear of the prevalent anti-Semitism generated by the Germans in this terrible war, the fear of having his little girl called a "kike" at school, and the fear of losing his directorship of the Summer Art School.

"Ma has all she can do to hold herself together, but I cried all the while she told me. His problems had nothing whatsoever to do with you, except of course that he didn't want me to marry you."

Outside the dining room window, chickadees sang in the hardwoods. Echoing. Calling. The sky was crystalline, the air sparkling with cold.

Abe laughed derisively at her last observation. "Well, my shoulders are big."

Like hell! He minded a whole lot that her allegiance to her father was blind. He minded a whole lot that she pre-judged *his* actions before she even knew the whole story. He minded a whole lot because he'd spent his whole life living on her encouragement, which she chose to withdraw. Now the trail had been too long and the rewards too short. Abe started with that old ache in his throat again—and he was tired of feeling that way.

Sarah stuck to her explanations. "You need to know that I admired my arrogant father. I was totally in shock the last time you and I were together in August—a broken arm, deceased father, Ma rendered helpless. I drowned in paranoia." Her voice caught with the heightening tension she felt from Abe.

"Yep," Abe agreed, bristling somewhat. "You were all of the above." He felt the strength of the stand he took, a mission of mind-bending pleasure and indulgence.

"It's different now. Ma said that the morning of the day he attacked us, he had just received news that his two younger brothers, who he's been trying to get out of Poland, were interred in Auschwitz, and they hadn't been heard from since."

Abe took a quick breath. "Christ, Sarah! That's a crematorium death camp. It's an end-of-the-road piece-of-shit real estate, a hell and horror." Abe's mind overflowed with imagery of pictures he had seen of concentration camp internees, standing inside barbed wire fences, their Hansel and Gretel bone-like fingers hanging onto the strung wire, gaunt skin pulled over their bones like loose rubber suits, eyes sunken and hollow.

"Yes, exactly. That's what pushed him over the edge. The pressure of hiding his religion and the practices prevalent to being a conservative Jew just about killed him. He was a proud man, proud of his nationality. Then, his brothers' fate proved too much for him to handle. I'm convinced that it really was me he tried to kill." She sighed wistfully.

"Don't ever think that, Sarah. Your father, even in his madness, wouldn't kill you. It was me that he intended to kill. Better that he had tried to convert me than to kill me. Max and I had many close moments. I may have been persuaded toward Judaism."

Abe stared vacantly out the living room window at the peacefulness of the neighbor's horses grazing in the thin winter snow cover of the field across the street. How inconsistent they looked compared to the information coming over the telephone.

Steadfastly, Sarah poured out her regrets. "Why didn't I rationalize the unusual foods in our home: mushroom soufflé in flaky filo dough crust, the endive and avocado salads, Manischewitz Concord grape wine on the table, and the fried balls of falafel?"

"Don't beat yourself to death over this, Sarah. Strange things happen."

"But Abe, I'm half Jewish. My mother is French. A 'goy,' as the Jewish community views anyone other than their chosen people." She sounded staggered.

"There's nothing wrong with that, Sarah. You're a beautiful woman."

Abe, over the last two years, had lost the heat of the chase, a chase he always lost, and the fine-tuning it required to magnetize two people. In spite of that, he knew he'd never forget Sarah, his first love.

CHAPTER TWENTY-SIX

Crossing the Straits of Mackinac, Abe felt renewed by the beauty of Mackinac Island and the deep blue Lake Michigan and Lake Huron water that surrounded it like a watery frame. It reminded him of the awesome trip he'd had with Doc the summer he graduated high school.

Doc. He felt kindly toward him. He would spend as much time as he could in his company this summer. Abe's last memories were of the funeral. He did not want to reopen those old wounds. He thought he'd die himself when Fabian passed on. Indeed, he wanted to follow, and wished himself dead.

When Farley phoned and advised him of Liz's death in early February, he recalled how he hustled, taking the first available flight to Escanaba. Bernard Tobin, on leave from his US Navy duties, arranged with Farley to pick him up.

"It was fast, Abe. It's a blessing that she didn't linger. After that diagnostic trip to Ann Arbor in October, she went downhill steadily. For the last month, Doc has had her in the hospital with around-the-clock care—just trying to make her comfortable." Abe noticed how rigid Bernard's jaws were.

"How's he holding up?" Abe forced himself to be stoic for Doc's sake. "He's pretty broken up, but prepared. I'm sure he knows more than anyone that it's a piece of good fortune that she passed on. She didn't even know where she was anymore, didn't remember anyone's name and didn't know the day of the week. Poor lady. Poor, dear, sharp, gracious, beautiful lady. When Doc found her down to the end of her energy reserves, he lay in bed beside her—that small hospital bed. He stayed right there by her side with his arm around her for forty-five minutes after she'd expired. Quigley called Bill Acker and Alan Mercier to come over to the hospital to get him away from her." Bernard's normally cheerful face was overlaid like a curtain, starched and firm. He'd fallen into a different persona for this temporary trip down Remorse Road.

A short silence ensued as Bernard collected his control, a silence broken only by passing cars on U.S.2. "Doc has chosen not to have her laid out at home, as has been the custom in Nahma. He said that he just couldn't bear the thoughts afterwards, knowing she had laid dead for public viewing in his own home. She's at the funeral home. We'll stop there and spend a couple of hours, and then drive on to Nahma.

"Walter and Anne are already there with him. They arrived yesterday from Florida. Trixie and I are staying with Clyde and his family. I understand you're staying with Farley and Norrhea." Bernie threw him a quick glance in the gathering dusk.

Abe turned to him reflectively. "Yes, sure, they've always been gracious and considerate about extending me the hospitality of their home." Abe only had today and tomorrow, then he would have to fly back for term finals. In the back of his mind prayers prowled that a fierce Siberian Express didn't swoop down upon him.

Bernard shifted in his cycle of information for Abe. "There'll be services tomorrow at St. Andrew's Parish, but the burial will be in Gwinn—up near Marquette. That's where both Doc and Liz are from. Doc's parents settled there years ago when they emigrated from England. He was about seventeen years old. Walter had already graduated from law school and was teaching at the university.

"Doc's folks worked hard and established themselves on a nice chunk of land near Gwinn, where they harvested tons of potatoes every year to the tune of one hundred sixty acres. They owned a whole section—six hundred and forty acres. Economically, the operation encompassed many facets. They raised oats, barley, corn and hay, in addition to harvesting timber. They did all right for themselves. I'm sure they were sorely disappointed that neither Walter nor Doc cared to carry on the family farming.

"However, they left Walter and Doc a fortune when they passed on." Bernard had pulled the car up to the curb near the Hallo Funeral Home in Gladstone, where Abe had been to arrange—a shit-kicking time ago—for Fabian's funeral.

His stomach knotted and burned with the thought of seeing Doc miserable, lost, overwhelmed with grief—his Doc, his giant of a man, his man of cultural refinement, his mentor. He pictured him sitting in the big oak chair in his home office, dressed in one of his Italian silk suits, beautifully tailored and pressed, as he crossed his legs in that manner that says, "I'm in control." Yards of oak bookshelves stood lined with New England Journals of Medicine and clouty-looking leather-bound reference books. Now they all seemed minuscule and insignificant. Absent from the heart of his home was his wife, the lovely Liz, who had always sat at the opposite end of the grand dining room table while guests' conversations skirted the length, candlelight breathing on their countenances.

Doc wore an ashen expression. "Abe," he whispered, hugging him— hugging him a long time, without words. Abe could feel Doc's body heat, his chest heaving. Saying nothing, Abe returned the embrace. *At last, at last,* he thought. He'd wanted to do that for so many years—wanted to hug him, wanted to feel the warmth of him, wanted to pat him on the back with an entire absence of words. Abe wanted to tell him how great he thought he was and what fine work he did for the community, but mostly how much he loved him and needed him, so he did that with his presence and a silent hug. There they stood—tall, strong men conveying a multitude of thoughts in reticence.

After what seemed forever, lost in time, Doc drew Abe over to the casket, where Abe knelt and asked his God to allow this lovely woman, who had never harmed anyone, to rest in peace. His tough facade wouldn't go the distance. Upon standing, he turned to Doc, his eyes flooded with tears, whereupon they collected each other in another grip. Doc uttered one terrible loud sob and their shoulders shook in unison. They wept together. The soft mauve lights of the funeral home gave a surreal ambiance to the room as banks of votive candles danced and flickered on either end of the bier. What had been a quiet room was now washed with untold respect for ravaging grief.

At the Funeral Mass, Abe sat next to Bernard and Trixie. Bill and Hattie Acker were seated in front of them, with Alan and Rose Mercier in the same pew. Dave and Rose Phalen tapped him on the shoulder when they entered the pew behind him. With the acknowledgment of his presence by the Secretary of the F. W. Good School Board, Abe lightened somewhat. This very man had paid for his "Track" pictures and signed his high school diploma, which he never in his wildest dreams thought he'd attain. Abe felt much more than a modicum of respect for these hometown icons.

"*Agnus Dei quitollis peccata mundi: miserere nobis, dona nobis pacem.*" The choir sang before Communion. He had to hang onto his self-control as never before when Earl Cousenault sang, "Amazing Grace" at the Offertory and "My Soul Is Longing for Your Peace" as the mourners shuffled up to the communion railing. "Lord, I am not worthy that you should enter under my roof, only say the word and my soul shall be healed," resonated throughout the standing-room-only service.

The Solemn High Mass was officiated by Father McKevitt and assisted by Father Epouffette, the Indian missionary priest, and Father Larsen from Gwinn. Their silver-colored silk, black-trimmed vestments shimmered in the reflection of the tall altar candles. "*Requiescat in pace,*" Father McKevitt intoned as he blessed the casket.

The two assisting priests intoned "Amen," six bars long, starting with pianissimo and ending in a forte that bounced off the high ornate tin ceiling.

It was a long, long day. Abe joined the funeral entourage as it drove to Gwinn for the burial service, riding with Bernard, Trixie and Mary Krutina, who kept up a constant chatter the entire distance of seventy miles.

"The flag is at half-staff in everybody's heart," Abe breathed to Doc as he left Gwinn that day.

Doc grabbed his elbow and shook his hand, his larder of words depleted.

*

During the rest of the semester, Abe concentrated on survival. The strongest survivors are those set apart with an excessive ability to live with denial and keep on plugging along. Abe kept on marching. Did he really deny the grief in his past life or did he find a niche in which to store it? He preferred to believe in the niche theory, but he prayed that the cubbyhole would stay closed.

After successfully marching through another year at UM, with a lot of help from his friends, he found himself back in Nahma for the summer. Abe waited a few days before allowing himself to drive over to Doc's. In the back seat was a large portrait of Liz as she sat in Walter's house last fall at the time she was diagnosed with a tumor. It seemed almost alive. The beige and gold damask drapes hung in soft folds in the background. The hidden lamp behind her chair sent fiery lights through Liz's blonde hair, giving off glints of honey. Her face lay partly in shadow, showing only a two-thirds profile. She outlined a study in complacency, her high cheekbones accented. With her right hand resting gracefully on the arm of the chair, her mouth was soft and restful.

"Abe! You're a dream for my doldrums. C'mon in." Doc smiled warmly, his head tipped to one side. "How've you been? Nice trip?" he asked, his eyes reflecting love and pleasure at the sight of the young man.

"Yes, everything's just fine and another school year is successfully completed." Abe produced a fake cough. "However, for the last two terms, I've been carrying a punishing schedule."

"Let's have a beer on that," Doc said, placing his arm more comfortably now around the back of Abe's shoulder, leading him into the living room. "A few beers never sent a man to hell yet, as far as I know." Early evening light streamed in through the big bay window and through the high narrow windows on each side of the fireplace.

Doc eyed the large, draped frame. "What in the world do you have there? I'll bet it's your new entry for the Summer Art School Auction." Handing Abe a frosty cold beer in the lovely leaded Pilsner glasses, Doc sat down and crossed his legs in that careless, intelligent, *I'm-all-here* fashion.

After taking a long draught on the beer, Abe unveiled his presentation to Doc, allowing the drape to puddle on the floor.

Generating an ever-so-slight lurch in his chair, Doc sat, speechless, and then stood as if he was nailed to the floor, mesmerized.

"Abe!" A long slow sigh escaped. "That is absolutely breathtaking. The colors are so soft. The kindness and beauty-of-soul it bespeaks." He choked down a sob, his voice a whisper. "I can't thank you enough. It's as if she's alive—palpable!"

Abe suppressed his *glad* smile, using only his not-quite-a-smile instead. "You're supposed to be happy about this. You want me to go out and come back with it for a new start?" Abe grinned his ray-of-sunshine smile for Doc. His eyes teased him.

"You better not," Doc said, "or I'll have your head on a stake." His elbows were on his knees now, still staring at the picture, wanting to glean more from its intensity.

Abe laughed. "Geez, I need to remember that one for the next time I run across someone like old John Pedo." His hand slapped the arm of the chair.

"So, you *did* do that!" Jolted, Doc jerked his gaze to Abe.

"You'll never know, will you?" Abe teased at Doc's perplexity.

Shaking his head, Doc arose and lifted the picture, gazing at it longingly, drinking it in, memorizing it. Abe followed him out to the foyer where he took down a great copper sunbeam sconce that hung in the focal spot below the open stairway. Beneath it streamed the customary vase, overflowing with seasonal flowers, now filled with bridal wreath, pungent and heavy with fragrance.

Abe watched as Doc caressingly hung the canvas above the flowers, stood back, and folded his hands in front of him. Staring, he pulled himself into the picture, resurrecting memories. He tugged a cigar from his pocket and absentmindedly lit it, the action mechanical and relaxed. As Doc dreamed, the strength of his face impressed Abe—the strong lines, the perfect part in his hair. Abe's heart ached for this man friend.

The heavenly scent of baked ham drifted through the house, just as if Liz were in the kitchen. "Geez, Doc, you sharpening your culinary skills now?"

"Uh-uh. Maxine Bedard, Stub's wife, volunteered through the goodness of her heart to come in late every afternoon and put some dinner into the oven for me. She just turns it on low and I have dinner when I get ready. With my profession, sometimes that's nine or ten o'clock at night. Being a doctor is an onerous job at best sometimes, but we have a commitment to society to assist the injured and the ill."

"You stay and have supper with this lonely old goat and we'll speak of sealing wax and fools and things that rhyme with cabbages and kings, or something like that." Doc led the way back into the living room.

"Sure, Doc. I'd be happy to do that. Remember me? Every time I cook, it's the worst dining experience in history, and that includes the Donner party."

Doc put on a recent Harry James record. "Supper can wait for a while. It'll stay warm. Maxine fixed potatoes au gratin and that's in the oven too, so we can have another beer and you can catch me up on everything that's happened to you these past two terms." The signature James trumpet expressed mellow, clear heart rending with "It's Been A Long, Long Time."

Doc sighed as he reclined with his fresh beer. "Speaking of a long, long time, what do you hear from Sarah these days?" His eyes flashed over his glass.

"She'll be back to open the house in a couple of weeks. That'll only give us about a month to talk things over and try to reconcile over our rift since Max's death. I need to be back in Ann Arbor the first part of August for pre-season practice." The last ten months had been like a long-term cease fire to Abe. "I don't really see much chance for us anymore. You know...distance...time..."

Doc could read the heavy pain behind the light words. "Don't let her slip away from you, Abe, if this is the woman you want for your wife. I suppose now that you're a big-man-on-campus football star, you aren't having any problems finding female friends." Doc smiled, his eyes twinkling.

Abe tried to suppress a smile at the thought, licking his lips. "Girls! I never knew those little coeds were such willing impish numbers. Besides that, word's out on campus that I'm the team stud, for cryin' out loud. I'm dubbed, 'Moose,' 'Gorilla,' and 'Stag.'"

"Nice analogy, Abe. I see many changes in you since you've been away, and all for the good. I hope you're using condoms with these one-night stands of yours. On a college campus there is all kinds of creepy crud."

"Well geez, Doc, I'm not screwing every girl I see. Sometimes I just fall into it, so to speak. That is to say...didn't really mean that as a play on words," he insisted.

Doc found it amusing. "Has Sarah seen a doctor about her sexual rigidity?"

"Probably not. If she'd go to anyone, it would be you. I'll encourage her." Even if *they* couldn't get things on, she needed to be sound for marriage and a future.

"Well, whatever you do this summer, just cool it. She'll make you a lovely wife, even if she's not terribly interested in your sexual advances. I believe that she *does* love you, and that's a heavily weighted factor in deciding who you're going to marry. She doesn't have to be a whiz in bed. Liz never was," he added.

With his legs crossed and his English accent heavy, Doc's words came easily, revealing none of the regret Abe had seen blossom and fade. "But I highly respected her, a lovely wife, cultured and knowledgeable. She wanted children desperately, other than that, she was pretty much unreceptive. It created some powerful tensions in me. She was aware that I had sojourns into the world of hired women. She simply acquiesced—tolerating playtime by a philandering husband. I'd have never left her. She was good to me, and never did anything against my best interests."

"You mean she *knew* you saw other women?" Abe asked with astonishment.

"Sure she did. You need to remember, however, that it's an enormous responsibility. One must be very discreet. I'd always go out of town—Chicago mostly—where I had the best contacts, best hotels and fabulous women, *mis enamoradas bonitas*. Most often, I'd get the same one." Doc's mouth molded into a smile of intrigue.

Abe hung on every word, his expression one of dismay, yet admiration.

"You could do that too. Sarah doesn't have to be the be-all and end-all of your sexual desires after you're married, even if she is your nexus with being a kosher husband. Someone else can satisfy that niche for you, while you're in a win/win situation—having a lovely lady for a wife *and* having someone on the side too. Think about it. It worked for me." Doc rewarded Abe with one of his rare big smiles.

"I can't get near her now. Poor girl. I forgot all the niceties of courtship. I nearly killed her, at least psychologically. I know the incident still colors her thinking."

Lifting his eyes to Doc's big bay window, Abe ingested the lingering twilight of June. Trailing streaks of coral, fuchsia and baby pink brushed across the sky.

Doc rubbed his face. "You know what to do, at least for this summer?"

Abe nodded a go-ahead.

"Whenever you're going to be alone with Sarah and you feel it's going to be an occasion of lust, visit Abbie first. That way you won't have a full head of steam and you can be more cognizant of her trepidations about sex. You need to control your libido."

"Maybe, maybe that would work. That could be the solution, at least temporarily. That's a good idea, Doc. I'll keep it in mind." He nodded his head, his smile fading with the realization that he'd probably not see Sarah alone all summer anyway. It seemed there remained nothing between them. Strange, she'd been his soul mate since the time they were youngsters in the sandbox, scavenging the beach, sharing classes at school. She'd been him. He'd been her. How does one lose that?

Rising from his chair and crossing to the window, Doc too scanned the skyline. "Now let's chow down, you and me. I might just have one more beer with my dinner. Join me?" Doc turned to him, his glass empty. Harry James played on with "I'll Be Seeing You," coiling the room in warmth and camaraderie.

※

Arriving home after the Fourth of July celebration, Abe found Ma and Sarah unpacking the car. "Hey, ladies, it's so nice to see you. I'll help with that paraphernalia before you break your little-lady backs!" He smiled with amused self-confidence.

"Hey, Abe, it's good to see you!"

Sarah looked even more beautiful than recent memory served him. Who could stay in the loop when you saw someone once a year? Much more sophisticated and self-assured, her dark brown eyes were a sea of wonder. Long dark lashes lifted to reveal eyes shining with warmth. She looked more radiant; she seemed to be grasping the tiller of her life. Like a doll, her head matched her perfect shoulders. Her waist curved in as if it were molded. And her hips—so round. She was too beautiful by half again as much. Abe sucked in his breath looking at long legs in short shorts! Damndamndamn!

Bumping through the house and lifting the windows, Ma made herself at home immediately. "I can't tell you how nice it is to be back. I forgot how lovely this home is. Thank you, Abe, for all your help. You'll have to come over and have dinner with us tomorrow night. I'll fix steaks on the barbecue Max built and we'll have a picnic." She brushed soft ringlets from her forehead—just like Sarah so often did.

That's that genetic thing Jan and Nancy were talking about.

Abe knew better than to accept dinner with them. He knew instinctively that the nearness of Sarah gave rise to a voodoo potion he couldn't handle. "Thank you, Ma, but maybe we can make it another time and give you a chance to get a taste of summer first."

Abe warmed to see the Savin's lights on again in the evening. They awakened a clarion of memories of his childhood—coming home at night after shoveling sidewalks for the Company and after the jackknife fiasco. The early evenings when darkness curled with cold and dampness, sometimes snowing and blowing. The Savin's yard lights welcomed him like a homing beacon. Maybe some things you never outgrow.

The suns of summer slipped away all too quickly as he ran the length of the beach every evening, sometimes out to the Indian Point Trading Post, lingering for dinner. He never allowed himself a spare moment and fell into bed at night exhausted.

Because of his time pressures, he hoped the quality of his art wouldn't slip. Working on two submissions this year, Abe felt pleased with the final flourishes on "Old Man and the Sea." The old man's blowing hair stood in relief, as well as the curling belly hair of his cocker spaneil . He had no doubt of the caption for the second one: "Peaceful Pastorate," featuring St. Andrew's Parish as observed from the north-northeast with just a hint of the cemetery in the background. He inserted Fabian's gravesite in the picture, but only Abe would know that. A gravel road ran down the length of the church to the cemetery, becoming less significant as it disappeared behind the building. Slightly ajar, the front doors revealed a radiant light shining from within. Reaching into an azure sky, the steeple appeared to pierce the whiff of clouds—one floating from the edge of the canvas. Abe felt a compulsion to meld into the picture physically, force the church door open farther and enter the exquisite bliss emanating from within.

On a hot and steamy day in the first week of August, Abe rolled the clackety-clack push mower back into the garage when he caught sight of Sarah in the yard, cutting her traditional table bouquet of flowers.

"Sarah!" he shouted. "There are only a few days remaining before I return to Ann Arbor. How's about we drive out to Farley and Norrhea's tonight and visit with them for a while?" *Can't hurt to devote time to her as a courtesy to the many years we were inseparable. Haven't paid her as much as a visit all summer*

"Sure thing, Abe. We never seem to have enough time together," she said, coming out her front gate with an armful of long-stemmed blue larkspurs. "The flowers are so perfect his year. Max would've been proud of his gardens."

Abe stood transfixed, wiping his sweating forehead with the back of his forearm. *What a picture! Warm weather ringlets clung to her forehead and temples; mahogany hair in a shoulder-length pageboy. How incredibly clear were her brown eyes, a dream with heavy lashes, all complemented by the delicate hues of blue and white of the bouquet. Click.* He captured the moment in a pigeonhole. He seldom looked her way, but swore at himself for knowing every move she had made all summer long.

He acknowledged that she contained a rare combination of wholesomeness, intelligence and beauty, but they couldn't negotiate a cease-fire. He could anticipate no peace pact returning them to the trusting relationship they had enjoyed since they were in Dick and Jane Readers. There were thick and heavy differences. Abe deeply resented how she clung so stubbornly to the causes behind her father's death.

Sitting on the back porch of Farley's home, facing the lake, the four enjoyed a leisurely early evening. "Farley, tell Sarah how you met Norrhea and married her. It's such an interesting story, and traditionally Sioux." Abe relaxed with Sarah as they listened to Farley's nostalgic legends, tales and traditions of his heritage. Abe unwound in a canvas, sling chair, wearing a pair of white duck shorts and navy and white striped shirt that barely hid his long lean muscles. His body was deeply tanned. He wore a pair of tire-tread huaraches, which he flipped on and off his heel. They'd stretched somewhat since Walter and Anne had brought them back for him after a winter's trip to Mexico.

"...so one thing led to another and I found myself married to my brother's daughter, right here at the Indian Point Mission." Farley indulged in rendering a historical accounting of Abe's people and what was socially acceptable to them.

"Glass of homemade chokecherry wine, Sarah?" Norrhea asked encouragingly. "I made it myself." She edged forward in her chair.

"Well?" Sarah hesitated and looked to Abe for approval.

He nodded and smiled. *That should give daddy's little girl a kick in the ass.*

"Sure. Thank you very much. I'd be delighted. I've never had homemade wine before. That'll be a treat, I'm sure." Although Sarah's words sounded trite and formal, her smile was genuine. "Do you need some help?" she volunteered as Norrhea rose and swept open the screen door to the kitchen, the coil spring inching its way out to full, complaining with the strain.

"No, no, no. Everything is under control. It's nothing, really." Norrhea's life would be meaningless without fussing.

Farley's tale-telling found no dampening by the interruption. "Families share their women with each other, with permission, of course." Farley nodded in deference to Sarah's tender ears. "The Plains Indians were nomadic and lived remote from any other culture. As a result, they looked within their own tribes for fulfillment. At Tribal Fire Councils, the practice of sharing their women with their best friends in a sort of pact or unwritten agreement is prevalent. They find no immorality in this. Sometimes I think the white man's culture is too civilized. Not enough sexual latitude is allowed."

Abe swerved his eyes to Sarah, catching the smile as it played around her lips, and was pleased that the Sioux philosophies seemed to make sense to her in the context Farley had presented them. Feeling his eyes on her, she tilted her chin up to better read him, but he avoided the contact by quickly returning his attention to Farley.

Crushed by his avoidance of her all summer, she collected her poise. Graciously, she straightened her petite le fleur dirndl skirt, smoothed her white peasant blouse and brushed her hand nervously over the three thin silver bangles she wore.

Abe was acutely aware of what a bastard he portrayed. He flirted with disaster. He knew that everything he'd wanted all his life could be found in her, waiting for her to take him to the Promised Land. He knew she could as no one else had ever done, yet she'd have to do some serious flip-flopping of attitude before they could get on with things, and that wasn't likely.

Stubborn bitch. If I Spend too much time with her and her prissy ways I'll probably end up opening a home for two-headed turtles instead of playing football.

Abe and Farley entertained their usual cold Schlitz. One led to two, and two led to three before the stories were all told and an August moon rose over the bay, competing with the last splendors of the sunset dying in the west.

"Thank you for the lovely evening," Sarah said graciously upon leaving. "I don't think I should've had that last glass of wine. I feel kind of woozy." Smiling brightly, her maiden brown eyes assumed a new depth.

"You're welcome, Sarah." Norrhea found this young lady completely disarming. "You tell Abe to bring you out here more often. He's too loose and doesn't share with us all the nice things in his life, such as you." She patted Sarah's hand.

Farley walked with his arm around Abe's waist. "Be careful on your trip back south." He had observed dramatic changes in Abe after his first two years at Michigan: strong facial contours, self-reliance and potency. He'd heard of the gift of the gods, but he viewed Abe as *his* gift *to* the gods, the gods of his ancestors.

"Thanks, Farley. I'll do that. Be sure to listen to the football games this fall on the Escanaba station. I'll be first-stringing it again this year." Abe's wide smile and perfect white teeth were breathtakingly spooky to his loving grandparents.

He looked so much like Suki. So much!

CHAPTER TWENTY-SEVEN

As he drove away, Abe waved to them, standing under the front porch light. It provided a fond memory he could carry with him to tweak and examine often. Driving the short two miles back to Nahma, Abe pulled off to the lakeside on the airport road. "Have to take a whiz. We can stop here for a few minutes." He shut off the headlights and the engine.

"Abe! That word!"

"Come off it, Sarah. Whiz-whiz-whiz!"

Her eyes fell at his smarting reply. She readily admitted that she had to do the same thing. "But I can't go on the beach like you can." She appraised the parking spot, looking for the shelter of some bushes.

"For Christ sake, Sarah, there's some beach scrub growth over there." He pointed behind the car. "Doesn't her ladyship know how to pee in the woods?" He laughed, but he remembered the time she was brokenhearted because the boys secretly watched her change clothes in the bushes at the beach. *Maybe she was the proper one and he was basically a mere lower primate.*

"Don't say that word, Abe. It's not proper." Her lips pressed together in a pout.

"You need to toughen your ears, Sarah. People *do* say words like that." He recklessly smiled at her inability to handle beach brush on her butt while she peed.

"Well, okay. I guess it's any port in a storm," she said reluctantly. Abe watched her wander to the tree line while he unzipped his shorts and stood rugged only yards from the car door to relieve his aching bladder.

Returning, Sarah found the car radio playing softly and the warm night air gently stirring. "Let's Dance," the radio announcer said, "is being brought to you by the National Biscuit Company on NBC Radio featuring Benny Goodman, The King of Swing and his classical clarinet!" The Goodman band broke into "Dream." "Things never are as bad as they seem, so dream, dream, dream."

Reclining back behind the steering wheel, Abe grew mellow. "You know, I heard that Benny Goodman has black musicians in his band, one of the first big bands to integrate blacks and whites. He said that if a guy's got it, let him give it, because he's selling music, not prejudice. That's the way Coach Kreiler is too. He has at least a dozen black players on the Michigan team all the time."

"What's more, Benny Goodman is Jewish!" Sarah exclaimed and brightened.

Looking over at her was like having to pay a penance. Her lips carried a glistening quality in the brilliant moonlight. He could feel himself slipping under her spell, drawn to her in inexplicable magnetism, as if it were manifest destiny. Intense heat prowled in his bones. He ignited such as this with no other women—only her. He silently cursed. It maddened him that she could stir his needs. He shored himself, knowing any further commitments would only lead to more heartache for him. Starting the engine, he turned the car around— knew he had to leave quickly to stay in control.

"Do you not like me at all anymore, Abe?" Her voice was small, a thread of curiosity. Hadn't she been distinctly let down and rejected?

He stopped, staring straight ahead. He reached down and turned off the engine, leaning his head on the steering wheel, and fought against desires he thought he'd squelched long ago, desires that prodded his whole body as if a thousand tiny demons poked him with minuscule pitchforks.

Sarah had observed so many changes in him this summer—the hard line of his jaw, the Sioux definition of his cheekbones more pronounced, also his aloofness and studied avoidance of her. After all these years together, was there someone else? She reached over and put her hand on his arm—lightly, ever so lightly—disturbing the curling hair that lived there. He quickly put his hand over hers, quieting the movement of her fingers.

"I don't know where I stand in your food chain any longer," she said, tilting her head better to see him, her eyes teasing. Should she say anymore? She wasn't going to beg, if that's what he wanted. She'd fry in hell first.

His anger at himself reached a feverish pitch as he pulled her roughly to him and brought his mouth down hard on hers, mashing her teeth; he'd penalize her for the anguish she'd caused him in the past two years. Instead, he found her mouth warm and soft, feeding his soul with a peace he only found with her. He groaned without releasing her, his lips becoming tender, seeking and drinking all she had to offer. He needed her so badly—her encouragements, her love, her warmth, her humor and her dependability. He wasn't whole without her. She was so right for him, he reasoned wildly.

"You still love me, Abe." Her voice conveyed the deliverance she felt.

He wrestled with the frustration of his thoughts, unable to sort them out. He thought he had his life all figured out without her. He needed her love, not another broken heart. Could he separate them? Her attitude over the past two years had been reprehensible to the point that he'd shut the door. Now, in just a few moments, all the old raw emotions ran through him—fresh, new, undeniable.

"I'd love to hear you say it, Abe. I need to hear you say it." Her voice caught.

The eyes he turned on her were decisive, warm. "Yes. I've denied it too long. I do love you, Sarah. You mean so much to me. I'm nothing without you. I've always been so proud to have you for my woman, but we need changes. You must put me first in your life. I refuse to be treated as a back-burner item. And you must stop over-valuing incidents that are out of our control." He moved his arm up over the seat.

She held his attention, continuing with contrition and confidence. "There's no one else in my life, Abe—just you. I admit that I've been unreasonable in the past year or so, and you've felt it more than anyone else. I love you too. I want to be your wife some day. Let's plan a June wedding in 1948, right after we both graduate." She found security in the thought. Abe had always been so protective and possessive.

"Sarah?" Abe returned his hands to his lap, resting his head, staring at the ceiling.

"Mmm?" she said softly, turning to him.

"I think that's a good date. However, I don't want your frigidity problems to escalate. You need to see Doc for some help." He was firm and clear, the pressure of this problem far outweighing others.

"I'm still thinking about it, Abe. That's a very difficult thing for me to do, a most debilitating decision to tell a doctor that it hurts to have intercourse. All the girls at school are intimate with their fiancées and have been for years. Here I am, still holding out." She put her head down, smoothing non-existent wrinkles from her skirt.

"Sarah?" His voice sounded hoarse.

"Yes," she breathed, barely a whisper.

His nerves taut, he persisted in his demands. It was now or never. "I'm not going to marry you under the present conditions. You'll need to get pregnant, sometime. And I think you know how to get yourself with child. So make up your mind. Do you want to keep what's left of your virginity, what I didn't already take, or do you want a happily married life with me?" He turned his head to her, meeting her surprised eyes.

Discontent surged through him. "I'm not going to settle for half a marriage. I want it all. You tell me when, and I'll provide you with an abundance of baby batter. When your tiny belly starts rising and I see for myself that you are pregnant I'll marry you." He wasn't smiling. With hands resting on his stomach, his eyes studied her face.

"Abe, you know I can't handle what you have! And don't say things like that. That's so crude." Her hand reached out to his.

Taking her hand, he leaned towards her. "Getting you pregnant is exactly what I want to do. Make no mistake about it. And it's not crude to say how I'll accomplish that. It's what I'm going to do the first chance I get. I don't care if it takes twenty...er, ah exposures. There, is that better?" He allowed the last words to be spoken just over her lips, his words not a threat but a promise—a promise not to be negotiated, but demanded. Sioux Culture measured a man's worth by the children he created.

His face advanced too near hers. She wasn't thinking clearly. Maybe it was the wine. "I'll make an appointment next week to see Doc, but will you tell him what my problem is? I just can't do that. It's going to be so humiliating. I wish you could be with me. I'd feel so much better." Her eyes flooded with tears of apprehension.

"Sarah, I love you. Sure, I'll tell Doc. He's my best friend, and already knows about it." He wrapped her face in his hands, kissing her eyes.

She pulled away. "What? You've been discussing me with Doc?"

He put his hand over her mouth and pulled her closer. "Nothing's private between Doc and me. I share everything with him. You understand that? He's my best friend. Remember that, Sarah. He'll make our lives much more compatible." Tilting her head up with his hand, he covered her small warm mouth with his.

"Mmmm...mmmm...mmm," she succumbed under the pressure of his kiss.

Slowly, her arm crept around his neck, running her hand through his short haircut. It felt so good. He smelled so good. She trickled her hand down over his shoulders, his furry arms. She moved slowly back up his arm, feeling his muscles and firm hard shoulders under her slim fingers as she circled his ear and cupped the back of his head.

He licked her teeth, nuzzling her mouth open, inserted his tongue, slowly and lightly, then more forcefully. Pulling her upwards against his body, she felt as supple as a wood sprite.

Sarah felt helpless to move from his vise-like arms. *The smith a mighty man was he with strong and sinewy hands. The muscles of his brawny arms were strong as iron bands.* "The Village Blacksmith." Longfellow skirted through her mind, drawn up from some unknown reservoir, teasing, for some quirky reason. Did she unconsciously make light of the situation, or was the situation so like the poem? She responded to his searching tongue with a twist of her own. Why'd she do that? Maybe it was the wine.

He made a throaty sound. "Christ, Sarah. You fill up my senses. You're hypnotic. Your magic keeps me trapped. Even when you're not near, I can smell you. Your chemistry is as clean as fresh sheets. It's intoxicating. I feel your softness and I glow; your voice brings me peace. I am hard hard-wired to you and only half a person without you; your presence is therapeutic." He struggled to stay in control.

"I feel confined. What say you we go lay on the beach in the warm sand. I have a blanket in the trunk." He was already moving to get out.

"Okay, but Abe..."

He turned back.

"Please don't force yourself on me." Her voice was small and plaintive.

"I won't. It won't happen. I've been curbing my libido. Doc told me I had to do that. But that doesn't mean I can't lay with you." He smiled reassuringly.

The blanket fell smoothly on the sand in the warm still night. Turning to Sarah, he found her reaching up on her tiptoes to kiss him. Pulling her toward him, he knew she'd find him hard and confident. He sought to leave her breathless.

"Ohhh, Abe. You have me tingling all over."

Grasping her bodily, he laid her down gently, kneeling beside her. She watched as he removed his clothing: shirt, slowly unbuttoning it, revealing a forest of black hair, never taking his eyes off her. She could see the worship on his face. She felt so loved, wanted and needed after a summer of neglect and avoidance.

The moon had machetied a swath across the lake, cutting through the intermittent clouds, walking right up to the shoreline and licking at the sand and water, greedy with the desire for license to navigate up to them. Almost as if it, too, was seeking Sarah, to implant her with its seed, creating a Moon Princess.

Christ, Doc, I'm doing my best not to devastate this woman. I want to ravage her. Eat her. He'd settle for less. Whatever he could get.

Bending near, he kissed her lightly, smoothed her peasant blouse from her shoulders. A lacy white bra held her small breasts apart. Moving her sideways, he unbuckled her bra. *Stay in charge. Faint heart never won fair maiden.*

He pulled the straps down over her shoulders—pure ivory in the moonlight— revealing small, perfect breasts that he fell into, fondling, kissing, nuzzling, biting.

"I love you," she whispered.

"I love you *what* Sarah?" His voice was raw with passion.

"I love you, Abe." Her hands were entwined in his hair, holding him in place.

"I love you Abe *what?*" he asked, nuzzling near her ear, his breath hot.

"I love you, Abe Miereau. I've always loved you," she sighed deeply.

Moving up, he feathered kisses over her cheeks, her eyes, her ears, her neck and back down to her breasts, which he tried again to devour. "What will your name be in June of 1948? Say it, Sarah. Let me hear it." His whispers floated over her mouth.

"Sarah Savin-Miereau?" she teased, her eyes twinkling.

"I'll give you *Savin*. It'll be Sarah Miereau, and that's the last we'll hear of that," he said as he brought his mouth down hard on hers, demanding, searching, and coaxing.

Sarah stiffened with apprehension at the thought of her previous experiences with him, hoping he wasn't going into one of his bubbles where he heard and saw nothing.

He tossed his white duck shorts aside, but remained in his jockeys, watching her turn away. *She is so spoiled, so sheltered. It'll be a cold day in hell when I can get this woman pregnant—fat chance.*

His chest covered hers as he lay back down beside her. Waves of crisp curling hair slid on her breasts. She squirmed with his aggressiveness. He hoped the ball stayed in play. Slipping his hand up under her skirt, he felt the smooth expanse of her thighs, the flatness of her belly, the belly he wanted swollen—his belly, his woman.

He didn't know if he could resist this without forcing action on her. He should have done what Doc suggested and gone to see Abbie this afternoon. He wanted her so badly he had tears in his eyes.

The lazy waves on the shore were hypnotic and arousing on this voluptuous summer night. Two prolific cell structures were in a cocoon of rapture. At the shore, the tiny waves played a sonata of the soul, lulling, soothing and embracing—playing their minds like a finely-tuned Stradivarius.

Abe whispered and cajoled, aching with lust and desire. He lay down next to her, disciplining his libido.

Why did this have to be so difficult? It seemed as if it was trying to open a safe without the combination. Other women would have been performing for him by this time. "How do you feel, Sarah? Are you okay with this?"

She looked up at him, her eyes reflecting the same distress and torment as his. "Yes," she whispered, at a loss for words at these wonderful sensations encircling her body. "Ohhh," she moved her hips.

My God! Maybe there was hope for this woman yet.

He reached down, cupping and touching her.

"Ohhh," she said as she jerked and arched her back.

This is where he'd made the Rose Bowl of all mistakes the last time and attacked her. Not this time. *Don't do it, Abe. Don't do it, boy. You'll be sorry. You'll probably not see her for another year, or longer.*

He crept up, straddling her body, his hardness holding high against her stomach, pulsating. *You're dead meat, Miereau. You're done for.*

She's still dessert, Fabian.

She's still dessert.

CHAPTER TWENTY-EIGHT

It was just a jacket, but Abe was so proud to be wearing it; just a dark blue jacket, the M Go Blue jacket, the letterman's jacket—*his* jacket. The memorable scenario was indelible—sitting in the bleachers as a freshman, working on his canvases, admiring the jerseys, the sweatshirts, the jackets, but at a price unattainable to him.

His old teammates had reported for the '46, '47 academic year at Michigan. They were enthused. Pre-season had gone smoothly. Abe and Bob Chapin hoped they were still the starting lineup receivers, with Bruce Hulk the quarterback starter, Bump Ness the fullback and Chuck Burgher at halfback. They were Abe's circle of friends.

He especially liked his choice of credit hours this year. Now he would get his teeth into The Themes and Symbols of Western Art, Art in America, Junior Pro-seminar, and Independent Study, his favorite, because it allowed him to study under an instructor in the field, and out of the classroom.

It was time again for Coach Kreiler's opening-game gusto pitch. Sitting this year in the upper levels with the Junior and Senior players, Abe heard only whispers.

The door opened. Kreiler blew on stage.

"All Right, you new Players! Pay attention! They call it a 'game' we're playing here—football—but it's a ruthless situation out there."

Ah-oh, here comes the tradition speech again. Tradition toned good, all the tradition. Being part of it stimulated a natural high.

"The quarterback is not trying to grab the center's balls when he sticks his hands under his ass. He's waiting for the football to be snapped so he can pass it to a back who will run for a touchdown in front of seventy-five thousand spectators, even if the NCAA rules don't permit him to have any spending money for froufrou."

No froufrou, no. Abe had received a football scholarship this year, as well as his art scholarship. He was attending college free! He couldn't believe the dumbass luck, getting a double chit to a first-class college most students couldn't even afford.

Coach Kyle drew on intensity. "Football is the supreme test of bravado in sports, but there used to be more dread involved. That's when the players didn't wear facemasks. I don't want to see anyone on the playing field without a face mask." Standing behind the podium, Kreiler tapped the eraser end of a pencil on the top.

"Contrary to popular belief, you can't be stupid and play football." Tap, tap, tap.

"If you're wearing an attitude of disregard, you'll sit on the sidelines. If you think you're Mr. Remarkable, you'll also rest on the sidelines." He threw the pencil up in the air for a loop, catching it without a hitch.

"For you players who've never left the State of Michigan, we'll be traveling to such glamorous places as Minneapolis, Minnesota at 40° degrees below zero and to Iowa City, Iowa where the wind whips into the stadium at fifty miles an hour. Football is ten percent glory and ninety percent work and high tolerance. To a person who isn't as big as all of you, it's a daunting experience." Kreiler flipped pages in his notebook.

"Few relics in college football cause more sensation than the Heisman Memorial Trophy, an award that is supposed to go to the exceptional player in the country each year, and sometimes does. It's usually a quarterback, receiver or ball carrier. We're dusting off the trophy shelf, getting ready for the Heisman. We have character, capability and grit on this team. That's what I'm talking about. You can't teach it. You can't buy it. But we have Heisman material on this team."

Character? They should've known Eddie Arsenault. He'd outrun half the guys on this team and still go eight rounds with his cousin in bed. Now that's character.

"There's a fixed gulf between college football and the pros. College teams rationally play football from September through November, whereas the NFL plays from early August until all the winter snow has melted from Khyber Pass. College football has scrumptious cheerleaders, marching bands and stirring fight songs."

No one oozed more scrumptious than Sarah. She had started her treatments with Doc—so far, just psychological tests. He'd finish them at Thanksgiving and Christmas break.

"I don't want to have to tell you again for the rest of the year that the following football *faux pas* will not be tolerated:

"One—failure to get off a punt." He paused, his eyes sweeping his fifty players.

"Two—poor snaps from center." Arrows were flying.

"Three—poor handoffs." He banged his fist on the podium.

"Four—a delay penalty...no excuse!"

"Five—a clip. Don't even think about it."

"Six—forget the snap count and go offside. For this I kill."

A fate worse than the charging of the bulls in Pamplona. At least you had a chance of out-running the bulls.

"Our university, as well as the whole country, is undergoing readjustment pains since the end of the war. You all know that freshmen have become eligible to play football during this time. More importantly, scores of veterans returning from Europe and the South Pacific are eager to resume their disrupted college careers. Resultantly, I had one hundred and twenty-five prominent varsity candidates from which to choose my fifty-man squad this year." Kreiler stepped down from the dais, put his hands behind his back and began pacing the room.

Wait'll I tell Farley. He'll be so proud of this Sioux Indian from Nahma. I need for him to know that his grandson passed muster.

"So your sheer presence at this meeting means you are the cream of the crop, the survivors, the meltdown elixer of untold hours of dedication. We'll work hard to mesh together this year, polishing our plays beyond mediocrity. Don't ever settle for that. You'll wind up like a slug. Trust me on this.

"We'll continue our single-wing offense and platoon system. The tactic will be a dizzying, rapid-fire series of fake handoffs, spins, reverses, pitches and passes, involving every man in the backfield, as well as the ends. We'll always leave a designated offensive back or end on the field when the defense platoon comes in.

"Offensive Team!

"Hulk! You're starting quarterback.

"Ness! You're starting fullback.

"Burgher! You're starting halfback.

"Chapin! You start as one of the receivers.

"Miereau!"

Silence.

I wonder how Doc is enjoying his vacation out west, hunting and fishing. He sure deserves it. Two months off to relax in the Dakotas and Montana. I miss him; *Doc is the nicest thing between the Sturgeon River and the end of time.*

"Miereau!" Kreiler launched a shot over the bow.

"Here!"

"Will you pay attention? You start as the other receiver, and I hope you're more alert on the field."

Laughter spread throughout the hall.

"Manny Mansfield at Center, Dick Riff at tight end, Bill Prita at tackle, Joe Sabol at tackle, Dom Tomm at guard and J. R. Black at guard.

"Let me burn this brand on your brain. You won the roll of the dice for starting lineup, but we have talent in flux, talent running deep if you lay up, lay off or lay down." He stopped in the center of the room, pausing, his eyes scanning each player.

"Defensive team! Roc, Wahl, Creel, Troll, Ruthles, Tyber, Dumore, Volvo, Mazda, Rowe and Hale. The same message goes for you.

"There will be no ethnic privileges or segregation at this University, neither tactical or by subterfuge. We don't need resolution to problems such as these, because we are simply not going to have them. Period. Back up halfback will be Gene Derry and ends Bob Lann and Lenny Dodge, who are African-Americans. Make them welcome on this team because they *are* welcome. And that's the last we'll hear on that subject."

☙❧

It dawned an unseasonably cold forty-degree day for the fans who wedged their way into Spartan Stadium for the Michigan-Michigan State Game. They didn't have to wait for the kickoff to get a clue that this game would be played at a high intensity level. While Michigan warmed up at the north end of the field, the Spartans came charging out of the tunnel. Two years earlier the Wolverines had meekly stood aside and let the boisterous hosts bolt through. Not this time.

Abe again took offense to a green-clad opponent who bumped him as they went through their calisthenics. Tense and savage, Abe recoiled and proceeded to deck the Spartan offender, and a full-scale but brief brouhaha broke out.

The atmosphere was anxious when Kreiler reprimanded Abe. "We get a bad aura over incidences such as this. I know you just retaliated and that the Indians really are the good guys, but try to count to ten more often." Immediately Kreiler turned his head to restrain a smile.

Abe caught the humorous flicker as Kreiler re-postured himself. For all the gruffness in the coach's voice, Abe was pleased that Kreiler was as happy as hell that he'd not taken the aggressive affront timidly.

Early in the game, State scored a touchdown and conversion point.

Now it was the third and three, a long field ahead of them, last of the fourth quarter, seven to zero, with Michigan in possession—the kind of play that induced Kreiler to chew his gum on the side like a rabbit. Hulk called a pass that he threw into the wide left flat. Abe was open, but the ball hung long enough for a defensive back to try for an interception. Abe saw it coming. He darted and side-stepped in front of the defender, leaped and received the ball with nothing but fifty-five yards of beautiful, unpopulated coliseum turf before him. Chapin ran by his side. Abe did his predictable Indian Sun Dance, bringing down the stadium with cheers. Game over! Score tied seven to seven. After the first quarter, Michigan defense with their three bad-boy black players held the Spartans scoreless throughout the game. Abe-mania grew like a strawberry rash.

Having been an underdog, barely squeaking by State the year before, the ensuing celebration by rooters of the Blue was worthy of a conference championship. Maybe Michigan hadn't beaten their East Lansing counterparts, but they hadn't lost either. That started the snakedancing down State Street. When the Michigan busses arrived on campus, they were mobbed.

The Thanksgiving game took place in Columbus, where the Ohio State Team awaited vengeance from last year's defeat. Little they knew. Along the Nahma beach, at least once each day during June and July, the tall wiry Sioux Indian had run through the white powder-soft sand. Wearing only shorts and hightop football shoes for the last three years, he had churned along those beaches at a brisk pace, made even more trying by weights he strapped to his ankles. Obviously, Abe Miereau liked to run.

So it unfolded no wonder that on that rainy afternoon at the Ohio State Stadium he slogged through ankle-deep mud and water and never seemed to tire. He assaulted the Ohio State defense time after time, singlehandedly controlling a championship game as no man would until super heroes started playing in the then-distant championship games called Super Bowls.

At six feet two inches and one hundred and ninety-five pounds, Miereau was not big by the standards of conventional-wisdom football, but as a wide receiver, he was as shifty as a halfback and had the dexterity of a deer. He could run a deep pattern, or run a quick slant across the middle. Either way, Miereau could bust a play for a touchdown. Many a beleaguered safetyman had to sacrifice his body as the last obstacle between Miereau and the goal line.

Instead of using his legs to mislead defenders, he would fake with his head and his shoulders. Maintaining his straight-ahead course, he would swing his head or drop a shoulder as if to turn or swerve, and more often than not the defender would be left bewildered, having missed the tackle or perhaps having been simply run over.

The two teams sparred for the first quarter. Repeatedly, Michigan's rushing game stood stonewalled by the Ohio defense. Soon Ohio's safeties were playing closer and closer to the line to try to contain the Michigan rushing game.

The Ohio team fell into the same mistake that many other teams had made in playing Michigan. In the second quarter, Kreiler told Hulk to open his passing game. The ball was slippery and the footing treacherous, but Hulk trundled back into the pocket and began throwing. Suddenly, the startled Ohio defenders were scurrying backward, trying to cover the Michigan receivers.

Hulk hit Abe for eleven yards, then again for sixteen more. Miereau teased the loosened Ohio defense, and Hulk could sense that his opponents were vulnerably indecisive. He called a pass play that sent Chapin across the middle, after a fake to Miereau running to the inside. The ball slipped on coming off Hulk's fingers as he aimed it at Chapin near the fifteen-yard line. This one seemed to stick as soon as it hit Chapin's fingers, however, and he came down with it, with no one around him. He quickly turned and blazed into the end zone. The Ohio State Team couldn't believe it. Michigan had used a play supposedly a specialty of theirs, and had scored against them. All that concentration on trying to stop Miereau had netted them zero.

At halftime, Michigan still led seven to zero. Hulk had thrown only nine passes, and although he'd completed five, he had twice been intercepted. Not wanting to risk costly turnovers, Kreiler shelved the passing part of his game plan.

On the other hand, Michigan's halfback, Chuck Burgher, had carried the ball on thirteen of the Michigan's twenty-four rushing plays. Kreiler informed Burgher that he would have even more work in the second half, as Michigan attempted to continue to control the game. Burgher had collected one hundred and twenty-one yards rushing for more than four times as much as the Ohio team total. For the Ohio team, their great passing quarterback had thrown for only five completions for merely forty-five yards.

The Ohio State attack was no better in the second half, though the rain finally ceased. The middle of the Michigan defensive line held the Ohio team to a paltry twenty-one yards rushing for the day. The team passing stymied them as well.

The game's only other touchdown came early in the third quarter when Abe, who had been left in to play defensive back, blocked an Ohio State low punt at the Ohio forty-yard line, scooped it up, and high-stepped it all the way into the end zone. Another Indian Sun Dance. The crowd went crazy…"Abe-Abe-Abe."

With the score now fourteen to zero and time on the scoreboard of only one minute, the University of Michigan made no pretense; it would be Miereau left in the game at defensive back, attempting to waste both the Ohio offense and the time remaining in the game. He did just that, by intercepting yet another pass with his lanky jumping, running it into the end zone for a deafening, standup, banner-waving mêlée as the stadium went wild. The scoreboard tilted crazily again with twenty-one to zero, a rout, under near-impossible playing conditions. That finished the day. The heavens filled with noise. "Abe!" they were hollering. "A-Abe!"

The team was made up of tigers. News crews boiled around. Flash bulbs popped.

Total yards gained by Miereau: one hundred and fifty-six of the team's total of two hundred ninety, a blocked punt and an intercept returned for a touchdown.

Kreiler had tears in his eyes and didn't scold Abe about his Sun Dance over the goal line. Jim Funt took a shower with his cigar still lighted. There would be no sleeping tonight, so the Michigan buses were boarded and they headed for Ann Arbor. The trek, no less than two hundred miles, was a riot all the way.

Abe read somewhere that success, in its sweeping path, is like a dependency drug; in triumph, it undermines your delight and in defeat, it deepens your despondency. Once you've tasted it, you're snared, and then you lie in bed, wide awake, seeing the other teams you will meet next week, next year, and constantly plagued by doubts.

܀

The post season, beached for the year, became history. It was crunch time for the rest of the term, especially for his three-credit-hour class with a private instructor in Independent Study. He tackled the mental picture he'd clicked of Sarah, holding the long-stemmed bouquet of larkspurs.

The early days of December descended upon Michigan with a cloak of gray and sudden early evenings. While working on his "Maid In The Mist" canvas of Sarah, Abe felt an urgent need to talk to Doc when the phone rang, jolting him as if he'd been shot.

"Abe! You've been heavy on my mind. How are you?" With the sound of Doc's voice, Abe re-visited the smell of his rich cigar smoke, the glow of his

The Taming of a Sioux

warm twinkling eyes, the sight of a rich Italian suit, shirt and tie.

"Pretty good, Doc. I was just thinking about you. I appreciated your calls from out west. You need to come to one of my games next year."

"You bet I will. We'll make a weekend of it. It'll be a nice respite."

"Well, I can't allow respite from Sarah. Have the first phase of her treatments been completed?" Abe had been building listening skills since sitting through lectures, and braced himself for an encouraging answer from Doc.

"It seems that her rejections are mental and can be allayed by continued visits." Doc spoke guardedly, not wanting to arouse Abe's fiery jealousy.

"That *is* good news." Abe had all he could do not to stop and do his Sun Dance.

"You tell her to call the office and set up some appointments. I don't want any unnecesary trepidation. It would be medical suicide. An oxymoron if I ever heard one."

"Maybe under that cool exterior rages a stream of magma!"

"Abe, you wouldn't..."

"Christ no, Doc! I got around third base, though, for the first time last summer. It seemed satisfying to her. Of course, something moved in it for me, too."

"Well, keep your distance until I've completed her series of office visits. So far it looks as if her condition can be relieved. I'll supplement her office visits with exercises. Maybe by the time you see her again she'll be just what the doctor ordered."

"Christ, Doc, will you stop being a comedian? This is serious business for me."

"Okay, settle down. You're only talking two weeks or less. Speaking of the Christmas holidays, I'd like to fly down and spend New Years with you."

"Why didn't you say so right away? You can come tomorrow if you wish. On second thought, you need to stay in Nahma long enough to give Sarah her treatments."

"Don't worry. Her treatments will be done before I leave. She's a beautiful woman, Abe, very attractive and put together well. But I have two somethings that I want to share with you. The first one is that the Clubhouse burned right down to the ground yesterday."

"No!"

"Yes. Turns, out, it was some bonfire. They're going to spend the rest of the winter clearing away the debris and rebuild in the spring. Maybe it happened for the best. That building dated back to 1923."

"Sonofagun! Lots of memories went up in smoke there!" Abe's heart called up many of his own—his licorice whip episode with ravishing Ruby Warren, the track team celebration, dances with Sarah, his auctions, graduations. His mind searched and sorted.

"I'll say, but shifting gears here, my second thing is going to be a total surprise. It's your Christmas present, and you're going to like it very much."

"Thanks Doc, but no presents. You've done enough. If you get Sarah fixed, that'll be my Christmas present for the rest of my life. Not to diminish your surprise, of course. Do you need a lift from the airport?"

"Thanks, but no. I'm going to rent a car because I'll have to run to various places while I'm there. I'll only be there the thirtieth, thirty-first and the first and flying back on the second. Oh, I've made reservations for New Year's Eve at the Allenal."

"You don't mean it!" Abe laughed, his warmth unmonitored. "Thanks, Doc." Abe ran his hand through his hair. *What was that "Christmas present?"*

❧❦

Early on the evening of the thirtieth, headlights beamed up the driveway. Abe bustled to lift the garage door as protection from the cold raw night. Logs crackled in the fireplace in anticipation of a conversation fest with Doc.

What the hell? There were two people in the car, one much smaller than Doc. It didn't take a Michigan Science Lab Full Professorship to deduce that he'd brought a woman with him. What now…?

Doc moved to the back of the car to hug Abe, his warm breath vaporizing in the cold air. With the smell of his tweed overcoat, the rich leather trim and a rich cashmere neck scarf, Abe warmed.

"Abe! Damn good to see you again." Doc wrapped an arm around Abe's shoulder, his eyes glowing.

Precious memories flooded Abe's heart. He knew it was an egregious mistake to underestimate Doc's wealth of capabilities to melt anyone's defenses.

Patting Abe's arm, Doc quickly moved to open the passenger door and bent to assist one of the most beautiful women Abe had ever seen. She was about Sarah's height, and wore shoulder-length straight black hair. Thick bangs complemented deep oval, dark-brown eyes. An exquisitely chiseled, well-defined nose and a smile wide and warm revealed to Abe cloud-white teeth that shone even in the dim garage light, her skin tawny like an island person, but somewhat lighter. She snuggled into a glistening brown mink coat. On her feet were stadium boots sporting dark-brown fur and laced up the front. Brown leather gloves covered her hands against the starkly cold night.

Abe couldn't stop staring. "C'mon in, fast," he said, finding his tongue. "It's freezing out here." He nodded at the exquisite woman and held the breezeway door open to hustle her through to the warmth of the kitchen.

Doc gathered her hand and ran into the house ahead of Abe, stomping his feet on the snow rug in front of the door, at once rubbing his hands together. Lady Mink Coat stood in the kitchen staring intently at Abe, narrowing her eyes uncertainly, but unable to hide the happiness dancing therein.

Doc paused, the heat of the home feeling wholesome and receptive. Something in his eyes made Abe think of mischief...but more, much more.

"My God, Abe, it's colder here than an Alberta Clipper. I thought you lived in the banana belt." His smile teased.

Abe laughed at the implications. "This *is* freakish weather for here, but we have to roll with it. The wind's been blowing all day, but we can sit by the fire and have a hot toddy." Abe knew he was rambling.

In a modality of "let's do first things first," Doc raised his palm in a halting gesture. "Abe, this is my fiancée. I want you to be among the first to meet her. We're going to be married tomorrow at St. Thomas the Apostle Parish on Elizabeth Street right on the campus. We hope that you'll be our best man. A son should be present to give his mother in marriage." Doc wore a playful smile, a small half grin.

Stillness ensued as a rueful countenance was entertained by Suki Miereau as she studied the impact on Abe, an air of indecision about her as to her posture.

"Abe, this is your mother. Tomorrow she will be Suki Whittaker, for which I am eternally grateful." Doc broke the hanging silence.

The color drained from Abe's face. Of all the psychic moments he'd had in his life, this time they failed him. He felt faint—made automatic movements while he continued in the kitchen, gathering coats scarves and gloves. In need of words, he stood silent, his mouth open, his heart racing. His eyes hadn't moved from this beautiful woman, who was still smiling at him. It seemed as if he were looking into a mirror—the same smile, the same teeth, the dark eyes, the black hair. He melted inside. He had listened greedily to the word "*mother*," but with stunned comprehension.

"Mother? Where? How did you...?" He paused, took a deep breath.

Doc was struck hesitant more than he'd anticipated to see Abe's guileless shock—the questions in his eyes. "That's why we came here tonight, to spend the evening with you so you wouldn't be so taken aback when we were married tomorrow." He had interfaced with this moment a thousand times in his mind. He knew it would be difficult, traumatizing, if not explosive. Abe had been reduced to a substance somewhere between Jell-O and marshmallows.

Doc professionally observed Abe's feelings of pure panic, his powerlessness to overcome the moment. "Here," he said with tenacity, "I'll take those coats for you and hang them up." Taking the burden from Abe, who had frozen in place, he led them both into the living room. "Come, you two and sit here by the fire. I'll tend bar." Doc felt at home and confident.

Reticent and in a daze, Abe took a chair across from Suki at the grouping he'd arranged comfortably around the fireplace. The drapes were drawn, muffling the howling wind. Ice crystals could be heard clicking against the large picture window.

Before sitting down, Suki rose, walked over to Abe, put out a small hand and addressed him cordially. "I'm so pleased to re-acquaint myself with you after twenty-one years." Her voice sounded low and receptive. "I know you're twenty-two years old, but I left when you were not quite one year old. I knew I couldn't continue my sham life with Fabian, living a lie, and betraying the love and trust he placed in me, so I left, secure in the fact that you had a very dedicated father who would care for you." She understood the coolness in Abe's eyes, accepting it.

"There was nothing in life in which he took greater pride than you. It's my fondest wish that someday, sometime, somewhere you'll find it in your heart to forgive that decision." Affection filled her voice, which sent a smile across Abe's mouth—not generous, but it wasn't derisive either. She would settle for that.

Abe searched for words. "Well, yes, I'm sure." Did he somehow recall this woman? Did he remember feeding at her breast, looking up into her eyes? What explanation could he attribute to this breathlessness he felt simply by being near her without ever having seen her before? He knew without qualification that she was someone he could trust and reach out to. Her voice sounded familiar, the resonance and timbre echoing through his bones, finding a home. Beauty is truth.

His glance darted to Doc, who was still standing in the foyer. At last words came stumbling out. "Forgive me for staring. It's difficult to get my bearings. Here I am rambling like some pigeon-headed parrot. You've been a spirit word to me all these years, a surreal dream." His tongue reached out and searched his bottom lip.

He watched as Suki walked to the fireplace. Her back turned to him, she studied the fire. She sighed, finding fault with herself.

The sound impacted him as if it were laden with remorse—regrets about irreversible decisions, lonely. Abe knew that nothing fell easier than fault finding;

no talent, no brain, no character is required to set up in the grumbling business.

"How about something to warm the cockles of your heart?" Doc asked, rubbing his hands together and smiling that half-smile that camped on his countenance.

Suki turned to face Doc. "Thank you, Danforth. I'll have some sherry, please, or chardonnay...whatever."

Doc nodded in affirmation as he swung his gaze to Abe. "I'm going to have Johnny Walker Red, Abe. How about you?"

Abe cut him a quick look, finding it difficult to remove his eyes from his mother. "Yeah, I need it, on ice, in a tub, a big one!"

Doc sat on the love seat that Abe had pulled in front of the fireplace when he had arranged the two wingback chairs on either side. Suki arose and joined him. Draping on either side of her crossed legs hung a navy blue pleated skirt. Navy platform shoes covered her small feet since she had come into the warmth of the house. Ever so lightly, a navy and white horizontally striped nylon sweater, with full-fashioned sleeves, fell softly over her firm breasts.

Puzzling thoughts clouded Abe's mind. "I assume you both got here today, from somewhere. I'm so lost, I can't think of an intelligent question," Abe said, gesticulating broadly with his arms. His Johnny Walker Red sat idle on an end table.

Doc's voice traveled alight with the excitement of the day. "I flew into Detroit Metro before Suki got there from Rapid City, South Dakota. I waited for her, then we rented a car, and here we are." His eyes were gleaming in the firelight. "In retrospect, that is hardly a fair or adequate explanation of the events leading to this evening. I think we both owe you that." Doc held his tumbler of scotch in both hands, leaning forward, his elbows resting on his knees.

Abe read his happiness and comfort level at a ten.

With a memory-retrieval sigh, he dropped his head back against the loveseat. "While I was out west on my trip last fall I visited the Badlands National Park. Of course, it would be difficult to go there and not see the Wounded Knee Monument where Farley's mother, your grandmother," nodding to Suki, "and Abe, your great-grandmother was killed. While there, I read the materials ascribed to the various exhibits, and a National Park Authority stopped to ask me if I was enjoying my visit. It was Suki! I hadn't seen your mother for a hundred years. But there she was, fresh, young, brand new and hardly changed from the last time I'd seen her!" Doc gave her a sideways glance, his eyes shining, patting her on the knee, his hand lingering.

It didn't escape Abe's notice. His eyes traveled from one to the other, studying and analyzing them.

"And did you recognize him, er...ah...what...what shall I call you?" He laughed nervously, splaying his hands wide of himself.

"Just call me Suki. I don't expect a patronizing name such as Mom or Mother. But I *would* like to be your friend, if you can acquiesce to that. And, yes, to answer your question. It took but a moment. We stared hard at each other. I was magnetized, hypnotized, swirling into his being like a fallen leaf circling a drain."

CHAPTER TWENTY-NINE

Yes. I knew him and warmed to him. It was Danforth Whittaker. We both said at same time, 'Aren't you...?' Suki laughed velvety and low, deeply in love, gazing up at Doc for reassurance.

He nodded, smiling. "And then I called her a few weeks after I got back, and asked her to marry me. Can you believe that?" Doc slapped his forehead. "Over the phone! It was totally unimaginative, but it turned out splendidly."

"And I said, 'yes!'" Suki squeaked. "After he left, I felt such a hole in my life. I hadn't seen him for more than twenty years, but I had missed him so. We talked non-stop for three days when he visited there. You were topical, Abe." She smiled, her eyes sparkling. "He told me what you were doing and about your powerful ability at painting and football." She made no attempt to disguise her admiration.

Abe smiled as he listened. This lovely lady turned out to be his mother! Abednego Miereau, you are one lucky sonofabitch! Yes, she was him. He was her. Other children digested this slowly over a lifetime, but the high-impact truth avalanched onto him in ten minutes.

She smiled at him, a warm and selfless beam. A sense of well-being pervaded Abe's body at rapid speed, as if by an injection. Maybe at some level it disturbed him, but he would not dredge up any ghosts. Old pent-up grudges were hedgerow upon hedgerow of battlements that disallowed growth.

Doc could feel Abe slipping into his bubble. "So Abe, what do you think of my luck at finding the most beautiful woman in the whole USA at the Red Ridge Indian Reservation in Badlands, South Dakota?" His senses were crying for comment on what had to be the biggest surprise of Abe's lifetime. The young man's faith must have been tested repeatedly, growing up without a mother, and feeling abandoned.

"I think. I think..." He swallowed. The realization of having a tangible mother after all these years had released new sentiments—one of ties, one of belonging, one of being wanted and loved after all. At the end of a long string of frustrations and lack of confidence, he was sitting in the same room as his mother! Unable to make further answer and embarrassed, his head slumped.

Doc arose and massaged Abe's head, his thick black hair, rubbing it sideways and flipping it back into place. No words were exchanged.

Gaining in composure, Abe lightened. "Thanks, Doc. You're a phenomenal Medicine Man; you made my mother appear out of nowhere, *poof.*"

Doc's countenance was sober, standing next to Abe, looking down. "The only thing that could make this evening more complete would be to tell you that I would've been proud to be your father, Abe. At least by marriage, I'll be your family."

"Doc, you've always been my family—always been there for me. Fabian would have been so proud." His voice teetered for control.

"Danforth, perhaps another cocktail?" Suki's voice was diminutive.

Doc looked up quickly. "Yes, of course. I'm sorry for letting it go unnoticed. Is it another Red for you, Abe?"

"Thanks, but no. My last one is dying from neglect, as is the fire. I'll get a couple more logs," he said, slapping his knees in a gesture of finality.

Both came back at the same time. Opening the glass fire doors, Abe gently inserted the new logs on top of the smoldering embers of the old fire. Flames licked up over the bark of the new energy source—yellow, orange, blue-green and red.

Extending an arm over the back of the loveseat, Doc coddled Suki in his grasp. They looked so natural to Abe. Kinda like God—always was and always would be. Doc bent over, nuzzled Suki's bangs up out of the way and kissed her forehead. She smiled up at him, her worship and love not withheld.

Abe already liked this woman. She would be good for Doc. Seeing them together conjured up cream with coffee, syrup with pancakes, and salt with pepper. It warmed him, viewing them from the distance of his chair.

He'd never once seen Doc make any public overtures to Liz. She was too proper. *Someday,* he thought. Someday, maybe he and Sarah could sit in front of a fire and look at each other that way. Damn! If growing up meant that you don't hurt anymore, than he wished to hell he'd grow up.

"I need to find the powder room," Suki said with a hint of shyness.

"Oh! I apologize." Doc pointed down the hall. "Need some help?"

"Danforth, will you stop that?" Suki was secretly tickled at his forever teasing.

As she disappeared down the hall, Abe wheeled around and clutched Doc's arm. "Christ, Doc! Don't ever do anything like that again." Abe grinned. "You'll never know the impact. It left me naked...without any armor. Congratulations are clearly in order. She's beautiful, and of all things, she's my mother! It's a resurrection, for Christ's sake!" The inadvertent play on words caused their eyes to lock and crinkle.

An energized wind swooped down on the house with another assault of ice and rain, making the living room feel wrapped in warmth.

Doc crossed one foot over the other knee, holding his ankle. "I simply couldn't believe it when I saw her there at the Wounded Knee Monument. She looked like a specter, an oracle. It struck us both at the same time, then the words tumbled out, one over another. We'd have to stop each other to say something."

Suki returned, looking bright and alive, yet preoccupied. "Well, I took a personal tour of this lovely home. You're so lucky, Abe, to have this nest while you're in college."

She lowered herself comfortably next to Doc. He took her hand, kissed it, lingering on her fingers, as the wind continued in its unrelenting madness, clicking at the windows with late December's wrath.

Waxing in the warmth and wholesome of the house, Suki cleared her throat. "What a perfect moment in time," she said, moving in closer to Doc. Her obvious demonstrable love was an element Doc had never known from the very proper Liz.

Abe gazed at them as if he were voyeuring, lapsing into a comfortable languor. He was so happy for Doc, and equally pleased to find his mother.

"Let's all have a nightcap before calling it a day," he suggested. "It's getting late, and the day started early."

"My turn to buy," Abe said, gathering the glasses. Refills accomplished, Abe found Suki had crossed to the front of the fireplace, her hand resting high on the mantle, scanning her two men. Doc yet lolled in the loveseat, his legs crossed in his take- charge persona—powerful, aggressive and confident.

"Here you go, my newly-found mother," Abe said, shifting his head sideways, looking at her in the dancing light of the fireplace.

Receiving the long-stemmed glass of sherry, Suki smiled fondly at this man in front of her—tall, virile, handsome. No thanks to her, except for his heritage.

"Thank you, Abe. You're even a nicer young man than I dared imagine. How lucky can I get?" She toasted her glass with his.

Abe, feeling tackled by tons of defense, clinked her glass. "Cheers to you."

"Gentlemen," she said, her voice loaded with incendiary seriousness. "I make a toast to my husband-to-be, my new-found son, and the father of my new-found son—you, Danforth." In her voice prevailed pained rawness at the revelation.

A stunned silence, rife with unspoken thoughts, filled the air. There were unanswered questions, fears, dismay, anxiety. The two men sat, stymied, eyes connecting, seeing each other for the first time as father and son. The explosive information settling in, they threw their glance to Suki, then again at each other.

Although Suki's breathing grew heavy, moving toward crying, she bucked up, eyes dry, taking a deep breath to go on.

Abe swore to himself that he couldn't handle any more of this cockamamie family stuff. His breath tore at his throat.

Doc sat like a piece of fulgurite, newly formed by a streak of lightning.

"Yes, Danforth, *you* are Abe's father, not Fabian. I happened to be already pregnant when I married Fabian, barely—just. Danforth, it was you, remember?" She sparkled with a knowing smile, making direct contact with Doc.

Doc's mind reeled, pulling labels off labels, punctuating his past with vagaries.

"I loved you so much. Our few encounters were like heaven. I'd have done anything for you, but it wasn't meant to be. You were committed, and I was engaged to Fabian. A Sioux does not renege; I had been promised to him for more than a year.

"I'll never forget, however, the sublimity of it all when first the Sturgeon River flooded and you came to help the Indian Point Mission. You provided inoculations and Red Cross assistance. Our few times together after working hard days with the homeless were etched in my memory forever. We melded so naturally in our love times. I only had three occasions to have conceived of your seed, and I did. I had been a virgin. I don't know how it happened so quickly, so irreversibly." Her face shone taut, as if she'd been beatified. "Abe is your child, your love child, not Fabian's. That's why I had to leave. I couldn't live a lie. I couldn't break Fabian's heart either. He loved his son. The situation seemed hopeless. I left with the bag of gold that Farley and Norrhea had given me as a wedding gift." She paused, her eyes flickering over both men appraisingly.

"I went all the way to Wounded Knee, got a job, furthered my education with a M.B.A. Degree and became director of the Badlands National Park. So the story comes full circle. Abe is your son, Danforth. Abe, Dr. Whittaker is your father." Her breath caught as if the very air was being sucked out of the room.

Her chin grew soft, quivering. "It hurts to open old wounds, wounds that have slammed repeatedly into my conscience, sometimes out of nowhere like a chill blast of arctic wind. Don't think it was an easy decision, leaving my beautiful child, feeling him yet at my breast long after I'd left, holding his tiny hand that curled around my finger while he fed, gazing up at me wide-eyed with trust, smelling his baby freshness. I can still see the little beads of sweat that formed on his forehead while he nursed, feeling the fullness and satisfaction of motherhood with him soft in my arms. It haunted me forever, until I thought I would lose my mind, but there was no turning back." Her eyes sparkled with the vivid memories, focusing now on Doc.

"But I cannot marry you without you having full knowledge and understanding of this, both of you." She cut her surveillance back to Abe.

An enormous undercurrent swept through the room, her message touching each one with its electricity, emitting almost measurable static.

She paused, unable to go on. Panic seized her very being at what she may have sacrificed here with the truth. The truth, however, was more welcome to her than its counterfeits. A marriage without the truth would bring indelible destruction to all of them. Sheltering her face with her hands, she succumbed to the tears that lay latent for the past ten minutes. Hurrying from the room, she sought the privacy of a bedroom. A rigorous remorse of twenty year's duration had surfaced in the telling.

Doc sat back, rubbing his face with his hand. He sighed, long and lonely. The mechanism in his mind ratcheted slowly, retrieving stored reference, clicking like a cog railroad crawling slowly up the mountainside. Yes, he remembered. There it lay, stored in a locked niche he had to open.

His body scrunched forward. Head in his hands, he posed a compendium of hopelessness and regret. He wept uncontrollably for the pain this woman had endured and his complicity in it. The struggles she'd had and the absence of knowledge of the fruit of his groin. He counted the lost days, months and years. For Christ's sake, he'd delivered his own son!

He'd sat and had a drink with Fabian while Suki slumbered after her difficult labor, delivering a child too big for her small anatomy. He'd given it no thought whatsoever—yesterday, when he was young. Suki had found his most sensitive pressure point, his intrinsic sense of responsibility.

Abe, with but a few deft movements leaned his head on Doc's shoulder. Once more they found an occasion to weep together. For the times they had shared. For the times they had not shared. This time for a million regrets, for a tsunami of water over the dam, for irretrievably lost days and for memories never made.

Abe made a strangling sound. "Go to her, Doc." His voice struggled out as a hoarse whisper. "Tell her you'll devote the rest of your life to her comfort and well-being." Abe stood up in unison with Doc, the same muscles flexing, the same hearts beating, and the same arms outstretched and supportive.

Doc's deep English voice quavered. "Well, I wish she'd have administered anesthetic with that surgery. She opened me up and revealed all the things I hoped I wasn't: selfish, insensitive and even ruthless. Yes, I remember the times we spent together like two magnets, young, in love, warm and carefree. Suki founded love. Liz delivered compliance with my past. I chose the compliance, and threw away the one great love of my life." Doc gathered his professionalism again, as if bringing together the raveled ends of a jagged cut, finely sewing the violated skin back into something wholesome and new.

"How could I not have known you were my son?" His voice cracked. "Look at the numerous similarities. Even the finely tuned camaraderie we've always shared. I'm so proud of you, and here you are my son. I'll never be able to make up for all the years I wasn't there for you, never, but I'm going to make one helluva an effort." He reached out and hugged Abe, felt the steel-like strength in his back, his arms. *His son!*

"Well now, just see to it that you do." Abe answered in an attempt to bring levity into the revelation. "If I had to choose a father for myself after Fabian's death, it always would have been you. I relied on you for everything." Abe felt his throat tightening with the old familiar kindergarten lump.

"I, admittedly, have loved you for years." Doc's chin shifted to offset, while he clenched his teeth for self-discipline. "Now I think that I'd best do damage control."

☙❧

On New Years Eve morning 1946, Abe took a woozy walk to the bathroom. He shouldn't have had that last Johnny Walker—potent stuff.

It all hit him again. There was a woman visiting in the house. *A woman?* His mother! Doc's woman was his mother! Good thing she wasn't around while he grew up. He'd have been locked into an Oedipus Rex Complex so damn tightly he'd have never left the house. He wondered how long it would take to get used to having a mother, and Doc as his father. *His father!* There were all kinds of similarities, warmth and love. How could he not have noticed?

Still hearing nothing from the master bedroom, Abe showered, dressed and opened his easel in the living room to lay the closing touches on Sarah's canvas, "Maid in the Mist." It grew on him. There she stood, the early morning fog rolling in off the bay. Freshly picked, muted-tone larkspurs of blue hues lay across both her arms. Her mahogany hair curled around her temples in wayward wisps. Deep brown eyes, slanted slightly, widened with honest love; a pensive smile enchanted her face.

Falling gently off her shoulders, a white peasant blouse revealed flawless shoulders. Fresh, young and vital, a fine mist moisturized her skin with a dewy appearance. On her ears dazzled topaz earrings that emulated the larkspurs. The hand securing the flowers lay long and tapered. From her delicate wrist lazily hung a gold chain-link bracelet, a stone of dazzling blue topaz set into each link. As he added a very minute dab of iridescence to the stones, he sensed someone behind him.

Looking over his shoulder, her hands clutched behind her back, Suki showed great interest. "What a magnificent picture, Abe. It's breathtaking. That girl looks as if you could reach out and wipe the dew off her face. Someone you know?"

What the hell? Suki looked more beautiful this morning than when she went to bed last night. She was wrapped in a warm chenille robe of teal blue, tied about her tiny waist. At first Abe wondered if he'd forgotten to hike up the thermostat, but he was sure he had. Frequently, he second-guessed himself because his bubble insulated him from ordinary creature comforts. This morning, however, he had rekindled the fireplace, kicked in the furnace, opened the drapes, and shifted into daytime modality.

"Morning, Suki. If I forgot to tell you in my surprise last night how welcome you are, let me do so now." Abe turned around to face her. My God, how he would have liked to gaze into this fantastic face all his life! His mother...he got lost in her eyes, as if looking into his own.

"Thank you very much. I do feel at home. There hasn't been a day I didn't wonder how you were and what you were doing." She spoke frankly, her eyes unwavering. "Danforth has given me a new lease on life. It was difficult for me to leave my job; it spelled security. In just a few years I could have retired with half pay, but Danforth assures me I'll have no worries; he'll provide just as well as my half pay."

She smiled down at him, reminding him again that was *his* smile. It takes seventeen muscles to smile, but seventy-two to frown. What made him think of that? For cryin' out loud, *carpe diem*!

She bent her head, examining a fingernail, at a loss for further words.

Abe, sensing her insecurity, jumped up to busy himself. "Well, now, I trust you had a comfortable night's sleep, in spite of that dismal wind howling outside. The hurricane has transformed into a spring breeze and crept off into another county, thank God. What would you like for breakfast, Suki?"

"Don't worry about us, Abe. I'll take care of Danforth, whatever he wishes to have. You go on working on your picture. Tell me who the girl is. Someone special?"

"Yeah, it's Sarah Savin from across the street. I want to marry her some day." He looked at the picture reflectively, remembering a quote from his Michelangelo essay: 'The true work of art is but a shadow of the divine perfection.'

"Yes, I remember the Savins, but they didn't have children when I lived there. She's a lucky lady to have someone like you in her life. Conventional wisdom would say you're everything a woman could want."

Her face was sculpted so perfectly; Abe knew he could get lost in it. "Thank you, 'Ma'. I had nothing to do with that, however. It's all in the genes." He smiled, the deep resonance of his voice as sweet and deep as fudge frosting.

Suki smiled, squeezing his arm.

Doc, appearing from out of nowhere, stood in the dining room archway, pouring juice, wrapped in Walter's bathrobe. "What the hell's going on out here? A guy can't even take a shower without having someone else move into his territory."

Abe stared at him in amusement—Doc, his father—and acknowledged what a powerful face he had—strength and leadership, clearly defined.

Doc approached, bending closer to the picture, holding his glass of juice. "Nice canvas, Abe. Nice. 'When love and skill work together, expect a masterpiece.' Ruskin. Wait until Sarah sees that. And Ma! They're going to go nuts. But I've never seen her with those earrings and that bracelet. They're quite splendid."

"Let me show you something," Abe interjected. Jumping up, he bounded down the hall to his bedroom. "Look at this," he said, returning. Reverently, he opened two gray velvet gift boxes, revealing topaz earrings and a bracelet he'd purchased for Sarah.

"Holy jumpin' Jehosephat, Abe! Those are nice. Did you pull a heist on a bank?" Doc was genuinely awed at the glistening pieces with their insets of semi-precious stone.

"You aren't going to believe this, Doc. After I got back to school in August, Coach Kreiler had swung an athletic scholarship for me, so I'm going to school for absolutely nothing now. Free! Everything is paid. Take this little dumbass kid kicking around Nahma, put him in the big city, and see what happens?" Abe couldn't conceal his pleasure. "It's pure luck. Anyway, that means I've been able to save a lot of money." Abe smiled shyly, licking his lips, but only slightly.

"Remarkable. But then, it follows, doesn't it? Hard work and all," Doc said, patting Abe on the shoulder.

"There's more." Abe stood taller, snapping the boxes closed. "I bought myself a new tan pinstripe suit at Jacobsen's. It's a Baker Brothers wool flannel with a beautiful press; also a new white shirt, new tie with brown, butterscotch and white stripes. Oh, there are some little gold balls flirting with the stripes here and there, but they're too insignificant to mention. It's all been a stroke of luck. I'll wear the suit today."

Doc, listening as Abe spoke, drew the imagery of Abe—tall, dark, his Sioux bone structure regal with his tawny coloring—striking in the suit

"At Jacobsen's is where I saw the two pieces of topaz for Sarah. I bought them on impulse. I'm hoping that maybe she can fly in to Ann Arbor and visit sometime this winter. Get this. I even bought myself some brown kid shoes. Soft as you-know-what...excuse me, Suki." Abe turned to her, nodding, still smiling shyly.

Waving him off with an *it's nothing* gesture, she smiled and turned to the kitchen to start breakfast.

Focused intensely on Abe, Doc zeroed in on Abe's new image. "I'll bet you're a knockout in those new clothes—girls chasing you all over the place."

"As a matter of fact, I had a setup for tonight with Bob Chapin, my friend from Milan; we find common ground on most things. But," Abe sighed, "I told him that I would be busy the next two days with out-of-town company. He understood." Abe felt a rush of lust thinking of Jan; he curbed it.

"We need to settle you down. I hope you don't end up with some dread disease." Doc acquired a peculiar liquid look to his eyes with a new set of concerns. This was a whole new ballgame now; he worried...about *his* son.

"You forget that you were his age once," Suki said from the dining room. "He has a good head on his shoulders." She had brushed back her dark hair, revealing the cultural lines of her large eyes, high cheekbones and full mouth. Abe thought of angels.

Doc gathered her into his arms, kissing her full on the mouth, pulling her tiny body up to the full length of him. *Lucky sonofabitch, kissing my mother! But he's your father, Abe! Oh yeah.* Suki was enchanting, so feminine and fragile. Liz had been tall and angular, but lovely in her own way.

After fixing eggs and bacon, Suki enjoyed her morning coffee. "We'll be getting married at four o'clock, Abe. That means we need to leave as soon as we finish getting dressed. There are still loose ends to tie up." Her mouth curved into *his* smile.

Doc, holding his mug, advised his new son. "We would like you to meet us there. After the ceremony, we'll go over to the Allenal for cocktails and a long leisurely dinner. I understand that they have one of the best big bands in the area playing there tonight for New Year's Eve. They do all the sounds—Dorsey, Miller, and James. Suki and I'll be staying at the hotel for the next two nights, but we intend to see a whole lot of you before we fly back up north." His look softened as he felt the flow of family around him.*He is the happiest,be he king or peasant, who finds peace in his home.*

⚜

Abe arrived at the church at three o'clock. Yesterday's storm had blown over and relinquished its hold on Washtenaw County. The sky was light blue, clear and dry, with only a nervous cloud lingering here and there. He figured that regardless, the weather always seemed to be eighty degrees and sunny when he was in Doc's company.

In the rectory, the parish priest stamped the marriage credentials provided by Doc and Suki's hometown parishes, as well as their license and blood tests. Holy Mother the Church was zealous in her thoroughness, resolving any problems they may incur through church laws regarding marriage.

Abe stopped at the statue of the Blessed Mother, glancing up at her kindly forgiving face. As in the Michelangelo paintings, it symbolized peace. He swam in one of his bubbles, his senses in harmony. Abe found solitude there, as well as in the stately church, restive and spiritual. It was as if being alone was not alone. Votive lights danced and bent in a draught of air as one of the wide church doors opened in back under the choir loft. The space at the open door shimmered with heat inversions.

Dead in his tracks, he stared, stunned. The woman who had just entered the back of the church looked oddly familiar. The idea seemed so absurd that he should know *anyone* entering this hallowed place that he shrugged it off as an on-vacation mind synapses. She wore a double breasted camel coat, her dark hair floating over the collar. Settled loosely around her neck hung a wool scarf, her feet finely shod in off-white, sling-back pumps. Leave it to a fashion-conscious woman to be out on such a cold day with no boots on her feet. Soft leather off-white gloves kept her hands warm, however. Almost soundlessly, she walked up to the front of the church, genuflected and knelt in a front pew. On the chapel side of the church, Abe stared incredulously. The woman had metamorphosed into Sarah. As an escape hatch for his wildest dreams, his mind blinked like a pinball machine. *His Sarah! His woman!*

He exited the chapel alcove and hurried to ask a hundred questions.

Her expression of wariness as he approached pressed him with her vulnerability. He waved his arms. "Sarah," he stage whispered. "It's me, Abe! Pardon my English, but where the hell did you come from?" He juggled the word; the happiness he felt rasped his throat.

Staring in the dimly-lighted church, Sarah adjusted her eyes to this very big man coming her way. He saw a raw shiver run through her. "Abe, it's you," she said in a thread of a voice. "I didn't know who you were; you look terrific." Standing up, she hugged him, just as the priest and the wedding couple came in from the rectory.

"Well, I see you two have discovered each other," Doc said. "We were hoping that we'd be here before that happened, but 'all's well that ends well,' someone once said." He raised one eyebrow, his eyes dancing with pleasure.

Abe cast him a mock smoldering gaze. "You planned this whole thing and didn't tell me. I hope that this is the last trick up your sleeve, Doc." Abe produced a withheld smile as a common thread of camaraderie wove through the small group.

Doc lifted his shoulders in a desperate shrug of "muffed up again." "Sarah will be here for the next two days, then she'll fly back to Escanaba with us. We thought we'd surprise you. Ma approved her coming along." Doc was excited to the point of abandonment; the anxieties of the last twenty-four hours began to dissipate.

The tremolo chords of the organ floated around them. "I Love You Truly," light as a butterfly, kissed their ears. Abe was reminded again that Doc didn't miss a trick. He did everything with such *savoir faire*.

Taking off their coats, the bridal party assembled before the priest for the short ceremony, consisting of the Offertory, Communion and the Wedding Vows. The altar and side altars stood proudly puffed with flowers.

Everything looked so festive to Abe. He wondered where Doc had bought his suit. Covering his athletic physique, the fabric glistened with conservative richness. Although black in color, it radiated an iridescent copper undertone that attempted to surface now and again in the varying light. Add a white shirt, copper and black silk tie, neat Florsheims, and the man looked like a mannequin.

In vestments of ornate white and gold, underlined with a crisp white alb, the wiry-haired priest intoned, *"Dominus vobiscum."*

"Et cum spiritu tuo," responded altar boys, dressed in black albs and white tunics.

Sarah, delighted to serve as witness to this wedding, knew these two were going to be sealed to each other forever. Thoughts rekindled of her flight with Doc over Lake Michigan from Escanaba to Detroit Metro. She couldn't believe that she'd been so apprehensive about the treatments. Quigley had been heavenly and had helped her through the worst parts.

"Agnus Dei, qui tollis peccata mundi..." the priest intoned the Communion ritual.

Sarah drank in Suki's ensemble. Complementing her dark shiny hair, she wore a winter-white wool dress with long tapered sleeves, jewel neckline, small belted waist, and soft A-line skirt. *She* made the dress, however. She wondered if Doc had given her that string of pearls and the solitaire-set pearl earrings. Suki was a vision— sumptuous—an understatement that shouted.

"May I have the rings, please?" Piercing blue eyes under scraggly, white eyebrows sought Abe's, his voice deep and resonant. The pinkish-white skin of the priest presented a scrubbed clean purity.

Abe retrieved them from his inside suit jacket pocket.

"Do you, Danforth Dean Whittaker, take this woman to be your lawfully wedded wife, for better or worse, in sickness and in health, until death do you part?"

"I do." Doc's voice was vibrant and affirmative, holding Suki's hand, gazing at her with something akin to worship.

Suki returned his gaze, her dark eyes warm, black eyelashes thick and heavy.

"You may put your ring on her finger now." The trace of a smile glinted in the pastor's blue eyes.

"Do you, Suki Marie Miereau, take this man to be your lawfully wedded husband, in sickness and in health, for better or worse, until death do you part?"

"I do," she said softly, her tone self-assuring.

"You may slip the ring onto Dr. Whittaker's finger now," Father Clearly-Irish said as he looked appraisingly at Suki.

Sprinkling holy water and giving his blessing, he declared, "By the power vested in me by Holy Mother the Church, I now pronounce you man and wife."

After the Communion Rite, the pastor addressed the wedding party. "My dear friends, let us turn to the Lord and pray that he will bless with his grace this woman, Suki Marie Miereau, now married in Christ to this man, Danforth Dean Whittaker, and that through the sacrament of the body and blood of Christ he will unite in love the couple he has joined in this holy bond."

"Thank you, Father," they said in unison.

So two cells joined; *he* and *she* were now we.

CHAPTER THIRTY

Only the wedding feast at Cana presented better vintage wine than that which Doc provided for their celebration of marriage. Dom Perignon graced their table in the elegant dining room of the Allenal Hotel. Filled frequently were long-stemmed crystal glasses.

"Your cheeks are as pink as wild cherry blossoms, Sarah," Abe teased, reaching over and tenderly stroking her cheek with his knuckle. She caught his hand and pressed it in place against her warm skin.

"I know," she said, her eyes cast down. "I don't handle wine very well."

"Don't let them tease you, Sarah." Suki reached over and patted her on the shoulder. "I don't either, my eyes get all sparkly and glassy like a koala bear." Turning to Doc, she added, "I think we better order Danforth before we lose Sarah to an early evening. It *is* New Year's Eve. I'd like her to have at least nine o'clock staying power!"

"Yeah, me too," added Abe with a growl. He kissed the back of Sarah's hand affectionately, his fingers smoothing hers.

The dinner cuisine was magnificent. Having thoroughly enjoyed the new adventure in dining, Sarah shared her own thoughts. I'd never be able to duplicate this cuisine in a hundred years." She cut a "But that's okay" pouty look at Abe.

"Well, then, we'll just have to come back again next year and do it all over again." Suki bubbled excitedly. Needless to say, when you come over for dinner, it won't be shrimp kabobs we'll have, or, *Danforth,* scalloped oysters marinated in brandy." She wrinkled her nose at him playfully.

Doc lifted his glass, twinkling at her over the rim. "I'm disappointed that it would be a knotty problem for you, my dear. I quite expected pheasant under glass every night!" He sipped a small measure of wine and shot her a quick salute, whereupon she lifted her glass in return.

"Happiness to the nicest couple in the whole world." Abe offered a toast, their glasses clinking softly. It never ceased to amaze him that love could last over the long haul of distance and indifference, yet resurrect to blossom again.

Whipping into more nocturnal melodies in lieu of dinner music, the band tuned up in transition. Over the din of the diners came an excited, officious voice. "Ladies and Gentlemen. May I have your attention please?" Diners turned to the band shell, where the hotel manager stood poised. "As a special New Year's Eve treat for our patrons, it's our good fortune to have with us tonight the director of the Philadelphia Philharmonic Orchestra, Mr. Eugene Ormandy. Dance and enjoy, everyone!" He bowed back, a man accustomed to providing only the finest.

The ballroom rocked with applause.

Incredible! thought Abe. "Doc, did you know that?" Abe carried on knocked out of his socks.

"Sure, of course. Only the best for my guests," he said, his eyes twinkling, his shoulders shaking with laughter.

"Sarah, would you like to come to the powder room with me?" Suki gathered her gold lamè evening bag.

"Sure thing." Sarah brushed her hair back off her shoulders and reached for her small purse, laced with seed pearls.

Doc and Abe rose as the ladies left.

There was no loneliness between the two men tonight, no sadness, but instead electrifying communication. There lay between them a bond of communion, a communion of souls, the closest they'd ever felt in their lives to another human being—the glue of father and son.

Abe didn't take his eyes off Sarah until she disappeared through the Exit. Leaning forward confidentially, he prodded Doc. "How did you reconcile the obvious hurt Suki felt? I wanted to ask you that all day." Abe's concern left him toying with the hem of the linen tablecloth.

Doc clenched his teeth on his cigar, rolling it to the front of his mouth where he bit it lightly between his front teeth before removing it. "It wasn't easy. She didn't acquiesce quickly as she has lived grievously wounded by that part of her life. But I think you and I can make it up to her, and she to us, by starting anew." Doc waxed philosophical, his voice growing a little husky with the telling.

Elbows resting on the table, the warmth of fire in his deep brown eyes, Abe folded his hands together. "It's a whole new ballgame, thinking of her as my mother and you as my father; it'll take time. We can't rewrite the last twenty years, but I love you both already." He leaned back, sighing slowly.

"And us, you, of course. But speaking of ladies," Doc said, casting a quick eye at the Exit. "I want to tell you before Sarah comes back that her treatments are all done. That wasn't easy either. She was like a frightened little rabbit. Quigley helped me through the worst parts."

Abe jerked forward at the mention. "You mean..." He held his breath.

"Yes, you big ape. You did some job on her when you forced entry; she has scar tissue. If she hasn't sufficiently lubricated naturally, you see to it." A great puff of smoke billowed up from Doc's cigar as he exhaled.

His tongue pushing at the back of his teeth, Abe's smile gave into an incandescent "Ooo-kay."

"How's Suki, Doc? ...You know..." Abe clasped his hands together on top the table, anticipating the answer as if he were dancing on the head of a pin.

Leaning his elbows on the table and curving his shoulders in somewhat, Doc confided, "She turned me on twenty-three years ago, and look what we produced." Doc's eyes were warm, his half-smile growing to a full, uninhibited show of love. He clamped his teeth on his cigar again, moving his jaw offset, thinking. It occurred to Doc that Suki would probably beat him with a stick if she knew he was sharing this intimate information with Abe.

On returning, Sarah was scooped up by Abe for a dance. A thrill of anticipation ran through him as "Rhapsody in Blue" filled his ears. He walked his fingers slowly around to the back of her waist, pulling her close to him; she fell into place like a puzzle piece. "What a wonderful surprise you are, my lady. In my wildest dreams, I never, ever thought I'd be spending New Year's Eve with my best girl," he whispered down toward her ear, smelling deeply the halo of her hair.

"I'm so happy to be here," she said quietly, looking up into his face.

"I didn't tell you how beautiful you are tonight. You should wear that color more often," Abe whispered again, this time more hoarsely. He could feel the longings she aroused. "What *do* you call that color—I need to copy it in my paints."

"This is palest ever peach, a surprise Christmas gift from Ma—kitten-soft Icelandic wool and angora."

The words fell sensually on Abe's ears. "It's like a baby blanket. You feel so good, so much a part of me."

"I *want* to be a part of you. By the way, that suit is very professional looking. You look like a Wall Street Bull!" She leaned back, studying his face.

"Nah, remember me? I'm your old friend, the Beach Road Bum!" He laughed, crunching her back against his confident body.

Ormandy whipped the orchestra into Tommy Dorsey's "Boogie Woogie." Abe and Sarah moved into it with the crowd of revelers. They'd been dancing since they were in the seventh grade, their movements anticipatory and tandem. After such a workout, Ormandy slowed the tempo to "Moonlight Serenade."

"I think I died and went to heaven, Abe. I'm so happy," Sarah's voice, soft and rich, lingered on Abe's ears.

He wanted to memorize the sound of it. Holding her against him, he could feel every move of her legs, every sway of her hips, which were a bit right of promiscuous. He didn't know how much longer he'd be able to stay this close to her and not be embarrassed. "Sarah?"

Leaning her head back, her eyes swept back and forth. "Mmm."

"I'm hoping to show you my home. It isn't far from here, only about five miles. Would you want to take a break and drive out there with me? Take a look around?"

"Yes!" Her eyes lit up. "Yes, I'd like that." Her eyes widened.

"Why don't you..." he whispered hesitantly..."why don't you take a change of clothes in case I can't get you back here until tomorrow?" His eyes begged her.

"I don't know, Abe. Ma wouldn't approve of that, and she trusted Doc to look out for my best interests." Her eyes shouted apprehension.

That figures. "Damn it, Sarah, you're twenty-one years old. You can make those decisions for yourself. You don't need someone *looking out* for you. *I'll* look after your best interests." His voice took on an edge of irritability.

"Well, okay," she conceded. The raw sound of his voice commanded compliance. "Give me a few minutes." She pulled in her lips and rolled her eyes as if she were about to walk through a haunted forest.

Returning to the table, Abe casually announced. "I'm taking Sarah out to Walter's, Doc. I want to show her where I live. Hope you don't mind."

Doc chuckled and said, "No, not at all." He motioned with his head that he wanted to speak to Abe alone. Excusing himself to Suki, he moved away from the table, guiding Abe's elbow for emphasis. "You be careful with her. Remember, she's very naïve for her age, physically and psychologically." He clasped Abe on the shoulder.

Abe shrugged, smiling. If he'd ever been happier, he couldn't remember when.

"Doc?"

"Yes." Doc turned back.

"Congratulations again. I'm so happy for you both. You don't mind us leaving you, do you?" A hint of indecision hovered in Abe's eyes.

"Go on. Get outta here. We're perfectly happy and content. We have a thousand things to discuss, including you." Doc looked at Abe with unspeakable pride, hoping he'd remember everything he'd told him, but his bubble was so damned unpredictable.

☙❧

An uneven wind whisked up. Frost could be felt in the air. The stars shone so big and bright in the clear Michigan night that they seemed close enough to touch.

"Brrr." Sarah shivered, adjusting her scarf more tightly around her neck.

Abe rubbed her shoulders through her coat. "I'll get you warmed up in no time. In fact, I'll bring some logs into the house from the garage so I can light the fire."

Sitting in front of the fireplace, the new logs snapping, Abe had a bottle of Schlitz. "Sure I can't get you anything, pretty lady? A glass of wine? A loaf of bread? Me?" Wearing his manners, he was eager to have Sarah relax. The fire twisted deliciously around the logs. Sparks flew against the metal mesh inside the glass doors.

"Isn't that the prettiest thing you ever saw? Kind of hypnotic—watching the life in it." Sarah sat dreamy in the loveseat with Abe, staring into the fire. "It's as if it's being swallowed into a dark world of busy little carnivores eating their dinner."

"Sarah! What an imagination. Nothing wrong with that, I guess. Here, I want to show you something," he said, rising and moving to the foyer where his easel rested.

"What do you think of this?" he asked as he pulled off the protective sheet that draped the easel and canvas, and waved it to the side like a magician's cape. "Voilà!" Without shoes, Sarah appeared even smaller and more vulnerable to Abe.

Her toes squiggled in the carpet. Wide eyes ran between him and the canvas and back again in quick darts. He saw in her face a measuring of him, of the painting, calculating the transplanted information from his mind to the canvas. She stood silent.

The Johnstown Flood washed over Abe. *My God, what if she doesn't like it?* When would the terrible uncertainties in life end?

Slowly she reached out, touched her face on the canvas, the swirling mist of fog in the air, the flowers bearing heavy dabs of dark blue, lighter dabs of pale blue, the long slender stems of the larkspurs blending from deep swamp greens to early-spring leafy green. She felt her childish innocent eyes on the canvas, the focus of the picture, clear, dark, honest and loving. Fighting down an overwhelming desire to cry, she saw in this work nurturing seen through his eyes. Wonder had to be the finest form of flattery.

"You could sell me your thoughts," Abe said softly, his confidence slowly ebbing.

The magnitude of her feelings wanted to explode; her throat tightened. She couldn't find voice or words for them. Instead, she turned to him, reached up and put her hands on both his cheeks caressingly, feeling his late-day beard growth coming through. Standing on tiptoes, she planted a warm kiss smack on his mouth. He responded, his arms encircling her easily, lifting her from the floor, as she returned his warmth.

"Ohhh, Abe, it's lovely! It says so much."

She likes it! He deliberately looked away for a moment—his face popping with such pride. "It's yours, milady, as soon as I get credit for it from my instructor." His eyes locked on hers. He thought he'd drown. "Now, how about I fetch you a glass of sherry? Suki said it is quite outstanding; it's from the vineyards of Jerez, Spain." *Until a few years ago, he hadn't known sherry from chipotle.*

"Sold!" She giggled enthusiastically, uplifted by the beautiful canvas.

Hot damn! He hoped this would loosen her up somewhat. He'd put on Glenn Miller too. Things were humming like a top. Here they were—alone!

"Bring your sherry with you, Sarah. I want to show you something." He whistled down the hall. "Right in here, little lady," he said with shades of John Wayne.

On the right side of his bedroom stood an over-sized walnut dresser with a mirror equally as large. From it, he retrieved the jewelry box that held the topaz bracelet.

"This is something special just for you."

She seemed to be hiding within herself, apprehensive, and only peeked out in slow small jerks, her eyes fluttering between him and the box. Opening it, she gasped. "It's dazzling, Abe! You shouldn't have," she cried, raising her eyes to meet his.

"Sarah, you're worth a fortune, two fortunes. Here's that bracelet's first cousin," he said, presenting her with yet another velvet case, his stomach doing flip flops.

Squeak, click, the box groaned from newness as she popped it open. "Topaz earrings too, Abe! They're absolutely breathtaking. They're the ones in the picture." She chattered with indulgence, warmed with the flavor of the gifts.

Abe's smile wrinkled in rays around his eyes. "You bet, milady. Allow me to put them on for you." His large hands working with the tiny clasp of the bracelet moved her. With the tip of his tongue he wet his lips, such a familiar mannerism, timeless, tracing back to when they were kids playing in the sand on the beach.

As she folded her hands together over her breasts, he kissed her lightly on the mouth. Turning to the dresser, he collected the earrings from the box. In his hand they looked like a lost, small glimmer. Brushing her hair back, he clamped the earrings onto her ear lobes rubbing them between his thumb and forefinger. Eyes closed, her lashes fluttered; she sighed. He paused uneasily, his stomach moving into thrill heaven. *Don't go too fast*, he admonished himself.

"I'll put some more wood on the fire while you count the sparkles in that bracelet," he said weakly, feeling himself moving in slow motion.

She joined him by the fireplace and sat on the floor, holding her wine on her knee. "This sherry is quite superior, Abe. I fancy the silky, light fruity taste." She nodded her head. There wasn't the slightest doubt that she liked this heady drink. Not the slightest.

He hoped she liked the kick too. He couldn't wait much longer.

"This is such a lovely home. I hope that someday you and I'll have one just like it." Her eyes flirted over the rim of her flute.

"I'm sure we will," he said, sitting on the floor beside her, stretching long legs toward the fire. "The firelight is becoming to you, Sarah. Your eyes light up like a timid forest creature."

"Well, thanks a lot! I hoped my eyes held more appeal to you than a little creature's." She laughed, rubbing his hair. "I like your haircut; it's good looking and machismo. You're so worldly. Ma tells me, however, that I don't have to be worldly.'"

He straightened, surprised by the gratification that filled him with her admission. "That means that you're being saved just for me," he gulped, feeling himself unraveling.

They were speaking in whispers, their heads close together. He stroked her back, her soft angora knit sweater. His fingers played with her earrings. She leaned into him, flexing with the glide of his hand, sipping the sherry.

"Abe?" she murmured quietly, adjusting her skirt and fingering her bracelet.

"Yes," he whispered in her ear. He'd dreamed of a moment like this forever.

"I love you," she said, breathing softly, her nose nuzzling his cheek.

A leaping thrill shot through him with her candor. He was more accustomed to the use of a ruse and patented overtures. "I love you more."

"If you are taking me to your bedroom, I'd like to take a bath first and have another glass of sherry. It's sooo good." She looked up at him, cuddling closer.

She couldn't have engineered a more perfect pose! Abe thought the heat from his body must be melting his belt.

"Your wish is my command," he said, pulling her to a standing position.

Her legs felt as light as hummingbird wings. A specter of well-being sifted about Sarah like an aura.

Another glass of sherry was just what the doctor ordered to relax this little lady recently out of Catholic College.

"You can use my bathroom, right off the bedroom. I'll get the sherry and another Schlitz for me."

By the time he got back he could hear the bath water running. She fussed with her overnight bag, which lay on the double dresser. He felt brutal and tireless. *Me gustaría hacer el amor contigo!* This was certainly no time to be a boy.

"Is that you, Abe?"

"It better be. There's no one else in the house."

"What are you doing?" she asked. Her back to the room, she glanced up through the large mirrors, but she only saw an empty bedroom and part of the bathroom.

"I'm tending your bath. You're my woman and you need to get used to things like that." Abe bent and turned off the faucets in the bathtub, bubbles overflowing the edges.

"Well, leave the bathroom while I take my bath, will you?" Her voice rose.

Glancing up, he appeared behind her, his arms around her waist. Reaching out, he picked up her glass of wine and lifted it to her lips. "You haven't touched a drop of this. I'm disappointed." A kick of conscience cut in, knowing he had used baiting tactics, but it always worked for him, eliminating any problems with refusals.

"Lift your arms, Sarah; I'll remove your sweater for you."

"No!"

Abe felt as if he were limping through heavy traffic.

"Please," he whispered. "I'm just trying to be helpful."

She obliged, exotic thrills chasing through her such as she'd never known. She felt his hands working her skirt off, which she stepped out of as she took another sip of sherry, which he encouraged.

"Relax, Sarah. We've waited forever for this moment."

Turning to him, he pulled her slip over her head; her bra unsnapped, her panties worked down over her feet. As he carried her to the bathtub, his lips gently feathered over her mouth, his eyes seeking to keep her relaxed. Gently, he laid her into the lush comfort of fragrant, warm water. "Now, don't make a move until I get back. I'm going to take a three-minute shower in Walter's bathroom." He smiled down at her. "I'll place your sherry right here within easy reach." Turning, Sarah found a chilled carafe of wine at her beck and call. Abe knocked back a long draft of Schlitz.

In minutes he returned, wrapped in a loincloth-style towel. The waving mounds of hair on his chest choked her into a loss for words, her porcelain facade fading fast.

"Now, my lady, I'll give you a bath." He smiled tenderly at his woman.

Her eyes flew wide. "No!" Sarah sat aghast, her eyes liquid.

"Yes!" he whispered, as he drew the washcloth over her, swirling currents of warm water against her relaxed body. The hard muscles in his arms and shoulders flexed as he moved over her breasts, the bubbles clinging to the heavy hair on his arms.

"Oh, Abe, that feels so good," she murmured, leaning back and closing her eyes. She wondered if she wasn't a bit of a chameleon, entering his home as a lady and turning into some kind of a harlot. Why did she not feel ashamed? Could she no longer differentiate between a white hat and a black hat? What's more, did she simply slice the truth by not admitting this was leading to fornication? Nonetheless, her mind refused to be rational in this oasis of serenity.

"That's how I want you to feel." He'd promise her anything right now. "I want to know you, in the biblical sense," he said gallantly. "Now stand up so I can finish. After all these years, I only have negligible data on you."

Abe gave new meaning to body language, and Sarah was delighted. His eyes grazed over her face, her neck, and her shoulders—the bareness of her. She shook with the emotions he aroused. His eyes were as dark as a sorcerer's, casting a spell.

Lifting her dripping out of the tub, he toweled her down and slipped his bathrobe over her shoulders. "Voilá!" he said, taking a deep bow. Abe's bathrobe fell around her like a drape from the Chicago Tent & Awning Company. Her toes were pink and bare, sticking out of the length, which folded several times over onto the floor.

Abe cracked up. "Good fit!" He stood near the closet, hanging her clothes, then his clothes. He built fantasies about what he now *knew* curved under that entire bathrobe. "You're getting better, Sarah," he mused. "You used to look away when I got down to my nothings," he said quietly. An infectious grin grew steadily across his face.

"Well, that's all based on the fact that I figure you're getting better to look at, now that I'm not afraid of you anymore. Doc told me to relax. He says that your love for me has endured, lasting and loyal." She wrinkled her nose at him. "That puts a new coat of clean on you."

"I didn't know my reputation had preceded me. Doc must think that I'm a campus peril." He held up his hands in mock surrender. "I'm just a plain man who loves one woman very deeply," he said, bending over her chair and kissing her lightly on the mouth. He kept his terry cloth loincloth on, surprising her.

"Mmmh." Just when she started thinking that perhaps she could revel in what he had after all, he kept it to himself. She smiled and waved him off. "I see Walter and Anne have some family pictures in their bedroom. May I check them out?" she asked, nodding in the direction of the bedroom across the hall.

"Yes," he growled, entertaining a prickly irritability. *Pictures, at a time like this?*

He found her in the master bedroom, holding a picture of Walter and Doc when they were young. He locked into her eyes, teetering on the brink of ravishing her.

Catching his gaze, she became apprehensive, stunned, embarrassed by his stripping stare. She shot wild looks about the room, looking for an escape route.

His approach sharpened steadily. Taking the picture from her and setting it on the dresser, he pulled the bow of her belt and loosened it, grabbed the back of her collar and jerked the robe off her shoulders, over her arms, and let it drop to the floor.

The next few seconds were frozen in time as a heart-stopping thrill ran throughout his whole body. He clenched his teeth. He wanted to remember the beauty of her skin—silky smooth, body chiseled by some maestro of perfection. Wings of delight fluttered in his chest as he stared at her childish breasts, her tiny waist... His lust clung to him like a dust-ridden fog—unshakable—bruising him with its impact.

A nasty nodule of wind from the north assaulted the house creating an almost imperceptible tremor to run through Sarah.

Abe felt like a circling turkey buzzard as he lifted and carried her to his room, nuzzling her head, which she had tucked into his solid shoulder, her fingers stroking the wiry hair on his chest, sculpting lazy circles that led downward to his waist. He gasped, fumbling for control.

"Abe, please don't hurt me anymore." Her voice churned plaintive and thin. "I love you so much. You're the only man who's ever touched me."

His good luck detonated, paralyzing him, bordering on the unbelievable. He knew this—felt certain. But to hear it! Her own lips spoke the words. His head pulsed with the pounding of his heart. He'd waited all his life to claim this woman, and now it was about to materialize.

He felt a surge of his Sioux brutality, insensitivity and ruthlessness. It had escalated to the power of ten. He reminded himself not to rush pell-mell into a miserable start. Blood pulsed through his veins like water forced through a too-small spigot. Discipline! He needed to restrain himself into a gentleman's facade, but there nestled a subterranean attack machine lurking in his depths, waiting to charge.

Lying her on the bed, her hair fell back; the topaz earrings shone a hundred points of reflection from the lamps. She was still wearing his bracelet. A punch of pride raced through him. Here was his woman, naked, wearing nothing but his jewelry. He viewed her as the mother of all possessions. Standing by the bed and locking onto her eyes, he slowly and deliberately loosened his wrap. Letting it fall to the floor where he stood, a portrait of Sioux masculinity, which spoke of countless conquests. There was no substitute for it. No one could challenge his manhood. No one. For several seconds they stared at each other; it seemed like an eternity. This time she didn't avert her eyes; but beheld him, powerful and manly. His hair, on leave from discipline, wandered untamed, his chest, his naval, his pelvis, his legs and arms... He gave rise to the term "Olympian."

She lifted her eyes to his with anxiety.

CHAPTER THIRTY-ONE

He had to take his time or he'd not validate the conquest. The last thing he wanted was for her to walk away from this experience feeling abused. But slowly...it would be a test of endurance that ended far from failure.

His heart stuttered as he leaned his head on his elbow, then bent and kissed her ears lightly, chewing on an earring, nuzzling her hair. He cupped her chin and turned her head to him, kissing her nose and mouth. Dampening his finger, he traced her mouth, which opened only slightly while his finger found the inside perimeter of her lips.

She responded! His eyes danced with the unprecedented success. The mystique and magic of this woman were immeasurable. There he dawdled, sweat beads forming on his forehead. This conquest brought immense pride to him, the lionization of a lifetime. It tugged at his conscience, but trifling. He laid his mouth full on hers, all encompassing. His tongue invaded her mouth, searching for acceptance, a safety valve for his libido. He knew he was shadowboxing with an unknown factor.

With Sarah accepting his overtures, he fought back the tendency to be surprised. Salivating, he gasped, coming up taking a deep breath. He dangled on the cutting edge of this sexual war they'd carried on since he was thirteen years old. She always had a fortress of objections for him to overcome. He'd carried some nasty scars over the damnable business; however, he would not fail this time, but succeed.

Something finally clicked inside Sarah, loosening, submitting, reducing her world to its basic common denominator, what she crafted on earth to accomplish: proliferation of the species. "I'm so happy, Abe," she whispered, gazing deep into his existence with sincerity. She at once dreaded this new experience, but at the same time she eagerly awaited the first invasion into her innocence.

His ego, bloated with body fluids, flooded with an unexpected surge of heat, a thousand volts of pent up energy. He had played this scene over in his mind a thousand times, but never anticipated it would be so sophomorically uncontrollable. He was twenty-two years old, successful, handsome and virile. He was used to being in control. What Sarah aroused in him, however, was overriding and unprecedented. His body incinerated with a thrill he'd never before felt so keenly. The semen train had left the station. In a last desperate attempt, he ordered it back with harshness, but to no avail.

He groaned long, his chest heaving repeatedly. His head jerked back.

"Sarah! I-am-so-sorry." He enunciated every word, his embarrassment palpable.

She made a move toward him, putting her arm around his neck, feeling his hot breath, the sweat pouring off his hair. "It's all right. We can try it again another time." Was it her fault? She knew little of such things. She lay rigidly beside him. The sounds of silence were deafening in the room.

Comfort surrounded him that she seemed to think him none the worse for being so uncontrolled. This poor performance on the field would have cost the team a penalty. He'd been worse than a child who indulged in licorice whips at the Candy Kitchen, with no discipline whatsoever. He wanted to cry, but then he'd be even more embarrassed. He dreamed of Sarah cooing how wonderful he'd made her feel, giving him kudos galore. Now this! He needed to learn to play smarter and stay longer.

"Well, let's not have a completely wiped out evening." He ran his fingers through his thick dark hair, feeling the situation inextricable. "I'll dial in Guy Lombardo and the Royal Canadians for the New Year's Eve Celebration from Times Square in New York City." Abe struggled to redeem himself from this purgatory. The grand Cavalier intended to show her the way, the truth and the light about sex, but he'd failed.

"That's a terrific idea, Abe. We don't have long to wait."

Turning on the console radio in the living room, there arose a swelling ocean of static. What else could go wrong? Did the fickle finger of fate always apply?

It settled down.

"Ladies and Gentlemen from the Great White Way in New York City, NBC brings you Guy Lombardo and the Royal Canadians to celebrate this New Year, 1947! From Times Square, we bring you the sweetest music this side of heaven."

The music layered mellow, heavy to base, as it drifted into the living room.

"May I have this dance, your highness?" Abe sucked up his sagging libido. This was no time to vacillate, even if it had been the wipeout at Little Bighorn, so far.

"I am pleasured to have been asked, Sir Wondrous Knight!"

They swept into each other's arms—Sarah in Abe's bathrobe, Abe in Walter's bathrobe, which fit too tightly, but it was warm.

"Sarah," Abe whispered as though someone else were listening. "Did Doc's treatments go well?" Talking would give him time and confidence.

"Yes, they did, and I practiced the exercises he gave me. By the way, he said that I am a very healthy young woman, and that my fears have no basis. So…I'm ready to try it whenever you are." Abe had always admired her ability to focus on the root of a problem, but her candidness struck him in the gut.

He felt himself rising to the challenge. Thank God for quick recoveries. A lurch of pleasure punched him. He would have thought himself fatally flawed had he not reacted to her again. The hair on his chest and stomach prickled. Bending down, he sought her mouth with his teeth, chewing on her bottom lip.

Feeling his desire growing against her stomach, she whispered, "You're a sumptuous male, Abe, very potent."

His ego returned like a blitz out of nowhere. Stopping in mid-dance, he stripped off her bathrobe, gazed at her perfect body, hungry as a starved elephant.

She blushed with color.

Spreading her bathrobe, he pulled her to the floor. The fire glowed warmly. Her bathrobe abandoned and her body beneath him, he leaned into her.

"Now," he said huskily. "Do you think we can continue where we left off?"

She thrilled to the authority in his voice, thinking that surely she'd been possessed by the devil himself to feel this relaxed. She smiled, feeling his ears, tracing her fingers over his arms and down his side, over his athletic hips.

"Christ, Sarah! This is so good." His voice shook. Stroking down her back, he felt it arch inwards, allowing his hand to wander onto her thighs. They curved as a smooth plane of God-given pastoral hills. As he pressed her to him, she complied, molding with his body. Slowly, he moved down her body, gazing at her breasts. She bent one knee. He hadn't had to fight with her to do that. He couldn't believe it. Like catching a long bomb, she came in on time and at the right angle. His touch moved down her belly, squeezing it, moving on.

"Abe."

"Hmm?"

"I love you so much. You make me feel so good, so vital." Her words flowed, unpracticed and hesitant.

"I love you more, I promise."

Their voices fell as svelte tissue paper, the sounds of their bodies moving on the bathrobes louder than their whispered confidences. The fire burned slowly, licking a high flame here and there and lowering its aims as if to hold a fine line.

She watched him with breathless attention.

Cognizant that this was her first time. His football training taught him to go for the endurance. "Relax, Sarah. Use the exercises Doc gave you."

Abe spiraled, lost in the timelessness of the moment. He felt the contentment she gave, the support, the faith, and his body became energized as never before. He felt fulfillment, even as he thirsted for more to the background music of Guy Lombardo's "Auld Lang Syne." He wore no condom.

Later, in the seclusion of his bedroom, he was reluctant to release her or return her to the Allenal. In time, he lay on his side and drew her close. He kissed her gently and folded her against him, knowing that he could be flawlessly happy lying quietly like this for the rest of his life. Moments later, he re-thought that image when he again thickened.

In the hours that followed, Sarah grew increasingly worn when her initiative flagged and the pleasures grew one-sided. Her hands weren't knowing, nor did they delve to learn. Nonetheless, Abe's boldness found further arousal in the aphrodisiac of her nearness. Insatiable he never thought of a condom.

Sarah lay limp as a rag doll; her energy poured out like a tumbled teapot.

Abe, restful by the heat of their bodies, sank into a sleep so deep that he didn't awaken until five-thirty. He awoke with a start. Sarah was there, unveiled in bed with him! Again, he ravaged the sweet Sarah. Again he wore no condom.

Sarah lay weak with lack of sleep, raw skin from five o'clock shadow, scalding between her thighs, burning and aching breasts.

Abe knew he'd had dessert—many servings. Fabian spoke the truth. She'd been worth the wait.

Some time after daylight of New Year's Day 1947, Sarah found herself ill. She emerged in anguish and nausea. "Please call Doc for me, Abe."

"My God, Sarah, what did I do to you?" His tone was that of a hoarse whisper.

Sensing Abe's alarm and distraught expression brought on a maelstrom of Sarah's tears. Overcome with weariness from all-night mauling, she gave in to her exhaustion, navigating to the bathroom where she became violently ill, retching until she fell faint.

Solicitous, Abe lifted her and carried her back to bed. "I'll call Doc." He saw teeth marks on her breasts. How could he have done that? Her body looked as if it had been sandpapered. He loved her so much! He never wanted to hurt her. He'd gotten lost in her, lost in his bubble. He didn't recall being rough with her.

"Dead meat, dead meat," Abe muttered into his hands as he doubled over the telephone.

"Doc!" Abe shouted with a voice up to a hundred decibels.

"Morning, Abe. Do you think I've gone deaf overnight?" Doc chuckled.

"It's Sarah. Sarah..." There lay hope, yet heartbreak, in his voice.

"What the hell's wrong, Abe? Spit it out, son," Doc's tone became stiff.

"Everything is wrong, Doc. We got up this morning..."

Doc interrupted. "You mean you kept Sarah there all night?"

"Let me finish, Doc. It's important. Yes, she stayed here all night, and this morning she's sick. She hurts all over, throwing up and fainted outright on me." Abe knew he sounded brittle and cracked.

"Abe, what did you do to that tiny princess now? I warned you how far she was from being physically mature." He needed to have a serious talk with this young man.

There was a long pause. "Well, you know, once wasn't enough."

"Abe, you made love the rest of the night?" Doc queried dryly.

"I did, and now she's not well," Abe managed to get out very succinctly.

"We'll be there in just a bit. I have my bag with me...I always carry it."

Watching for their arrival, Abe hastily ushered them into the house, taking coats in a whirlwind. In Abe's bedroom, they found Sarah as white as the sheet with which she lay covered. Her small china face seemed to be sealed closed. Her large brown eyes looked embarrassed and held no more shimmer than cold dishwater.

"Morning, Sarah. I understand you're not feeling very well?" There was extra warmth in Doc's voice, this man of gentle genres, so cosmopolitan and cultural.

"No," she squeaked, taking a shaky breath, struggling for some degree of dignity.

"Well, let's see what we can do for you," he said gently, easing the sheet down.

Suki gasped, seeing the raw skin, beautiful brown eyes dimmed with tears. Wide-eyed, she turned to Abe with a stare of disbelief.

It was all too much for Abe. Flooded with remorse and penitence, he floundered in a world where his dreams had become a nightmare.

"I say there, you two, I don't need three patients in here." Doc showed no signs of anxiety or concern and rarely flaunted visible indicators of such. "Look," he said cogently, "do me a favor and wait outside while I see what I can do for the real patient."

As the door closed behind Abe and Suki, Doc removed the sheet entirely from Sarah. "I would surmise that the bedding rubs on your skin and burns." Doc reminded himself that, theoretically, anything could happen when Abe was alone with a woman. Not that it soothed the seething annoyance he felt for him right now.

"Yes," she sniffled, slipping a tissue from the box. "My whole body burns."

"I understand. Have you been able to relieve your bladder this morning?"

"Only somewhat, and that burns badly." She gulped deep breaths like a disillusioned child who had missed out on the tooth fairy. "I'm sick to my stomach, too."

"Did you drink any wine after you left the hotel?" Doc had one eyebrow raised.

"Yes," came the quiet reply.

"How much?" Doc was young once himself. Yes, he remembered it well.

"I don't know. I lost count—glasses and glasses." Sarah cried with the acknowledgment. Now Doc would think her a fallen woman, ready for the streets.

He stood by the head of the bed. "That could have an enormous influence on your nausea. However, we're going to have to get you to the bathroom and encourage bladder function." He peered at her cheerfully, making the best of an awkward situation. His sense of humor had pulled him through many a sticky situation.

Her eyes looked suddenly opaque again, tucking herself away behind some indefinable fortification.

Observing how she had struggled between staying forever as she was or submit to the burning release of her bladder with some element of composure, he grasped her wrist and busied himself with her pulse rate. "I'll have Suki run some warm bath water; the ambience should do the trick. It's going to seem like a heaven of relief."

"Okay," she acquiesced, still blubbering as she moved slowly toward the edge of the bed with Doc's help, her skin scathing on the sheet.

"There, that's fine. That's far enough." What the hell! That crazy Indian did more than make love to this woman. The raw redness of her skin showed that he'd been pervasive, Abe not missing any part of her. He needed to instruct that young man about practicing discipline instead of bestiality. *Here was the woman he wanted to marry some day?* "Hmph." Doc, in a foul mood, snorted. He'd see to it that Abe wakened to a new year with fireworks all right.

"Okay, Sarah. Here we go." He felt her body stiffen as she arose.

Oh, how she loved this gentle man. But aloud, she quietly said, "Thank you, Doc. You've been so kind...so good to me...so patient." She bawled some more.

"You're going to be just fine, Sarah. Unlike living in the shelter of your home, the waters of the world are filled with sharks. Sometimes we need to swim with the current, gotta get tough just to get through." A mental image of Abe in action flashed across his mind. "I'm going to apply salve to your thighs and the surrounding area to ease the burning sensations." He carried on a steady banter with her, his usual conversational swing with an edgy patient. He felt her body relaxing. "These problems you have with Abe are not inextricable. They're just entanglements that need to be disengaged and solved," he said as he applied jell.

"This treatment will work wonders." Contrary to his pleasant tone of voice, his thoughts were becoming deranged. He may just throttle Abe with his bare hands. "I want you to know that there is nothing wrong with your mating capabilities. Even an experienced woman would have a hard time handling Abe for an all-night stint. Did you take precautions as I instructed you to do?"

"Yes, I did." She sniffled.

"Every time?" He applied the healing balm.

"Yes," she said softly, struggling for composure.

Abe would make a king lion seem right friendly by comparison. Anger rode on Doc's eyebrows.

The room, bathed in early morning sunlight, lent some cheer to Sarah's muddled mind. "He kept waking up..." She cried again, falling apart with the renewed recollections, her confidence and dignity slowly slipping away.

Doc had increased difficulty maintaining his professional aloofness. His shoulders wilted with the weight of responsibilities he'd not carried when Abe was yet a lad.

"Suki will run a bath for you. Afterwards I'll have her massage you with ointment. We need to get your skin settled down for the flight back tomorrow.

"Now, young lady, this experience will take time to sort out, but I wouldn't make any hasty adjustments in your life over this incident, Sarah."

It hurt to move her legs. It was the first time that energy had been so flagging.

"Don't write him off," Doc encouraged.

Sarah did not respond.

※

Abe stopped believing in such nonsense as "desserts" and "unconscionable sins," even though he believed that his sins were many. It had been his experience that his catechism conscience always kicked in too late to warn him of his misdeeds. Gone were the days of childhood when his little fingers dug through licorice whips or Cracker Jacks for treasures such as a plastic whistle, BB game or cricket clicker. That was for fools. One minute things move along good, the next, the breeze blows your ass to trash.

And speaking of breezy, this mid-March day sported a raucous wind and the phone jangled off the hook upon Abe's arrival home from classes.

"Abe!"

"Yeah."

"How the hell have you been?"

Bill Acker! *What the...?* He hadn't called Abe at school in three years.

"Just fine, Bill, just fine. How's everything at Nahma, and the mill and the lumber camps? I could go on and on."

"Couldn't be better. Everything is running like clockwork, except for one little glitch." Abe knew Acker as a man who could be hard in business matters, yet soft in matters of art and culture.

"I'm afraid to ask." Abe chuckled.

"I met with the Summer Art School Board of Directors last night. We've been struggling these past two years to fill Max's shoes as director of the six-week affair. It was suggested that we enlist your services this summer for the directorship. Of course all the board members, including Doc, wholeheartedly supported your nomination. We feel that with three year's study at one of the best art schools in the USA, you're the candidate of the hour. Who better but Max's own protégé?" The excitement in Acker's voice sizzled.

"I hardly know what to say, Bill." Abe had difficulty concealing his pleasure. "I'm secure enough in the arts to feel comfortable with the job, but I've only had two terms in administrative processes. I need another term of organizational skills before I meet the requirements of a directorship."

The questioning in Abe's tone hung heavily on Acker. "Screw it." Bill had this uncanny capacity to instill confidence and trust in people. "If management is your only worry, perish the thought. The board of directors concern themselves with that. Because the new clubhouse is not yet built, we're going with a tent city in the lot behind the new construction. It'll be a camp-like experience, creating a bourgeois atmosphere; the artists will enjoy the blue sky ambiance."

"That sounds like an *added* attraction to me. There is another thing. I'll need to leave for Ann Arbor on August 7; that's a week before the Summer Art School is finalized." Abe wound down, this being the last, but biggest obstacle.

"I can get Dave Phalen to run the art auction. He has a line of mischief a mile long. That's really the biggest event of the last week."

"I can hardly say no then. This will be a learning experience for me too. I'll use it for my thesis next spring." Abe wanted to leap in the air and click his heels.

"Here's some more good news. That position pays five hundred dollars a month. That's considerably more than your salary at the office." Acker's voice rose with the revelation.

"Yeah, many times as much. Thank you, thank you," Abe could only mumble incoherently. Even accidently, Abe's tongue rolled no orations.

"Don't mention it. You'll be on the payroll as of the first of June."

"I won't even be back there on the first of June." Abe's eyebrows shot up.

"That's okay. We aren't going to quibble over a few days here and there." He amused at the young man's deep concerns over his responsibilities.

"Thanks again, Bill. See you in June."

"You bet. Congratulations, Abe. We are proud of what you've accomplished in your lifetime. Some people fold with adversity and some people, like you, fly."

"Thanks. Let's hope I can live up to your expectations." Abe knew virtue lay in hard work, but he hoped he hadn't out-walked the gangplank this time.

❧❦

Golden summer days had arrived in Nahma by the time Abe returned. The land dozed in a haze of summer light beneath blue skies and slow moving clouds. Abe found the town peaceful and undemanding after the hustle of the school year in Ann Arbor.

The Summer Art School obligations were incredibly overwhelming, especially stepping in without prior insight into the official capacity of the program. Abe found there were many players on the team with a committee covering every aspect of the effort. Resultantly, he stayed in the trenches as the Public Relations man—a warrior chairman, the nexus who tied the activities together.

In the potpourri of responsibilities, he didn't forget to run out to Farley and Norrhea's regularly, where his Indian Heritage metamorphosed into a profound heritage. His people were proud; they delighted at Suki's return. With regards to her past, they never ceased to be incredulous.

Abe visited often with Doc and Suki.

"Hey, Suki," he called from the front door, never knocking anymore. "Are you having pheasant under glass for supper?"

Laughing, she met him in the foyer and gave him a great tiptoe hug and kiss.

"Doc's not home yet?"

"No, but he should be soon. C'mon in the backyard and have some lemonade. I'm just sunbathing." The weather in the late afternoon was perfect. A few puffer-belly clouds looked portentous, faking their way across the sky.

They descended the back steps to the lawn furniture that surrounded a splashing concrete fountain large enough to sit in. Doc had built her a five-foot-high woven fence so she could have privacy from passersby.

"I understand from all reports that the Summer Art School is faring just fine under your fantastic directorship. I'm so happy for you." Her gentle voice always mesmerized Abe. She owned a master's degree in casual conversation—straightforward and abreast. People understood and liked her.

"Yes, yes it is." Running his hand through his hair, Abe smiled happily, content in her presence. "We're only about ten days into it, but I've never seen things go so smoothly. The enrollment is filled. The hotel is full, and private homes are bursting."

Suki sat across from him on a chaise lounge, her knees bent sideways, juggling her glass of lemonade. "I just can't believe how well this has worked out for you."

He took a ragged breath. "Well, I've pretty much committed myself to the project. I've done little else this summer. Sarah's home now. She and Ma opened the house last week. It's nice to see lights on there again."

"How is Sarah?" Suki asked over the rim of her glass of lemonade, the question as loaded as the bottom of an iceberg.

"Yes," Doc's booming voice reached them from the back porch, "how *is* Sarah? Hang on; I'll be out in a minute. Want a beer, Abe, instead of that old lady's lemonade?"

"Thanks. Sure. Sounds good."

Abe's lean handsome face did not register the volatile mixture of thoughts and feelings in his hidden places regarding Sarah. He stilled his hands to betray nothing. He tried to control his nerves and facial expressions. Living with the New Year's Eve catastrophe strained like walking around with compacted tin cans tied to his ass.

"So, I say, how's Sarah, Abe? I haven't seen her since last January, just before she went back to school." Doc's eyes softened.

Abe jerked from his bubble to respond. "She's fine. I've only talked to her over the fence, but she looks terrific. Like a little kid, sometimes I don't know what to say to her or how to answer a simple question. I wish I could simplify my life in that respect." Abe felt as if he needed a hat in his hand that he could twist around and around.

"Maybe you never will," Suki commented. "Do you fall apart whenever I talk to you, dear?" She turned lazily to Doc; her head leaned back against the chaise.

Silently, Doc turned to Abe and winked. He emitted a long, controlled sigh. "Let me just say that I'm glad you're not one of my patients. I'm afraid I'd be most unfaithful." He rubbed his mouth and chin, chewing on the moment.

With the bantering, Suki was uncomfortable with the boys. "I'll leave you two to your man talk and get a head start on supper. Please join us, Abe."

"I'd like that, and I have the time. Thank you." Abe smiled warmly.

"By the way," Doc said, assuming an advisory mode, "I examined Sarah before she left for school around the tenth of January. Everything seemed to be restored to normal. You're one lucky sonofabitch that she's not pregnant. No condoms... She's totally frightened, and I'm really sorry about that." Doc found empathy and swelled with unanticipated pride as Abe's father, but how could he reach that remote cavern of his brain that so often drove him headlong into trouble?

"I know you think the world of her, but I'd be surprised if you even got near her this summer." He shrugged slowly, collecting the empty beer bottles and going back to the house for more.

Abe had expected a blizzard of criticism from Doc on this matter, but he had been admonished in such a fashion that he felt like a cockatoo instead of a cockroach. He needed to remember that Sarah was fragile and tender. The nature of man would never change. Lust was Abe's favorite sin. He applied this instinct to envelop a woman, to master her, to make her his slave. That would never change. But along the way, he had to remember she graced the more ingenuous counterpart of him.

❧

The summer, lush with greenery and wildflowers, fled on wings of Icarus. Abe had no time to do a single canvas, which gave him a good dose of frustration.

So did Sarah.

He walked with her, swam with her, played some tennis and worshipped the ground she walked on, but never got farther than a kiss from her, and *then* she backed off, frigid and uptight. Always there were uneasy silences and stifling tensions. They never touched the New Year's debacle again. It remained a stalled storm front between them.

"I'll miss you when you go back to school, Abe. You've kept my summer entertaining. I loved every minute of it. Thanks a million for the lovely portrait of me too. Ma says that you have a talent—that of capturing the souls of people in their eyes."

With her head down, Sarah walked along the beach with Abe. The early August evening had turned the beach to gold as the sunset lingered lazily over the horizon. "It seems like we're always saying goodbye." There arose a catch in her voice.

Abe managed a slight smile. "We *are* always saying goodbye."

A soft breeze played with the leaves in the beechwoods. Mother Nature, in a diplomatic mode, softly laid the waves upon the sandy beach.

"Sarah," he said softly to the top of her head.

"Yes." She raised her deeply-inquiring brown eyes that devastated him.

Abe cleared his throat. A cold, clutching fear gripped him. He languished in such a stygian stupor, but the words came out remarkably gentle. "Will you still marry me next spring when we graduate?" He stopped walking and held her hands.

Screeching, the seagulls weaved and soared like Abe's thought waves.

Deliciously wanting and loving this man, Sarah considered what kind of life could she expect with octopus-attack lovemaking? Could she ever satisfy him?

Her eyes darted across his face, but she managed to sound casual. "Abe, I've known no other man." She flushed with the admission. "I don't want to know any other man. What I would hope to do is spend another evening with you sometime between now and next spring and see how things go. We need to be together more often, alone. Alone so we can rediscover each other— alone so you can become cognizant that I am someone far inferior to your strength. She gave him a fierce hug, and was glad to discover that he did not have …well, she never settled sure what to call it.

He held her close—his treasure. Taking a moment to savor how good life was, he breathed deeply and listened to their hearts beating in unison. Viewing the wide, endless sweep of the bay, he witnessed a lightning glimpse of his future with Sarah in a haze-like reel of fast-moving images. The revelation lodged intellectual, but communicated a comfortable aura, tinged with tangible love and tinted with nurturing. There existed a future somewhere out there. He wasn't sure just what it held, but he was ready to take that first step with Sarah. So grateful for her reply, he ached.

He slept fitfully that night. He dreamed of rolling wheat fields in which Sarah stood on the other side of the forty and he thrashed about to reach out and walk to her, but his feet were stuck grotesquely to the ground by overwhelming gravitational impulses.

He'd never get there.

He awoke in a fierce sweat.

CHAPTER THIRTY-TWO

While expending much sweat in his three football seasons, Abe had risen the fastest in his class. He was a paradox in terms of neophyte beginnings, and he didn't fit the general rule of talent potential at first. However, the frog turned into a prince.

By the start of the fourth year, the team realized that all college football players fell into two categories: the *haves* and the *have-nots*. Abe was a *have* after being named All American in the 1946 NCAA football program, an appropriate way to end a bizarre season. The team had won most of its games by squeakers, but vaulted to second place in the country, Notre Dame being first. For the team, in its fourth season now, and for Abe, in his final year, there had been summits, gorges and weird dances with fate.

The difference between the *haves* and *have-nots* was often small and slanted, but it was also right there for everybody to see and make assessments. During the week, the *haves* wore starter-status blue jerseys or one of the other major colors—light blue on offense and dark blue on defense; the *have-nots* wore white jerseys. The *haves* get press write-ups and made public appearances around town. The *have-nots* were nameless.

The *haves* and *have-nots* suited up alongside each other in the locker room. They got parallel treatment from the coach during practice; they jogged onto the field before games and blended near the benches. During games, however, the *haves* traversed the narrow sideline and played. They gathered bashes and laurels. They swaggered. They attracted the stunning women. The *have-nots* tread the sideline, careful not to get in the way of a frenetic coach explaining something to a *have*. The *have-nots* hung around. They gathered corrosion. Women weren't as easy to come by for them.

One of the difficult parts of football was being struck hard without actually being punched, those mental blows to confidence. Other than during the games, the sport Americans seemed most ardent about was not fun. Not even close. Practices were long, hard and brutal; the coaches oftentimes were brusque on the field and remote off it.

The season began on August 7th at six-thirty in the morning. The first game of the season was on September 23rd, with Michigan State once again. Kreiler had the killer instinct at pre-game. Abe sat relaxed in the top deck with Hulk, Chapin, Ness and Burgher. Kreiler's bully pulpit no longer intimidated him as it did at one time. He'd found that Kreiler was really a sweet William, and not the tiger lily image with which he portrayed himself.

Inviting Doc, Suki, and Sarah for the Ohio State, Thanksgiving weekend game was a coup. Abe wanted them there for his last game, the grand finale.

His class load this term was relaxed: Nineteenth Century Masters, Chinese-Asian Studies, fulfilling his philosophy requirements, and Arts and Letters of China, American Culture, meeting his humanities requirements, and Spanish Art: El Greco to Goya.

He may have stretched his time parameters with that private instructorship he took again, but he needed the extra credit hours to graduate next spring. No longer would he have time to go to Old German, Metzgers, Preketes or the Pretzel Bell with the guys. However, in this nice weather, he treasured the time to sit in the Diag and study, or daydream—watch a dog sniff the air, gaze around among the guitar players and observe students idle in and out of the library.

"Miereau!"

"Yo!"

"Will you pay attention? I feel as if I'm talking to a wall when you drift off like that. Put a cap on it! You, Chapin, Ness, Burgher and Hulk are going to be my Magic Wolverines this year, so listen up."

Abe shifted gears, listening with enthusiasm to the ring of "Magic Wolverines." It sounded symbiotic to him—one for all and all for one.

"When I came to the stadium this morning, and I have been here since this morning, as opposed to some of you hoo-hahs who get here a mere hour before the game, traffic dragged tediously. It was burdensome, with men who must convince other men that they need a gym membership or a new roof or a new truck or who must solve an air conditioning problem or an assembly line lag, and there is not much difference between them and us. All of life is rife with competition. Some of us will perform well and some will not, but we'll all be evaluated by only one thing—the end result." A pause ensued, followed by more silence.

"The result, gentlemen! The result!" Another heavy silence followed.

"The difference between winning and losing is economic, social and prestige. I–like-the-prestige!" he said, enunciating every word slowly and clearly as he paced near the podium, tossing a piece of chalk from his right hand to his left. "Slapdash effort and limp opposition are like menacing diseases. They can contaminate a whole team."

"Stay loose out there. I want every nerve fiber tingling with anticipation. You've been through a hundred agility drills, on-call running forward, backward, to one side or the other to further loosen those muscles. Keep 'em movable, particularly you men on the offensive team. Stands to reason you're the ones who tighten up because you go out there and block, run and pass without restraint if you're going to move that ball."

"Chapin! How long have you been running hurdles?" Kreiler tossed his chalk in the air.

"Sir. Since Junior High." A stirring could be observed in the underclassmen.

"What's your best time in the hundred yard dash?"

"Sir. Nine point nine seconds." A low rumble. Aroused whispers.

"Miereau!" Silence. "*Miereau!* Do you need an engraved invitation to join us in this dissertation?"

"No sir. Sorry, Sir."

"How long have you been running an obstacle course practicing for track events?"

"Since high school, Sir."

"And what did you use for hurdles when you practiced?"

"Old piles of washed-up driftwood on the beach." Abe heard muffled laughter.

"Tell us where you placed at your track events in the Upper Peninsula."

"All Michigan for two years." The laughter subsided and sounds of appraising sighs circled the lecture room. Round-eyed lower classmen turned around and stared, their mouths opening and closing like a fish's.

"And tell us if you will, your best time at running the mile in competition."

"Four minutes thirty-one seconds." All heads were now on swivels, their eyes wider. General stirrings were mingled with low conversations and excitement.

"For you freshmen, Abe Miereau never played the game of football until he came to the University. It was a fluke that we even found him. He was painting on a canvas in the bleachers, and turned into our very own Renoir Warrior. He's not intimidated by bullying defensive backs. When we throw to him across the middle and he is belted, he gets right back up. I knew from the start we had a good receiver here." Kreiler placed both hands on the edges of the podium.

"Chapin is cut from the same redwood. He's quick and a great actor on the fakes. His stride is deceptive. We have a formidable offense this year. By the way, Miereau, see if you can't get through this season without laying an opponent flat before the game even starts." An air of pride lingered in the remark, tongue-in-cheek. "Recidivism is not viewed as healthy for the team…"

Ripples of laughter sounded. Freshman could be seen getting information on the Miereau muggings of the past.

"I want to see good hustle and robust, hard-hitting plays. Every team we meet this year will be coming to knock your blocks off. Remember that. I want every move you make power-packed and accurately timed. I want you all-aggression and shatterproof because we *are shatterproof.* This is the year. We've been fine-tuning for three years. This is our year of *perfection!* We're primed. It is 1947, and that is *our* year, and if you're not cognizant of this fact, you are out of the loop." Kreiler slammed his notebook shut and left the dais, pacing the floor in front of the podium.

"Michigan and Notre Dame are the clear-cut kings of college football. We just may be in a league of our own this year—a *universe* of our own. I have a feeling that no other teams on earth will compare this year. The quality and depth of the talent amassed at Michigan and Notre Dame is staggering!" Kreiler's blue-green eyes shone like mica.

"We're only playing nine games this year. By conference rule, only three of the nine games can be played against non-league opponents. A new policy of the Michigan Board mandates that Michigan State will get one spot, while the other two will be filled by Army and Iowa, thus there will be no place for a Midwestern independent such as Notre Dame." Winking, he flashed a knowing look to Jim Funt.

"I want you to remember that all football coaches have at least one thing in common; they all have huge egos. The greater the football coach, the greater the ego. I have a *big* ego. The unimaginative and the uncertain don't stand a chance in this evolution. The coach who enjoys great skill and certainty must make sure his players know it, and they must believe in themselves with every thread of their being. I want you to do that too. You must firmly believe that every one of you is far superior to those opposition players. It's a timeless mentality that is entwined into every coach and every winning football team. We walk with a strut. We are the kings of cool. *Just do it! Just be it*—*the greatest team of the year!*"

They came out of the tunnel to the deafening roar of seventy-five thousand fans. Abe never did get used to that sound—tumultuous, like a sudden violent whirlwind.

Michigan State drew first blood—a touchdown and a point after conversion, bringing the score to seven to zero, in favor of State.

On the first Michigan offensive play of the game Abe made a great leaping catch right down the middle, and Michigan reached first and ten on their thirty-seven. Burgher picked up two yards. Hulk threw. With a State defensive back on his tail, Abe leapt and caught, dropped, rolled, jumped up and drove for two more yards.

Michigan chalked up the first down on their forty-one.

A Michigan tackle picked up State's blitzing weak-side linebacker. Another tackle took the strong-side blitz. Ness beat his man, creating another first down. Michigan sat on State's forty-seven.

Chapin, gaining a great block by a guard, ran away from one man and pivoted around another. Michigan stood on State's thirty.

Miereau ran a perfect zigzag-out and Hulk fired it right into his hands. Michigan camped on State's twelve. Ness picked up five. Michigan had a second and five on State's seven, and they were in great shape.

Then they were set back a yard.

It was third and five now. Hulk faked—dropping back. Chapin ran, his man beaten, caught it and ran out of field as he went into the end zone.

The reward was a field goal and a conversion. With the score seven to seven, the game was all tied up.

The fourth quarter found the same score on the board. With fewer than four minutes remaining, Kreiler appeared jumpier than a Mexican flea.

Abe made an interception while staying in for defense; a *thop* sound could be heard. He wedged it and blazed right past Kreiler down the sideline. He took it all the way to States eighteen.

The time read thirty-six seconds remaining.

Michigan rushed for five. The ball was stationed on the thirteen and Hulk knelt on the twenty-one. Michigan had just one-point-five seconds from the pass-back to the kick. That's all Michigan needed. The ball rose up between the end posts, absolutely true, and sailed into the end zone stands. The referee's arms flew up, signaling the positive kick.

With thirty-three seconds remaining, it was State seven, Michigan ten. The kickoff carried to State's twenty-five—second and ten. Seventeen seconds left.

State attempted a long bomb to the flanker, but the throw was too wide, and he had no chance on it. There were twelve seconds left.

The State quarterback threw out-of-bounds across the other sideline, with four seconds left. On a screen, he let it go to his left halfback, who received it and ran to his right toward Michigan's sideline. Lenny Dodge, one of Michigan's great black defensemen, closed in, hit him and they went down.

The gun went off and it was over.

The air split with a thundering noise.

"Abe!" came from the bleachers. "A-Abe!" in a cadence.

"It's some kind of heady, hard-to-handle experience to hear your name by thousands of people!" Abe shook his head. "I can taste the noise."

Hulk and Abe were elated.

"I'm pumped about Kreiler's accelerated offensive game," Hulk shared with Abe in the shower. "When I returned in August and Kreiler said he intended to be wide open on offense, pass happy as no one had ever seen, I thought I'd jump right out of my skin. That's our game, Abe." His voice shook with excitement.

"Sure thing. I'd like to reach the pros. It's looking more favorable all the time, but I'll never get used to seventy-five thousand people shouting our names. I just get out there and do my best...forget everything else, and try to use focusing disciplines I learned when I was a kid. It's a crazy fucking life. You just gotta take 'er around the block and see how it runs. Nothing ventured, nothing gained."

September 30, 1947—Michigan vs Iowa.

Down in the corner of the end zone, Abe had made a touchdown catch for the all-time highlight film, but he lost the ball as it hit his fingertips, then it rolled off his back and, as he and an Iowa defender hit the ground, miraculously the ball came to rest in his hands. Even sweeter, Michigan, after the extra point, led one of the previous season's hottest teams, finally winning by twenty-seven to three.

October 6, 1947—Michigan vs. Army

The onslaught started after back-to-back fumble recoveries by Michigan— one of them by Abe. In short order, Hulk ran fifteen yards and then flipped a pass over the middle to Chapin from the opponent's five yard line for his third touchdown pass. Number four was a gift from Abe, that can-you-believe-it catch.

Incredibly, there followed a number five. Hulk got credit for it, but did nothing more than toss a short pass to the much-heralded Miereau at Michigan's forty-eight yard line. Abe weaved his way fifty-two yards and into the end zone. Kreiler stood, stunned. The rout was on, adding another victory for Michigan. The Wolverines snarled tonight.

October 20, 1947—Michigan vs. Northwestern

Abe reversed the flow, first with a fifty-five-yard punt return for a touchdown while staying in for defense, and later with an acrobatic fifty-three yard catch of Hulk's air-out, exhibiting magnificent qualities in the chant of "Just Do It!" Michigan won, forty-nine to twenty-one.

October, 1947—Michigan vs. Minnesota

The game was as consistently powerful as a coach could hope, winning by a score of thirteen to six. Hulk passed eight times, completed five for ninety-one yards and two touchdowns, both scored by Abe.

Kreiler's dynamos would, once or twice each game, wipe out the one-second pause required after a shift, but Minnesota did it only when it needed a few yards near the opposing goal. Result? They'd catch the rival linemen drifting to adjust positions and bean 'em when they were off-balance. Kyle relied on the weakness of human nature, figuring the officials would say, "Oops, twas a fast shift!" Then, while they nibbled their squawkers in uncertainty, they'd add, "Oh well, they've been straightforward up until now. Let's wait and see." But there wouldn't *be* a next *time*! So Kyle succeeded.

November 3, 1947—Michigan vs. Indiana

Michigan put on a show beyond belief. The offense scored on its first possession and scored again on its second possession. Hulk hit Abe in the end zone from eight yards out, then scored again on third possession. Very quickly, it got even better. Abe dashed forty-seven yards on a reverse for a third quarter touchdown and made an over-the-shoulder catch of a forty-five yard Hulk pass in the end zone for a fourth quarter touchdown. It ended in a thirty-five to zero rout. The Mad Magicians were carnivorous.

November 17, 1947—Michigan vs. Wisconsin

Michigan sailed straight ahead as they watched Wisconsin busy themselves with thudding in the line that caused five fumbles, four interceptions, twenty-five incompletions, assorted bobbles, confusing time-outs, sideline arguments and a total of twenty rushing plays that lost yardage. Final score: Michigan, forty—Wisconsin, six. Kreiler and Funt made eye contact—speechless, lest the magic spell be broken.

The WWJ Radio Announcing Team analyzed, "The thing about Miereau is, he's not just large, he's agile, and he's not just speedy, he's on the ball. He's not just robust, he's got a sixth sense, and he's not just tall, he's rangy. We understand that Miereau has raised his grade point average to three point zero, and you never can undervalue intelligence in any walk of life. It's those hands of his, of course, as we've mentioned on other occasions, and those strong shoulders. It's rare to find a kid as fierce on the football field who finds time to paint. Kreiler has dubbed him the Renoir Warrior. Miereau thinks *t-e-a-m* all the time. Now that is *character,* and not just any Jock McStrap. Wolverine partisans believe that the Mad Magicians—Miereau, Hulk, Chapin, Ness and Burgher—are the greatest offense since the Four Horsemen."

Thanksgiving—Michigan Vs Ohio

The excitement for both the team and the fans began building Monday. By the time over two thousand assembled on the Diag Friday afternoon to hear Kyle, Abe, Hulk, Ness, Chapin, Burgher and the rest, the fever burned out of control, the electricity overwhelming. It surpassed any week the media had ever experienced. No one spent a quiet night, and few students made many classes.

During the weeklong study of tactics, the coaching staff had noticed a quirk on the part of Ohio halfback, Bo Renn. When he moved into his stance, he put his right hand down if the play was to go left. Conversely, the left hand would be down if the action was to go right. This signage would play major havoc in the game, with Kreiler using the information to call defensive signals throughout the afternoon.

Abe needed this last big game to vault him as a contender for the Heisman Trophy. He wanted to live the aspiration a little longer. Even dreamier pastures, Karen Kreiler arranged for Doc, Suki and Sarah to sit with her near the sideline.

Yet dreamland is a hallway sometimes, or so it seemed to Abe as he bustled toward the squad room in the early afternoon of November 24, 1947. He tore around a corner and there, right in his pathway, he found a figure that might have caused anyone else to fall through the floor. Socially, Abe fit the part of the absentee thinker in his class, but he spoke the proper words. "How are you, Mr. President?"

"Nice to see you," President Truman, thirty-third President of the United States replied. "Going to the same place I'm going?" A manta ray would have been as out of place as Mr. President, who struck such fear and awe in Abe.

Yes, the president *was* going to the squad room, but his escort, Coach Kreiler, had been temporarily sidetracked, so for several tongue-tied and wonderful moments there were just the two of them, Abe and President Truman, chitchatting. Not that they were alone. Near the Secret Service Agents were the University of Michigan Public relations men with news cameras recording everything for future generations.

"What's your name?" the president asked.

"Abednego Miereau."

If his face or his voice offered no hint of nerves colliding inside, Abe died with visceral tightness. No one but his father and Sarah ever got away with calling him *Abednego*, not without a knock-down-drag-out confrontation. Regardless of the circumstances, Abe's smile grew wide and genuine and his greeting changed to a casual, "Abe Miereau, usually. I work with the wide receivers." No dramatics fell into Abe's tone—nothing that might remain even for an instant in a president's mind, yet Truman mentioned particulars about Miereau when Kreiler arrived a few minutes later.

Kreiler could smell victory and felt glorious in introducing the President of the United States as a surprise to the full team when they gathered for pre-game instructions. A standing round of applause greeted him. Truman spoke briefly of solidarity and used as an illustration his experiences with A-Bomb detonations, ending World War II. "Know the organized game plan and be ready and gutsy enough to deliver it."

In the strong presence of the president, Kreiler was subdued to the point that he was brief. He used his pulpit again to instill enthusiasm and unadulterated aggression. "We've got to be our best to even stay with 'em today. I want to see you out there like a band of Argonauts off on a quest; defeating Ohio is the Golden Fleece! *They* want this game badly. I want to see you plow them under and lay them fallow until next year! I've never met a victory I didn't like. Let's do it!"

A biting cold wave had howled out of Canada and anesthetized the Great Lakes region the day before. The University of Michigan Alumni Association forked over more than seven thousand dollars on nine thousand bales of hay to cover the field to save it from freezing. Over the hay they swathed a shielding canvas, only to observe in alarm as masses of snow released from the sky, forming a squashing third layer.

On the morning of the game, with the thermometer hovering well below the freezing mark and the wind shipping about the vast stadium, some three hundred volunteers removed the snow from atop the field's shielding covering, then they heaved the hay insulation to the sidelines, revealing the playing arena in what had come to look more like a Winter Land kiddy park than a football stadium.

Despite the burdensome precautions, the field had iced up, which gave the Ohio State team a hands-down advantage. They had brought along sneakers to give better grip on a frozen field, whereas the University of Michigan players had only cleated football shoes. Kyle Kreiler appealed to the Ohio State Coach, and he finally agreed that his team would play in conformist football shoes. He declined to rescind the order, even after his players complained of the hazardous field during the pre-game warm up. That decision alone may have sealed his doom.

The weather influenced more than the result of the game. On warmer days in Ann Arbor, University Stadium had accommodated as many as seventy-five thousand spectators. On this brutal late-November Saturday, it held slightly less. The steam from the spectators' breathing floated cumulatively straight up into the gray overcast day like tentacles of a thousand squid.

The added significance of this game was sharpened because the Ohio game would be the final one in Michigan Stadium for Hulk, Miereau and Chapin. They were honored by Michigan fans during pre-game ceremonies.

Abe waved to Sarah and her party. She looked so beautiful in her Teddy Bear coat and hat. His heart swelled to think she'd been his girl since she'd been a wee cub. There she stood, all honey-beige except for her mahogany hair and dazzlingly white teeth. Abe got soft and weak. She could light up the darkest of his moments with only one smile—a private smile aimed just at him. He wondered if he'd ever be able to break down the barriers he'd created last New Year's Eve. Had he poisoned the well?

Abe grew with pride because his Nahma people were in the stands for his finest moment in four years of seasoned play. Damn, Doc looked good in his stadium jacket—handsome, handsome as hell! Suki wore her mink wrapped up to her chin; her matching headband glistening when she moved.

It was almost game time. The National Anthem swelled on the sidelines. Perched high atop the bulk of the bleachers, the American flag waved and flicked steadily in the cold twenty-mile-per-hour wind.

As the Michigan team stood shoulder-to-shoulder, Kreiler approached Abe from behind. A network of wrinkles surrounded his eyes. "I hope to hell that you aren't going to be waving to sweet Sarah during this game. You blow this one and the team forfeits its year-long, no-loss record. Damn it, for now, stay focused."

"Yeah, sure thing, Coach." Abe, a graduate of the bump-and-bruise trail, hassled with a hammer that pounded him to persevere and stay focused.

The spiffy, national-award-winning Michigan band struck on the Star Spangled Banner. For Abe, this was a tough part of the game; he always got choked up deeply by this show of patriotism. When the band crescendoed to "The rockets' red glare, the bombs bursting in air," he felt that kindergarten throb in his throat that he couldn't control and his eyes teared over. Hulk blasted him with an elbow to the side, his camaraderie sealed so tightly that he could read him like a map. Abe sometimes swore that Hulk lived inside his mind.

Some daft things helped determine that game: a goal post on the goal line, a pass from the end zone that hit the posts and the rule that such a pass was a safety if it bounced back into the end zone. The next year the tainted rule saw massaging, and some thirty years later the goal posts were moved to the end line.

After driving to a first and goal on the Ohio eight yard line, Michigan breached the goal line, won the conversion, and augured up by seven-zip.

Limbaugh, the Ohio quarterback who had dangerously damaged his ribs late in the season, participated, all but sheathed in iron bands for this game. The Ohio coach did not want him to play, but Limbaugh prevailed. On the Ohio first possession, he botched moving the club and did not compete with his hands-on self. Nonetheless, he called the plays when Ohio moved the ball after the Michigan touchdown.

On the first play, Limbaugh called for a straight snap into the end zone, facing as if to punt the ball. Actually, Limbaugh intended to pass, but the ball smacked his cold hands and fell to the turf. As the Michigan linemen moved down on him, he quickly retrieved the ball and thrust it toward the sidelines, far from any logical Ohio receiver or Michigan defender. The referee's horn protested, and the Ohio State team saw reprimand by half the distance to the goal line for deliberately grounding the ball.

Even with the ball inside his three, Limbaugh dismissed any thoughts of punting. He figured that he could get his team out of its predicament with a quick crossing pattern to either end or running back. He was right. The running back promptly broke into the secondary and was available when Limbaugh straightened to throw.

"I had a damn touchdown," he said of the play. "That back was clear out there, but I couldn't get as much on the ball as I typically did. We were moving against the wind in that first quarter, and as soon as I delivered the ball, up came a blast of air and lifted it right into the crossbar."

"Damn!" he said as soon as the ball hit the post. Limbaugh was upset about not completing the pass. He had no idea about a safety until the referee signaled, but he oozed with more anger at missing a touchdown than at Michigan getting two points.

The score now stood nine to zero.

The play ended with Limbaugh's last significant one of the day. He again injured his ribs and after the first quarter gave up the ghost, having completed just one of six passes for a squalid seven yards. The Ohio team deeply ached for Limbaugh, not only on offense but also on defense. He was a superlative safetyman, a sure tackle and a shrewd strategist who read the opposition's offense as though he were supervising it.

Starting with a thirty-nine yard-punt return by Abe with about five minutes left in the third quarter, the Michigan Wolverines made the scoreboard flicker like a pinball machine out of whack. Abe did his Indian Sun Dance before spiking the ball.

Fifteen—zip.

Kreiler fiercely chewed his gum. It was so cold he didn't know how the guys were holding onto the ball, much less catching it!

The Michigan place-kicker lined up to kick the extra point, but as his toe smacked the ball, an Ohio tackle nibbled it with his hand and left it bobbling toward the goal posts. The ball struck the crossbar and hung there for an instant, as if indecisive as to what to do. Ultimately, it dropped over for the extra point.

Sixteen to zero.

Clearly, it was not the Ohio team's day. Their famed band was queued to participate in the half-time show, only to find that its reeds and brass had iced up.

In the fourth quarter, Hulk got his Abe-ignited offense rolling again, crowning a drive by passing to Miereau down the middle and over the Ohio jumping-jack backer, who had two interceptions this day, for the touchdown. This time, Michigan's extra point drove a clear miss, sailing well to the right.

Trying to overcome the twenty-two to zero lead, the Ohio quarterback passed fifty yards to his receiver on the Michigan six-yard line, then screwed about on the next play, resulting in an eleven-yard loss.

Twice during the last quarter the Ohio quarterback steered his offense into scoring position. The first time, he managed it to Michigan's thirty-one yard line. The gusting wind ceased as he lined up the kick, but no sooner had his toe met the ball than the wind fanned furiously again, progressively pushing the ball to the side until it missed moving through the uprights for at least two points on the score board.

A few minutes later the same quarterback connected on short passes, moving the ball to Michigan's thirty-six yard line, but this time the field goal try blustered far short. So, too, were the Ohio efforts for a fourth national title in ten years.

The final score was twenty-two to nothing.

The cold, for which the Ohio players had been equipped with their sneakers, might have been a benefit if they had gone ahead and worn the rubber-soled footwear. The wind, which blew Limbaugh's pass into the goal posts and the field-goal attempt wide, penalized the Ohio team more than the Michigan team. Yet weather, which is fundamentally beyond man's control, somehow escaped culpability. It was the rule on safeties that angered the Ohio State administration. It took their Board of Regents exactly twenty-seven days until the next rules committee meeting to have that rule amended. It turned out, after all, easier than reforming the weather.

Miereau became a prime offensive threat in his senior year, when he performed impressively enough to be a top draft pick of the Green Bay Packers at the conclusion of the 1947 season.

To this day, Michigan and Notre Dame both claim the 1947 National Championship as its own. Officially, Notre Dame garnered the honor, as it finished first in the official determinant of the day—the final, regular-season Associated Press Writers Poll. The coaches' poll had not yet begun. Had the debate been settled on the field, college football records for attendance, scalping, wagering, hype and partisan zealousness could have been obliterated.

In the victorious aftermath, the coaches entered the showers one by one. Lady Abundance had left her cornucopia in the Michigan locker room. Jim Funt did Abe's Sun Dance in the shower. Kreiler led a most stirring rendition of "The Victors," his voice resonant and strong. Roses were tossed from player to player as they realized that for the first time in fourteen years a Michigan team would be in Pasadena on New Year's Day.

Things were just as crazy in downtown Ann Arbor as fans spilled out of homes, bars, dorms and apartments to dance with strangers in the freezing cold. Roses were thrown freely in the streets. In the reception area for families after the game, players posed together for snapshots with their families.

The tough times of his years at college seemed nil: Abe learning the game from scratch and not doing all that well at first, trying to make the grade in his classes but lacking reading power, being yanked for a while as a junior because of disciplinary reasons. He was caught with a girl in a dorm room, along with Chapin, and he was involved in a fight outside a bar one night. He was whomped twelve months probation for that.

Nonetheless, how magnificent the turnaround had been! After graduation, Abe left Michigan football with every important single season and career-receiving record. His shtick was running, and run he did, better than anyone he faced. He was fairly certain of making the upcoming NFL draft, along with Chapin and Hulk, so he insured himself for one million dollars! But he didn't tell Sarah that right away.

In a few minutes, Abe pulled free from the flocking crowd and found Sarah walking toward him. "Hey, Miss Sarah!" he said, still playful as he extended his arms.

She whispered, "I'm really proud of you."

He made no response. His head tucked down into her hair and smelled that clean fragrance of a fresh shampoo. He ached all over for this woman.

"I've always been proud of *you*, Sarah. I can't wait to show you off to everyone at the hotel tonight. We're going to celebrate at dinner!"

Upon leaving the stadium, Abe was excited with the promise of meeting Doc, Suki and Sarah at the Allenal, that is as soon as he could change clothes and get back to the hotel where they were staying. This was a seminal moment and there was no time for shilly-shallying. Wearing the look of someone who hears distant music, he considered the perfect football season. Maybe the Heisman! NFL Draft coming up!

Smiling, incredulous, he tapped the steering wheel in beat to "*You Could Be Swinging On A Star*" "Hot damn, but life is good!" he said aloud.

CHAPTER THIRTY-THREE

Abe, in anticipation of the celebration, was super-charged with the fact that he'd bought himself a new suit—camel-colored gabardine—this time at Saks. An ivory-hued shirt and a rich, brown/beige/rust tie with matching pocket handkerchief rounded out the outfit. Further indulging himself, he splurged on a pair of tan bucks that caught his eye.

How he had smiled as he passed the sweater vests, turned around as one called out to him, shook his head, moved slowly away, then came back and succumbed to the temptation. He decided on a cable knit in variegated shades of tan. What a dude! He felt like a walking ad for an expensive Irish whiskey.

He hoped that it turned Sarah on. It had been almost a year since he'd been able to get close to her. Of all the blessed women running around and available out there, it had to be his lot in life to love that woman beyond all imagination. He seemed to start where she ended. His love never slept; it floated like a persistent insomnia. Maybe...just maybe... Yes! While at Saks, he'd get an engagement ring to spring on her after the game Saturday. His savings account was healthy. His expenses had been minimal.

But what if she turned him down? What if she thought him a raving lunatic to entertain such a thought? He remembered the hesitation in her eyes last summer. After he'd painted her love all over his heart, what if she'd decided not to marry him? She hadn't said for sure, but she had hinted that she wanted some time together. It seemed like their relationship had more interference than a stumble-fumble offense. This was no time to be second-guessing himself. *Faint heart never won fair maiden.*

Abe spent the better part of an hour looking at rings and asking questions. He finally decided on a briolette, a pear-shaped diamond cut in long triangular facets. He found that it literally danced with a thousand gimlet points of light.

"Excellent choice, sir! That'll be $150.00, plus the nuisance luxury tax of ten percent with which we're still stuck since the war. How would you like to pay for that, sir? We have an easy monthly installment plan for students." The jeweler sniffed a nasty-nostril stance of superiority he reserved for dealing with the bourgeoisie.

"Cash," said Abe, reaching for his wallet and retrieving two one hundred dollar bills.

"Yes, sir! Very good, sir! Is there anything else I can do for you today? How about gift wrap?"

"No to all the above, thank you. I'll just be on my way." A knot had returned to his stomach as he recalled the arrogant treatment he'd received from the funeral home director when he'd made burial arrangements for Fabian. Fabian only owned one suit all his life until his burial. Abe's grief poured over him in a surprise attack.

"Sonofabitches!"

Cash always brought out the best in these kikes. He'd probably go straight to hell for thinking that. In addition, he must have a sprained brain because he remembered that Sarah's genetics were half-Jewish. Well, they were still a strange breed.

"Pardon me, sir. Did you say something?"

"Yes. Britches."

"Britches?"

"Freeze your britches—cold as hell out there today. Oh, by the way, I changed my mind; I *do* want that ring gift wrapped. No charge."

"Very good, sir. Happy to do that for you!"

The department store memory faded into a haze of gauze while the successful football season usurped his mind. In his wildest dreams, never had he anticipated a moment as grand as this. It launched as the lost-and-found of his wildest imaginings. He couldn't sluice away all the deprivations of childhood, however, when the waters had been choppy and his fragile boat chafed against life's wharf—the instants he shivered with the cold; the stretches he dragged himself home through the dark and snow, counting streetlights with trepidation until he ran out of them on the beach road; the ever advancing storm of taunting kids because he was a slow learner; being dry-docked in the seventh grade while his classmates sailed on, too big for the desks, too old for the other kids, too tongue-tied to speak clearly and the naysayers who shook their heads.

Through the aegis of a caring ship of state, he overcame all obstacles and foibles and was now sitting on top the world. How much he owed Doc! The secret to surviving he traced to this surrogate father. Abe concluded that his gift of a fantasy bubble meant more to him than any other talent on which he may ever warm his hands. It had taken him through all his bad times, yet the seabirds screeched his nemesis: "Sarah."

Unabashed, he fantasized. Contemporary society would say that he'd given a smashing performance today. Maybe now she would consider him a suitable husband.

The price of her soul was immeasurable. She was cultured, intelligent and beautiful; she could have ten men like him. Maybe he was chasing a frivolous dream and should deal more in tangibles. Abe's face lost all expression as such thick thoughts rushed upon him. Maybe he should walk away from heartbreak while he still could. It was No Man's Land between the mind's wanderings and reality.

He obsessed while he dressed. Looking into the double door mirrors on the closet, he saw a worldly man—suave, debonair, successful, confident and prepossessed with an inner power and drive not known to many men. His eyes bespoke intelligence with but a hint of covert savagery, barbaric, with high levels of testosterone. God hadn't slept late on the day Abe Miereau was conceived.

Slipping the gift box into his new camel suit's inner pocket, he ran his hand back over his already groomed hair, which glistened darkly in contrast to the lighter color of the suit, the French vanilla shirt, Joe-campus vest, and Windsor-knotted tie. He wore his success like a badge. At long last, here stood a man ready to take his place in the world of responsibilities, disciplines and success.

Tonight he would see Sarah and derive *some time* with her. Maybe he and she could sneak away for a private conversation. *Sayonara* to the thought that he'd ever get her back out to his house. Maybe they could sit in the lobby for a while. Fat chance she'd ever invite him up to her room. He'd really blown it. Abe had an enduring impression of his *last* time alone with her. He'd never forget how afraid and hurt she was when she left. If disillusionment had a face, it was hers.

He had memorized a quote from Confucius that affected him with many truths. Although reluctant to step over the threshold, Philosophy turned out to be a most wholesome class for him.

To put the world right in order,
We must first put the nation in order.
To put the nation in order,
We must first put the family in order.
To put the family in order,
We must first cultivate our personal life;

We must first set our hearts right.

Tonight he'd set his heart right. He'd get Sarah to commit to him. She *had* to marry him. He envisioned his life as only whole with her in it. He could no longer look and not touch. Admittedly, that loomed as a simple solution for a complex problem. He swore he could smell her when she wasn't present, feel her soft skin when she was hundreds of miles away. His thoughts were like a spider's, spinning its web.

Although there had been no fresh snowfall since last night, the clouds rolled past the waning moon and the unrelenting wind stirred the white powder into snow devils as Abe drove the short five miles to the hotel. The Allenal bustled with reservations for the Mt. Olympus of football games. He checked in at the receptionist's desk. "Would you call Dr. Whittaker's suite, please?" he said to the desk clerk who mentally ran an unmistakable appraisal of Abe, readily identifiable in a college town as *Miereau,* one of Kreiler's Mad Magicians.

"Yes, sure, of course, sir, right away."

"Thanks." Abe rested an elbow on the desk and turned to observe the hectic activity of the richly appointed lobby, hanging with Waterford Crystal chandeliers and deep, black-leather upholstered furniture scattered in talkative tightness. He spotted two brilliantly lighted Tang vases displayed behind thick glass. One sat on either side of the arch that led to the dining room. Abe figured late Tang Dynasty, probably 800-900 A.D., a vastly wealthy era touted for its encouragement of the arts and literature.

The desk clerk cleared his throat. "Dr. Whittaker said to come up; it's seven-four-seven. Sir...I wonder if I could bother you to get your autograph for my son, Timmy. He idolizes the Michigan team—especially you. He plays football in junior high."

"No bother at all." Abe scrawled his name across a blank sheet of hotel letterhead stationery, adding, "To Timmy, from Abe. Don't stop trying. November 24, 1947."

The situation stirred Abe to chuckle. What a crazy roller coaster life he'd had! And this had been a no-complainer day, And it was not over yet! *But he'd need a St. Christopher medal to carry him through this evening with Sarah.*

"C'mon in here, champ." Doc's voice conveyed warmth and pride. "Can't tell you how glad we are to get a few minutes alone with you. What a ball game! Smashing! I still can't believe what a ball handler you've become, with no formal training in high school. We're so proud of you, son." Doc had his arm around Abe's waist.

Abe steeled himself, afraid he might be headed for a downfall.

"Suki, Abe is here and you're still puttering. What are you doing?" Doc questioned in the direction of the bedroom of the elegant suite.

"Hey, fella, you look absolutely gentlemanly in that soft-spoken suit—really all together. You're quite a turnaround from this afternoon. You wear the look well. I see that you've treated yourself to a little retail therapy," he added, his eyes traveling the polar directions of Abe's lean, muscular frame. "It looks as if you had a blowout shopping spree. When I have too many things to buy, I fall into shopping tedium, so I curb my needs into small doses." Doc had a cocktail in his hand—a dry martini, up.

"Can I interest you in a drink, Abe? The bar is stocked with anything your little heart may desire." He stroked his mustache.

Abe felt impulsive. "I've never had a martini. I'll try one, too, and thanks for the compliments. These *are* all new, just bought them for tonight. I need to put my best foot forward for Sarah." Abe took a sip of the martini and choked. "Holy hell, Doc, one more of these and I'll be laid flat! How do you handle them?" He nearly choked.

"Very carefully, son, very carefully." He smiled at Abe as he moved to a silver and white striped upholstered captain's chair, one arranged on either side of a large window overlooking Huron Avenue. He gestured for Abe to take the other one. Sitting, he crossed his legs in a *take-charge* manner, his richly shod feet shining in black leather. Taller than Abe, his weight commensurate, he sported a fine Savile Row suit of the deepest blue and looked the part of the man who *made* the clothes. If Abe had not had a life-long association with him he'd feel out of depth in his presence.

"How's your financial status this winter? Need anything? I know that you're not undervalued at this school, but a doctor's son can't be running around the campus like a penniless pauper." He smiled, the warmth reaching his eyes, teasing, yet caring. "A man has to leave something more meaningful than a house and a car when he departs this world. You're *it* for me. Suki and I won't be having any more children. How could we possibly top the power and prestige of our first attempt?"

"Uh-huh, I quite agree." Abe did not wriggle at this personal revelation, but did laugh at the intended humor in it. He took another sip of his martini and looked at Doc with steady eyes. He respected this man very much. It showed.

"You've been my *it* for years now. I'll try to live up to your expectations. I'm really doing okay money-wise. Of course, since my shopping trip, my account is a little lower, but that job I had last summer as Director of the Summer Art School really put me over the top in financial comfort." His face broke in a grin. "Thanks again for your support in getting me that position." Abe leaned back confidently and inadvertently crossed his legs in the same manner as Doc. It hit him that he did it without thinking, so naturally, part of his gene pool.

"I need to ask you for some advice, Doc. Maybe I did something foolish and delusional. I bought Sarah an engagement ring to present to her tonight. It's dazzling." He paused, sipping his drink as the angst built. "I wanted her to know how much I care. I have no assurance that she is any longer interested in marrying me. We've not been intimate since last New Year's Eve when I pummeled her." He cleared his throat. "I planned to present it to her after dinner tonight in the dining room, with you and Suki. Do you think that's a shabby idea?" He was distinctly respectful and solicitous, while he studied his hands folding and unfolding with the telling.

Doc brushed his face with his hand. "No, it's not a bad idea, and I *don't* think that the time or the place is inappropriate. I *do* think, however, that you need a commitment or a cutoff. It's said that those who marry in haste live to repent in leisure, but that can hardly be twisted to fit your situation. You've known each other for years. You'll both be free agents, so to speak, next spring, and it's time you had a declaration from her." Doc hesitated in his shepherding of this young man. He didn't want to be the cause of any *faux pas*.

"I know you've told her in a hundred ways how much she means to you. She *is* good wife material, and a quality wife can be of inestimable value throughout your lifetime. Maybe it's smart to make a move now, instead of hanging out to dry for another six months." Looking over the rim of his martini glass, he added, "It's time to push the envelope. She could put you off forever being a *securocrat*."

"Thanks, Doc. I've had a ton of second thoughts about it, especially now that the proposal timeline is drawing near." Abe grinned largely at this fabulous frame of a man, constructed as if by design. *His father!* He still couldn't believe it! He took yet another draw on his martini. "Potent little things, aren't they? I've only had three sips, and I can feel the kick. You're a better man than I am to handle these!"

"Nah, I've just been at it longer than you have." Doc's smile trailed off, his jaw line hard holding that ultra-handsome look—rugged, intelligent and pensive.

Abe could smell Suki's cologne—Channel, statemental and prohibitively expensive—as she entered.

"There you are, you fabulous, fantastic football star!" She swooped down and gave him a kiss on the ear, her voice every bit as melodic as he remembered—a Beethoven symphony to his ears.

Doc stood at the bar, mixing Suki a small martini on the rocks. He cautioned himself to mix it lightly, very lightly. He didn't want her head spinning so early in the evening. He'd be less than honest if he didn't admit that later, maybe later, her head could spin, definitely later.

"Suki, look at you. You're good enough to make me drool, and beautiful as a twenty-year-old. You are a centerfold's centerfold. What do you do with yourself to account for all this youthfulness? Is it a potion, an old Indian Shaman rite?" Abe was smitten with her, dressed in an oatmeal-colored sheath, with a brown velvet bolero jacket over her arm, her shining black hair pulled back into a chignon. Below a turtleneck hung a heavy gold link chain; a matching bracelet she held loosely in her hand.

Waving away Abe's bamboozle, she turned to Doc. "Would you fasten this for me, Danforth? Somehow I can't manage to attach clasp bracelets with one hand." She smiled up at him. His eyes drank in her face, warm and adoring, approvingly.

"Anything for you, Milady," he said, kissing the back of her hand.

Tap, tap, tap at the door.

"Look who's here! It's Lady Marian!" Doc smartly waved Sarah into the suite.

Whah! Was she for real? A walking, talking dream? Abe felt as if he was wound tightly. A misty angel in an ice blue wool Pendleton dress, long sleeves, deep V neckline over her small breasts, and full skirt falling in gentle folds around her long slim legs that seemed to start where her earrings stopped. Periwinkle-blue suede shoes completed the Cinderella look—slim and sprite-like.

Abe stood transfixed, simply staring at her. He needed a bulletproof vest to deflect cupid's arrows. He felt glued to the chair—a room decoration. Slowly, he stirred himself to move to her, taking her hand and moving her over to one of the chairs near him. He tried to think of something appropriate to say after his obvious, tripping on-the-tongue inspection, but his throat thickened with the awesome aura she exuded.

What was it about her that kept him running on hot? She wore his topaz bracelet and earrings! Maybe, just maybe, she'd accept his proposal. Abe, at this point hung onto any small straws. It didn't sound like his own voice when finally he whispered, "Sarah, you're prettier than a silky Thanksgiving pumpkin pie."

"And you, Mr. Miereau, are as handsome and warm as the kitchen in which it was baked!" Her smile lit up the room and wove together the threads of love in his heart.

Suki drank in the young couple—the scarcely hidden love in their eyes. The trust and teamwork, albeit in their downhome dialogue. She savored their banter and their shining youth, feeling younger by association. They were so natural together, so beautiful, so complementary to each other. She hoped they could find happiness and compatibility. She'd never heal if Sarah weren't her daughter-in-law, and she had every confidence that they could make a marriage work. Suki found that she was filled with such emotion that she couldn't speak.

Doc broke the momentary silence. "Sarah! What a sight you are, simply a vision for these old eyes." Doc kissed her on the cheek and winked at Abe.

Damn it! If Doc kissed her one more time, he'd be dealing with disaster. Abe knew that Doc warmed to this woman. What's more, he hadn't kissed her yet himself, so Doc had better back off! Abe's eyes snapped in vitriolic aggression, which he tried desperately to conceal.

Sarah curtsied and laughed that rich, smoky sound that drove Abe right out of his mind. "I'm sorry to be running a little late. Karen Kreiler called and I chatted with her for a while. She wants us to meet her and Kyle in the dining room. They're here already." The sparkle of the topaz had set residence in her eyes.

Now what was he to do with the Kreilers at the same table? Did Abe need an entire advisory group to instruct him on the presentation of the engagement ring?

The Kreilers had reserved a table in the middle of the dining room. Candles flickered in the quietly lighted arena. A low murmur of voices became audible as the foursome entered, adjusting their eyes from the bright lobby to the restful light of the dining room and dance floor. Kreiler waved them over as if he were directing traffic.

When the order of aperitifs was delivered, it took an entourage: a waiter with a silver platter of cocktails, a waiter with a magnum of Dom Perignon, a waiter with a dozen American Beauty roses, and a waiter with a deep vase and plant stand.

"That must all be for you, Kreiler, for your successful season as a football coach. You're the best!" Doc stretched around, awed at all the attention. Heads turned as the roses were placed into a vase and the champagne into a deep ice bucket.

"Uh-uh, that must be for Abe's successful season. *He's* been my vanguard for three years." Kreiler offered a salute. "Abe and my lucky rabbit rock, together we pulled it off." Reaching into his pocket, he produced the smallest ever rock with two outgrowths for ears and a polarized nub emulating a tail. "Why not, I ask you? Samson had his hair, Patton had his spirits, Luciano his dark glasses, and me, a pet rabbit!"

Abe, sitting on the opposite end of the table from Doc, grinned as he hunched over the table and leaned closer to Sarah. Gently, he reached out and picked up her small hand in his, kissing the back of it. If his karma were correct, she should be getting some reaction from his action. Incendiary, Abe viewed his queen. If she would consent to marrying him, his kingdom would be complete.

Four people asked Abe for autographs "for their kids." He forgot how great it was to be anonymous. He wasn't comfortable with the publicity, but realistic enough to concede that the world worked this way. Abe, never having been caring-impaired, had an innate gift of seeing the best of most situations.

Ten minutes later, a waiter approached with yet *another* dozen American Beauty roses. Heads turned. People buzzed.

"What the hell..." Abe said, startled.

"Well, this is the Dinner of Roses before the Tournament of Roses, it appears," Suki bubbled. "I ordered a dozen roses in commemoration of such an exciting event." Her tone was congenial, inspiring love with her self-effacing characteristics.

"And I ordered roses to honor the season of hard work," Karen added, laughing, her eyes dancing with mischief.

Surrounding diners stirred with the infectious amusement of the riot of roses.

A regular Yamaguchi Harvest of Japanese cuisine, cooked for them at the table over high flames that licked and seared the small slices of chicken and beef, shrimp and scallops, followed. Their chef chopped vegetables with the rapidity and accuracy of highly sophisticated weaponry, throwing knives in the air, catching them and never missing a beat, all the while carrying on a staccato chatter to the rhythm of the slicing knives, leaving everyone entertained, but breathless, with his mechanized performance.

Abe looked up. Yet another dozen roses were delivered, selling memories to last a lifetime. "What the hell!" he said again, tickled to his toes. He remembered when he couldn't afford to *smell* a long-stemmed rose, and now there were three dozen strewn around the table like a slightly overdone High Tea. It was always feast or famine.

In a small, timorous voice, Sarah injected. "Well, it's like this. I was so proud of all of you that *I* ordered roses too. An event such as this doesn't come along every day!" She flushed, smiling shyly.

Abe leaned over and kissed her cheek. She needed to be touched. Her delicate, parchment-like beauty readily showed her sensitivity among these pillars of Abe's life. He wondered how much she'd blush if she knew what made his eyes so hungry.

"They're the nicest roses of all, but I like the roses I see in your cheeks better," he whispered, his eyes grazing her face. "You've been enjoying the champagne, I see," he said, not being able to resist the opportunity to give her a rub, and sitting replete with the return of her smile. He wanted to loosen his tie, but thought better of it.

Sarah found him studying her peripherally, even apprehensively, as if trying to draw some conclusion from her very countenance.

Somewhere between dinner and afterglow, diners passed by their table, offering congratulations and extending best wishes. The whole dining room seemed to be celebrating the upcoming Rose Bowl game that would feature Michigan and the Unviersity of Southern California. It registered in everyone's eyes, on their tongues and in their hearts. Abe felt that perhaps a person could sit on top of the world with all this adulation, but *he'd* just played the game the best he could.

The rich aromas of the dining room danced in the air like explosive dream puffs—the leather chairs, the beeswax candles, the roses, the expensive colognes and rich wool fabrics, the sizzling of steaks as they passed by on broiler platters. Corks popped on champagne bottles, people conversed from table to table with live abandon of gracious dining room decorum.

Abe, making extraneous eye contact with Doc, noticed Doc's nodding approval. His hand slid inside his suit jacket, removed the cache from his inner pocket and slid it over to Sarah. His heart raced. His mouth went suddenly dry, but a light of whimsy danced in his eyes—another journey to the top of the mountain. This had to be the mother of all presumptions. The silence pounded as Abe swallowed at Sarah unwrapping the small box. *Open it, open it!*

Her eyes glistened with tears. "Oh!" She gasped as she raised them, searching Abe's face. "This is outstanding, impressive. It's beautiful. I'd never thought..." Taking her table napkin, she dabbed at her eyes. "I never dreamed of a diamond ring as part of your shtick. Topaz,...yes, but not this..." Her voice cracked.

She smiled only slightly, retiring into herself in a way that Abe found disconcerting. What filament danced in her head? Was that a *yes* smile or a *no* smile?

Had he tapped a hot wire? *Faint heart never won fair maiden.* He had to make his move. Fabian had preached that he should trust his instincts in reactive situations. Was he heading for a three peat of heartbreak and headache? No! No! No! She had to say yes. Had to. Their relationship idled to a near stall. Why had he done this? Was any part of his brain living? His mind collapsed into small enclaves of yeses and no's.

Made impetuous with the cocktails, good food and good company, he shot up and waved for quietude at the table, raising his enormous wide-receiver hands.

"I have an announcement to make," he said with confidence, his voice resonant.

Heads turned. People hushed.

Filled with whimsy, he gave a great sweep of his arm, bowed in front of Sarah and said. "My good Lady Sar-ah," he enunciated with great care. "Your M-Go-Blue Wolverine in shining helmet kindly requests the honor of your hand in marriage. Today, I have slain a dragon just for you!" His hand on his heart in knightly fashion, Abe kept his head bowed, his toes curled as if there were a pebble in his shoe.

Angst broadcast itself, audible. A riffle of whispers quickly spread throughout the dining room. Eager anticipation built and spread. Abe was in too deep to back out now. Herein lay a time when logic played no part in his life. There was one evident constant: Insanity. He was sure of it. An ancestor had handed him a hi-jinx.

He became a tower of babble. "I shall be your dedicated servant from this day forward," he went on with great flourish, raising his eyes to meet hers, "should you choose to accept my heartfelt offer." Getting down on one knee, he held her hand, slipped the ring onto her finger and kissed it, afraid to look up and read the message in her eyes. Abe juggled in a bubble of absolutes. She had to say *yes*, or had to say *no*. He couldn't handle *maybe* any longer.

She couldn't say no. He loved her so much; she couldn't say no. He'd promise not to hurt her any more. He knew he trod on shaky ground—fallen into a trough of restless second-guessing. A subterranean feeling of relief struck him suddenly as the diamond ring picked up magical beams from the candles. They flashed hypnotically, entrancing blue, green, gold, pink. *"Whenever you see glints off the water, stars twinkling in the sky..."* Fabian! Stillness engulfed the dining room, a moment when time stood still. Abe had no body, but instead felt that he levitated on sheer energy.

The posture-perfect headwaiter explained the developing situation to a riveted band that had ceased playing all of a sudden, sensing that they were not in the loop.

Sarah gave Abe an I'll get you for this" look, bent her head down and whispered, "'Tis but a short distance from your lips to my heart, brave knight. Your offer has all but made me swoon. How can I but accept?" She flushed again, and smiled down at him, her eyes soft and shiny-like.

He drowned in her beauty, then it occurred to him that she actually had *accepted* his proposal. Life was too short to comprehend why. A great joy spread through him. He wanted to shout, to laugh, to do his Indian Sun Dance—so he did.

Oblivious to time, place or who observed, he did then and there do his Sun Dance and finished by spiking a spook ball. Lifting Sarah from her chair, he raised her clear up into the air, holding her up as if she were a pocket person. He wanted to soak her up, drink her in, and inhale her. She was his!

"Yes! Yes!! Yes!" he shouted, his eyes taking on a telling intensity.

The spell was broken. Diners laughed and applauded. The band struck up "To Each His Own." Abe released her where she smoothed her dress, trying to collect herself from his delirious outburst. To add to the chaos, the Kreilers and the Whittakers were out of their chairs to congratulate Abe and hug Sarah.

Abe drew Sarah onto the dance floor, where, through deference to the newly-promised couple, they were rewarded with the dance floor all to themselves for a few minutes. A strong tenor worked the mike. Abe listened and savored the words.

A rose must remain with the sun and the rain,
Or it's lovely promise won't come true.

"Promise me, Sarah, you'll always be mine," Abe whispered.

To each his own, To each his own, And my own is you.

"Yes," soft as baby's breath. She pressed close to his body.

Your touch means too much to me.

"Your touch means everything to me, Sarah, more than myself. I want to give you children and a home," he breathed into her hair.

Abe's big hand held her tightly to him, first squeezing her shoulders, then sliding his hand to the middle of her back. He felt joy spreading throughout his body, the old familiar heat building in his groin. His hand slipped down to her waist, back up to feel the smoothness of her back.

Being with Sarah was...well, he didn't know...like slipping into a pair of old blue jeans. She provided grist for the mill, water for his thirst, the gentle balm of Gilead for his restless soul. She was his Sioux equalizer—rendering him peaceful and non-aggressive. When not in his life, he acted as rugged as rawhide. He loved her ingenuousness, yet she shouted intelligence. He loved her infectious laughter, yet she could give him a serious ear. Abe felt a synthesis of their chemistry.

"You are *my* rose tonight, Sarah. Winning that game meant a hundred times more to me today because you were there. You're beautiful tonight, and your earrings show such good taste!" He looked down at her as she pulled away, laughing. Drawing her back, he put his hand on her head, gently nudging it against his shoulder. "I want to be part of you," he whispered poignantly, dancing closely. "Come out to Pasadena for the Rose Bowl. We can have time to make plans for the future." Abe felt his brain bouncing like a ball from such a bizarre day. "I'll be out there for a week and I can make all the arrangements." Abe again possessed complete paralysis with the fear of her refusal.

"I'd like that, Abe. My next semester doesn't start until January 14. That will give me plenty of time for travel."

He was speechless, his brain sizzling. "Let's go somewhere where we can talk privately—perhaps in the lobby?" *Lobby, hell! Maybe she'd ask him to her room.*

She reached up and lovingly pinched his cheek, gazing at his finely chiseled features. She'd always wanted to do that. He was so handsome—he was *her man*. With almost uncanny communication, wordlessly, she mouthed, "my room."

CHAPTER THIRTY-FOUR

Abe explained to the Kreilers and the Whittakers, taking charge of the situation. "We have a few things to dicuss, so we're going to find a quieter place to talk." The two couples registered professional politeness, accommodating the absence of these beautiful young people, remembering, sympathetic. As they left the dining room, again spontaneous applause broke out.

"Why are they doing that, Abe? They already applauded your proposal."

"They probably think I'm going to get laid," he said with abandon.

"Abe!" She shook her head in resignation to his coarse locker room word list.

Handing him her key on the fifth floor, he opened the door for her and stood back as she entered into a sea of roses, raucous glades of roses and another magnum of Dom Perignon chilling in a silver ice bucket.

"Who... whhhaaat?" they said in trembling breathlessness—both in an advanced stage of permanent surprise. Sensuously, they inhaled the redolent air.

This had to be Doc's handiwork; he knew they'd come up here! Did he have to anticipate every move Abe made, and read him like a road map? He'd go to the bank on the fact that Doc was relaxing in the dining room, chuckling. *Just wait until I see him...*

Sarah flung her arms wide and tucked herself into his.

He held her close, rocking, while he mentally devoured her: the beauty of her, the slimness of her, the nearness of her, and the smell of her. *Now* he could put his hands on her hips and did, pressing her to him, chauvinistic, presumptuous and prepared. Sarah did not pull away. Lord, he wanted this woman so badly! She must have read the signs, the trail of bread crumbs spread so conspicuously.

Her voice thickened and trembled. "I'm so happy. I *do* love you Abe, very much." She untangled herself and moved away to the champagne bucket. "Come open this, please." She watched him move, his warrior vitality evident, his strong jaw and cheekbones showing his roots, validating his authority. The darkness of his beard showed just under his skin, stirring her strangely. Was she pitting time against another tragedy? No, quite appropriately, he'd shave.

By rote, Abe busied himself with the task at hand. He understood that they needed to discuss family—children, many of them, with Sarah as their mother. He'd always wanted them, more than one—not an *only child*. How would he explain that to her? She always put him off when he mentioned it. He would use honesty. He would offer her anything to conceive his children. This was the time for a showdown on this issue, not two years from now.

Handing her a long-stemmed flute, she took a sip of the rich wine. "Hmmm, every bit as good as I remembered." Her arm slipped around his waist under his suit jacket, and felt the corundum muscles surrounding his rib cage. Her fingers traced them, up and down. "You're a beautiful man, Abe, so strong, virile, tall and masterful. Have I told you lately that I love you?" She smiled up at him, her eyes shining.

Stirring with wonderful impulses, he must talk to her about gender specific duties.

"Sarah, come sit down. We need to share some ideas." He would approach it as a family thing. He reached out and tucked her hair behind her ear, as he leaned over her chair near the heavily-draped window, before seating himself across from her. *Just cut to the chase, Abe.* "I can't wait for you to have my babies. All the boys will look like me, and all the girls will be as beautiful as their mother." His voice sounded deep and mellow, his eyes dark searching her face. A hint of a smile tiptoed around his mouth.

Subtlety was not his forte. He watched for signs of consent as she distilled the message. Over the rim of the glass she looked at him long, then, setting it down on the end table, her shoulders softened, resting her hands on her lap. "Abe," her voice caught, "maybe some time in the future. I don't see it as an immediate possibility. I want to have a career in management, maybe my own art shop. You could help me choose the inventory with your expertise." Her enthusiasm built, showing without apology.

Deflated but not defeated, he carried on. "No!" he cried, his voice a runaway fire. "I want children right away. You don't have to work. The NFL draft is coming up in December, and it appears that I'll be taken within the first five rounds. We're secure for the rest of our lives, Sarah. I'll take care of you forever."

Her heart stuttered. She needed to explain, use the language to reach him, be a wordsmith. Waddling around, per se, carrying babies for ten years—it was nothing less than masochistic in her estimation. Besides, from all reports, labor reputed to be very painful, and she did not care to go through *that* ordeal even one time.

She walked over to him and sat on his lap. "We'll have plenty of time for that Abe. I'm sure we'll find a niche for babies after we've been married for a while. Once you have children, they are all over the house, constantly encountered. I have visions of them popping out of closets at random, scaring me, spending hours in the bathroom. In addition, they're an enormous liability in terms of constant care for eighteen years. I just can't see myself being confined to the kitchen and the nursery for the rest of my life!

"A kitchen, Abe. I hardly know my way around a kitchen; it's a never-never land for me." She slapped her hand to her forehead in mock desperation. She knew she'd better tread lightly here. She couldn't bear to gain everything precious and then lose it over a silly argument about children, children that were never going to happen. The situation was too similar to living on the edge, bearing children like Abe who needed tutoring and constant encouragement. No way. She kissed him on the ear and snuggled.

Abe rubbed his football calluses against Sarah's arm. He didn't know that she had any say in this. A good Sioux Indian should be able to accomplish conception in no time flat. Yes!

"Sarah" he whispered, pulling her closer to him. His peripheral vision caught the V-neckline of her dress opening. This woman drove him right out of his mind, so he could hardly think, at least with his head. He saw her breast under a low-cut, spaghetti strap chemise. The fertile fields of his mind ripened with acres of thoughts. He wanted to see his newborn son suckling there. The campus farm provided him with all the women he needed to alleviate his lust, but Sarah would breed his children. He felt the echoing footsteps of his ancestors, his ancestors with parallel values.

Her beauty and allure proved no match for Abe's determination. "I'm *not* going to marry you *until* you're pregnant, very pregnant, noticeably pregnant, markedly pregnant, so everyone can see that I've made it with you. I want you great with child when we get married!" He stood strong, cool and confident in his delivery as he nipped on the Dom Perignon, withdrawing none of his demands. He felt he could conquer the world right now and eat anyone who got in his way. He balked, as unshakable as Mohammed's mountain.

"Abe, gentlemen don't do that; it's so rural. You wouldn't! I'd be so embarrassed; my family would be shamed and worst of all, I'd have to deliver that child. I just can't anticipate myself doing that. It's totally too painful—far too painful. I simply refuse to do that," she responded, mildly nettled.

"You'll do it just fine, Sarah. You're a healthy young woman." He kissed her mouth, her eyes, her beautiful eyes—eyes that made him melt every time she fluttered her long, dark lashes. She flooded him with overwhelming desires such that he could turn down the invitation in any woman's eyes when Sarah was present.

"Yes, sure, I'm young and healthy that's true, but still..." her voice trailed off as he kissed her mouth. Sarah felt adamant, but she knew she'd said enough for now. He thought he'd won the battle. Let it go, Sarah. Was she, however, to be at war over this issue forever? Unrestricted thoughts swamped her. She would not bear his children, even if she had to hire two bodyguards named Nuke and Bubba.

Abe's mind rolled. Sarah didn't really know him anymore. What she didn't know could fill Michigan Stadium—the other women, the fights, the bruises and knocks on and off the field, toughness born of experience. No, she didn't know him. He would have children, and she'd be the mother. His mind darkened with determination.

Pulling her to him hard, he pressed her breasts against him, his other hand on her thigh. "Mmm. This is so good. I will never get enough of you, Sarah, never. We're together so seldom." Aggressively, he slipped his huge hand inside the deep V-neckline of her dress. So small, but it would nurture his son one day. With the promise of marriage, he felt entitlements as he zealously unzipped the back of her dress, pulling it down over her shoulders and arms, along with the filmy chemise, baring her upper body. She shrunk into him shyly.

"Ohhh," he groaned. Heat rushed through him with such immediacy that it crowded out all other thoughts, all other brainers. He just wanted to love his woman, become a part of her, make her a part of him the way he always knew they were—bonded, one in the same, always were, and always would be.

Sarah felt his aggressiveness. "Whoa! Maybe we're rushing things."

"No slower. No way," he breathed heavily, his sexual appetite insatiable, exhibiting not a thread of logic. It far surpassed football days and Allenal nights.

Slippery fear cascaded over her skin. What if he'd had too much champagne, and she couldn't handle him? What if he worked her over as he had last New Year's Eve? She challenged herself not to look under that rock again, and then not to worsen the situation by rejection. It was best she played into the general scheme of things, at least for right now.

His regal Sioux features were strained, his eyes glossed as he lifted her bodily off his lap, rested her feet on the floor, and with shaky hands proceeded to unbuckle her belt and pull her dress down over her hips. Her half-slip slid off easily; her panties posed no problem. He stepped back to worship his goddess.

"Oh, Sarah," he said, barely breathing. "How could I ever forget how gorgeous you are? So perfect, shaped as a piece of sculptured art, and you're promised to me," he whispered. Kneeling in front of her, he kissed her soft belly. This is where she'd incubate his son. "You smell so good. Are you still *my* woman only? Has there been no other man?" His lips feathered the words over her abdomen.

"None, there has been no other, ever, Abe, only you."

His eyes had drifted to her face, locking onto her deep-sea dark eyes. *His woman.* Staring at her naked body, he'd felt something go straight to his solar plexus, hot and searing. He tightened. With all his philandering, she'd had no other man!

"Oh my God, you're beautiful and still all mine." *Lucky bastard, after all the carousing you've done!* "You're a fine piece of porcelain, Sarah, translucent, white but better than quartz and feldspar; you're fired to perfection." Still fully clothed, he reached out and gathered her to him, as if in protection and sanctuary. The whole room seemed to hold its breath, the air charged.

The scent of roses still permeating the ambiance, he swiped the bedspread down in one deft movement and loosened the top sheet. There he laid her gently onto the bed, then pulled the sheet over her. "I'll join you in a minute."

"Can I help you?" Sarah asked teasingly from the bed as she watched his every stance while he removed his clothes, recording it on her memory tapes.

"A little more champagne and you'd have had to do it all by yourself. Now, imagine how frustrated you'd be trying that! If you're going to be married to me, Sarah, you'll have to learn that I'm a very basic person. What you see is what you get, and is it all that bad?" His voice elevated.

"No. I like that part of you—your honesty, your upfront candidness."

He approached the bed shocking in his nakedness, his body dense with hair from neckline to pelvis, then starting again on his thighs. She could feel her body tingling. A tiger lily blossomed inside her belly, unfolding with desire.

Abe pulled her to him, fitting her into place like his childhood teddy bear. She was about the size of an angel, with a humming bird soul. He smiled down at her; he kissed her forehead. "I thoroughly expected you to come to bed wearing your flannel pajamas, Sister Sinless." His voice resonated with a rhapsody of teasing and sleaziness.

She closed her eyes; she could handle the babble. It varied so deeply from her lifestyle that it again stirred the blossoming tiger lily. Even if he doesn't know enough to close the bathroom door and breathe the words of a gentleman, Sarah loved this man. She ran her fingers slowly and lightly down the length of his back and then up to his shoulders, feathering his skin. Rangy and muscular, her own Zeus, she allowed her fingers to slide through his hair, his beautiful hair, so like his mother's. She sank into the fur of his chest, reviving impressions of Doc, who had the same fleece visible from his shirts. Abe seemed so different tonight, somehow. In charge? In charge.

His body shuddered convulsively with the steady advance and retreat of her hands, her gentle fingers. Hiking her up, he kissed her mouth and pressed the length of her body to him. She felt soft, warm, and she fit him so well. He wanted to know this body better, this *terra incognita*. He'd do as he wished. She was his, and she *would* have his babies. She would suckle his son. Her non-acceptance drove him wild; his fixation became fanatic. It mattered to him, very much. Yes, it did, it did. There remained no indecision. There lived no doubt. It grew to be an incipient epiphany.

He allowed her to continue tracing his body with her fingers for long, long minutes, while he reflected the many times she had gotten up during the night when last he made love to her almost a year ago. Why had she not conceived at that time? He pondered. He'd been prolific and virile. He'd not worn a condom. She'd been exposed three times and once before that, years ago, why had she not become pregnant? It was tearing at him—searing his soul.

He could feel her breath, as warm as a baby's, on his neck and chest. His whole body bubbled hot and responding to her advances. She was getting good at this. Every nerve in his body responded in tune. He abandoned his concerns as he kissed her breasts, fondling them. He was moved by the way his hand covered both of them easily. He imagined his son pulling at them. He would make sure of that.

"I love you more than words, Sarah. They're inadequate to tell you how I feel. I'm only replete when I'm with you." He kissed her mouth deeply, lingering. She responded, sending great waves of excitement through his abdomen. He salivated. He couldn't biologically control this when in the act of breeding a woman. It seemed inherent to his physiology. What the hell, it came in handy too. He smiled to himself at the thought. He kissed her velvet-soft belly, *his belly,* his proving ground for his heirs.

Tearing the sheet back, he moved to the foot of the bed. Through a subliminal sharing of spirits, he moved in harmony with this woman. The long terrain of her legs curved smoothly under his hand. He felt vital, energized and boorish, and he needed to get between the goal posts. His objectives were certain, his path hazy, operating on senses long ago established by his nameless ancestors.

"Loosen up," he whispered heavily. She was harder to access than a wild throw from Hulk.

Her mind was muddled with the demands of her body versus the dictates of her soul. Should she be allowing him to do this, if, indeed, she did not want children? It did not agree with the precepts of her church. Torn between two demands, she permitted herself the latitude of enjoying the dream-like maze of the dilemma.

Hold on, Abe! Remaining cool had become an art form to him, giving him lasting power. He retained the caresses she liked, the hunger, the voracious exploring.

"Ohhh." She heaved and swallowed, her body lurching.

Slowly, he moved over her body, the length of him drowning her as if in an eclipse. His chest came to life, with electrical impulses warming his whole body.

She no longer argued with her brain, but enjoyed his brawn.

He was gone—gone in his biological bubble of self-indulgence. He disappeared in an incredible emotional whirlpool, thrusting himself down into delirium with pleasure.

They lay quietly, recovering from their frenetic fulfillment, breathing heavily, her skin as rosy as the flowers, her cheeks as red as the blooms—his love as rich as the fragrance.

He hoped for a love child.

&

A plucky rain plundered the windowpanes, the sky a solid mass of gray on Christmas Day. With Abe's flight to Los Angeles leaving tomorrow morning from Detroit Metro at seven o'clock, he prudently packed his bags. Early flight time required that he set his alarm for four o'clock in order to make the team buses for the airport. He glanced at his watch. Abe knew Kreiler would personally choke anyone who arrived late.

Since Thanksgiving, his life had been a parade of playing catch-up with his class work, getting his first canvas of the school year completed for his private tutorial, interviewing with NFL representatives who never stopped sleuthing him.

He had chosen to paint a picture of himself in the end zone doing his Sioux Sun Dance. A plastic football helmet sat perched on his head in his hand a Sioux War Bonnet. He wore a football uniform, but an Indian ancestral ghost and the ghost's ghost danced in an infinity of mirrors in the end zone, wearing only loin cloths. He longed for it to be the *magnum opus* of his college career.

How great Walter and Anne had been during these long four years. Feeling parental and supportive, they were flying out to Pasadena for the Rose Bowl. Abe knew he could never have made it this far without their limitless generosities. He had spent early and late summers in Ann Arbor, the grass thick, the birds in abundance to warm his heart, the blazing sun to warm his body, Anne's wild-flower gardens, and polar air to freeze his ass, but never did it get as cold as it was in Nahma when he shivered as a kid.

Doc, Suki and Sarah would fly out of Detroit Metro on Tuesday, the thirtieth, land in L.A., and take a Huntington Hotel airport limousine to Pasadena. Good thing he knew where they were staying, because they sure as hell didn't know where he'd be bivouacked. Kreiler had kept a tight lid on it.

Karen Kreiler did a great job at routing reservations at the Huntington. She and Kyle were staying there too. Seemed they couldn't even get *close* to a reservation in Pasadena without the help of Karen's sister, who lived in San Marino and owned the Casablanca Ceiling Fan Company.

He packed knock-around clothes because he knew they all wanted to go to Anaheim to tour Disneyland the day after the game. Abe felt as close as skin to Doc, talking to him often, and he had advised also taking a suit for better dining. He found himself grumbling that he'd have to drag half the house with him.

Warming him, however, were the memories of Sarah's visit. It had been a bit embarrassing, coming down from Sarah's room after the celebratory dinner. He thought he could make it through the lobby without being detected; however, Doc and Kyle were just returning from the restroom and spotted him. Flashpoint!

"Hey, Abe!" He heard Doc's voice. "Where's Sarah?"

"Well, she said she was tired, so she decided to go to bed. She said to say goodnight to all of you. I'm pretty beat myself—thought I'd head for home," Abe responded, clicking his car keys. He found himself searching for words as he read *a likely story* look on Doc's face, the raised eyebrow, the knowing smile.

"What the hell..." Kyle said. "My star receiver can't go home and leave us to party all by ourselves. At least come sit and tell us what you and Sarah hashed out tonight. I don't want anything on your mind before the Rose Bowl Game."

Abe brooded a bit, startled at the idea, but knew that tone of voice meant, 'Just *do* it.' He sat with the Kreilers and the Whittakers for another hour. Never could keep up with those two hoo-hah's, to paraphrase Kyle.

"Sarah said to say thanks, and I do too, for all the roses in the room *and* the champagne. It was a total surprise!" Abe confided in the guys as he stood up.

"So, that's where you were. Never dreamed of looking for you up there," Doc said, smiling and patting Abe on the shoulder. "Hope everything went well for you, my son," he said, laughing—a knowing light glowing in his eyes.

He'd get him for this, but he was too tired to care now. He felt leathered and weathered out. He must look like a football with two eyes.

"Is Sarah going to the Rose Bowl?" Kreiler inquired with forthright candor.

"Yes. She said she'd do that. Makes me happy." Abe smiled warmly.

"Well, I'm not letting you out of my sight the night before the game, so forget about seeing her on New Year's Eve. I want you to stay focused, and that's pretty hard to do with a beautiful woman such as Sarah close by."

"Thanks, Coach. Isn't she a gem?" Abe's eyes sparkled with love and fulfillment, Kreiler's comment making him feel enormously important.

Doc's psychic comprehension was incredibly quick. "You met with success!" Abe wished that these guys could be a little more circumspect with their ribaldry, but he accepted them as they were. He loved them both. Having them aware of his star power with Sarah made the blood course through his veins like the Bay de Nocquet Lumber Company runaway Percherons. He'd need to pack twenty lunches and hike through a desert to find better people than this.

"That's good," Kyle interjected. "I've seen firsthand what your quick temper can trigger when you get up-tight."

Karen cringed, stunned. "Kyle!" She reprimanded him, her eyes big and round, shaking her head as if to clear it. "You can't interfere in someone's personal life." She laid a restraining hand on his sleeve.

Kyle blinked, tweaking Karen under the chin. "Try me." Kyle knew few nuances when it came to victories and losses. Neither could be re-captured.

Although Abe found the conversation disconcerting, it flowed among them like a chattering stream, wending its way to the river. He smiled and committed to nothing. However, he struggled for humility. His maneuvering Sarah into a marriage commitment bonded the confluence of his life's dreams and hopes. It gained him the ultimate in unshakable confidence, the kind you find in intelligent, undefeated people, people with purpose and the poise to effectuate it. He knew he could be victorious, therefore he was.

With the regular season having ended, it didn't take long for the individual honors to start pouring in to South Bend and Ann Arbor. Abe reflected that he had won the major awards for football. He was named outstanding senior player of the year. LaJeunesse of Notre Dame and Miereau of Michigan blew away the field in balloting for the Heisman Trophy. LaJeunesse won it with seven hundred and forty-two first-place votes to Miereau's five hundred and fifty-five. Michigan and Notre Dame were well represented on the various All-American Teams as well, while Kreiler beat out Notre Dame's Letty for the National Coach of the Year Award.

All these honors only fanned the flames of the Notre Dame-University of Michigan debate. It'll never get old; it'll never die; it'll never go away! It embraced the spirited story around the country. Who's better, the Wolverines or the Fighting Irish? Seemingly, everyone had an opinion. Michigan had one last chance to win over the masses, as the Wolverines were heading west to play Southern Cal in the Rose Bowl on New Year's Day. The Southern Cal Trojans had proven no match for Letty's Irish, so this game would be viewed as the yardstick for comparison.

In the meantime, NFL Scouts had been reporting on Miereau for the last two seasons. The Green Bay Packers were steamed about getting him. It'd be the salt in their stew, having him on their offense—good for team chemistry. Before the annual league draft meeting in early December, the Packers had their own staff meeting, and each of them had read reports on hundreds of players and graded each man.

Although their principal need for the future called for a receiver, they were not going to put one at the topmost of their list as their number one or number two choices. The first and second choices were going to be the best cast list they could draft in spite of position, and they calculated that each year there ordinarily were only about thirty top-notch college players available. The Packers finished in fourth place in the league, but that still gave them three picks within that first thirty options. They reckoned if their need did happen to be a receiver, and it was, and there surfaced one who listed in the top thirty, and they were fortunate enough to gain him, they then would have achieved two things: They had drafted a top-notch football player, and they had filled a need.

In a hotel ballroom in Chicago they started sign-up and the names went up on the display board adjacent to the names of the teams. Then they started eliminating them from their list. If, after two rounds, the guy held fast, he may last the third round, so they would get on the phone and call his coach. Maybe he had a bad ankle they knew nothing about, or maybe he had already signed with the other league or in Canada. There was a twenty-minute time limit for decisions, so they had to secure information in a hurry.

They made some gambles. They'd devoted over fifty thousand dollars and a lot of sweat in the scouting for those four or five they dreamed would end up on their schedule this year. But Dick Boris, the Michigan Scout, had shadowed Abe for the last twenty-eight days and never lost sight of him until he had his autograph on a promissory, with a contract execution at post-graduation. Although Abe persevered as an unknown factor in the pro football leagues, Curly Lambeau approved the reports he'd had from Boris. In fact, he had attended the Michigan-Ohio game two weeks ago. The young man came across as gratifyingly good.

Back home in Green Bay, Lambeau looked around the locker room at the cubicles, each with a name card, one new one for Miereau. The gold pants were hanging inside on the right, the green jerseys and blue warm-up sweaters on hangers on the left, the floor of each compartment covered with six or eight pair of football shoes at sixteen dollars a pair. The footballs needed inflating with thirteen pounds of pressure, but that could wait until next pre-season practices. The hats were above the stalls. *Miereau*, he'd better be goddamn good! He had sacrificed an excellent back and promised him a contract for fifteen thousand a year, plus putting his neck on the chopping block.

One thing Lambeau knew he wouldn't have to do was to teach that kid to run to daylight. It was always advantageous to run to a specific hole, but it couldn't be cut in concrete; players needed to run to the opening. Abe did that. He was a vertical runner, and Lambeau wouldn't change that for a minute, because it was his style, and he got back up as soon as he got hit. He could tell that as a receiver, Miereau's greatest ability was to relax. He had great deception and great moves. He measured six feet two inches, one-hundred ninety-five pounds of perfection. Lambeau carried on, determined to go to the Rose Bowl to watch his new horse.

CHAPTER THIRTY-FIVE

He'd talked to Sarah before leaving. "How are *you*, my little lady?" The air around Abe was filled with smoking anticipation.

"Just fine, Abe. It's so good to hear from you. I'm looking forward to our trip to Los Angeles and the game." Her voice sounded eager.

"So you're feeling very well? No morning sickness?" He held his breath.

"No, not at all...?" Her voice trailed off. "I'm not pregnant, if that's what you're asking. All is well, now that I know we'll be married in the spring. What do you think of June, maybe around the twentieth or so?"

"Sounds good to me, but remember, you need to be pregnant for us to get married." His expression came across as annoyed and smug.

"Abe! I will *not* be pregnant. Not then or maybe ever." Her tone was emphatic, with no wriggle room for wrangling.

He felt the silence of the dead, his self-confidence badly bruised by her balking. "Yes, you will. You *will* have my children." He *would* dictate the terms of his marriage, as any good Sioux Warrior would do when accessing personal property.

Sarah fought with indignation—him flaunting his superiority, muscle and all. "Oh, nuts, let's not argue about such things now. That's a *tomorrow* subject." She laughed, bringing magic to his ears and finality to the conversation.

Abe threw bunches of stockings into the suitcase, a pair for every day and a few more *for the road*. Sarah's lack of fertility attacked him like a psychological paralysis, burdensome and mischievous.

He'd call Doc. Maybe *he* could shed some light on this dilemma and relieve an ache so deep it placed a cramp in his bowels.

"Merry Christmas, Doc." Abe rallied somewhat on his own enthusiasm.

"Well, same to you, my boy. How are your travel plans? Leaving soon?"

"Uh-huh. We leave tomorrow to allow ourselves scrimmage time. Thank you very much for the generous Christmas check; two hundred dollars is a whole lot of money. I can't tell you how much I appreciate it."

"Your're welcome." A strange choking invaded his throat every time thoughts traipsed before him of the many years Abe needed him and he wasn't there for his needs, physical and spiritual.

"There *is* something that I need to ask you. It's been puzzling me that Sarah and I have been intimate on several occasions, but she doesn't get pregnant. Do you think that there's something wrong with me?"

Doc hooted with the mirth of a nation. "Abe, I'm laughing at the fact that you'd think anything could be wrong with you. You're the quintessential of virility."

"Well, I just can't figure this out. I've called her, and she said that she's feeling just fine. Something is wrong here."

"It could very well be that I'm the one to blame for that. She asked me how to avoid the risk of pregnancy, and I suggested that she abstain. I thought you'd like that." Doc cracked up at Abe's discomfort. "Abe, you make me feel brand new."

"Sonofa...you didn't!" Abe was confounded by Doc's situational delight.

"Sure I did!" Doc spoke, amused. "Actually, I advised her to cleanse as soon as possible after every exposure to you. You won't be married until next summer. Wouldn't you want to wait until after that?" Spirited dismay rounded Doc's question. He toyed with a pen on his desk, spinning it around and around distractedly.

Abe felt himself paling. "No, I don't want to wait! I feel very strongly about it. I'll take care of her. My contract with the Packers starts July first, so we aren't really talking any financial crunch time here."

"I wasn't aware of your desire for instant children, Abe. I'm sorry if you think I've interfered with your family planning. It was inadvertent, rest reassured." He dropped the pen, stopped, and sighed at the ceiling.

"Perish the thought, Doc. I'm not blaming you for anything. I'm glad, however, to find out what's been the wrench in the works. I look forward to seeing you next Tuesday at the hotel—not Wednesday, however. Kreiler won't allow any of the team out of his sight before the big game on Thursday."

"Take care, Abe, and stay warm. Suki sends her love; she's sitting right here beside me. We can't wait to love your children."

When Abe hung up, he knew he would start exercising his conjugal marital rights *now*, even though they wouldn't be married for five months yet.

He smacked the phone on the wall and started putting a plan in place.

Landing in Los Angeles, the captain announced the ground temperature at eighty-eight degrees, unseasonably warm. For the first time, he witnessed the shimmering chiffon of heat inversions coming off the tarmac like restless souls. Abe put the city of Pasadena at the head of his list for places he liked to be. No football stadium that he'd ever seen had such a breathtaking backdrop as that which was provided by the San Gabriel Mountains, bathed in the late afternoon sun.

In the few days prior to the 1948 Rose Bowl game, the team suddenly witnessed their All-American Renoir Warrior come up lame, pain flaring suddenly, hot as coals. He limped toward the sidelines.

Jim Funt raced to meet him halfway. "What's wrong, Abe?"

"It felt as if someone slashed my thigh with a knife," Abe said, gritting his teeth.

Jim quickly found the break in the muscle and went to work. "It's not like a football injury at all, but more like a track sprinter would experience," said Jim.

Abe attempted to lie down when they got to the clubhouse.

"No. No. No. You can't lie down. You have to sit with your leg over the table."

For the next four and a half hours, Jim prodded Abe slowly to extend his leg, although it was extremely painful. He was inundated with a startling orbit of contradictory emotions. He'd play anyway. He'd not be able to play at all. *He'd never* get better. The fog of this hard-hitting handicap would not clear away.

Jim continued treatment over the next two days, while the press had a field day guessing whether Michigan's key to Kreiler's single-wing offense would face USC.

Tuesday evening, Abe and Kreiler took the Maryland Hotel's limousine service to the Huntington to visit with Doc, et al. Abe was relieved to leave the team location of their domicile for the duration. He felt more as if he were being cloistered *in* than for the real purpose of keeping other people *out*.

"You're looking mighty Californian tonight, Abe. Cant' find a single fault line on you," Kreiler teased on the way over. "Nice press on those trousers. Behold the jacket! Yes, sir, I've always wanted a corduroy jacket with leather patches on the elbows," Kreiler said with a lean laugh as he stretched his legs out in the backseat.

"Thanks, Coach. Just an ornamental something I threw together." Abe waved his enormous hand in a noxious show of effeminate grace. "I need it to gather women."

Kreiler looked at him, speaking under his breath. "And if I believe that…"

It was only a ten-minute drive to the Huntington Hotel at 1401 South

Oak Knoll Avenue, and they were already pulling into a vast circular drive where tall royal palms stood sentry. Abe floated in a surreal world. The hotel stood as an imposing piece of architecture that couldn't be encompassed with a glance, but instead had to be swept for one hundred and eighty degrees, seven stories of pink and tan perfection, boasting three hundred and eighty-three rooms and a village of cottages that edged the periphery of the twenty-three acres. The grounds, gardens, pools and promenades were breathtaking in aesthetic beauty, as well as in their dimensions.

They found the Whittakers, Karen Kreiler, and Sarah lounging near the pool.

"Ain't this ever livin'," Kyle said, bending down and kissing Karen on the cheek. "It looks to me as if you aren't having any problem adjusting to sunny California in the dead of winter. I suppose I should brush the snow from this chair before I sit down." He swished, creating a whiskbroom of his hand.

"Yeah, and we had to follow the snowplow all the way from our hotel in order to get here," Abe added, his spirits high. He placed his arm around Sarah's shoulders, chucking her chin. "Bring an extra bathing suit with you, Doc? I didn't pack one. It was the farthest thing from my mind," he said, smiling broadly.

Rising, Doc moved to leave. "You bet. Let's go up and you can change."

"'Tis a beautiful place, Doc. It's beyond belief! Everything is different—the stucco, the vegetation, the clothing, and even the people. It's like being in another country—a Utopia with an eternal summer where the livin' is easy." A smile crept slowly about the rugged mouth of the All-American wide receiver. "If I lived here I'd get very practiced in the reduction of my surplus wealth." *Yeah, sure, Abe, lots of surplus wealth you have! Well, maybe someday.*

As they passed through the lower lobby, an exhibit caught Abe's eye. Within a large, glassed-in pier he observed a brilliant geode, its cavity lined with gold ore. The inscription read of removal from Sutter's Mill in Calaveras County in 1848.

"Whah, now that is a chunk of gold! And I thought the nuggets I received from Farley and Norrhea and your Krugerrands were a treasure." He nodded to Doc.

Abe couldn't help but notice in the foyer the well-tended Zen garden, restful with earth, rock, gravel and chunk deposits of granite, gneiss and quartz. Curiously winding jade trees bowed in honor to passersby. Abe felt like a piece of standard issue jack from the Bay de Nocquet Lumber Company camps deep in the forests of the nation's mid-section. "This place must be made of gold! I see dollar bills everywhere I turn!"

Doc shook his head. "Not to worry." He reached and patted Abe on the shoulder. "I see you harvested your whiskers before you came," Doc said approvingly.

"Hell, yes! I don't want to go through that again!" Abe turned to him in a total meeting of their minds. He found himself standing stark still for a moment upon entering Doc's suite of rooms on the fourth floor. "What the hell! This is fantastic. Take a look at all the windows and the floor-to-ceiling French doors, and the floor-to-ceiling sheers and drapes." He paused, noticing the draperies hanging longer than necessary creating a puddle of lush fabric on the floor, giving a subtle indication of wealth.

"And this patio...even turns the corner. Talk about the lap of luxury. The view looks like a movie backdrop. There's more room in here than my whole house in Nahma—two bedrooms too!" Abe's voice became softer, as if he was in awe of such magnificence and luxury. *Clumsy bastard, how'd he ever rate coming here?*

"Tidy little place to hang my hat, ay?" For emphasis, Doc had mockingly added the Upper Midwest Canadian influence to his statement.

Together, they returned to the pool. Abe dove into the water with a tremendous splash, drops flying clear up to the basking sideline guests.

"For chrise sake, Miereau," Kreiler said, wiping his face with a towel. "You just hiked the water level in the pool by six inches."

"Whale in the water!" Karen adlibbed, the laughter as contagious as measles.

In the pool, Sarah and Abe cavorted like two porpoises, he so big and masculine, she the china doll, fragile and slim, her long legs lapping the pool. In the curve of the kidney-shaped pool, sparkling with late sunset glints on the water through the skylight, Abe could be seen making aggressive passes at Sarah, but she successfully eluded him. Light reflections in the water danced with macabre delight. Her smile would have brought out the oleander blossoms in December, and indeed, it very well might have, because many were blooming, blood red, delicate pink, fuchsia and white, in generous profusion. The heated pool water felt fantastic on Abe's pulled muscle, but Abe delighted mostly in watching Sarah's mouth, how the corners curled up before she actually showed her pleasure in a word, in an occasion, as if she had to go through a series of gears to get to full power.

The San Gabriel Mountains were off to their north, as well as covering the scope of view to the east and west through the glass full-domed windows. A spectacular orange-red ball of fire, the sun wound down.

For some time Abe and Sarah lay on chaise lounges, the friendly humidity of the pool and late sun licking their bodies. Abe's pulled muscle said a heated *thank you*.

"Sit in the spa for a while, Abe, and let the jets run on your leg. It'll keep it loose." Kyle, concerned with Abe's injury, would be hard-pressed to fill the gap in his Mad Magicians without Abe on the field of play on Thursday.

The six people lazed in comfort, watching the *kids*. At times, Sarah completely disappeared as Abe floated on top of her, assertive and aggressive. For him, it was like hunting at the zoo. For her, it gravitated more as whistling past the graveyard. Somehow, she always managed to surface on the other side of him, blowing bubbles, wiping her eyes. The glissando of her laugh grew contagious. The deep mahogany of her hair and eyelashes spoke of youth and health; her skin shined with an estrogen glow.

"That girl is unstoppable," Kyle remarked.

"Tough nut to crack," Karen said, laughing.

"Indomitable," Walter added, enjoying the word game.

"Impregnable," Doc said under his breath.

"What did you say, dear?" Suki inquired.

"Nothing, really, I was simply talking to myself."

They ordered dinner served at poolside. "Good grief," Walter said with dismay. "There's enough food here to last through the Yalta Peace Conference, and then some."

"I don't think so, Walter," Anne said laughing. "Roosevelt, Churchill and Stalin didn't have it this good!"

The counters continued until long after sundown.

Because Abe had his bags delivered to Sarah's room when he and Kyle had arrived, none the worse was thought of them for catching a few moments together, especially in view of their historic, long separations.

Changing into a shirt and trousers for a soda with the rest of the crew before curfew, Abe reflected on his annoyance with Sarah's refusal to have his children. Damn, he was furious with her roundabout route, always coming back to the same spot. It was a vicious circle ending in an impasse.

"Sarah, have you given any more thought to having children?" His timeless Sioux features set upon her face as he pulled on his jacket.

"We'll wait on that, Abe. I simply don't want to spend all my young years tending to children and their constant needs."

His eyes chilled at her response, her contented smirk. Her dark eyes barely concealed irritation at the very suggestion. Burning disappointment seared his soul and reached the same depth where he'd locked away all the hurt he'd suffered after Fabian's death, and Eddie's death.

"You can't mean that, Sarah," he said, his voice strained, his hands working in frustration. Did she enjoy hurting him? Leaving his life in disarray?

A fixed gulf of old, ugly specters hovered between them and built in enormity as they stared at each other in a strange setting of drawing a line in the sand. Minutes of absolute silence ticked away in the wake of her agonizing announcement. Perhaps this was Fabian's warning—a strained muscle and a pained relationship.

A smile stayed on her lips as if she'd enameled it there. "I've never lied to you about that, Abe. I thought we could live with that. We love each other, and that should be enough." *Why does he keep hammering away at this old chestnut? He's California dreaming if he thinks I'm going to spend the rest of my life steppin' and fetchin' with kids hanging all over me. Not this girl.*

Adamant and restless, Abe crossed the room to stand at the French doors, gazing at a crescent moon as it sliced its way over the San Gabriel Mountains, his right hand in his trousers pocket, jostling some coins. "I thought that we had a love deeper than that, something less superficial. I imagined that our desires were sealed together for an endless time, leaving children to carry on after we're gone." Turning back to her, his eyes grew hard, sending signals of impending truculence. "Up until this moment," he went on, holding his emotions in check, "I thought that fate had emptied her cornucopia at my doorstep. Instead, I have a crushing problem of immense proportions." Energized, he walked determinedly to the luggage holder and retrieved his bag. There was no accounting for warped values, but he didn't have to live with them for the rest of his life.

"Abe! What are you doing?" Her stomach became a bottomless pit, taking a quick breath in between breaths.

"I will not marry you, Sarah. I want more fulfillment in life than you can offer. You've burned me as dry as the Mojave Desert. My joy of harmony in the home has just moved from the penthouse to the outhouse." He closed his bag with a click of finality that somehow reminded her of a phone being hung up in her ear.

"It seems that we have irreparable differences in what we expected from married life," she said, gaily clad in a plum wool dress for their trip downstairs. "You ask too much of me. The whole scenario is inconceivable. I've spent four years gaining a degree in management to stay home and rear your children? It's too demanding. I can't possibly consider it." She settled in a provocative stance, hands on her hips, but felt her spirit waning, as if she were bodily melting away like the Wicked Witch of the North, no longer a viable entity in this life.

"I'll stay with Doc and Suki tonight. I won't expect to see you again, ever. I've been dangling for too long." Highly stung, he straightened his jacket with an angry jerk, staying in command and on course. "Your rationale is damned convoluted for a woman who is supposedly in love. When and *if* you ever grow up and decide to be a woman, I'd be glad to re-negotiate this contract. I want a child, a boy child, and until you're ready to give me one, we have nothing further to discuss. Maybe that's forever; it's up to you. Think it over," he suggested in a frosty voice, striving to cover his hurt—his simmering Sioux temper. Emotional fireworks surged within him like short-circuited synapses.

"But Abe, how can you..." She reached out in a gesture of supplication.

Standing with his overnight case, he flung an arm in despair, his dark eyes making a final search of her face, trying to find a flicker of hope that may be written there. He found nothing but the firm set of determination around her mouth, in her chin. Recognizing the futility and sadness contained in his voice, he couldn't control it any more than he could control this woman standing in front of him, whom he thought he knew but didn't know at all.

"Don't take too long to reconsider, Sarah. There are a whole lot of other women out there who would be happy to have me as the father of their children. It's not asking too much, in my point of view. You're being extremely selfish in this matter. It's no way to start a marriage." Opening the door, he left without glancing back, the door closing behind him with a soft click. Then he was gone. She knew.

Her hands came up to cover her face. "Carpe diem," she sighed under her breath. "And for what?" Changing her clothes, she put on pajamas and went to bed, similar to any other night at school. Why had she held herself the epitome of virtue all these years? Just for him? Just to be rejected? He was an imperious clod and not the Abe she used to know. Why did she ever come out here—twenty-five hundred miles from home? A shudder of dread ran through her. She lay on the bed, abandoned like a rag doll. He'd never be able to make amends for these drastic measures.

Such anticipation she'd had—spending nearly a week with Abe, seeing the Rose Bowl Parade and game, watching him play football and feeling pride in his successes, only to have it end like this. And she'd only just arrived! She'd call the airline tomorrow and switch her ticket for a fast flight back to Michigan. Who needed a Rose Bowl game? Pain engulfed her such as she'd not known since Max died. She reeled from the depth of the wound he'd inflicted. And she'd thought he loved her, but all his desires were for an incubator!

Having a baby boiled down to nothing but an experiment in terror. Besides, she knew the child would have *his* learning disabilities, and she'd have to struggle for years, as she had with him. No way. He'd never understand that, never. Nor could he convince her otherwise. After all the years of dedication to each other, their relationship had been severed with but a few words. He punished her because he couldn't call all the shots. He'd been intolerable since he'd become a football star.

Incredible! Well, she wouldn't allow herself any meaningless hopes of his hasty return. How fragile a package love wrapped. Does one measure it in days of happiness before it cracks and disintegrates? Does the shine of it attrition out, or do people pass in and out of it like a time warp? Maybe the gods on Mt. Olympus allow and disallow it at will, with mere humans being pawns in the game of love. Whatever it was, the pain of it was almost more than she could bear. She wept with the futility and finality of it all. Should she kneel down and pray for intervention from above, or stand up and shout her wrath? The situation was much too late for either of them. Sleep only came in the half-world of consciousness, where she re-fought all the struggles of their early years to have it end like this. How would she explain this to Ma, to Doc, to Suki?

༄༅

Strange behavior, Doc thought, *Abe joining them alone in the lounge last night.* From his suite, he stood gazing out over the gardens. The pools and the cottages, far out on the acreage, looked like thatched-roof Hawaiian Hukilaus, all tucked in with topiary hedges and gates. Now Abe and Kreiler had left for their prep time at the stadium. He'd not see them again until Thursday night. Sure, he'd said Sarah was tired and made her excuses, but Doc knew him too well not to notice how weighted down he appeared.

Then Abe had moved into Doc's suite and used the other bedroom when Sarah lived and breathed in the adjacent suite—alone! Something threw his main switch. She didn't show up at breakfast, either. Then there came that earth-shaking phone call that he had intercepted from the airline, advising that there were no cancellations for her early-return flight request. Had he not put both rooms in his name, he'd never have known.

"Suki," he called into the bedroom. "I'm going to see if Sarah is all right while you go to the pool with Anne and Karen. I'll join you later." He sounded preoccupied.

"That's a good idea, dear. I've never known Sarah to require as much privacy as she's been demanding since last night. Maybe she isn't feeling well." Suki came breezing out of the bedroom, her black bathing suit covered by a splashy cruise skirt fastened around her waist, and Indian-jeweled sandals decorating her feet.

Doc smiled. "You have a good time. The sun is nice today; you ought to use the outdoor pool until the sun goes down." He stroked her cheek.

"I think we will, yes. Anne mentioned that, too." She gathered her canvas tote and whirled out the door, smiling over her shoulder.

Opening the lanai door, the unseasonably warm air funneled in, furling the sheers that hung to the side of it. Doc stood for a moment, breathing in the fragrance of the Cape jasmine, blooming abundantly in shrubs and trees, with their glossy green foliage and large, fragrant, white flowers. Looking down the lanai, he observed Sarah's French doors open and her sheers softly billowing inward through the doors, inviting and warm. Tapping lightly on the open door, he walked into the suite, finding Sarah seated at the desk using the phone, her back to him.

He tapped again, gaining her attention as she swung around, her eyes wide. "Yes," she said. "Yes, that's correct. I would appreciate it. Thank you."

Hanging up, she turned in her chair to give full attention to her caller. "Doc! It's so nice to see you. Come in. Come in."

As she walked into the sun near the window, golden light streamed over her shoulder, making her look like a golden goddess.

"I turned the couch around so I could get a better view of the mountains. They're so beautiful and timeless." She fussed, plopping pillows over to the side, making room for them both. "Thank you very much for the lovely suite. It gives one a pampered sense of grandeur—the beautiful appointments, the view and all." She wound down, then started up again with renewed vigor. "The bathroom and bedroom are large, bright and airy, all done in soft gold and vanilla. Come see," she said, jumping up to lead him into the bedroom that ran laterally off the sitting room.

"Take a look at that Karastan rug under the bed. I never saw one quite so large. Look how all the tassels are combed out carefully, as though each were straightened by hand. And the colors, all subtle mint, mauve, gold, beige and white."

Doc caught her by the shoulders, spinning her around. "What's wrong, Sarah? It's me you're talking to. You're vibrating like an over-wound top."

Tremors bolted through her body like a jumble of fire ants. She stared up at him in silence, her dark eyes glistening, fearful.

"I know you're trying to get an early flight back to Michigan," he said softly. "The airline called. Mind explaining? Can I help?" One dark brow jutted upward; a faint smile grew on his face and warmth radiated from his dark eyes.

"Oh, Doc, Abe left me. He said he never wants to see me again," her words strung out, her chin quivering. Her lovely eyes became a well of water.

Doc gathered her to him, resting her head against his chest. "Look, Sarah, nothing is as bad as all that. Let's talk about it." He led her back to the couch. "I'll order up some light wine; it'll make you feel better. You need to relax before you spin right out."

Sarah heard from what seemed a long distance. "Yes, California vineyard chardonnay, chilled please. Yes, it's Whittaker in 417. Thank you."

Returning to the couch, he sat lightly on the edge of the cushions taking her hands in his. "Now, young lady, let's you and I have a little heart to heart, right now."

She looked at him like a frightened rabbit. He wanted desperately to touch her. She had beguiled him deeply years ago at Abe's seventeenth birthday party, burrowing inside him like a permanent houseguest. He was drawn to her headlong, as if it were manifest destiny. He evaluated her, his smile turning sad. Doc didn't know how long it had been since he'd seen such unadulterated grief. Silently and with liquid movements, he reached out and ran his thumbs under her eyes, wiping her tears.

With pain and sincerity, Sarah gazed up at him. "He started on the children conundrum again. He wants to have one hundred eighty of them. I know nothing of children. Pregnant! I don't want to go through labor and bring his child into the world, especially a child like Abe." She tried to hide her fear of the future with a trembling smile. "You know how he lollygagged as a kid. I'd have to spend the rest of my life pulling the cart of education for the children, and I don't want that. I love Abe, that's why I worked so hard with him, but I don't intend to do it all over again. He's asking too much from me." She knew that she was blubbering.

With a light tap at the door, room service delivered the wine. Doc jumped to his feet, signed for the bucket of chardonnay on ice, nicely toweled and set into a tripod. "Thank you. No, that'll be all." Sarah heard the door close softly behind the young man.

Carrying two flutes, Doc approached the couch. Adroitly, he poured the wine, talking, his voice smooth with verbal persuasion of brighter days, consoling her.

She admired how suavely he did everything and how classic he looked in his shorts and shirt, the knit collar falling conservatively, but loosely enough to reveal the myriad of chest hair that wrestled its way out to daylight. Somehow, it moved her, making a statement of masculinity and stability. Blood pounded in her ears like the thundering surf at the Nahma beach.

"Sarah, this is not an impossible problem. Abe must have been terribly upset to walk out on you. I know he loves you very much. But the heart is wayward and unpredictable; one never really knows the workings of another's yearnings. It's a kind of protection we give ourselves—a defense mechanism. Yes, Abe did have a difficult childhood and I have complete empathy with your concerns." He reached out and lightly pushed her hair back over her ear, studying her face.

She closed her eyes, feeling his touch to her toes. There was nothing like anguish to make one acutely alert to another's sage advice. Maybe a sip of wine *would* do her good. Yes, she opened her large brown eyes slowly to meet his. The air sighed from her lungs in weariness.

"I have a suggestion that might help." God, she was so young, wholesome and radiant. She made Doc feel brand new. How could Abe remove himself from her? He hoped she'd listen to him, as he took another sip of wine, looked down for a moment and placed the glass on the coffee table. Inhaling deeply of the warm, heavily perfumed air from the lanai, he looked at her to make sure, to try to anticipate her reaction, test the water. Her large oval eyes shifted back and forth on his face expectantly.

Listen, Doc. You had better think this over. Remain detached. You're a smart guy, smarter than the average bear, and richer, too. Do you really want to propose this to her? You have Suki to think of, and Abe. You've stayed out of trouble all your life. Are you going to start dumbing up now? There's no fool like an old fool. Think about it. She's a beauty, however—fresh, peachy, ripe. A hot torrent of emotion welled up in his throat like a rushing surge. No one could ever know the effort it took to keep his hands off her when the core of him burned painfully with desire for yon maiden.

He felt confident, buoyant and young again, being with her, alone, her gaze warm and receptive. He turned slightly to retrieve the chardonnay from the holder, pouring more wine into their flutes. The developing of his proposal made his pulse race. Small hammerings were revisiting him with a heat he hadn't felt since he'd married Suki. His eyes became more direct, pinning her to his wavelength.

Sarah waited, watching hypnotically at the way his lips curled under his mustache as he spoke, the physical beauty of his posture, the confidence and worldliness he exuded. She felt the muscles in her throat tightening. She took a sip of wine. She couldn't possibly feel this way about him. Hadn't she prided herself on her virtuousness? She felt a croak escape from deep within her inner being. Intrigue was alive from simply being near him, sharing his ideas and philosophies.

She raised the flute to her mouth, all the while fixing her eyes on him.

CHAPTER THIRTY-SIX

Reining in the beast inside him, he fixed on some verbal tiptoeing. He lifted his head and gazed off into the distance for a moment before resuming. "If your biggest concern is the incestual deficits in Abe's genetic code, have *my* baby," he said abruptly, the words veritably jumping out of his mouth, on fire. "I *am* Abe's father." He paused as he observed her shoulders stiffen, the fabric of her sundress pull tightly across her small breasts, sending fingers of desire running rampant through his chest. Sipping slowly, he went on. "Any similarities will be passed off as procedural replication. You'd have a semblance of Abe's child, but without the learning disabilities—the physical debilitations he suffered as a child."

"Of course, you'll need to be exposed to him within a short period of time after my insemination, perhaps by simply telling him that you've changed your mind, and now desire to have children. Pride is a lonely bedfellow, Sarah."

His eyes searched her face for comprehension and acceptance. If the offer suffered somewhat from the untamed emotions he entertained, he hoped his voice didn't betray him. She *had* to accept. God, he couldn't believe how he lusted after her.

Staring up at him, her eyes shone unreadable, starry and wondering. "But…how…when…I don't fully understand," she breathed, her voice smoky soft. It wasn't the first time in her life that Sarah maddened at the social system cast upon women—the duplicity of moral codes for men as opposed to those imposed upon women. Men were considered devilish and intriguing with their casual sexual affairs, but she recognized the shame that would be brought upon a woman who exhibited such behavior. She hadn't wanted this attraction, but there it was again, alive and well.

Doc wanted her so badly that he was afraid to touch her, afraid he couldn't stop. But what about his medical ethics? Oh, how different this cast. In this instance, he could apply situational ethics, which passed his moral bar.

"Sweet Sarah, I already possess corporeal knowledge of you; this will be no stranger with whom you're mating. It will only work, however, in your vulnerable time." He noticed she hadn't sipped on her wine at all since his proposal. He lifted the glass to her lips. The manner in which she possessed the stemmed glass with delicately tapered fingers caused sweat to break out on his chest. He settled back into the couch and drew her close to him.

"I'm...susceptible right now," came the words, barely whispering.

Tipping her chin, he read her lips. "Well, that answers the *when*. The *where* is here. As far as *how* is concerned, I think you know how the hell a woman gets pregnant." Unbiddingly, he rasped his eyes, seducing her. It didn't go unnoticed by Doc's trained observations that her respiration betrayed her increased excitement.

She could have found the proposal preposterous, but surprisingly, she did not. Was there something wrong with her mind? Why did it sound so reasonable? Why was she so drawn to him? She'd always loved him, been fascinated by him, his English accent. He'd always been a hypnotic element in her life—an admired icon. Where did that surge of heat come from in her abdomen? She couldn't be feeling this. How could she turn to him so quickly after Abe's departure?

"Do you love me?" she whispered, ignoring the wine for a moment, as if she couldn't possibly handle two actions at once.

There was no way she could know how her sultry voice raised the hairs on his neck, his arms. "Yes," he said simply. He knew he shouldn't be saying these things to his son's woman of choice, but he couldn't curb himself. "It happened a long time ago. I've never stopped loving you. In this way, I can keep you in the family as Abe's wife, and continue to love you and keep you near me. Perhaps it's not right, not moral, but it seems like the logical solution at this moment."

Slowly, she turned her eyes away from the bright Pasadena sunshine. She fought back rationale. Carefully she set her wine flute on the long table in front of the couch, reached out and captured *his* glass of wine, never removing her eyes from his. Slowly, she turned the glass in her hands, her finger tracing around the rim, her lips finally coming to rest on the same spot where he had drunk. She sipped slowly—small intakes—a message locking into his eyes, the hot taste of liquid desire in her mouth.

Doc felt potent, an electric power surge, the surge of arousal; he wanted to growl, beat his chest. His hand gently stroked her cheek as she continued sipping. The caress was undemanding, but it was foreshadowed with hints of great promise.

"All right," she said, removing her lips from the flute, wet, parted and ripe. She wasn't too young to know that this meant more than a simple afternoon rendezvous, but she found no fault in it. Instead, Sarah felt a lifelong commitment. The biggest shame she felt persisted in that she felt unashamed. His eyes stayed locked on hers until Sarah felt herself floating away in the deep recesses of his soul, a shared communion in a commonizing thought process. The roll of evening tide washed gently on the beach of her inner being.

His arm hooked itself around her tiny waist as he drew her to him, slowly lowering his mouth onto hers in a kiss deeply tender. A leaping thrill thrived within her. The drama followed with everything she'd dreamed; his mustache swept her with its masculinity and brittleness, yet soft. She knew the experience of being near him, to feel his professional touch, but never ever came near guessing the compelling magnitude of emotions that pervaded her with his first kiss.

Easing his mouth from her lips, he wisped it across her cheek, whispering to her of the magic she worked on him.

The susurrations warmed her, his breath a kiss of its own on her ears, her neck.

Standing, he pulled her to him with a hint of roughness, framing her upturned gaze in his large hands, his thumbs grazing the pastures of her throat, kissing her again, this time more deeply demanding. Had he ever wanted Liz or Suki this badly?

Reaching down, she lifted the wine glass, dipped her finger in it and traced his lips, never moving her eyes from them. "You kiss beautifully, Doc. Is it like that every time you kiss?" The words emitted rigorously shaky, hoarse.

"No, not every time. It gets better," he said, smiling, licking the wine from his lips as she watched the action of his tongue, imagining the movements, anticipating the taste of it. He gathered her in his arms and carried her into the bedroom, snuggling her breasts to his chest protectively, as if they were too small to be out by themselves.

She allowed her hand to slip inside his shirt, feeling the coarse hair growing there. She felt his chest heave. Lying on the bed, she reached up and pulled him down, wanting more—his chest, the smell of him, his skin and the hard roughness of him.

His voice was a masculine vibration on her skin, in her ear, on her hair, as his fingers grasped the pasteurized cream of her shoulders. "I've waited so long—too long." His features were strained, his breathing constrained. "Bear this in mind, my child. It's what I want to give you, this gift to your happiness with Abe, a gift to me to enjoy in my older years." The consequences of his actions were of small significance to him compared to his all en-compassing need for her.

A soft gasp escaped her. Never had she felt so alive, so vital, so much a woman, a woman in complete abandonment of time and place and self. She was fully aware of his male self as she felt the pressure of his hips, his demands were growing stronger.

He knew what he wanted, knew what he'd wanted all along...what he wanted to create—the trail he would blaze for Abe, who knew not what he had. Abe, who soared too quick and heated to arouse his woman to fulfillment. Abe, who was too impulsive to negotiate. His nostrils flared at the fresh scent of her.

"I love you, Sarah," he whispered as he pulled her full against him. "Do you want me to pull the drapes?" He could feel the heat coming off his body. His eyes squinted.

"No," she said thickly. "I want to see you, all of you. I've dreamed of a moment such as this with you, too, of course only in fantasy, never really expecting it to happen." Tears glistened in her eyes. "I love you, Doc." Her eyes fixed on him and she beheld the exquisiteness of his manhood—his powerful shoulders, his broad chest circled with dark hair, his naked biceps and forearms firm with muscle and capable hands with professional, long fingers. She opened her mouth, then closed it, speechless, but her dark eyes spoke volumes.

Lying beside her, he again kissed her gently, then deepening the aggression. "Call me Danforth, Sarah. Say it. Call me by my name—Danforth. Do it, Sarah."

"I love you, Danforth," she breathed as he pulled her closely to feel flesh on flesh, heat against heat, her softness crippling him, drawing him into a bewitching circle. The sound of his name on her breath inundated him. He lurched. She took pleasure in his physical reactions. "Danforth, you've given me so much to look forward to, given me your son to love, given me the wherewithal to let him love me.

"In the meantime, I have fallen in love with you too. You're important to me, Danforth. Don't leave me. Abe lacks the security and stability you offer." She shuddered as her body ebbed and flowed inside with the bay wash. "If I conceive of your child, I shall marry Abe and be devoted to both of you." She squirmed against him, demanding more, never ever feeling more receptive.

Sensing her excitement, he kissed her repeatedly, his lips moving from her mouth to her eyelids, her beautiful eyelids, her ears, her nose, her cheeks, down her neck where he nuzzled while she grew in excitement. Danforth was an expert in recognizing the signs of ovulation and its resulting emulations. His body grew hard and rigid as he massaged her belly; his trained fingers traced her lower abdomen.

Gazing down at her, his whole body became in accord, seeing her cheeks in flame, her eyes bright and her respiration up. He knew she was vulnerable and used his professionalism to nudge her into cooperation. In a heartbeat, he explored the adventure of her, the moist, soft, warm enclosure of her, where he'd been before but never to these depths or in this manner—undreamed—unattainable—a fabled fantasy.

They lay in velvet silence, their bodies speaking an unspoken language, in complete harmony. Without ever considering the situation as the result of what transpired, she slipped into the bigger impulse to go with the feeling, the feeling that sought her inner soul, the feeling that brought her out of the commonplace into the sublime. She rode the surge of a wave until she gasped, "Danforth."

He knew. He knew. The sensing was primitive. The throbbing peaked more than he could handle, the demands more than he could explain.

She saw the urgency in his eyes, the excitement, the darkening of his countenance. "I've never wanted anyone so much, Sarah. You must have me. You must conceive of my child, our child, our love child. We'll never have any regrets about this. It's your future, my future. I want you so desperately." His face gleamed with the wonder of it all, the love of it all.

He didn't have to tell her. It must have been meant to be. A small sound erupted from her with the complete fulfillment of herself. She lay enamored with how he accommodated and worked with her. The rhythm was in concert, the tempo slow with compassion and love, as he pleasured her beyond her wildest expectations. He seemed weightless as compared to Abe in his bubble of gratification.

"Danforth," she whispered. She felt a surge of sensations, indescribable, her fingers dug into his shoulders, her head lurched back, her breath held. Her satisfaction excited him intensely. They reached rapture as the waves crashed on the beach again, a rapture unknown but to love mates, together, alone, in another world where time hung meaningless.

Afterwards, lying in his arms, she felt sleepy and content, but she heard his whisperings of endearments. "Sarah, what can I say? This has been an irreplaceable experience, indulgence, a time without dimensions. I'll stand by you, always."

As fate would have it, he stood by her again on Thursday night after everyone else had retired...the same rapture, the same enthrallment, the same commitment. He drowned her with his kisses and caresses as she sank into the quicksand of his love, the meek Pacific breezes drifting through the opulent sheers hanging at the French doors through which he had come like a phantom in the night.

※※

Magnificence is synonymous with the Annual Tournament of Roses Parade.

Early on New Year's Day, the Whittaker party scampered onto the viewing stands at eight o'clock. Seated on the west side of Colorado Boulevard, the morning sun smiled warm and glorious in a cloudless sky.

Sarah felt her presence with these people slightly bizarre in view of the fact that Abe had unceremoniously dumped her Tuesday night. Unsuccessful were her efforts to exchange her airline ticket for an earlier flight back to Detroit. There were no accommodations for four days, and in as much as she was scheduled on a flight back Sunday anyway, she dropped the effort as futile.

Nonetheless, the Fifty-Ninth Annual Tournament of Roses Parade touted a knockout program, and Sarah listened politely as Suki read from her program.

"The parade theme is *Our Golden West* featuring a five-mile-long route and consisting of nearly sixty flower-covered floats, a great number of California's outstanding marching bands and hundreds of the finest riding horses adorned with silver mounted equipment. Floats depicting highlights of the western United States in the past, present and future, such as the pony express, and stagecoach, or present day highlights of industry and developments in the golden west assure the public of a very beautiful parade and at the same time one with a great variety of floats."

"Over a million people will view this parade today. It will be photographed by professional cameramen and newsreel cameramen from all parts of the United States and from foreign countries."

"KTLA in Los Angeles is televising it. Can you believe it?" Her eyes raked the group.

"And listen to this," Karen interjected.

"Each float must conform to certain regulations in the areas of height, width, length and thematic design. When construction is completed, the float is transformed through the use of natural and organic materials. The entire surface must be covered using a variety of flowers, seed, bark, leaves and other flora. Most floats are controlled internally and are entered in the Parade on behalf of a corporation, city or organization."

"I see the President of the parade this year is Louis R. Vincenti, and General Omar Bradley is the Parade Marshall, but what I'm interested in is who in the world is the Parade Queen?" Doc queried.

Suki rose to the occasion. "Okay. Okay. I found it here in the program. It's Virginia Goodhue, a Pasadena girl. So there, ask and thou shalt receive." Suki stayed abreast of events.

"And you, Sarah, what do you enjoy about the parade? You're so very quiet today." Doc's tone of voice was solicitous. Her normal enthusiasm seemed washed away, as if caught up in some especially painful memory. He hoped it wasn't him.

"The marching bands," she replied quietly. "They are quite outstanding and include as many as *three hundred* marching instruments in a single unit. I can't believe how terrific they are," she replied, working at even small voice inflections. She met the wise doctor-eyes. They were empathetic, but twinkling. Nothing of her inner agitation did she allow to flow out to him.

"Here is the Michigan Marching Band," Anne cried, as applause sprung up along the parade route. "Hail to the Victor" sounded across the parade route.

Karen was alive with energy and excitement. "All this, and remember, my sister wants us for lunch in San Marino by eleven, then to the game at two!" She smiled widely at the thought. How it satisfied her to see her sister, have Kyle named coach of the year and his team in the Rose Bowl. Her cup runneth over.

She bubbled with more information. "Via Kyle, Curly Lambeau has invited all of us to view the game from his box. 'Sure would like to meet Abe's family, as long they're here,' Curly told Kyle...no hesitation whatsoever. 'The Packers team is close; we make a point of knowing the families and having outings together.' Can't wait for that game! M Go Blue!" She virtually squirmed, sitting on the bleachers.

✶

The team was suited up and attentive in the locker room. Kyle paced the floor, head bent, and hands clasped behind his back, looking every bit like a worried professor. He said nothing, just paced. The longer he paced, the quieter the room became. It was a clever mind game.

Stopping suddenly, he projected in a strong voice, "You can't say, 'This-is-only-a-game.' *It's not.* It's a *Poll Game!* Which means it's more important than life or death. We're talking about *football* here! A Poll Bowl is a crucial confrontation, a battle of Goliaths, a super shootout where the cheese stands alone when it's over! There is nothing ambiguous about it... no two ways you can describe it. We're talking about *football* here!

"It's sometimes a Game of the Year, occasionally a Game of the Decade, and in rare instances a Game of the Century. This is the Game of the Century! The whole country is watching us. The winner of this game will make national headlines. Poll Bowls never die. They are emblazoned into the memories of the winners and losers forever. It's an unforgiving sport—football. In Poll Bowls, people with names like Thorpe, Grange, Harmon, Doak, Lujack and so forth get to do amazing things and become immortal.

"Schools win national championships in Poll Bowls. A Poll Bowl between Notre Dame and the University of Southern California once drew one hundred twelve thousand people in Chicago's Soldier Field, and this event was far removed from your anticipated television that we keep hearing about, which is not going to invent football or Poll Bowls.

"In case no one told you, the first live Los Angeles telecast of a college football game is taking place today by KTLA. *You* are playing in a most historic game. The Rose Bowl Game registered a sell out last year for the first time. It's also a sellout this year. Last year, the first game played under the Tournament's exclusive agreement with the Big Ten and Pacific Coast Conference. This will continue to be a featured championship between the top teams of these two conferences." Kyle's icy blue eyes snapped as he included all the players in his scrutiny.

Warming now, his voice becoming gentler, he went on. "I want you to know that I was very proud of each and every one of you yesterday at the Kickoff Luncheon that was sponsored by the Pasadena Kiwanis Club. It saw attendance of approximately two thousand persons and broadcast over a nationwide hookup. Besides the competing teams, there were nationally known coaches, sports writers and other celebrities attending.

"It brought a great honor to have General Omar Bradley as the keynote speaker. With my affinity to military strategy, it pleases me to no end to know that General Bradley will also be in attendance at today's game." He leaned an elbow on the podium, crossing one foot over the other, showing only a profile to half the players.

"In case you've forgotten, I want you to know what a prestigious event this is," he reminded them imperiously. "The game is most affectionately called 'The Granddaddy of Them All.' It is played in a granddaddy, horseshoe-shaped stadium, built with a seating capacity of fifty-seven thousand in 1922 and deeded to the City of Pasadena by the Tournament of Roses Association. TOR volunteers raised two hundred seventy-two thousand dollars to fund the stadium, which was named 'The Rose Bowl.' In 1928, the Rose Bowl Stadium was enlarged by nineteen thousand seats, increasing its capacity to seventy-six thousand. In the late 1930s another seventeen thousand seats were added. I think that I can safely say that there'll be well over ninety thousand people out there in the stands watching your asses at work." He turned, leaning to the other side.

"I want to give each of you my bountiful thanks for a very splendid year. It's been fantastic. But don't let your guard down. Are we up for this opportunity? Listen. I'm counting on you, *all* of you. You've never been better prepared for a challenge. USC is going to come at you like murdering mutts, besiege you like nomadic Bedouins. I don't want to run this into the ground fellas, but I can't emphasize it enough—watch your backs out there. Buckle up for the hard hits." Putting both hands on the podium, he leaned back, pausing. "Whatever you do, don't go out there onto that playing field *expecting* to win. That attitude can kick the hell out of any victory we may get. Now, let's get out there with panache and make some serious noise!" The confidence he exuded collided with the chaos he felt inside, the anxiety only a coach could know.

When the team came through the tunnel, the cacophony of sound they heard was unimaginably loud. A biblical invasion of locusts could not have been more overwhelmingly noisy. Abe was awed with the out-pouring of support for the Michigan Team, two thousand miles from home. Where did they get fans such as this? He felt minuscule in the general scheme of things.

Jim Funt needn't have worried about Abe playing. He played alright.

With Jim looking on, fingers crossed, Abe set a Rose Bowl record with catching a combined twelve passes for two hundred seventy-nine yards in total offense to lead the Wolverines to a forty-nine to zero rout of the Trojans before a crowd of ninety-three thousand in Pasadena. The Wolverines amassed nearly five hundred yards of offense in handing the Trojans their worst loss in school history. Abe lead the team in rushing to electrify a nationwide following. His eighty-four-yard touchdown scamper set a new bowl record as the longest run in history. He gained recognition as Michigan's quintessential receiver, a six foot-two inch artist dancer in pads. Kreiler said afterward that the '47 Wolverines were the greatest team he had ever coached.

The following day, Jim Funt got almost as much ink as Abe. Newspapers across the country heralded the Michigan Mad Magicians, carrying pictures of Abe running, along with his stats for the game and for the year.

Kreiler paced once more, however, when with 3:49 remaining in the game, USC got the ball back one more time and advanced it to the crunch-time dilemma of fourth and eight on Michigan's twenty.

The USC coach called time. He considered a field goal, but then changed his mind. "Let's go for it. We're never going to make progress if we're going to start hoping they're going to make a mistake. We'll just take a deep breath and go for it."

The go-for-it decision was what the coach called "kind of a publicity stunt play," a fake screen pass to a back and an actual pass to the tight end over the middle. USC quarterback Spike took the ball from the center, dropped back, and faked a short pass to his wide receiver. Turning, he was surprised as hell to find a defender all but draped over his intended receiver—a senior tight end.

Trailing and being obliterated down to what could have been his last play, and with the teammate to whom he intended to throw this rally-making pass on fourth and a bunch not close to open, the situation seemed bleak. Instinctively, Spike pulled the ball back toward his body and initiated a run. At first slipping on the grass, he then dodged a couple of tacklers and kept the drive alive. Needing eight yards for a first down, he jostled for thirteen. The place went wild because it added up the first time USC had done anything all day. Ecstatic, as he returned to the huddle and received slaps on the back, Spike had shown the creative skills that made him so highly desirable.

Now first and goal, Spike got half the yardage necessary on the first play. He then bulldozed for two more yards, and on third down, for another. On fourth down, USC still lagged a yard bashful of the end zone.

This time Spike set the ball in the halfback's belly and then took it away. Michigan did not fall for the fake. Spike's initial tackle came from Abe, who had been left in to play defense when the platoon changed. With other defenders joining him, Spike turned cold—losing ground. Abe's effort could be seen in the picture that the school paper ran of the crucial play. With twenty-seven seconds remaining in the ball game, there remained no time for USC to rally.

Pandemonium broke loose before the clock ran out.

Abe could outrun half the backs on the Michigan team. One of the most famous pictures in Michigan football lore is the shot of Abe loping alongside Chapin during Chapin's record-breaking dash.

"To my amazement," said Chapin, "I had broken through the line and found myself in the open. Our off-side linemen had leveled their defensive backs, and I stretched out my long legs and huffed and puffed my way into the end zone after a fifty-four yard rumble. I felt pretty good about myself until I saw the movies and watched Abe barely exerting himself, sauntering alongside for the final forty yards. There I was, running at full throttle, while Abe loped about at half-speed. It was embarrassing."

In addition, it was pretty embarrassing for their opponents, who found they were staring up at the sky after being run over by a sprinter who could tackle them.

Abe exhibited a punishing defensive back who lived that day for the sheer thrill of clobbering enemy ball carriers. He came off as wild and aggressive, beyond the pale of normal boundaries. Kyle pulled him twice before penalties were called.

After the game, Curly Lambeau couldn't stop re-hashing the Wolverines and the Mad Magicians. "That quarterback, Hulk, is a master at getting rid of the ball under duress, and when his receivers were covered, he had the rare talent of throwing, if just a little astray, so it could neither be intercepted nor called intentional grounding. He threw few interceptions and he seldom had to chomp the ball. In addition, he varies the time interval between those 'huts' when hecalls the plays so no one could predict the snap of the ball. It keeps the offensive line on-side, and the other people honest.

"And *Miereau!* He's downfield thirty yards before Hulk lets it go. He wants to be sure the flanker is open, but he has to foretell it, because if he waits until he sees him open, that's freebie time for the defensive man. When a flanker makes that good feint and gets that one-step lead, he has such long legs and such velocity that it takes the defensive back three steps to just catch up." Lambeau stuck his hands in his trousers pockets, shaking his head, smiling, as if he'd just seen a hero-never-dies film. "I noticed too that he's great at spotting defenses," Lambeau remarked.

"That recognition of the defense is difficult to coach, for me anyway," Kreiler added, "so it's difficult to learn because receivers must perceive it on that first step across the line, at the same time that the defense is trying to conceal it.

"You know as well as I do, Curly, that receivers must make their open interval between two point five seconds and four seconds. That's all they have— one point five seconds—and it's all the time the quarterback has to be hopeful of, but there's a logic some receivers have about getting open, and Miereau is uncanny about it. He says that he can interconnect, soak up and understand the quarterback, as if he's viewing the corner pages of a Little Big Book. Crazy as hell, like a phenomenon. Maybe it's Abe with his paintbrush or Bach with his originality, and there's your creativity. That's what Abe has. You have it or you don't." Kreiler laughed. "We'll miss him sorely."

Lambeau agreed, with a nod. "That's why we were so desperate to get Miereau this year. We're using more of a wide-open passing game next year. I've seen too many of my men suffer injuries, bad injuries, in the rushing game."

"Did you happen to observe how Abe runs under the ball and doesn't leap for it?" Kreiler rapped into it with Lambeau; he energized by talking football with a pro coach.

Curly nodded. "That's good, damn good for a college kid. While they're in the air, they're losing time gained on the ground." Curly sighed, kicking some sod, pleased with his draft choice.

The Associated Press would not drop the issue of which team was best— Notre Dame or Michigan. Acting on the request of the *Detroit Free Press* sports editor, Lyle Smith, the AP decided to conduct an unprecedented post-bowl poll of sports editors of all member papers nationwide. The poll was simple: Pick Michigan or Notre Dame, and forget about everybody else.

The AP announced the results of the special, unofficial poll on January 6. Michigan won it handily, taking two hundred and twenty-six first-place votes to Notre Dame's one hundred and nineteen. The Wolverines drew their greatest backing in the Midwest. Support was more or less from both coasts, while the Irish were the overwhelming pick of the South.

"The men who voted couldn't have made a mistake if they had picked either team," Kreiler diplomatically responded.

Letty, too, was especially praiseworthy of his rival coach and school. "I'm thoroughly convinced that the 1947 Michigan team will go down in football history as one of the greatest intercollegiate squads ever assembled. I have a very healthy respect for coach Kreiler. There is no better coach in the business."

CHAPTER THIRTY-SEVEN

Sarah thought the game somewhat mindless with Michigan scoring time and again, even with Kyle putting in depth from the lines. No wonder they were called the Michigan Mad Magicians. She wished she had the magical power to make Abe disappear from her memory. Letting go would be her biggest obstacle, unless she ate humble pie and confessed her readiness to have his child after all.

"Time and determination overcome most difficulties in the end," she remembered her mother saying. It worked for *her* after Max died, bless her heart. Sarah's eyes clouded over. Wait until she disclosed to Ma that Abe called off everything—the engagement, the wedding. She'd be ultimately shocked and embarrassed.

Sarah managed to keep her eyes dry, but she couldn't swallow the swell of anger that rose in her throat. Since he'd had such a successful year, he'd forgotten how to communicate except by dictating. He didn't even know how to compromise anymore. He just bellowed like a bull. That's exactly what he seemed like—a self-centered bully. She'd had enough. She felt confident that her mental condensation and digestion of feelings were highly accurate. What an loathsome prig! She'd been born twenty years too late. She would love to have had Doc, er, Danforth for her husband. She found herself stricken at the enormity of the agreement with Danforth.

"What a game, huh, Sarah?" Doc patted her on the shoulder, identifying with her emotional vulnerability, but added nothing and asked nothing. His voice was low and fell on her ears as more of a caress that a question.

Sitting with her hands clasped together as if being prayerful, she looked up at Doc. "Yes, outstanding. What a nice way to end a successful season," she replied, biting her tongue. In all likelihood, no one would be able to talk to Abe now. He'd stopped listening and only looked for personal gratification.

She sighed heavily. His prosperity had brought nothing but forgetfulness of what a nice guy he used to be. She knew her mind temperature dropped thirty degrees every time she'd thought of him. She pressed her fingers to her temples, rubbing them lightly.

There seemed to be no answer for her anxieties. They raised a frightening dilemma, diverse with a dozen intricacies, but he wouldn't listen to her fears. Did she want to devote nine months to incubating a child with all the discomforts, the worries as to health and possible disabilities? She flinched at the horror stories she'd heard about the pain of childbirth, and shuddered at the tied-down world of young mothers she'd known, feared having a child born with Tay-Sachs disease, so dominant in Jewish children. How could she marry a man who refused to listen to her concerns.

On the short drive back to the hotel, dusk had settled in, and the lamps were glowing up and down the streets. The city nightlights were like fine pieces of jewelry, decorating an already beautiful lady. "A penny for your thoughts," Doc whispered.

Jarred out of her reverie, Sarah physically lurched. "I slipped a thousand miles away. I'm sorry." She gibed at herself for being thrown off her stride.

☙❧

The victory dinner dragged on, noisy and replete with steady congratulations from the other hotel guests, many from Michigan. Sarah wore a pale pink cotton sheath dress with shades of pastel embroidery on the bodice, simple but accentuating her full hips. Polished clam jewelry was her only accent other than a pearlescent pair of pink heels.

She swallowed hard with the need to possess staying power. She could hardly bear to sit there and pretend that everything was hunky-dory, but she demurred at the aplomb and glory being doused on Abe and Kyle. Participating with a warm smile, she wished she could abracadabra her way to being alone with her thoughts.

Finding it difficult to breathe normally anymore, she found a solution. "Well, guys, if we're going to Disneyland tomorrow, I need my beauty sleep, so I'll say goodnight to all you nice people," she said, making a haphazard move to leave. "I'll see you in the morning." She smiled as she left, pushing in her chair.

Doc covertly watched Abe's eyes drink in her perfection for the full distance of the dining room as she walked away, her buns balanced neatly into the darts of the sheath. Heads turned as she passed, exiting like a brief comet whose intense light thrilled everyone she passed. Doc sensed that Abe ached, burning in his self-imposed celibacy. His eyes turned the color of deep winter, wretchedly bitter and disillusioned.

He acknowledged that Abe and Sarah's relationship had worsened into serious trouble. His deductions were sound but how could he be of assistance without sharing that he possessed knowledge aforehand? He sighed and cautioned himself not to meddle. They seemed to have their personal battleground: a mini Anzio. Let it go.

He'd run over and see her tonight when he went up to the suite. The airline called twice with cancellations she could've had. She'd never know that he'd turned them down.

☙❧

The drive to Anaheim took well over an hour, the conversation strained. Once on the grounds, however, everyone grew engrossed in the state-of-the-art entertainment provided and the beautifully appointed gardens. They frolicked through Disneyland like orphans on a holiday. Watching Abe and Doc stuff their frames into the tiny teacups was worth the price of admission. After four hours of the Matterhorn, Frontierland, Haunted House and Jungle Cruise, they returned to the Huntington Hotel in Pasadena.

Needing rest for their shopping trip to Hollywood the next day, all the ladies retired early. Resultantly, Doc, Kyle and Abe went down to the lounge for a thirsty night. Walter decided he'd had it for the day.

"What'll it be, gentlemen?" The bartender appeared cordial and courteous, his keen blue eyes looked out from heavy eyebrows that stuck out here and there like cactus spines giving him a, "Dona-foola-rounda-widda-me" look. His broad shoulders hinted at hidden strength.

"I'm going to have one of those dry martinis," said Abe, "on the rocks."

"Ah ha! I have you hooked on those already?" Doc inquired. "You need to be careful; they can knock a guy on his ass, but quick."

Abe turned to him and laughed, nodding. "Well, I haven't had a cocktail since Thanksgiving, so I decided I'd go for the gusto."

"I'll have the same, but leave mine up after you've shaken, but not bruised it." Doc expected his cocktail after a dusty day at Disneyland.

Kyle, not a drinking man, had a primitive instinct to survive with these two. "You badasses aren't going to make me wimp out. Make me one, too, up, like Doc's."

And so it stemmed that they were off to a short start on a long evening of fast-talking. The football game was replayed with enthusiasm and Disneyland revisited with the incredible animations they'd seen there. That called for a second martini.

Abe leaned on the bar, his head bowed, waltzing his martini glass in slow circles.

"Hey, boy, after the last two years you've had on that football field, you must be the happiest guy in the whole USA!" Kreiler had learned to love this young man.

"It's been a dream, totally unbelievable. I'm the one that's living in a Magic Kingdom. I thought I had my queen chosen, but I've had to write her off and start over again." Thoughts of Sarah had an incredible habit of bouncing back. His eyes were full of hardness, and something more—something more dangerous.

For a brief moment, Doc let his eyes widen in amazement. Maybe he should ignore the danger signs, but often dangerous waters stirred up solutions. "What say you?" Doc asked with feigned alarm. "You wrote off Sarah?" He winked at Kyle, both knowing all week that something was wrong. "What happened now?"

Emotion quickly spread over Abe's face, through his eyes, and then disappeared. "Snafu. She told me directly that she is uninterested in having children right now, and maybe not ever. Any wife of mine is going to give me a son, at least. So I walked out on our relationship, finished it, kaput." He made a popping sound with his mouth.

"Let's sit at a table over there," Doc suggested, with a twist of his head. Abe obviously needed some nurturing and privacy. He exchanged a knowing glance with Kyle. In addition, a round table offered greater comfort to speak freely.

"No goddamn wonder she tried to get an early flight back to Detroit," Doc breathed, leaning back in his chair.

"She did what?" Abe asked, surprised, exasperation in his voice. *Who the hell did she think she was to abandon his big game?* Storm clouds hung over him.

"Wednesday I took a couple of calls from the airlines, advising that they had two cancellations, but I told them that she no longer had an interest. What she doesn't know won't hurt her. You and Sarah have laid a whole lot of common ground in your lifetime. I can't believe that you performed that kind of radical surgery on your relationship." He *had* to get them back together. His heart slammed in his throat.

Abe's face lost its guarded look, the first Kyle and Doc had seen for days. "Well, it's been a problem for a while now. I pushed her for a *yes* or *no* decision, and it was *no*. So I just walked out—ended it. It's time to shoot the dog. Our association had gotten badly crippled anyway." He toyed with his graduation ring, rubbing it with his thumb.

Doc slipped this information into perspective. "Crippled, then, but not dead?" he asked, encouraged.

"Something like that." Abe flipped his hand in kumsee kumsaw. Abe pushed back from the table as he clasped his hands in front of him, as though deep in thought. Admittedly, he still found her highly desirable. His tongue licked out over his bottom lip.

"There has to be a resolution to all these problems, Abe," Kyle advised. "So why did she say she wasn't ready to have children?" He was attentive and deliberate, a master of tactical solutions. Perhaps this was only a skirmish and not a battle. He shot Abe a brilliant smile of reassurance.

"She says she's afraid, that children terrify her. Stupid!" His hands flexed in and out, the movements obvious to his observers, involuntary to Abe. He'd never had a woman reject him so soundly in all his life. "She's apprehensive about going through childbirth, but that's what women are made for." Abe was adamant, looking directly at them both candidly, certain and inflexible.

Doc and Kyle exchanged concerned looks.

"It sounds to me as if all her fears are legitimate," Doc said slowly, not wanting to trespass on his son's convictions. "Bloody hell," he shot out. "It can't be easy to commit nine months to carrying around a small body in your belly, and then push it out of a narrow passageway, especially her. I can understand her fears. Did you discuss them with her, so she has a sounding board—a sympathetic shoulder, someone who can share the load along the way?" Unflinching, Doc looked squarely at Abe.

"No, I didn't. It just seemed to me that all those petty reasons were just excuses without a basis." He spread his hands in frustration while his mind stretched tightly with the vagueness of his convictions, as opposed to Doc's and Kyle's.

"But they aren't, Abe, if you don't mind my saying so," Kyle interjected. He leaned forward, folding his hands. "When people hide these fears, they become phobias—gnarly issues. You need to be reasonable." Kyle knew they were finally getting to the crux of the matter—his inability to empathize.

"Then she told me that she doesn't know how to care for children, and that frightens her, too." Abe's exasperation with the whole affair was intensified by the rebuttals of his two mentors. The dark hair on his chest appeared to press against his shirt, as if in total defense of his position.

Kyle put his hand up before Abe could say more. "You don't want to lose such a lovely woman, Abe. Sarah is a lady who will never lose her luster." He signaled for the bartender to bring another round. "You'll be making big bucks with the Packers; you can afford to hire help for her if she provides you with a son. It's a compromise." Kyle's vivid green eyes spoke volumes with passion. "We negotiate. We arbitrate. You might have shot yourself in the foot by throwing the baby out with the bath water, excuse the analogy." Kyle was obviously concerned. He had to rescue this kid from ruin.

Abe rubbed his hands over his eyes in a weary gesture. The anti-arguments being tossed at him created knots in his stomach. "Well, how about the fact that she can't tolerate the pain of childbirth? What in the hell is she talking about? It's a naturally occurring, biological incident. I told her to grow up." His voice was heavily tinged with anger, the hurt in his eyes like an open book.

Again, the two men exchanged time-to-say-something glances. Whatever happened to the nice young man they used to know? "Have you thought of adoption?" Doc was searching. "It would solve the knotty issue of childbirth," he said softly. Doc sought new doors to open, but he knew which door he *wanted* to stay open.

Kyle sipped on his fresh drink. "She's a keeper, Abe. I wouldn't throw her away so hastily." Suddenly, his eyes sparkled with the mischief of a new thought. "What the hell, maybe you're right! Who needs to dance to a foolish girl's whims and worries? Who needs her looking at you with eyes that love and worship you? It's pesky as all get out. What kind of a moron wants her touching him with gentle hands and rich laughter that blows your mind? It's not you, for sure. Any woman can stir your lust and desire the same way that Sarah causes tingles whenever she's around—around to give you a special smile, to make you feel like a king. After all, with the status you've reached in life, why should you bow to the frivolous demands of one woman? What's worse, why should you entertain the thought of apologizing for being a bit pompous when you have every right to be so?" His expression carried ill-concealed amusement.

Abe heard the strain in Kyle's voice and showed rankling at his obvious negative parallels. An annoyance played around the corners of his mouth. "You know what I really think?" His eyebrows knit together. "What I really, really think?" He leaned back, searching the faces of these two grand men. "Now I truly *believe* this. I think that she doesn't want to have my children because I'm Sioux Indian and the kid might inherit my problems." His voice gave out on him—emotions running high—clearly rattled.

Doc heard promise in Abe's grating pain. His vintage eyebrow shot up. This kid carried some torturous baggage! He'd hit the nail right on the head. He knew he and Kyle were witnessing a breakdown of composure and he didn't want Abe plagued with self-doubt. Doc knew Abe had handled it all his life and he sure didn't need any more.

"Now that just isn't like her at all, Abe." He startled at the limits to which his son had taken this baby issue. "She loves you very much. Underneath her strong facade these last three days, she's probably been crying inside. Have you ever given any thought to her worries about *her* genetic background?"

Abe had worked up an undeniable obsession in his confession. He shook his head, not conceding any high-risk drawbacks to her genetic background. Dark determination spread over his countenance.

"It's not good." Doc nodded. "The Jewish community is plagued with Tay Sachs Disease. The incidence of Tay-Sachs in the United States is one in thirty-six hundred live births among the Ashkenazi Hebrews. This is in sharp contrast to the incidence rates for those not of Hebrew descent: a carrier frequency of one in three hundred and an affected incidence of one in three hundred and sixty thousand live births!"

"What the hell is Tay-Sachs disease? You gotta talk my language, Doc." Abe flummoxed with this new information.

"The Tay-Sachs baby usually appears normal for the first five months of life. Even in this early period, however, he may exhibit an exaggerated alarmed response to sound. As the baby ages, even the softest sound alarms him. By eight months of age, the infant may look sleepy or less alert. Examination at this time or shortly thereafter may show poor muscle and head control. In about eighty percent of Tay-Sachs infants, examination of the region of the retina reveals the characteristic cherry-red macular spot. Cerebral degeneration is progressive. The infant loses all the skills previously developed, becomes blind, and usually dies prior to the age of four. This is after Sarah would have carried him for nine months, given painful birth, nurtured and loved him for four years. He would most certainly die." Doc paused.

Abe had never seen this sternness in Doc, his eyes darker than dark, the fires of warmth absent. A muscle twitched in his jaw, but he held firm.

"Now, then, do you yet think that she's worried about carrying a child of Sioux Indian descent in view of what *she* could pass on to that child? I don't think so. I think she learned to embrace the identity of your heritage a long time ago. You should have walked with this ball for a while before taking it over the end zone." Doc hoped he had coded the disparities in Abe's rationale.

"Damn, Doc, that's a heavy load to carry around! I guess that I haven't been listening." Abe's face became a mixture of enlightenment, bewilderment and the last threads of annoyance. He thrust a worried hand through his hair. "What can I say?"

"I'll tell you what you can say. '*Mea culpa, mea culpa.*'" Doc delivered his frank opinion. "I'm not dunning you for this, Abe." Doc groaned. "Sometimes, when you're twenty-three years old and everything is going your way, you tend to kick in the teeth those you love and cherish the most. You've given Sarah some bad times in your lifetime, but regardless, she has remained true to you through thick and thin."

Doc wasn't done. "If I were you, I'd get down on my knees and beg her for forgiveness, and try to work out an equitable solution to this problem. I think adoption sounds good, and the nanny idea is excellent. It's time to tell that lady what a horse's patoot you've been. You'll be lucky indeed to even have her reconsider you."

Abe studied him as he talked—confident, handsome, intelligent eyes and quick humor drew Abe's admiration. Not many men would have had the moxey to stay so calm in the face of the caliber of provocation Abe had delivered.

"I agree," said Kyle. "The take-back-to-your-room-message is this: one is a lonely number. The task might seem daunting for a man of your talent and stature, but it's time you make the move. Apologies are always difficult. It's not a boy's exercise—it takes a man."

Did Abe hear a snarl in Kreiler's voice?

"You'd better punctuate your apology with a few kisses and tender hugs. If you leave here this weekend with your engagement broken off after only one month, you'll have gained nothing...megazilch. You might as well start entertaining thoughts of making an appointment with the Arroyo Seco—the Suicide Bridge on the other side of town." Kyle's fist came down on the table in emphasis and finality.

Doc nodded. "That's right, Abe—everything he said. Tread lightly and try listening and hearing." Doc reached out and covered Abe's hand. "Now, I think that I, in my enormous capacity to drink martinis, have reached my point of super saturation."

Abe covered Doc's hand and then rose to leave. "Thanks, guys. I don't know if it's changed my mind, but you've made many valid points."

∽•∾

Saturday bloomed like a daisy chain of endless sunshine and flowers. A mild breeze sprang up from the south, layering the air with softness. Sarah pinched herself with the reality of it all on the drive to Bullock's Department Store, where the hotel limousine transported them for their morning shopping trip. Choosing to sit by the pool and relax, Anne had declined the outing.

"Is there anything special you want to pick up today, Sarah?" Suki asked. "It might be a good time to select something for your honeymoon trip, wherever you might be going." Suki's glance warmed with solicitousness.

Abe's rejection drummed so closely under her skin that Sarah could conceal the hurt no longer. The veritable time bomb she'd been carrying around for four days finally exploded. She blurted, "There's going to be no wedding. Abe's called the whole thing off." Her voice was barely audible, filled with self-doubt.

"What did you say? He called the whole thing off?" Suki bristled.

"Yes." Sarah breathed the word—uncontrollable tears cascaded from her eyes.

Suki and Karen made eye contact and sat stunned.

"Here, dear, here's a tissue," Karen offered, feeling inadequate. "What seems to be the problem? Ultimately, I know he loves you very much. He talks about you all the time. In fact, I couldn't wait to meet you after tutoring him for two years. I had built myself a minds-eye version of what you looked like, and you're just like that picture, too, it turns out." She smiled weakly, shifting her glance to Suki.

"Can we help?" Suki held Sarah's hand. "This has to be something very silly."

Karen fidgeted in her seat. "That's right, we're here for you. You don't have to talk about *anything if* you don't want to, but we'd like to help and want you to know that." Karen found no comfortable position or posture in this awkward situation.

"He wants me to have a child right away. Maybe I never want to. He told me to grow up and be a woman. Can you believe that?" Her shoulders were shaking, her hands trembling. "His only barometer of a woman is whether or not she's pregnant. He's been crude and crass." She put her hands to her face, crying harder now.

Karen's back stiffened. "Men *are* by nature crude and crass, dear. I believe, however, he's gone way beyond the boundary in questioning your womanhood because you want to be in charge on having children. That's your right. Kyle and I have two children, but it's because it was a mutual agreement." Karen was livid, her eyes snapping.

Suki knew how Abe felt on this subject. She also knew he'd use everything at his disposal to control Sarah. "In Sioux Indian anthropology, it is culturally a fact that a wife is to serve her husband in all things. You deflated his ego by refusing to have his children, that's all. The Sioux believe that the road to immortality must be paved with their offspring. After Fabian died, Abe spent a vast amount of time with Farley and Norrhea, and I'm afraid they were very influential on his thinking. He has been deep into Sioux tradition. I even sense an animalistic aggression about him at times, and that is a very Sioux orientation." She paused with the sense of wonder that came over her in the revelation of her son's strong convictions, too strong. Her heart thumped.

Angrily, she went on. "He *has* lived in the Whiteman's world, however, and will do so for the rest of his life. He'd better get with the program and realize that white women aren't born into slavery. He's going to find himself dead at the hands of his mother! What a bunch of idealistic drivel." She broke off breathlessly.

Suki's voice trailed off, remembering the heartbreak of leaving Abe with Fabian when she made her way out into the world, but a baby had no place in a life of hopping on buses, working crazy hours, keeping a roof over your head. That was no existence for a child. Fabian loved him so much and had been defensibly proud of him.

"I don't know what to tell you, Sarah." Suki waxed conservative. "Maybe it's best you dissolve the association. He's given you more than a fair share of *les miserables*. Sometimes the warnings we get during our courtship are underlined in red, twice, and as in your case, many times." Suki wanted them both to be happy.

She put her arm around Sarah, whose crying had calmed. They were on Lake Street now and Bullock's came into view. Suki would make every effort to amend to Sarah for her son's stupidity, and she knew that was simply a euphemism—asshole was a better word! She'd like to take a magazine, roll it up and whack him with it.

Sarah's tears turned to absence of feeling and burrowed deeply within her. It was a magnificent California day, and she would make the best of it. Her gaze filled with wanting—wanting more happiness, wanting an end to problems, and yes, heartbreak.

Over the intercom, the uniformed driver advised, "Ladies, when you're ready to return to the hotel or want to go anywhere else, just call the office. I'll return pronto."

Entering the wide front doors of the store, Karen tensed with excitement. "I know what to do. I know! Allow us to buy you a new dress to wear tonight, Sarah. One that'll make him absolutely crawl the floor for you. And then I'll tell Kyle that he needs to ask you to dance with him. Abe'll go right out of his mind." She laughed, her eyes twinkling. Her lips tilted in vast amusement.

"Capital! And I'll have Danforth do the same!" Suki was amused and more. There lived a lump in her throat for Sarah. "No immature modest overtures, either. The moves will be so amorous that Abe will growl like a bear fresh out of hibernation."

"*Au contraire*, Suki. To be precise, roaring like a Catholic alligator charging out of a swamp filled with fat frogs—on Friday!" Karen rollicked with this new plan, slapping her knee. "The best defense is a good offense! We'll show him that you're not a second-draft choice." Her eyes were wide with excitement.

With an enormous effort, Sarah brought her crying under control, but found she operated on autopilot. Her two Fairy Godmothers were setting out to work wonders with their magic wands. Together, they chose an off-white cotton-acetate dress that sported cut-away shoulders and a high collar line that blended into generous lapels that rolled open right down to her waist, her tiny waist, cinched with a self-belt inhabited by an over-sized gold oyster-shell-shaped buckle. The skirt of the dress formed a perfect circle, which would look scrumptiously seductive on the dance floor as she moved, glided, or even walked. They added polished walnut earrings, the definition rings of which cascaded in threesomes over each shoulder. A double walnut-ring bracelet graced her right arm. The shoes took some doing to find, but when spied, they hit all of them at once. They weren't glass, but you'd never know they weren't; they were the shining pale bronze of highly-polished hardwood floors. Sarah could see herself in them.

Oh happy day! What fun! Suki and Karen were in a riotous frame of mind, tickled in the belly. Suki paused in the middle of an aisle, exclaiming, as if a light suddenly blinked above her head, "Wait-just-a-darn-minute-here! Let's, let's, well Sarah, what would you think of having your hair lifted into a chignon high on the back of your head?" A lopsided grin sprang onto her face. "Wouldn't that be a knockout with your tiny features and your big brown eyes? Abe will drop dead when he sees you!"

As if reading her mind with the imprint, Karen added, "Capital!" She liked that word and didn't mind copying it. "Capital! And we'll add a small tiara-style comb in honey-beige polished bone. He's going to go nuts with jealousy. Isn't this fun? I can't wait." She was already studying a store schematic, seeking a salon.

"You need to do that." Suki caught the contagious moment. "You'd carry that hairstyle so well. This is so exciting! Are you game for it? You'll be at the zenith of your beauty." Her face lightened with anticipation—the anticipation of watching macho Abe suffer through the delirium of her desirability, while the other men published their pleasure sharing her company.

"Hmm," Sarah beamed. "There *is* a nice flavor to the idea." The music of her laughter floated on wings for the first time in four days.

Suki could hardly wait to share their plan with Doc. She covered her mouth, giggling with the trickery of it all.

CHAPTER THIRTY-EIGHT

The guys had a foursome for tennis and spent the day sweating. Abe, now showered, lay in the sun. His recent anxieties began to coil like a roll of barbed wire.

He mulled the advice he received last night from Kyle and Doc and suspected that it made sense. He never doubted that he loved Sarah; it was an unending thing for him. Since he'd cut off the engagement, he'd felt as dead as yesterday's chicken. He drifted in a nowhere abyss, lost—bereft of feelings and shut down. He hadn't quite placed Sarah into a niche in his heart next to Fabian's, but she was well on the way.

He ached when he thought of her being someone else's wife. *Wife.* There was music in the word—a symphony in sync with his very being—in sync with his lifelong aspirations for family and home. Thoughts of her wrapped him in a soft blanket of warmth. But he could not, would not change his point of view on children. He couldn't consider adoption as an option. It had to be *his* child.

The nanny he thought sounded like a brilliant idea, but that would mean nothing unless she agreed to have his child. There were a thousand good reasons to marry her, yet this one—the rejection of his children—outweighed all of them. His temples began to tighten, as if his ancestors had slipped a war bonnet on his head.

It would take a bigger man than him to admit fault in his demands. He lacked the wherewithal to stomach it. Mutiny rose in his throat at the thought. Him. Abe Miereau. Apologizing? For-get it.

Doc sat in silence next to Abe, reading the *Los Angeles Times* and basking in the sunshine. The splash of a softly flowing fountain made the day pleasant. Glancing at Abe, he could feel in his bones that he was immersed in concentration. He turned the pages quietly so as not to disturb the gentle giant in his silent deliberations. If only he could transfer by telepathy the arsenal of his life's lessons into Abe's consciousness.

Kyle and Walter snoozed on the other side of him, breathing the rhythm of a sleeping cocker spaneil.

So they walked through the beautiful January day, blessed by a high blue sky and bashful breezes.

ಸಃ

"You and Abe go on ahead to the dining room," Suki interjected from the bedroom. "I'm not quite ready, Danforth, so I'll wait for Sarah to stop by and gather me on the way down. It won't be long." Suki kept her voice light.

"Sure thing. Maybe we can winnow Kyle out into the hall to join us. Can I do anything for you before I go?" Doc had difficulty being casual, treating this as simply another dinner with the Michigan football victors.

For Doc's solicitousness of Suki, Abe was grateful, grateful they'd found each other. Never had he felt more secure in his whole life. Since breaking off with Sarah he'd been lonely, but not alone. As they moved down the hall to Kyle's suite, a tremor ran through him with the highs and lows he experienced in the past week: the successes, the heartache, the heartburn, and the indecisions all a-muddle in his mind.

"I hope you don't mind my camping in your tent while we're here." Abe moved next to Doc like a cloned tandem, heaving a weary burst of trapped air.

"Don't give it another thought, Abe. It's remarkable the funny tricks life plays on us all. The moments of happiness and disappointments we feel take us all by surprise." He recalled the happiness by which he'd been seized the day he married Suki, a whole year ago now, and the happiness he knew with Sarah. He closed his eyes, clenching his teeth. She *had* to marry Abe. Maybe tonight would set the stage.

"Sarah!" Suki exclaimed upon opening the suite door. "Look at yourself! You're going to gun Abe down with grandeur." She stood grand bait, the quarry a known factor.

Sarah was ravishing in the vanilla ice cream dress, her porcelain-like skin glowing from her shoulders and arms. Her décolleté neckline opened seductively as she moved; the high collar rolled back against her neck. Swirling around her knees, the skirt flowed gracefully. The rich brown walnut earrings swept gracefully just above her shoulders—the perfect touch for her mahogany hair pulled high into the chignon, showing her tiny ears, accenting her big eyes. Tiny wisps of hair curled incorrigibly about her temples and ears. Undisciplined wisps wandered into her neckline.

"All you need is a scepter and crown!" Suki was ecstatic with the results of their plotting. With hands on her hips, Sarah leaned nonchalantly against the doorframe impersonating a pose she'd seen of Betty Grable. She laughed, her nose crinkling in good humor and self-effacement.

"Lordy, behold the sacrificial lamb," Karen exclaimed upon arrival. "You're going to stir that young man carnivorous. His blood pressure will shoot right off the charts!"

A flicker of hope rose in Sarah's eyes; her legs grew unsteady. Whole rolls of cotton batting tightened inside her. Were they wads of excitement or apprehension? She vacillated between the two emotions in an electrical flow of synapses. "I can't help but feel that something's going to go wrong, as if a big black spider is going to bite me!"

"No spider is going to sit down beside you and frighten Miss Muffet away. But Abe will get close. Better believe it, and then you *should* feel frightened. He's going to be out of his mind with desire!" Karen warmed with the challenge, her face alight.

The ladies hesitated at the dining room, searching for the gentlemen when the maître d'hôtel came to their assistance. As they approached, the men stood to seat the ladies. Abe reflected simultaneous looks of suppressed elation, rejection, enchantment and enthrallment, and, lastly, disciplined rejection. As the mixture of emotions flashed over his face in readable phases, his jaw hardened; his eyes shadowed over.

"Whew! Look at how beautiful you ladies are. Would you be so kind as to join us lonesome, worn out men for dinner?" As prearranged, Doc, seated at the head of the table, pulled out two chairs on his left for Sarah and Suki, while Abe sat across the table from them both. Kyle held court at the other end of the table, he and Doc presiding like a couple of moneyed maharajahs.

Sarah observed that Abe deliberately ignored her, conveying a message of complete disinterest, if not disdain. She glanced at Karen, sitting next to Abe, a look that spoke of concern with his apathy. Shifting uneasily, she arranged her full skirt and toyed with her bracelets. She perceived a surge of something so inherent inside him that she ached with hopelessness.

Doc rubbed his hands together, smiling. "I think you ladies need a cocktail. Name your poison, and I don't want to hear old hemlock. This is our last night here, and it calls for a victorious celebration." Doc thought he finally discerned the flavor of the young people's disagreement: the establishment of a pecking order in the marriage. Desperate conditions require desperate measures. He'd deeply place a punt into Abe's territory so as the kid would have a spot of bother to not play it out.

While the women indulged in sherry wine, the men moved deep into the martinis again, in spite of their morning-after dues. Doc engaged Sarah in entertaining conversation not audible to the rest of the table. Doc squeezed her hand in a show of complete engrossment in every word she said. "*That* dress is a howitzer, princess!"

She exulted in the helpful glow of rapture on his face. "Danforth," she whispered conversationally, oblivious to the delight and buoyancy she instilled in him by using his given name. "Let's hope this works. It looks dubious right now." Her eyes were soft, searching his for encouragement. She gazed at Abe under lowered lashes. He wore his dress-up manners and gray ensemble of charcoal trousers and light gray sport coat, with a white turtleneck.

Abe sought Karen's attention while staying on his private wavelength, frantic to appear nonchalant. He fought his subjective state of mind—fought pain, yes. Rejected love, yes. The pleasure he always found at seeing her, yes. Anger. Yes anger at his being unprepared for her sudden display of grandeur.

Sarah felt a shiver of apprehension. The golden glow of the exquisitely appointed dining room melded into hazy characters on stage, as if she were watching from a distance. The chandeliers glittered; the candles spoke softly in bending confidences; the background chattered of silver on china.

Dinner was served up in gourmet fashion, the wine glasses never empty. Abe and Doc inhaled a chateau Briand, medium rare, along with Idaho bakers stuffed with sour cream, delicately flavored Bermuda shallots and lightly sprinkled with cilantro. An oval platter containing asparagus covered with salsa cheese sauce arrived on a sizzler.

The ladies gravitated to seafood and pasta, served with lightly grilled slices of squash brushed with butter. Kyle savored baked salmon in saffron sauce, while Walter and Anne chose chicken valdestona, the thick cheese sauce piquant. All went with the house special Waldorf salad—the celery crisp, the Spanish nuts adding the zest of salt. For dessert, they were shown selections of pistachio pudding swirled with whipped cream in tall flutes, Black Forest torte, German chocolate layer cake, cheesecakes with berry sauces and pies that boasted apples, raisins, and mixed berries.

Sarah wilted inside, dipping scallops and clams from her thick linguine in cream sauce. She couldn't shake the black spider scenario creating a burning at the back of her throat. She squeezed her stinging eyes to keep tears from telling all.

"And what will you do next spring when you graduate, Sarah? Got anything on the front burner?" Kyle grew solicitous.

She cleared her throat, hoping she didn't come off sounding like a frog. "I'll probably stay in the Milwaukee area. It's a folksy city. It'll be a management position I'm looking for. Job interviews are held in April at the college, placing ninety-five percent of all Mount Mary graduates. Come June I shall have been educated, graduated and liberated!" She didn't know how she managed to keep her voice light and confident, laughing with the delivery, albeit shaky.

"That's impressive," Kyle agreed. His smile and attention tilled like a gift.

Doc captured Sarah's hand and kissed the back of it, raising his eyes to meet hers. "If she were a nurse, I'd capture her talents in a minute. What say you, lovely lady, that we have this dance?" His eyes mated with hers in assurance.

Sarah's breathy laugh hurt Abe's ears. He shot her a quick glance, surprised at Doc's obvious advances. The band swung into, "It's Been a Long, Long Time." Quickly, he saved himself from staring by inviting Suki to dance. He allowed his strong hands to feather over her back, having missed the warmth of a woman for too long.

Doc held Sarah tightly, her body fitting up against his like putty on a pane as they moved nimbly to the music of the band. "You are an absolute knockout tonight, Sarah!" he whispered down at her. His voice held a brace of huskiness. "Do you think we're making any progress?" he murmured softly, bending and breathing on her neck

"Unlike his usual self, he's being hard to read. So far, he seems unscathed." Sarah felt Doc's warmth. Somehow, she liked it—his pleasure excited her as if his large warm hands had encircled her heart, squeezing it.

"You are *so* seductive. Strange how having you has oxygenated my desire for Suki. But *you* too I would support in style, Sarah. Abe wants you, however, so I need to cease that line of thinking. So you see I have an ulterior motive in mending the fences between you and Abe." He smiled down on her, his voice caring.

She felt at ease with this man, her friend. She fought a sinking desire to lie with him again, beyond the bargain they had struck. Maybe she'd have less heartache as his lady-in-waiting than with Abe taking his pleasures at no heed to her own.

"You'll do just fine, Sarah," he said with a rueful smile. She persevered as someone with whom a man could fly away and get lost for all eternity. "I thrilled making love to you, Sarah," he breathed against her ear. "Politics, power, money, sex and scandal are historical bedfellows. I would willingly share them all with you," he announced, with that wry twist of his lips which endeared him to her. Hit suddenly by an overpowering revelation, Doc realized that the clock ticked on his dream of many years. He was gripped by a stab of sorrow as deep as a grave.

He knew well that Abe was cognizant of the fact that Sarah was now a free agent. He was equally disturbed, however, as to whether this commenced the beginning of something for him or the end of everything. If this ran revenge for the girls, it triggered trouble with a capital "T" for him. He had entirely too much at stake in this game.

Abe watched in his peripheral vision as Sarah returned to the table and arranged her flowing skirt before sitting down, sharing a whispered confidence with Doc. Suddenly, he felt a possessive indignation coarse through him, the caveman defending his domicile. He wished now he had a spare arrow in his quiver, but he'd shot them all. He raised a brow in lofty disregard.

Sarah sensed him studying her—felt the faintest gleanings of cautious optimism in terms of the electricity emanating from him. At oneness with his soul, she felt his emotions, sometimes second-guessing his actions before he made a move.

Abe clenched his teeth. He'd chosen to exit this relationship. She wasn't his any longer. Goddamn right she wasn't! She hadn't even worn his topaz tonight. It would have looked so nice with that dress. His engagement ring must be sitting abandoned on her dresser, because she sure as hell didn't have it on. His eyes were dark and dangerous. She'd probably thrown the fuckin' thing away. She'd cut the ties, as he had when he walked out on her. Walked out on her, thousands of miles from home and family. Perhaps he could disappear into the Pasadena morning mist tomorrow.

He found himself a compilation of mixed emotions as he observed Kyle posing Sarah to dance. Moving her chair back, he assisted her rising and drew her to the dance floor while sharing a close comment.

Abe now shot a quick glimpse at Doc, who watched the couple with intentness born of interest and admiration. Abe felt that old visceral savagery that engulfed him whenever someone else looked at Sarah. Like the time he nearly killed Neil Izcik for undressing her with his eyes—ogling her breasts!

"Would you like to dance, Karen?" Abe hissed softly, but politely. A turnabout is fair play. The effort was strange and cumbersome to him, to ask another man's wife to dance. He was hesitant, his mind a tangled mess, but he managed to pull it off.

The raw feelings in Abe's voice startled Karen, but since she had plotted as one of the culprits subtly manipulating him, she agreed. "That would be so nice, Abe. Thank you." She had the distinct feeling that he walked a tight rope ready to snap. She lowered her eyes, delighting in the wealth and comfort of victory.

He flashed his best incandescent smile. Karen, his mentor, stood probably not more than five feet two inches tall, but as warm and cuddly as a fuzzy bear. He knew that Kyle worshiped her. They had such a nice relationship. "I'll Be

Seeing You" played slowly with mellowness, the haunting lyrics the product of the war. He refused to take his eyes off Kreiler, his head bent close to Sarah's, where they conversed intently.

Abe's eyes took on a strange darkness. He'd need to have ice in his heart to not care. His stomach churned with primitive jealousy. He considered it too late to avoid the pain he'd inflicted upon himself, but why in the hell did it get worse instead of better? To his remorse, he still wanted his childhood sweetheart. Desperately. What's more and even worse, he still loved her. Deeply. A great ball grew in his throat.

Doc studied him covertly, astonished at how rapidly Abe roared to flash point. He had handled jealousy himself, and not always very well. He judged this the first example, however, that he'd actually observed the emotion in his son. He estimated it time to stop this charade before Abe's Sioux inclinations gave way to something violent. He might not want her, but by God, he wanted no one else to have her either.

As they sat down, "Moonlight Serenade" struck up, the plaintive clarinets and sax reaching deeply into Abe's memory reserve of the many times he and Sarah had danced to that song. It stirred him irreversibly. Without a word, he pushed back his chair, walked around the table and wrested Sarah by the wrist with a come-along assertive jerk, wrenching her out of the chair, her feet hardly keeping up with her legs.

She tucked her free hand into the folds of her skirt to hide the fact that it shook. In total surprise at the caveman effrontery, her mouth dropped open, but her sense of isolation and abandonment underwent relief. But did she really want to dance with him? So much hurt had crowded into her life, her body became electrified and adrenaline flowed to stave off further attacks.

Abe took no delight in feeling her frightened body trembling as he escorted her to the dance floor. Folding her softly and gently into his arms, he made a slight sound from deep within himself. His woman. She felt so good. "What are you remembering?" he asked in a dangerously soft voice, breathing hard into her hair, his eyes imploring.

"All the good times we had dancing to this song when times were better and we were more understanding of each other."

She didn't want to cry. She wouldn't cry. She bit her lip.

Abe mentally gathered together all the disintegration of the past five days. The fallout created a whirlwind of dust and debris of broken commitments. He felt her close to him, fitting him like a packaged set of bookends, felt the vitality of her heartbeat, the warmth of her body and saw the beauty of this miracle he held. How he'd waited for her, fought for her, thrilled with the wonder of her. He released her and looked into her depthless brown eyes. What he saw was hurt. All the hurt he'd heaped upon her in the last week. "We're going back to the table. Get your bag. We're leaving."

"What?" Her tone skeptical, she knew him for what he was—fiery, vindictive, and impulsive. She met his gaze and glimpsed guilt rising in his wonderful eyes.

"Just do it." His words were hard and demanding.

Again he clutched her by the wrist, dragged her back to the table as if she were the prize steer from the county fair. Without a word, he allowed her two seconds to grab her purse and keep up with him as he dragged her from the room. Abe wasn't sure how to proceed with reconciling with his lifelong love, but he had done nothing so far, and sure as hell, nothing wasn't good enough.

From those remaining at the table there raised a burst of applause. Abe never stopped, hesitated or looked back. Sarah jogged, hard pressed to keep up with him.

"The Quiet Man," Suki said, looking around the table for confirmation.

Nodding, Kyle said, "'Come into my parlor,' said the spider to the fly."

"Allow me to show you my etchings," Karen retorted, getting into the word game.

"Near-naked Neanderthal." Doc grinned, rubbing his face.

Sighing deeply, he looked up to heaven, for the coldness of the grave had deserted him as quietly as it had arrived.

CHAPTER THIRTY-NINE

Sarah secured firmly by the wrist, Abe remained silent on the elevator, tormented as a rabbit with an earache. With a smooth swish, the doors opened. The lift softly chimed upon reaching the fourth floor. As he led her down the long passage to her suite next to Doc's, she dragged at his hands as she moved through a vacuum of soft carpeting and hushed aura. Did he lead her to her death? Shakily, she pilfered her purse in an attempt to find her room key, when she caught the wall behind her as Abe pinned her, sending the purse and contents flying across the hall. She could read the anger in his eyes as he leaned hard into her, his mouth coming down on hers in a claiming kiss, wantonly working his mouth over hers, taking and taking. He worked his hand into her hair to better angle her head, pressing it against the wall. All you could see of Sarah was her bouffant skirt.

She squeaked a protest, but it was too late. His mouth stayed closed over hers, cutting off any objections she may have proffered. Hot, wet and invasive, his tongue slid inside, to another squeak. Sarah's eyes flew open upon hearing the primal sound, and realized it had emerged from deep within her own being.

It broke Abe's bestial attack on Sarah, coming up for air, his eyes at half-mast. She ran the back of her hand over her mouth, wiping away with disgust his presumptuous kiss, expecting all to be forgiven at *his* time and *his* pace. He retrieved the key from the floor and roughly opened the door. Retrieving her purse and contents, she had a clear and present feeling that had the door not opened readily; he'd have broken it down.

It couldn't be. Dèjá vu! Scattered about the room bloomed dozens of roses and a chilled magnum of Dom Perignon.

Once inside the room, Abe slammed the door shut, driving home the bolt and chaining it. Staring, grim and dark, he grabbed her hard, her head snapping back, maneuvering her against him, making demands with his penetrating mouth.

Releasing his hold, she shoved him heavily away, her hand sliding across her mouth once again—her hand that he caught by the wrist.

"What is this, Sarah?" He breathed with a theatrical sigh. "You no longer find my kisses tasteful? Is this whole thing a plot...roses and champagne?" His eyes were on fire. "Huh? Tell me! All I've done is kissed you. That's not even half of what I want to do."

His emotions were a hurricane of intense jealousy, joy, anger and apologies. And love. Although he had a jackrabbit temper, she had to know how much he loved her. She had to know how much he cared. He wanted her so badly that he ached all over. *But did she know? Did she really know? Have you ever bothered to tell her? How would she know? You're such a stiff ass.* He opened his mouth to come to terms with her, but never gained that latitude.

Without as much as a by-your-leave, she made a fist and punched him in the stomach. Hard. She'd been breathless when he released her. "It wasn't a scheme in the dark terms you mean!" A half-sob escaped her lips, staring terrified up into his eyes. "I didn't know about the roses and champagne!" she said, gesturing wildly. Would he enter into one of his bubbles and tear off her clothes? Was *he* the big black spider?

Holding his stomach at all the sizzle and no meat in the lightweight punch, he blanched at the terror in her eyes—unconcealed, daunting terror—of him. She backed up to an end table where she grasped a heavy glass ashtray. Before she could wield it at him, he advanced receiver-fast upon her, encircling her arms with a firm grip, pulling her to him again. His mouth gained on hers in contrition.

"Christ, Sarah. I'm not going to beat you, if that's what you think." His voice was thick with passion, and distant, as if coming from someone else. "I've been so concerned about you that I can hardly focus on anything else. I don't know how I got through that game Thursday," he whispered, not trusting his voice. He could feel her breasts cushioned against his chest, her body quaking like the aspens at the Nahma beach.

She backed away from him while she could, her eyes glaring, her heart doing gymnastics from real or imagined jeopardy, but he caught her hand, kissing the palm and lingering, his eyes raising to meet hers.

His eyes. What did she read in them? Disbelief at her rejections? Anger? No. Maybe amusement? This aroused stifling indignation to a point of stiffening. With concentration, she moved to the champagne but clutched the heavy ashtray in her hand.

Her unfeigned fear had him completely stymied. A lump choked back in his throat and a tear held near overflowing at the bottom of each eyelid. She feared him! Just below the surface, he felt the tremors of terror flowing like a spring creek. How could he quell this hostility he'd created? The problem was his alone to solve.

"Will you open this Perignon," she said to distract him, measuring the distance between her and the phone. "I think it's so terrific. Doc did this for us again," she said, her lightness a lie. "Think so?" The room swam with sensually perfumed reality. Her eyes swept the nuances of magenta, white, pink, fuchsia, yellow and coral roses all over the room, and back at him, checking his stance. Was it relaxed or panther-like?

Without a word, Abe opened the magnum. She found herself magnetically drawn to the flex and fall of his muscles rippling through his sport coat as he went about the trivial business, pouring two long-stemmed glasses of the sparkling wine. Masculinity and assertiveness proved spicy as an unexpected flood of warmth encircled her body. Could fear be diluted to become passion? She gripped herself tightly.

"Sarah. You sit over there," he said pointing to a chair directly across from him near the French doors, and I'll sit here, because when I get close to you I lose my good judgment. We need to do a little thawing. I don't want to ever again give you cause to look at me with such terror. What I want for the rest of my life is to have you look at me with the love and warmth I used to see in your eyes." The reverberations of his voice forced from a choked throat.

He watched her sit in the chair, her full-circle skirt embracing her legs and thighs caressingly and her bronze Cinderella slippers accenting her gazelle ankles. He wound up nuts again. Concentrating fiercely, he jousted her right into his bubble where there hushed complete silence. Total silence. Just him and her and total, complete, engulfing silence. He wanted to float away with her to some Wonderful World of Oz where there were no worries, no cares, and no differences. No Ice Ages. His fantasy bubble had gotten him as far as he was today. Why shouldn't he capture her and take her inside with him, reinforce the sides and never let her out?

Passing her a glass of champagne, he continued his white knight gallantry. "Your servant, Milady. Talk to me of your qualms about marriage and children." He sat, crossing his long legs in a confident manner, exhibiting a servile attentiveness. He'd best not make any sudden moves or she would fly out the door and he'd lose her forever. He knew that all right, and he observed how her fingers shook as she lifted the flute, horror hidden in her eyes. He fought the urge to fall upon her, protect her, and remove the stricken storm clouds from her eyes.

Wary and observing him over the rim of her glass, she became nonetheless smitten with his cocky posture, her eyes wide with wonder. Uncertainty surrounded her as to the depth of his nurturing staying power. In dribs and drabs she spoke, giving only surgical slices of her real feelings—bracing herself for a tirade. Her embryonic smidgens of information poked only a small hole into the dam of her pent up emotions. She quivered with the slimness of the thin ice on which she skated. Would he become volatile and slam out of her life once more? Had he become inflexible to her feelings?

As she proceeded, without interruptions from him, the dam slowly cracked, and she spilled forth her fears and anxieties, while he listened—he *listened*. He listened to her fear of carrying a child for nine months—her terror of childbirth. He listened to her chilling at never having a minute to herself. He heard her horror and dread of Tay-Sachs disease. He understood her logic of having devoted four years to a degree in Business Administration and never getting a chance to spread her wings and fly. Until, at last, her throat lumped over, making it impossible to speak.

Only someone as unresponsive as a doorknob, like himself, could not have heard what she'd been trying to tell him forever. Settling his glass on an end table, he smoothly moved to her, kneeling on the floor, pulling her closer to him, resting his lips on her forehead, and stroking the warm curls near her temples. Sensually, he ran his thumbs into the soft spot behind her ears.

"What would it take, Sarah, to make you love me again as you did before?" His voice was tight with tears he was ashamed to shed. "Can you ever forgive me for being such an ass?" he whispered, struggling with words. "You're my life. You're my daily need, like bread. I understand that I've been starving our relationship with a complete lack of understanding. Please say you'll forgive me and wear my ring again." He should have *felt* the truth of what she spoke, felt it in his heart.

He inhaled the sweet fragrance of the dampness forming near her temples, in her wispy curls. He looked straight up at the ceiling for a moment to gain his composure. Then, pulling away and holding her by the shoulders. "Give me another chance," he sighed, his eyes heartbreakingly beseeching.

She nodded her head, too at-odds to speak, too afraid to test her voice. She heard the yearning in his voice, saw it in his eyes.

Hurting tears flooded her beautiful eyes. His eyes. The light of his life. He put his hands to either side of her face and kissed them. Kissed her lightly and pleasantly on the mouth without pushing or demanding. "I want you, Sarah. Forever. You're mine."

"I don't know, Abe..."

"Where is it?" he asked, holding her from him while yet kneeling on the floor. "What did you do with it? The ring? You didn't throw it away?" He was aware that his voice reached a feverish pitch, the words tumbling like marbles out of a bag.

She nodded toward the bed stand. Opening the drawer, he found the ring in its original box, tucked neatly back into its crevice, radiating with a regal measure of happiness—flawless. Like Sarah. A thrill ran through him, a hypnotic thrill, one holding great promise, mesmerized by the shining facets of the ring.

Kneeling again in front of her, he slipped the ring onto her finger, kissing it, kissing her hand, kissing her arm, collecting her finally to him in a rush, and whispered. "Sarah, will you marry me anyway—even after all my stupidity?"

She shook her head yes, not yet trusting her voice, still dabbing her endless tears with a tissue. He physically lurched, laying his head in her lap, where she stroked his hair, his beautiful black hair. A satisfied groan escaped from deep within him. His breath felt warm on her legs. His hands ran up the length of her hose, feeling her ankles, her knees, her thighs. "I love you so desperately," he murmured as if to himself.

Pulling her to her feet, he had her out of the chair, crushing her to him. Then leading her, he moved to the bow window to show her where the moon had crept up over the San Gabriel Mountains, when her heel caught on the carpet and she foundered. She caught at him for support, which he readily held available for her, experiencing incredible pleasure at her need of him. So pleasured, he swooped her up and carried her. Sitting on the window seat, his long legs stretched out, he placed her in between them. Her back to him, his arms around her to share the moment of mystical moonlight and forgiveness that swelled within him. But oh, he knew where his treasure lay now.

"God, how I love you Sarah! You are my fifth appendage, my indispensable one," he whispered softly against her ear as they watched the rounded summits become defined with the moonlight. Soft, wayward clouds hazed the edges of the picture at will. He'd never forget the scene—engraved indelibly on his eidetic memory. *Click.*

His encircling hands moved to her face, felt her eyes, still wet, lingering on her ears, her lips tender and puffed from crying because of the pain that he had interjected into her life. With a sense of wonder, he reminded himself how lucky he was to have her back, to have had her back so many times when they had distanced themselves from each other all due to his unbending values. *The world according to Abe.* In a wild, cascading surge of love, he laid his forehead on her back, groaning with unconcealed love, contrition and endearment.

"Sarah," he said, his voice raw, "you could have me at your feet, begging for forgiveness every day for the rest of my life." He whispered, nuzzling beneath her ear.

She shook her head slowly back and forth, unable to get words past the lump in her throat. As if reading her mind, he kissed her hand, holding it to his cheek. His large hand slid onto her shoulder under the bodice of her low-lapelled dress, massaging her with his fingers. The heel of his callused hand pressured her breast. At first he pressed lightly, promising himself to be gentle, then clutching more firmly as bolts of pleasure broke through his body.

Turning to look at him, she found his eyes alight, his smile soft, melting away a ton of ice, which had built up in her reservoir of disfavor of him. This time, the lump in her throat ran second place to the giant leap of her heart.

"This dress has been driving me out of my skull all night. Every time you moved, your lapels gapped and all eyes were drawn to the enticement. I didn't miss any of it. I was so sinkin' jealous," his teeth gritted. "I wanted to knock them into the middle of next week! I don't want you to ever wear that dress again." His eyes grew dark.

"Abe. You don't mean that!" She wondered, however, how bad his thoughts were when they stirred something inside her—something magical, exotic and welcome. She felt his warm breath in her ears, his hair against her cheeks.

"Damn it, Sarah. Don't ever do that to me again. I nearly went nuts, sitting there pretending that it didn't bother me. You're my woman, just mine. I don't want someone else preying on you!" He shouted, surprising himself. Never had a woman made him so angry. "Every time I think of Kyle and Doc dancing with you as if you were open market goods, I want to knock them both silly." He reached for her chin, nudging her face back toward him where he could taste her cheeks, her ears, gaze into her beautiful eyes.

Her heart pulsed like quicksilver deep within her, feeling his groin growing warm on her back. Her blood pressure skyrocketed—her breath coming in short spurts. "Abe, I want to take a shower after dancing all evening. Maybe you could shave—that is, it might be a good idea. You have five o'clock shadow already. That is…if you don't…" Her voice searched, not wanting to nettle him.

"For cryin' out loud, Sarah," he laughed, deep and hardy. "I get the idea. Okay, I'll shave while you're taking a shower," he said, laughing, chucking her cheek and chin.

While Sarah fussed with setting out her nightgown, she watched him remove his clothing, hanging them in the closet next to hers. His sport coat, his trousers and his shoes "plop, plop." His shirt and tie were removed with masculine and masterful artistry. Sarah felt quaintness in his tidiness and the nuance of the moment as an aphrodisiac. A persistent feeling of pleasure began to pervade her as thrills darted the length of her legs and into her lower abdomen. For the first time in their relationship, she really wanted to give of herself.

Stepping out of the shower, her body warm and receptive, she felt richly atmospheric, her heart rising into her throat. When she came out of the bathroom, wearing her pale-pink chiffon nightgown, he'd be able to see her silhouette with the bathroom light behind her. With the thrill of it all, she knew she must be shameless.

Deep brown eyes devoured her as she moved to have another glass of champagne while he took his shower. The layered gown flowed as she walked, transforming her into a gossamer goddess, her hair released from the chignon.

This is what it was all about. You take the gift wrap off your woman and she's even more beautiful. Clad only in a pair of jockeys, he wanted to run and tackle her, bring her down and hold her until someone pulled him off and called excessive force. After all these years of knowing her, his hunger had never been greater. He thirsted so powerfully that it made him as taut as his childhood slingshot.

She listened to the lulling sound of the shower, the bathroom door open as usual. Abe never explained his actions, but he never complained when she opposed them either. He delivered himself in all situations—a study of dynamo energy in motion. The guise of anything other than what he was would have been a betrayal of his very spirit.

He came out of the shower, silhouetted in his stark nakedness, unashamed.

In the half-light of the room, Sarah gazed at him—the forest of hair on his chest, fading to timberline near his waist, with reforestation over his abdomen. His big hands and the coiling hair on his muscled rangy legs curled her anticipation.

Moving to the Perignon, he joined her in another glass of the magnum.

"To us, Sarah, to us forever, you and I. The way it's always been and always will be." He lightly toasted his glass to hers, his body within inches of her, so phenomenal that she shrank into the chair.

Into his dazed eyes, she raised her splendid glance, shining warm and delicious.

Thrills coursed through her with his need, thrills like a million searching tentacles.

He should never have found fault with this beautiful nymph. "No other woman lights a fire under me like you do, Sarah," his voice was a heated whisper.

"Abe," she said, sulking, "I prefer that you stop seeing other women." Her eyes registered disillusionment.

"I can't, Sarah. It's a virtually impossible task. I'm not celibate; I need to have a woman regularly. It's a release for me. They're all fleeting pleasures, whereas you're the keeper. I heat to 'cook' just looking at you. I want to love you. Roll you up and put you in my pocket. Keep you like a dog burying a bone, which he can dig up repeatedly."

"Abe! That's not a very flattering analogy."

"Probably not. But you're this dog's favorite."

Reaching out with one hand, she carefully and lightly touched him with her index finger. The winds of passion had whipped Abe into a ferocious boil, alive and pulsing. His head flipped back, gasping.

She withdrew her hand from this frightening new territory, practically uncharted.

"I need you to be my wife and lover. Don't say no ever again. Say yes, yes, yes," he whispered.

She thrilled to his heated entreaties.

"Let's slip into bed," he groaned from deep within his throat. "I want your whole body near me." He took both of her hands, assisting her out of the chair. Burying his face in her neck, he was unable to speak. His hands feathered the satin of her skin while he worked at her lustrous shoulders under the straps of her nightgown, his breath warm on her ears as he sucked them between his teeth. Effortlessly, he lifted her and carried her into the suite bedroom. Drawing down the top sheet with one hand, he placed her beneath him.

Studying him closely as he walked around the bed, she thought maybe this would be her last chance to run, to fly to Suki or Karen, to find help. She'd had no satisfying bodily common cause with him so far. It had been too forceful—too frightening.

"C'mon, Sarah. I'm not going to hurt you. I'll lie by you, that's all," he said, as if he were reading her mind. In a moment, she found herself beside him, his tawny skin warm, provoking her pendulum of productivity into spasms swinging rhythmically across her abdomen, measuring time and space deliciously. Gathering the pink fluff of her near him, he drew her over to lie in his arms. She smelled so good—clean—soapy. So soft.

He kissed her hair that fell softly around her face and chin. Finding her mouth, he kissed her lightly, her ears, her forehead, her cheeks and then her mouth again. Wrenching his mouth away, he whispered under his breath as if someone else were listening, all the while his hands sent messages up and down her spine.

After a long and thoughtful pause, he whispered, "Love you, babe." That was an understatement; he craved her. "Need you all the time." His lips lightly brushed her mouth while mouthing words she needed to hear. She tasted sweet, the way he remembered her, had remembered so many times, like sustenance. "I'm sorry, so very sorry for all the pain I caused you this week." He surprised himself that he found the courage to humble himself. "How beautiful you are. I'm so Goddamn jealous of you, Sarah. Don't push associations with any men. I'll fucking kill them." His lips were on fire, moving to the corner of her mouth.

"You were my special treasure at the Rose Bowl—no one else was as important to me as you." His tongue grazed over her cheek, her ear, making a wet sound. "I want you more than anything else in the world. Nothing else matters, just possessing you." His hands caressed her skin, like a merchant testing the tensile strength of a bolt of silk.

Words ran from him like flimsies of fantasy, one following the other. He found the corner of her mouth again, sticking the tip of his tongue in lightly. He lingered at her neck, feeling her pulse beating wildly, his hands caressing her body, working her chiffon nightgown over her thighs, clumping the fabric, smelling it. "I do love you." He managed a smile as he smoothed her hair back over an ear. Palming the privacy of her, his breath came fast. "I've loved you forever." Spreading her arms wide, he tongued the length of her arms, leaning his chest on hers teasingly, the hair barely brushing her upper breasts.

"You'll soon be Mrs. Miereau," he said from deep within his throat. "Mine."

The words sent heady titillations under her skin where he kissed, his tongue making whorls, his thumbs making circles. The thought of being Mrs. Miereau relaxed her beyond anything he could have said—relaxed her to a surrender of high caliber proportions. She loved having her arms spread out for his conquest. Big hands that could hold a football, paint a picture, protect her, were slowly setting her body on fire.

He sought her mouth with his tongue, seeking satisfaction. Thrusting. Searching. Exploring. Working a rhythm. He pulled the spaghetti straps of her gown off her shoulders. She shook with desire, with anticipation. A guttural sound tore from her throat.

She lurched with the sensations spreading throughout her whole body and hoped that she didn't start shaking and embarrass herself with the outward signs of her enrapturement. She breathed rapidly, her nostrils flaring, her cheeks red.

"Sarah Miereau?"

"Hmmm?"

"You *will* suckle my son with these breasts. You *will*. You *will* be my wife, bear my son, and nourish him like a good mother. And you *will* love every minute of it."

"Yes, Abe. Yes!" She steadied in a burning flow of unstable magma, warm and responding to his aggressive lovemaking. She pushed her body into his, swaying sinuously, making her marriageable to him.

Abe was bewitched. He'd thought that he would have another Armageddon on his hands tonight. She'd been harder to reach than Hulk's air outs. What a woman! He might be staying home after they were married after all. He'd been resigned that she would be the mother of his children, but he'd need to get good sex somewhere else.

He groaned with the joy of her flooding him. He'd disciplined himself with the control to be patient. No longer could he wait. "Sarah, you taste so good. You smell so good." He pulled the nightgown over the top of her head. His voice hoarse and low, he murmured, "Now, Sarah."

Surprise sprang to her eyes. "Ohhh," she gasped as she worked her hands into his chest hair, running it between her fingers. He reached for fulfillment in a state of unbridled abandon, occupying another planet, a planet of exotic pleasure and thrills. No one else existed. No one else in the whole world ever gave him an experience such as this woman. He rambled on in half sentences, "Marry me, Sarah. Wear my ring. Be my woman. Incubate my children. Unnhh," he grunted in Precambrian fashion.

The anxieties of the past week washed away and he felt the peace of fulfillment.

"I love you so much, Abe," the words choked from her, "but please take good care of me. You frighten me so at times."

Slowly he rolled her to her side and lay near her, her head warm against his chest. His heart raced wildly—the denouement of his angst came full circle to resolution. It was as if the seed he broadcast tonight had been predestined.

"How long will you lay here with me, Sarah, before you wash away my son?" He whispered in her ear, still breathing hard. The deepest part of him feared a reply.

"Just five minutes." She spoke softly but firmly, spinning back to reality.

"Then I'll take the five minutes," he said, holding her tightly against the length of his body, the adamancy of her convictions settling in.

Silence fell upon the room. The fragrance of roses permeated every corner.

"Abe?"

"Yes," he said quietly.

"I'm exhausted. I'm getting terribly sleepy. I think I'd better move now and not wait five minutes," she said, snuggling into his shoulder.

"Shhh, Sarah, lie still. Five minutes isn't very long, babe. I love holding you next to me in this moment," he said, gently kissing her cheek.

"Mmm." The somnolence and security of his voice lulled her to sleep.

In minutes, Abe heard the regular breathing of her asleep in his arms.

He quivered with wild imaginings as he held her closely, his whole body protecting what he had planted. If he had to lie there all night in that position, he would. Every minute counted—the longer the better. He slowly and carefully raised the back of his hand to wipe away the tears, which freely flowed down his cheeks. His Sioux Indian spirits had intervened to create for him the higher ecstasy of creation.

His son. Yes! His very own son!! He kissed her forehead. His woman... Never had he known such happiness.

Never.

CHAPTER FORTY

June 18, 1948

How excited he'd been when he'd called Sarah in February just for a chat. Yeah, sure! Not that he hadn't called her before that. But by now, well...she should be ready to kill him or acquiesce to her situation, which, he hoped would be positive.

"How are ya, little lady?" His John Wayne delivery had never been better. "I hope you're staying warm. It's cold as hell here—snowing and blowing, and I'm tired of living alone." His eyes darted from one side to the other, wondering, getting wider with anticipation by the minute.

"I guess I am too, Abe, but I'm still not as alone as you are. This place is wallowing with women. It's almost time for me to graduate. *If* I graduate," she added.

"I sense a problem. Anything I can do to help?" His eyes slipped to the corner then rolled, an amused wildness leaping into them.

"You, my good man, have done enough already! I'm pregnant! A tidal wave of nausea washes over me in the morning. I'm walking through my classes as if I'm caught in a cobweb. I'm hoping no one notices how dragged out and listless I am."

Abe felt as if he was strangling. A harsh, choking sound erupted.

"All I want to do is sleep, and it's your fault, Abe Miereau!" Her voice was stiff.

A muscle in Abe's jaw flexed violently, but her words spread over him like pleasant rain on a hot day. As it concerned him, the only rebuttal shouted *Yes!* Instead, he opted for propriety. "I'm sorry you don't feel well."

She was with child! He knew he could do it, if he could get her to lie still long enough. He viewed it as somewhat crummy, the way he'd carried it off, but a guy had to do what a guy had to do. He'd anticipated that she'd explode into a diatribe of blue-air. So far, so good.

"I want you to know that I'm fired up by your pregnancy, however. How many monthly cycles have you missed?" *Abe, you can count?* He scolded his gut. Yeah, but he needed to encourage her conversation, show some interest. He held his breath.

"Two, so it's definite. I'll see Doc during Easter break. He'll confirm it and give me a due date. This is so embarrassing, Abe. Would you consider getting married before June? We could just meet somewhere and make it official."

His heart expanded and warmed. "No way, lady." He rolled his head around his shoulders with pride. "I want my bride to look pregnant on our wedding day. I want everyone to know that I claimed you a long time ago, and planted a boy seed. It's my privilege as a Sioux. I want everyone to look at you as my property, so I can puff up my chest and beat on it!" The last he added with his rich laugh, albeit blasé.

She could imagine his rascally smile, his dark eyes ablaze, his joy jumping all encompassing and unrestrained.

"Scratch it, Abe. Be serious." A few beats separated the words. "It's going to be embarrassing for my family and me. We don't practice your cultural beliefs. A white wedding gown is even out of the question." Her voice clearly sagged with the admission.

He knew she was sulking. "What's the difference what color you wear, Sarah? The important thing is that I love you, and we're going to be married!" He felt as if his stomach had been girdled and tied.

"Abe, I love you too, but I really don't know why. You're a bully and a tyrant." Through the telephone lines, he could visualize the pout on her face—her eyes snapping.

"Ah, but honey, you like it that way, don't you? I'll call again soon. I can't tell you how happy I am." His toes curled up with pleasure. The spirits of his dead ancestors kept his determination alive, and he would now continue his lineage. The ancient Sioux lore was alive and well, and he could easily buy into what the mystical visions had revealed to him.

※

Now home in Nahma and getting wedding-ready, reality settled in. He had a future filled with fantastic football, a baby boy on the way—and a beautiful wife. He had built himself eternal reminiscences and savored the thoughts like fine wine, the after-taste as good as the vintage.

He wished Fabian could see all this. He'd never believe it. He moved onto the front porch. A fresh breeze circled the porch and crept inside his shirt, stirring the collar against his neck and billowing the shoulders and sleeves like God's own coolant.

Suddenly, he found himself distracted. In his peripheral vision, he saw a movement—a sea gull feather ethereally floated to the ground, gently landing on the curious summer grass. With ghost-like carriage, he retrieved the feather, caressing it, bringing it into the house and pressing it between the pages of Fabian's Holy Bible.

He was here.

I've had dessert, Dad, he communicated with Fabian. The quiet quality of the thoughts arrested him. *It was delicious. She's a day in May for the rest of my life. She's mine. I'm glad you approve.* Abe felt the brutal stab of grief that accompanied the memory of his loss. Not able to quite lock it away and seal it, Abe stood quietly, his thoughts screaming around him. After more than six years, the intense pain of Fabian's loss ate at him like a cancer cruising on healthy pink cells. He heard himself swallow, as famished and empty as the day his father had died. He dried his eyes on a kitchen towel.

Examining his surroundings, he grew pinioned with a stab of gratitude for Mrs. Hebert, who had cleaned the house. Everything sparkled. He found fresh sheets on the bed, and the curtains washed and starched. The windows were squeaky clean.

Upon arriving home late Monday night, Abe was greeted by the smell of fresh-blown lake air—the house alive with the far-reaching fragrances of early summer. On the kitchen table, in one of Fabian's mason jars, he spotted a large bouquet of lilacs just like when he was a kid. The years melted away as though he'd never left. He felt that kindergarten choke taking charge and imagined the smell of fresh coffee perking on the back of the kitchen range.

Abe sped upstairs to his old bedroom drinking in the flood of memories—memories of waking at four in the morning in the throes of a dream about Sarah, and wondering what in the hell had happened. His heart jammed his rib cage as thoughts washed over him with the anxieties of youth. If time existed as the fourth dimension, then he'd slipped back into a warp of realism he didn't imagine possible.

The sound of Fabian's voice in the morning returned to him, the radio announcing World War II in tones that chilled his very being, raising the hair on his arms. The Saturday Night Barndance out of WLS in Chicago was playing. His fingers pulled up tightly to form a fist.

Old Beach Road was cheerful, a fruitful land bathed in radiant benevolent sunlight, a landscape painted by a peaceful artist. Dressed in a bright red shirt, chinos and sneakers, on Tuesday morning, he had sought out the Savins. Running up their front porch steps, he caught a cocktail of flower scents from the planters that sat staggered on the porch railing, filled with alyssum, moss rose, and petunias.

Hearing his thudding feet, Sarah had the door open. My God, she was beautiful, vibrant and alive. He did a quick mental review of the number of months since last he had laid with her. He expected to find her great with child, but she hardly had any tummy at all. A dampened sense of enthusiasm settled upon him.

Sarah grew uncomfortable under Abe's scrutiny, her eyes worried. There hovered about him a strain of metallic, the bleed-through of his people's tragic history. She needed to talk to Doc about that.

Abe remained strangled in his own umbilical cord of pride, tied to this woman, in the fact that she carried his child, but she didn't even *look* it. What the hell happened?

Ma and Sarah were enthusiastic in their greetings; hugs and kisses prevailed. Abe squeezed Sarah's arm with enthusiasm, his face glowing. This was the first time in years that he'd been so well received in the Savin household without the deeply lined face and the wild white hair of Max looming feral.

He settled in a kitchen chair with the air of someone who had dropped in to pass the time of day, clasping his hands on the table. Early morning sunshine filtered in through the large kitchen window. From the white birch in the yard, dancing patterns played on the cupboards and floor. Ma and Sarah both talked at the same time, bringing him up to speed on the wedding day plans.

The wedding breakfast for more than one hundred out-of-town guests would be held at the Clubhouse immediately following the ceremony. In addition, the Who's Who of the town itself would be there, which Abe decided included nearly everyone. That count beefed up the chow line to more than two hundred and fifty, he guessed. His eyes widened when he encompassed the enormity of the plans.

The four o'clock reception and buffet would take place at the Clubhouse also, followed by a dance in the gymnasium, which had already been decorated by Sarah's high school friends, Betsy Hebert and Mary Nolan, who were her attendants.

"Where are your groomsmen, Abe?" Sarah's eyebrows rose.

"They'll be here Friday. Bob Chapin and Bruce Hulk will both be staying at the hotel, returning downstate on Sunday. I arranged to have their wedding duds delivered to the hotel." He had difficulty averting his eyes from Sarah's belly.

"I'm very proud to have you for my son-in-law," Ma said, giving him a hug. "So many arrangements you've made by long distance, but everything is falling right into place." She smiled warmly.

Not accustomed to hearing praise from the Savins applied salve to the wound he felt at Sarah's slimness. Doubt grew in him. Maybe, just maybe, there *was* no baby on the way! Sometimes, what *should be* is not in reality what *is*. He felt somewhat like a voyeur, sneaking glances at her midsection. His hand massaged the back of his neck.

He returned Ma's conjectures with sincere eyes. He couldn't believe that he'd pleased her so tremendously by simply tending to necessities. His mind came alive with echoes of long-ago memories when his approval rating had generated zip at the Savin's.

"It seems that everything is under control except the bar," Ma said. "There should be limited liquor at the breakfast, but full accommodations at the reception and dance. Maybe you can arrange to have that done, as well as see to the bartenders. That is usually the groom's responsibility," Ma Savin advised with calm assertion.

Damn! Abe thought. *What do I know about the anatomy of a wedding?* Social discipline was not his strong suit.

He'd see Doc.

Wound up like an eight-day clock, Abe waited until five o'clock before visiting Doc and Suki. He hadn't seen them since returning from the Rose Bowl trip and felt a solid thrill navigating the steps to their front porch and ringing the doorbell. He strived not to become undone. Here, too, he found window boxes sporting bright red geraniums, fragrant white alyssum and trailing vines.

"Abe! Great to see you." Suki rushed from parts unknown with a hug.

"Suki, if I change my mind about marrying Sarah, would you marry me?" His voice coaxed, electrified at the sight of her. She radiated a beauty unmatched by anyone else Abe knew—tawny, dark-eyed, lithe and supple. His body responded. Well, he was no goddamn chunk of coal. He'd known that since he turned twelve. Suki could bushwhack him anytime with just one look. Just one smile.

"Now, young man, you know I'm too old for you, and it could be the source of bad habits for someone so young, tender and inexperienced." That brought a round of laughter, including her own, that gurgled like the Sturgeon River running toward Big Bay de Nocquet, tumbling and dancing.

In her heart, where she had little doors just like Abe, she tucked away a special place just for him that opened on her intermittently. She had slim recollection of him as anything but a man person, and that thought kept nudging out fallow thoughts of him as her child. Sometimes the concepts crowded together, choking her. But why shouldn't she have these thoughts? He featured Danforth's child, and behold how she loved Danforth.

Abe fidgeted. "I need to talk to Doc about some things."

"Yes. Of course," Doc interjected, approaching and shaking Abe's hand.

"Suki, will you bring us a couple of drinks, please? What's your heart's desire, Abe? I took the rest of the week off. A doctor from Marquette is filling in for me until next Monday. I felt there were just too many things to do before your wedding." His eyebrows shot up. "Let's have a martini, you and I. What say you?" Doc rubbed his hands together in a gesture of anticipation.

"Sounds good to me." Abe sank easily into one of the big leather chairs. "It's good to be home and have college behind me. I know that I didn't reveal how hard it was. It's taken much help from a whole lot of people to get through these four years."

"I graduated with a two-point-nine GPA. I guess it's nothing to write home about, but quite an accomplishment from my humble beginnings, and all I wove into that time period." He moved his elbows to rest on his knees, his chin in his cupped hands. "It's been a struggle, carrying a football regimen as well as an academic schedule. And *you* know that when I started, I'd have been lucky to graduate with three point zero *without* football." He managed a laugh, rubbing a hand through his hair.

On a silver tray, Suki delivered two martinis with double olives.

"Hey, I've never had a better-looking drink anywhere, Suki." Abe glanced up at her, winking, his voice somewhat husky.

Suki smiled and disappeared quietly.

"I think you've done just fine, Abe. You bet you've had a heavy load. None of us anticipated the athletic interference in your degree. We're all sorry that you can't take over the Summer Art School this year, but we understand your time imbalance." Doc smiled brilliantly. "As it is, you'll only be around for a week or so before signing in for pre-season practice July first."

Abe scooted to the edge of the chair and placed his head in his hands. "Doc, I know I'm shifting gears here, but I need to know why Sarah doesn't look as if she's pregnant." His voice drifted away, travel-worn and hesitant.

"Are you open for business?" His whisper hung as a shout, laden with true Sioux trepidation.

"Certainly I am. For you, anytime!" Abe had doubted the prognosis?

"What happened?" His voice mused intense. "Did you examine her? I expected to see her looking like the Hindenburg, but instead she looks like Minnie Mouse." His voice shrunk to the carriage of a five-year-old featured soloist.

"Abe," Doc laughed indulgently, wiping his hand over his mustache and mouth, "I appoint you the Vice President in Charge of Doubting Thomases. You have this woman pregnant, and that's not enough, you want her to look like Santa Claus for nine months? It doesn't work that way. She's only about twenty-three weeks into this pregnancy. Although that's better than halfway, she may not show much for another month or so. I've had women in their eighth month that you would hardly even suspect of pregnancy. It's the nature of the individual."

"You're sure she's pregnant though, huh?" Abe settled down and leaned back, understanding the situation intellectually, but not emotionally.

"Take my word for it, Abe. She's definitely pregnant. How you accomplished that with her adamancy toward *not* having children, I'll never know, but my hat's off to you. You must have charmed her into it." Doc searched Abe's eyes.

"Nah. The gist of it is, I *slept* her into it," Abe laughed. "I held her my prisoner in bed until she fell asleep, and by then it was a done deal. If she thought that she were spending a week with me in Pasadena on a fling, it turned out to be a high-risk one. Be dammed if one of my little swimmers didn't plunge right between the goal posts! There's more to us Whittakers than good looks," he said, his eyes dancing with warmth and laughter.

"Abe, I don't know how you ever became engaged to such a beautiful, intelligent woman with your Neanderthal ways. It's been the "*Seduction of Sarah*" ... good name for a movie. She's hooked on you." Doc's spirits were lifted in this conversation with his son. *His son.* Yes. He could see himself in Abe's eyes.

"Yeah," Abe said with a slow chuckle, taking a measured draw of his martini.

Doc thought of all the things this young man may lack, but it wasn't veracity, love or sincerity. "I examined her for the first time at Easter at an interval of about twelve weeks pregnant. She was doing just fine then, too. I understand she had a bad time at first with nausea. She's so proud—never asked for help." Doc spread his hands, palms up. "I don't know how she ever crept through this semester. You have an intrepid lady there, Abe. I'd bet no one at Mount Mary knew she was pregnant. She certainly concealed it well." Doc's eyes smiled over the rim of the martini glass.

He remembered Sarah's Easter checkup as if it were yesterday. Yes. Not a day passed by that he didn't remember. She wore a crisp, white tailored blouse, unbuttoned at the neck, which caused his blood to race. He recalled the clean smell of her, the feel of her, and the electricity of her touch. There was mysticism in the moment. Damn! When would he stop thinking of her—coveting her?

Abe's interruption of his thoughts sent him a jolt. "Have you seen her since then? I don't want anything to happen to her or my baby." Abe's words washed one over the other heavy with concern. "Do you think it might be a boy?" Once he'd put voice to his deepest desire, he felt prep school and illiterate.

"For Christ's sake, Abe, let's slay this summer evening with only good tidings. Yes, she's doing very well. Yes, I've examined her since she's graduated. No, I don't know if it's a boy." There was a faint twinge of sadness in his answers. "I hope, for your sake, however, that it is indeed a boy, because I don't think you're going to get a second-go-around with Sarah falling asleep in your arms." Doc offset his chin, rendering Abe an indulgent half-smile. "You needn't question the care Sarah is getting. No one loves her more than I do." Having said so, he put on an embarrassed countenance.

"Doc, don't you even look at her crossways. I'll have your head on a spear. Remember that!" Abe laughed

"Probably in another month or so she'll start looking pregnant. I've measured her pelvic structure; it's of a size and nature that accommodates delivery very well. Sometimes small women surprise us in their capabilities and endurance. Your mother labored for more than thirty hours and was exhausted when you finally arrived in the world, howling red and angry. Fabian stood so proud of you."

Silence fell while Doc's emotions transitioned into a still solid ball. "I still fall apart whenever I think of it...my own son..." Doc trailed off, quietly pensive. "Sometimes a man's hormones supersede all caution."

"Don't dwell on it, Doc. It stirs up too many hard-to-handle emotions. I don't know why I didn't realize long ago the similarities between you and me." Abe shook his head as if removing cobwebs. "It's uncanny. We both overlooked it. There were times when I felt we were in such sync that I had crawled inside your mind with affection. There. I've said it. That should earn me another martini." Abe wasn't sure, but it seemed Doc's mouth tightened.

Doc, recovering, leaned forward, reaching out. "And I, you. And there, *I've* said it." There were tears hanging on the brim of his eyes. "And I shall have a grandson on or about the first week of October, very early October. Are you and Sarah going to move to Green Bay immediately, or is she going to stay the summer with Ma?"

"Actually, she'll be staying here for the summer." He'd lived in this town all his life, mostly as an orphan, and no one had ever let him down. In his self-perceived insignificance, he granted people a greatness they had not earned. Sometimes he felt as if he'd been sprouted from a white pine, fed at the breast of a sugar maple in spring, and securely harbored by Big Bay de Nocquet. Sarah would fare well here.

"But we're going to go to Green Bay soon to find a temporary rental until we can afford to buy a place of our own. The baby needs a home. I'll drive home on weekends. It's only three, three and a half hours. That's decent. Besides, she wants the baby born here. You know that, don't you?"

"That's what I would prefer," Doc said, trying not to show his great relief. "I'm glad to hear it. She'll need to make monthly visits to the office until September. After that, I want to see her every two weeks until the baby is born." He rubbed his damp hand on his knee. "She'll have all the care and attention of a queen in this hospital. You're so lucky, Abe, even if we did set you up for the fall in Pasadena with a trap-the-wild-game maneuver," Doc said reflectively, slapping his knee.

Abe caught his jovial tone and kept his gun in his holster. "Don't ever do that to me again! That had to be the worst night of my whole life! I thought I'd go crazy, watching her with such longing and not touching her, loving her and not speaking to her, you and Kyle moving in on my territory, too proud to admit anything, too proud to say anything until I was steaming inside." He gazed at Doc, his eyes enormous. "You're lucky I didn't drag her off by the hair, like a caveman!"

Now they were both laughing.

"Where are you going for your honeymoon, Abe? Made any plans?"

"Nah. It's so good to be home, I thought that we'd just stay right at my place on the Beach Road. I had Mrs. Hebert clean the whole place for me; it's shining. Besides, we can't afford a whole lot before I get on the Packer payroll. Things will fall into place, and we're happy with what we have." Abe drained his second martini.

Suki appeared, with cold salmon and snack crackers, iced shrimp and crab salad, along with thick slices of French bread.

"Just in time, Suki. These martinis are mellowing me right of out of my mind," Abe said. "No more nostalgia." Gazing up at her, he brushed her hand lightly.

"Don't touch my wife's hand," Doc said, mimicking a frown.

Suki waved him off. "You guys are getting mushy." Her smile was double dazzled as she faded her way out.

Doc's mind roared with warning at Abe's non-honeymoon plans. "I don't want you to stay in town the night of your wedding," he remarked, concerned. "You'll be sorry, very sorry. There'll be people harassing you all night with brouhaha— cat calls, pebbles at the windows. It's nonsense."

"It's going to be a long day. You should leave the reception at about five o'clock. That's courtesy time to have greeted everyone with *savior-faire* and made a socially proper day of it. After that, you owe no one anything, except your wife, who will be exhausted. Remember, she's carrying that little one; you dare not overtax her." Doc knew his views were colored by his deep caring in regard to Sarah's welfare.

"Resultantly, and I hope you don't mind, I've made reservations for the both of you at the Grand Hotel on Mackinac Island for five days. That'll give you ample time to get back here, drive to Green Bay and choose a *domicile* before pre-season practice."

Abe couldn't see into Doc's mind, but he felt that he delicately rode the edge of interference. His old feeling of not being good enough, adequate, or correct swept over him, but the wind chimes in his mind were soon soothed.

Doc spread salmon onto his French bread. "You'll have a two hour drive to the Straits of Mackinac, hop a ferry and be on the island by nine, ten o'clock at the latest, allowing you a little time to relax. By then, it'll have been a long day for you both." Doc hurried, bending syllables and sincerity to fit his presumptuousness. "I know. I've been there. It gets burdensome. I'll make your excuses to anyone who inquires as to your whereabouts." Doc paused, scanning Abe's face for acceptance.

"You've got to be kidding, Doc. Mackinac Island! The Grand Hotel? I can't afford to smell that place. It's close to fifty dollars a day to stay there, plus whatever amenities you choose to use. Besides, Esther Williams just made a movie at the Grand, and the place is in a state of stampede. Thank you for the thought, however." Abe chowed down a rye cracker, heaped with seafood salad.

"It isn't just a thought, Abe." The words rolled out more slowly, finding he danced on the head of a needle. "I've arranged everything without cost to you." Doc reached for a small plate onto which he spooned some seafood salad.

"My God, Doc! You mean it? You're talking serious money here." His eyes alight, the next cracker stopped in mid-stream to his mouth.

"Abe, I've never meant anything more in my whole life. You take Sarah out of here early on Saturday and move on to the rest of your life with those five days at Mackinac Island." Doc delivered the statement with finality.

Abe knew better than to object. Although Doc hadn't said so, he'd conveyed a sound message; he did it out of love and not imperiousness. Abe's tongue felt swollen and thick. He *could* blame it on the martinis when no words came out.

"By the way, I've also arranged for the entire bar activity for the weekend both at the hotel and at the clubhouse. It's the obligation of the groom's family to provide that service. Ma insisted on the catering; she can't be swayed otherwise." Before he dissolved in a sea of takeover, he needed to hurry on. "She said Max would roll over in his grave if she didn't pick up the tab for the wedding expenses at church, and the catering." Doc's mouth shifted from side to side with the delight he took in his ability to be generous at this grandiose time in his son's life.

Abe faded into his chair and slapped his forehead with the heel of his hand. "My God, Doc! You can't pay for all this to-do that I've created." Sweat formed just inside his hairline, threatening to roll down his temples. "Some day I may *really* need some assistance from you—then you can help." He froze, as still as a cigar store Indian.

"If it'll make you feel better, you can pick up the tab for your groomsmen's stay at the hotel." This placed a niche sculpted into the day over which Abe reigned lord of the manor. He'd spent a lifetime in problem solving. Efficient problem solving. Successful problem solving. Now he wanted to make everything right for his son.

"Please," Abe demurred, "I need to do that. It makes me feel better. You need to be measured for a straight jacket right now. You know, I've never had such a wrap of security as I've had since you've entered my life. But, if the old axiom is true—*goods and services are paid for only with goods and services*—I owe you a bundle." His jaw clamped tightly shut as his tongue turned into that certain wooden Indian.

"In you, Abe, I've found my second existence. I enjoy doing this for you. You owe me nothing." Their eyes met momentarily, connecting, melding as one in the communion of time and space. "Call it my wedding gift to both of you," he added.

CHAPTER FORTY-ONE

It truly was good to be home again on Beach Road. Abe sang in the shower, "For Me and My Gal." His dinner jacket and black trousers, with satin stripes down each side, hung behind the door in his bedroom, along with his deep crimson cummerbund—the color of Sarah's bridesmaids' gowns.

The last semester had raced by in a blur. He couldn't believe the valleys he'd descended, the craggy crests he'd climbed, or the defeats in his life. There were victories too; he even got the right to vote as a Sioux Indian. Today he would claim the bride he'd longed for all his life. He'd been in love with her since before kindergarten.

With the windows open, a curling current of air blew across the Old Beach Road, lifting the perfume of the lilacs and bridal wreath up to him. The same breeze made castanets of the tender green leaves of birch and maple trees.

The Savins. He wondered if Sarah slept at all, with people coming and going half the night. He hoped *she* trotted herself off to bed early, because she wasn't going to get much sleep tonight, not if he could help it. Life was good.

It would be nothing like the night he'd called Sarah and found out she was pregnant, though. At the thought of it, his very being became encircled by pleasant and exciting whirlwinds of positive emotion. Toweling down, he leapt in the air, then buried his head in the terrycloth, rubbing hard to dry his hair.

"Abracadabra!" he shouted aloud. He'd done it.

Abe remembered the spark that struck the night when he thought he'd lost her forever. Out of control, he became a flaming fire storm—and if she hadn't fanned the flames... A little more of her and he might start staying home nights.

The robins singing reached his ears. The perfectly rounded notes had to be for him, and for Sarah. In the trees and in the grass, they answered each other, busy in their sojourns for food and nesting materials.

The seating capacity of the small parish, stuffed at one hundred and fifty, was filled to bursting by nine-fifteen. Doc's four guest bedrooms were occupied by Walter and Anne, Kyle and Karen, Curly Lambeau and his wife Ruth, and Bob Chapin's folks, Warren and Dee from Milan. Abe couldn't forget the extraordinary hospitality he'd had while he was a guest in their home on the four Christmases he'd spent alone—and lonely.

Because there were only fifteen available rooms at the Nahma Hotel, reservations had been made weeks in advance. The Allan Merciers, Bill Acker, Rudy Jehns and Peanuts Sargents left their names at the hotel to take the overflow. The Clyde Tobin family, the Frank Hruska family and Dave Phalen family had many children, but their houses seemed infinitely inflatable when space was needed. Abe sucked in air, glad to learn that Bernard and Trixie had arranged Navy leave time for his and Sarah's big day.

A warm sun shone out of an electric blue sky. With a clarity only known on clear, summer days, the church bells rang at ten o'clock, sending reverberations of never-ending rings of happiness into the forest, the town, over the cemetery, out to the lake and into infinity. Pulling the bell tower rope was thirteen-year-old Billy Hardwick, a dedicated altar boy from the Indian Point Mission, who bent and rose with the pull and yield of the rope, his cheeks puffing, his white smock billowing and flowing.

Doc, asked by Ma Savin, the pillar of propriety, to give Sarah away, stood regal in his formal wear, outside the church with the bride. The attendants lined the stairway. Sarah trembled, gazing at the height of him—taller than Abe.

Doc steadied her elbow. "You need to settle down, Sarah. You'll have nothing to do the rest of the day but look beautiful. Abe is so lucky." His mental alarm had been ringing before he ever left home. Doc knew this would be a tough day for both of them. Her, pregnant and all, perhaps plagued by regrets and recriminations about her decision to have *his* child. He wanted no such regrets entertaining her on this day. It had been a mutual decision—one in which they shared the responsibility equally.

She was so young, her skin as transparent as a new apple on the tree, a different and rare apple, a perfect apple. As tempted as Adam, he bit into the inner core of her, finding her satisfying and tasty through and through. He treasured the fluffy ringlets of undisciplined hair that curled around her temples as it did now, the wonder of her wide brown oval eyes that tilted up at the corners, and the long thick lashes that swept over them, the dazzle of her teeth and lips, the manner in which her flesh smoothed over her cheekbones, her throat. He regained a new title to his youth when he was near her, yet he was hopelessly wanting in his ability to share that with her. He couldn't. He wouldn't.

Sarah somehow knew that her security would always be entangled with this man among men. She'd never forget his salvation when her romance with Abe wilted at the Rose Bowl. Fascinated with the findings in his face, Sarah was surprised at the reach of his gentle hand at her neck, the upsweep of her illusion veil as he pulled her to him, sweeping her off the ground, his mouth coming down on hers for the last time before betrothal to his son. She could feel the outpouring of love and tension.

His mouth smoothed over her face, recording the taste. He knew he loved this woman as deeply as he loved his wife. He admonished himself for harboring such thoughts. *Foolish old man.* Her veil back in place, Sarah looked up at him through the blusher, the brilliant June sun striking the nylon threads like spun silver, creating an angelic aura about her. This moment was going to take some mind-mending, but could he ever relegate the memory to vague and fuzzy? Uh-uh.

Strains of the traditional "Wedding March" by Mozart from the Marriage of Figaro called to them. For the first time in his life, he resented the melody and all it imbibed. It punctuated a point of no return. He led Sarah down the aisle.

Abe stood, hypnotized with the illusion floating down the aisle on the arms of his father. The two people he loved most in life. *Click!* His eidetic memory recorded the picture forever in the annals of his mind to transfer to canvas. Sarah moved as a dream in a cloud of off-white slipper satin and poufy tulle. Her gown featured long, tapered sleeves ending in tatted lace; the bodice boasted pearl passementerie on a woven nylon inset to the neckline, which ended in peaks of matching tatted lace. The straining empire waist fell to a gently flowing skirt with tulle insets that swooshed about her thighs.

Sarah feared that she had walked her whole life one step at a time, trying not to think of the span of a hopeless road. The long train moved in small jerks, pacing, a-swish, a-swish, a-swish. She wore her hair down, the way Abe liked it, in a simple pageboy, with a Juliet skullcap holding a million small seed pearls, and a fingertip illusion veil pulled over her face. Although she wore three-inch heels, she was nowhere near as tall as Doc, who treated her with the fragility of a delicate lady's slipper.

Reaching the altar rail, Abe stepped forward and received his bride from his father's hand. This was going to be tough. He didn't know if he could hold up through all this tradition and pomp of the Whiteman's culture. His hand shook annoyingly when he touched Doc's, allowing it to linger there for a moment, then giving a firm squeeze, which was returned. His stomach lurched at the drawn look of Doc's expression. He wished he could lighten his countenance, brush it with blush and sunshine, as he did on canvas, but he dared not make an overture in this religiously correct setting.

With the wedding couple kneeling on velvet cushioned kneelers in the wide expanse in front of the altar and the attendants kneeling at the communion railing, Father McKevitt opened the wedding ceremony with the Entrance Antiphon and proceeded to the Opening Prayer, his black wavy hair streaked with gray, his vivid blue eyes smiling.

"Father, you have made the bond of marriage a holy mystery, a symbol of Christ's love for his Church. With faith in you and in each other, they pledge their love today. May their lives always bear witness to the reality of that love. We ask this through our Lord Jesus Christ, your Son, who lives and reigns with...one God, forever and ever."

"Amen," said Abe and Sarah.

After two readings, the priest read the Holy Gospel, while the congregation stood.

Abe wanted to get out of the *"Amens"* and into the *"I do's."* The service had just started, and he itched for it to be over. How would he know he was married if he didn't go through the beauty of the ceremony? He simply wanted to nail this down so Sarah was legally his woman.

"A reading from the Holy Gospel according to Mark. 'At the beginning of creation God made the male and female: for this reason a man shall leave his father and mother and the two shall become as one. Therefore, let no man separate what God has joined.' This is the gospel of the Lord."

Father McKevitt then asked that all stand, including the bride and groom. "My dear friends, you have come together so that the Lord may seal your love in the presence of the Church's minister and this community. He has already consecrated you in baptism and now he enriches and strengthens you by a special sacrament so that you may assume the duties of marriage in mutual and lasting fidelity. And so, in the presence of the Church, I ask you to state your intentions."

Now they were getting somewhere!

"Abednego Fabian Miereau and Sarah Marian Savin, have you come here freely and without reservation to give yourselves to each other in marriage?"

"I have."

"Will you love and honor each other as man and wife for the rest of your lives?"

"I will."

"Will you accept children lovingly from God, and bring them up according to the law of Christ and his church?"

Abe wondered how she'd answer this one. He thought he could comfortably change that word to "child."

"I will," from Sarah in a tone as thin and fragile as a wafer.

"*I will,*" Abe proclaimed loudly.

"Since it is your intention to enter into marriage, join your right hands and declare your consent before God and his Church."

Abe and Sarah joined hands, Abe squeezing and releasing hers.

"I, Abednego Fabian Miereau, take you, Sarah Marian Savin, to be my wife. I promise to be true to you in good times and in bad, in sickness and in health. I will love you and honor you all the days of my life."

You're one lucky beach bum, buster. I know. I know.

"I, Sarah Marian Savin, take you, Abednego Fabian Miereau, to be my husband. I promise to be true to you in good times and in bad, in sickness and in health. I will love you and honor you all the days of my life."

She did it! She said it! She's mine! Where'd a guy like you get such stupid-ass luck? Abe's mind drifted and dreamed in a constant state of flux.

"You've declared your consent before the Church. May the Lord in his goodness fill you both with His blessings. What God has joined, men must not divide."

I would dare someone to come between us. I'd knock them clear off the planet. Dona teasa the gorilla!

"Lord, bless and consecrate Abednego and Sarah in their love for each other. May these rings be a symbol of true faith in each other, and always remind them of their love, through Christ our Lord. Amen."

I can't wait to get her alone for five days on the island, a cornucopia of marital bliss. Sleep all night with Sarah snuggling beside me.

"Abe...Abe!" Father McKevitt whispered.

He jerked, then blinked.

"The ring...it's time for the ring." The words drifted in the air between them.

Bob Chapin reached out with the ring, barely concealing a breakdown laugh, being accustomed to Abe's wool gathering at the most unexpected times. Abe clearly expected to hear the resonance of Kyle Kreiler: "Miereau! Would you care to join us?"

Abe and Sarah placed rings on each other's fingers: "Take this ring as a sign of my love and fidelity, in the name of the Father, and of the Son, and of the Holy Ghost."

It played out like the classic story of Boy-Marries-Girl-Next-Door, come to life. He had the greatest prize of all. Abe Miereau had the girl from across the street.

After the Lord's Prayer, Father McKevitt turned to the congregation. "My dear friends, let us pray that the Lord will bless with his grace this woman, Sarah Marian Savin, now married in Christ to this man, Abednego Fabian Miereau, and that through the sacrament of the body and blood of Christ, He will unite in love the couple He has joined in this holy bond."

This is it! I'm married. She's mine! In the midst of this the most solemn of ceremonies, inappropriatky out of place, Abe smiled. *Why couldn't he take the road less traveled and just get the hell out of here?*

Betsy Hebert lifted Sarah's veil and fluffed it to the back of her head. Abe gazed directly into his bride's fathomless brown eyes for the first time during the ceremony without the veil overlaying her long lashes. He was completely enchanted—in one of his bubbles—as he grasped her greedily around the waist, pulled her to him and kissed her soundly in front of God, the priest and all the witnesses to the wedding.

"Congratulations, Mrs. Miereau," Abe whispered seductively. A round of applause broke out from the parish. The priest smiled, showing his impish Irish humor.

Sarah composed her veil and gown. She knew her husband was incorrigible and impulsive; yet in this somber stillness, she loved him deeply and terribly.

The priest then extended the Solemn Blessing. "May God, the eternal Father, keep you in love, so the peace of Christ may stay with you and be always in your home."

Abe wanted to carry his woman out to the car, scream the tires on the June-hot tar, and say goodbye to the rest of the day—just sail away where they could be alone.

"May your children bless you, your friends console you and men live in peace with you."

He knew, however, that he'd have to stay the rest of the day to be polite and socially correct for Sarah, but he couldn't dismiss his urgent feelings. After all, you can't make a goldfish out of a sow's ear, or something like that.

"May you always bear witness to the love of God so that the afflicted and the needy will find in you generous friends and welcome you into the joys of heaven."

If this ceremony doesn't end soon, I'll tackle someone using excessive force.

Advancing to the pulpit, Father McKevitt addressed the overflowing church. "It's my rare and unusual privilege to inject a note of family ties into the ceremony at this point. In my many years of service to Holy Mother the Church, I've never had this occasion arise, but it is fitting and proper that it should culminate at this time."

Nodding to Dr. Whittaker, Father McKevitt relinquished his presence at the pulpit and sat in his Bishop's chair at the right side of the altar.

Seemingly standing seven feet tall, Doc Whittaker, sartorially elegant in his black cutaway drifting diagonally from the waist and forming tails at the back, arose from the front pew and ascended the steps via the side altar to circumvent stepping on Sarah's long train. Standing at the pulpit, one was immediately aware that this icon had never been an off-stage presence. He slowly previewed everyone in the church as though measuring his audience and their receptiveness, his magnetism powerful and drawing.

Click. Abe recorded another irreplaceable image deep within the recesses of his mind. *Wonder what Doc's got on his mind—never rehearsed this.*

Doc's voice projected throughout the church as if he had tutored with Diogenes, enunciating each word with his conspicuously clean English Accent. "Conduct your affairs with humility and you will be loved more than a giver of gifts. Book of Sirach."

Abe and Sarah looked hard to their left, for the pulpit stood almost in direct line with their kneelers. They were shaken with the angst Doc displayed and the self-control he pressed upon himself. Playing around his eyes and mouth were distinct lines of tension. An errant sunbeam highlighted his dark hair, his mustache and his eyebrows as if in silhouette. Steady and enduring, his eyes offered not a hint of his thoughts.

"Today I am humbled in the presence of the Church, and you my friends of many years." A tear coursed down his cheek unashamedly, glinting brilliantly in the same morning sunbeam shooting through a side window.

"Some things take a long time to sift and settle." He paused, braking on the reins of his runaway thoughts and assuming casualness like a diplomatic veneer. "The time is appropriate to confess to everyone in this community an indiscretion I committed twenty-four years ago, and tell you that Abednego Fabian Miereau…is…in reality…my son."

The fragrance of wild roses hung heavily following the explosive announcement.

Stifled murmurs hummed through the church like Morse code through the wires—on a hot day—in July—in Death Valley.

Doc wiped away another tear with the back of his hand.

"'The deliberations of mortals are timid, and unsure are our plans.' Book of Wisdom. I grow old too soon and wise too late. My deliberations have been timid and uncertain. Without ever inquiring into her welfare, I heedlessly left Suki Marie Horse carrying my child, alone, to marry another man, who in turn raised my child." The last words ragged. It was as if someone had saddled him with the last straw.

Silence. Abe found his eyes burning at the pain he witnessed. He soon recovered and flicked a quick look at Sarah, whose stricken eyes were overflowing.

"This revelation was presented to me a year and a half ago, and yet I chose not to make this information public. My negligence has been difficult, at best, to admit. I realize that this measure is not a cure-all, but it *is* a reveal-all, and I stand before you a humbled man, contrite, with a thousand regrets."

Air sucked through the church. Wooden pews creaked. People shifted uneasily.

Holy lady-be-good! Abe never thought he'd do it. He just cut to the chase and admitted everything. What a guy! Could he have done that? Through his faith, Abe thought, Doc opened his soul like the peonies in Sarah's yard opened to the sun, showing their full glory and splendor.

"'If a man decides to build a tower, will he not first sit down and calculate the outlay to see if he has enough materials and money to complete the project?' Gospel according to Luke. I decided twenty-four years ago to build a tower without giving a thought to the materials required, or the cost, or the hurt it would create." Grasping both sides of the podium, his head bent to his chest as if in deep meditation.

"As you all know, I have now married Suki, my first love, and would choose to propose to my son, if he will have me, to add my name to his in a renewal of his Baptismal vows, christening him Abednego-Fabian-Miereau-Whittaker." The last words he delivered with a belying ounce of composure reserves, his voice breaking on his name.

Abe viewed in Doc a premier person. Rising from his kneeler, he hurried the short distance to his father, where he embraced him wordlessly. Together they stood in the silence of the church. Robins' song drifted through the window transoms; a bee, laden with golden bags of pollen could be heard buzzing in the bridal wreaths and orange blossoms bedecking the altar. Handkerchiefs drifted to eyes in the congregation.

Pulling loose ends together, Father McKevitt gestured for Abe to position beside his bride. With holy water, Father McKevitt sprinkled Abe's Head. "The church blesses the addition of Whittaker to your baptismal name:

Abednego-Fabian-Miereau-Whittaker, in the name of the Father, the Son and the Holy Ghost."

With sparkling tears, Sarah beheld the men she loved.

"The mass is ended. Go in peace and love to serve the Lord."

As they descended from the altar, the organ boomed to the triumphal Recessional Hymn. With Sarah on his arm, Abe released her so she could hug her mother. Abe stopped and kissed Suki in the front pew, along with Farley and Norrhea.

Click. Another irreplaceable shot of the grandeur, strength and pride of his heritage, standing tall and honorable—*together.* They were indeed a compliment to the Crazy Horse ancestry: Sioux survivors: his people, his culture. He would embrace it forever.

At all costs.

CHAPTER FORTY-TWO

Abe and Sarah were pleased to have caught the eight-thirty ferry out of St. Ignace, arriving on Mackinac Island shortly after nine o'clock and sharing the debarkation point with another ferry carrying freight.

Two thickly lumbered crates swung precariously from a boom aboard the second ferry. Out of the corner of his eye, Abe caught the movement, jerking quickly back to catch the scene again as the netted freight swung wildly over the dock, rapidly approaching the figure of a man walking briskly, swinging a cane smartly to his cadence. Abe's measured precision of distances told him the man would not out-walk the crate coming at him with deadly force.

Without a moment's hesitation, he sprinted as never before, tackling the man and throwing him to the dock as the crates swung violently over their heads. Abe felt the breeze of the cargo course. Pounding like horses' hooves, the heartbeat of the man beneath him pumped into finish-line speed, as his own finished second.

Why had he taken such a chance? They could have both been killed. Why does someone climb an insurmountable mountain? The shorter man mumbled thanks, most appreciatively. Abe thought him dapper: thinly shaved mustached, impeccably dressed, snapping dark eyes, thin mouth. He was surprised that the man was not as old as he'd first perceived—probably in his thirties, late thirties, Abe determined.

"Thank you," he said, his mouth gaping somewhat. "I say there," he said, clearing his throat, "thank you many times over. A daunting thing you did there. Yes." Reaching out, he shook Abe's hand. "What an exquisite gesture. Let me present you with my card," he said, his hand reaching inside his nautical, double-breasted sport coat.

Abe read: Neville Chamberlain II, International Institute of the Arts, *See The Erection of Eros*, Piccadilly Circus, and London, England. The phone number was inscribed in small print at the bottom.

"You're welcome. Nice to meet you, ahh, Mr. Chamberlain, I'm sure." Abe smiled brushing down his khaki trousers and cotton button-down shirt. "Couldn't believe my eyes when I saw what was about to happen! There was no time for a warning." He solicitously bent, touching Chamberlain's elbow. "You okay?"

"By all means. Fit as a monarch, thanks to you," he smiled. "And your name?" He studied Abe, viewing this giant standing before him to whom he surely owed his life.

"Abe Miereau. Here for five days with my new bride. Sarah!" He gestured for her to join them from where she was yet frozen to the spot. "This is my new wife, Sarah. This gentleman is Neville Chamberlain."

"Pleased to meet you," Sarah said, finally smiling. "You're a lucky man, Mr. Chamberlain. That was a close call." She sighed, rolling her eyes to heaven.

"Yes it was. I'm delighted to have made your acquaintance." He shook Sarah's hand, the look on his face one of admiration and pleasure. "Perhaps I will be so lucky as to see you again before I leave the island." As he departed, he waved to them kindly.

A four-seated surrey waited to take Abe and Sarah clop, clop, clopping up the winding road to the hotel. Sarah, still white around the mouth, sighed. "Oh, Abe, you were absolutely awesome, saving that man."

He gave her his weak wrist wave-off, fluttering his eyelashes.

"Stop that, Abednego Fabian Miereau-Whittaker," she said tersely as they rounded a curve and saw the majesty of the Grand Hotel looming in front of them. "Have you ever seen anything so awesome?" Sarah swept the length and breadth of the Grand Hotel, with its softly lighted front portico stretching from here to eternity, her arms widespread. She drank in the Greek gothic columns that staggered the entire length, supporting the porch as if it were some great entranceway into heaven.

Abe leaned back in the surrey, hands behind his head, watching the fringes on top circle and sway, reminding him of the pasties on a stripper. He fantasized. He smiled. Threw her a glance out of the corner of his eye.

Abe did notice that the hotel was neoclassical, as seen in the work of John Nash's Regent's Park, London. Bay windows, balconies, and eclectic design characteristics abounded. They were both surprised at the distance the hotel stood back from the lake, high on a hill, reserved and withdrawn behind its wide expanse of perfectly manicured lawn. It was not so much that it peered over the lake as that it did hold court there.

There existed no wait. A red-jacketed bellboy gathered their luggage and had them settled in their room without even checking in at the front desk. The spiffy All-American Joe-college bellboy wore a hundred dollar smile that awakened warmth.

"This suite on the fourth floor is especially for honeymooners and privileged guests," he ran on, unpacking their suitcases and hanging their clothes in the closet. "Go ahead and do a little exploring. I'll be right with you," he said, slipping their Samsonite luggage, graduation gifts for both of them, into the far end of the closet.

"This outer room will provide all the daytime pleasantries one needs, including a refrigerator and wet bar. The couch is a hide-a-bed, which you may use anytime," he smiled, flicking a glance up at them, then withdrawing his eyes again. "You have an efficiency desk complete with stationery, pens and stamps, compliments of the hotel."

In the bedroom, the whole room sprung to life with indirect lighting, seemingly by the hand of a wizard. An oversized bed rested off center of the far wall, dressed in an elegant satin comforter and flounce of white dazzled with broad-leaf fichus. Elongated cathedral lamps hung from the ceiling on either side of the bed, softly illuminating the bedside stands. A mirrored vanity at least eight feet long decorated the wall on the right. Dressers with delineated mirrors stretched on either side of the entrance door, a bi-fold of wide, walnut louvers. Off to the left there was a bathroom that could have held their wedding breakfast guests.

Straight ahead and to the left of the bed were French doors opening onto the lanai, overlooking the Straits of Mackinac. The view sucked Sarah's breath away. The lanai bespoke relaxation: two bamboo chaise lounges with pads carrying out the bedspread motif, two captain's chairs done in the same mode and two round bamboo tables with glass tops. Soft lamps hung on the building on either side of the lanai.

The bellboy observed Sarah's wide eyes. "I don't know the good Samaritan who provided the accouterments to fine living, but here you have a bottle of Chivas Regal," he said, pointing to one of the bamboo tables where an ice bucket and two crystal glasses bearing an intricate design of diamonds awaited them.

"In addition, the late-blooming lilacs were hand-picked late this afternoon. I'm assigned to help you in any way I can to make your vacation with us pleasant." He smiled his fresh young smile, looking appraisingly at Sarah. "Also, all gratuities have been built into your initial room fees."

He reminded Abe of the Nahma public pump—they both ran on

incessantly. It didn't escape Abe's Sioux pride in ownership of this woman. "I think that will be all," he said with a commanding presence. "Thank you," he said heading to the door with confidence that the bellboy would follow.

Well-trained to know when the courtesies had been extended and the guests curried to feel they were of the utmost importance to the hotel, the bellboy nodded politely. "Enjoy your stay," he said, again drinking in the splendor of Sarah before he closed the door, a mocking smile playing at the corner of his mouth.

"Good thing that bastard left when he did. I didn't like the way he gave you the once over!" Abe's eyes snapped, his mouth tight.

"Oh, Abe, he's just a kid, probably only sixteen or so," she said casting her hands palm-up to signify the triviality of the matter.

"I don't care how young he is. He appreciated you!" A puckered smile of contrition appeared around his mouth.

"Look at this, Abe—by the bed! A chilled bottle of Madeira. Whenever the girls from school went out to dinner, that's what we always ordered. It took all of us pitching in. It's made on the Madeira Islands off Portugal, in the Atlantic Ocean. It's usually thought of as a dessert wine."

"Dessert?" Abe said astonished. "Dessert wine?"

"Yes. It's a mite heavy, but it has a bouquet that makes it palatable for hours."

"*Dessert?*"

"Yes. My goodness. What's the problem?" she said, her laugh smoky.

Abe lifted the bottle from the bucket—the ice disturbed, grumbling in the urn. He wondered if Fabian did it through mental dynamics. He'd willed it. Abe had learned more in college than the Pythagorean theory. Thought transference. *It's dessert time, Dad.*

"Let's sit on the lanai, Sarah. It's a beautiful evening; it's young and it's ours."

The moon, on its journey to fullness, hung low in the east, puffed up and deep orange. Their room, angling west, gave them a complete one hundred and eighty degree view of Lake Huron to the east, the Straits of Mackinac in the middle, and Lake Michigan to the west.

"Abe," Sarah whispered, afraid if she spoke aloud she would break the spell, "isn't it magic?" Her voice held a breathless quality.

"Yeah," he said in the same tone, concluding that it was a given. "Pure magic. Unreal, Sarah. Unreal," he stopped short, his voice running just north of the breaking point. "Think I'll have a glug of this Chivas on the rocks," he said, studying the bottle label. "Could I open the Madeira for you, little lady?" He looked deeply into her soft eyes, saw the love that Kyle had spoken of, the love he almost threw away. It put a fright in him. He concluded that there lay upon them a magical power, some mystical prowess that touched their skin, their hearts.

"Please. Yes. This is unreal! I feel *nouveau riche.*" Settled into one of the captain's chairs, he realized that she looked right at home surrounded by luxury. Someone who *should* know luxury. Someone who complemented luxury.

"Now just what does that mean in French? You know I studied only Spanish." He disappeared into the bedroom to access the wine.

"Newly rich." Elevating her voice somewhat, still not wanting to break the spell.

"*Si. Es oro!* Yes. It is gold! Someday we'll own a penthouse in New York."

She laughed richly. "Or a townhouse in London."

"Or a villa on the Riviera," he concluded the banter, reappearing with a glass of wine for her. "Come, sit near me, Sarah, and look at that lake. Isn't it absolutely eerie, yet grand?" *Click.*

Getting hazy, the lake emanated a mist-like genie in fluffy little curlicues, circling and testing for a place to rest after a long hot day. The lights of St. Ignace twinkled and danced in the distance through the heat inversions off the water—lights that you could almost reach out and touch—up and down the shoreline as far as you could see. Pleasure-boat lights twinkled and moved in the straits. Giant iron ore boats, strung heavily with ghostly lights, slowly navigated the commercial waterways—east to west, north to south—creating a busy junction with the ease of an experienced traffic cop.

"My gosh, Abe. Look at those Northern lights off over the mainland!" In an electrical light green, pink, blue and yellow, the cosmic dance of color and energy swayed and glowed, appearing and disappearing in a perfect rhythm, tantalizing, beckoning, mesmerizing and hypnotic. Abe wondered what the price of admission would be if he had to purchase a ticket. "Unusual to see the Northern lights this time of the year. It must be a show just for our honeymoon, Sarah," he said, chuckling.

The ice clinked in Abe's glass as his stream of consciousness rounded the corner to how grateful he was, to Doc, to Sarah, to Fabian, and to God. Then, as if by some great decree of release, he breathed a deep sigh and allowed his shoulders to relax.

Flipping on the radio that rested near him, he listened, enveloped by the soft and haunting strains of "Laura" by Johnny Mercer, reaching out like the mist over the lake.

"Laura is a face in a misty light, footsteps that you hear down the hall. She gave her very first kiss to you..."

Yes, she did, you lucky bastard, and her last one, and the one before that, too.

Building another Chivas with water, he returned to the chaise lounge, kissing Sarah on the top of her head.

She was taken with his new attitude of late—his command, his confidence, his swagger. The kind of strut that said "Step Aside" as boldly as if he were wearing a message T-shirt. He was a study in self-assurance and chutzpah, the very soul of imagination, creativity and efficiency.

"Abe."

"Hmmm?"

"I love you."

The words thrilled him, curling his toes. Every time she said his name it turned to music, and she *loved* him. It had been a long time. He'd been a long, long time, alone.

"Sarah," he said sitting up straight, "we're lucky to have survived these four years of tugging and pulling at each other's patience. The absences alone should have knocked the pins right out from beneath us, but we survived. You're everything to me—everything. I love you very deeply." He saw the lanai lights reflecting on the plains of her face—her forehead, her nose, her chin—and he wanted to taste her. Taste her skin. Smell her hair. "Allow me to pour you another Madeira."

She laughed. "Are you going to be able to keep me in Madeira and yourself in Chivas? I'm expensive..." she drawled, looking up at him bewitchingly.

"I'll take it out in trade," he replied, nonplussed. "You'll get everything you want, if first I get everything I want." He shot her with his finger.

A dog barked, the sound rising through the evening mist that circled the prevalent island cedars and whispering hardwoods. They were struck repeatedly by the heavy redolence of lilacs blooming profusely on the island.

"You get the Madeira. I'll don my new peignoir from Ma. I need to wear it, you know. Memories of honeymoons include thoughts of peignoirs, on or off the hangers," she added, teasing.

"Sounds good to me, but you know what *I* like you to wear." His voice trailed off.

"We have *cause celebre,*" she tossed at him as she disappeared into the grand hall of the bathroom. She knew how good it played out to be his friend, as well as his love mate. What she had not previously realized, now manifested itself clearly; they were a matched pair, a chunk of intergalactic particle that drifted apart from a mother planet, only to swim in time together, forever.

A soft humid breeze circled its way into the bedroom from the open French doors. Abe would have been content to remain isolated on this island for the rest of his life, just Sarah and him. He dare not let her know the extent of his love. Somehow, he would be regarded as less significant, less virile, if it were known how big a part she played in his life. Chapin and Hulk would never stop reminding him. As it were, before he'd left Nahma, they'd razzed him about lugging at the end of a chain. All he could do now was bark harmlessly—no more bite.

Abe admitted that nothing else seemed worthwhile, just her. Maybe he should practice some hocus pocus with the voodoo of crawling roots, chicken bones and humming bird eyebrows to keep her magnetized to him forever. His brows began to relax.

"Abe," she murmured softly from over his shoulder. Turning in his chair, he beheld an oracle from heaven, standing in layers and layers of billowing chiffon in a hue of almost-not-there pale green, her silhouette back-lighted from the bedroom. A small satin rosebud held together the neckline where white piping ran its course. Triple layered cap sleeves ending in white piping lightly kissed her tanned arms.

"Sarah," he whispered without intent. His first inclination tended toward ecstatic shouting, but it couldn't break the circuit between his brain and his tongue. "My God, you're beautiful!" His eyes were as hot and burning as coals in the dim twilight. "You've been beautiful all day, first as my beautiful bride, and now as an illusion. Come fluff yourself onto the lounge by me." He devoured every last bit of her with his eyes. Sweat broke out on his chest as white hot flames swept through his body.

Lowering herself onto his lounge, she rested her Madeira on the round glass-topped table and snuggled in close. He pulled her into his arms, smelling the incense of her linen-like cologne, her hair. It was fatal, throwing his heart into wild humming.

How do you treat a pregnant woman? Abe remembered Doc's lecture: be careful—don't over-indulge—make sure she has a nap every day. *Lord, how can I not imbibe?* He wanted to rush her to the floor and crush her with his weight, carry her inside and try out the carpeting, and that's all before he even got her into bed. His blood coursed through his veins like a leaf caught in an early spring runoff. He wanted to absorb her by some kind of heavenly metamorphosis.

"Abe?"

"Hmmm?"

"I'm so happy."

She was happy! *He* was the Chief Executive in Charge of Insanity.

"Sarah?" Pausing, he put both his hands on her slender arms that looked like they had been molded by Aphrodite herself.

"Yesss," she whispered, the chiffon of her peignoir spilling over the chair and onto the floor. Her eyes locked onto his mercilessly, the same eyes that had mesmerized him since before kindergarten.

"Are you feeling okay? Are you still nauseated? Do you think we could make a little whoopee?" Abe barely spoke above a whisper, his mouth in her ear, licking the hair away—languishing on her lobe.

With effort, she drew back, studying, her head slanted. "Certainly. I'm not fragile. Doc said I'm a healthy young woman. And the child I'm carrying is healthy, too. He boxes with me every day." She laughed, rubbing his nose with hers.

"Come inside with me while I shower. I don't want you to be far away."

"I'm hardly going anywhere because we're on an island, remember? Besides, I love being near to you, Mr. Abednego Fabian Miereau-Whittaker."

He reacted with a wash of passion and pride at the sound of the words.

"Don't you think that this is just the most nefariously black night we've spent together? It doesn't seem right. When do you think we will get acclimated to this?"

Sarah giggled with the newness of it all, but knew she would never forget that Abe came into her life permanently during the summer equinox of 1948.

"Abe. When are you going to learn to close the door for privacy?"

"Never, Sarah. That's me. You're stuck with it now. Besides, there's nothing wrong in admiring God's handiwork. And no, I don't think we're being nefarious; we are going to have some legal sex." His voice reached her from the distance.

Appearing from the bathroom in the persona created by his many successes, Abe was casual in his nakedness.

Sarah cowed at the size of him and the animalistic contours of his muscled body.

He seized her from the chair, crushing her into him. "This is the completion of the years of our promises and trials. I love you desperately." He could feel the tantalizing warmth of her, smell the freshness, taste the goodness, and breathe the essence of her. The soft breeze encircled the room stirring the redolence of lilacs mingling with the moist smell of the lake.

Her head bent back, he kissed her neck, cheeks, her beautiful brown eyes, tiny nose. Her battlements down, he felt her arms closing around his shoulders, his breath catching in his throat. Damn! What this woman did to him! His tongue attacked, coercing her mouth open, feeling her body soften. Although recessive, he coaxed her tongue into responsiveness and went wild with the taste, the feel of her.

Maybe all she'd ever needed was his name. Could he ever figure out women? She knew damn well that he'd always loved her. He had been prepared to accept her purely as his wife and the mother of his children, even if he had to get good sex somewhere else. Maybe she'd be all things to him.

He groaned aloud, the sound slipping from deep within. His glance traveled from her soft lips to her eyes, then back to her lips. "I love and cherish you, Sarah, but I don't have one honorable thought on my mind right now," he whispered huskily. He unclipped the little rosebud on her peignoir; her outer layer of chiffon peeled to the floor.

He recorded forever her shoulders, perfectly proportioned to her body. She was sinuous, lithe, supple, curves and turns, winding. She was flawless!

"That Old Black Magic" sounded from the radio on the lanai, its volume turned down low. "Down and down I go, round and round I go..."

Lowering his hungry mouth, he edged the outline of his body into her stomach.

Her breathing stopped in mid-intake. The baby lurched.

"What *was* that!" He pulled back, his mouth open surveying her in askance.

"You jostled him—your son. He's protesting," she said with a soft, low sound.

"Holy hell, Sarah, it's alive! It's moving. It's mine!" His breath came in short gasps. Would he have to duel with this new little person between them? He kissed the wispy pirate curls at her temple, her hair, her eyes, seeking to stamp her with his love.

She couldn't doubt his love—she had to know how badly he needed her. He pulled a nightgown strap over her shoulder, fingers massaging, smoothing—then the other. It didn't fall off as on previous occasions. He worked the straps down slowly with his demanding hands, revealing her breasts.

"Sarah," he breathed so close that she felt his moisture, like a welcome bay mist.

"What happened to your breasts? How big they are." His eyes asked soundless questions of her and then allowed his gaze to drift down the wonder of her new figure. In his aggressive state, he captured them both.

"Unnhh," she said, bowing her head. "They're sensitive, Abe." Her voice stayed in his ears, plaintive.

"I'm so sorry, Sarah. It's just that I can't believe they're so nice, so large. Your breasts have always been tiny and pliable to my touch." To relate to her tender breasts when his body insisted on release presented a great difficulty. "Don't move away, Sarah," he said as she sidled backwards for relief. "Just stand there." Scooping up her nightgown, he pulled it over her head, her hair flying back.

She shook her head to allow her wealth of mahogany hair to fall back into place, standing naked in front of him in the soft lighting of the bedroom, the French doors standing open, the night riding redolent in the moonlight.

"Ohhh," he breathed, his eyes traveling the distance of her deity, her legs, her arms, back up to her face. His woman. He knelt down, reached out and touched her belly where a firm, round ball protruded, very evident to him now. His son again protested his touch. Surprised, he pulled back, tears in his eyes. He caressed her belly with his accurate football-receiver's hands, holding his future right here, his son. Sinking his head into her abdomen, he kissed her belly, lingered, and breathed the humidity of her skin that emanated her own sweet fragrance. Overcome with the wonder of it all, he knew he worshiped every square inch of her.

Standing, he swept her up, pulled down the coverlet and gently placed her upon the bed, lying down beside her. "Sarah, I love you. Everything is just beginning for us. I'm sorry that you became pregnant when you didn't want to, but I had to do something to create my son." He kissed her new breasts lightly. "I didn't think you'd *ever* cooperate voluntarily." Kissed her belly thoroughly. "I'm going to make you the happiest woman in the whole world. I'm going to reach out and be better, quicker and faster and put my talents as a football pro to the test. Everything I do will be for you and my son. I can't tell you how much I think of you for keeping the baby."

"I need to get you on canvas in full pregnancy so life can imitate art. I love all of you, even more beautiful in the bloom of motherhood." His voice bred low and raw.

Softened to his advances, she welcomed his deep kisses, his tongue searching.

"Dream" drifted on a soft waft of air from outside, "When you're feeling blue, Dream that's the thing to do. Just let the smoke rings rise in the air..."

"I can't wait any longer, Sarah," he groaned.

"Abe," her hands wrung into his hair, feeling the stirrings of his caresses filling her soul, her body. "Go slow, Abe." Her voice lulled in his ear.

"You ask too much."

"God, how I've missed you, Sarah." He hauled her to him, encouraging her to join with him.

Her anticipation of jolting pain stiffened her hands on his shoulders, her heart beating rapidly. "You're going to move the baby," she said shakily.

But he didn't hear in his heated state of being.

She reached up and smoothed the hair from his forehead. She'd derived small pleasure from his fulfillment. Up so tight, she felt like a fence post. Perhaps she'd get used to it. Maybe. Maybe he'd get better. She'd hope.

Quietly, Sarah lay corrupted in bed, naked. As she drowsed, she reflected on her beautiful wedding day: The memorable church service, Doc's public declaration of Abe, the smilax woven into the decorations at the Clubhouse. Streams of sunshine punctuated the umbrella of a giant oak tree to dance in broken patterns on the crowd as they milled about on the campus in front of the Clubhouse. She memorized the dozens of roses in honor of Abe. Amazing were the white table coverings on which sat buffets of cornucopia. Even the ice cream had been formed into shapes of the bride and groom. Kosher lamb and rice was served up, as well as desert tuber truffles sautéed in butter and onion, heaping platters of fruit, philo pastries and a giant maraschino cherry wedding cake, at Abe's request.

Gift boxes heaped on the tables with the bridesmaids in attendance, telegrams from well-wishers, and, of course, the eternal paparazzi! Strange, how dry the champagne tasted in mid-day as opposed to how good it tasted in the evening.

As she drifted off to sleep, she could still hear the whirlwind words of the wall of people…"man and wife…congratulations … just gotta kiss the bride … beautiful … lovely wedding … let me introduce you … gorgeous bride … blushing … could you come here a minute?" She ached all over as sleep overtook her, nonetheless feeling her presence in her wedding bed to be of clandestine nature.

When finally he crawled into bed after calling Doc, Abe drew Sarah's sleeping body close and listened to the gentle June breeze whispering about the lounges of the lanai. Whispery conversations carried on, murmuring of the love in the room.

He invented every man who ever had loved—every man who ever had found pleasure in a woman—every man who ever had felt alive, productive and indispensable to someone who needed him.

He'd be there for her … the rest of his life. Forever. He fell certain.

Cares unknown would not be cares entertained.

Tonight.

CHAPTER FORTY-THREE

Riding in a surrey around the island, Abe quipped, "Did you know we're sitting on a piece of God's earth that barely measures two by three miles? It says here in the brochure that the island is a gem and almost as unspoiled as it appeared when the first Europeans arrived here some three centuries ago.

"The cannons still boom at the island's fort. One yet must get around either by bicycle or by horsepower, and a blacksmith still uses a glowing forge to fashion the horseshoes and wagon wheel rims." He glanced sideways at Sarah to reassure himself that he had her full attention. Smiling, he put his arm around her.

"Interesting..." Sarah was captivated with this small piece of real estate as their surrey driver pointed out various attractions. "Well, as we can see, it's still popular with visitors. But tell me," she said, addressing the driver. "Did you see the display of Northern lights the other night?" She leaned forward.

"Yah. Nice they are. Darn tootin'. But it's unusual seein' them in June. Usually late in August through the winter months we see 'em, dancin' out over the straits from Lake Huron all the way to Lake Michigan. My Grampa, right from Finland, used to say they were the Norse gods in the great halls of Valhalla, fighting one another over who owns the horizons. Yah. You betcha. They're mighty majestic and scary even sometimes. Ay." With the reins in his hands, he clucked to the two horses.

Indulging the driver, Abe winked at Sarah and read with intrigue. "The Island has several inns, including the elegant Grand Hotel, which is said to have the longest porch in the world. Oh. And listen to this." Abe laughed. "Visitors return year after year, but only after they have sampled the delicious product of one of the many renowned fudge shops on Huron Street are they considered to be true "fudgies" as the islanders like to call visitors." Abe chuckled.

All week, under a sky of porcelain blue with feathery cirrus clouds, Abe and Sarah viewed miles of surf licking at the island shore. They found themselves involved in an adventure of people-watching on the promenade. Various and sundry personalities strolled the porch, holding conversations in cozy twosomes, a raucous rounder of four heading for the golf course, tennis players in short pleated skirts whom Abe watched until they were out of sight. The clinking of the wrought iron gates leading to the pool area became a familiar sound. June drowsed good-naturedly around them.

"Let's dress for High Tea today at four o'clock," Sarah suggested. "I've wanted to do that all week. We leave tomorrow, and don't know when we'll get back."

"All right. But I'd like to know just what the hell I'm supposed to do at any High Tea ritual. You've heard of the bull in the china shop." He grunted.

High Tea was served in the grand drawing room immediately off the lobby area. The largest *white* grand piano they had ever seen sat in splendor under a bank of windows. A commanding presence, the instrument was played by a genteel gray-haired blue-eyed gentleman in coat and tails. Waiters dressed in full array of sparkling white jackets and gold braid moved about with trays of drinks and hors d'oeuvres, in addition to trays of steaming Earl Gray tea in translucent china cups. Scones and toasted crumpets sprinkled with powdered sugar exhibited on delicate doilies graced china plates. Crustless cucumber sandwiches held crisp eye appeal.

Through a wall of bi-fold louvered doors left ajar, the scent of honeysuckle drifted from the side portico.

Looking down at his four o'clock cocktail—*screw the tea*—Abe did a double take of two dark-green jade lions resting on either side of the portico doors; their curling manes and snarling teeth could mean only one thing: Fu Lions out of the Imperial Palace in Peking during the Boxer Rebellion. He stood near the doors with the sun trickling through the cedars and watched the motion of ethereal light over a vacuum of stillness where nothing else moved. Transported into a plateau of time layers, he stood as demonstrable as the statues, as if he'd loved and touched them at an earlier time and place in this same extra terrestrial glow.

"What the hell!" He shuddered. He tossed a glance at Sarah, who had obviously felt or saw nothing. "Look at those, Sarah," he said nudging her along over to the open doors. "I've only seen pictures of these. They're supposedly in London somewhere. These are either the real thing or a damn good imitation. They're magnificent. Look at the detail of the fur, the curl of the tails, the girth of the hips, and the strength showing in the shanks. Outstanding!"

"Excuse me, sir."

Abe, surprised, turned around and found the man from the brief dock experience. He was surprised to see him again and was struck by his deep resemblance to Hollywood actor David Niven—an imposing figure, with every hair in place, a manicured mustache above his exacting mouth and discerning gray-blue eyes. An air of political arrogance encompassed the man. Slightly built, neat to a turn, he was dressed impeccably in a tailored navy blazer and gray trousers with custom-made gold sea-lion cuff links clinching the sleeves of his dress shirt.

"Arthur Neville Chamberlain II of Great Britain!" Abe exclaimed, grinning, having been impressed by the usage of the man's complete name on his calling card.

"Abe! It's you! I say there. How awfully decent it is to run into you again. Good afternoon to you too, Sarah. You perhaps heard of my father, Neville Chamberlain, former Conservative Chancellor of the Exchequer and prime minister in 1937. He died eight years ago, in the middle of the war. I couldn't help but pick up on your ballyhoo about the Fu lions." He smiled, but only slightly, his eyes studying Abe.

Grasping Chamberlain's outstretched hand, Abe gripped it firmly. "I just graduated with a Bachelor of Fine Arts Degree, and these Fu Lions caught my eye. They're outstanding replicas. Quite unbelievable, really."

"Bully! They're indeed the real thing! I personally made the trip here from England to present them to the hotel ownership. That's what those crates contained that nearly did me in back a few days. Years ago, my father befriended Adolph Hitler, believing him to be a very gifted statesman. He never realized what a rigidly circumscribed, fanatically agendaized individual Hitler was. On one of his visitations to Berlin, Hitler presented my father with these lions as a token of his friendship." He cleared his throat, pulling himself taller.

"They've been in the family since that time. I wished, however, to have them out of the country and into a new home; they have too many memories attached to them. I felt this would be a proper resting place in such a grandiose ambiance, rich in British history." He made a delicate fist, putting it to his mouth to smother a stage cough.

Abe was awestruck, but in his element. The *real thing* and *he* hadn't wanted to come to this High Tea! "What a fine gesture," he said.

"Would you like to see a genuine Reynolds? I had one of *them* shipped also. It arrived only a few days ago." He paused for effect, looking into his glass.

Abe thought he'd died and gone to heaven. "Yes. Absolutely." Leading the way, Chamberlain helped himself to a fresh glass of chining blanc wine from a waiter's tray.

Abe followed suit, passing one on to Sarah first. "You're not a high tea drinker, either, er, ah Mr. Chamberlain?"

"Call me Art." Pinching his nostrils, he said quietly. "No, a spot of hot tea on a stifling June day, that I don't relish." His accent sounded so much like Doc's that it put them both at ease with the English nobleman.

Unlocking a door to a private dining room of elegant appointments and floor-to-ceiling windows hung with rich burgundy-colored velvet draperies, Abe immediately saw the large painting hanging over a giant fireplace at the far end of the room. Underneath, on a bronze plaque was engraved, "Sir Edmund Burke, by: Sir Joshua Reynolds, 1723-1792. English Portrait Painter."

"My God!" Abe exclaimed, his dark brown eyes warming with delight.

"This was also a gift from Adolph Hitler to my father. No one wants the memories of what happened. My father was instrumental in the policy of 'appeasement' of the Axis powers that culminated in the Munich Pact in 1938. Of course we all know what happened after that. Subsequently, my father seemed to die in pieces, disappointed in his statesmanship and allegiance to Great Britain after the outbreak of the war."

"I'm sorry about your father—being so well-intended and all. What a cache of art he left you, however. I'm familiar with the works of Reynolds and eighteenth century art in Europe. He is considered historically *the* most important English painter, raising the artist to a position of respect in England."

Chamberlain agreed tacitly with a wink. "He was a bit of a wit and charming company, taking London by storm. His portrait commissions ran in the megabucks. He had his own gallery and earned election to president of the Royal Academy in 1768."

"Awesome!" Abe adjusted his shoulders, squirming in the good fortune of previewing these historic pieces of art of which he'd only read and seen in pictures.

Chamberlain smiled conservatively. "Yes. Precisely. This particular portrait of Sir Edmund Burke I thought would be of special interest to Americans. He was an Irish-born British politician who lived during the Reynolds era. He pleaded in parliament the cause of the American colonists. All this happened about the same time this island was colonized by Great Britain. So you see, it all falls together."

"I can't tell you how pleased I am that you appeared on the scene when you did, Art." Abe was nearly delirious. "I viewed my excursion into the four o'clock tea custom as a moment in time that I devoted to my new wife, for her pleasure. Turns out, it's been *my* pleasure. I can't thank you enough."

Abe knew he had a guardian angel. It was as if he received these pervasive seismic shifts in the middle of nothingness. Fu Lions, Reynolds originals, here, on Mackinac Island! He smiled to himself, indulging his bubble.

Chamberlain, caught up in the young couple, reached out to them uncharacteristically. "Look, would you do me a favor? Let me take you to the lounge and buy you a decent drink, then join me for dinner as partial repayment and appreciation for saving my life." He raised his eyebrows inquisitively.

Abe nodded in pleasure at the invitation. "Thank you. We'd enjoy that," he said, gazing again at the splendid piece of art refinement for the hotel.

In his clipped accent, Chamberlain declared, "Bloody nice of you to share your time with me."

And so it came to be that Abe and Sarah began their married life with yet another Brit—a Brit who would strongly influence their future.

⇜⇝

It happened during the days of Indian summer when autumn gently asserted itself on Big Bay de Nocquet, which lazed in the warmth of falling leaves and rising harvests.

Ma became adamant. "You can't wait one minute longer for Abe to arrive from Green Bay. You need to go to the hospital. Now! I insist."

Nauseated, dizzy and experiencing intense labor pains, Sarah didn't argue. The calendar read October 2, a Tuesday. Abe should have been able to leave Green Bay quickly, but there was a sudden storm. An idyllic day until eleven, the sky succumbed to clouds that draped over the bay and rolled in like the wrath of God.

After Quigley admitted and secured Sarah into a private room at the hospital, Sarah heard torrential rain, driven by a warring wind, hammering at the window. Curious, how she thought of Max at a time like this. He used to tell her that southwesters had the fury of a Machiavellian monster manipulating the powers of darkness.

Sighing, she reviewed the long summer she'd had carrying this child. She'd gone to the beach every day—did the backstroke regularly—found the water supportive to the baby's weight. She thought back now, however, to a month ago when her uterus grew so large that it pressed upward into her stomach and her heartburn became diabolical.

Her back ached constantly. "The ligaments and fibrous tissue that normally lock your joints firmly together become more elastic during pregnancy, Sarah,"

Doc advised during her mid-September office visit. "This is to allow your pelvis to expand at the moment of birth. The joints of your spine endure particular stress, because during pregnancy they come under additional tension.

"The growth of your uterus shifts your center of balance and your posture changes, so even standing for any length of time can result in a non-specific backache." He wore an expression of concern, sitting behind his desk at the hospital, his elbow on the armrest, his forefinger curved across his mouth in an absorbed nod.

"It's really bad now," Sarah explained, sitting across from him. "The pain is shooting down my left leg." She didn't want to. She wouldn't. She couldn't, but she caved, crying uncontrollably, exhausted. Coping grew to be impossibly complex.

He sucked in his breath, his face a study in compassion. Rising abruptly, he circled the desk, drew her off the chair and folded her in his arms. "I have loved you for an eternity, Sarah, and would like to tuck you away somewhere so you wouldn't hurt anymore. Overtly, I cannot show you how much I care. Painful as it is, you belong to another man, and I'm so glad it's my son." His voice grew soft and reassuring, his hands gentle on her aching back. "Your discomfort distresses me to no end."

"I've loved you for an incredibly long time too, Danforth. You're never far from my thoughts, not for a day, not for an hour." She sighed, tears rolling down her cheeks. "I pray that it's your child I'm carrying." She felt secure in his arms.

He physically reacted to her admission with a total body spasm. The frown lines between his eyebrows were as deep as battle scars. Smoothing the hair back from her forehead, he kissed the top of her face, thumbing back the wispy curls at her temples.

"You'll have medication for that pain. It'll make the going easier, but you need to lie down intermittently. Your due date is close. You could deliver anytime." Whispering gently, his voice vibrated through her skin.

"The sooner the better." The tears continued to prickle against her eyelids.

"No one gets more attention from me than you do, and that will never cease. Now we need to go over a few things so you don't enter into labor in a state of apprehension." Doc held her at arm's length, smiling down at her, warm and sincere. At fifty-two years old, he felt the same drives he had when eighteen.

"The pain you're describing is sciatica," he said, returning to his chair behind the desk. "Some fluid that your body produces during pregnancy is stored inside nerve tissue, which makes the sciatic nerve become slightly swollen.

The swollen tissue then presses against the bony channels of the spine. Sciatica pain may radiate from the back and down the legs, such as you're describing. I want you to take these pills as instructed." His head dipped, writing on the small white dosage envelope.

"When will I know if I'm in labor, Danforth?" Sarah asked suddenly, her breath coming in short bursts.

"You're in labor right now. Throughout pregnancy, the uterus contracts in preparation for labor, although these contractions are usually not noticeable until the last weeks of pregnancy. If you have contractions, but they're not accompanied by any other signs and don't increase in frequency, you're probably not in labor. When you've passed your mucous plug that has formed a barrier between your uterus and vagina during pregnancy—it will be a good show—then you're moving on." He looked at her possessively, his soul aching with her unattainability.

"Does that have to occur before I come to the hospital?" She found it difficult to think clearly. Her brain must be in idle. She'd been like that lately—one minute with the program and the next minute befuddled.

"Not necessarily. Your amniotic sac may rupture. This will be a slow trickle of fluid from your vagina or you may have a sudden gush. But I want you here as soon as you determine your labor pains are coming at regular intervals. I want to monitor you closely. You're carrying a very large baby for a woman your size. I'd say it's roughly around eight pounds. But we might have expected that with a super sire such as you've had," he said, smiling, raising one eyebrow, tongue-in-cheek.

❦

She remembered that the days dragged on after that last visit, but she remained encouraged by Doc, who made her feel dear and important to him. Thank God, she had him. Needing Abe so much, anxiety prevailed without him. No longer able to come home on weekends, since football season had started, she hadn't seen him for two weeks. She reminded herself that she had known that when she married him—that his first love rested in the economics and competition of football. She needed to understand that and *grow up*, as Abe said. Her facial muscles were up tight with the preponderance of adjustments in her life. She wondered why life seemed so imperfect at times.

What started out as a lazy drizzle grew into a raging rain slamming against doors and windows with a vengeance, snarling and howling, blowing the bushes alongside the building topsy turvy like papier-mâché mockups.

"When did the labor pains start?" Doc asked anxiously as he arrived, seemingly out of nowhere. Viewing him from her bed, he looked bigger than ever.

"Only a couple of hours ago, but I've had cramps since yesterday," Sarah said, gritting her teeth against a new contraction. "I'm so glad to see you; I hurt so badly!"

Doc laid his hand on her billowed belly, felt the hardness of the contraction and sucked in his breath. "Okay, Lady Sarah, it looks as if we're in business. Quigley will carry out some routine prep steps to avoid infection."

Categorically, Sarah rejected the announcement. "What? No one mentioned these things." Her eyes rounded with displeasure and objection.

"Delivering a baby isn't written under a column entitled "Glamorous." However, we find in our business that the heavenly and the pits of hell often occur simultaneously. You're going to have a beautiful baby to take home, if I ever allow you out of this hospital." Bending over, he kissed her on the forehead. "Hold tight."

While being prepped, she heard water splashing—the clatter of metal stirrups being mounted, the rattle of instrument trays being prepared in the surgical room across the hall where babies were also delivered. Doc had called in Ruby Brimmer, his midwife nurse assistant. Sarah knew her as a less-than-slender alternately somber or cheery creature in her early thirties, dark-skinned, with enormous brown eyes, dark-rimmed glasses and a quicksilver wit and smile.

Sarah shuddered, running her hand through her hair, now wet with the sweat of labor. No longer could she think of all the metaphors she'd heard during her pregnancy that she'd found so humorous: a bundle of joy, found in the cabbage patch, the stork delivers, swallowed a watermelon seed. They were worn out and beaten; this was real and extravagantly unpleasant.

A violent clap of thunder shook the building as if the complete lumberyard had collapsed, an earsplitting noise, as the lightning flashed and the wind increased in intensity. Sarah heard the pine tree outside her window crack and pop.

"Okay!" Doc returned in his scrubs and smacked his hands together. "Let's see what we have here. I need those gloves, Quigley. He spread Sarah's knees only enough to check gently. She clutched Quigley's arm and groaned as a great gush of water spurted over Doc's gloved hand and the bed. "Ohhh, I didn't mean to do that. I'm sorry," she cried in embarrassment as the contraction relaxed.

"Of course you didn't mean to do that. Your sac of amniotic fluid just broke. Your first stage of labor is over Sarah. I can't believe it. You must have had some hair-curling cramping at home," he scolded. "You've nearly reached full dilation with the opening of the cervix at about 9 cm—nearly four inches in diameter."

"Oh-oooh-uh," she screamed and rolled sideways with a fist of pain beyond endurance. She pulled a pillow over her head until the contraction released itself.

Doc eased the pillow away. "There," he said tenderly. "Take some deep breaths like you practiced with Suki. She'll be here in a few minutes to help you." He toweled her forehead, further instructing her to breathe in quick pants.

"When the cervix is fully dilated there is a transition period between the first and second stages of labor. You'll be relieved to know that in some women labor seems to come to a temporary halt at this point." His eyes were as heavy with compassion as the low-hanging clouds outside.

Abe's voice in the hall brought more tears, tears of relief one felt to find salvation. Yet, at the same time, it brought stuttering giggles, the ones that bubble up from nowhere, impossible to suppress.

Quigley quickly greeted him and closed the door. His shoes, wet from stepping in puddles of rainwater, sounded "squish, squish" across the floor. Rushing to Sarah, he found tears rolling down her cheeks. He bent and kissed them soundlessly. Closed tightly with that old familiar lump, his throat blocked words he'd rehearsed to say. Touching her gently on the cheek with his knuckles, he worried.

"I'm sorry to be slow arriving, but it's so black and storming out there that you can hardly see the road. It's been bearish. But I'm here for you now, Sarah." He breathed her name softly, like a child's breath. Seeing her in such anguish sent wooziness creeping over him like a colony of fire ants.

"You're looking like a dime store skeleton, Abe," Doc said. "Don't you go fading away." He shook Abe's elbow.

"Ohhhhhmmmm," Sarah writhed with another seizure of naked pain, placing the pillow over her head again.

"Breathe, Sarah, breathe." Suki had come in, dressed in scrubs, too.

"So glad to see you, Abe," Doc teased, giving a grimace of mock despair. "A diller a dollar, et cetera. Before you touch a thing, go in the next room and get on a suit like mine. There's one laid out for you. Wash your hands well and come back. You're the only father ever allowed in my delivery room, I want you to know." Doc stood back for Abe to leave, his gesture sure, certain; he was in charge.

"Now, Sarah," Doc advised with patience, "you can't get adequate oxygen with a pillow over your head. You don't want to deny your little one its healthy blood supply," he said, his voice commandingly coaxing.

"I don't want to wake up everyone in the hospital with screaming and groaning," Sarah bleated, leaning over to throw up as Quigley rushed with the kidney-shaped basin.

Doc rejected her concerns. "Don't you give a single thought to who hears you scream. Labor can get damned awful. Your contractions will become more powerful and they will be accompanied by an urge to push the baby through the birth canal. Quigley will administer a combination of gas and air during your contractions."

Suddenly she lurched, her whole body consumed with strapping pains encircling her whole body, her back shrieking for relief. She screamed long; her voice echoed in her own ears from far away.

"Try panting during the contraction, Sarah," Suki encouraged, holding her hand.

Doc nodded to Quigley to be ready with gas for the next contraction.

Spreading her legs wider, with no protest from the now-anaesthetized Sarah, Doc knew she'd birth this baby in a field of hay just to have it done with. He re-examined her, feeling her abdomen for the next contraction, which crunched within a minute.

"She's ten. Let's do it!" he ordered.

CHAPTER FORTY-FOUR

Like clockwork, Quigley set the gurney in place as she, Doc and Ruby moved Sarah in between contractions, and wheeled it across the hall to the brightly lighted delivery room.

Sarah thrashed with pain. It never stopped now, a penance of burning hell. Sweat flowed off her forehead, her hair soaked. Childbirth remained a terror, a nightmare of odyssey proportions. She screamed silently this time—she thought—being in some kind of frightful, endless fog.

Abe entered the room.

In Sarah's tribulation, a dam broke. "Ohhhhhmmmm. How much *more* damned awful is this going to get?" She gasped, clutching Abe's smock in her fist.

He looked at her helplessly, then at Doc, then back to her, not knowing what to say. "It'll be over soon and the pain will be gone." *I don't know why I demanded she have this child. This is it. Oh Sarah, I love you so much.*

Seized with another fierce pain, she breathed deeply of the gas, coming out of it and wretching again, not caring what they thought of the unladylike posture of this experiment in dread.

Doc positioned her for birth, applying soothing lubrication. Ruby wrapped her legs and feet in sheets.

"Make it all stop, Abe. Just let's not do this. I don't want to have this baby. I changed my mind." She screamed long and hard again, her head moving back and forth, trying by sheer will to shake away the pain.

Abe slumped onto a nearby stool, elbows on his knees, his head hanging low. "Doc, can't you do something to help her?" Abe's questioning eyes teared over.

With compassion, Doc looked at him over his mask, and shook his head *no* with the unspoken truth. "She has a big baby to move, Abe. We'll need her to push soon. Besides, it's dangerous for the baby to be under sedation at this point. Sorry." Doc looked as handsome as an early June morning in his scrubs and mask, which did nothing to conceal the firm set of his jaw.

"How're you doing, Sarah?" Doc asked.

How am I doing? she thought. How can he ask? How can he not know how I feel? For the first time in her life, she snarled, rejecting his solicitation of concern completely. "I'm dying and no one cares," she sobbed, her voice choking. "I'm done with this," she cried, going blind with pain. She begged shamelessly. "Some more gas, please, Doc. I can't breathe anymore. I can't push anymore. Everything hurts so much!" She screamed again, she could hear it—*doesn't sound like me...can't be me.*

"Okay, Sarah. Push!" Doc grew excited. "Push! Try! Imagine this miracle that's passing from your body into life's stream, the new little beating heart, the sucking for air; it's up to you, Sarah. Push!" Doc's voice carried the right message.

She screamed from somewhere off in space and pushed, took a deep breath and pushed somemore. A burning sensation escalated and seared her vitals. She felt she must be someone not in control, some wandering soul searching for peace, delirious. She was being drawn and quartered. She threw up again, knew not where or on whom—maybe she'd choke and die. Wouldn't that be wonderful!

"Push, Sarah," Doc encouraged. "Just one more time!" His voice held command and excitement. Doc saw the beginning of the end and became elated.

"Unnnnhhhh. No more, can't..." her voice faded into nothingness. Smudges of fatigue covered her countenance; deep shadows camped under her eyes.

Doc caught Quigley's eye and nodded to put her out. He could finish the job himself now. He gestured a *come here* to Abe and Suki to behold the miracle.

Abe saw a little head of black hair between Sarah's legs, slowly ejecting from the birth canal. Doc applied ample lubrication. He looked surprised; it appeared as if no episiotomy would be necessary.

Abe watched in fascination as the head was delivered. A crawling feeling started at the hackles of his neck, sped down his back, shook his shoes. Doc waited, his hands in position, the room in total silence. The shoulders slipped out quickly in another spasm. The hips and legs delivered so quickly that they fairly exploded out.

"Just look at the size of that baby...baby...baby boy!" Doc shouted. The excitement was contagious. Everyone soared, ebullient, laughing, a catch in the throat, looking at the newly delivered prize.

The newly delivered treasure wailed as loudly as Sarah had been screaming. Ruby took him and laid him on Sarah's belly, while Quigley removed the anesthetic mask, allowing Sarah to return to the land of the living, groaning, squeaking, gasping hysterically, "No, no, no, no. I don't want to wake up. No, no, no, never!"

Abe leaned over her. "Sarah! We have a great big baby boy! He's beautiful!" His voice cracked as tears rolled down his cheeks, and he kissed Sarah's wet forehead.

Lifting her head, she groggily looked down at the blustering bundle on her belly; a wonder stare of impossible magnitude appeared in her eyes and passed quickly into a smile—joy flooded through her such as she'd never known. Her son!

Abe bent down and kissed her, kissed his son, and wept. "Thank you, Sarah, for the greatest gift in the whole world, my son. You're the best, babe." His voice split with emotion, but he didn't care—didn't care who heard, didn't care who saw. He had a son!

The umbilical cord had been severed and tied. To speed the process and to prevent excessive bleeding, Doc pulled gently on the cord while pressing on her abdomen with the other hand. All the while, he watched Abe caressing Sarah's hairline, whispering to her. He ached. He ached with love for this woman and love for his son, and God only knew, for this his second son. He ached for never knowing the joy of having his own child, the lost years, the misdemeanors of his life, the felony of abandoning his real love and only son, and vowed that Abe would never know that this wasn't his own son, if, indeed, it wasn't.

He administered a hypo of medication to prevent excessive bleeding. Doc had a picture-perfect birth. No hang-ups, no emergencies; he breathed a long sigh of relief. He always expected the unexpected. The impossible would take a little longer.

"I have a few small tears here that need to be sutured. I'll freeze the area locally, Sarah. You'll feel a little prick." Doc was solicitous in his kindness.

"A little prick I can handle after what I've been through," she said softly, her arm around Abe's neck, looking up at him, happiness radiating from their eyes like two beams of searching light. There sprung a wide, crazy smile on Abe's unshaven face, declaring this his finest moment.

"I'll just get this little guy cleaned up, Sarah, then you can hold him again," Ruby said over her shoulder.

"What are you going to do with him?" Sarah asked, concerned about having the child out of her sight.

"First I'll check his backbone for defects, then Ill check his mouth for a harelip or a cleft palate. I also check his genitals and anus for working order. His genitals!" she cried. "Holy blue blazes, look at the size of this kid's balls! Did you ever see anything like that, Doc?" she asked, holding the baby up to show them. "We got any blue ribbons here?" She laughed while she finished checking the feet and the legs for proper bone structure. "This kid is going to make some woman happy." She continued laughing.

Doc looked at Abe. Their eyes locked in mutual understanding for a full minute before they joined in the laughter.

Sarah had returned to a sound sleep, exhausted, drifting away into that land of rewards after a hard day's work. Deep circles under her eyes belied how peaceful she otherwise looked.

Abe hadn't noticed until Doc stood up that he was spattered with blood. He took off his glasses, crinkled his eyes and rubbed them. He rarely ever saw Doc wear glasses. It showed him as a different man—professional, discerning, prudent.

"Quigley," Doc ordered, "give Sarah a shot of the God Morpheus, and let her get some rest. I want her checked often for hemorrhaging. She lost a lot of blood after the delivery, although I have it down to a normal flow right now."

Abe observed how pragmatic Doc could be in the face of intellectual solutions. He never seemed to become unzipped about anything, either. Whatta guy!

The wind gusted to a renewed gale, driving and scraping the bushes against the outer wall of the delivery room. The night was black and violent—unrelenting.

Ruby and Suki *oohed* and *aahed* over the new baby—couldn't wait to show it to the waiting Marian Savin, who had no desire to witness the birthing.

"Abe, let's you and I go home and have a stiff one. That was hard work for us, don't you think so?" Doc laughed, grasping Abe's shoulder. "We can unwind a little. Two showers are in order, and we'll both be done at the same time."

Prepared to leave, Doc poked his head into Sarah's room to check on her one last time; Abe accompanied him in tandem. The women were tucking baby boy Miereau-Whittaker into a bassinet near Sarah's bed.

Kissing Sarah's face in the repose of sleep, Abe turned his attention to his new son—dark hair, lots of it, fat squishy face, eyes that fought to open and tiny fists that flailed the air. He'd finally stopped crying now that he was securely wrapped in warmth.

"Fabian Danforth Miereau-Whittaker." *What a handle for such a defenseless child.* "We'll just call you Fabe," he said, bending over the child's bed. "Yes, Fabe it is! Run, Fabe. Catch the ball, Fabe. Hut, hut, hut." Abe provided his Sioux Sun Dance in the crowded room, ending with a victorious spike of the fabricated ball, to everyone's amusement. "Yes!" He declared.

Doc shook his head at the whimsical antics of this new father, his son, his eyebrow raised, that conservative half grin re-born. "I'll leave the garage door open, Suki, so don't be long. A warm fire will be roaring in the fireplace by the time you get there. I can suddenly hear rain again, drenching, a downpour."

"Thanks, Danforth. I just want to stay a short while with little Fabe, Sarah and Ma and help Quigley finish up here. I won't be long." She smiled warmly at her handsome husband, her diamond-in-the-rough son, filled with new tenderness at the addition of yet another young man in her life—all virile Whittakers.

∼∽

In one of the most imposing homes in the village, Doc and Abe found solace as rain streamed over the eaves in long silver threads. "What a nice gesture this is, naming your new son after Fabian and me. I'm pleased and flattered." Doc set the firewood in place and ignited it with a "poof," closing the metal mesh, leaving the glass doors open. The fire sprang to life, licking hungrily at the teepee of logs.

"That's always been it, Doc. No doubt about it. That delivery room scenario was awesome, but for a while I wanted to wad it up and throw it away. You were in an element in which I've seen you but few times. It's a curious feeling, as if viewing a person for the first time, one you don't know. It kind of got to me, right here," Abe said, pointing to his heart. "If that were a stage performance, I'd give you a standing ovation." Abe accepted the martini Doc poured for him.

"Thank you, Abe." Doc could see the joy, disconcertion yet fascination written clearly on Abe's face. "Delivery rooms and surgical theatres are an isolated part of most people's lives, shaky ground to many. I'd have been terribly disappointed had Sarah decided to birth baby Fabe in Green Bay. What a big moment that achieved for *us* too." There was the sound of repleteness in Doc's voice, satisfying and profound.

Lightning flashed in the big bay window of the living room as they heard the back door close—Suki arriving home. Fresh and drippy from running from the garage into the house, Suki sailed into the living room. "A few more days of this rain and the toads will drown," she said, giving Doc a big kiss on the head. She sought the depth of his eyes. "Danforth, what a wonderful guy you were in the delivery room. That is an unforgettable experience for me; you were absolutely impressive!"

"*Merci beaucoup.*" Doc said, smiling, rubbing his mustache.

Leaning down and giving Abe a squeeze, she turned effusive. "Congratulations, Dad. What a beautiful child—just perfect. Sarah is a good cook and *you* were a good provider of the necessary ingredients for a perfect product!"

Abe preened, his pride showing in the immediate smile that lit his whole face. "Thanks, Suki. That was my very own Manhattan Project! However, that's the last time we're cooking. I can't believe what she had to go through to bring that child into the world. She is quite a lady." His eyes stirred with pride.

"Yes, she is. I made a bigger to-do than that when *you* were born. I'll never forget it, ever. It was the pits. You see that I've had no further children, either. Once around on that is plenty." She flashed Doc a big smile. "Even if the father were stalwart and strong and available, I'd have still backed way off...well...maybe...if the opportunity had struck. Who knows?" she said, tossing her arms into the air.

"Ah, but look what you got," Doc said, teasing Suki. "My son. I don't allow just anyone to be the mother of my child!"

"Oh, stop," she said, waving him off. "Wish to hear a little Vivaldi?"

Doc nodded, his eyes closing for a moment at the thought of it. Quickly, the clarity of the lutes and strings trailed the sounds of happiness.

"See you guys later. I'm going to take a shower and go to bed. Congratulations to you both. You did an outstanding job, Danforth. I'm so proud of you." Her soothing smile warmed them both.

"Well, life has changed in a heartbeat for you, Abe. Now you have the responsibility of a little one and a wife who needs you. You need to remember to love the woman in her, and not treat her like a wife and mother only." Sometimes Doc felt the warnings to go slowly with Abe. "Wary" was the word that came to his mind.

"Yeah, I don't think I'll ever forget that. Every time I thought of Sarah out there in the working world and having other interests than devoting her time to me, I'd go crazy—have nightmares, my oldest enemy. Now she'll have her hands full."

Doc took a deep breath, wondering if Abe really heard what he said.

Sometimes he simply didn't use the right words to reach him. Sarah's a woman, not a commodity. Doc shook his head, as if settling the dust of his thoughts, a few minutes of actual time, but twenty-three years of memories.

"Shifting gears here. How do you like being a Packer?" Doc poured them both another drink. The fire crackled, Vivaldi lifting their spirits—rain beat relentlessly.

Abe's eyes lit up with a new vigor and intensity. "Do you know that the Packer-Bear rivalry is more than what meets the headlines? It's crazy. Last week the Bears played at Green Bay, as you know, but what you don't know is that they traveled by bus and stayed in Appleton for overnight lodging. From there north to Green Bay, the drive was a four-lane highway through rolling farmland. But the thing is, you can see huge, stuffed, black bears...five feet tall, and with a face that looks very much like the logo of the Bears. They have them hanging from maple trees, apple trees, whatever, with ropes tied around their necks, maybe forty yards from the shoulder of the road. And just as the Bear buses sped by, two-three kids in the yards took to beating on the stuffed Bears. It was wild!" His voice resonated with enthusiasm and a robust quality to his voice with the telling. Strong muscles in Abe's shoulders flexed and moved, his gestures showing the strong chest curving around to his back. "It has to be nuts, elevated to stimulating. Can you believe getting that carried away with Packer fever?"

Doc laughed. The anecdote sprung to life in his mind. "The support for the Packers in Green Bay is absolutely awesome." His English enunciation curled around the word as if he could savor it. "They're a bunch of born ballosauruses."

Abe's eyes widened, laughing. "Good one, Doc. And did you know that Packer fans tailgate at Packer Stadium? You walk from your car through parking lots full of bratwurst-cooking tailgaters. Two rules about being a Packer fan: You gotta love brats, and you gotta hate the Bears." Trembles of excitement flowed physically through him, finding the rivalry rousing, yet a little scary in its encompassing dimensions.

"You walk through the parking lots of Packer Stadium and find that it's tailgate heaven. It surely is. I don't know what else you could call it. It has to be the greatest smell of all time, the bratwurst and the crisp fall air and the leather from the footballs whacking off the cars. No one can ruin that." His eyes were glowing as brightly as the early morning sun on dew.

"Nope, you can't," Doc replied. "It's the sights and sounds that infiltrate the fans' senses to make it Packer Backer time. There is completeness to the whole scenario. They all come together at Packer Home Games like a spiritual ablution as warm as a bowl of hot soup on a cold day. Packer fans find a kind of music to the word 'Packer.'"

Abe nodded in agreement. "Exactly." His voice grew a little tight, not wanting to sound arrogant. "I've averaged five catches per game. Of course, it's only been two games, but it's a nice start. Curly is happy." He studied Doc's gaze on him. "Am I talking your head off, Doc? I get so excited. I guess I'm all wound up with the new baby and pro ball..." He gestured with a slap to his forehead.

"No, you're not talking my head off." Doc laughed warmly. "I like to hear about your life, Abe. It's very different than mine. I could only fantasize about a day in your life. You know the old saying—the grass is always greener, etc. My mind had to hurry to keep up with your pictorial descriptions, so vivid, so now, so real." Doc became pensive again. His elbow rested on the arm of the chair, his finger bent over his mustache and mouth—Abe's favorite memory of him.

"You're so fast, Doc. You're always way ahead of me. Sometimes I don't even have to finish what I'm saying because you already know what's coming next. Reminds me of Fabian's old blue enameled coffee pot—always spoke to me of home and warmth—always tasted dependably the same." His voice declined as he put his finger to his lips as if the words just occurred to him with the delivery. "You're a one and only."

"Well, your one-and-only wants you to have something for new baby Fabian Danforth Miereau-Whittaker." Doc stood up and walked toward the foyer, then swung back. "You'll have to promise me that it will stay in the family as a keepsake." Abe could hear him in his adjoining office, moving items on the shelves of his bookcases.

Doc returned in a minute, carrying the case of twelve Krugerrand, each softly bedded into a velvet notch under glass. Without a word, he presented them to Abe, who sat with his shoulders rounded, his hands between his knees, containing himself until Doc's return. Abe shifted his gaze from the case up to Doc, his eyes wide, marveling at such largesse. *Is he serious? There must be easily five hundred dollars worth the gold in there.* He released an audible sigh. "Doc, you...you can't be serious! I know how proud you are of this collection. It's one of the first things you showed me—long ago, on the night I came to you seeking advice on Fabian. And now you want little Fabian to have it?" An unusual rawness showed in his voice. There raged in him warmth over which he had no control, a hot core with radiating memories to support it.

Doc, still standing over him, nodded. "It's for him. You keep these. They'll be secure seed money for Fabe's college years. Each piece contains one ounce of solid gold, their value enduring and appreciating forever." His eyes focused on Abe, but he seemed to reach far beyond, or perhaps he searched within himself, seeking...solace? But then it withdrew. "When you get to Green Bay you need to rent yourself a safety deposit box at your bank and store them. Unless, of course, you feel you have a secure place for it at home such as I have in my office. It's just a suggestion," Doc said, his voice trailing off as he went to the kitchen to get snacks for the two of them.

Returning with a cheese board of double-cream Brie and thick slices of Italian bread, he continued as if he'd never left. "You see, Abe, everything a man works for all his life is the final accumulation of heritage for his children. It's my fondest wish that little Fabe has this insurance for his future, probably long after I'm gone. Who knows?" Abe caught a brief peek into something burning in his eyes, a reflection of a firm commitment, pre-determined and culminated in this gesture.

"Well, thank you so much, Doc. I never dreamed these Krugerrand would be resting in my hands one day. Unbelievable." Abe's words became strangled. He felt as if he were a kid again, wrestling to get words out that were plugged up somewhere between his head and his heart and his tongue. The parallelism he felt with this man was incredibly sweeping. "I don't want you to ever leave me, Doc. You gotta stick around until Fabe grows up and goes to college and plays football, just as I did," he ground out huskily. All the gratitude and love of a lifetime was laced into the simplicity of his message in Abe's glistening, rich-brown eyes.

The howling wind and rain outside seemed to be getting threadbare in its insistence, hopefully having maxed itself out.

Doc shifted his eyes to the fireplace, wanting to give Abe a measure of dignity time, acknowledging that it was *he* who knew gratitude for Abe gracing *his* life—knowing it was *he* who had neglected the boy dismally all his childhood, knowing that it was *he* who would do anything for Abe. "You owe me no debt of gratitude, Abe. It's what I want to do for you and your new family. It makes me happy to be able to do so. Suki and I are very proud of you." Doc's hand opened and closed, flexing.

"You know, it's funny." Abe tried an offhanded laugh, but it came out more of a chortled choke. "Often times I want to just show everybody how much I belong there in the big time, seeing as I've come all the way from this little town, but when all is said and done, I'm still small town. There are nights when I just sit home in the practical place I rented, pitifully lonely. I'll be glad to get my family moved down there." He spread the Brie on a slice of bread, closing his eyes to enjoy the superb cheese.

"No one is, Abe. We all have times like that. Sometimes I get lonely in a crowd. It's curious, isn't it?" Doc sat quietly, reflecting. The living room fell into silence except for Vivaldi, who had slipped into a sassy sonata. The instruments talked to each other—arguing, appeasing, making love. The anxieties of the long day began to dissipate.

"What the hell, Abe. Let me fix another pitcher of martinis, and you just stay overnight here in the guest room. No sense in going home to a chilly house. We'd be delighted to have you, my son, sleeping in my house. I want you to make a habit of it too. That grandson isn't going to be a stranger around here!"

Seated again by the fire, Abe talked excitedly about colorful Curly stories. "Do you know what that guy did? You won't believe it. One day, four of his players reported late to practice. There is a regular fine of five hundred dollars for missing practice, and Lambeau decided to levy the hefty fine on all four guys. He ordered them all to draft checks for five hundred dollars to the Packers, posthaste and forthwith."

"I'm cashing them, too," he said, "before you can stop payment."

"If you do, I'll kill you," one of the offenders snarled.

"Wouldn't do any good," Lambeau said. "I'll just hit you with another five hundred dollar fine." Abe laughed, languishing in his deep well of humor.

"Hard sonofabitch! I never saw that in him." Doc laughed. "I guess he let them know who's on first. Apparently he's *par excellence* and *persona extraordinaire*," he said with a smile that swept farther than his eyes.

That's you, too, Doc—all that." He pulled on his lower lip thoughtfully. The length of the day caught up with him like the daylight reaching for the early morning sun, but bowing out at the end of the day.

※

Sarah was confined in the hospital for a week, then at her mother's home for another week before Doc discharged her into the custody of her husband and his son. A cool nip hung in the air; the leaves were off all the hardwoods, the bleakness of winter a definite promise.

His heart lurched—he hurt all over. He'd had the complete dominance since last June of this woman he loved with such fierce protectiveness. It was difficult to let her go. No, not difficult—devastating. However, he loved her so much that her happiness and that of Abe's took precedence over his emotions. But how could he blow off responsibility? Did he care? Did he care! How much, posed the better question.

Fabe, who had weighed in at eight pounds four ounces and a whopping twenty-three inches long, created the picture of contentment in his mother's arms as they stopped at Doc's on that early Tuesday evening, October 16, just two weeks after Fabe had been born on that terribly stormy night.

Abe had bought a new 1948 Hudson four-door car, forest green and gleaming. "Doc, when I traded that 1942 Ford at the garage in Green Bay, I felt as if I should be playing taps and as if I were betraying Eddie's memory. That car has been so good to me...took me through thick and thin. But it had seventy-six thousand miles on it, which was overplaying my hand. Now that I have a wife and son, I need more security."

"It's a beauty, Abe. It puts my mind at ease too, knowing you're driving a new car. Be careful on the trip back to Green Bay. You should be there by nine o'clock at the latest. If you need anything, anything at all, call us. Suki and I will try to get down to Green Bay to visit you yet this fall before the snow piles up too high."

"Thank you, Doc, for everything. You've done so much for both of us. All the gratitude we could ever convey would never be enough." Abe embraced his father, then hugged his mother. Doc flinched, feeling his mind close down in self-protection.

The face Sarah turned up to them from within the car shone with love and longing, her eyes glistening at the thought of leaving them both, but filled with the future and her new life. She had known a measure of tears and was moved to numbness at leaving Doc and Suki. Fabe lay nestled in his blankets, sleeping soundly.

Reaching through the car window, Doc touched her face, gently patting it, bringing a dazzling smile from her. His mouth went dry, dwarfing anything he'd ever experienced in loneliness.

And they were on their way to their new life.

"May God go with them," Doc said under his breath. Suki turned to ask him what he'd said, but thought she must have just heard the soft susurrations of the wind. Going inside, he lit a cigar, watching the blue-green smoke wisp through the warm air. He felt a visceral tightness in his stomach—emptiness. *Somewhere over the rainbow with your fantasies*, Danforth, he thought.

CHAPTER FORTY-FIVE

The next four years whistled by in speedy locomotion of busy seasons in Green Bay for the Miereau-Whittakers. In May 1952, Abe knew he had the world by the tail—plus tax. He never could figure out, why him? Here he lived ensconced in a beautiful home on the Fox River—a dream, only a dream to most. He sipped coffee on the front patio, the sun warming the early morning chill. Heavily wooded near the street for privacy, his front lawn swept out to Riverside Drive. The breeze in the birches and sweet maples reminded him of his home in Nahma, and brought the fresh smell of dissipating dew. But that's where the similarity ended.

He placed his elbows on his knees, encircled the mug with both hands, and leaned forward, the warmth of the hot coffee seeping through. He had all this: a red brick home with white Doric columns fluted at the tops, a *porte cochere* on the side, over which an immense deck rested where Sarah sunbathed her skin to a flawless chestnut. His second floor master bedroom gave onto the deck, connected with high, wide French doors. Max would have a flood of fits to see what he'd done with his life—the penniless half-breed, not fit to marry his daughter. He'd blown right past the line in the sand Max had drawn. Laughter rippled again, this time gently.

Abe reviewed the pleasant evenings he spent in the backyard that sloped gently down to the Fox River where his dock stood sturdy, anchoring a forty-five foot pleasure boat, powerful enough to take out into the bay. He owned groomed-gardens of annuals like tulips, crocus, hyacinth and daffodils in the spring, right down to the last blaze of chrysanthemums in the fall. Max wouldn't believe that either.

It was hard to believe that Fabe was already three years old, four in October. He wished he could convince Sarah to have another child. Fabe needed a brother. Not that he wasn't a happy little guy, a stunningly beautiful child, rather serious though. Abe was proud of his husky Fabe, his abundant black hair, dark eyes and generous genitals. Proud of the child's studious intensity, his exhibited keen interest in Grandpa Danforth's medical "stuff." His half smile lighted his eyes—funny how *contagious* genetics were.

He could hear Fabe now in the kitchen with Sarah, ordering up his breakfast like an English nobleman. "Pancakes today, Mom. Lots of syrup, please." *Gotta talk to that kid. Sounds as if he stayed up all night making the damn decision of what to have for breakfast!* In the background, Abe heard WFRV and Sarah humming "If You Got the Money Honey, I Got the Time." Could he have wished for anything more? Maybe he had sold his soul to the devil.

In another hour or so he should be getting a call from Doc that the moving van had arrived. He'd walk down Riverside Drive and help Doc and Suki move into their new home on the Fox River, only minutes away, here in Allouez. Their new mansion! Five bedrooms, four baths, and unique as hell with its stone facade, Tudor design, tennis court and swimming pool. Abe understood that the house had been built in 1850, at a cost of at least a hundred thousand dollars, by a lumber baron and had been conscientiously maintained over the years, possessing a quiet understatement of wealth and dignity.

It didn't seem possible that the Bay de Nocquet Lumber Company shut down their operations in Nahma—cut their last logs. That meant that Doc's services were no longer needed. Could it have been a stroke of luck?

A thrill of excitement ran through Abe as he thought of Doc's new clinic being built near the Packer Stadium, on Ashland Avenue: a clinic, an athletic club, complete with workout equipment and racket ball. *His resources seem to be limitless!* And...and it must have tickled him right down to his essentials when Bob Chapin committed to a partnership in the clinic as soon as he completed his internship in orthopedics.

In addition, Doc strung together a group of his old cohorts from Michigan. They, with their accumulated degrees in general medicine, internal medicine, orthopedic medicine, neurology and obstetrics & gynecology, would attract most, if not all, of the Green Bay Packer families, as well as all of the game-related injury referrals.

God only knows, the Packers needed a good referral unit for adaptation and recuperation from the tumultuous injuries on the field—Doc, Bob et al, could handle them all, plus provide a physical therapy program at the new clinic. Abe felt a shot of excitement at using the state-of-the-art gym. Doc's popularity, respect and demand would grow with the city and the Packers, as it had done in the village of Nahma.

Abe arose and leaned against a Doric column, still holding his coffee mug.

Beyond his wildest dreams, Doc convinced Bernard Tobin to commit to being his athletic trainer for subscribers to the private athletic club. Tobin's service in the Navy had seen a four-year-stint, and then his commitment to the new consolidated school district drained all his energies. Now, he'd live right here where they could have them over for dinner to make up for the many meals Tobin provided when he was a kid and starving to death!

Abe bit into his memory of the last four summers. He couldn't believe how good Doc looked, young, virile at fifty-six years old and Suki at forty-nine, both as flawless as hell. Abe knew that they had negotiated successfully with the Bay de Nocquet Lumber Company to buy their Nahma home for summer getaways. So while Abe and Sarah enjoyed their modest home on Beach Road in the summer months, the Whittakers continued to enjoy their magnificent home on the boulevard downtown.

Abe reclined again in his chair, stretching out his long legs. Crossing his feet at the ankles, he placed his coffee cup on the patio table and hooked his thumbs under his chinos. He yet excited at visiting in Ann Arbor. The five of them flew from Green Bay across Lake Michigan to Ann Arbor to spend the Easter Holiday with Walter and Anne, who returned from Florida for the event. Kyle and Karen Kreiler attended on Saturday for a cookout in the Whittaker's rambling backyard.

Then there was Hulk, drafted the same year as Abe and went to the great George Blanda years with the Bears, remaining a pain in the ass to the Packers. "You guys'll never beat the Bears," Hulk called over his shoulder.

"And you guys'll never know the glue that holds the Packers together. We have dedication. The Bears are too much into personal agendas," Abe replied.

"Call it what you want, we're making it; we're winning," The never-ending but loving thorn in his side, Hulk liked the time they spent together.

At a post-game mixer, Abe had introduced Bruce Hulk to Julie, a wide-eyed, Irish and Polish school teacher, who had relocated to Green Bay from Peshtigo.

Hulk chose to pursue this little gem. Peshtigo had strong ties to Nahma, both being lumbering towns, both having been burned to the ground at one time. Abe knew Hulk had chosen Julie from a family that had sheltered her very closely. This fact remained a high-water mark with both of them. On their nights out alone, they chewed on the ins and outs of being a football star, and the gratification of choosing for their mates creme de la creme virgins. After all his philandering, Hulk slid to a stop and drilled down roots.

Abe was overjoyed at the thought of how his home filled with friends from Nahma on Packer home game weekends. Kenny Ritter and his wife Betty came often. Kenny worked at the mill after the war until it closed in '51. Doc delivered two children to them before leaving—a little boy and a little girl, just a year apart. Now they lived in Escanaba, where Kenny worked for Mead Corporation, located on the Escanaba River.

Del and Mary Nolan-O'Brian visited as often as Del could get away from managing the Nahma Golf Course. "Abe, while you're home in the summer, come out to the course. You and I can knock off eighteen easily in four hours." Abe did.

He felt a stirring in his abdomen when he included Sarah in his memories. He continued to worship *his woman,* and swept her into his arms to dance to "Moonlight Serenade." Fabe pretended to be an airplane and danced around the room with them. Contentment flourished and grew in the Miereau-Whittaker household. Curious, Abe thought, that his philandering spirit rarely went farther than the visual or verbal since getting married. Questions in regard to his physical integrity to Sarah circled his mind like moths under a streetlight. Did it stem from respect? Allegiance? Convenience? An inherent Boy Scout dedication? Hell, who knows?

Abe noticed the azure of the sky this day in May, the breeze getting warmer. At this time two years ago Harriet Acker died of lung cancer, leaving Bill a lonely man until he struck up a rewarding relationship with Ma Savin, who came into his life and made it sing with a resonance unknown to him before this time. Thereafter, whenever Abe and Sarah were in town, Bill and Ma had them over to the grand house on the boulevard that used to scare the hell out of Abe as a kid. Bill demanded that she be addressed as *Marian,* as well she should be. Max had flippancy about his relationships with people.

Abe went into the house and poured himself more coffee, observing Fabe, sitting at the table in his booster chair, manipulating his eating utensils. There lay on his face and in his hair smidgeons of syrup.

"Where's Katie this morning? There's no need for you to trouble yourself with Fabe's table training, Sarah. I've hired her to do that for you. I don't want you to get discouraged about child rearing," he said, delivering wicked smiles.

"Dad-dyyyy!" Fabe wailed raucously, hanging onto the last note.

"Hi, big guy! How ya doing today, huh? Are you daddy's best buddy?" Abe bent near Fabe. As Fabe reached out to touch with his syrupy hand, Abe jumped out of reach, thanks to his quick skills as a wide receiver. "Oh-no-you-don't. Daddy will play with you later." Fabe stared at him, his eyes full of wonder.

Frowning, Sarah looked at her watch. "I told Katie she could come an hour later because we'll be gone all day helping Doc and Suki. I never thought it was this much of an enigma feeding Fabe in the morning. It's worse than his baby night time feedings," she said, returning his smile, squared; his double meaning didn't escape her notice.

Abe's head snapped about to lock her in his gaze. He approached, touched her face, brushed his fingers over her soft mouth, looking into her eyes, questioning. He couldn't discern anything. *I wonder? Would she consider?*

"Dad-dyyyy!" Fabe beckoned again.

"Okay, okay, Fabe. Get cleaned up and Dad-dy will take you out on the swing." Fabe slapped his fat dimpled hands in his plate, grinning, syrup trickling out the side of his mouth, his tongue trailing after it. Abe shuddered, shook his head, and left.

Strolling out onto the patio, he leaned a shoulder against one of the large white columns at the far end of the front promenade and returned to his reveries. He'd saved all his press clippings for the past four years. His favorites weren't even about football.

"An immensely popular player, Miereau will always be known as one of the nicer guys in sports history. The yard of his home in Allouez is always filled with kids playing, often with Abe at the bottom of the pile. He volunteers for every charity he can. And what a team player. Find a teammate who doesn't like Miereau and you've found a teammate who doesn't like apple pie."

His next favorite read:

"Abe Miereau-Whittaker has made the number one position in the annual receivers list his personal preserve."

He wished Fabian were alive to share the successes of his life—Eddie, too. Abe felt a void as wicked as the storms of November out on the bay. He wished he had more children, too. *What the hell, Abe. You won't get Sarah to consent to another child.*

The telephone jangled. *Doc.* His first reaction jolted him from the searching dialogue with himself. How bright the future looked with the prospect of having Doc and Suki living just minutes down the street.

�❧

JULY 1954

"What the hell's keeping you, Sarah?" Abe paced the foyer. "We're supposed to be over at Doc's by now." He shouted up the stairs. "Remember? He said he needed some help to crank up the outdoor barbecues for the Clinic Employees Picnic."

"Here I am," she said from the top of the long, curving stairway.

He was breathless—saw her seventeen years old again, beautiful in a bronze-colored sundress, with a dazzling sweep of orange birds-of-paradise running diagonally from her right breast to the left hem of her skirt. Thin straps crept over her tanned shoulders. As she moved like a soft breeze down the stairs, he couldn't be sure he was breathing real air. Tan leather sandals lay caught between her toes.

"My God, Sarah, you're nothing if not an illusion. I can't believe yet that I'm so lucky as to have you for my wife. I'm going to try to stay virtuous all day at the picnic, but wait until we get home; you're going to preview my vices first hand!" He chucked her under the chin, his eyes a reflection of the love in his soul.

"My oh my. It's a silver tongue you have today, Mr. Miereau-Whittaker," she said, shooting him a teasing smile that rendered him as soft as warm butter. He could feel his heart beating as raggedly as it ever did even in tight pinches on the playing field.

Taking her hand, they walked slowly up Riverside Drive to Doc's new mansion on the Fox River. Katie, the nanny, had left with Fabe an hour ago.

"Would you marry me?" Abe asked, his eyes glinting with mischief. "I want you to be the mother of my second child." The words were as much a surprise when they exploded from his mouth as when the corks had ejected from the Dom Perignon bottles. Immediately, he became uneasy, knowing this injected a hotbed of controversy.

Her mouth went dry. Without thinking, she pressed her hands to her abdomen in an attempt to squelch the fear that filled her whenever he mentioned more children.

"Now don't shut down on me again, Sarah. Today would be a beautiful day to make a new baby. Besides, I have black lace fever." Suddenly, he drew her close, his mouth closed down over hers, pressing hard, demanding. Releasing her, he continued. "How do I begin to tell you how important it is to me to have another child?" A fierce intensity filled his voice. Licking his lips, he flashed his blue-ribbon smile, boyishly.

She never could resist his demanding an answering smile, which she had always provided since she'd been four-years old. But would he misinterpret it as a positive response? There lengthened considerable mileage between his question and the warmth of her smile. How long could she put him off? How would she dissuade him? Fear of going through the whole ordeal of pregnancy and childbirth again sent icy fingers creeping over her chest.

"I don't know if we'll ever hear the end of this difference we have about bringing another child into the world." She put her head down, talking to the sidewalk. "I don't want to have any more children, Abe. I wish we could be happy that we love each other." Her response metered somewhere between a laugh and a sob. "I've a notion to stop your love potions!" A short laugh emitted again.

Stopping, she looked up at him—the hurt she saw—his eyes wet with anguish. Then a louver closed over the pathway to the core of him. Eyes that had moments ago danced with warmth and love turned as lifeless as the brown marbles they had played with when they were children. He had gone from indisputable lover to a stranger in the speed of sound. She knew the blankness in his eyes meant subterranean anger. Perhaps she'd put him off too long— five years. She felt a pervading apprehension taking control.

"I've been hit with harder balls, Sarah, but I don't know when." His voice crawled with barely a whisper. Reaching up, she put her fingers on his mouth, her heart brutal with panic. He might leave her again. The church would consider it grounds for annulment to deny him a child. It would kill her she knew, to go through that again. The logistics of having another child were lost on him, lost in his cultural need of creating a family. She knew how stubborn he could be when he drove this route of thought. Sometimes she thought he'd see her crash and burn if she didn't cooperate.

Wordlessly, they walked up Doc's front sidewalk and used the flagstone path to the backyard, where they heard whoops and shouts from the picnickers. Laughter curled through the afternoon like cigarette smoke. Unobtrusive sprinklers in the front yard were moving robotically with a-shoosh, a-shoosh, a-shoosh, and from the distance of the sidewalk it gave a cooling effect. With shafts of bright sunlight piercing the umbrella of the hardwoods, it appeared a fairyland of dancing shapes and forms as people moved about, some playing tennis, horseshoes, milling around in conversation. Abe viewed it as a watercolor mist, dreamy and pastel. *Click.*

"Dad-dy!" Fabe called from the swing Doc had tied securely to a gnome-like old oak.

"Hey, big guy! C'mon over here and give daddy a Packer-size hug." Abe knelt down to receive five-year-old Fabe in his arms, lifting him in the air, his feet swinging out.

"High in the sky, Dad!" He laughed until his belly shook while Abe hoisted him onto his shoulders, holding his yet baby-dimpled hands in the security of his own, so large and skilled.

"Let's go help Grandpa and that crazy bachelor, Bob Chapin, with the barbecues. They'll like that, especially if *you* hand them the hot dogs."

"Yeahhh. Hot dogs!" Fabe shrieked, galloping Abe along with his hands under his chin. His long strides took him down the campus of Doc's lawn to the fire pit, now banked and laid over with extensive grillwork.

Sarah, trying to get her mind off the dreadful diatribe with Abe, busied herself with table covers that rippled in the breeze, tucking corners here and there as if it were a major commitment. Conversations drifted around her like a multitude of radio waves, all tweaking their turn to be heard. Giving warm hugs, Bill and Marian found Sarah. Under the oak by Fabe's empty swing, Farley and Norrhea sat collapsed in lawn chairs and waved a c'mon-over-and-join-us to her. All were houseguests of Doc.

Constant kibitzing hung in the air, ringing the lawn. "Suki, this is so nice! What a great day for a picnic. You must live right to get this nice weather. Who ordered this Chamber of Commerce day? Have another beer…over there on tap. Yes, hot dogs, hamburgers, brats and chicken all down on the grill. Doc and Bob are cooking. Dixie cups are in the coolers on the patio. Who's for volley ball?" Loads of laughter swirled through the afternoon heat with guys winding up on shop talk.

A soft southwest air stream blew in off the water, smelling of riverbank growth as Sarah approached the cooks with their tall white barbecue hats. Abe turned his head as she approached. For a brief moment she saw through the coldness of his gaze to a thread of love, and then he shut down again. She thought perhaps he'd acclimated to her insistence on no more children, but instead she'd seen a drastic escalation to his demands. The day lost some of its shine; his shutdown she knew amounted to a shutout.

"I love you," she said, trying to make up for his dashed hopes. She heard his sharp intake of breath as he returned his gaze to her, staring for what seemed like forever, but not long enough. In his eyes she read the wretchedness of a man who discovered he had but one solution to his problems. That choice was agony—a surrogate.

In a moment of absorption, Doc studied them, felt the pain himself. He had learned long ago to trust his instincts and intuitions and divined that something was off kilter. The depth of his deep brown eyes showed considerable concern. Sarah stood like a statue, rigid and frozen. She sighed. Doc could hear the sob in it. It pained him; all he ever wished for her was abundant joy, not the deep December of disillusionment.

Just as quickly as Abe had turned to Sarah, he ignored her. Putting on his party manners, he turned to the guests, appearing unimpressed with his *haus frau*, and chatted hospitably. She swung her eyes up to Doc on the other side of the grill, casting signs of readable apprehension. Both knew Abe's capacity to rage like a cornered coon.

❧❦

The sun hung like a molten ball of flaming magma over the edge of the Fox River as it slowly made its way offstage for another day, the sky around it brittle blue without the relief of a kiss of cirrus. Sun-drenched picnickers had started drifting away about an hour ago, and their numbers slowly attritioned to a boisterous few at the beer barrel.

Abe wandered into the house to use the bathroom, two of which were downstairs. He so much enjoyed meandering through Doc's immense castle that he took the stairway to better encompass the wide expanse of the foyer. From there, he viewed the swimming design of Mexican tiles on the floor, the sinking of his feet into the plush carpeting on the stairs, and the feel of satiny wood under his hand of the black walnut banister.

He wondered if he hallucinated the entire scene as he glanced back down over the splendor of it all. It gave him a dimension of time and space back to the mid 1800s, when this home had been built with the lumber baron's big bucks he'd derived from the metamorphosis of thick slashings left in the woods after a cut of the big timber. Slashings meant pulpwood. Pulpwood meant paper. Paper converted to millions and millions of dollars. That smell along the river from the paper mills equated to the smell of *green*—conversion of acid-bathed pulpwood to paper—to millions in the bank.

Moving along the hall upstairs to the left, he knew he'd find an empty bathroom off the guest room where Fabe slept over as often as they'd part with him. He loved sleeping at Papa Doc's house. Here Fabe had a closet full of clothes and toys. Abe closed the door in deference to the tender eyes of little ones running all over the place today. *Seems to me I heard voices in Doc's suite when I went by—sounded like Doc. There lay a depth of concentration to his voice...intriguing. Wonder what's up?*

Heading back along the hall with long strides on the soft carpeting, he reached the door to Doc's bedroom, which lay in the middle of the upstairs, with large windows and French doors, giving him a sweeping view of the river sunsets. He and Suki were so lucky; they sat in the evening on the deck built over the downstairs patio and surveyed the panorama view like two monarchs. He found himself happy for them.

Yes, that *is* Doc...speaking low...*Sarah?*

She sounded upset. "He's a basilisk breathing fire again about having another child. I can't put him off any longer. He's determined, Danforth."

Danforth?

Urgency and desperation rode the thermals of her voice. "I'm afraid he's going to walk out on me again." Her voice caught.

"Abe wouldn't do that to you," he said, a slightly raised eyebrow his only facial reaction to her deep concern. "You need to stop worrying. Now just settle down, Sarah." Doc's voice sounded solicitous. "He emanates a tough armor, but you've always been able to find the secret to scratch through it." He smiled down at this wondrous stroke of Kismet that had crept into his heart years ago never to leave again. Reaching out, Doc knuckled Sarah's cheek. "You need to put Abe's leaving you way down at the bottom of your worry list, my dear. Would a man leave his treasure? That's where his heart abides." He smiled reassuringly, his eyes filled with love.

"You don't understand," she rushed on, glumly, avoiding his warm gaze. "It wouldn't take much for him to get an annulment of our marriage on the grounds that I refuse him children. I simply don't want to go through that ordeal again. Fabe was such a happy answer for us. I think we could pull it off again without arousing his suspicions." Seeing the misery on her face, Doc ached to take her in his arms and keep her there forever. He thrilled to see traces of love on her face.

Sarah rushed on. "He cherishes the little guy as much as you do, and never questions the fact that he looks so much like you—the eyes, the jaw, the quick half smile, the confident little swagger—beautiful child." Her eyes returned to him, finding it difficult to look away from his easy graceful presence. The quiet relaxation and soothing understanding she found there held her transfixed.

"I'm sure he chalked it up to atavism, his genetic code." Doc's expression hadn't stirred from its original calm.

Her head fell into her hands. "I'm afraid I have no other choice but to oblige him," she admitted, then sighed wistfully. Doc leaned close, grasping her wrists, then brushed his mouth across hers. Looking into his eyes for assurance, she found it, resting her head on his chest.

She even smells young, he thought, with a growing feeling of being sautéed. The eiderdown in his head slowly circled up the chain of reaction. The revelation came to him like the fused fragrance of rosemary and sage from Suki's herb garden out on the lanai as it drifted into the bedroom on an early evening draft. His hand involuntarily smoothed down to her hips, pulling her closer.

"When, Sarah?" he whispered sotto voce. "Now? In a month or so? I'll accommodate, but you know it has to be the right time, like it was in Pasadena." His hand moved the texture of her hair, lifting it gently, allowing it to fall, and his lips moved to within fluttering distance of hers, his breath warm. "And yes, I've known since Fabe was just hours old that he was *my* son. You are O negative. I'm A-positive. The child is A-positive. Abe is AB positive." He brushed his lips across her mouth again, her cheeks, her ears. "I've missed this so much, Sarah." Her name came out a ragged whisper. "I discipline myself constantly to stay away from you. You've been a wonderful mother."

The radio from the lanai drifted with the strains of "You'll Never Know Just How Much I Love You," spelled by a soft, magic sax accompanied by an unobtrusive poco piano and soft drum brushes, casting its own spell. Embers long buried glowed again as he pulled her to him, sweeping her off the floor, his mouth curling over hers.

In his professionalism, Sarah knew Danforth to be much tougher than his soft core revealed, just like the hard lines of his mouth were always so surprisingly soft and warm as they were now. She tore herself only inches away, drawing in a deep breath. He stirred her—warm, gentle, tender and prolonged. "Now," she said. "Now or in the next couple of days." Her voice was sensual. He laid the back of his hand against her cheek, running it up to her tilted eyes, back to her hairline.

"Now," he said. "It may be too late if he gets to you tonight. I can't wait to give you a new little life." His voice came from deep within—jagged—communicating his love, promising to endow her with the gift of his seed. He felt his blood stirring, a strangling sensation in his throat. Anticipation. A splendid aching. What this woman did to him was inexplicable. She aroused feelings he hadn't experienced since last he bedded her. He loved Suki so very much, but never had he experienced what he felt with Sarah—vital, needed, powerful, providing and young.

Before she could back out of his reach, he grazed the backs of his hands on her silken tanned shoulders, allowing his rough hair to graze against her soft skin. The action continued down her arms with scintillating electricity, tracing the curve of her elbows, her wrists, catching her hands in his gentle grasp, as she leaned her head sideways and sighed to the thrill of him. She'd forgotten what a master he was at this art of lovemaking, arousing in her a need that surpassed anything Abe had ever brought out in her. She closed her eyes to absorb him more intimately, thrilling to his every touch.

His hands traveled gently and loosely down her back as his mouth feathered over the corner of her lips, raking them over her ear. His hand wisped the length of her spine, gently indenting along the vertebrae, his other hand clutching the back of her neck, his mouth whispering over hers salaciously. "I love every inch of you, Sarah. I covet my son's wife shamelessly and desperately. You're so special to me." His mouth came down on hers, his control lost in the last touch, his kiss this time raw and invasive.

CHAPTER FORTY-SIX

Abe, standing outside the partially closed door, knew now that the niggling he'd had in the back of his mind—the one he could never quite rein in, the one that he couldn't quite put his finger on—had suddenly grown hair. He thought at first that he'd screamed aloud. A groan tore from his throat; time stopped as he suppressed it with his hands pressing against his face, his breathing coming in double time. The icy horror of shock he endured at Eddie's death poured over him like a galvanization process, feeling less need of an invitation on the second visit. Blindly, he kicked the door open to see with his eyes what his ears had heard: Doc and Sarah standing silhouetted against the copper-ball sinking sun in an embrace so deeply involved they didn't hear anything but the splinter of the door. They both turned their faces to him, dazed, their eyes glazed from the sensationalism of consensual imbibing love.

A struggling breath escaped Sarah's lips. She stared aghast at her husband. Doc froze, yet stayed in control.

Abe's leaden feet moved toward them with the efficacy of an elephant, his fists working in and out, his face white and rigid with scarcely controlled lunacy. His expression went through a series of changes, looking crazily as if he were solving something enigmatic, but the haze in his brain would only allow limited trespass.

"Is it true, Sarah?" The words sprung from deep within his belly, a tortured groan barely controlled through clenched teeth. "Fabe is not my child?" He raked the words in indignation and disbelief. "Is it true that Doc's the father?"

Sarah froze. Her hands flew to her mouth, her eyes gaining the best of her face.

Doc lifted his hand in a gruff gesture for Abe to "hold on" there just one minute. The brusqueness drew bile from Abe. Jerking his head around to Doc, he fairly grated, "Don't-you-shut-me-up; I'll get to you later." His eyes disdainfully danced over the length of him, as if seeing him for the first time.

Turning his gaze back to Sarah, he drilled her with burning quality to his words. "Is it true?" His voice was pure malevolence, demanding, his lips thinned in anger.

She nodded, realizing that he could unexpectedly strike her at any moment. "Yesss," she yielded, hanging onto the word, backing up.

Dead silence slammed the air, as if oxygen had suddenly bolted from the room.

Abe walked through an emotional mine field. His face wore the fibrous lines of fury. His eyes flashed feral. Her one-word response sliced through him and cut him into pieces, slashing like a cat-o'-nine-tails. He came out of his cautiousness, and a strong picture formed in his mind. "I'll kill him! I'll kill him," he roared. "I'll...I'll see your head on a stake," he spat at Doc, producing his jackknife, holding it in his fist.

Stunned, Doc stared vacuously at his out-of-control son.

Sarah's eyes rounded and darkened in apprehension.

From somewhere deep within Abe came a sound of pain so terrible it was animalistic. His shoulders shook with sinking sobs more agonizing with their silence.

In the name of God, to what depths had she pushed the man she loved! What had she done? *The devil never sleeps, Sarah.*

Doc's eyebrows drew together in a straight line. His thumb and forefinger came together to massage the bridge of his nose. The seconds ticked away like drugged slugs.

Abe's ship of composure foundered in the storm of his wrath. He listed about, as his pulse beat a tattoo in his ears. A raging Minotaur, his closed fist came up and without warning, he smashed Doc on the cheek, snapping his head back and sending him crashing onto the floor to within inches of sailing out onto the lanai, slamming the French door against the radio table, the radio skidding along the floor.

Something in Abe had broken, realizing Doc's culpability in this. The betraying glow of a natural killer showed in his eyes. Crying guttural sounds and shaking with rage, he went after Doc again while he lay on the floor, stunned. "You sonofabitch! You fucking sonofabitch! You denied my father his firstborn child and now you've denied me my firstborn child. You're nothing but a goddamned black hole of iniquity!"

He hoisted his long leg back and kicked Doc in the ribs with a terrible thud, and flipped the large blade from his jackknife. "You'll never get another woman pregnant. You know what circumcision is, don't you Sarah?" He raised eyes that bulged as primeval as a ground-hunting scavenger and his voice as guttural as a rusting machine clogged with grime. "Well, wait'll you see this circumcision!" he yammered while cutting away at Doc's picnic shorts.

Suddenly, a zenith of nirvana encompassed his very being with brilliant light shining upon him radiant in its coruscation and dimensions. Abe became infused—prickled with an eeriness he'd felt before in moments of madness. *Fabian.* Abe's heart swelled with the warmth and protective shell of his presence. A great feeling of calmness lay over all, flowing and gentle. As if he were in a dream, gossamer light settled about him, yet he knew his whereabouts and who he was. Abe knew nothing of clairvoyance or parapsychology, nor did he realize its powerful implications. All he knew was that Fabian materialized before his very eyes. Not the deathbed Fabian, but Fabian, young and vigorous, his voice soft, yet authoritative.

"You haven't walked barefoot through hell all these years to settle for prison. Leave murder and madness out of your life. The torturous culture of the Sioux is as foul-smelling as ptomaine and twice as rotten. Such insanity is out-of-date. There are advantages in the love of a family. Allow forgiveness to live in your soul." A light of such love shown about Fabian that Abe waxed to the spot, his arms still in the air in the act of raising Doc and slicing his knife where it would count. The light faded, then receded, not with a pop or a blip, but slowly, leaving Abe wanting more.

Aggressiveness dissipated. Images of a jail cell, a funeral cortege, a collapsed public image, and a fatherless family roiled in his mind, settling into smooth layers of wisps, and it was replaced by a wonderful peace that flooded his soul.

Sarah had never seen Abe like this, his beautiful head jutting belligerently, his finely groomed hair bristling with magnetic electricity, and then suddenly his physique returning to normalcy, as if he'd been taken apart and put back together again. She watched him approach with fluted nostrils, a streak of white on either side. His mouth disappeared completely as he grabbed her wrist, leading her from the bedroom.

Observing Doc's dazed look of dismay, Abe bristled like an outraged porcupine. "You detestable piece of shit!" he said.

"Come," he said to Sarah through grated clenched teeth.

The only sound came from the soft rustle of leaves in the evening breeze, ebbing and flowing with the faint static of the radio, now tediously off-tuned.

Abe wondered if he were going to wander forever through fields of broken dreams, his head full of *clicks*—a whole album of them—*clicks* of his walk down life's road with Sarah. Now *clicks* of Doc and Sarah together— maddening, denigrating *clicks.*

Leading Sarah with determination, Abe met Suki on the front verandah. "Keep Fabe overnight for us. Katie has him in the backyard." Curt, brief, abrupt his delivery.

"Yes!" she said, sounding excited. A ripple of pleasure passed through Suki's eyes at the thought of having Fabe overnight, all cuddly in his little pajamas and tucked into the bedroom next to theirs. The familiarity in the child's directness—his inquisitiveness—gave her a second chance at being a mother. She loved the way he put his hand in hers with such trust. "I love you, Granny," he'd say and look far up at her with wise brown eyes. Cherubic and ingenuous, Fabe belonged to her for a while.

However, Suki observed that Sarah wore an expression of sheer terror, her sandals snapping against her heels in rapid succession as Abe pulled her down the front steps, barely suppressing his rage. *What's gotten into Mr. Macho now? Has to be another beauty of a bug up his ass.*

Marching her down the street like a wayward child, her feet stumbling, Abe fumed. "Why, Sarah? Why?"

Her body felt lifeless, as if it were someone else's. Fright deeply consumed her.

"Why? Goddamn it! I asked you a question," he jerked her arm, moving up the sidewalk to their home, the twilight lingering long and hot in a Fourth-of-July sky.

"We thought...we thought..." she turned away unable to speak, sobs rushing into her throat. Was he going to strike her? Slap her down and kick her as he had done to Doc? Was there no one around to help her? If she screamed, would anyone hear her?

"You thought what? I fail to believe you thought at all." There lay dismayed detonation in his voice. *Had the heat of the day affected him? Was he going to explode?*

Taking a shaky breath, she gathered her determination. "We thought to give you a healthy child. A child engendered by Doc remained in the family, but one without your genetic problems." She stopped, trying to untangle her voice from the sobs, her telling fragmented in free-fall. "When you left me in Pasadena, I knew you wouldn't come back without the promise of a child, so we sought to give you one." Her stomach lurched, bringing on sweatiness, fever punctuating her essence.

Reaching home, he closed the front door behind them and hauled her up the stairs to their bedroom. "Wait a minute," he said. Then, with exaggerated slowness, "Wait—a—minute. So *my* baby wasn't good enough for you! That's the be-all and end-all of the whole affair, isn't it? You didn't want any part of my Indian heritage. Marry the college all-star football player, but don't love the man...love his father instead! You're as bad as he is! Sins committed in hell don't have angels as accomplices."

He wound up again. Should she try to run back for the door, she wondered, casting her eyes at the distance between herself and the hall.

Following her line of vision, he stepped between her and the route she'd mentally drawn for him. "For a while I thought that maybe in his suave worldliness he'd seduced you, but the concept was your idea in the first place, wasn't it?"

Sarah's eyes grew larger and rounder, shaking her head *no*. She turned her face to her shoulder to wipe away the tears. Anger-inflated, she knew he'd believe nothing she told him now. Perhaps she should look forward to the disintegration of their marriage. Whatever happened to the *joie de vivre* she experienced with him? This Abe and the *joie* Abe were two very dissimilar people. She grew weary of his mindless perceptions of her explanations, but lamented of her decision for having children by Danforth, breaking into tears again.

Perhaps she should have taken a chance on Abe's offspring. She could feel caving ground beneath her feet, making it hard to walk, her legs heavy. What were his intentions? Whatever they were, she didn't want to go there, didn't want to face it. Her toes squiggled nervously over the ends of her sandals in the soft pile of the carpet. Thoughts of her death grew imminent. She turned her face to him. Whatever manic thoughts ruled his mind, at least she could see the onslaught.

His hands seized her arms just below the shoulders, dragging her bodily to him. He tried to control his rage, but he couldn't manage it. Not now, not before, not ever. "I don't know what part I play in your life anymore, Sarah."

Her mind registered his anger, his hurt, his firmly set jaw, his eyes shutting down on her again. She gasped a protest as he put his hand under the strap of her sundress.

"Why did you wear this dress that I paid for, huh? Too look pretty for Doc?" He ripped off the strap, fixing his eyes on hers. Holding her hair with his hand, he ripped away the other strap.

"If it's got to be *now* that you conceive a child, it'll be mine. You hear?" He pulled on her hair, snapping her head backwards.

With his free hand, he sadistically grasped at her dress, ripping it down the front where it fell to the floor in a puddle, leaving her standing with only her panties and shoes on. His blazing eyes traveled the geography of her—the white areas created by tanning on the deck, a deck he provided, the areas that only he should see, but oh, she willed to have Doc see them. He flamed in fury again, grabbing both her wrists with one hand, pushing her back against a wall. With superior size and power, he quickly found her mouth, his hand entwined in her hair, possessing, owning.

"You're mine, Sarah. If it takes the rest of your life to learn, that's up to you. Learn the hard way." He snarled, leaning into her. "Now that I know you're a whore, I'll just take you against the wall, because I'm just a man, subject to all the feelings and flaws of my gender."

"No, Abe. Please." Hysterical, her voice became hardly perceptible, her face wet with tears. "You know you've been the only man in my life except for Danforth."

"How many times, Sarah? How many times in the past? Every time I'm out of town on away games? Every time my back is turned? How long, Sarah?" His voice angry, projected demanding urgency.

"Twice! Just twice. In Pasadena when you left me. He hasn't touched me since then. You must believe that, Abe. For you we planned Fabe." Her words came in short bursts as he pressed her, suffocating, against the wall.

"And you expect me to believe that?" Picking her up, he carried her to the bed, dropping her there from his full height. She cried in abject fear as she landed, her teeth tormented. Standing near the bed, he removed his clothing daring her with his eyes to make one false move. The memory of seeing her in Doc's embrace couldn't be dispelled.

He shook his head. "Do you really expect me to believe that you had Doc's child for my benefit? You can't hide the love I saw between the two of you." His voice was low, vicious. The hurt and hate in his darkened eyes were more than she could harbor.

Hauling her up farther onto the bed, he twisted her onto her back, removing the scant remainder of her dignity. Sandals that *he* had bought her, panties that *he'd* paid for. A roof over her head that *he* provided, but she wouldn't have *his* babies! A rumble of emotion came from the farthest reaches of his soul as he straddled her. "You love me, don't you, Sarah? Tell me you love me and look at me the way you were looking at Doc. Lies! I've been living with lies. Tell me again how much you love me. Your lip service has reached a level that I can't live with anymore," he said, leaning back.

"Please Abe, not like this..." she protested, fear filling her every fiber.

"Yes. Like this." His mind told him to be done with her, but his heart tore deeply inside him at the thought of living the rest of his life without her.

Why did she suddenly see him as a curious collection of despicable junglism? She put her slim delicate hands over her face. "Please, Abe. Don't let me see you like this. I don't even know you." Her chest heaved with sobs of sorrow, of fear, of hysteria.

"No. You've never known me, Sarah. This is how I've found relief many times. No. You don't know me. You don't know half the things I've been through—the trials by fire—the debilitating struggles with learning—the faith I placed in you. You were my mainstay, my salvation, just you, my chosen one, the mother of my children. Now this!" Emotions too raw to define and sort ran through him like licking flames from hell.

Tears slid down her cheeks and trickled into her hair. Did she just for a moment see a flash of regret on his face? He looked up at the ceiling, but carried on. "That's all in the past. I'll leave you with this parting gift, from me to you. A nice little Catholic girl like you wouldn't abort a child conceived in her marriage bed, now would she?"

He made no effort to alleviate the vast discrepancy in their sizes smothering her breath. She tugged at her bottom lip to keep from screaming, or was it from throwing up? He disregarded her comfort, her pain, her dignity, just as he'd done when she was so young and unused. *It doesn't make sense*, she thought. *None of this makes sense—he's barbaric and Godless.*

He passed the seed of his loins into Sarah's soft nursery, but not with any degree of satiation. Hastily, he arose, a strangled sigh escaping him as he dressed.

Moving to arise, he seized Sarah by the wrist and held her to the bed. "Oh no you don't. You aren't going anywhere. Don't even think about it."

Her stomach did a convulsion, nauseated. "Please, Abe. I'm vulnerable right now, and you used no protection." The soft fervor of her voice assaulted him.

Although he scrutinized her raw pleading, her agony, her need, he postured unrelenting in his need to punish her. *Just let her lie there for an hour or so.* His conscience was as obstinate as her blatant sins against him and their marriage vows. "No. You-aren't-going-anywhere. You'll just lie there while I pack the few things I'll need to live elsewhere. I'll send for the rest." His voice grew stronger now with conviction—sinister, quiet.

She pulled the sheet over herself in her nakedness and her shame. Never had she felt so violated. He had cut her heart out and left her there to die unmercifully.

Noisily opening and closing dresser drawers, Abe knew this was not a high point in his life, and he wasn't proud, but he probably would do the same thing again. Glimpses of his past crept up on him and lit in mind-flicks: random images of losses and gains, the losses always outnumbering the gains. "I wonder," he said, "what part tonight plays in love. I once heard someone say that all is possible in love as long as you're audacious enough. No, that's wrong. It was General Patton who said that about war. But I guess it applies in either instance; sometimes I can't tell the difference. I'm trying to figure out which of us has been the most audacious. I always thought it was me—until tonight." He walked over to the bed where Sarah lay crying and curled up in the fetal position, her face flushed and looking ill.

"This is just one bitter pill for me to swallow in a long series of bad prescriptions but there won't be any more. When I love someone, it's not going to be in doled slices, but all the time and forever, and you don't fill that bill, Sarah. It's time to call the game because of darkness." He managed to keep his voice free of the sinking loss he felt. *Did she compare us? I should have killed that bastard.*

Returning to the closet, he hauled out suitcases and tossed clothes in with reckless abandon. Maybe he should assume some mutual guilt here, but he wouldn't. He couldn't. Why didn't he stick to his guns in Pasadena? Everything pointed to her fault. He'd use this moment to allay his guilt by punishing her.

"From now on," he said over his shoulder; "I'll hang out with the guys. We're a bunch of pirates seeking what we want and grabbing it. It's worked all my life. Enemies walk the plank, enemies like you, Sarah. I'll leave you the house for you and my *half brother*. You already have your own car. Maintenance on the home and the car you can find on your own. No judge will award you any support money from me on a child that isn't even mine. What's more, don't expect a divorce to be forthcoming. Nice life you'll have. Men are free to run and roam, but a woman is restricted in social outlets."

He descended on the bed for his final declamation, shaking her by the shoulders for attention. "I'm going to forget that I had a difficult childhood and that poverty surrounded me every day I walked the streets of Nahma, often hungry and cold. I'm going to forget that you ever helped me through a bunch of rough patches. You've been paid back in spades. I'll now think of myself as a fine, free citizen, a productive part of a new community, and not a bad fellow after all." His deep brown eyes opened onto her for a brief second, doing a slow reading of her face. Something flickered there, something sad, something craving, unfulfilled, as he watched her sobbing—he never could handle that. He shut down again. "You understand what I'm saying to you, lady?" His voice cracked unexpectedly, belying the vehemence of his words.

"Yes," she replied, a whisper as light as the evening breeze.

Hoping that he wasn't going to strike her, she stayed hidden under the sheet until she heard the garage door open, the car start and leave, the sound drifting away in the quiet night. Then, and only then, did she release a long sigh. *This is how love ebbs and dies: anger, violence and silence.* Hurrying to the bathroom, she completed tasks on demand, then threw up, after which she sat on the floor with her body bent forward in despair until she had to throw up again. She lay on the floor, crying, holding her churning stomach, not knowing the hour or the day. She flooded with the reality that whatever the future held in store for them, they would never be the same again. Her love languished, her marriage failed and her future teemed tentative and all because she surrendered to a stealthy sin of the flesh to produce a fine healthy child for Abe.

After a shower, she pulled on pink baby-doll pajamas before patting down the stairs to sit in the living room and gaze at the empty chair where her husband had spent so many happy hours reading to Fabe and enjoying his home. Tears edged down her cheeks, her breath coming in gasps. Ma had told her long ago that you could measure the quality of a person by their absences, by the vacuum they leave behind when gone. Admittedly, Sarah had never known such devastation.

❧

Doc rang her doorbell; his pulse picked up. What would he face? A yet-terrorized Abe? Sarah tied up in rawhide? Someone came—Sarah! There, through the sidelights, she approached. Damp tendrils of hair curled around her temples. God in heaven! Did he grow eager to see her? Hurriedly, she swung the door open, and for a moment they stood transfixed, communicating in that first single gaze of intense caring. He gravitated across the threshold with a crazy impulse to take her in his arms.

"Sarah, I can't tell you how sorry I am that this happened. It's so bizarre. Are you all right? Did he hurt you? Is he gone?" Closing the door and moving through the foyer, his height seemingly dwarfed the room as Abe's always had.

"I'm okay, I guess. Yes, he's gone and didn't hurt me, really, but he *did* pillage and plunder. He forced himself on me in such a wretched manner, as if I were a street person he'd picked up under a lamppost somewhere. Said he's never coming back. And what's worse, he didn't allow me to get out of bed afterward for over an hour, so I don't know what's going to happen." The tears spilled down her cheeks again as he enclosed her in his arms where she fit so gratefully. She needed his rock-solidness.

Why did he feel so amazingly cheerful at Abe's leaving? He had to knock that down. She needed Abe; he knew she loved him. But it seemed so easy to forget when he held her—him at sixty years old, but feeling sixteen. He could taste her youth and vitality. Holding her at arm's length, smiling, he emanated tender warmth encircling her burned-out shell. "Let's have coffee and get caught up," he suggested, taking charge.

As they entered the brightly lit kitchen, she gasped at the ugly split on the side of his face and the growing purple bruise gerrymandering up into his eye. "Danforth," she whispered, reaching up and touching him gingerly over the devastated area. "It's so awful. How're your ribs? He went crazy! I thought he was going to kill you!" Her eyes yielded deep concern.

A swelling grew in his throat, her touch like silk, producing an indescribable heaven. Taking a deep breath, he stayed in control. "Oh, I know those ribs are there, but I'm breathing okay, so I know there's nothing broken." Adjusting a chair, he observed her fatigue as she put the coffee in the Pyrex filtering system, the heated water climbing its way up the glass tube slowly, making a gurgling, sucking sound, then faster until it bubbled over into the coffee reservoir, filtering through and back down into the cylinder.

"Sit down, Sarah, I'll pour the coffee," he said, taking two mugs from the tree. "You look as if you've been drawn and quartered."

She felt the pressure of his solicitations, but he did not pry for some reason. "Not physically, unless you consider the backstreet mating; it was brutal. I never knew he could be so barbaric." The tears slid down her cheeks again. Passing the filled mug to her, his fingers lingered. Her glance shipped up to him, the memories flooding back to more than six years ago when he had loved her with such tenderness and care, the stimuli striking yet in her mind. Never had she been so aroused, loved so thoroughly—until her whole body begged for relief. She looked at him and saw the look of authority, the look of salvation—the look of Abe. Both of them were unrelenting in their pursuits, both athletic, and she now knew from tonight's experience, fiercely competitive.

Moving to the coffee pot again, he held it out inquiringly, but she held her hand over the cup. He poured himself a warming dose, adding, "Fabe is just fine. He's been sleeping for more than an hour already. He's a beautiful child, Sarah, simply beautiful. I'll thank you for him as long as I live. What a gift. I wish that Abe could view it as such. Instead, he'll choose to build himself some brittle sheath where he can hide any real feelings he has for the child now—put himself in some kind of purgatory without redemption." He mulled it over in his mind, staring into his coffee mug, sitting across the kitchen table from her.

"*He* doesn't think so. He sees himself now as some kind of American icon—a Golden Boy." She still sniffled and could discern that Doc wasn't exactly following what she said; maybe she wasn't sure herself what she was saying. "The sum and substance of what he told me is that love is perfect trust, and he couldn't trust me anymore."

Her voice lowered. "The best he predicted for me is some kind of black bombazine fabric to wear in my newly cloistered life of no social activity because women can't mix in the world like men do. He hoped that would be my punishment." She attempted kindliness by not painting him too harsh, but here and now, she lacked even the slightest vestige of goodwill. "He wants my heart to remain asleep for the rest of my life. Ma told me that there would be days in my married life that started out as magic and shift modality in midstream to becoming mocking nightmares. Today is it. The worst. I feel like an inanimate object, empty and cold." The last words barely tumbled out as a squeak before the tears flooded her eyes again. With both of her elbows on the table, she put her head on her folded hands and bawled until her shoulders shook.

"Dear, dear Sarah." Doc slid his chair back with a scraping sound, hurrying around the table to comfort her—massaging her shoulders. "So much love and patience with your *Golden Boy*, and so rarely rewarded. Abe will not cause interference of any kind with his focused plans, especially from his wife, whom he expects to be loyal and obedient. You need to set your sights on something, something to assuage yourself. Time matters here. If you are indeed pregnant, we'll all help see you through that time. If you're not, you should pursue that commercial venture you always dreamed of having, maybe out on the Door Peninsula—out near Sister Bay or Ephraim. You'd be so successful at something such as that—arts and crafts. Think about it. I'll help set you up there financially. Your dreams are mine," he said softly, care creeping through, his pride in her immeasurable. "You can close the door on this part of your life."

She nodded, unable to speak.

Turning the chair around, he lifted her tenderly and carried her upstairs to her bedroom, hoping she could dismiss the terror she had suffered there only hours ago. "I'm going to tuck you into your bed so you can get some rest. I brought along a sedative." Safely in bed and covered, she could hear him running water from the bathroom, bringing comfort to her to swallow a small white pill.

He pulled a Chippendale boudoir chair, upholstered in bright pink and silver stripes of chintz, close to the bed and sat near her. Folding her hand in his, he felt the delicate bone structure, the long slim fingers, the talented tendons that cared for Fabe, that glissandoed up and down the piano keyboard, fragile. His fingers stroked the heartbeat circling within them.

"You're beautiful, Sarah—beautiful, intelligent and capable. You don't need him. You can't be living with his idiosyncrasies for the rest of your life; they're too unpredictable. The guy seems to swerve and veer at the slightest inclination. He's a Sherman Tank in a No. 14 Packer jersey. I want you to wake up tomorrow morning to a new day. Go out into your garden and watch the sun turn the dew to mist; count your blessings for the brilliant new life you'll have. I'll always be here for you," he whispered soothingly.

She drifted away, hoping he wouldn't note the tremors running the full length of her body. Gliding softly away with the buoyancy she only felt when she was pregnant with Fabe or floating in the warm waters at the Nahma beach, warm, tranquillizing, hypnotic. Doc's voice hovered from far away.

"Today's celebration was another howling success except, of course for you and Abe. But I guess," he offered teasingly, "that could be considered the consummation of a coup—depends on how you view success, hmm?" Doc observed Sarah's irregular breathing meld to somnolence, then to deep sleep while he spoke of better days. He knew how long nights could be when your soul lay burdened by the ebony thoughts of the day. He'd call Marian to pack an overnight bag and stay with Sarah for security.

Closing the front door after himself, he sat on the verandah, waiting for Marian to arrive; fireflies flickered in and out of the bushes and thick grass, a lulling conference of crickets connected with his spirit in the hush of the evening. Shaking his head, he drew deep breaths to abstain from crying, but from pitifully deep inside the sobs exploded non-stop from his internal grief. Now that he was alone, the tears flowed freely, tears of a desolate, abandoned child resurrecting in the man. Tears that weren't only produced from today's sorrows, but for all the hurting Abe had heaped upon Sarah as far back as he could remember, and for the part *he* had played in it.

With all the discipline he could muster, he pulled himself together when he saw Marian and Bill coming up the long sidewalk from the street, enjoying the beautiful evening. Looking at him curiously, neither verbalized the questions that danced just beyond their eyes. Doc breathed softly, eternally grateful for their social aptitude.

"Sarah and Abe hit a rough spot in their road of tranquility tonight," he explained. "Abe has left, says he's not coming back. I gave her a light sedation. She won't hear a thing until morning. But when she wakes up, I know she'll be glad to have your company instead of being alone."

Bill and Marian nodded, dismayed, but understanding.

They knew Abe.

That's exactly what Doc wanted—rest for her, deserving rest, peaceful rest. God, how he ached. How he loved this wondrous white flower growing in the cracks of his life. She could make him blind and deaf with needs. It appeared that she was his responsibility now, his impossible dream.

He knew.

CHAPTER FORTY-SEVEN

Abe still couldn't erase Doc's 4th of July celebration. The pain he put himself through—the torture, the loneliness. He hated this when he mulled over the incident and always arrived at the same conclusion: he lived like a man without a country.

Sarah took Fabe and went back up north to Nahma to spend the remainder of the summer months with Bill and Marian, and he didn't even know where they were for more than a month. He never asked, never intended to give them a hint of how much he cared. He presented to the public a package of contentment, bliss and disinterest. Doc took the month of August off and opened the home on the boulevard in Nahma.

By the middle of August, the heat became unbearable and sultry in the city. Getting time off from Curly, he needed to talk to Doc—had to see Sarah and Fabe. His heart pulled for their presence. Arriving in Nahma, the cool air off the bay descended right from heaven and opening the house on Old Beach Road gave him time to think, time to collect his thoughts. How could he ever have forgotten his humble beginnings here in the home that looked now to him more like temporary housing for seasonal workers, small and inadequate, but it had meant everything to him at one time: security, love, sustenance and shelter. Sitting in Fabian's wing-back chair, he folded his hands behind his head, stretching out his long legs.

Thoughts flowed of how he had stolen his first kiss from Sarah on the beach down at Stony Point. He remembered dancing with her in the kitchen after the Sadie Hawkins's Day Festival, "Moonlight Serenade" playing with such fulfillment. How he had undressed her—saw her naked for the first time, the breathless thrill that shot him through. He shivered. What a bully he'd been after the '43 graduation ceremonies. If she had any feelings toward him, they would have been dissipated. But no, she had still loved him with unbelievable tenacity.

The paintings. How he had painted! The beach sweet peas, the school, the sunset over the burner, the dream team series, the lumber camp, the church, Farnsworth Park, Sarah as the Maid in the Mist, Sarah as his bride, Farley and Norrhea in the front pew, Doc speaking behind the pulpit at his wedding, Farley standing tall in church, the moon over the straits of Mackinac, all the canvases from college, and one of the latest, Picnickers at Doc's Fourth of July Party. And Fabe. His Michelangelo cherub. Fabe's image hung all over his den. The football field and players, in addition to himself, danced in the end zone. It had all started here. It all started here with a small palette from Max and two photographer's lights from Fabian, lights that he knew Fabian couldn't afford in a million years.

Now he'd been asked by Neville Chamberlain II to exhibit his work next spring in London—he'd provide the gallery. Lucky bastard! He made a mental note to ask Bernie if he could use his sweet peas picture for the exhibit. He doubted very much that he'd ever get Sarah's picture of the Maid in the Mist from Marian, even on a lend-lease, especially in view of the fact of how shabbily he'd treated Sarah.

He had only four days in Nahma, four days to reclaim the rest of his life. It had been six weeks since he'd acted so violently to Doc and Sarah and seen Fabe! God, how he missed that child! *I don't care whose child he is by blood. He's mine.*

The next day he sat on the beach in the warm sun, listening to the sound of waves licking the shore and sucking back out, hoping to see Sarah, but no such luck.

He looked in the mirror late that afternoon before he called on Doc and Suki. Still acceptable, he reassured himself, wider than average brown eyes, cheeks high with a broad quicksilver smile, his teeth gleaming. The abundance of his dark hair showed no signs of receding; he'd checked.

Now or never, he decided. "*It takes a man to apologize,*" he remembered Kreiler telling him once. If that's what it took, he'd strive for that goal, because he wasn't proud of himself or his demeanor of six-seven weeks ago.

"Abe!" Suki answered the door smiling uncertainly. "Come in. Doc'll be glad to hear from you. It's been so long! You okay?" she asked, thrusting her hands wildly into the air, then reaching up and kissing him on the cheek.

"Yeah, sure." Abe had his hands in the pockets of his denim shorts, his short-sleeved polo shirt of navy and white stripes showed the outlines of his angular frame. As always in the summer, he wore canvas deck shoes. "Think I need to talk to Doc alone for just a few minutes. No offense, Suki. I just need to tell him something." His shoulders hitched. She kept her eyes on him, inquiring, listening with her eyes.

"Sure. Come on in. Come through the house. He'll be glad to see you. And no offense taken. I'll start putting dinner together for us. I'm just going to cook on the grill tonight. Please stay," she said with the same old enthusiasm.

"Sure thing. Sounds good." He met her gaze evenly, finding the love there. Oh how he needed that! His throat caught.

"Abe!" Doc said, looking up from the *Escanaba Daily Press*. He rose slowly from his chair but made no approach to meet Abe halfway, still holding the paper open with his index finger to the page he'd been reading. A smile of relief wreathed his face, however, relaxing his eyes. "Come sit down and enjoy the sun."

Abe's confidence waned. "Thanks, Doc." If he had a fedora to hold, he'd be twisting it in his hands, around and around and around. He fumbled, doing it in his mind anyway. He sat, placing his elbows on his knees, hands over his nose prayerfully, looking for the right words to negotiate a renewal of friendly terms.

"I don't know where to start, Doc, but I wanted to simply say how sorry I am for what happened at your party. I lost my mind." He put his hands down, still folded between his legs. "I couldn't handle the information overload." He turned his head to look squarely at Doc, making an effort at fearlessness, but he only showed the complete breakdown of his defenses. "The hurt of all I overheard and observed hasn't faded. I've been injured, but the personal attack I made on you and Sarah was ludicrous and could have been murderous. How I wish that I had approached the solution of my immediate problem in another fashion. But it doesn't change a dawgone thing. What a schmuck! I owe you so much for many years of selflessness. But I didn't feel I owed you my wife, *until I realized that she wasn't my wife—she wasn't even my betrothed.* I had called the whole thing off, abandoned her, when you stepped in with your quarterbacking. Of course I still view it as a bad means to a good end, but it worked. We *did* get married."

Doc silently observed and listened, folding the newspaper and setting it on a cane patio table. "Don't worry about it, Abe. Life teaches us strange lessons. It never stops. I had no right to play God in your life. That had to have been a kick in the ass for you learning that Fabe was actually my child. I think of that often, too. I've never touched Sarah since then until you found us together, planning for another child."

"It's too bad people don't come with warranties, like washing machines, but there are no assurances for people's actions or reactions. When we skid the stone across the water we have no idea how much water it displaces." He bent forward, cupping his hands between his legs. "Suki knows nothing of the incident. I'd appreciate your not telling her any of this. I told her I ran into the French door of the patio and injured my cheek. You and I need to keep the bigger picture in view." A faint smile brought relaxing lines around his mouth.

Leaning back again and crossing his legs, he continued in his "take charge" modal. "Have you seen Sarah yet? She's staying with Bill and Marian. She and Fabe are having a nice summer—no pressures, just long sunny days. She says she misses her piano, however. Marian's thinking of buying another one so when Sarah visits she can play for her. She has a blessed touch with her musical talent."

The remark served to remind Abe of the finely molded woman he'd had. It slso served to remind him of what a scuzz he'd been...treating Sarah with ownership rights.

Doc slapped the arm of his padded cane chair. "Forever more! Where are my manners? Can I get you something to drink, Abe? A gin and tonic with lime? That's what I'm going to have!" Doc stood to go into the house.

"Sure nuff. That'd be fine. Thanks." Abe stood and put a hand on Doc's shoulder, squeezing it, saying more than all his words had done. Doc's eyes, wet, he turned before his emotions ran away with him.

Abe envisioned how urgently he wanted to talk to Sarah, but was reluctant to go over to Bill's. How could he ever explain how he had treated Sarah—so lowly? Maybe she hadn't told them; it wasn't a pleasant thing to tell, her own subordination to a Native American nut and her own rationale to incubate a child without learning problems. He'd try the beach again. Eating crow was a caution.

If...if...if...

He felt like yesterday's spaghetti, lifeless and unappealing.

※

Friday. How lucky he was. Nice day. Hot day! Not a breath of wind. On the beach by one o'clock so he wouldn't miss Sarah, he situated himself considerably west of where she usually spread her blanket. His heart went wild when at last he saw her show up, just before two o'clock. But what entered her mind to wear that skimpy bathing suit? She's a married woman! Two pieces! The bottom was fashioned with a tied knot over each hip, revealing a long expanse of leg—tanned leg—silky tanned leg. A matching large knot was tied between her breasts. Were her breasts larger? Or was he imagining it? And look at Fabe, so husky and brown in his little drawstring trunks. She was such a good mother. Abe watched as Sarah sat in warm wading water and Fabe splashed around her. "Gitchoo, Mama. Gitchoo." He laughed and shrieked.

Abe's memory of the day returned so clearly and sharply that he could hear the cry of gulls floating on the afternoon heat inversions. Working up enough courage to approach Sarah was a frightening thing, he a Packer staple, awards and such every year. Fans cheered his every move, calling his name in unison. Sports writers found him their number one topic of Packer glory. Yet he maintained fear of talking to this five-foot-four-inch woman. Life had taught him that dear ones could be fleeting things.

Face the problem head-on, Abe. Faceit-faceit-faceit. Finding his feet, he headed down the beach and approached Fabe and Sarah, now building a sand castle. His feet in cast iron and his knees on rusty hinges, he arrived, casting a shadow onto their work, causing Fabe to look up at the great height of him. "Dad-dy!" He jumped up and ran rough-and-tumble into Abe, hugging his legs. "Dad-dy! Where you been? I missed you. Mama said you went away. Far, far away?" Abe swooped Fabe onto his shoulders. People around them smiled and nodded at the happy family.

Sarah stood hastily, backing off from Abe. A look of terrible fright prevailed in her eyes, now round with terror. Her mouth opened, but nothing came out. In the presence of a populated beach, she measured her words. "Put him down, Abe. Don't hurt him, please. I love him very much." Her arms were extended in supplication as the words were voiced to meet only his ears.

How he had hurt her, he remembered. The pit of his stomach churned, crippled by doubt. Aching, he reached up, removing Fabe from his shoulders, sitting in the sand near her blanket and holding Fabe in a hug between his knees. "I love him too. I'd never hurt him. Don't think that way, Sarah. I'm not going to hurt you either. I need your forgiveness so badly." He had willed it not to happen, but there was a sob in his voice. "There isn't a day or an hour that passes that I don't think of you both. Thinking of the way we were. What we had. I want back into your life, forever. Do you think you could at least consider that?"

He still hugged Fabe, who clung to him as if he were his favorite teddy bear. Abe ran his hand over Fabe's thick black hair, cradling him against his shoulder, feeling his heart beat rapidly against his chest, the warmth of his skin, strong muscles growing along his ribs, the sturdy little legs. It was all due to Sarah's nurturing. He couldn't remove his eyes from her beauty and perfection, struck by her bareness—the way the sun highlighted the walnut and pecan highlights in her hair. Considering the way he had walked out of her life, how could he account for these feelings commingling in the very depths of him, the temptation to reach out and touch her? There were all kinds of words he'd rehearsed to convince her of his sincerity—words he wanted to propel out of his very soul, but they stuck somewhere in the vitals of his pride.

"No. No, Abe. I'll not be considering allowing you back into my life," she said quietly, not wanting to create a scene. "You've turned my hopes into nothingness for the last time. My life lay in shambles after you left. Just as you said, I didn't have the outlets *you* had for distractions to my loneliness. I faced day after day of dreariness, and a forever of flip-flop nights. The emptiness gnawed at me always." She stood there, the sun in her face, her hand sheltering her eyes drinking in the scene of her husband and her child in a caress. It seemed so right.

"I'll not deny you seeing Fabe, however. I know you love him." Abe would be out of her life, but she'd always be reminded of him by his constant visitations with Fabe. In addition, now she'd missed two menstrual periods, knew herself to be pregnant again with his child, but she'd not give him the satisfaction that he'd been successful in planting his seed within her by his vile act of brute force. She sat down on the blanket, her back partially to him, but she could feel his eyes probing her profile.

"I guess I can settle for that." Abe's voice came out husky and hurt. "But I'll keep asking you the same thing over and over again. I'll never let this die. The regrets I carry around with me are astronomical. I need your forgiveness desperately. Just knowing you will try to erase the memories of that night would help me get through the days ahead. Are you pregnant, Sarah?" He was direct.

She felt a feistiness creep into her very being. "That is no longer any of your business, Mr. Miereau-Whittaker, nor will it ever be from now on. And don't come bellyaching to me about getting through the days ahead. You don't even know half the pain I've had. After you left the house of our dreams, the one that beckoned to both of us, the one we had dreamed of while yet in college, it was merely an empty shell. The same house that drew us magnetically to have and to hold from that day forward became a prison." She took a deep breath to go on, her eyes protected.

"Everywhere I turned there were your canvases—in the halls, on the end tables, in the kitchen, all your watercolors and oils. I had constant reminders of their excellence—happy dimensions without end, luminous light, depths that had no explanation, me as a happy bride, my eyes reflecting the love you saw there. The 'Winter Forest' you painted while you were in high school is so real that it makes me lonely for the deep woods around Nahma. The large canvas of the lumberjacks on a cold morning, their breath frozen in midair; it is enough to make me run for a sweater.

"I remember the first time I saw one of your paintings, how I raved to Max about it—it was just a water color done in the third grade. You gave it to me and I kept it in my room where I'd sit on my bed and study it for hours, all pastel with floating flowers, sunshine, clouds and boats with sails on the bay. The sun fell so brightly on the water that it billowed in sparkles—breathtaking. I don't know now what became of it. It just disappeared, like your love." She gestured widely, sweeping both arms.

Her mouth tightened. "That house seemed like a mausoleum, heavy with a silence so deep I could reach out and *touch* it, *hear* it, *feel* it." For a brief moment, there came no sound in Sarah's life, only the careless invasion of the soft surf, riding in and crawling out into its labyrinth of sand beds as if it had changed its mind as to its direction. Glancing back at him, she saw that black marble thing in his eyes again, watching, weighing. No! She would be always frightened of him. Forever.

"I promised myself that I would never get into the heart of a home again. Everywhere I live from now on will be just a house without the three dimensionalism of love, dependability and security. Despite the nights of sleeplessness, I got through it. I staggered with disillusionment and disbelief; it all transpired as if you'd died. Thanks to my faith and my imagination, my thoughts searched enough to find hope. Brick by brick, I built a wall around myself and solidified my objectives, and they don't include you!"

"Sure, there were many times I felt inadequate without you, but it wasn't because I lacked education; it was because I had depended upon you so completely...so unreservedly...so unquestioningly." Sarah surprised herself—pleased that she could get all that out without crying. Every sentence had hurt deeply, drawn from the despair she had carried with her for the last month and a half.

Abe's voice resonated with emotion. "I'd like to take care of you again, Sarah—you and Fabe. I think that during our seven years of marriage we connected, laid some good foundations. Now you want to put the end in sight, to my complete loss and desolation. I'm sorry, so sorry. I'll not fail to support you, either."

He had turned Fabe around and set him in front of the sand castle, which he proceeded to build with dollops of wet sand. "Daddy, you coming home?" Fabe asked, sitting back, looking with wide brown eyes at Abe. "Grandpa Bill has a swing in the backyard. Come push me high in the sky, Daddy." Fabe sat back on his heels, laughing, his stomach muscles rippling with the joy of it all. "High in the sky," he squealed.

Abe thought his heart would break—thought he'd break down and cry right there on the beach. He knew she spoke frankly. The fractures in their marriage had occurred over time, cruel times created by him, verbal lashings heaped upon her that she'd never forget. But it was all moot now, rendering him denied of pushing Fabe on a mere swing.

"Not tonight, Fabe, but when you get back to Green Bay Daddy will take you to the park often. We'll try Friday afternoons, if it's okay with Mama." A smile curled around the edges of his mouth, ready to furl into full bloom. He knew he'd just cornered Sarah into seeing her at least once a week.

"I guess that'd be okay," she breathed. "He starts school the day after Labor Day, but he'll only go in the mornings for this year," she said, wiping her hands one on the other to remove the wet sand.

"In which school did you decide to enroll him? Doty or Parkview? They're about an equal distance from the house."

"It'll be Doty. I like the staff. Besides, other Packer children are going to school there, giving me the advantage of Packer wives to share my time."

"*I'll* share my time with you, twenty-four hours a day," he said looking at her with a yearning that she'd never seen before, his nerves jumping like sand fleas. He hadn't tried to conceal it—no louvers closed this time.

"No thank you. *You* I can do without very well. No thanks." She moved to the blanket, her back to him. Her fine back, straight, bronzed. He wanted to reach out and touch her, run his hands through her hair, feel her golden shoulders, the softness of her, the warmth, the *all* of her again. It pained him until his throat became just a small opening, without room for words to pass. "Sarah," he whispered. "I don't want to be a quasi-husband and father any longer. Do you want me to beg? I will."

She rose to her feet like a goddess, the sun radiating an aura around her, the silk of her hair shimmering in the sun. "Don't you even consider that, Mr. Miereau-Whittaker. It won't work!" she said, her head shaking gravely in defiance.

"I want you to know, too, your-royal-highness-big-shot-Packer, that I don't need your support money," Sarah taunted. "Keep it. Fabe and I are well off. My trust fund from Max matured this month: fifty thousand dollars. It'll keep us just fine until I find a business to buy—perhaps next spring. I'll get a nanny for the children."

"Children?" Abe gasped loudly—forgetting where he stood.

"Well, now you know. Yes, *children*. I'll care for them both. We don't need you." She kept her back to him, talking to the surging water.

Abe must have stretched clear up to seven feet tall. This time *he did* it. She was pregnant—his child! But her not needing him tore at his guts. He needed her to need him—to need his presence—his supportiveness, his money, his fatherliness, his protection! What kind of a bum was he? A wife and two children that he made no effort to support? He had, indeed abandoned them. *And now, even from the grave, Max is reminding me of what poor husband material I am! He has to support his daughter, even after she's married!* The sorrow in his life became immeasurable, returning at unexpected moments and sticking like cockleburs.

CHAPTER FORTY-EIGHT

August and September had crawled by on narrow track until the Packer/Bear game. He had the game of his life that bright, early-October day. His heart had soared to unprecedented heights. Doc and Suki, Sarah and Fabe, Bill and Marian, and Farley and Norrhea were all there behind the players' bench. Curly played Abe on offense and kept him in as a retaining player on defense.

Fabe continually shouted, 'Dad-dy!' Abe thought that he'd virtually burst with pride. So proud. He had a son who loved him deeply, but he was denied his full-time presence because he'd been such a jerk.

The temperature at kickoff was fifty-two degrees, with a puckish wind that pushed and prodded now and then, but was never of any great significance. Abe's gunslinger quarterback, Duke Daily, needed his sights sharpened at the onset. The Bears scored off an interception by a corner back who ran it back for a touchdown.

Daily called "Miereau," and Abe made a spectacular twenty-nine yard catch over a defender in the end zone for the Packer's first score, the big difference: seven-seven. Then Daily dropped the ball on one of his daring scrambles. The eager and poised Bears jumped on that turnover for a ten-seven lead.

Eventually, the winds and the Packer fans calmed down, and so did Daily. After his dreadful two for eight, sixteen-yard first quarter, the Packers played smash-mouth football and routed the Bears thirty to thirteen.

Daily, suddenly finding his rhythm and a powerful Miereau-Benning running combo, drove the Packers seventy-one yards for a fourteen to ten lead. They then scored on the next four series, building a thirty to thirteen lead against the Bears weary three-four defense. The Bears were forced to rely almost totally on Hulk's arm when their rushing attack stalled, sending in a deep pass in a disastrous final minute of the first half.

Miereau pulled off an interception at the Green Bay thirty-nine.

Daily scrambled and threw to castoff Benning for twenty-three yards, then he fed Miereau an inside route for twenty-five yards, on which the defender Bears were penalized an extra ten yards on a late hit. The Packer kicker booted a thirty-one-yard field goal for a seventeen to ten lead with ten left in the first half.

The Packers dominated the game by running from four receiver sets and passing from power sets and rushed for two hundred and one yards. Miereau gained ninety-nine receiving yards, which was expected. Benning finished with a gaudy eight yard average on ten snaps, which wasn't expected. The one Bear's sack on Daily's ill-advised scramble-and-fumble, was credited as a team sack.

In the third quarter, Daily arched a delicate screen just over the linebacker's reach. Miereau took it fifty-five yards as a safety over-pursued, and the fullback smothered the corner with a great block.

With the Bears squeezing their linebackers inside, Miereau scored standing up on a short ten-yard pass, for a twenty-seven to thirteen lead. He danced.

What a day, thought Abe. The exhilaration of the Bear defeat had him walking on air—until he attended the reception at Curly's that night.

༒

What a night for a party! Abe had been instrumental in winning the game—riding high. Every light in Curly's house shined brightly. He'd removed furniture from his recreation room in the basement and created a dance area and bar—tables and chairs spread around the perimeter, Chinese lanterns hung crazily around the room. A fantasy fling for Packer players, the gathering included their wives and close associates.

Yeah, sure, Abe invited Sarah to attend with him, but she declined, saying she would accompany Doc and Suki. He said he didn't mind, but he minded. He'd still be there, but he had to remember to play it cool—after all, he was Joe Big Guy.

Sarah showed up as a knockout—a drop-dead knockout. She wore an off-white wool suit with a short waist-cut jacket, long lapels covered in black velvet. A sheer black blouse made its presence known under the jacket as she moved and gestured. Black suede shoes with a conservative heel sported her feet. Dangling ever so slightly from her ears were onyx earrings with diamond insets.

Now where did she get those? My blue topaz would be pretty with that outfit, but not nearly as pretty as what she's wearing. Every time she moved, the diamonds coruscated with her smile. Bob Chapin stood possessively by her side. *Chapin!*

Out of his peripheral vision, he found that she wore no wedding ring, no engagement ring. Nothing that *he'd* given her. Maybe he'd not been attentive enough while they *were* having their happy days. *Happy.* Such a simplistic word to blanket all the love they'd had for each other. Maybe he should have showered her with all the thingamajigs that make a woman happy and cared for, things he'd overlooked in his selfishness, notoriety and stardom. He'd treated her like a shadow.

Abe caught himself double-clutching on his breath as Chapin took her in his arms and danced with her. Teammates and wives were stunned, heads jerking around for second takes. He didn't like his proprietary air, his possessiveness, and he didn't like the way Chapin kept his arm around her when they talked to people. He gidn't like the way he never let her out of his sight or away from her side, solicitous and caring.

Nor did Abe know what to do, so he just inclined his head, meticulously polite, as she passed in front of him. It was extremely embarrassing. He didn't know that the team knew of his marital difficulties. They knew now, and he was at the mercy of a fraternity that took no prisoners when it came to fair treatment of family.

"For Christ's sake, do something about this, Abe." Curly approached him, a drink in hand. "There's enough hot-air gossip floating around this room to fill an air mattress! I've never seen two people more matched than you and Sarah, and you just let some other tiger invade your jungle? Your first line of defense is to go fight for her!" His eyes blazed blue; his partially gray hair cut short, curled around his head with no sense of direction, and his eyebrows knit together over an exquisitely chiseled nose.

From across the room, Sarah wondered if Abe had any feelings at all the way he kept them reined in. He reminded her of Hans Christian Anderson's *Ice Prince.* She watched with peripheral vision as he raised a cup of punch to his mouth. Immediately, she knew it was fatal—it caused her eyes to travel the distance to his eyes, which almost on command met hers. She felt a surge of heat in her temples, willing it to stop-stop-stop. With all her misgivings, the magnetism could not be removed. She tried to bury the feelings as devil's doings.

His fixation stayed on her face, searching, a flare of yearning lighting his eyes and simultaneously an element of irritation that the yearning was so evident. As she crossed the room to the punch bowl, she looked all creamy, soft and slow-moving. Poetry reflected in the flexing of her knees and the pitch of her hips. Sarah graced with the redolence of jasmine in the spring, the feel of spun silk on the bolt and the taste of a fine wine on the palate. Possessed with her glow and iridescence, he noticed that her eyes, under the uncannily long lashes, were almost opaque brown against the whitest of whites. On either side of her nose, small flutes flared with her speech.

Why am I doing this to myself? With all the partiers having a good time, I'm analyzing what I had—what I should still have—what I'll never have again. There was no chance for them now. None at all.

She laughed at something Bob said and her nose wrinkled. She was the embodiment of the finest award a man could ever attain, and he'd thrown it away. The faux pas fumble of a lifetime. Probably no one but Abe would notice the subtle flare to her hips making a cradle for the child within her. His child.

Abe couldn't believe it when Glen Miller turned over on the music selections. "Moonlight Serenade." It tore his heart out—the memories, the longing for her, the fighting for her all of his life. Tapping lightly on her shoulder, she turned around, her large dark eyes seeking upwards to his great height, the long lashes appraising him. His muscles knotted worse than a three-hour practice session. He was surprised to hear his own voice. "Could Milady's First Knight have this dance?" he asked, bowing ceremoniously, bringing a smile to Doc's face as he stood nearby.

Unexpectedly, she flashed him her big smile, the one she always kept just for him. "I'd be decadent to turn you down, my knight. You have fought the good battle today. You have staved off the dragons." He held out his strong receiver's hand, the one on which he wore an award white diamond on the little finger. Shyly, she put her hand in his as she had done in grade school. *I should have told him no, firmly. Why can't I? Something compels me to hold the door open a crack.*

He wanted to touch her so badly. It was hell being with her and not being able to kiss those smiling lips, taste the honey he knew waited there. He turned his full attention on her, holding her away from him, trying to see her better. He couldn't trust holding her too closely. He gazed at his woman as any other man in the room might have done, as any laborer, as any park bench observer.

He gathered her closer; his heart hammered in his head, his throat suddenly as parched and hot as a freshly planed board in the Nahma sawmill. He thought he'd never survive until the end of the full plaintive notes of "Moonlight Serenade." It completely captivated him. Her small body jelled inside his, as it always had. With his chin tucked down and resting on top of her head, he thought, *how strange—how content he felt to be near her like this—to feel the rightness of it.*

I love you, Sarah, he wanted to whisper into her hair. Instead, he startled himself saying, "Sarah, listen to this psalm. *'Come back to me and fill my heart. Don't let fear keep us apart. Long have I waited for your coming home to me and sharing fully our new life.'* That's only a part of it, but you see, even in biblical times married people had problems and separations and were given second chances." He held her out slightly, visualizing her understanding, hoping for forgiveness.

"I can't, Abe. You've taken me to hell and back and left me with numbed expectations. Bob has asked me to marry him. He would be an excellent husband and father for my children, and I do believe that he loves me. He knows I'm pregnant. He never asked me whose child I was carrying. He accepts me as I am. That has to be caring and love. I think I can buy that, accept it, live with it. I've extended to you all the forgiveness I can. You need to accept that and move on with your life." She leaned back, looking up into the indescribable hurt in his eyes.

He blanched, as if he'd been hit by a freight train. "Sarah. You haven't..."

"No, I haven't, and he's not pushed it. I think he knows it's too soon, and you and I aren't divorced." She could feel his whole body relax from the building tensions he felt with her message. Stillness encompassed them—silence followed, each consumed with their own thoughts. The years of loving, longing, providing and planning, all swept away by his violence. Would he survive this?

⁂

The ground lay heavy with snow. It was his birthday, December 14. He visited his house—Sarah's house. Five and a half months pregnant and she'd already put up the Christmas tree! This woman was incorrigible.

"Daddy!" Fabe came running into the foyer. "Dad-dy!" What a kid. Dressed in tight jeans, a chambray shirt and shaker sweater, he looked like a six-year-old king of the hill. Fabe jumped up on Abe. "Daddy! Stay with us. Santa's coming here!" He danced his way over to the fireplace, stooped down, placed his hands on his knees, and peered up the chimney. Abe melted. He wouldn't be part of all the hoopla with Fabe. He didn't care any more who in the hell's kid he was. He was *his.*

At first she'd met him at the door with a grim gaze—decision making—must have thought of him as an orphan coming in off the street. They sat in the living room of her house, *his* house, and watched the dazzling twinkling lights of the Christmas tree, and listened to carols while Fabe hopped around showing Daddy his school work, his Little Golden Books, his birthday toys. "Carry me to bed, Daddy. Read me a story. My new one...Dr. Suess: *Horton Hears A Who.*" Sarah nodded her assent, smiling. *Damn! There she sits in her terrible pride, her strength. Will I ever break through again?*

Abe swooped Fabe into the air, landing him squarely on his shoulders, carrying him up the stairs to his new bedroom. "Nice room, Fabe. Mama fixed it up nice for you—new bed, big kid's bed. You don't fall out?" Abe lifted him off his shoulders and set him gently in the middle of the youth bed. "No. See. I have sides I can pull up so I don't roll off," he said, laughing again with that belly shaker of his.

"Daddy, I don't love Uncle Bob like I love you. I want you home again, or just come more often. Where do you go? What do you do while you're gone? Mama says you're busy. Would you be busy with me? When's my turn?" He reached up and put his arms around Abe's neck, smiling, his red lips parting, showing little pearls of kindergarten teeth, his trusting eyes beaming love at Abe.

"Soon, Fabe. Soon I'll be back. You and I—we'll do lots of things. Let's take the boat out next summer. Won't that be nice?" He studied the child he loved.

"Yeah. You and me, Daddy. You and me," he breathed, winding down, his long lashes curling over his cheeks in restfulness.

❧

Christmas. The excitement of Fabe. Doc invited Abe to join them for the day—Doc, Suki, Bill, Marian, Farley and Norrhea, all over at Doc's. The whole day was handled by a catering service. Doc's big home rang with cheer, trimmings, pine boughs from Nahma, mistletoe and holly, a fifteen-foot tree in the living room, outdoor decorations blinking and dazzling, even at midday. A light snow fell, dressing everything in an Upper Midwest fantasy. Abe, always impressed with the affluence of Doc's lifestyle, had no idea how much his father was worth—must be millions. Millions!

A light buffet was served throughout the entire day, with oyster en brochette, Swedish meatballs in rich gravy, tiny Pulaski Polish sausages in hot sauce, Kaukauna cheeses, Brie wedges, Swiss gruyere cheese, baskets of fresh fruit, fresh vegetables on ice, wispy philo confections rolled in powder sugar, stuffed mushrooms. Abe, fidgety to an extreme, was glad to see that Bob Chapin hadn't been invited. *Thanks, Doc.*

Sarah was breathtaking in a forest green velvet dress with a tucked bodice that fell full away from the midriff. He thought he saw her gasp upon seeing him there, but she immediately recovered her poise.

She felt suddenly like a child, filled with a deep warmth after she'd gotten everything she wanted for Christmas. *But, remember, Sarah, he may not have had a thought about you at all.* Her body stiffened and her eyes brightened with tears.

Abe thought he'd spare her the bother of saying hello and nodded curtly. And wasn't it ironic that he'd worn his dark green Pendleton single breasted blazer with the patch pockets and charcoal-gray, wool blend slacks. He was as sure his hair stood on end as if she were sending out electrified particles.

Had he read too much into what *he* wanted, and misread her feelings? He stood motionless, conscious of a sense of loss that pumped him empty. Until he had lost her, he had not recognized that in her, his hopes were all tied together. In her presence, a lapping of synapses spread through the entirety of his senses. It annoyed him. How much longer could he restrain himself with the desire to reach out and touch her, pull her to him? *Keep it together, Abe. Stand down. She's not yours any longer.*

Dinner was served promptly at six, with Doc presiding at the head of the table as if he were holding court. Suki, at the other end of the candle-bedecked table, reigned, adulated and revered by him. Often Abe could feel the intensity of the two of them, their longings, she echoing his feelings as if by telepathy, pulling them together. Ostensibly, she satisfied him with her Sioux culture more than any other woman could. Doc kept her closely guarded, not wanting to share her with anyone. Abe experienced a roiling rancor with his inability to experience the same association with Sarah. What did it take? *Maturity, Abe. Grow up.*

Doc seated Fabe in a youth chair to his immediate right, with Sarah next to Fabe and Abe across the table on his immediate left. Fabe looked like the picture of decor as grace was recited, his round cherub face gathered in thought. As Papa Doc carved the turkey, however, he commenced to roll his eyes and rub his belly, laughing in delight as if he hadn't seen food for a month, annoying Abe to no end.

"What's the matter with that kid?" he asked, cutting his glance to Sarah. "Don't you feed him at home?"

Sarah, crestfallen, parted her lips slightly, but no words came out.

Doc shot Abe a don't-start-with-her look, which forewarned of bad timing.

Suki studied her son's profile, pained by the Sioux hardness she saw in his cheek and jaw line, and the warrior feelings that he kept deeply repressed.

Christ, Abe! What's the matter with you? Why did you say that? Fabe is the picture of health—chubby, pink, happy, bright-eyed. Can't you squelch that burning blackguard for even one day?

The turkey, carved and steaming, was served with all the accouterments. The after dinner brandies were served in the living room, where Sarah entertained with carols on the Kawai baby grand, the rich tones contained well within the room, the puddling draperies providing the acoustical values. Fabe scrambled onto the piano bench to play a duet with Mama, adding nothing to the selections but sour notes.

Doc, standing against the fireplace mantle, clamped a cigar between his teeth in preparation to lighting it. "I wonder, Sarah, if you would allow Fabe to stay here with us tonight—to enjoy him in the morning," Doc asked, his tone reward-seeking, his eyes shifting from Abe to Sarah. A brutally intense need to have the child near shot him through. "You had the pleasure of him this morning; we'd all like to see him with *us* tomorrow morning. Isn't that right," he nodded to Bill and Marian, Farley and Norrhea. A resounding ad-lib of "Yeses" circuited the room.

"Yes, of course, Fabe would love it, I'm sure, but don't spoil him. He's getting to be a little rascal." She laughed that deep misty laugh that turned Abe inside out. Involuntarily, he jerked his head toward her. A longing such as he'd never experienced darted through him, vicious and unanticipated, leaving him looking vulnerably at her.

Doc didn't miss the expression; his heart went out to his son. Christmas. His dreams unfulfilled. He had everything, but he had nothing. Doc would never stop blaming himself for this grief visited upon Abe. *Don't meddle, Doc.*

"Little rascal. Little rascal." Fabe cavorted around the living room like a wood sprite, stopping at Papa Doc. "Little rascal, Papa Doc!" He exclaimed, laughing.

"No way, Fabe," Sarah admonished.

Running to Bill Atkins, Fabe grabbed his knees. "Rascal, rascal, Grandpa Bill!" Fabe's belly shook with laughter.

"No. Not Grandpa Bill either!" Sarah shook her finger at him.

Running to Abe, Fabe looked up at the tall length of him, his eyes dancing with mischief. "Dad-dy. Dad-dy. Rascal, rascal, rascal!" The room turned quiet. *Out of the mouth of babes,* thought Abe. Placing things into focus, he lifted Fabe and hugged him. "Yes. You're just like daddy, rascal, rascal, rascal!" The strained quality of the room settled to Yule warmth, the awkward moment having passed.

"So, I wonder Abe, if you'll take me home," Sarah asked without hidden meaning. "I walked over here, but it's dark out now and shivery, probably slippery, too, with this light snowfall." She smiled up at him from the piano bench.

"It would be my pleasure, little lady," Abe baritoned in his best John Wayne mimicry. He walked over, picked up her hand and kissed the back of it, bringing smiles of encouragement from the full contingency of the houseguests. He caught the bright glow of delight that flashed across her eyes, but shielded by the lowering of her lashes.

Abe smiled to himself, but he knew he skated on thin ice and queued far from fool enough to think that she would accept him back in her heart.

CHAPTER FORTY-NINE

The lawn looked like a bolt of deep cotton batting as Abe escorted Sarah down the long sidewalk to the front door. He stood in the foyer, his mind racing for some means to suspend time. "Let me build a fire for you in the fireplace before I leave, Sarah. You should have some traditions of your own and a fireplace fire is a good place to start on Christmas night." He raised his eyebrows, looking down at her from his towering height. Smiling his dazzling best, he captured both her wrists. "Please say yes!"

"Well, all right, Abe."

When she looked up, that old heat rushed through him as if he were thirteen years old, stealing a look at her breasts for the first time while out digging clams at Stony Point.

"Would you like coffee or a nightcap, Abe?" she asked as she hung her coat.

"I'll have Crown Royal in a snifter, if you don't mind. No rush." *Don't hurry, Sarah. I have nowhere to go. Nothing to do. Just emptiness lays ahead of me on this Christmas night.* He checked himself as he found himself nodding involuntarily, in complete compliance with his own thoughts.

She returned as the fire snapped into play, Abe's small teepee of kindling dry enough to set the house afire, topped with white birch and sweet maple.

"So pretty, Abe. I rarely ever light the fireplace. It feels good tonight, with the snowflakes drawing to the windows like moths to a flame. I know that's an illusion, but it does seem that way. Thank you," she said, handing him the miniature fishbowl-on-a-stem snifter. "Sit down, Abe, anywhere. I think I'll sit right here on the floor in front of the fireplace and let my mind wander with the flames. Aren't they fascinating?" She rocked back and forth, getting comfortable. He stood staring at her as she glanced up at him with that supernatural sublimity she bore at times. His same sweet Sarah.

"I'm sorry," he said. "I'm sorry you found me staring." He decided he had to use this time to erase yesterday's images. He couldn't undo what had been done, but could spend the rest of his life making it up to her. His life wasn't the wonderful freedom he'd thought to possess. He had to breathe life back into his marriage.

Leaning against the fireplace with his snifter, he put one hand in his trousers pocket, looking every bit the man of the house. "What do you want from me, Sarah?" His face registered concern. "I'll give you anything. Don't shut me out. *You* are Christmas. It flourishes in your face." He knew he fumbled over the words, using them as they popped into his head. He never was good with this word business. "I promised you happiness. Let me give that to you. Let me *try* to give that to you. I veered way out of line in my treatment of Fabe's revelation."

She caught the flicker of pain in his eyes that he wasn't quick enough to conceal. Her heart leaped into her throat at his words. She tried to push his voice aside, the words aside. She needed to squelch this feeling of tenderness and compassion. She shifted her gaze to the long windows on either side of the fireplace, watching the swirling flakes lift and lower, never quite making it to the windows.

"Do you not have even the remotest love for me at all?" His voice died softly. He realized that his eyes were blurring over.

She observed him standing at the fireplace, the bigness of him. She shrank there, sitting on the floor, hypnotized by the leaping firelight, observing the intensity of his dark eyes, the muscles working about his temples. Something fell apart—all her resolutions. This was the Abe of her childhood, the Abe in need and the Abe she'd nurtured all her life. Her heart melted at his misery. His longings, yearnings, his pain, they were all hers. Yes. She still loved him.

"Yes," she whispered. "I care." Her voice caught. Her stomach muscles were so intense that she found herself breathing only shallowly. How she had fought being around him to avoid this attraction she felt. Now he had crashed through her shell.

He stared down into her eyes at her words, words that fell melodiously in the swelling of his heart. Words that satiated him with a fierce knightly protectiveness of his lady. Had it been six months since she'd shut him out of her life, or six years?

Excitement surged through him, crowning in his splendid face. Setting his snifter on the mantle, he quickly reached down and pulled her up to him as if he'd been endowed suddenly with Herculean powers, his eyes still misty, and this time with joy.

She set her hand between them to stave off being pulled into his arms. In the next millisecond, his mouth buried in her abundant hair near her ear, his voice grew husky. "That's all that's important to me, to hear you say you care. Love can grow again. Just care for me, Sarah. Just care," his voice was a blend of sobs and joy. A seed of a smile grew in his dark brown eyes and spread to his mouth, showing his perfect white teeth in his tawny skin, the skin that Sarah admired. The face she loved relaxed, the hard marbles gone, non-existent. The sound of his deep, resonant voice in her home once more made her heart thump.

She pulled back, having second thoughts, her delicate hands on his chest where she could feel the beat of his heart, her eyes searching, examining and testing. She was angry with herself for trembling with the cravings he had affected.

He turned her sideways to better have the firelight play on her, tilting her head back and re-memorizing her face, running his fingers lightly over her eyebrows, her cheeks, her lips, her nose, along her throat. He feathered his mouth over hers, tasting, dipping, moving on, not getting enough of anything, his eyes smoldering, traveling.

Why did he look at her like that? What was he thinking? She put her hands to her cheeks to stop the blushing. Why did she feel this way?

"I've been dead, Sarah," he whispered, as he continued his journey around her head and neck. "I haven't known a minute's happiness. Sometimes I can't eat; nothing will go down. I sleep only when I'm completely exhausted, and then I wake up, clutching the sheets, searching for you, realizing you're gone, forever. I tell myself to get over it, that you're just another woman, but that doesn't work. Nothing works. Only you." His voice fell soft on her ears as he pulled her hair back and twined it between his fingers. "I thought maybe I had fallen into a permanent state of grief—worse than when Fabian died—when Eddie died. I can't live without you in my life." The Westminster chimes sounded the hour on the mantle clock—nine o'clock.

She felt so alive as she closed her eyes and succumbed to the pleasure of having him hold her again, the pleasure and security of his arms. She hadn't always known happiness with him, but now she felt herself surrendering to this moment in time when she forgot everything else and enjoyed the love he offered. Maybe her future wouldn't be bright, but with all certainty, it had been bleak without him. Shall it always be? *It's up to you Sarah. He's offered.* It was as if someone had just blown reveille.

"Please don't say no, Sarah. Just say you'll consider my offer." His voice thickened with emotion. Abe could feel the knots in the depths of his stomach starting to uncoil. He hadn't realized he'd been holding himself so uptight, awaiting her reply.

She eased away from him, drifting quietly to the glass-fronted fireplace to stare down at the story-telling flames, first one then the other leaped to its feet to tell a tale. "Lasting love is scarce, Abe. Lasting *true* love is scarcer than hummingbird eyebrows, as Max used to say." She shrugged in a hopeless fashion, lifting her shoulders, her vulnerability endearing to Abe.

His eyebrows shot up in sharp question. Did she say that there was a forever-and-ever kind? That he had a chance? Taking charge, he approached deliberately. A second later the deep pools of her eyes were looking up at him, locked on him. In the firelight, he could see the wetness of them. Neither knew who moved first. She framed his face with her hands; he held her to him, feeling every line of her body, his hands not stopping. He thought his heart would break in losing her, but now it ached with a joy that left him speechless. With an ill-concealed groan, he gathered her closer as if he could make her part of himself where she could never again get away. "You're so beautiful," he said, afire. She leaned into him, satisfying the demands of his arms.

His caressing hands stroked up and down her bare arms, sending a firestorm of heat through her. The hungry urgency of his kiss fanned the inferno. A sound came from deep within his throat again, making her respond with a lack of reserve she'd never known, pulling his head down hard onto her mouth. Sarah's clothing articles disappeared. His mouth and hands were exploring, reassuring, and pressing the softness of her, the roundness of her. "Oh God! How I love you, missed you, missed all this."

"I know," she said. "I know." She clung to him, moving her fingers up over the inside of his jacket, feeling his rangy firmness as she dug her fingers into it. The muscles rippled in his chest as she drew her hands around it, tracing, lingering. She felt no cold, but she grew pink with his aggressions. He pressed her closely, taking gulping breaths, his mouth warm and his breath hot in her ears. "You're so beautiful." He trembled with control, dark brown eyes smoldering, locking her into him. "What am I thinking? You must be cold," he said sweeping her off her feet and carrying upstairs to *their* bedroom, tucking her under the comforter.

She watched as he removed his clothes and hung them in the closet where they rightfully belonged, never taking his eyes off her. He shook the enormity of what she had said—that she still cared for him! Naked, but not ashamed, he moved toward the bed with determination and exaltation, a sublimation of soul and body.

Pulling back the coverlets, he groaned from deep within. His long dry spell caught up with him as he lay down beside her. His passion had him massaging his fingers into her back, feeling her belly, *his* belly. He placed his hands on his child, growing there in her belly. The child lurched. He felt excited. It had to be a boy! His hand slid down the length of her thigh. "God, you're beautiful, my wife, my Sarah!" His breath caught on her name, lingering there, savoring it.

He wanted her to need him, to enjoy his love making, to make this memorable—a firm commitment from him. "You'll never know how I tried to forget you," he breathed, his voice coated, "but you were always there, even on the football field in the most detailed of calls. You were there when the Angelus rang, carrying its message daily on the heavy air. You were there when I climbed into bed. It never stopped. Endless-endless-endless," he whispered agonizingly. "I love you so dearly, Sarah. You are me—I am you." Nothing lay hidden in his message; the warmth in his eyes harvested her breath like a sudden whip of wind.

"There was no rationale for the things I said to you last July, Sarah. At the time you conceived of Fabe, I had left you high and dry. There was meanness in my mind, wanting to hurt you. It was a disaster to think that I'd never know your love again. It's been a hurting six months."

"Shhh, Abe. We need to move on with our lives and try to forget the ugliness of that night." Yes, she cared for him. She had prayed to God to relieve her of this longing for him. Now, she thrilled, electricity pumping through her.

Her gentle hands that he loved so much curved around his neck, tracing her fingers into his hair, approving his love. She smiled, that *just-for-him* smile, enchanting him with the slow outward flexing of her lips. As the light wind clicked snowflakes softly against the windows, he wanted her. God, how he needed her!

He was consumed with such enrapturement that he knew he must be damned for the rest of his life, needing her. The thought thumped his soul pleasantly. He moved gently, not tearing his eyes from her, her cheekbones that seemed to laugh when she did, her small mouth that surprised him constantly with her dazzling full smile, her determined chin that told him without a word when he was out of line. They lay together in sated communion, breathing in unison as if someone had written the score, their silence a stronger declamation than a million words.

"I love you more than anything in the whole world, Sarah. Oneness with you is all I ever want." Why? He could have any woman he wanted; he prided in that fact. *What bewitchment she works on me, until I'm not whole without her.*

Her response, quiet and unexpected, rhapsodized him. "We'll see, Abe." The corners of her mouth curved in a ready smile, but the words came out, tortured, weary.

He knew he'd not broken through her secondary yet and he'd have to back off again. Holding her dearly, he ran a finger down her cheek, his face a study in love.

෴

The calendar on the bedside table read March 21, 1955 when the telephone jangled. It's the phone, Abe—answer the phone. *What in the hell time is it, anyway?* 6:00 a.m.! What the hell? "Hello." Muffled, foggy. Abe was never afflicted with insomnia; he always slept like a gas station hound.

"Abe, this is Doc. Wake up. I just brought Sarah to the hospital to induce labor. She'd complained that the baby had become somnolent lately, so I drew some amniotic fluid from her and found red blood cell antibodies were abundantly present, so we can no longer risk allowing the child to be invaded with these anti-bodies." He paused. "Are you listening, Abe?" Doc's voice resonated, concisely feeding him information.

Abe looked at the receiver as if he were holding a talking testament to the latest news of the day, none of which he absorbed. "Yeah, but I'm not quite following you. So Sarah's at the hospital. I assume Bellin. Did she ask for me? Or is this *your* idea that I be there?" Abe's tone could curdle milk.

"It's *my* idea, sure, but you should be here. You *are* the father. You have a right to be here, even if she didn't ask for you, and she didn't. But maybe this baby will make all the difference as to whether she reconciles with you or not. It's been a tough nine months for her." Doc knew he was pushing the envelope to insist on Abe's appearance, but maybe it would work. "Bob Chapin will be here for her, and he is one charismatic man with a brilliant mind. You know he's been relentless for her to marry him. If there is even a vestige of hope for you, you should protect your home turf."

The hair on Abe's arms tingled, showing small goose bumps on the surface. *Chill out, Chapin. You're not going to get her. She's mine—always has been.* Abe searched his flight-or-fight emotions. He'd fight.

None of this would have happened had I not left her. He sighed deeply. "It'll be an hour or so, that is if I don't get held up by the Main Street drawbridge. Thanks for calling, Doc."

"All right, but take care." For some reason, Doc didn't feel the comfort he should at Abe's agreement to be present. The two were still polarized. However, now Sarah wouldn't allow Abe back into *her* life. Every time he tried to act as an intermediary, she uncovered every venial sin Abe had ever committed against her.

Abe set the phone softly into the cradle, staring off into space, the sheet covering only the bottom half of him, his rug-covered chest breathing softly in and out. He grew anxious as he moved out of bed in his one-bedroom condominium at the corner of Packerland Drive and Hazelwood Lane. He fit very well here where it was quiet and away from the hubbub of busy streets, yet not too far from the stadium. The large windows on either side of his headboard showed him the first smoky quartz of dawn, highlighting tender green silhouettes in the copse of hardwoods behind the condominiums. Birds called, examining the morning. He found it uplifting.

What a mess he'd made of things at thirty-one years old—things he took out and examined meticulously: the silt of his life, the toe-stubbers, knee benders and *mea culpas*. The memory of arguing with Curly a couple of times over trivia. Curly, who had taught him a wealth about football when he thought he already knew it all. Abe shuddered. He had missed so many things. Fabe running through the house, laughing, eyes dancing with indisputable love. "I love you, Daddy," came echoing back to him through the silky sheerness of time.

So many times he'd tried to shake off those thoughts, but they jumped back on him, clinging. Then there was the comforting sound of Sarah puttering around the house, playing the piano in the living room. His ears were hearing on their own, as if they were separate entities, the sentimental strains of Debussy's "Clair de Lune." The fantasies she wove with the melancholy of Beethoven's "Moonlight Sonata." It reminded him of moonlight over Big Bay de Nocquet in Nahma, rich and stirring. When Perry Como recorded "Till the End of Time" back in '45, the meaningful melody had a way of haunting him. He hummed it now in the shower.

Making up his bed, he fluffed the throw pillows as he tossed them over his regular pillows and thought of how often he'd assisted in making the bed in the seven years they were married. Seven years of pleasure and fulfillment, all tossed out the window like yesterday's newspaper. He heard a shouting in the back of his mind that he could no longer dislodge: *jerk, jerk, jerk*. He quickly dressed in tan bucks, khaki chinos, green soft-knit shirt and an off-white bulky sweater. Heavily, his feet hit the stairs from his loft-style bedroom and bathroom. *I'd marry her again, no matter whose baby she carried. So would Chapin.* Abe felt the old tensions returning. The same old shit he'd been projecting for months, and it didn't smell any better with the passage of time.

Grabbing corn flakes in the small kitchen, Abe captured a bowl, spoon and milk—juggling all of them as he hurried to the table. He recognized that the choices he had made in life had left embattlements that extended far beyond what met the eye.

The years washed away, familiar voices drenching his memory bank, surfacing into the present like transient images. The voices were places, and the places were people living again—exhumed, floating in the flow of his consciousness. Farley, relating the abuses suffered by his Sioux ancestors: *"I can hear the whinny of the horses, smell the smoke of the cooking fires, and thrill to the shrieks of Indian children at play."*

Children. Kids teasing him at school when he was young: *"Let dumb Abe do it,"* the jibe of the day. His speech problems because of a tied tongue, salivation problems, all of which Doc cured. He glimpsed Fabian's death and the grief for which society had little patience to endure with the bereaved. Never knew he could miss another human being so much, never, until Eddie died. *"I'm going to join the army and drive a jeep in circles around those Kraut tanks until they're dizzy!"* It still hurt. Max's tirade: *"A half breed,"* he called me, spitting out the words as if they were dirty. Just think, Abe, you paid for some of your college with gold, the gold bought with the lives of your great-grandparents. Then there was ugly old John Pedo—now dead John Pedo—who died incoherent and insane: *"Come into my home for a penny."* Abe, crunching cornflakes, shuddered again. No mother. No attention—the soft, warm kind. *Nada.*

Abe's solution to the nefarious Neil Izcik problem: *I can still hear that kid's head pop like a ripe melon.* *"Can always get a woman around here,"* drifted back to him from Doc's conversation, overheard while shoveling snow at the hotel, hungry, cold.

"You're a good boy, Abe. I'm proud to be your father." Fabian. Fabian, with his egregious terrors of WW II.

"No, Abe, I'm not that kind of girl." Sarah. Lovely Sarah. How mean he'd been to her. Yes, mean. *Hard to admit, huh, Abe? Why?* No one he loved more. The lecherous Levine's: *"Just how do you intend to pay for this funeral?"* Liked to have knocked him on his ass. Then Sarah going away to school. *"Won't be back all summer either..."* How his heart broke. *"Some of the jacks save their money all winter to go into town in the spring and have a knockdown drag-out fling, go back to camp broke, and start saving all over again."* That was Alan Mercier. Can't imagine ever having to live like those

jacks. Bleak! So cold that you have to kick at the frozen-shut caboose door to get back in at the end of the day. I can still smell the wet stockings hanging by the barrel stoves. Sarah's sweet, velvet voice: *"My family will be so embarrassed if I get married great-with-child, Abe."* He'd been an insensitive selfish ass, all me-me-me.

Anxiety clutched him as he pushed his chair back from the table. Strange, how weak and watery his legs felt from the terror and torment of his self-admissions, as if a spotlight had been thrown on his failings. What you didn't get back for what you put into life, you raped and stole for it. You thought there was a proper balance between grief and remaining joys. *Well, you've blown it. There is no equality between pitfalls and victory trophies. Try bending with the breeze.*

Negotiating the two short steps to the living room, he snapped on the TV while he held the bowl of cereal, spooning it vacuously, pleased at the early morning sports news. "What folks see when they come to Packer games is the love affair between a town and its football team." *It's March, and the sports news is still Packers!*

"Packer fans don't care if others think a cheese sculpture of Curly Lambeau is funny. Packer fans laugh along with the jokes about the team with undying love." The announcer paused, laughed, then went on. "Question: How many Packer fans does it take to change a light bulb? Answer: Three. One to screw it in, and two to sit around and reminisce about what a great job the old bulb did." Abe broke out in laughter. Yes, this was a great town. You just didn't play football here on contract, you were adopted by the city and you damn well better shape up. The whole city rolled up the streets on Packer home games—time stood still.

He thought of it now, while he turned off the TV and grabbed his trench coat. Upstairs. Yes, that's where it was—one of his old jerseys, number 14. He'd take it to the hospital and give it to Sarah for their new son. Gotta be another son. He already gave one to Fabe, who wore it around the house like Peewee from the Popeye Comics.

Running out the door, he stuffed the jersey into his pocket. *Our new little guy will be baptized at the Resurrection Parish over on Hilltop Drive. That's another thing I like about Green Bay. Where else would you find such strong identification of players with the team and the area, and the traditional values of religion, family and civic virtue? Just since I've been here, our team has been rescued by the community from financial crises three times.* Abe felt drifty, like a canoe launched onto the Sturgeon River in July, taking him downriver on slowly moving currents.

The Taming of a Sioux

Driving Lombardi Avenue, he made an easy access onto Broadway North. Abe found it hard to believe that Curly had started this team under the aegis of the Green Bay Acme Packing Co. *Even harder to believe that I'm here playing football.* He was still averaging over five passes a game and one and a half touchdowns, leading the league in yardage. *Curly's happy. I'm happy. Now I need to convince Sarah that she's happy too.* Maybe Doc's right. Maybe this baby will do it. He needed to test the water—look for the vital signs, maybe a small flicker in her eyes. His heart stabbed, remembering how she used to look at him with such worship and love and trust. *I know this baby is mine. Has to be mine...timing's right. Glad that Main Street drawbridge is down.*

Moving onto Webster, he headed south for about a mile to Bellin Memorial Hospital. After turning off the ignition, he sat for a while, eyeing a developing fizzy drizzle from out of nowhere. In late March, it wasn't April showers, but close enough for a taste of spring. *March 21st! Fabian died twelve years ago today!* There arose a rainstorm, a granddaddy blowout. Sighing, he opened the car door and ran as only he could from the parking lot to the front door.

The elevator opened as quietly on the fourth floor as it had on the first floor. "You'll have to wait a while, Mr. Miereau," the charge nurse looked directly at him with piercing blue eyes that didn't fool around. "The waiting room is at the end of the hall," she said, pointing with her pencil. "We'll call you when she's ready." Finally, a smile.

Abe sank back into a leather upholstered chair, placing his elbow on the armrest, extending his forefinger over his mouth, his long legs sticking out straight.

"Abe!" Doc walked in, startling him.

Abe started. "What in the world is wrong in there? Why can't I see Sarah yet? Has she refused to see me?" Questions shot pompously, reflecting the tightness Doc observed in his shoulders.

"Take it easy, Abe. I haven't even told Sarah that you're here. I don't control the scenario at this hospital as I did in Nahma. However, I did arrange for you to be present in the delivery room so you can see your new baby born. They don't do that for fathers here. I advised them, however, that you had witnessed the birth of your first child, and that you held up just fine, so they acquiesced." Doc looked sartorial in his chocolate brown suit, white shirt, gold, tan and flamingo tie. His soft leather oxfords were designed of interlaced leather strips—Italian, no doubt. Abe never knew him to be more in his domain than anywhere in the medical modal. His dark brown eyes measured and equated constantly.

"Doc eased into a chair near Abe. "I need to tell you about your blood incompatibility with Sarah's. Mine is incompatible, too. But for the first delivery, this usually is no problem. The trouble arises in subsequent pregnancies. Sarah is O negative and you're AB positive. This occurs in only a small number of pregnancies. The Rhesus incompatibility is a sort of war between the blood groups of the mother and the developing baby. Obviously, she's carrying a child of your blood type."

While Abe sat back in his chair, his back to the window, arms folded across his chest, Doc sat on the edge of his chair, sideways, to better make eye contact and read understanding of the information he conveyed.

"When any baby is born, some of the baby's blood enters the mother's circulation. An Rh-negative mother's body reacts to the baby's Rh-positive blood as foreign material and produces antibodies to combat it. Because this usually happens as a delayed reaction after the baby is born, the first baby may not be harmed. However, the mother will continue to produce these antibodies after delivery, and in any subsequent pregnancy, these antibodies may pass from the mother's bloodstream into that of the developing baby and will start to destroy the baby's red blood cells, *if* the baby has Rh-positive blood. Your child does," Doc said succinctly.

Abe listened—eyes widening—his mind sucking hard at this new knowledge.

"About fifteen percent of the white population of the United States has Rh-negative blood. Slightly greater than ten percent of marriages are between an Rh-negative woman and an Rh-positive man. However, updated diagnosis and treatment have made the problems of Rhesus incompatibility rare."

Doc arose, pulling at his lower lip, and paced. "Rhesus incompatibility produces no symptoms in the mother. When it occurs, the baby may develop hemolytic anemia and neonatal jaundice at birth, or in extreme cases, it may be stillborn."

"You mean dead?" Abe nearly shouted. His voice conveyed trauma as he, too, stood, approaching Doc, as if the comprehension would be easier.

"Yes. These risks increase with each Rhesus incompatibility pregnancy." Doc's tone awakened thoughts of losing Sarah in a far different manner than her refusal to reconcile. *What if my baby dies? What if she dies? What the hell is going on here?* He blanched. "Dead?" He clasped Doc's shoulders, his eyes questioning and alert.

"Yes. It's insidious. If ignored, the child could die within the womb. Given my awareness, I commenced regular blood testing. Two days ago I took an amniocentesis of the amniotic fluid that surrounds the baby in the uterus. It's positive. Sarah's antibodies are beginning to affect the baby's blood adversely, so we induced labor. You can expect that after the delivery your baby will have jaundice, and if this is severe, he or she may need a total blood exchange. This hospital, thank God, has a specialized unit to deal with the diverse problems of ill and premature infants. We would not have had that benefit in Nahma. It takes the larger city hospital to deal with isolated problems such as this." They looked at each other, exchanging knowing looks.

Abe stood wide-eyed, his breath coming in short gasps. His baby, his very own child. A child he'd wanted since he was seventeen. Now he was thirty-one and dealing with the possibility that he would have no child of his own. Somehow, he understood everything Doc had told him, and more than that. He understood as if it had been willed that he do so through some medium; metabollization had spun the words into Abe-onics.

"Don't leave me now, Abe, after I bragged to everyone how staunch you were." Doc pressed on Abe's shoulder to get him to sit down. "We're all working for you. I'm going to check Sarah one more time, and then I'll be leaving for the clinic. Dr. Moreno will be assisting me in the delivery, and if it's any comfort to you, he's an obstetrician. Usually, any pregnancies I refer immediately to him, but not Sarah's. I wanted this one for myself. I hope you don't mind, Abe. I only have your best wishes at heart."

"I know, Doc, but I wish they'd let me see her. I just want to talk to her. Maybe, just maybe she'll come around." Abe pulled his hands down over his face, sighing.

Doc looked down on him, pausing. *This kid has hit some potholes in his life, but this one must be the Grand Canyon.* "I wish you the best, Abe—always wanted her for you. I think the violent incidences you've had in your life have arisen from the fact that you love her so much that you're obsessed, but she doesn't see it that way. I'll try to convince her that seeing you is the right thing to do, you being the father and all. I'll be back out in a short while."

"Thanks, Doc." Abe sat with his elbows on his spread knees, his hands folded between them, head down. *Me, the father and all. Yes. Goddamn it! I am the father. You'd better put some skids on your imagination, Abe. Sure, you're the father, but to her you're out of the picture. You might as well be standing behind a bush! You being the father is of no significance to this wonderful mother.*

Into his bubble again, his whole body lurched at the sound of Doc's voice. "It's okay, Abe. You can come and see her now." The past did a quick fade. "She's actually in labor—the drip IV worked, and she's experiencing contractions—seems to be in a good frame of mind. May God go with you. I know you love her, but so does Bob, and he's willing to give her *anything* and already has showered her with attention and gifts. But you *can* be competitive here. She accepted your gifts long before he came on the scene. Take that ball and run with it, because as soon as Bob hears Sarah's in labor, he's going to appear and stand by her. You can go to the bank on that. You could outrun Bob at the Rosebowl and you can out-run him here. Remember, she loved you first. This is *your* child she's delivering today."

CHAPTER FIFTY

Abe felt awkward and cumbersome as he walked into the birthing room of a woman who feared his presence. It was close to ten o'clock, and the IV had been dripping for three hours. As he walked in, she writhed—a contraction. He hurried to the side of the bed to hold her hand, which she withdrew. He wanted to console her, to tell her how much he loved her, how much this child meant to him. He swallowed hard.

Grasping the back of the bed, she sighed as the pain withdrew. "Abe, Doc said you were here. How thoughtful. I'm impressed. The pains are coming harder and faster than they did with Fabe. Those started so slow and easy, but this IV has started them furiously. How have you been since Christmas?" Seeming to have second thoughts, she held her hand out to him uncertainly.

Responding involuntarily, he moved forward quickly, grasping her hand. "Just fine, fine. But nothing is greater than this, Sarah. Would you marry me?" He teased, yet sounding disconsolate. "I'd marry you a hundred times over. What can I promise you—a pilgrimage to the Milky Way, an odyssey to the Aurora Borealis? Yes, allow me to promise you that," he said as she went into another contraction. This time he clutched her hand and wouldn't let go, watching the sweat roll off her forehead and into her hair.

"Could we ask you to wait in the expectant father's room, Mr. Miereau?" A middle-aged round-faced nurse asked. "Dr. Moreno needs to examine your wife, and sometimes it is awkward for the father. Thank you." Behind steel-rimmed glasses, the nurse's eyes were kindly as Abe shifted his gaze from Sarah to the stiff white uniform the attendant wore.

Abe found himself again lodged in the waiting room as if he were some unneeded appendage of a major undertaking. He looked at the clock on the wall with its slow, herky-jerky movements, and with nothing better to do than to antagonize expectant fathers. Ten-thirty. *Sarah's been here since six o'clock.* It must seem like an eternity to her. After all he'd done to her, couldn't he at least help alleviate her pain?

Pulling on his bottom lip with his thumb and forefinger, he thought he'd lose his mind when Chapin walked into the room. Bob looked just as startled. "Abe! I didn't know you were here for this Coming-Out-Party." He smiled his kid-next-door grin.

Abe didn't appreciate the euphemism, whispering hoarsely. "Yeah, I'm here. And I'm staying here for the duration, whether you like it or not, my friend!" His brain traveled through a synapses overload again. A chill as cold as his childhood winter's night walk home struck him full in the face, in the gut, in the heart.

Immediately, Bob's sensitivity swelled. "Whoa, old buddy," he said raising his hand to flag down Abe's inclination for explosive reactions. "I had no idea you were here. I didn't want Sarah to be alone, is all. We've been friends for too long, Abe, to interfere in each other's personal lives. If you're going to sit with her today I'll leave and check in by phone later." Bob looked as if he'd just had the wind knocked out of him. "Okay, fella?" He extended his hand to Abe and shook it, his freckles dancing across his nose in that way Abe always found down-home.

"Sure thing, Bob. Sorry to have reacted that way. Yes, I'm staying. And yes, it'll be forever, if she'll have me." His voice betrayed his sinking hopes.

Reaching out, Bob jostled Abe's shoulder with a good-natured fist, turned on his heel and left, calling back over his shoulder, "Good luck to you, Abe, and Sarah, too. I think you know that I care about you both." Bob intuitively gathered that it was time to *fold* and not *stay*. His fallen face saw shelter from the closing of the door. The room immediately lost its energy with him gone. Abe ached for his old friend and cohort.

"*Mr. Miereau,*" a nurse called. "You can come in and sit with your wife now. She's doing very well."

Pulling a chair close to the bed, Abe sat down and entwined his fingers with hers, a small smile pushing at his cheeks. "Sarah," he whispered, kissing the palm of her hand. "Are the pains still coming hard and fast?" he asked, not really knowing what *hard and fast* meant in terms of labor.

Glancing at the clock, Abe realized that she was at least five hours into labor, the clock showing noon. "Yes, I knew it would be painful and I psyched myself up for it, but it's still more traumatic than I remembered. It's terrible, Abe. My back hurts so much that I think it's going to break."

The starched and pinned nurse came in and administered a hypo in Sarah's upper arm. "This will help relax her," she said to Abe, as if Sarah were a non-entity.

"Thanks so much," Abe said, then turned his attention back to Sarah. "Here, let me rub your back, little lady," helping her to roll to the side. "I'll massage it."

His eyes filled with a tenderness she hadn't seen in a very long time. His hands stroked her back with warm firmness. *Yes, Abe, I want you to rub my back with your big hands, say thanks for having this child and tell me you haven't lost that old love.*

Abe wanted to be everything for her, her oasis where she could find refreshment. The rain continued slowly wiggling down the windowpanes toward the casements.

By three o'clock great fists encircled her body like steel bands on a barrel, ever tightening, gripping. With each contraction Abe continued to stroke her pain-ridden body, now over her belly, which turned into ripples of hardness with each contraction. Bending over, Abe kissed her belly, nuzzling, while this terrible nightmare repeated itself without her consent, without her doing, without her approval. How could this have happened to her? To her! Graduated cum laude—voted most likely to succeed.

Doc walked in without warning—jarred at the familiarity exhibited between these estranged people. "I'm sorry!" A flame of excitement swept over him—all consuming. "I should have tapped at the door. I'm so sorry, Abe."

Abe, reluctantly extracting himself from the communion he'd been sharing with his wife, held up his hand. "It's okay, Doc. I just got carried away."

Dressed in scrubs, Doc said, "Let's see what we have here. You can stay, Abe," he nodded as he pulled on latex gloves. "Yes, yes, about a nine. You're doing just great." Shifting his gaze to Abe, he shook his head. "The baby is large, I'd say close to nine pounds. You'll need to keep her breathing and panting with the contractions to excise it."

Sarah gritted her teeth with the examination. Her head, her back, her belly, her vitals, they all ached. How much longer could she hold out? Another shot in the arm. She didn't know who stood around her, but she didn't care. Abe leaned over the bed and held her with desperate concern. He, at last, admitted to himself that he loved his wife more than she would ever love him, but he was willing to accept that.

"Doc, do something for her." His distress was a study in compassion.

Abe felt his shoulder being patted. "She'll do just fine. It's time for you to get into a set of scrubs and join me in the delivery room. I have them all ready for you in the doctors' lounge just down the hall. In the meantime, I'll get her into the delivery room; Dr. Moreno will join us there. She's close to delivering." Looking at the clock as he left, he saw that it was four o'clock. Where had the day gone?

Abe shook his head as if to clear cobwebs from his mind as he hurried back down the hall to the brightly lit delivery room. When Sarah screamed, "No more, no more," Abe dabbed her forehead with the coolness of a wet cloth. Her beautiful mahogany hair lay strung out in her tears, the sour stench of vomit and saturating sweat hanging over all. Hunkered against the merciless pain, she looked like an abandoned scrap of refuse. She cared about nothing now, but drifted off when she was given a moment's respite from the onslaught. She floated, her thoughts bobbing on a wave of woven tapestry, its length being shaken out in ever decreasing ripples, ending in a lasting levity without an anchor. Moistening her dry lips with her tongue, she hiccupped, a biological afterthought of her terrorized body.

This shaded almost more than Abe could bear. His personal effrontery of her nine months previous rushed in upon him with cold fury, tearing at his soul, his countenance a study in compassion and anxiety.

Sensing Abe's inner hysteria, Doc schooled his own face to reflect confidence. "Push, Sarah, I can see the baby crowning. Push!" Doc encouraged.

Moreno's worry printed boldly upon his face as he turned to Doc, the stethoscope in his hand. "She must move this baby, Danforth—its pulse is slowing."

Sarah didn't respond—didn't talk, didn't scream, just turned her head back and forth, slipping away from sheer exhaustion, her intake of breath intense, a look of surrender covering her fine small face, and her eyes now large pools of hopelessness.

Abe softly toweled her face, his breathing as ragged as Sarah's.

Slipping away, she thought how gentle his hands were, the same hands that carried a football so adeptly, the same hands that painted exotic pictures, held Fabe, chopped wood for the fireplace...

"One more time, Sarah! Just one more time, and we'll have it." Doc shouted, excited, yet concerned with the turn of events. How his heart beat seeing new little entities emerge into the world. It was a miracle every time for him. *Please God. Don't let anything happen to her—to the baby.*

She emitted nothing as her energy leaked away. She didn't twist her head anymore, but lay rigid, white and unresponsive. A flood gate opened in her mind, permitting happy thoughts to flow in, the ghosts and wavering images of her life, better moments with Abe, days at the beach, wild roses growing in fragrance and beauty, pearlescent in color. She saw them unfolding like time-lapse photography—mellowing in her mind. The squishy, warm sugary sand seeped between her toes just inches from the waves rolling in from the bay. Bright orange poppies bent on long stems in Max's garden, lupines grew on the hillsides, wild, profuse, blue and green.

"She's sinking—pulse rate dropping!" The anesthesiologist shouted.

"Unit of blood! Stat." Dr. Moreno was no longer an assistant.

Abe, standing by, could see the small head of black hair at a standstill — not budging. A look of panic swept over the handsome terrain of his face. Shot with adrenalin, his gaze grew bright; his eyes searched those of Moreno's over his mask, deducing nothing from his studied professionalism.

"Episiotomy!" Doc ordered gruffly, using only the one word, holding up his hand as a scalpel was slapped into it, glancing up at the anesthesiologist for a nod. Doc caught out of the corner of his eye Abe's collapse as he groaned, folded and dropped to the floor. Moreno stepped around Abe as emergency teams answered the code call. Forceps were slapped into Doc's hand. Gently, he inserted them into the vaginal cavity, grasping the child's head, carefully assisting it to emerge from the birth canal, followed by copious bleeding from vaginal tears and uterus weakening.

Moreno worked on Sarah's abdomen, ordering a hypo for quick contraction, while Doc slowly encouraged the placenta to deliver. Still the hemorrhaging, the uterus weak from carrying the large child, from being in labor for so long, muscles fatigued, refusing to contract. The IV drip, drip, dripped. The transfusion drip, drip, dripped.

Doc observed the child a—boy, that was all—as he worked to save the mother. The placenta, fragmented, passed in pieces. *Merciful God, thank you. Thank you. Amen.* An anesthetic syringe was quickly passed to Doc to freeze the incised area. Steadily he sutured, stemming the flow of at least some of the precious blood that was draining away.

"She's shocking!" the anesthetist counseled. "Pulse increasing. Blood pressure dangerously low!"

The baby crying huskily.

Sarah, quiet, happy, content, seemed to be slipping farther and farther from grasp, and happy to do so. No more of this horseshit! Did she really think horseshit? No more pain, just that bright light, that enticing, magnetizing bright light of forgiveness, serenity and solitude where she could rest, have refreshment and reprieve from pain. "Yes, yes," wrenched from the dungeon of her soul. A calm, peaceful serenity descended.

Abe returned to the land of the living after being maneuvered by the staff who were urgently trying to save Sarah and care for him in addition. He found himself lying on a gurney. Dizzy, but aroused by smelling salts, he was infused with a heavenly shot of energy. He fought to get up and move to Sarah. White and rigid, her mouth lay open in a horrible gape, oxygen being applied, her arms flung east and west with an IV in each, her legs in stirrups, her life's blood flowing yet unstemmed.

The crash team pushed him aside, then applied the defibrillator, once—flat line. Twice. Nothing.

Ice flowed through his broad chest like a constricting vice grabbing, tightening, squeezing all of life's air out of his lungs. He bowed his head, thought he'd choke, clenched his teeth and closed his eyes. Nothing went away. His hands doubled into fists as fear flailed at his chest. It seemed as if three footballs hit him in the head at once, taking a while to register, but when it did a guttural scream escaped from deep within his volcanism. "Sar-ah!" He could hear the magma of his scream, flowing on forever like eternal hell, in the sterile whiteness of the room.

What he couldn't forgive in himself were the shared memories that had grown devalued and depreciated by their separation. What happens to mutual memories that are no longer durable? Wouldn't the birth of Fabe be less dear when remembered alone? Weren't Fabian's and Max's deaths less real if only he recalled it? Wasn't the tragedy of Eddie more painful, his childhood fears more fearful, and his early-year humiliations more dreadful, when suffered alone? And what of the lonely years of separation we suffered together, the successes counted, and the complex understandings of mysterious forces form the past? The realization caused Abe's world to tilt and smear across time.

Slowly, he turned around and pasted his forehead against a cupboard door. Struggling for a full order of air, a cloak of realization spread over him. Abe, in his earthly agony, witnessed that eerie yellow-green-white light approaching. Dazzling. Coruscating. Surrounding him completely with a cocoon of warmth. *Fabian!*

"Abe! You need to call Sarah to come back. She's leaving. Call her, Abe! She's crossing over." Fabian's voice curled strong, commanding, and thunderous.

"Sarah," he shouted, to everyone's dismay, drawing raw looks from the delivery room team, the crash team. He caught her by the shoulders and gave her a harsh shake as he rebuked her angrily. "Come here. Don't leave. I need you. Here, Sarah. Stay here! Don't go! Please don't go." *Please don't go Sarah. You have too much to live for yet, too much laughter, too much gusto. Let me make up for the bad times.*

Doc had witnessed many strange events in his lifetime with fathers. Some made fools of themselves over the new baby, some threw dignity to the wind as they worshiped their wives publicly, and some were braggadocios, passing out cigars before the little woman was even sutured from her splitting delivery. But he'd never seen anyone try to communicate through sheer determination—insistence—commanding his wife to return to the land of the living. Sarah's eyes stared wide as Doc approached Abe.

She couldn't remember when she'd ever felt this resplendent and restored. Being pulled magnetically into the sucking waves at the Nahma beach, it felt so good. The dampness soothed as it swirled and eddied around her in cooling comfort. *Abe's calling me! Where has he been? Gone for so long. He sounds in trouble. Abe? Maybe he wants to swim underwater with me. Come with me, Abe. Come with me—experience the softness of the flowing water, beckoning my bones, mesmerizing my mind, saturating my very soul. Experience...*

"Sarah! You hear me!" Abe shouted furiously, bending over her, his eyes demanding. "Come back. Don't go. Come with me, Sarah! We'll get married again and go to Mackinac Island." He pulled on her arm, jerking the IV, startling the staff who hurried to waylay him, assuage him—he'd flipped out. "I miss you so much, Sarah. Don't go!" His voice resounded in every corner.

The dazzling whiteness engulfed her now, endless in its dimensions. She felt nothing and cruised with that numbness, with peace. *Abe! I can't get there. I'm too tired. If I could just float back, maybe a large wave could carry me, carry me, and carry me, yes!* She could feel his powerful hands pulling her to him. *Feel it, Abe? I'm washing back ashore! Catch me, Abe. I love you, too. Yes! We'll get married again.*

She shipped out. Doc understood. He'd loved her so much. She succumbed. What a life she'd had with Abe. This breathed life into her reward—a promised land. Doc's jaw tightened as he put his arm around Abe to assist him out of the delivery room, getting a last long look at Sarah, her hair wet and stringing in death, her life over. He didn't want Abe to hold a last vision of her like this—in her last struggle with life.

Abe seemed not to hear, never turned to leave with Doc's encouraging nudge. This remained the last picture in his triptych of holes in the heart. Fabian, Eddie and now Sarah. If she were gone, he might as well pack it in right off the Main Street Drawbridge!

"Sarah, please come back!" he shouted again, burying his hands in her wet hair.

Beep, pause, *beep,* pause, pause, stutter, pause, *beep,* the heart monitor virtually sonic-boomed to everyone in the room, explosive, miraculous. "Pulse! I have a trace of a pulse here!" shouted the anesthetist. "It's getting stronger. Go! Go! Go!" he shouted as Dr. Moreno hurried to Sarah's side, massaging, oxygen flowing.

Abe sucked in his breath, ripping a glance from Sarah to Doc, his whole body experiencing an electrical impulse of magnificent magnitude as the heavenly light dissipated. "Sarah! Come back. Stay with us. I'll catch you. See? We'll all catch you. Come back—all the way, Sarah, all the way!" His heart roared in his ears.

The staff hushed in amazed silence, eyes shifting from patient to monitor as it became stronger and stronger. The bleeding diminished, the uterus contracting on its own with the additional timely injections of the hypo. She was not out of the woods, but she was back. Not conscious, but gaining color.

Abe wanted to see her tip her head back and laugh, that smoky sound he loved so much. He wanted to confiscate her, abscond with her, and keep her safe, hidden away with him where she could never be hurt or violated again. He had never felt such sorrow. *What a weak word, what a stupid word, sorry.* His defenses were nil as he grabbed Doc and wept like a child, his chest heaving, emotionally drained. Crying like his newborn son, naked and angry with the world, crying lustily during his routine checkout, his feet and hands flailing.

Doc wore his best professionalism to rally for Abe—to be supportive after this near-death experience. Why hadn't he given her a C-section? Why-why-why? "It's over now, son." His voice soft, barely perceptible. He pulled Abe to him, closer still, rocking him gently. "She's done with the pain now; the rest is all recuperation, good care, getting the baby through the next few days. It's okay," he said, still whispering. "I'm sorry for the bad time she had. She just had too big of a child to deliver. I should have given her a Cesarean Section, but I thought she could do it. You have a very gritty wife and a handsome little son. We'll monitor him very closely over the next week. A blood exchange will be done if need be. Fine-looking baby. Nine pounds two ounces. A bouncer. It's a rite of passage—your own son." Doc's voice soothed him, as Abe continued to shake with sobs. Weariness, bone-deep and mind-numbing, gripped him.

Trance-like, he pulled back, looking at Doc as if he were seeing him for the first time. *Look at him—he looks like hell. I've always only seen his virility, his youthfulness, but look at the lines around his mouth, that crepey constancy to his skin lurking around his eyes and his mouth. It's time you get beyond the myth of him and capture the man living there, Abe.* He realized, although stricken, that Doc had tried to uphold an upbeat attitude in regard Sarah and the baby. He knew it wasn't strawberry fields forever. He had a long way to go before he could redeem himself in Sarah's eyes. Life seemed to be a long series of connecting the dots. *Go for the field goal, Miereau. It's the bird in the hand.*

While they spoke, the delivery room staff and Dr. Moreno busied themselves with cleanup, carefully monitoring Sarah, who appeared to Abe to be an alien now attached to tubes and wires in the foreign world of medicine. It boggled his mind.

"We'll leave a catheter in her for at least twenty-four hours. She'll have to be monitored hourly for urine output. Kidney failure is always a problem with shock patients," Moreno advised, sensing Abe's bewilderment.

"Ohhh," Sarah moaned gutturally. *Beep, beep, beep*, the heart monitor sang with regular rhythm. The whole staff applauded. The very air in the room lightened. Her long lashes remained closed, her breathing still irregular.

Doc leaned over her. "Sarah, do you know where you are?"

"Hmmm?" She responded with barely a sound, her long lashes fluttering.

"Who am I, Sarah?" Doc prodded, fearful of oxygen deprivation to her brain when her heart had stopped. Slowly she opened her eyes, confused.

Doc now tugged at his skullcap and mask, pulling them off. "You've been away. We missed you." He looked at her with an outpouring of love and gratefulness.

"Doc," she whispered, the sound reedy. The familiar face did not relate to where she had been, but it looked compelling enough to stay here.

"Yes! Yes! It's me. What's your name?"

Her eyes weren't focusing well—burning, swimming. Her stomach ached, her chest ached, the back of her chest ached. "Sarah Savin." Another whisper.

"Say it again?" Doc reached out, touching her arm soothingly.

"Sarah Savin Miereau-Whittaker," running out of breath, her look softened with his need to be recognized.

"Abe!" Her voice became an inch stronger, yet bird-like. "Where's Abe?" She asked, locking into Doc's eyes, alarmed, every word panic-stricken.

Before the last coherent syllable left her mouth, Abe bent over her, cupping her face in his gentle hands, depositing tear-laden kisses. He hadn't meant to touch her, but he couldn't resist in his grief, in his joy, in his thankfulness. Anxieties he had suppressed since six o'clock in the morning came pouring out. He didn't care who knew how much he loved his wife. He could feel her tremble with debilitating weakness, tears streaming down her cheeks. It almost seemed to him that he could lay hands on her—allow his life to flow into her, his electric energy excesses soothe her soul, feed her body. He wanted to tell her all those things that he'd never said before because he was too macho, because a man never allowed anyone into his heart that deeply, because he'd probably never been a *man*, he thought. He squeezed her thin fingers reassuringly.

Her gaze re-focused with effort. Yes, it *was* him. He had caught her! His gentle brown eyes glowed in response to her return.

He took a deep breath, wanting to say so much, so fast, so full, but instead he simply exhaled slowly. "I have a surprise for you, Sarah," he whispered, releasing her face, which he yet clutched. "You just wait right here," he said, laughing. "Don't go away, hey?" Sarah felt his humor, somewhat twisted, but the sentiment was beautiful.

Abe breezed by Doc, who lifted his shoulders in bafflement at the delivery room crew. Abe knew he shouldn't be doing this—now he wouldn't be sanitized; he'd get chewed on, but it seemed a small price to pay for her, the one who had done so much for him. Sprinting down the hall, he retrieved his number fourteen, green and gold jersey from his trench coat, hurried back to the delivery room, the lights again blinding him with their starkness. Rushing to the naked child, he wrapped *Danforth Abednego* in the jersey and carefully carried him to the delivery table, measuring every step as if the child were a basket of fresh eggs, and carefully laid him on Sarah's now-empty belly, the child waving his arms wildly with small cries of protest at his relocation. Abe's eyes were as bright as any light in the room, speaking to her of love and caring and pride.

Sarah heaved with the desire to touch the child, but she had both hands still taped to the IV boards. "Oh, Abe. Don't let him fall." Her voice was anxious. "It has to be a boy for you to be carrying on so. We'll keep the jersey forever as a memento. Does he have the Whittaker...?"

"Yes, he does," said Doc, standing on the other side of the table, wearing a full smile, or was it a proud grin? "The bloodline continues—what is known as value added." He beamed. Now he knew it was his turn to kiss her heartily, right on the mouth, warm and filled with the happiness he felt for them.

❧❦

It was ten o'clock before Abe and Doc felt safe to leave the hospital. The nursery had brought *Danny* in to sleepy Sarah to start him nuzzling at her breasts, encouraging the flow of milk, which would be in ample supply within two to three days. Doc helped her put the child to her breast, which Danny grabbed immediately.

Abe laughed. "That's my boy, all right."

It even raised a smile from Sarah, her eyes burning with fatigue as she gazed at this blessed miracle, her son, so perfect—so complete. But he wasn't sucking well; he kept slipping and sliding. In her weariness, she felt tears stinging her eyes.

"Well, let's see what's wrong here," Doc said taking out his pen light and laying Danny on Sarah's belly. "Ah-huh!" he cried. "Look at this Abe!" Bending down, Abe could see the small strip of flesh under Danny's tongue, holding it down so he had limited action. Standing up, Doc snapped off the light, eyes locked onto Abe's, both of them laughing with the recognition. "Now, whose son do you think this is, Abe?"

Both grabbed each other's shoulders and embraced. "We'll snip that tomorrow for him, Sarah...just a little tongue-tied. No problem. You'll have great care here, so we'll leave you alone to gather some well-deserved rest after that long struggle."

Sarah produced only a small smile. "I'm not made of spun sugar and I won't collapse into a thousand pieces when I fall on bad times."

"Well, if you do, I'll be around to pick up the pieces, Sarah," Abe said, clasping her arms with no uncertainty.

❧

As Doc and Abe left the building on the 21st day of March, swirls of magenta and violet bordered on purple where the sky spread over the rest of the land. They found the air ripe with the pungent smells of the paper mills, but re-quantified by the fragrant promises of spring. A heady mist hung in the air, giving the city sky a healthy glow not unlike that held in their hearts. The lazy rain had finally stopped, promising a warm tomorrow, and maybe some crocuses and daffodils in Sarah's garden.

Abe felt a new confidence as he walked tall, disappearing into the depth of the parking lot with Doc at his side, the hospital looming lordly behind them, lights dancing through the windows to brighten the night.

The wily warrior practices of Grandfather Crazy Horse would live on in today's world with eternal mid-summer Sun Dances to express his thanks. Abe would hold his little family together with baling wire, if need be...whatever it took.

EPILOGUE

Here's how Abe's receiving total measured against those of his contemporaries in his last ten years of play.

	Rec.	Yds.	TDs
Miereau, Green Bay	499	7991	99
Benton, Cleveland	190	3309	33
Malone, Washington	126	1801	11
Masterson, Washington	126	1697	13

Miereau was almost three times as prolific as his peers were. No other player in football annals can make that claim. Certainly, Miereau was helped by Lambeau's attentiveness to the pass, but if you're going to categorize the best players of all time, you make some assessment calls. Naming Miereau to the top spot is one of them.

On offense, he most often had double coverage. Great hands, hard to tackle, Miereau could out brawl defenders for the ball all over the field. And he was fast. He continued to average five point zero catches per game. The top three receivers of all time—Art Monk, four point five; Steve Largent, four point one; and Charlie Joiner, three point eight—couldn't touch him.

Curly Lambeau was forever amazed at the shockers Abe handed him week in and week out. "He's the most deceptive receiver in football. He changes configurations to fit the situation. It's almost as if the quarterback says to him in the huddle, 'Just get yourself open, and I'll chuck to you.' He's the master of monkey business. He runs pass routes on the team that I've never dreamed about."

Miereau was a specialist in touchdown receptions, leading the NFL eight times in his eleven dominant seasons. In 1948 he caught seventy-four passes, more than four teams amassed in total. Miereau's record of ninety-nine career touchdown receptions stood for thirty-one years; Steve Largent finally broke it in 1989.

In 1952, Curly Lambeau and Abe watched their old team play the New York Giants at Yankee Stadium for the NFL Championship. The Packers dominated the Giants for the second straight season, winning 16-7 before a crowd of sixty-five thousand.

"Not that many people live in Green Bay!" Curly laughed.

"And its sixty-five times more people than live in Nahma!" Abe tittered.

In his last season, 1958, Miereau scored nineteen points in the second quarter of a rout of Detroit; he finished the season with a league-high forty-seven catches. When the Pro Football Hall of Fame elected its inaugural class in 1963, he was a charter member.

He saw a brand new stadium erected in Green Bay in 1958—Lambeau Field, and he was honored at the dedication ceremonies with Curly, both with tears in their eyes.

"Damn it, Curly, why is it that we never get used to things like this?" His chest heaved, his voice was cut short.

"That's because we're just two kids who can't shed the small town basic ethics of succeeding with hard work." Curly wiped his eyes with the back of his hand.

Abe would remember this moment at Curly's funeral in 1965.

The torch passed to Vince Lombardi (1958) and his team of giants, kicking off their Glory Years.

In 1958, at thirty-four years old, Abe was appointed as the youngest Director ever of the International Association of the Arts, being strongly supported by Neville chamberlain of Great Britain, whom he had met those many years ago on Mackinac Island while on his honeymoon. In such a capacity, he could keep his home in Green Bay (Allouez), his summer home in Nahma, and still travel extensively to fulfill the disciplines of his new responsibilities.

That first year of his retirement from football, he traveled to the People's Republic of China for an International Art Festival in Beijing. Accompanying him on the great odyssey were his grandparents, Farley, now eight-two, and Norrhea, eight-one. Their family bonding grew ever stronger in love and faith, renewing Abe's gentle spiritual connections with his ancestors.

While on a tour boat in Hong Kong Harbor, Abe couldn't believe running into Mary Krutina, his old high school mentor, on a group tour offered by the State of Washington Education Association. They spent long hours reminiscing before her tour prompted other paths.

Fabe, ten years old, walked to school every day with the little girl from across the street, Katie Lauren. Whenever her name was mentioned, his eyes grew soft and warm. Abe made a point of not teasing Fabe about her, remembering all too well...

Content to follow Abe's career and tend to Danny after her difficult delivery, Sarah revitalized herself with hand and foot attention by Abe. When Danny was three months old, they did have a second honeymoon on Mackinac Island. Doc and Suki cared for the children. Abe always made her feel needed and important in his life; he even settled down and stopped chasing women!

Sarah's college-day aspirations to own her personal business vaporized in the resplendence of Abe's love and devotion. The days flowed like the timeless Sturgeon River out to Lake Michigan, which swallowed up years like a black hole. The exhilarating sureness of Abe's love and devotion lay as steady as a rock.

The Easter tradition of a trip to Ann Arbor continued. The Walter Whittakers and Kyle Kreilers virtually adored Fabe and Danny, their eyes flooding with emotion upon reuniting each year.